I0831841

The Lords of Dûs

Other books by Lawrence Watt-Evans:

Legends of Ethshar

Night of Madness
The Misenchanted Sword
With A Single Spell
The Unwilling Warlord
Taking Flight
The Blood of A Dragon
The Spell of the Black Dagger
Ithanalin's Restoration (forthcoming)

The Obsidian Chronicles

Dragon Weather
The Dragon Society
Dragon Venom (forthcoming)

The Lords of Dûs

The Lure of the Basilisk
The Seven Altars of Dûsarra
The Sword of Bheleu
The Book of Silence

The Three Worlds Trilogy

Out of This World
In the Empire of Shadow
The Reign of the Brown Magician

Other Works

Touched by the Gods
Crosstime Traffic
Celestial Debris
Nightside City
The Rebirth of Wonder
Split Heirs (with Esther M. Friesner)
The Nightmare People

The Lords of Dûs

Lawrence Watt-Evans

WILDSIDE PRESS
Doylestown, Pennsylvania

The Lords of Dûs
A publication of
Wildside Press
P.O. Box 301
Holicong, PA 18928-0301
www.wildsidepress.com

FIRST OMNIBUS EDITION

This Collected Edition is dedicated to Robert E. Howard

Polar Continent
The Cold Seas
N
Northern Waste
Ordunin
Bay of Ordunin
Kirpa
Gulf of Ypri
Sea of Mori
Skelleth
Yprian
Archipelago
Yprian
Coast
Plain of
Derbarok
Ur-Dormulk
Therin
Annamar Pass
Lagur
Derbarok
Mormoreth
Sland
Eramma
Dûsarra
Kholis
Ilnan
Nekutta
Orûn
Orgul
Tadumuri
Yesh

Book One: The Lure of the Basilisk

Prologue

"I am weary of all this death and dying."

The speaker was a huge armor-clad figure almost seven feet in height, standing at the narrow mouth of a small cave near the top of a snowy and rubble-strewn hillside; even from a distance an observer would have seen the fading light of the setting sun glinting a baleful red from his eyes, marking him as something other than human. He was speaking to a bent, crouching creature clad in tatters who stood inside the cave's mouth, at the edge of the impenetrable gloom of the interior, her face and form only faintly visible in the dim twilight; she was hunched and humpbacked, shriveled and bent with age. Her face was twisted and broken, her teeth gone, one of her golden eyes squinting horribly, yet she was plainly of the same race as the tall warrior.

"Death is everywhere;" the decrepit creature replied.

"I know that, Ao; I would it were not so." The hag addressed as Ao merely shrugged, and the warrior continued, "It makes life pointless to know that I and all I know will die and pass away, as if I had never been." He paused briefly, then went on, "I wish that it were possible for me to perform some feat of cosmic significance, to change the nature of things, so that all would look back millennia from now and say, 'Garth did this.' I wish that I could alter the uncaring universe so that even the stars would respond to my passing, so that my life would not be insignificant."

Ao moved uncomfortably. "You are a lord and a warrior, whose deeds will be recalled for a generation."

"I am known to a tiny corner of a single continent; and even there, as you yourself say, I will be remembered only for a century or two, an instant in the life of the world."

"What would you have of us, my sister and myself?"

"Is it possible for a mortal being to alter the way things are?"

"That, it is said, is the province of the gods; if the gods are the baseless myth some believe them, then it is the role of Fate and Chance."

Garth had apparently expected this reply; there was only the slightest pause before he said, "I would have it, then, that if I cannot change the world, at the least the world shall remember me. I would have it that my name shall be known as long as anything shall live, to the end of time. Can this be?" He stared at the misshapen hag, his usually expressionless face intent.

She gazed back impassively and answered slowly, "It is your desire that you be known throughout history, from now until the end of the world?"

"Yes."

"This can be done." Her tone seemed curiously reluctant.

"How?"

"Go to the village called Skelleth, and seek there the Forgotten King; submit yourself to him, obey him without fail, and what you have wished will be."

"How am I to find this king?"

"He is to be found in the King's Inn, clad in yellow rags."

"How long must I serve him?"

Ao drew a deep breath, paused, and said, "You weary us with your questions; we will answer no more." She turned and hobbled out of sight in the darkness of the cave, the darkness that concealed her sister Ta and their humble living facilities.

The warrior stood respectfully motionless as the oracle withdrew, then turned east, toward where the last rays of sunlight lit the iced-in port of Ordunin and the cold sea beyond, and started thoughtfully down the hillside.

Chapter One

The village of Skelleth was the northernmost limit of human civilization, a perpetually starving huddle of farmers and ice-cutters; it shrank with each succeeding ten-month winter. Its existence depended equally on the goats and hay of the farmers and on the declining trade in ice to cool the drinks of wealthy nobles to the south. This trade brought to the decaying community those many necessities they could not obtain from their own land, but was less each year as fewer of the ice-caravans survived the ravages of brigands and bankruptcy.

Although Skelleth was universally acknowledged as the limit of human civilization, both humans and civilization could be found further north. The humans, however, were either the goat-herding nomads of the plains and foothills or the barbaric hunters and trappers of the snow-covered mountains, who were all too fond of banditry and murder and could hardly be called civilization; while the civilization was that of the overmen of the Northern Waste, driven there by the Racial Wars of three centuries before, and they were most assuredly not human.

It was because of these last that the Baron of Skelleth had seen fit to make the North Gate the only portion of the crumbling city wall to be guarded, although none of Skelleth's meager trade passed through the North Gate, even the wild trappers preferring to use the more accessible gates to east and west on their rare trading expeditions. At any hour, night or day, one of Skelleth's three dozen men-at-arms could be found huddled over a watch-fire in the shelter of the one remaining wall of the fallen gatehouse – assuming that the man assigned had not deserted his post. This cold and unrewarding duty made a convenient punishment for any guard who chanced to run afoul of the moody Baron's whims, and so was usually the lot of the younger and more cheerful among the company, as the Baron was prone to consider it a mortal offense should anyone be happy when he himself was sunk in one of his frequent and incapacitating fits of black depression.

Thus it was that Arner, youngest and most daring of the guard, was ordered to stand twenty-four hours of guard duty without relief at this unattractive spot; and it was scarcely surprising that the youth should abandon his post and be asleep in his sweetheart's arms when, for the first time in memory, someone did approach Skelleth down the ancient Wasteland Road.

Thus it was that Garth rode into Skelleth unannounced and unopposed astride his great black warbeast, past the wide ring of abandoned, ruined homes and streets into the inhabited portion, his steel helmet glinting in the morning sunlight, his crimson cloak draped loosely across his shoulders. His gaze was fixed straight ahead, ignoring the ragged handful of villagers who first stared and then ran at his appearance in their midst.

Although Garth's noseless, leathery-brown face and glaring red eyes were enough to evoke horror among humans, it was quite possible that some of the villagers did not even notice him at first but ran from his mount, thinking it some unnatural monster of the waste; it stood five feet high at the shoulder and measured eighteen feet from nose to tail, its sleek-furred feline form so superbly muscled that the weight of its armored rider was as nothing to it. Its wide padded paws made no more sound than any lesser cat's and its slender tail curled behind it like a panther's. Like its master, the warbeast did not spare so much as a glance from its golden slit-eyes or a twitch of its stubby whiskers for the terror-stricken townspeople, but strode smoothly on, unaffected, with the superb grace of its catlike kind, triangular ears flattened against its head. Its normal walk was as fast as a man's trot, and the relentless onward flow of that great black body moving in utter silence through the icy mud of the streets was as terrifying in itself as the three-inch fangs that gleamed from its jaw.

As the screams and shouts of the fleeting villagers increased, a faint frown touched Garth's thin-lipped mouth, though his gaze never wavered; this noisy reception was not what he wanted. He slid back his cloak, revealing the steely grey breastplate and black mail beneath, and slid his double-edged battle-axe from its place on the saddle, carrying it loosely in his left hand. His right hand still held the guide-handle of the beast's halter, a guide that was more a formality than a necessity for a well-trained warbeast. Garth knew that his mount was the finest product of Kirpa's breeding farms, the end result of a thousand years of magically assisted crossbreeding and careful selection. Still, he kept the handle in hand, preferring to trust no creature save himself.

As Garth approached the market-square at the center of town, he found himself the object of a hundred curious stares. His lack of offensive action thus far had allowed the villagers to gather their nerve, and they now lined the street to watch him pass, their earlier shouting giving way to an awed silence; he was by far the most impressive sight Skelleth had seen in centuries. They gawked at the size of his mount, at his own seven-foot stature, at the gleaming axe in his hand, at the dull armor that protected him and, incidentally, hid the black fur that was one of the major differences between his race and humanity. He could not hide his lack of facial hair, his lack of a nose, nor the hollow cheeks and narrow lips which all combined to give his visage, to human eyes, much the appearance of a red-eyed skull.

Garth was not impressed with Skelleth. It certainly failed to live up to the ancestral tales of a mighty fortress standing eternally vigilant, barring his race from the warm, lush south. Although the outer wall had plainly once been a serious fortification, he had seen several gaps in it as he approached, crumbled sections wide enough for a dozen soldiers to walk through abreast if they were willing to clamber over loose stone. He could see why the wall went unrepaired; the village guarded by this quondam barrier was scarcely worth the trouble of taking that walk. Quite aside from the foolishness of the crowd, even in the parts not utterly ruinous, the half-timbered buildings that sagged with long years of harsh weather and ill care were no better than the poorest sections of his native Ordunin – rather worse, in truth, and the people, dirty, ragged, and flea-bitten, were worse still. But then, they were merely humans.

There was a murmur among the villagers as half a dozen men-at-arms belatedly appeared, their short swords drawn. Garth looked at them in mild amusement, dropping his gaze at last, and halted his mount with a soft word.

To the northerner, this pitiful sextet appeared as harmless as so many geese; he had feared he would be confronted by cavalry in plate armor, or at the very least a few pikemen, not a handful of farmers in rusty mail shirts carrying poorly-forged swords half the length of the broad blade that hung at his side. Surely his ancestors had fought mightier foes than these? It was clearly not just the wall that had decayed over the years since the overmen had withdrawn into the Northern Waste. Still, these were plainly the town authorities or their representatives, and it was necessary to treat them diplomatically if he were to go on about his business unhindered. It being the guest's duty to speak before the host, he said, "Greetings, men of Skelleth."

With some hesitation, the squad's captain – at least, Garth assumed he was captain, since his helmet was steel rather than leather – replied, "Greetings, overman."

"I am Garth of Ordunin. I come in peace."

"Then why is your axe unsheathed?"

"I was unsure of my reception."

Hesitating once more, the captain said, "We have no quarrel with you."

Garth slid the axe back into its boot. "Then could you direct me to the King's Inn?"

The man gave directions, then paused, unsure of what to do next.

"May I pass?" Garth asked politely.

Well aware that, should the warbeast decide to pass, he and his men would have no chance of stopping it, the captain motioned his subordinates aside, and Garth continued on his way to the broken-down tavern that had been known for longer than anyone could recall as the King's Inn, despite the utter lack of any connection with any known monarch.

As the guard captain watched the looming figure of the overman recede, it struck him that he had not yet fulfilled his whole duty; two details remained. "Tarl, Thoromor, we must inform the Baron at once," he said. Ignoring the unhappy expressions of the two chosen to accompany him, he pointed to those not named and went on, "And you three will go see whether that monster killed Arner or whether the young fool deserted his post, and report back to me" The trio saluted and marched off as the captain cast a final glance at Garth's back, sparing himself a moment to envy the overman's armor and weapons before hurrying toward the Baron's mansion. The pair he took with him followed reluctantly, muttering over the unpleasant likelihood that their lord would be in one of his notorious fits of depression.

It was a sign of Skelleth's poverty that the Baron could afford neither palace nor castle, but made do with a house that was referred to as a mansion largely out of courtesy, facing the market-square and blocking a few winding streets that perforce ended in a short cross-alley along the rear of the Baron's home. Once these streets had been thoroughfares leading into the square, when Skelleth had a less immediate government; but the first Baron had erected his domicile and seat of government with an utter disregard for anything except the appearance of its unbroken façade. Thus the alley that had once been an unimportant cross-street became even less important as the streets leading into it were cut off, and sank into a state of filth and disrepair unequaled anywhere in the kingdom of Eramma. It was on this alley that the King's Inn faced.

Garth's face, having no nose to wrinkle, showed no sign of disgust at his unhygienic surroundings as he led his mount into the stable beside the tavern, but he was disgusted nevertheless; no community of overmen, he told himself, would ever allow such feculence. Trying to ignore his environment, he made sure the warbeast was as comfortable as could be managed, removing the battle-axe from the saddle to prevent chafing where its haft slapped the creature's flank and cleaning the beast's catlike ears with the wire brush designed for that task. The creature accepted these attentions silently, as always. That done, the overman leaned the axe and his broadsword against one wall of the stall, as neither was suitable equipage for a visit to a tavern; his only weapon would be the foot-long dirk on his belt. Looking around, he spotted the stable boy who had tremblingly refused to approach the monstrous beast, and strode over to him. The frightened youth cowered, but stood his ground.

"My warbeast will need feeding. See that he is brought meat, as much as you can carry, raw, and as fresh as possible. If he is not fed before I return, I will let him eat you instead. Is that clear?" The lad nodded, too frightened to speak. "Further, if any of my belongings are disturbed, I will hunt down and kill whoever is responsible. Here." He pulled a handful of gold from the pouch on his belt and dumped it in the boy's hands. The youth's eyes widened, his fear forgotten, though he remained unable to speak. Garth realized that he had probably just given away as much gold as the entire village possessed, but the thought did not bother him; he had plenty, and could expect good service if he were generous. Leaving the boy staring in disbelief at the wealth he held, the overman strode out of the stable toward the tavern.

Stepping inside the taproom door, Garth stopped for an instant in astonishment. Despite its ordure-coated, crumbling exterior, the King's Inn was as clean and orderly within as a well-kept ship. The floor was well-scrubbed oak, worn to a velvet smoothness by countless feet and shaped into hills and valleys that showed the tables had not been moved in generations; the walls were paneled in dark woods kept polished to a reflective gloss; the windows, though the glass was purple with age, were spotless and unbroken. The tables and chairs were solid, well-made pieces of the woodworker's art, worn, like the floor, to a beautiful softness. Most of one wall was taken up by a stone fireplace where a friendly blaze danced; opposite it stood the barrels of beer and wine, their brass fittings polished and bright. The far wall was partially obscured by a staircase leading to an upper story, and various doors opened to either side.

Though it was too early in the day for even the lunchtime drinkers, half a dozen customers were sitting about; they had been talking cheerfully, but all conversation died when the overman entered. All eyes save two turned toward the armored monstrosity that stood in the doorway, blinking in surprise; the two that did not belonged to a figure that sat alone at a small table in the corner between the fireplace and the stairs, a figure bent with age whose only visible feature was a long white beard, the rest of his face and form being hidden by the tattered ruin of a hooded yellow cloak that he wore.

As Garth's moment of astonishment passed, he spotted this lone shape and wondered briefly why he did not look up as had his fellows. Perhaps he was deaf and had not noticed the silence, or blind, in which case he had no reason to raise his head. Both infirmities, Garth knew, were common among extremely aged humans. He returned his thoughts to his quest and realized that this ancient was the only one present fitting the oracle's description. Although the other customers, apparently all farmers, were far from well dressed, none were in rags. Only the old man wore yellow, the others being variously clad in grey, brown, and a paler grey that must once have been white. With a mental shrug, though outwardly impassive, Garth crossed the room to the shadowed corner where the old man sat, and seated himself at the other side of the table.

The old man gave no sign that he was aware of the newcomer.

The other customers, after following the overman across the room with their eyes, now turned back to their own conversations. Garth was unsure whether his sensitive ears had caught the phrase "Should have known" being muttered at another table.

After a moment, when the old man remained utterly motionless, Garth hesitantly broke the silence by saying, in a low voice, "I seek one called the Forgotten King."

"Who are you?" The voice was little more than a whisper, as dry as autumn leaves, horribly dry and harsh, yet clear and steady.

"I am called Garth, of Ordunin."

"Your title?"

"What?" Garth was taken aback.

"What title do you bear?"

"Tell me first of him whom I seek."

"I am he; answer me your title."

Reluctantly, the overman answered, "I am Prince of Ordunin, and Lord of the Overmen of the Northern Waste."

At last the old man moved, raising his head to gaze at Garth. The overman saw that his face was as dry and wrinkled as a mummy's, and his eyes so deeply sunken that they remained invisible in the shadow of the dark yellow hood. Garth had a momentary uncomfortable impression that there were no eyes, that he was looking at empty sockets, but he dismissed it as a trick of the light.

"What would you have of me?"

"I have been told, O King, that you can grant me a boon I desire."

"Who has told you this?"

"An oracle."

"What oracle?"

"One among my own people. You would not have heard of them."

"They have heard of me."

Unwillingly, unsettled by those darkened eyes, Garth replied, "They are called the Wise Women of Ordunin."

There was no reply.

"They have said that you alone may grant what I ask."

"Ah. What do you ask?"

"I am weary of life as it is, in which decay and death are everywhere. I am tired of being insignificant in the cosmos."

"Such is the lot of all, be they man or overman." The dry monotone was unchanged, but Garth thought a glint of light touched the hidden eyes. He was comforted by this proof that there were indeed eyes there.

"I would not have it so. O King, I know my place in the cosmos, I know I cannot change the stars nor alter the fate of the world, although I would like to; that is not what I ask. If I cannot change the world, then I would influence the dwellers therein; I would have it that my name shall be known so long as any living thing shall move upon the earth or sea, that I shall be famed throughout the world."

The figure in yellow stirred. "Why would you have this?"

"Vanity, O King."

"You know it for vanity? There is no other purpose?"

"There is no other purpose possible to such a desire."

"Think you not that your desire exceeds reason, even in vanity? What will it profit you that you be remembered when dead?"

"Nothing. But I would know while I yet live that I shall be thus remembered, for this knowledge will comfort me when it comes my turn to die."

"So be it, then, Garth of Ordunin; what you wish shall be yours if you serve me without fail in certain tasks. I, too, have an unfulfilled desire, the realization of which requires certain magic I do not now possess, and I swear by my heart and all the gods that if I achieve my goal with your aid, then your name shall be known as long as there is life upon this earth."

The old man's face had slipped back into shadow as he made this speech, but Garth thought he detected a smile as he said, "I shall serve you, O King."

"We shall see. I must first set you a trial of sorts, for I dare not send an incompetent about certain businesses. I must also be sure I will not be bothered unnecessarily."

Garth made no reply as the hooded face sank back to its original contemplative position, so that only the thin white beard showed. It was some ten minutes before the dry voice spoke again.

"You will bring me the first living thing you find in the ancient crypts beneath Mormoreth."

"Mormoreth?"

"A city, far to the east. But details can wait. Fetch me food and drink." The ancient head rose once more, and although the eyes were as invisible as ever, the wrinkled lips were twisted upward in a hideous grin.

Chapter Two

It was almost two days later when the overman remounted his warbeast and rode toward the East Gate. Much of the intervening time had been spent deciding what he might need and making sure he had it; although he had come from Ordunin equipped for most eventualities, he had not prepared for bringing a live captive of some sort back across plains and mountains. He had no idea what the first living thing he would encounter in the crypts would be, and had to consider every possibility from insect to elephant; he could only hope that it was not a dragon he was being sent after, although even that possibility was provided for as best he could manage with an asbestos blanket and several heavy chains. His first inclination had been to acquire cages of various sizes, but he quickly realized that that was impractical and settled on a single cage big enough for a large cat or small dog, but with a wire mesh so fine it would hold most insects or spiders. Should his quarry prove to be larger, he had several ropes and chains of various weights, and a short bolt of grey cloth which could be used for binding or muzzling. He had determined to make do with his usual three weapons, axe, sword, and dagger, rather than weigh himself and his mount down any further with more specialized gear; as with restraints, he could only hope he was not being sent after a dragon.

Besides these special preparations, he of course made the usual ones, checking and refilling his canteen and water-cask, obtaining food that would not spoil, and making certain that both he and his beast were as well-fed and healthy as he could contrive.

The Forgotten King watched all these preparations in silent amusement, refusing to offer any advice or assistance other than a repetition of the original charge and directions for reaching Mormoreth, which were absurdly simple inasmuch as an old highway ran almost directly thither from Skelleth's East Gate, requiring only that a traveler know which fork to take at each of three turnings. He also consumed, at Garth's expense, an amount of food and wine astonishing for one so old and thin, but prices being what they were in Skelleth this did little to deplete the overman's supply of gold.

While these preparations were being made, there was some stir in the village over a local event that did not strike Garth as being in any way relevant to himself; a man named Arner had been sentenced to decapitation by the Baron, who was said to be in an even fouler temper than was customary in the spring and to be behaving most erratically. When Garth overheard this, whispered by villagers torn between excitement at the prospect of a public execution and anger at the harshness of the decision, he shrugged it off as yet another manifestation of the difference between the cultures of Skelleth and Ordunin, an event that could only happen among humans. Unfamiliar as he was with human emotions, he did not notice the resentful glances invariably cast in his direction when the subject came up. He remained calmly unconcerned about the entire matter, riding through the village streets and out the gate unaware of the hate-filled glances he received, most especially from the Baron's guards, the companions of the doomed man. The hatred of his own kind was never visible in face or manner, but only in words and actions, so that he was utterly incapable of seeing the human emotion for what it was. Nor would he have cared if he did recognize it, for he thought little better of men than he did of dogs.

His journey was uneventful at first, a peaceful ride down a well-used highway where the snow had been pounded flat and hard by the feet of farmers and caravans and was only beginning to show signs of melting into the muddy slush it would soon become. But with his turning at the first fork, the way became much worse, as no trade passed along the road to Mormoreth and he was beyond all but the furthest farms. The road here was buried in largely untrodden snow, its presence discernible only because of the relatively large spaces between the struggling trees, the greater-than-elsewhere number of tracks, both human and animal – the human, as often as not, made by bare feet; the locals must be either very poor or very barbaric, Garth thought – and the irregularly spaced milestones, which were often buried, only a mound or small drift in the even snow cover indicating their presence.

The snow actually did little to slow the warbeast, whose padded paws and long legs had been intended for all weather, but the difficulty of being sure of the road's location caused Garth to keep the beast's speed down and to stop every so often to reconnoiter. As a result, it was a full week before he crossed the hills onto the Plain of Derbarok, a distance he could ordinarily have traveled in half that time. That week included two brief delays to allow his warbeast to hunt its own food; even had he wanted to, it would have been impossible for Garth to carry with him enough meat to feed the immense hybrid, especially in view of its preference for fresh meat. Instead he loosed the beast every third evening after he had made camp. Ordinarily it would have been back by morning, but the poor hunting the region allowed had kept it away until almost noon on both occasions so far. Entering the open plain worried the overman slightly, as he knew nothing of what wildlife was to be found in such terrain. Although the beast was normally superbly obedient, if it became hungry enough it would run amok, willing to devour even its master, and Garth had no misconceptions as to how dangerous the creature could be. Even with axe and broadsword, he had grave doubts that he could handle a starving warbeast.

It was with great relief, therefore, that he caught sight of large animals grazing in the distance. They disappeared over the horizon before he could decide whether to loose his mount or not, but he knew that where there was any wildlife at all his beast would be able to find sufficient prey. This weight lifted from his mind, he rode on calmly, meditating on his appointed task, wondering what manner of living thing he would find and running through every contingency he could think of, to be certain he was equipped as well as he could manage. The matter of feeding the warbeast was ignored, as it had been only two days since its last meal, the normal interval between feedings being seventy-two hours.

Having decided that he was indeed sufficiently well prepared, Garth pondered the purpose of his mission. The most likely products of his quest would be serpents, rats, or spiders, and he could see no point in the capture of vermin. The Forgotten King meant this errand as a trial, so there would be difficulties encountered; it would appear that his intended quarry was not mere vermin, then. But how could the old man be sure that the quarry he wanted would be the first living thing that Garth found? It seemed unlikely in the extreme that he had been to Mormoreth himself recently . . .

His thoughts were interrupted by a low growl from his mount; its catlike ears were laid back, as if in preparation for battle. Clearly, something had disturbed the great black beast. He looked at it questioningly, but it gave no indication of the direction from which danger threatened. Instead it stopped dead in its tracks, its nostrils flared, its head lowered as though ready either to receive a charge or launch one itself; yet the head wavered slightly from side to side. The beast was plainly as unsure of which quarter the threat lay in as was its master, and Garth thought it was unusually uneasy.

He unsheathed his broadsword and held it at ready; his own senses had as yet detected no sign of danger, but he trusted the keener perceptions of his mount. It had saved him before.

His eyes swept the plain, a vast expanse of drying mud, the winter snow melted on this side of the hills; it seemed empty as far as the horizon ahead and to either side, while behind lay only the barren, unthreatening ridge. He could see no danger. Closer at hand he saw no snakes, no pitfalls that could account for the warbeast's actions. Thoroughly unsettled, he sat unmoving upon his unmoving mount for perhaps a minute; when no threat manifested itself, he cautiously urged the animal forward, his sword still in his hand.

The beast took a single step, then froze again; Garth did not need to wonder why. He himself sat utterly motionless for a few brief seconds that seemed like long, slow minutes as he struggled to accept the evidence of his senses.

He was staring into the face of a fur-clad human, not fifteen feet away.

The face had not approached, not slid in from the side, not swooped down from above, not risen out of the ground; it had simply appeared!

Attached to the face was a lean body wrapped in grey furs and seated upon a beast thoroughly unlike Garth's own, a brown beast with a long, narrow muzzle, great round eyes on either side of its head of a brown a shade darker than its hide, a shock of long black hair starting between its ears and running down the back of its neck.

Garth took this in instantly, without any conscious reaction; indeed, the image of that bizarre creature and its barbaric rider burned itself into his mind to the momentary exclusion of all else.

The rider had skin burnt brown by the sun and wind, but still paler than the overman's own. He had dirty, ragged black hair trailing to his shoulders; his features were contorted into an expression that conveyed nothing to his inhuman observer; and his right arm was raised above his head, clutching a long, curved, dull-gray sword, which was sweeping down and to the side, a motion that, when combined with the forward charge of his mount, would bring the blade sweeping into the eyes of Garth's warbeast.

This all flashed before the overman in seeming slow motion as he sat frozen in astonishment; then time started to resume its normal pace as he brought his own blade up to meet and parry the attack.

It was only after he heard the clash of steel on steel, heard the warbeast roar in anger, felt it moving under him as it swung its head aside, and felt himself slipping from the saddle that he realized the attacker was not alone; at least a dozen of the strange animals and their barbaric riders were approaching from a dozen directions.

The combination of utter unbelieving astonishment, the sudden thrashing of his mount, and his own sideways lunge in parrying the first attack did what it would ordinarily take several men to do; Garth lost his balance. Rather than fight to regain it, which would waste precious seconds, he swung his legs free and slid to the ground, standing beside his beast. This action also served to guard his rear, as the furry bulk of the animal was almost as impenetrable as a stone wall at his back.

Fortunately for the overman, his opponents were disorganized, attacking without any order or plan; when he hit the ground he found one facing him all but motionless, while the others remained out of reach. Never one to miss an opportunity, he drove his sword forward with all the power he could manage at the extreme reach necessary to hit a mounted warrior; it was sufficient. The point of the blade ripped through the man's fur jacket, through the rusty mail underneath, and into his chest. He let out a gasping moan, and his eyes sprang wide. Garth guessed he had pierced a lung. His face grim, the overman withdrew his blade, unleashing a gout of blood from both the wound and the man's gaping mouth. The barbarian fell forward and to the left, tumbling messily from his mount, which shied away in terror, eyes rolling.

Even as the man died, Garth heard two screams, one human and one hideously inhuman; the warbeast was defending itself. Its low growl could be heard as the screaming subsided, but Garth dared not take the time to look to see what was happening; he was again beset, this time by a yelling maniac charging at him with saber swinging. Not caring to risk the strength of his sword's metal against the swooping arc of the saber, Garth ducked low and thrust his blade at the man's mount. The saber whistled over his head; his own weapon slashed open the animal's belly and was almost torn from his grasp by the momentum of the creature's charge. The thing screamed, horribly, then fell, flinging its master aside; Garth could spare no further attention for it as two more mounted warriors approached, much more cautiously.

This pair showed the first teamwork the attackers had displayed; approaching from opposite sides, they swung their blades in unison, both aiming for the body rather than the head. The overman parried one blade while attempting to dodge the other, but was not totally successful – his breastplate took the blow he had attempted to dodge, the sword scraping across it, bruising his body beneath, while his parry locked with the other blade, notching the overman's weapon and requiring three vital seconds to untangle.

Thus delayed, Garth was unable to defend himself against a second blow from his other antagonist. Seeing the blade approaching, he attempted to dodge again. He was lucky; the blade became entangled in his cloak, grazing his shoulder lightly. Awkwardly, Garth dropped his left hand from his sword hilt and drew his dagger; maintaining his guard as best he could with the broadsword on his right, he turned his attention to the left and hacked with his dagger at the hand that held the entangled sword. The man released his weapon, his wrist gouged messily, and Garth turned his attention once again to the right.

Throughout this exchange Garth could feel the warbeast moving about behind him, and a constant accompaniment of growling, screaming, and shouting filled the overman's ears. Rage began to overcome him, and rather than continue the defensive, cautious fighting he had been using up to that point, he went on the offensive. Depending on his vastly superior strength and reach, he drove forward, blade swinging.

From that point on, things happened too fast for Garth to follow consciously: he hacked down at least two more warriors, one mounted and one on foot; at least one sword broke before the fury of his onslaught; blood spattered his cloak and armor, some of it his own, but mostly human.

Then, abruptly, the fight was over. A cry went up calling the retreat, and Garth found himself standing alone, ten feet from his mount, with dead and dying men strewn about him. His rage subsided abruptly, to be replaced with revulsion; he did not approve of unnecessary bloodshed, and this gory mess seemed definitely unnecessary.

Disgusted, he looked about, ignoring the handful of survivors fleeing to the southeast. Nine men lay unmoving around him, and three of their strange beasts. Three of the men were obviously dead, their throats ripped out by the warbeast; two of the animals were the same. The third downed animal was the one Garth had gutted with his sword; the overman was not certain whether a trace of life remained or not. Since he obviously could do nothing for the creature if it still lived, he killed it as swiftly as he could with his sword.

Of the six men still more or less intact, investigation showed three dead of sword wounds, one with a broken neck resulting from being flung from his mount, one with a slashed wrist and a gash across his chest who was unconscious from loss of blood, and the last, his leg trapped beneath his fallen mount, still alive and struggling.

His struggles grew frantic as Garth approached, then ceased when he realized that he could not free himself. The overman looked at him and, seeing no obvious wounds, decided the man could wait. Ignoring the barbarian's terrified cringing, he motioned for the warbeast to stand guard over the trapped man. The creature padded silently over and stood motionless, its fearsome, blood-soaked jaws directly above the man's face, dripping gore on the mud by his ear.

Garth then turned his attention to the unconscious warrior; stripping off the man's armor and clothing, he used the cloth linings to improvise bandages and bind the wounds. He was displeased to see the dull white fabric turn bright red in a matter of seconds; the cuts were deeper than they appeared. Momentarily leaving the man where he lay, he fetched his own medical supplies from the pack on his mount's back.

The trapped barbarian asked hesitantly, "What are you doing?"

Garth did not bother to answer, but returned to his patient and carefully removed the bloody bandages. He cleaned the wounds as best he could, applied what healing herbs and drugs he felt he could spare, and bound them anew with fresh wrappings. When he was satisfied that he had done all he could, he arranged the warrior as comfortably as he could on the man's own furs, covered him with furs from one of his dead companions, and placed a sword beside the man's right hand so that he could defend himself, against any carrion-eaters that might wake him.

This done, he turned his attention to his own wounds; none were serious, but there were many of them. He had undoubtedly lost at least as much blood as the unconscious human he had just treated. Upon realizing this, he realized as well that he was very weary and that his entire body was laced with pain. Still, he drove himself to complete the dressing of his injuries and then to turn at last to his conscious captive.

Standing beside the warbeast, looking down at the pinned barbarian, Garth demanded, "Are you in pain?"

"My leg hurts."

"The trapped one?"

"Yes."

The overman muttered a command to the warbeast. It growled softly, then reached down, grabbed the dead animal's ruined neck in its teeth, and lifted the creature's front half off the ground as if it weighed no more than a mouthful of hay. The barbarian quickly pulled his leg free, and the warbeast bit down, so that the animal's body fell heavily to one side while its head fell to the other. Garth watched as a curious grimace crossed the face of his captive. He had had too little contact with humanity to realize that the man was struggling to keep from vomiting. The barbarian turned his head away from the grisly ruin of his mount and the unsettling sight of the warbeast chewing contentedly, and asked his captor, "What are you going to do with me?"

"Does your leg still hurt?"

"Yes." The man made a half-hearted attempt to get to his feet and failed. The overman stooped, and felt the damaged leg.

"It's broken; lie still."

It took the overman some time to locate a usable splint, but eventually he broke the haft from an axe he found among the scattered debris of the battle and bound it in place with leather from the reins of the man's mount. As he checked the bindings, the man said, "I am Elmil of Derbarok."

"I am Garth of Ordunin."

"What are you going to do with me?"

"I have not decided."

"What about –"

"Wait." Garth did not want to answer questions; he had not yet finished his self-imposed task of cleaning up after the battle. Ignoring Elmil temporarily, he systematically stripped the seven dead warriors, leaving them lying naked in the icy mud, then sorted through their belongings, and added those items he thought might prove useful or valuable to his own pack. The remainder he dumped in a heap beside the unconscious man he had earlier bandaged. Elmil watched these actions in confused silence, then demanded, "Why do you leave them naked?"

"As easier prey for carrion-eaters, so that your living companion will have more time to recover."

Elmil made no answer.

"Are the men of Derbarok honorable?" Garth inquired.

Elmil was astonished. "We are bandits and thieves who use magic trickery. How can you even ask?"

"It is said there is honor amongst thieves. I want to know whether I may take your word of honor rather than tying you up while I sleep."

"My word of honor?"

"Your word of honor that you will not escape, nor harm me nor my warbeast."

"But you have no way of knowing whether my word is good or not, save my word."

"This is true. But if you break it, you will die. If you escape, I will hunt you down. If you harm me, my warbeast will hunt you down."

"Then why do you ask?"

"I would have your word so that you will not feel compelled to attempt escape despite the consequences."

"I don't understand."

"It is not necessary that you understand, merely that you either give your word of honor that you will neither escape nor attempt to harm me, or permit me to bind you." The overman's faint tone of annoyance failed to register with the barbarian, but he had exhausted his objections.

"I could not escape with a broken leg in any case; I will give you my word."

"Very good. Then we will rest." It was scarcely sunset, but the overman's loss of blood had tired him. As he was preparing to bed down, himself on his bedroll and Elmil a few feet away on furs that had once belonged to his fellow bandits, the warbeast growled hungrily. Garth called to it, and it began contentedly eating what remained of Elmil's dead mount.

The action reminded Garth of a question. "What do you call those animals?"

"Do you mean the horses?"

"Horses?" Garth had heard the word before; to the inhabitants of the Northern Waste, horses were a vague legend. They were not suited to the climate and had long since died out in the northern lands, but they apparently still throve further south.

Elmil paused, then asked a question of his own. "What is your beast's name?"

"Name?"

"What do you call him?"

"Nothing. It is my beast. It needs no name of its own."

Elmil paused again, musing, then said, "I will call him Koros, for the Arkhein god of war."

Garth remarked absently, "It is a neuter, not a male." He considered briefly, then said, "It is a good name. Hear you, beast? Your name is Koros." The beast growled in answer as Garth rolled over and went to sleep.

Chapter Three

Garth awoke at the first light of dawn, and was gratified to see Elmil still asleep nearby. Had the man fled during the night, Garth's quest to Mormoreth might have been delayed for as much as a week in tracking him down and killing him.

Although it was not yet light enough to travel, the overman began packing and loading; there was not much to be done, and he finished in less than ten minutes. The sound was enough to waken Elmil, however, and the bandit lent what aid he could in tying the furs he had slept in over the immense pack on the warbeast's back. As he did, Garth noticed him glancing frequently at the creature's monstrous head and at the scanty remains of his horse. When the loading was complete, Garth said, "You never saw a warbeast before."

"No."

"Nor an overman?"

"No; I had heard tales of overmen, but never have I heard of such a beast."

"They are bred by my people in the valley of Kirpa; the first were an admixture of panther, dog, and ass used in the Racial Wars three hundreds years ago."

Elmil studied the beast. It was plainly descended from some great cat, and its disproportionately long legs could be from its donkey ancestry, but he could see no trace of the canine. Its huge, sleek black body bore not the slightest resemblance to the scruffy wild dogs he was familiar with. But then, overmen were said to be derived from humanity, and the seven-foot horror he had fought the previous day had not seemed in any way human.

His thoughts were interrupted by the overman's voice. "How did your band appear so abruptly yesterday?"

"By magic; we approached you while invisible."

"How was this magic worked?"

"Khand, our chieftain, had a talisman called the Jewel of Blindness. I do not know how it worked, save that it turned us all invisible, inaudible, and intangible when we touched it."

"Where did your chieftain get this? It would take a mighty wizard to make such a thing, and such a wizard would not be leading bandits."

"He got it from Shang."

"Who is Shang?"

"Have you never heard of him?" Elmil was plainly surprised.

"You had not heard of warbeasts," Garth reminded him.

"He is the mightiest wizard in Orûn. He came from the far south, and took Mormoreth for his own. All Orûn fears him."

"Why did he give Khand this talisman?"

"We had a bargain with him; in exchange for the talisman, we were to stay out of the valley Mormoreth lies in, and slay any who tried to approach it."

"Khand still has the talisman, then."

"What?" Again, Elmil's surprise was obvious. "Khand lies dead, where you slew him."

Garth looked where the bandit pointed; the corpse indicated was one of the men Koros had killed. Without further comment, the overman strode to where the unconscious barbarian he had bandaged the preceding day lay, and retrieved one of the furs he had been wrapped in; in doing so, Garth noticed that the man had died during the night.

The fur he had recovered was a bloodstained vest, which the overman remembered as coming from Khand's body; a quick investigation located a concealed inner pocket, which held a hard object perhaps the size of a walnut. Being careful not to touch the object, Garth opened the pocket and peered inside; it contained a pure-white gem that glittered in the dim morning light. Without comment, he carefully dumped the jewel into his own cloak pocket, still without touching it, and tossed the vest aside. Then, turning back to where Elmil stood dwarfed by the warbeast, he announced, "We go."

"Where?"

"To Mormoreth." He grinned as Elmil started to protest. "I intend to give Shang back his trinket."

The bandit thought better of further objections and permitted the overman to lift him, broken leg dragging awkwardly, onto Koros' broad back, like a child being placed astride a pony. Garth himself remained afoot, not wishing to overload the beast, and thus they set out along the muddy path that was euphemistically called a road.

Perhaps a quarter of an hour passed before either spoke; then Garth inquired, "Does Shang live in the crypts?"

Startled, Elmil asked, "What crypts?"

"You said that Shang dwells in Mormoreth. Does he live in the crypts beneath the city?"

"Shang lives in the palace. I know of no crypts."

This answer both relieved and troubled Garth. He was relieved in that he had not considered the possibility of being required to capture a powerful wizard, and was glad that he apparently wouldn't have to; but he was worried by Elmil's ignorance of the crypts. It occurred to him that he might well have to search the entire city to locate an entrance, a prospect that did not appeal to him in view of Shang's presence there.

They continued in silence, and the day passed without incident. They made good time, considering the fact that Garth was on foot, as here on the open plain there was no mistaking the road. Further, Elmil was thoroughly familiar with the terrain, having spent most of his life riding across it with his fellow bandits.

Shortly before sunset, Garth noticed that several sets of hoof prints had converged on the road, bound in the same direction that he and his captive were taking. His suspicions were corroborated when Elmil remarked, "These are left by my comrades; I recognize the bent horseshoe mark that Dansin's mount Eknissa makes."

Garth made no reply for several minutes; then he asked, "Does this road lead to your home?"

"No; our village is well to the south, along the old highway to Kholis. This road leads only to the Annamar Pass."

"Then why would your band take it?"

Elmil looked troubled, though Garth did not recognize what the change in expression signified. He replied, "I don't know. The Pass leads down through the hills into Orûn, through the valley of Mormoreth, and we have sworn not to trespass there. Perhaps they will turn aside, seeking a cache of supplies such as we have secreted along all the roads."

"Do you know of such a cache between here and this pass you have mentioned?"

The bandit's worried look deepened. "No."

The overman made no further comment. In renewed silence the trio of man, beast, and overman continued into the gathering darkness.

They made camp late that night and arose early, getting underway once more while dawn was still a pale glimmer in the east. Elmil wondered as to the reason for this, but decided against asking. He had begun to realize that Garth was reluctant to speak with him, though he had no idea why this was the case. He put it down to his status as a captive.

Garth, meanwhile, was wondering whether it was really worth keeping this foul little thief around. He could make much better time without him; also, the human had a rather unpleasant odor, and his appearance was hardly endearing. The overman wondered what use a nose was, and how men saw through such pale little eyes. He had never had much contact with humans, and was not particularly enjoying it. His brief stay in Skelleth had given him a very low opinion of humanity, and this barbarian had done little to raise it. However, he had wounded the man and separated him from his people, which obligated him to look after his welfare, at least until the broken leg was healed; and the man could provide much useful information about the area, as well as being a possible hostage should his tribesmen attack again. This last item seemed important, since it appeared that the bandits did indeed intend to ambush him, probably in the Annamar Pass. Why else would they take this road?

He considered altering his route to avoid such a possible ambush, but decided against it; he had no desire to get himself lost in strange country, and doubted that Elmil would be much use as a guide once they were off the plain. Another possibility was to attempt to use the talisman he had taken from Khand's corpse, which Elmil called the Jewel of Blindness; but that held little appeal. Garth distrusted all magic, as he distrusted anything he didn't understand, and did not care to risk the possible consequences of misusing such a powerful charm without a much better reason than the possibility of an ambush by a small band of vengeance-bent bandits that he had already defeated once.

In the end, he decided simply to proceed as he had planned, keeping a wary eye out for any possible ambuscade or sharp-shooting archers. The latter seemed unlikely, as he had seen no bows nor other long-range weaponry in the bandits' possession, nor found so much as a simple sling on the corpses he had stripped; but it never hurt to consider all possibilities.

For example, it had not escaped him that the bandits might have gone seeking reinforcements, perhaps even the aid of this mysterious wizard, Shang. It seemed of rather low probability, given the abject fear of the magician displayed by Elmil, and even less likely that Shang would give aid if asked, but the eventuality should be considered. Thus, Garth considered it, and concluded that he was simply too ignorant of the ways of wizards to devise an appropriate course of action. There were no wizards among the overmen of Ordunin, nor had he met any human wizards, unless the Forgotten King was such. He had seen minor exhibitions of so-called magic which appeared to be little more than sleight-of-hand, but he could not totally discount all tales of sorcerous doings as such simple trickery. In fact, he had once seen a roaring thunderstorm appear from a clear sky, supposedly the work of three wizards working in concert, to aid a pirate raid on Ordunin. The raid had failed, and three of the five pirate vessels had been sunk; the storm had had no significant effect on the battle.

It was also said that the breeding farms at Kirpa used magic to make possible hybrids that nature would not permit, such as his own warbeast. In fact, according to legend, the entire race of overmen was the result of a wizard's experiment some thousand years earlier. Garth was unsure how valid this latter rumor was.

In short, without a doubt his most direct contact with magic to date, and the most powerful magic he had ever received reliable word of, was the invisibility charm used by the bandits in their initial assault. That now lay safely in the pocket of his cloak. However, in all likelihood that was not Shang's most powerful device; if it were, he would hardly have entrusted it to a barbaric group of thieves.

Therefore, Garth concluded, he did not want to combat this enchanter. Truthfully, he did not even want to meet him, let alone risk antagonizing him; but it seemed inevitable that they would have some sort of contact.

The problem, therefore, was to keep all contact with Shang as amicable as possible. And that was not something that could be prepared in advance, but must be dealt with when the moment arrived. Thus he put aside consideration of the matter, consoling himself with a reminder that in all likelihood the bandits had no intention of seeking Shang's help after all.

So it was that Garth spent the remaining three days of the journey across the Plain of Derbarok alternately running through the same arguments mentally and relaxedly watching the rather drab scenery slowly inch by. The road became progressively muddier; some stretches were so lost in the mire that Garth mounted the warbeast behind Elmil until they were past, rather than struggle through on foot with his boots filling with the knee-deep and still cold muck. The animal, which Elmil insisted on calling Koros at every opportunity, did not seem to object. Its own huge padded paws moved as smoothly and gracefully through these morasses as the oars of a well-run galley through the sea, and its pace remained constant regardless of load or terrain, save only when it slowed to accommodate Garth's less rapid pace. The overman began to appreciate how wise he had been to accept the creature in lieu of further tribute from the colony of overmen at Kirpa. It was clearly worth more than the token annual payment of grain it had replaced, even considering Ordunin's perpetual near-starvation. Prior to embarking on this quest Garth had rarely ridden it, since he had done little casual traveling and had fought no wars save by sea, against the depredations and occasional raids of the pirates of the Sea of Mori; he had had no opportunity to observe just how indomitable the beast was. There was, indeed, something more than mortal about its serene confidence in its own power, and he had to admit that naming it for a war-god seemed fitting.

When the overman sent the warbeast off to hunt its twice-weekly meal on the third night following the battle, it returned shortly after midnight, well fed, as it had not in the forests west of Derbarok. Garth was pleased by this, as he was rather fond of the monster as well as impressed by it. Elmil, however, reacted with revulsion the following morning when he woke to find the only physical evidence of the hunt a pool of drying blood that had dripped from the animal's jaws during the night. Despite the bandit's admiration of Koros' power and grace, the beast both frightened and horrified him.

It was on the fourth day, shortly before sunset, with the eastern hills – which were actually good-sized mountains, in Garth's opinion – looming before them, and Garth riding and musing on his mount's virtues, that Elmil let out a sudden cry.

"Look! On the hilltop!"

Garth turned his gaze to follow the man's pointing finger, but saw nothing. He looked at him questioningly.

"I thought I saw a man."

"Was he of your band?"

"I think he may have been. I'm not sure."

With a wordless noise, Garth sat back in the saddle, scanning the horizon and ignoring Elmil's worried expression as the bandit twisted around to look at him. Seeing nothing, he glanced at the ground; seeing that they were past the pool of mud that had driven him to mount, he swung himself off Koros' back to resume his weary walking. Elmil continued to watch him worriedly for several minutes, but said nothing, and finally turned his attention back to the approaching mountains.

To Garth, the sighting plainly indicated that he was indeed walking into an ambush in the Annamar Pass; but, having already decided his course of action, he merely continued on as before. His only concession was to stand watch half that night while Elmil slept, then sleep whilst Elmil watched. Garth would have waited up much of the night in any case, as once again he let Koros hunt, rather than risk being unable to find game in the mountains. By referring to it as "standing guard" he allayed much of Elmil's growing uneasiness. He used Koros' return, shortly after midnight, as the signal to change the watch, and was mildly amused to see, as he dropped off to sleep, Elmil watching in horror as the warbeast licked blood from its curving front claws, claws that glittered red and bone-white in the moonlight.

It was still an hour before dawn when Garth awoke again, his light slumber broken by Elmil's first snore; despite his fears, the bandit had dozed off. No harm was done, though; rather, it merely meant the day would have an early start. After burying the ashes of their campfire and repacking their supplies, the overman woke his captive just long enough to get him perched firmly astride the warbeast, and set out toward the hills as the barbarian fell asleep again, bobbing gently in the saddle.

By the time Elmil woke fully the sun was visible above the mountains and the road was slanting upward enough to make walking difficult. By noon the party was well into the mountains, and the road was again level. This was the Annamar Pass, several hundred feet above the level of the plain, but thousands of feet below the peaks on either side.

It was here that Garth fully expected an ambush to occur, and his wary alertness gradually changed to a growing apprehension as no attack came; why were the bandits so slow to make their move? Was there, perhaps, something up here that had slain them and now lay lurking somewhere, ready to kill him as well? Or were they merely biding their time, to relax his vigilance?

Elmil, in the meantime, seemed utterly unworried. He had little to fear from any possible ambush, since the ambushers were his own tribesmen; although he felt no particular need of rescue from his inhuman captor, he had no objection to such an event. Garth had not mentioned the possibility of an ambush to him, but Elmil was not so blind as to miss the significance of sighting one of his comrades apparently standing lookout the preceding day. In fact, since it provided an acceptable explanation of why the bandits had taken this route, it relieved much of his earlier uneasiness. Thus he was highly amused by Garth's reaction when some small animal cracked a nut somewhere behind them. Far more nervous than he would ever have willingly admitted, the overman whirled at the sharp sound and stood with drawn sword at ready, glaring back down the road. Relaxing slowly, he turned forward once more and carefully sheathed his blade to find Elmil attempting to smother a grin and Karos waiting impatiently. Embarrassed, he said nothing, but merely marched on.

When sunset arrived they were perhaps two-thirds of the way through the pass, and the road had begun to slope downward. Garth had finally decided that there would be no ambush and relaxed somewhat, though he was still worried by the mystery of why the bandits had taken this road. He considered discussing the matter with Elmil, but decided against it.

Elmil, meanwhile, had decided that his tribesmen were planning a midnight assault, the standard method for dealing with well-armed caravans; he debated mentioning this to the overman, but decided against it. Despite Garth's mercy in letting him live and even bandaging his leg, he was still at least nominally an enemy. Besides, the idea was so obvious that he was sure the overman had already thought of it.

That Garth had not in fact thought of it was a sign of his inexperience; in the past his only battles had been by sea, against pirates unfamiliar with Ordunin's waters, who dared not move at night for fear of ramming one another or running aground on reefs and rocks. He had not yet adjusted his thinking to allow for a new enemy, despite his presence in a new land; in truth, he had done very little real thinking of any sort since his decision to seek out the Wise Women of Ordunin, but had been allowing himself to be swept along by his determination to fulfill his quest for immortal fame.

Thus when they made camp Elmil carefully arranged his sleeping-furs well away from the fire, and well away from both overman and warbeast, so as to avoid being accidentally caught up in the melee. Garth noticed this, but guessed it to be merely a result of Elmil's distrust of Koros and failed to see its true significance. He had no objection, especially since it put the bandit further downwind. He sat up for a few hours but decided that a proper watch was unnecessary, particularly in view of how little sleep he had managed the preceding night, and went to sleep shortly before midnight.

It was three hours later that he was awakened by a growl from his beast. He was instantly alert, reaching for his battle-axe, which lay in its accustomed place close by his side. As his eyes adjusted to the darkness he saw three men on horseback, armed with lances, standing on the road perhaps fifty feet away.

Koros was awake and wary, standing over the supplies and growling; Elmil was still asleep, and a fourth rider had dismounted to stand over him with a spear at his throat.

"I'll watch this traitor. You three kill the animal, and then we'll handle the overman." It was the man on foot who spoke.

Not wishing to lose either mount or captive, Garth leapt to his feet, axe in hand, and charged toward the intruders. To his astonishment, he was stopped short perhaps two yards from his bed, rebounding as if from an unseen wall. One of the horsemen laughed nastily, and all grinned as Garth groped his way along the barrier, to find that it extended in a full circle some eight or ten yards in diameter, bringing him back to where he began, facing the bandits. It extended to the ground throughout, regardless of the irregular terrain, and higher than he could reach, though when he leapt with one arm extended upward his hand met no resistance. When he tried to pull himself up the invisible wall, he could get no grip. It was as if the barrier slid out from under his fingers, dumping him rudely, still trapped inside. He dismissed any thought of jumping free; he could not possibly clear the mysterious barrier without a running start, for which he had insufficient room. He glared impotently at the bandits, who sneered back.

"All right, enough fun. Kill the beast." Once again it was the man on foot who spoke, apparently the group's leader.

The trio moved to obey, but reluctantly; Koros was fully as formidable an enemy as its master. The first raised his lance and urged his horse to a gallop. The warbeast batted aside his charge as a kitten bats a ball, of yarn, flinging the man screaming from his horse, his lance snapping against the beast's flank without leaving more than a scratch.

Elmil was awake now, watching helplessly as the other two approached more cautiously, looking for an opportunity to plunge their weapons into the warbeast's vitals. They separated, circling the monster in opposite directions, making it impossible for Koros to face them both; realizing what was happening, the beast went on the offensive and sprang at one of them, claws out, smashing the man off his horse against a rocky hillside. The other flung his spear; it stuck in Koros' shoulder, but failed to slow the beast as it ripped the throat out of the fallen bandit.

"Stop!" cried the apparent leader. "Overman, call off your beast, or I'll kill Elmil!" Elmil looked pleadingly at his quondam captor as the bandit's spear hovered over his heart.

Garth took perhaps half a second to consider, in which time Koros had pounced again, slashing at its remaining attacker without unhorsing him, leaving a bloody corpse to slip slowly from the saddle.

"Down!" Garth roared, and the warbeast suddenly stopped, as docile as a housecat, to tend to its wounded shoulder as best it could, licking at the oozing blood and brushing at the shaft of the spear while keeping a wary eye on the bandit leader.

"Why should I care if Elmil dies?" Both bandit and overman ignored the panic that appeared on Elmil's face as a slight jab kept him from protesting.

"You apparently have some use for a captive."

"No more. I kept him as hostage, but it appears you care as little for him as I do."

The bandit was disconcerted, and hesitated before saying, "Let us negotiate. Perhaps we can avoid further bloodshed."

"As you wish."

Unsure of himself, the bandit went on, "I fear we have made a mistake in attacking you."

Garth said nothing.

"Therefore, although we have wronged you, we ask that you pardon us, and we will go in peace."

Garth waited before replying, but the bandit could think of nothing further to add; so, finally, the overman said, "You will not bother me again, nor harm my beast."

"You have my word."

"You will leave Elmil alive and in my custody, and receive him back willingly when I free him."

"As you wish."

"You will remove this obstruction, and answer my questions."

"Very well."

"Should you renege on any of these promises, I shall track you down and kill you."

It was the bandit's turn to say nothing.

"Remove this barrier."

Hesitantly, the bandit said, "I must first have your word for my life, and for the lives of my companions . . . if any still survive."

"I give you my word that neither I nor my beast shall slay any of you without further provocation."

"Very well." The bandit turned away and fumbled with something under his vest; Garth felt the air in front of him, and found that the invisible wall was gone. He strode over to where Elmil lay and the bandit leader stood.

"Who are you?"

"I am Dansin of Derbarok."

"You are the leader of the bandits?"

"I was, from the time you slew Khand, our former leader, until now. I do not know if I can be so called any more."

"How did you create that barrier?"

"It is controlled with a talisman given me by the wizard Shang."

"Why did the wizard give you this charm?"

"To subdue you."

"How did Shang know of me?"

"We went to him for aid when you slew our fellows, and told him of the battle, and that you rode toward Mormoreth."

"You could not know whither I rode."

"The road you followed leads only there; the highways to Lagur and Ilnan have been abandoned, and all traffic thither takes other routes."

"So you told Shang of my approach; and then?"

"We asked him for powerful weapons, for magicks to slay you with to avenge our comrades and protect Mormoreth. He refused, saying that such were not necessary to stop a lone adventurer, and that he could not risk letting such as us use them. Instead, he gave us the charm of the invisible wall."

"I would see this charm."

"That was no part of our bargain." The bandit drew back.

"As you will." The overman thought briefly without striking upon any other questions, then said, "Let us see to your fellows." He failed to notice Dansin's surprise when he so readily abandoned his claim to the magical prison.

Fitting actions to words, Dansin, Garth, and Elmil found that of the three other bandits the first was unconscious from his fall but appeared otherwise unhurt, while the other two were quite dead. Next Garth removed the spear from the warbeast's shoulder and treated the wound as best he could. It was not deep, as the point had been embedded in a fold of hide rather than in muscle or bone. The warbeast seemed indifferent to its injuries, save that it licked at each scratch once or twice.

This done, Garth said, "You may take your comrade and go in peace. I ask, however, that you loan Elmil and myself your two extra horses, since you no longer need them. I will return them in Elmil's keeping when I release him."

"Very well." Thus it was arranged, and minutes later Dansin vanished into the darkness, riding his own horse while leading another with the unconscious bandit draped across it, and leaving Garth, Elmil, Koros, two horses and two corpses scattered about the faintly glowing remains of a campfire.

Within minutes, Garth and Elmil were asleep again, while Koros nibbled on one of the corpses.

Chapter Four

They awoke late the next day, well after dawn, due to the interruption of their sleep, and were not under way again until almost noon. Now Elmil rode upon one horse, the other carried part of Garth's supplies, and Garth himself rode in comfort astride Koros once more.

The day passed without incident, and their next camp was made at sunset on the edge of the valley of Mormoreth. The towers of the city glittered on the horizon, tall spires of white stone bright against the deepening blue of the eastern sky.

The air was warmer on this side of the mountains, as well, and the valley was green and lush with the spring. There were very few trees, as the entire area was farmland; instead, the crops and grasses lay like a thick green carpet in the shadow of the mountains. Garth had rarely seen farms before, being a city-dweller, and never any so rich; the scene was beautiful in a way he had never known before, for in his homeland the only beauties were those of sleek animals, carven stone, and glittering ice. Even in summer the lands were dull and barren, covered only with sparse grass where the overmen's diligent efforts could bring forth no wheat; he had never before seen so much green, nor such a rich shade of green.

However, something looked wrong, even to his untrained eyes; the young corn and wheat did not stand in neat rows, but were scattered about, and grass and weeds grew unchecked amid the crops. These farms were untended and abandoned. He wondered why.

He wondered also at the towers of Mormoreth. What were they for? Ordunin had a single tower above the harbor, where a perpetual watch was maintained for the benefit of both the trading ships carrying out furs, ice, carved bone and new-mined gold, and the port itself; the pirates in the region had several times assaulted Ordunin when unsatisfied with their take at sea. The port's other buildings were but one or two stories in height, or at most three; beyond that, stairs became too wearying. But here, amid a vast peaceful valley with land to spare, humans had built a city with a dozen towers, each a good hundred feet in height. Admittedly, the towers were very beautiful as they glowed in the setting sun; the architects had been excellent indeed. But building for beauty alone was something Ordunin could never dream of; mere survival took too much effort.

Contemplating beauty and the significance of beauty, and the further significance of abandoned farmlands, Garth fell asleep, to dream uneasily of the desolate beauties of winter in the Northern Waste, where drifting snow and pinnacles of ice would gleam in the setting sun like the towers of Mormoreth.

The following day Garth awoke once more at dawn, to find Elmil carefully separating his belongings from the overman's. He watched for a moment, then demanded, "What are you doing?"

"I am preparing to wait here while you go to Mormoreth."

"I intend to take you with me."

"I swore never to enter the valley."

"I am compelling you to break that vow."

"I will not."

Garth was momentarily speechless. Until now, Elmil had been a timid creature, with little will of his own. Garth realized he must have underestimated the man's terror of Shang, or else the man's sense of honor. In either case, it hardly seemed worth arguing.

"Very well. I said I would release you, and although I had not intended to do so so soon, I shall. You may go, and take the horses with you."

"Thank you, lord."

Reflecting that he had gotten little use out of his captive and might as well have released him long before rather than wasted food on him, Garth made his own preparations, and shortly thereafter, two very different figures rode in opposite directions from the campsite, Garth astride his warbeast, riding down the overgrown path to the valley, Elmil on horseback, making his way back up the pass into the mountains, leading the other horse.

The sun was warm, and it was not long at all before Garth found himself sweating under his armor; even the black hair stuffed under his helmet was damp, and his body-fur was matted and sopping. Fur was all very well in colder climates, he told himself, or even in warm weather if one wore nothing else, but with the mail and breastplate trapping the heat, he felt as though he were cooking alive. He considered removing the armor, but did not want to expose himself to attacks from Shang's hirelings and followers, who might easily be lurking hidden in the thick plants alongside the road. He compromised by removing helmet and breastplate, keeping his mail on and perching the helmet on the saddle in front of him where it could be reached and donned in seconds should danger threaten.

It was midafternoon when he neared the city gates, and Garth was moving slowly and cautiously; he was apprehensive, as the untended fields seemed indicative of something very wrong in Mormoreth. He had passed dry and broken irrigation ditches and farmers' cottages standing open and empty; nowhere had he seen any sign of life. Had he not been told that Shang yet lived and ruled Mormoreth, he would have taken the city to be deserted. Instead he was forced to assume that the population, probably greatly reduced, somehow managed to survive without ever leaving the city walls. He theorized either vast stockpiles or some magical means of supplying food.

As he approached the walls he saw several small but comfortable-looking stone houses built outside the gate, most likely the homes of farmers and those who dealt closely with farmers-smiths and the like-which also stood abandoned, with open doors and broken windows. Garth was not surprised; it was in keeping with the deserted farms. Undaunted, the overman rode directly up to the west gate, a huge brass-trimmed wooden portal standing at least fifteen feet in height. The walls themselves were of white marble, clear and unveined and spotlessly clean, that gleamed in the sun. Garth marveled that mere men had built such a thing, and wondered that they had used marble instead of the harder and more common granite. Perhaps the builders had been more concerned with beauty than efficiency, a thought that bothered Garth with its implications of affluence; it was not in keeping with the world as he knew it.

After a brief pause to see if the gatekeeper would admit or challenge him without being hailed, Garth bellowed, "Open!"

His shout echoed faintly from the polished stone walls to either side of the gate, but elicited no other response. After a decent interval, the overman called again, with as little result, and finally for a third time.

When this last shout was met with a renewed silence – even the chirping of birds and insects stilled in response to the noise – Garth slid from his mount's back, slipped his breastplate and helmet on and pulled his battle-axe from its boot. Standing braced, his feet well apart, he swung the axe against the weathered wood of the portal.

The blade buried itself in the oak, spraying splinters to either side, but the door did not move. Garth pulled it free and prepared for a second swing, but froze as the sound of laughter trailed down over him from somewhere above.

Stepping back, he looked up to see a figure atop the battlement, a large man who seemed somehow to be in shadow despite the bright sunlight that shown full upon him. With a start, Garth realized that the shadow was in fact the man's skin color, that the man laughing had skin darker than his own, so dark as to be almost black. The overman had not known humans came in such a wide range of hues; he studied this apparition carefully. This curious figure appeared to be well over six feet tall, and Garth guessed his weight at perhaps as much as three hundred pounds; he had an immense barrel chest, a belly to match, and arms and legs as thick as trees. He wore a flowing black robe worked with elaborate gold embroidery; no other ornamentation, no jewelry was to be seen. His face was innocent of any beard, and his hair; as black as the overman's own dead-straight shoulder-length mane, was clipped close to his skull. Garth could see no sword or other weapon in evidence; since no guardsman would be unarmed, this strange man was clearly no ordinary gatekeeper.

The apparition atop the wall was the first to speak.

"Greetings, overman." The voice was deep and resonant, tinged with amusement.

"Greetings, man. I have come in peace. May I enter the city as a friend?"

"So you come in peace? Is it peaceful to bury your weapon in my front door, to hack at my city's defenses?"

"Your pardon, man, but I received no answer to my hail."

"Could you not then accept it that you were not welcome, and go your way?"

"I have business in Mormoreth."

"You have no business in Mormoreth, nor does anyone save myself."

"I regret contradicting you, but I do have business within – the performance of a task set me."

"Ah, a quest! For what?" The voice was plainly mocking now.

"I seek to capture the first living thing I meet in the catacomb beneath the city."

Further laughter greeted this explanation. "Pray, who set you this impossible task, and for what? Do you seek the hand of some princess? But no, that would not be in keeping with an overman's nature. Wealth, then? Is it for gold you perform this errand?"

"My reasons are my own."

"Oh, come! Who sent you here?"

"I serve one called the Forgotten King, who dwells in Skelleth."

There was absolute silence for a long moment; then, slowly, the man asked, with every trace of humor gone from his voice, "You serve the Forgotten King?"

"So he calls himself."

"Describe him."

Although he wondered why this man, who was apparently Shang himself from his references to "my city," would ask such a thing, Garth responded as best he could. "He is an old man who wears yellow rags. I could not see his hair or eyes when I spoke to him, so I do not know their colors, but he has a long white beard. He is tall and thin, for a human, with . . ."

"Enough!" The interruption was harsh, as though the speaker were suppressing anger. "Overman, you are unwise. Abandon this quest and have nothing more to do with this . . . this so-called king."

"I have made a bargain."

"Listen, overman, you do not know what you do. Although I have no love for you or your kind, I warn you, I give you my word, that only destruction can come of serving this man."

"I gave my word that I would serve him." Although Garth's voice betrayed no emotion, Shang's words worried him; he wondered just what goals the Forgotten King was pursuing.

"Then argument of your master's treachery will not sway you? Let me warn you then, that your task is impossible. There is but one living thing in the crypts; the king-lizard, known as a basilisk."

Garth had never heard the word. He asked, "What manner of beast is a basilisk, that its capture is impossible?"

"Ah, I forgot; overmen know little of human legends. The basilisk is no natural beast, but the Lord of Reptiles, and the most venomous creature known to science or sorcery. Its breath slays instantly; to touch it is to die; to meet its gaze will turn a man – or overman – to stone. Should one somehow approach within reach and strike it with sword or spear, its poison runs up blade or shaft to kill the wielder before he can pierce its armored hide. It exists only as a result of the blackest magic and serves the Death-God himself. No, overman, you cannot capture this beast and carry it hence, and it can only be fatal to try."

"Nevertheless, I am sworn to do so."

"Fool! Why? What incentive is there, that you give up your life to serve a man, one not even of your own species?"

"I have made a bargain."

"But . . . overman, what is it you are to receive in turn? I am myself a powerful wizard; perhaps we could strike a better bargain."

"It was a trusted oracle that sent me to the one I serve; and though your words sound sincere, I cannot put more trust in you than in the oracle." Garth honestly regretted the truth of his statement; Shang's obvious concern contributed to his own growing discomfiture.

"Very well. Fool that you are, I will let you seek your destruction – but be warned, overman, that should you somehow contrive to succeed, I shall slay you myself. Neither I nor indeed any other can afford to risk allowing the so-called Forgotten King to obtain the basilisk's venom. He could use such a poison to work magicks like none known for centuries; he could cause limitless destruction. Much of my own magic derives from scrapings of floors the basilisk has walked upon; to give the monster itself to the King in Yellow is utter insanity."

"It is not my concern what he does with it; I am merely to bring it to him."

"Then die, like the fool you are, in the attempt. I will neither aid nor hinder you. Although ordinarily I would slay you merely for having trespassed upon my valley, I do not care to become involved in your doom. If the Forgotten King has indeed sent you here to die, I will not help him by killing you."

"As you will; then open the gates, that I may make my attempt."

"Oh, no; I have just said that I will not aid in your destruction."

Garth snarled in annoyance at this petty delay; he raised his axe and hacked again at the gate as Shang vanished from atop the wall. Splinters flew and he struck repeatedly, until at last he had chopped a hole big enough for him to squeeze through. He did so, and once inside he unbarred and opened the ruined gate to admit Koros; the beast had stood impassively throughout the assault on the portal, and now strode into the city with its usual smooth, graceful gait.

Replacing his axe in its place on the saddle, Garth flexed his arms to remove the tenseness as he looked about at the city of Mormoreth. He and his beast stood in a small plaza, perhaps a hundred feet across, its sides lined with merchants' stalls and with a street opening from the center of each side, save where the gate occupied one. The merchants' stalls were as empty and deserted as the farms Garth had passed outside the city, and the three streets were also uninhabited. An unnaturally complete silence hung over the scene; the overman's footsteps on the packed dirt of the market and the snuffling of the warbeast were the only sounds.

Curious, Garth crossed to one of the abandoned stalls and saw that the goods the owner had hoped to sell still lay spread out for the customer's inspection, a thin layer of dust hiding the details of the embroidered cloths. In the next booth an assortment of pins, needles, and bodkins lay strewn about in disarray, while a statue stood almost lost in the shadowy interior, a life-size figure of a man seated cross-legged, with dust obscuring the folds of the carven garments.

Leaving this unprofitable investigation, Garth led Koros into the street directly opposite the shattered gate, and proceeded cautiously deeper into the city.

The buildings, although dusty and falling into disrepair, were beautiful and well built, mostly of the same white marble as the city walls. Although most were two or three stories in height, Garth could see three of the dozen towers he had admired from across the valley, but still saw no indication of their purpose. Elaborate fountains, now dry and silent, and gardens and planters, now dead and brown from lack of watering, were common; the homes and shops were graceful and elegant even now. Innumerable statues stood on balconies, beside doorways, in gardens, even placed apparently at random in the streets, or blocking doorways; such a profusion of statuary seemed the only lapse in the exquisite taste of the city's inhabitants. Garth wondered once again what had become of them; had Shang slaughtered them all?

Investigating more closely the oddly scattered sculpture, Garth saw that all were of an amazing lifelikeness; were it not for the uniform grey of the stone, many could be mistaken for living people. Nor were they limited to the usual gracefully posed noblemen of most Orûnian art; the statues represented merchants, housewives, farmers, and children. Glancing down a side-street, the overman saw a cluster that represented gaudily clad young women whose low-cut dresses and curled hair clearly marked them as ladies of pleasure – as Garth knew from his stay in Skelleth. Ordunin, of course, had no need for such, overmen being what they were.

The unbroken stillness was unsettling; further, Garth realized that he had no idea where an entrance to the crypts might be found. To search the entire city for one could easily take weeks, and although Garth himself had no objection to such a delay, he knew that Koros would be hungry again in a day or two, and that it was most unlikely it would find game in a valley of farmland. Having no wish to risk letting the monster go hungry, Garth had no intention of resorting to a systematic search; instead, he determined to find an inhabitant and question him or her. Surely Shang had not wiped out everyone!

Upon brief reflection, Garth decided that the most likely place to find either living people or other useful indications was in one of the towers. Thus he entered the nearest, to be confronted with a sight that confirmed what he had subconsciously suspected but refused to admit. Seated in a chair, poised over a table as if to eat, with spoon in hand, sat another perfect statue. The only questions remaining were whether it had been Shang, the basilisk, or some hideous mesalliance of the two that had turned the people of Mormoreth to stone, and whether any had escaped.

Appalled, Garth explored further. It was as he gazed sadly at a child, petrified while clutching a doll that had remained untransformed, that he heard a noise.

He froze. Again he heard it. The sound was in the street outside, and approaching. Moving as quietly as he knew how, Garth crossed to the nearest window; he was still on the ground floor. He peered cautiously out, and to his astonishment saw a man approaching; the astonishment was not so much that a man was walking the streets of Mormoreth, but that Garth recognized him. It was Dansin, the bandit.

Seeing in the bandit leader as good a source of information as he was likely to find, Garth sprang through the window, scattering shattered glass across the street. Before Dansin could do anything but start in surprise at the noise, he found the overman's drawn sword at his throat.

"Man, I would know where to find an entrance to the crypts."

Dansin stammered, "What crypts?" His hand crept toward his vest, but Garth moved faster, and drew forth an intricately carved wooden rod, perhaps an inch in diameter and a foot long.

"I take it this is the device you used to imprison me at our last encounter. How does it work?"

"I . . . you swore not to harm me."

"I swore I would not kill you; nor shall I. However, should you refuse me, you will lose your right hand at the wrist. I want two things: the location of the crypt entrance, and the means of using this talisman."

"I know nothing of any crypt, I swear by the Fifteen!"

"You do know how to use this rod."

"Yes."

"Then explain it."

With much hesitation, the bandit did so; it was worked by pressing various of its carved surfaces in certain sequences. Garth kept Dansin within reach while he tested this information, and was gratified to find it accurate.

"Very good, thief. Now, why are you in Mormoreth?"

"I came to warn Shang of our defeat and your approach."

"How did he respond to your warning?"

"He laughed; he said he would meet you at the gate, and permitted me to stay, so that you would not meet me on the road. Then but an hour ago he returned to the palace in a rage and ordered me thence."

"Very well, then; you may go your way." Garth sheathed his sword, and in an instant Dansin was fleeing toward the gate as if pursued by demons.

Garth watched him go, then turned his own steps in the opposite direction. He had now been reminded that Shang dwelt in the palace; further, Shang had admitted that he derived much of his magic from the presence of the basilisk. Therefore, it seemed likely that there was an entrance to the catacombs somewhere in or near this palace. If the palace in question were the only one in the city, which it appeared to be from the manner in which it was referred to, then in all likelihood it lay in the center of the city, there being no high ground in this flat-bottomed valley. Thus, Garth headed for the center of the city.

He called for his beast, and Koros appeared from the alley where Garth had left him. Leading the monster, he strolled on at a casual pace, mulling over possible plans for invading the palace without again confronting Shang.

Chapter Five

Before he had gone very far Garth sighted his objective. The street he was on was very nearly straight, an oddity in human cities, with only a single curve in it perhaps a mile from the gate; after rounding this bend the overman found himself looking down a broad avenue that opened into a large square. On the far side of the square, its door directly in line with Garth's gaze, was a large and well-made structure some three stories in height, built of gleaming white stone, like most of Mormoreth, which was plainly the palace that Shang had appropriated. It was still perhaps a quarter mile distant. Garth paused to consider his approach. It was clearly impossible to attempt any kind of stealth with Koros in tow, so he led the beast into a convenient forecourt, out of sight of the square, and tied it loosely to a hitching post; he was well aware that the rope would scarcely begin to restrain the monster if it wanted to leave, but it would serve to reinforce his verbal instruction to stay. He could only hope and trust that he would be back before Koros got hungry enough to disobey him.

Leaving it standing there placidly, still saddled and loaded in case a rapid departure was necessary, he gathered what he thought he might need and proceeded as quietly as he could down the shadowy side of the avenue. His supplies consisted of his broadsword, his dirk, his battle-axe, and a sack containing ropes, chains, hooks, and two shaving mirrors appropriated from dead bandits after his first encounter with Elmil's band, in addition to the two magical talismans he had acquired and such staples as purse, canteen, and a wallet of provisions. In his belt were flint and steel as well as a prepared torch.

Reaching the corner where the avenue met the square, Garth looked about. The open area was clearly a marketplace, with taverns and inns standing dark and vacant on all sides, the canopies and tents of various merchants scattered in the dust before him. It was a good fifty yards square, perhaps more; the dusty and disarrayed awnings and such numbered in the dozens.

Almost the entire opposite side was occupied by a single building: the palace, glistening white marble that remained spotless despite the city's current depopulated condition. It had a single great door in the middle of its façade, a gem-encrusted expanse of beaten gold at the top of three steps of some rich red stone; the ground floor had no windows or ornaments except this portal, set in the smooth, blank marble.

Upper stories were another matter; half a dozen evenly spaced slits served as windows for the second floor, while the third had a dozen broad casements of elaborately leaded glass. The gently sloping roof was edged with innumerable gargoyles, carved of the same white marble as the walls.

Garth studied the situation. Shang was in there somewhere, presumably, but the structure was large enough that most of its interior would undoubtedly be out of sight and sound of the door. Unless the wizard were lying in wait for him, the odds were he could simply walk in the front door unnoticed-unless there were some sort of alarm. If there were, he would hear it, and could simply turn around and walk out again.

Although the boldest course, this was also the simplest, and therefore most likely the best; he had no way of knowing where in the palace he might encounter the wizard, so one point of entry was as good as another, making it foolish to risk climbing in windows where he could easily slip and break his neck.

His course of action decided, Garth strode across the square, dodging the collapsed tents. The sun, setting somewhere over his right shoulder, glittered redly on the gems that studded the palace door. Marching up the three steps, he grasped the handle and pushed; nothing happened. He pushed harder; the door still refused to yield. He could see no sign of lock or bar, yet it gave no more than would a mountainside; either the palace had been designed to withstand a siege or there was sorcery at work here. In either case, Garth did not care to press the issue. He considered trying to cut through the door with his axe as he had the city gate, but he rejected the idea. If anything would annoy Shang, the ruination of his front door would. Furthermore, the noise attendant upon such a proceeding would be vastly greater than that of his intended surreptitious entry, so that even if the wizard were in the far corner of the palace he might hear it.

Therefore another entrance must be found. Garth descended the red stone steps and turned right, to make a circuit of the building. This led him through a rather malodorous alleyway perhaps six feet in width, where he found the south face of the palace to be as totally blank and featureless on all three floors as the front was on the first. Then, some forty yards along, he found himself in a broader, more wholesome street at right angles to the alleyway. The back of the palace, he saw, had the same casements and gargoyles at top, the same slits on the second floor, the same smooth façade at ground level, save that where the golden door was in the front, the back had a large arch, perhaps fifteen feet wide and a dozen high, filled with an oaken gate.

A brief attempt showed that this barrier was as solidly closed as was the golden portal, if not more so, and the arguments against hacking it down still held; so Garth continued to the northern face, into an alleyway of perhaps eight-foot width, which was almost black in the gathering twilight. Here the palace was again utterly blank and featureless.

Emerging once more into the market-square, Garth realized that daylight was fading rapidly and that he could not afford to waste much more time if he wanted to be able to see what he was doing; therefore he discarded his consideration of such possibilities as concealed doorways, lock-picking, tunnels from adjacent buildings, and other unlikely means of ingress, and set his mind to reaching the third-floor windows . . . One, he could see, was not closed completely; perhaps an inch separated the metal casement from its frame.

A single attempt convinced him that the palace walls were not readily scalable; the smooth marble provided no hand- or toeholds, nor did he care to waste time and energy noisily making such holds with his axe. He did not care to attempt lassoing or grappling a gargoyle and clambering up the rope, because he doubted either the gargoyles or the rope were strong enough to hold him, and knew that he was no expert at either throwing or climbing ropes. No, the best approach, he saw, would be to get onto the roof somehow and lower himself down to the window from above, with two or three lengths of rope securely fastened to whatever could be found.

Since the palace itself was unscalable, he would have to get onto the roof from one of the adjacent buildings; to the right was an inn some three stories high, almost as tall as the palace, with overhanging eaves that Garth doubted he could get past, while to the left stood a house of two stories, the upper floor overhanging the lower so that its roof ended not more than two yards from the palace wall and perhaps ten feet below the level of the palace roof. That might serve as a jumping-off point, though the jump itself would be a difficult one.

Reaching that first roof, however, would be easy; an unfallen merchant's canopy sloped away from the house, supported by a fairly substantial wooden frame. Without further consideration, Garth grabbed the lower edge of the canopy, mere inches above his head. Moving as quickly as he could, he swung himself up onto it. The cloth gave, straining dangerously, and a cloud of dust arose, making his eyes water, but the canopy held – at first. He scrambled rapidly up the sloping homespun, feeling it give as he did so; the cloth was tearing loose from its framework. He rolled sideways onto the cloth-covered wood, only to hear the frame creak and feel it start to sag under his weight; but then he was at the top, clinging to the rough facade of the house. It was not rough enough for a proper hold, however, and he knew his grip was insufficient to save him if the rickety canopy were to collapse. Although the fall would probably not hurt him, it would ruin his planned approach to the palace, as well as make a considerable and undesirable racket.

He waited for the swaying and creaking to subside, spreading his weight as best he could, as he considered his next move. The eaves would be within easy reach if he were to stand up, but such an action would undoubtedly bring the tattered merchant's stall down in complete ruin. Perhaps if he could get a toe into the wall of the house he could let that carry the strain; there was an opening between two badly cut stones almost an inch high and four inches long. Carefully, slowly, he brought his left leg up and wedged the pointed toe of his boot into the flaw.

Thus anchored, he pulled himself up the wall a few inches at a time, his right leg resting on the wooden frame, until he was kneeling, his left leg braced against the wall, his hands, with all four thumbs digging in, clinging to the wall above his head. Then, in a single sudden surge, he flung himself upward, catching himself with his arms up over the eaves almost to his shoulder, then swinging his leg up onto the roof. From that perch he pulled up his other leg as he saw the canopy frame below him pull loose from the wall and slowly, quietly fall to the ground, the cloth forming a sort of parachute that both broke the fall and muffled the inevitable clatter.

He paused briefly to catch his breath but dared not wait, lest Shang had heard the noise; the collapse could have been caused by wind or wear, but Garth still had to get out of sight. Wasting no time in preparation, he stood and ran for the roof-edge facing the palace, and launched himself into the short gap between buildings. His run had been hindered by the slope of the roof and he had not fully caught his breath after gaining the rooftop, so the leap was short and sloppy, but his outstretched fingers reached one of the projecting gargoyles and wrapped around it automatically. To his surprise, the carving held; he had underestimated the local masons.

Carefully, he worked his fingers up across the stone until his hold was less precarious; then he swung his feet forward to press against the smooth white marble of the palace wall and give him sufficient traction to shift his grip, so that he could once again swing a leg up. This time it took two attempts to hook a toe over the parapet behind the grinning sculptures; Garth blamed it on the rapidly fading twilight rather than admit that he was tiring already. He was not as young as he once was, having lived more than a century. Though overmen could anticipate a lifespan of about two hundred years, Garth had long since lost the first bloom of youthful vigor.

Having finally gained the security of the palace roof, he moved well back from the edge, out of sight of the market-square if he kept his head down, and rested. Looking about him, he realized that the palace, which he already knew to be almost square, was a hollow square; a large courtyard occupied its center. Though he could not be seen from the market, he was in plain view of a third-floor open gallery that ran the length of the courtyard's opposite side. He crouched lower instinctively, though he knew that there was nowhere on the roof he could conceal himself completely; even the various chimneys were low, little more than holes in the roof. He lay motionless, waiting for a sound that would indicate Shang's whereabouts.

None came.

He remained where he was for several minutes, considering his best course of action; it would be much easier to enter the palace by dropping down into the courtyard or lowering himself into one of the galleries or balconies that adorned it, than by climbing in the front window. In ordinary circumstances it would also be less likely to be noticed. However, circumstances in Mormoreth were far from ordinary; the city was apparently uninhabited except for Shang, and Shang lived in the palace. Therefore, it was quite possible that at any given time he might be on a balcony, in a gallery, or strolling the courtyard, perhaps where he could watch Garth's descent while Garth was unable to see him until it was too late. On the other hand, an approach to the front window would be visible only from the marketplace and the room immediately inside. Shang was not in the marketplace, and could be seen and avoided if he were; and the odds against his presence in a single room on an upper floor were much better than the odds on the courtyard. Garth's original plan of action was still clearly the best.

Reaching into his pack, he brought out three ropes. He looped one around one of the low chimneys, and tied it as best as he could in the gathering darkness – which also recommended the front window, as glimmers of reflected firelight, presumably from torches and lamps, could be discerned in the courtyard, while a careful peering over the gargoyles showed the open window to be dark. A second rope was placed around a gargoyle, Garth's faith in them having been increased; and the third rope, since no other anchorage was available, was tied to the head of another gargoyle adjacent to the first, just behind the thing's batlike ears – it had no neck.

The three ropes were loosely braided together, and lowered carefully over the edge; then Garth lowered himself and climbed cautiously onto the dangling cord. To his relief it held, showing no signs of undue strain.

Once below the level of the carvings, it was a simple matter to reach out, swing the casement open – it was well oiled and swung freely without squeaking – and hook his legs over the sill. Then he was inside, sliding the rope carefully back over his shoulder so that it would not slap noisily against the wall. He regretted the necessity of leaving it dangling there, but with any sort of luck at all it would remain unnoticed until morning. Garth hoped to be out of the palace, his task done, by morning.

The room he found himself in was an unused bedchamber; a vast canopied four-poster occupied most of one wall, while directly opposite stood an ornately carved wardrobe and an elegant full-length mirror. Tapestries covered all the walls, divided here and there to allow draperied doorways. There was only the single window.

Moving carefully around the room counterclockwise, Garth peered carefully through each doorway. The first led to an indoor privy with a complex array of plumbing, which Garth would have liked to study further but could not by the feeble light available. He considered lighting his torch, but decided it was an unnecessary risk. The second door revealed a storeroom of some sort; the third a hallway; the fourth, which had a line of light surrounding the rectangle of drapery, Garth bypassed temporarily; and the fifth and last led to what was apparently a dressing room, with racks of women's dresses along either side. Returning to the fourth doorway, Garth used all his stealth and caution in peering past the velvet curtain. It took his eyes a few seconds to adjust to the light.

He was looking at another room of approximately the same dimensions as the bedchamber, furnished with a desk and an assortment of chairs and couches – a sitting room, apparently. It was not lit itself, but on the far side a wooden double door stood wide open, revealing many-paned glass doors through which torchlight poured; they apparently opened onto one of the courtyard galleries.

He had two choices: the darkened hallway or the torch lit gallery. The decision was simple; having rejected the courtyard route once, he saw no reason to risk it now.

Cautiously, he slipped past the velvet drape into the darkness of the hallway beyond. He could see almost nothing of his surroundings. There were neither windows nor skylights; the faint trace of light, far too little to be of any use, seeped in from the rooms and chambers to either side. As best the overman could determine, the hallway extended for perhaps a dozen yards from where he stood. At least two other rooms opened off it, detectable from the pale-gray glimmer in the blackness made by their doorways. Inching almost soundlessly, his feet cushioned by rich carpet, Garth moved down the corridor.

When he had passed the last pale seepings of light and worked his way a yard or two into the stygian dark beyond, his forward foot suddenly missed the floor; he was at the head of a staircase. Finding his way entirely by feel now, he moved carefully, step-by-step down the spiral until he emerged, long minutes later, on the ground floor. He had bypassed the intermediate level without hesitation, and only regretted that the stairs did not continue into the cellars, or better still the crypts themselves.

The final step deposited him on soft carpeting again, and by the feel of the air and the tiny echoes of the faint rattling of his armor and weapons, he knew himself to be in a large chamber. Although it did not yet seem the proper time to ignite the torch, he decided that it would be appropriate to risk a light; he had a few dry splinters of wood in his belt-pouch, as well as flint and steel, and carefully struck a spark to one of these. It caught almost immediately, to his relief, and smoldered a dull red, casting little light but enough for Garth's purposes.

The room he was in was indeed large, and richly furnished; although he could see little detail, he could see that the floor was lost beneath overlapping carpets, the walls shrouded in tapestries that caught the light where gold had been woven in, the great oaken table that stood in the center of the room elaborately carven and its chairs luxuriously upholstered. The room was apparently a dining chamber of some sort. Heavy wooden shutters covered what Garth decided must be openings into the courtyard, most likely equipped with outer doors of glass like the ones he had seen upstairs. A cavernous fireplace occupied the far end of the chamber, and to his left two large wooden doors led, presumably, to other parts of the palace. It was under the nearer of these portals that a light suddenly sprang up; instantly Garth dropped his glowing twig and crushed it underfoot while reaching for his sword hilt with his other hand. He waited as footsteps sounded dimly through the closed door, approaching slowly and casually. When they paused he realized he was holding his breath, and let it out carefully. There came the sound of a cabinet opening, the sound of its latch and the squeal of its hinges too high-pitched for a full-sized door. Something was moved about, then the cabinet was closed again. Through this Garth stood motionless, alert and ready for whatever should happen. At last the footsteps sounded again, retreating this time. The light grew dimmer, then went out, leaving Garth once again in utter darkness.

Slowly, the overman relaxed. That was as close as he cared to come to being discovered by Shang. He considered his next move carefully; he knew that Shang made use of the basilisk's venom in some way, from the wizard's own words, and he had just heard him either obtain something from storage or restore it to its place. Therefore it did not seem unlikely that the next room was where the basilisk venom was kept, for what could the wizard be moving about other than magical apparatus? Also, what point would there be in storing such a dangerous commodity further than necessary from its source? Quite possibly the entrance to the catacombs lay very near, beyond the door he now faced. If not, it was not unreasonable to think that a clue to where that entrance did lie might be found with the basilisk venom. It seemed plain that that room bore investigating. Shang had just visited it, and so would presumably not return immediately – though he might, of course; care was necessary – so that time should not be wasted. His decision made, Garth crossed to the doorway, finding his way by touch and memory, and groped for the door-handle. He found it and worked the latch. The door began to swing open of its own accord. It had apparently been hung badly. However, since it swung silently, Garth made no move to stop it; instead he stepped through when the opening was wide enough. After a moment's thought, he caught the door and swung it closed again, catching the latch and lowering it soundlessly in place; although this cut off one possible route of retreat, or at least put a delay in it, that seemed less important than leaving such an obvious proof of his presence should Shang investigate this room while Garth was elsewhere.

The room he was in was dark, though not so black as the dining hall; traces of light slipped in under half a dozen closed doors on two sides of the chamber, and shuttered windows on a third. He was apparently very near indeed to that portion of the palace Shang used for his personal quarters. Garth's eyes were already adjusted to the dark; after closing the door and turning away from the lit cracks, he had little difficulty in discerning the contents of the room. He immediately realized how wrong his assumptions had been.

He was in a kitchen; Shang had merely been obtaining a snack. One wall was lined with cupboards and cabinets, with an open arch in their midst that must lead to the larder and pantry. Around a corner must be the scullery, to judge from the pans that lay near. One wall was taken up mostly with assorted ovens and a huge open hearth. Tables and counters were scattered around, and the air smelled of vegetables and cooked meat.

Garth accepted his error with a shrug; he should have expected the next room to a dining hall to be a kitchen, and he had not. It was a mistake, but it was past and would not be made again. He was where he was, and would have to make the best of it. In fact, he told himself, this was a good place to be. The crypts were, of course, under the palace; therefore the palace cellars were a likely place to find an entrance, and the kitchen was the natural place to find an entrance to the cellars. Unquestionably one, or maybe several, of the many doors opened on stairs to the cellars. The only question was, which door?

Well, it was a safe assumption that the cellars were not illuminated at the moment, which eliminated from consideration those doors that showed light; that left three doors in the main portion of the kitchen, and perhaps others in the pantries and scullery.

He began to inch his way across the room toward the nearest of the unlit doors. His boots scraped slightly on the flagstone floor, so he switched to slow, careful strides, lifting his feet straight up, advancing them, and placing them gingerly down. He was perhaps halfway across the darkened kitchen when his moving foot collided in midstride with a kettle that lay on its side where it had been flung by Shang – who was rather a sloppy housekeeper. The copper pot rolled aside, rattling, when the toe of his foot struck it; he was thrown off balance and caught himself only at the cost of a loud thud as his foot hit the floor and his hand grabbed at a nearby table. He froze.

The kettle had scarcely stopped rolling when he heard the wizard's approaching footsteps. His right hand fell once again to his sword, while his left slipped inside his cloak, seeking the pocket where he had put the so-called Jewel of Blindness, as he told himself that if ever he needed magical aid it was now.

Groping, he found the pocket; he did not dare take his eyes from the general direction of the lit doorways, as he had no way of knowing which one was about to burst open and admit Shang. Being unaware from what direction the attack was to come, he could not afford to be looking the wrong way when it arrived. His three fingers fumbled about, his thumbs hooked over the pocket's edge to catch anything that fell. He felt the hard lump of the gem, and started to draw it forth.

A door slammed open, flung back against the wall.

The wizard stood framed in the doorway, a black silhouette against the torchlit room beyond. Garth was blinded momentarily by the sudden light, but nonetheless his sword was drawn and ready by the time the door had stopped its abrupt movement; his left hand was also held out before him, the Jewel of Blindness clutched tightly in his fist.

To his astonishment, Shang ignored him; he said nothing, made no threatening move. Instead he peered into the gloomy kitchen as a drunkard would peer into an empty bottle, as if he had expected and wanted to see something that wasn't there.

Not yet accepting his good fortune, Garth held his breath and stood ready, the slow realization that something was wrong seeping into his brain; be could not see the end of his sword, which should be well within his field of vision. Had he drawn the dirk by mistake? No, the weight difference would have told him of his error. He looked down, to be suddenly overwhelmed with a most peculiar form of vertigo; he could not see his hands, nor his legs, nor any other portion of his body or attire; his sword was as invisible as air. It was a very strange and unsettling experience, as if he were somehow adrift in midair; yet his other senses told him that he still stood with his feet firmly on the ground, with sword in hand.

Chapter Six

Shang stood in the doorway for a long moment, staring into the seemingly empty darkness. Then, with a shrug, he stepped back a pace and reached to one side, his hand disappearing around the doorframe to reappear almost immediately, clutching the stub of a torch. Casually, as though he had dismissed the possibility of an ambush, the wizard strolled into the kitchen and looked about. Seeing the kettle where it lay by Garth's now-invisible boot, he crossed the room, picked it up, and placed it on the table with a slight frown. Garth stood utterly unmoving, not even daring to breathe for fear he should be detected somehow. The wizard's hand passed within a few inches of his foot, and the overman wondered what would happen should Shang touch him. Elmil had said the jewel rendered the user invisible, inaudible, and intangible; then would the wizard's hand pass through him? Would he feel it? Would it harm him?

He had no opportunity to find out, as Shang did not happen to touch him. Instead, the thaumaturge, after restoring the kettle to its place, used his bit of torch to light a hanging oil lamp, then tossed the stub into the fireplace, where it was lost amid a shower of grey ash. The lamp flared up brightly for an instant, then subsided to a smoky and malodorous glow as Shang began opening and rummaging in various cabinets; he placed a plate of cheese on the table beside the kettle, then continued, apparently searching for something. Finally, with a noise of disgust, he slammed the last cabinet and crossed to a door, the same door Garth had planned to try. In the flickering lamplight the overman noticed that a heavy padlock held the door shut. He carefully considered, as quickly as he could, what this could signify; why would one door be locked when others were not? It guarded something valuable—perhaps the crypts, where the basilisk lived?

He had no time for further thought, as Shang turned a massive key in the lock and swung the door open; if he was to get inside that door speed was essential. He ran through the door a fraction of a second before the wizard himself stepped casually through, pulling it shut behind him.

Unfortunately, the door opened on a narrow landing at the head of a staircase; Garth lost his balance as a result of his mad dash and stumbled awkwardly halfway down the long flight before he managed to grasp to rail and halt his headlong progress. To his astonishment, he felt no bumps or bruises from his numerous impacts with both stairs and railing, nor did he make a sound; the silence was, in fact, rather eerie and horrible, as if he no longer really existed.

As the door slammed, shutting off the dim light from the kitchen, a bright little flame suddenly flashed into being; Garth saw with a curious mixture of fear and fascination that it came directly from the wizard's finger. Shang used it to light a torch that stood ready in a bracket above the landing, then extinguished it with a gesture and picked up the much brighter torch.

Looking around, Garth saw that he was more or less at the midpoint of approximately two dozen steps, hewn of some dull grey stone. On one side of the steps ran a wall of rough blocks of the same stone, while on the other there was a black iron railing to which Garth was clinging. Beyond the railing there extended a sizable wine cellar, with damp stone walls on either side and intricate, ancient stone vaulting overhead, its limits lost in the darkness beyond the torch's glow; in the portion that could be seen stood countless old and bewebbed wine-racks, some full, some empty, some in intermediate states. The light shifted, and Garth turned his gaze upward again to see Shang approaching. Not caring to risk a collision, he backed hastily down the steps, keeping a few paces ahead of the wizard until they both stood at the bottom, where Garth stepped aside and permitted Shang to move unimpeded to the nearest rack of bottles.

As he did, Garth was reprimanding himself for making another unjustified assumption; it was much more natural that Shang would seek a bit of wine to go with his cheese than that he would go prowling unarmed into the catacombs.

As if to confirm that the overman had acted hastily, Shang said loudly, "Ah! Perfect!" He drew forth a cobwebby bottle, dark liquid visible through its murky glass, then turned back toward the stairs. Garth remained where he was, attempting to plan his next move.

Although Shang's visit to the cellar had been in no way connected with the crypts, it was still perfectly possible that an entrance was to be found somewhere amid the wine-racks; since Garth was already down here it would do no harm to check. Therefore he would let the wizard leave, investigate, and then leave himself if he found nothing. It was only when he heard the padlock clicking back into place that he realized he had forgotten about it. He would either have to wait until the wizard was thirsty again or use his axe to hack open the door when it came time to depart. He felt rather foolish.

However, since there was nothing he could do about it, he would make the best of the situation and carry on with his intention of searching the cellar. Fortunately, Shang had not bothered to douse the torch, but had merely stuck it back in its bracket, still lit. Garth wondered if this meant he would be returning shortly. Presumably he would be, in order to restock the wine-cupboards in the kitchen. Therefore it would be advisable to work quickly, so as to have the torch back into its holder when Shang should return. Garth decided he could count on only as much time as it took a man to drink a rather small bottle of wine, which left no time for delay. He hurried up the steps and reached up to take the torch from its place. He closed his fingers around it and tugged. It did not move. Startled, he pulled again; again, the torch remained as motionless as the cellar wall. Garth removed his hand, then replaced it and tried again; still the wood refused to budge. Perhaps it was enchanted? It seemed rather unlikely that the wizard would bother with ensorcelling a torch in a wine cellar. Perhaps his invisible fingers were in the wrong place, and he was trying to move the bracket? But no, he distinctly felt the rough grain of the wood.

Studying his invisible hand, a horrible thought suddenly struck him: where was his sword? He felt where its hilt should be, and found nothing; his left hand still clutched the Jewel of Blindness, but his right hand had been empty since he staggered on the stairway and grabbed at the railing. He must have dropped the weapon, either in the kitchen or on the stairs; he could see no trace of it. Either it was still invisible, or it lay now on the kitchen floor as clear proof of his presence. It occurred to him that it was very well indeed that it had been the sword he had dropped, rather than the gem, which was his only means of restoring himself to visibility. To avoid any risk of losing it as well, he carefully tucked it into a pouch at his belt, a rather tricky proceeding while invisible. With both hands free, he then reached up and grasped the torch again, carefully feeling its shaft where it met the iron bracket. He could detect no latch or other impediment. He applied his full strength, which should have torn the entire bracket from its mountings; the torch did not so much as flicker. Either it was indeed enchanted, or this was some side effect of his intangible state . . . probably the latter. After all, could intangibles such as fear or courage lift a torch from its resting place? He descended the stairs once more and chose a bottle at random; he could not budge it, any more than he could lift the torch. Likewise, he realized, even if he found the door to the crypts, he would be unable to open it. Well, he decided, such details were best left until actually encountered. He was unsure he would be able to resume his invisibility once he broke it – assuming he could break it – and did not care to abandon his best protection against discovery until the last possible moment.

He wondered again what had become of his sword; wherever it was, it was apparently still invisible, or else Shang would have come back seeking him upon finding it on the kitchen floor. It struck him that he would have heard it fall, ordinarily; the inaudibility the spell conferred apparently affected the user as well as everyone else. In trial, he attempted to shout, and discovered he could not hear himself do so. No wonder the bandits had been so disorganized in their attack; it was a wonder they had been as well grouped as they were. The result of long practice, no doubt. Well, at least he could still feel; the intangibility apparently wasn't that complete.

It was complete enough, though. He couldn't move the torch, so he couldn't very well search the walls with it. He remembered the torch stuck in his belt and, groping, found it; that he could still handle. He drew it forth, climbed the stairs once again, and held it to the flame of the lit one. Nothing happened; no flame appeared. He started to feel for the oiled tip, and burnt his fingers in doing so. It was afire. Naturally, though, the flames were as invisible as the torch, casting invisible light.

Garth found himself wishing he knew the names of some appropriate gods to swear by; profanity seemed the only response in such a situation. Unfortunately, he did not. Like most overmen, he was an atheist, or at least an agnostic, refusing to listen to the babble of competing priesthoods without tangible evidence of the existence of the countless gods and goddesses they espoused. As a result of this widespread attitude, there were no priests of any description to be found in the Northern Waste.

He carefully stamped out the invisible flame with his invisible boot, and caught the odor of invisible smoke. He wondered if Shang would be able to smell his presence. He had no idea how well humans could smell; it would seem that such prominent noses should be fairly sensitive but, recalling the foulness of Skelleth, he decided that the appearance must be deceiving.

It seemed that the only thing to do was to search the walls as best he could in the dim light, working mostly by touch despite his inability to lift so much as a fallen leaf. He could still sense textures, though a silk drapery would give no more than a stone wall under his intangible fingers.

To his surprise, he found that in a way the darkness was comforting; he didn't expect to see his hands or feet in the dark, so their absence was much less distracting than in the light. He found his way without difficulty to the slightly damp and noticeably cool stone wall, and began cautiously feeling his way along, dodging around wine-racks when necessary, and likewise around cobwebs, which were as unbreakable as steel mesh to him now. Enough light trickled through the frames to keep him from actually colliding with anything. The miscellaneous projections he encountered were visible as patches of more complete darkness. No sort of detail could be made out, however; his explorations were of necessity tactile rather than visual.

He gradually became absorbed in his task, noticing and mentally cataloging an intriguing variety of textures in the stone and losing all sense of time. It was only when he reached a corner and decided to take a brief rest that he noticed he was now in complete darkness, even the glow of the torch lost amid the intervening wine-racks. He had systematically explored at least a hundred feet of wall, inch by inch; it must have taken hours, he realized in astonishment, yet Shang had not returned. He had no idea of the time, but guessed that the sun must have risen.

He rose from his comfortable crouch and strode back toward the far end of the cellar where the stairs were. As he did, he saw that the torchlight was dimmer than before. Breaking into a trot, he arrived at the foot of the stairs and saw that the torch had burnt down to a stub, too short to be held. In a moment it would go out. Further, there was nothing he could do to prevent it. He wondered whether some ill had befallen Shang, or whether he had merely forgotten about fetching more wine. It made little difference. As Garth watched, the flame flickered and died to a dull red glow that slowly faded.

A slight uneasiness touched him briefly, but he shook it off. If something had happened to the wizard, he would have to break the invisibility spell in order to leave the cellar; if he could not break the spell he would be trapped indefinitely. Of course he would not die of thirst, but he thought it doubtful that an overman could live for very long on nothing but wine. It did not occur to him that he would be unable to get at the wine in his intangible state. Also, his mount still waited for him in the city outside; it would be hungry if no one fed it within the next day or so. Well, the warbeast could take care of itself; he had his own worries. He turned his attention back to the cellar walls.

It was a long time later when he finally came across what was undoubtedly a door. The stone ended, there was a wooden frame, and set in a few inches was a wooden panel studded with iron spikes such as were used to discourage trespassers from attempting to break doors in with their shoulders. It was the first trace of anything other than solid stone he had found anywhere in the walls. Investigating further, he felt what were undoubtedly hinges; although he knew it was useless, he pushed against the opposite edge. It refused to yield. It would seem, he decided, that now was the appropriate time to try to turn himself visible once more. He reached into his belt-pouch and found the gem. Carefully, he tried to pull it out.

It caught; one of it edges had snagged in the pouch's lining.

Annoyed, he tugged at it. At first it held, then suddenly it sprang free and flew out of his grasp. Panic-stricken, Garth fell on his knees and groped for it, but found only dust. Without thinking, he yanked out his flint and steel and tinder and struck a spark, forgetting that the flame and light would be invisible.

The tinder caught and flared a bright yellow in Garth's perfectly normal, visible hands. He snorted with relief as he realized that he had somehow broken the enchantment while fumbling with the gem.

Quickly, before the flickering tinder could die, he pulled out his torch and held it to the flame; the oils, sooty and no longer fresh, took several seconds to catch, but flared up at last in smoky red light.

Pocketing flint and steel with one hand while the other held the torch, Garth saw that he had used the last of his tinder; he could not afford to lose the torch, his only source of light. A glance around showed him that there were other torches, long unused and covered with dust and cobwebs, mounted high along the cellar walls. He lit the nearest one, so as to have a second flame if he lost his first, then systematically collected himself an armload of unlit brands from the other brackets and distributed them about his person. This done, he turned his attention to the door he had found.

It was a massive thing, with three heavy black hinges supporting what appeared to be braced and layered oak, fit to withstand a siege and studded with a myriad of inch-long spikes. It was held shut by a heavy latch, secured with a massive bolt lock – a lock to which Shang undoubtedly held the key.

Reminded of the wizard and his works, he glanced around for the Jewel of Bilndness, but didn't see it. He shrugged. It had served his purpose, and he didn't care to spend the time to search for it; he wanted to get the basilisk above ground before Koros became hungry enough to go hunting. He turned his attention to the latch and lock, holding the torch as close as he could without igniting anything.

The latch was of little consequence; it could be worked from either side, apparently. The lock was the only difficulty. Nor did he have to worry about bars or locks on the other side, as Shang would be as unable pass them as he – probably. He was unsure as to whether such things could be manipulated magically. There was the possibility of a protective spell of some sort, but he would deal with that if it became necessary and not before.

The door fit its frame reasonably well, but close scrutiny revealed a narrow crack an inch or two above the lockbolt; through it Garth could see light glinting on the shiny metal of the bolt itself, proof that it had been recently worked and the rust scraped off. Putting aside the torch, he drew his dirk and found that the narrow blade fit into the opening. He forced it down until he felt it scrape on the bolt, then pried sideways, moving the bolt a fraction of an inch. He repeated this several times. Then, while holding the dagger-tip where it was, he peered into the crack. He could not be certain, but the bolt appeared to have moved perceptibly and not slid back completely. He continued; with a dozen more prying motions something snapped, and his dagger sprang free. He saw, to his disgust, that the point had broken off; however, a careful study of the crack seemed to show that the broken tip had worked its way between the lock and the frame. With the blunted end of the blade he pried once more.

There was a loud click, a sort of "thunk," and the lock was open.

Working the latch, Garth pushed on the door. It gave, slowly, with a harsh scratching sound where the tip of his dagger was wedged between the lock and the frame. He pressed harder, and it swung abruptly open, precipitating him forward into the darkness beyond.

He tumbled awkwardly down a few steps, then caught himself. He was on a narrow stair which descended further than he could see by the dim torchlight, with walls of solid stone on either side. The walls, in fact, appeared to be natural uncut stone; he could see no seams or mortar. The tunnel and stair were hewn from the living bedrock of the valley.

A breath of cool air wafted up to him from the invisible depths below. He had found the crypts of Mormoreth, he was quite certain.

Caution was called for from here on; at any moment he might encounter the basilisk. His only means of ensuring that he would not be petrified in such an encounter was the shaving mirrors he had brought, taken from the dead bandits. He found one of the two mirrors in his pack and stood it on his shoulder, holding it in place with his free hand; then he turned his head and angled the mirror so that he could see the reflection of the descending steps in it, and twisted his helmet around on his head so that its earpiece blocked his view. As long as he looked toward the mirror be would be unable to see in front of him, except by reflection. It was an awkward and uncomfortable arrangement, but he thought it would probably do.

Thus equipped, he returned to the head of the staircase, retrieved his torch, and pushed the door to, being careful not to let it lock. He returned his broken dirk to its sheath, then turned and descended, holding the torch high and finding his way entirely by the image in the mirror.

Chapter Seven

The stairs curved somewhat back and forth, with a sinuous grace; they continued downward for perhaps a hundred steps, perhaps more, and ended in a small chamber with a corridor opening from each side. The air was cool and dry, free of any movement or breeze. Garth had lost his sense of direction on the long, curving staircase, but that mattered little so far underground.

The corridor walls were astonishingly clean; there was no dust, and not a cobweb to be seen. Likewise, the antechamber was completely empty, nothing but a stark cube of stone with three corridors and the staircase opening from its four sides. There were no stalactites, nor niter deposits, nor any other sign of age, of growth, or of decay. It was as if the tunnels were newly bored. Still, there was an indefinable something, perhaps a scent in the air, which made the overman suspect that the catacombs were very ancient indeed, ancient and somehow evil. Certainly they were totally silent; there was no dripping water, no rustle of mice, no scratching insects, and the silence seemed somehow oppressive and ominous.

Moving slowly and carefully, guiding himself by the dim reflections in his shoulder-mirror, Garth advanced up the left-hand corridor and started his search for a living thing. He had hoped that despite Shang's warning he might somehow find some minor vermin, perhaps a fly or a rat, before coming across the basilisk; but having seen the utterly dead and sterile corridors, he all but gave up on that idea. His footsteps echoed from the blank walls like the booming of a drum, and he was quite sure that the buzzing of a gnat or the swish of a lizard would be magnified to audible proportions if such a thing dwelt anywhere nearby. He began to wonder how it was that he could not hear anything of the basilisk.

As he proceeded, moving through the complex web of corridors, Garth began to realize that he should have brought a thread to find his way out by; the crypts were a labyrinth of branching tunnels, echoing chambers, subtly-sloping floors and identical passages which might well have been designed to confuse an intruder. He wondered what their original purpose had been, but could think of nothing plausible.

As time passed he began to feel strangely tired, and perhaps a trifle nauseated. He shook his head to clear it, and paused in his patrol. In so doing, he noticed that the echoes of his footsteps could still be heard, resounding and reechoing, for long seconds after he stopped.

Why was he tired and ill? True, he had not slept in a day or two, but that was not unusual, and he had always been able in the past to go without sleep for as much as a week without difficulty. Perhaps it was hunger? He found a strip of dried meat in his pack and devoured it; it made no difference. In doing so, however, he noticed a peculiar smell, and realized that it had been present for some time and growing steadily stronger. It was a dry, reptilian smell, rather horrible; it could only be the odor of the basilisk, and the monster's poisonous breath was undoubtedly what was weakening him. It meant he was drawing near his goal.

Gathering himself together again, he adjusted his shoulder-mirror and moved on. His progress was necessarily quite slow, navigating by reflection; still, it was with surprising suddenness that he found himself looking at a low, humped shape that lay resting against the wall of a good-sized chamber. There could be no doubt that this was his quarry.

He took a step further, so that the sleeping shape was lit by his flickering torch; it was a dark, rich green, some seven feet long, counting the thin, pointed tail, and somehow forbidding in appearance. As he studied its reflected image, it awoke, raised its head and peered at him.

It had golden eyes, slanting, slit-pupiled eyes, eyes that caught Garth's; he froze, and tried to tear his gaze from the mirror. He could not. His eyes were dry; he could not blink. He stared fixedly at the monster's reflected face until his crimson eyes ached. Finally, the creature moved, rising to its feet, and the spell was broken. Garth closed his eyes and held them tightly shut, afraid to meet that baleful gaze again.

The image of the basilisk's eyes remained, even with his eyes shut; those hideous yellow orbs were like nothing Garth had ever seen, deep and hypnotic, tinged with an aura of knowing, timeless evil, an impression of a ghastly malign intelligence. Its stare had been the unrelenting, immobile, and utterly emotionless gaze of a serpent or lizard – and of course, the basilisk *was* a lizard. Just a lizard, Garth told himself.

Its stench was strong now; it held all the rot and decay that the catacombs lacked. It was a dry, burning smell, the smell of something long dead, or of death itself. Garth steeled himself and opened his eyes again, trying to avoid meeting the thing's reflected glare.

He looked at it as it stood, unmoving, perhaps twenty feet away. A golden ridge ran the length of its graceful, sleekly powerful body, ending in a crest atop its narrow head in the shape of a seven-pointed coronet. It had a long, narrow jaw, lined with hundreds, perhaps thousands, of small, needle-sharp teeth; a long black tongue flicked silently. Two slit nostrils breathed out a cloud of venom, a pale-silver ghost of vapor in the torchlight. It had four short, sturdy legs with long, clawed toes and, save for its huge size, much the shape of any lesser lizard. Its abominable eyes were unavoidable, though; Garth found his attention being drawn back to them, sucked in by that glittering golden smirk. He tore his gaze away once more, and felt his helmet shift. Fearful lest he should meet its eyes directly, he closed his own and this time kept them shut.

He wondered how old the thing was, and how long it had dwelt beneath Mormoreth; its eyes seemed ageless, as if they had watched the dawn of time with that same unchanging evil. He wondered also what it fed on, here in the empty, lightless, and lifeless crypts, and decided he would rather not know.

He heard a swish; the basilisk was moving. Having more respect for his life than his dignity, he turned and ran helter-skelter down the nearest corridor, only remembering at the last instant that he must not fling aside his stub of a torch; instead, he clutched it tightly as he fled.

When at length he paused, Garth carefully drew forth and lit a fresh torch from the glowing stump he held, licking at his hand where it had been slightly scorched by the flame. That done, he tried to relax, to stop the trembling induced by the sudden burst of adrenaline he had triggered; he breathed deeply and raggedly. If there were gods, he told himself, that creature did indeed serve the god of death, the one whose name was never spoken aloud. He was frightened of the basilisk as he had never before been frightened; its mere gaze induced more fear, more abject terror, than anything else he had ever seen.

He began to think that Shang was right, that the basilisk could not be captured. Further, he admired Shang's courage in entering the crypts to gather its venom, knowing what the basilisk was.

Suddenly he stopped his trembling and admonished himself fiercely that he was panicking, letting fear run away with him as if he were some mere animal, like a rabbit or a human, rather than a thinking, reasoning, and therefore supreme overman. There was nothing that could not be dealt with, he told himself sternly. He had to approach the problem objectively. He needed to capture the monster and bring it back alive; that was the basic requirement. He had to entrap it somehow, yet not touch it – as he had been entrapped in the Annamar Pass. Then his only problem would be getting it out past Shang without looking at it.

Clearly, the carved wooden rod he had taken from Dansin was perfect.

He had lost his mirror in his mad dash from the basilisk; it lay somewhere on the stone floor behind him. Fortunately, he had another. He delved into his pack and drew forth both the magic rod and the remaining mirror. He reminded himself to be more careful with these. They were almost all he had left; he had lost his sword, lost the Jewel of Blindness, broken his dagger, and now lost and most likely broken one of his mirrors. Such carelessness was inexcusable.

He had fully regained his nerve. Cautiously, with the mirror held in place with one hand while the other gripped the rod, he advanced back up the corridor, leaving his torch on the floor behind him, so that his shadow lengthened before him as he walked.

The basilisk had moved, apparently in casual pursuit of the fleeing overman. As he approached, it slid out into the corridor, its rich green armor faintly iridescent in the dim torchlight. Garth glimpsed it from the corner of his eye and turned away hurriedly before it looked at him; not caring to risk even the reflected image if he could avoid it, he closed his eyes and began fumbling with the talisman, working by feel.

When he had completed the sequence that was supposed to establish the magical barrier, he cautiously opened his eyes and studied the scene reflected in the mirror. The basilisk was still moving toward him, with a slow and regal pace as befitted the king of lizards. Abruptly it stopped, its advance halted in mid-stride. It hissed angrily, and Garth felt dizzy and ill from the monster's noxious breath. It explored to either side, and still encountered resistance; rearing up, its lighter colored belly scales flashing in the torchlight, it seemed to climb in thin air, only to slide back awkwardly. It could not climb the barrier, lizard or no.

Apparently that barrier, which could not be budged from the inside, could adjust to outside pressures, since it had narrowed to fit inside the corridor's dimensions.

Garth was satisfied. He turned his back on the basilisk and went to recover his torch. He was extremely pleased with himself; he had captured the creature, fulfilling his quest and defying Shang with the wizard's own device. All that remained was to transport the basilisk safely back to Skelleth. Of course, that might be a bit difficult. He still had to get the thing out of the crypts and beyond the city without encountering Shang. It was a great pity that he had lost the invisibility charm; even with its various disabilities, it could be useful.

He stooped and picked up the torch, then turned far enough to see the basilisk's reflection. He froze. It had come further down the corridor; it was scarcely as far away as it had been when he turned, though he had walked a dozen yards.

To his inexpressible relief, it stopped short, just as it had done before, and at the same distance. He had forgotten that the invisible wall would move as he moved, maintaining a constant distance from the generating talisman.

He caught a glimpse of the monster's eyes in the mirror, and an involuntary shudder ran through him; the calm evil in its gaze had been replaced with hatred, an emotion so intense that even Garth could not mistake it. Its regal air of detachment had vanished; its muscles were tensed with fury. The overman tore his gaze from the mirror and turned to face directly away from the monster again. Carefully, he removed the glass from its perch and wrapped it in a bit of cloth before putting it in his pack. He did not care to look at his catch again, either in reflection or directly; he reluctantly admitted to himself that he was afraid to.

The capture itself accomplished, he now had to get out. Again, he regretted that he had not thought to equip himself with a thread. Instead he would have to find his way out from memory, and without ever looking behind him; this latter necessity was stronger than any bargain or geas, it was a matter of personal survival. Yet as he began to walk he found himself possessed of a growing urge to turn and look, to make sure that his prize was still there, still secure – and no closer. Further, the thing's infernal gaze had a fascination all its own, and it took an effort of will not to seek it out.

It took him several hours to find the stairs leading up to the wine cellar; he repeatedly made wrong turns, only realizing that a corridor was unfamiliar when he had traversed half its length and having to carefully retrace his own steps backward, pressing the basilisk and its magical enclosure back-for the basilisk, though it willingly moved toward him, refused to retreat under its own power and had to be pushed along. This was done by moving the wooden rod that controlled the cage with force sufficient to move the monster, which must have weighed a good two hundred pounds. This dragging, when combined with the poisonous fumes the thing emitted and the corrosive trail its venom left on the stone floors, made any doubling back an ordeal, leaving Garth tired and weak. By the time he finally stumbled upon the steps he was exhausted and sick, his boots worn almost through by the venom-stained floors. He collapsed onto the staircase and rested for several minutes.

Rising at last, he started up the steps, and proceeded without difficulty up the first thirty or forty; then, abruptly, he lost his balance and fell back, as if an invisible hand had grabbed at him and yanked. Only by closing his eyes immediately did he avoid looking back at the basilisk. As he fell, he could hear the monster hissing angrily. Then something caught him, just as something had thrown him off balance, and he realized what it was; the talisman, which he carried in his belt, was responsible. The basilisk had followed willingly as far as the foot of the staircase, then balked. It was when the rear of the invisible cage collided with two hundred pounds of braced basilisk that he had been thrown off balance, and he had been caught again by the rod when the front of the cage encountered the basilisk, which had refused to retreat just as firmly as it had refused to climb the stairs.

It appeared that he would have to drag the creature up the winding staircase step by step. He wished Koros were here to do the hauling, though of course the huge warbeast would not have fit on the narrow stairs. Again he felt weak and sick. But telling himself it was necessary, he clambered to his feet, eyes still closed, and renewed his climb, this time moving slowly and carefully so as not to overbalance again.

As he started upward, he realized that he had lost his current torch; he opened his eyes on complete blackness. He shrugged. It mattered little, since he could scarcely go wrong from this point on. All it meant was that he was safe from the basilisk's gaze. Without thinking, he started to turn for a glance behind him. It was only the superhuman speed of an overman's reactions that stopped him in time when, as his head came around, he caught a sickly greenish glimmer; the basilisk had some luminescence of its own. Unable to resist, he rummaged in his pack and drew forth his remaining mirror; in it he saw that the creature's scales had a dim, silky blue-green phosphorescence, while its golden eyes glowed with an unnatural light that seemed as bright in the stygian gloom as the full moon at midnight. The glow enhanced the hypnotic spell of the monster's gaze. Garth had no idea what happened nor how much time passed from his first glimpse of the eerie illumination to the breaking of the mesmeric spell when the basilisk, unable to pass the protective barrier, gave up and blinked.

Instantly, when that blink came, Garth shut his own eyes and turned again. Then, after a moment for rest and recuperation, he proceeded, managing to drag the monster up onto the first step only by exerting every ounce of his remaining strength. Fortunately, the basilisk itself was unable to move the barrier, no matter how little resistance Garth provided; this was one distinct advantage the magical device had over any more usual net or cage.

Weakened as he was by the poisoned air, Garth found he had to rest several minutes after each step was surmounted. He began to lust after the scent of fresh air as he had never before lusted for anything, save in the sexual fit induced by an overwoman in heat.

To his immense relief, just as he thought he might be unable to reach the wine-cellar before losing consciousness completely and probably permanently, the basilisk gave up its resistance and began to crawl reluctantly upward under its own power. Apparently, now that it was out of sight of the crypts proper, it had decided it preferred cooperation to the tiring and probably painful struggle against the unseen and impenetrable wall that had pushed it so far. It still lingered at the lower end of the cage, but now moved upward at the first touch of the advancing barrier. Garth knew that this was the turning point, that he could make it the rest of the way now.

It was not very much later that he felt in front of himself only to scratch his outstretched hand rather painfully on one of the iron spikes set in the door that divided the crypts from the wine cellar. Upon close investigation, he noticed that there was a faint trace of light seeping in around the edges of the portal. He paused, but decided against waiting for it to vanish; it was most likely another torch accidentally left burning. Furthermore, even if Shang were just beyond, he doubted he had the stamina to wait for very long in the poisonous air of the crypts. The element of surprise would undoubtedly be on his side if he emerged immediately, and any delay could only weaken him further.

The decision made, he drew his broken dirk and worked it into the crack he had left between the door and its frame. With a slight tug, the portal swung inward. As soon as the opening was wide enough, he sprang through into the wine cellar, barely able to keep from falling headlong in his debilitated condition.

He was blinded temporarily by the sudden blaze of light after his long sojourn in complete darkness; when his sight returned, he found himself facing a wine-rack as if to impale it upon his blunted dagger. He crouched in a fighting stance and looked about.

The cellar was brightly lit, not merely by comparison with the crypts but in fact; torches flared cheerily in every bracket, though he knew he had left several of them empty. Also, it seemed that there were more empty wine-racks; less than half of those in sight held so much as a single bottle. Something had happened.

Befuddled as he was by exhaustion, the bright light, and enough basilisk venom to kill a dozen men, it was several minutes before he thought to look toward the stairs that led to the palace kitchen. When he did, he saw Shang standing at their head, leaning casually on the iron rail and watching the confused overman with sardonic amusement.

When the wizard saw Garth's gaze turn toward him, he laughed, a long and loud laugh. "Well, overman, you would appear to have survived," he said.

Garth made no answer.

"Are you ready now to concede your task impossible and to depart in peace?"

"Perhaps." Garth's voice was hoarse and unpleasant. He tried to clear his throat, with little success.

"It was rather careless of you to leave your sword cluttering up my kitchen floor, you know."

"Ah." His voice was little more than a croak. "Is that where it was?" It took an effort to make any reply at all, but his own self-respect demanded that he not let this upstart human verbally dominate him.

"I take it that your stay in my little catacomb was less than pleasant. You look quite bedraggled."

Garth did not answer; instead he began to wonder what Shang meant to do.

"It was careless to lose the Jewel of Blindness, too; at least, I assume you lost it. By now, even your slow mind would have remembered it, if you still had it, yet I can still see you."

"You speak, but make no sense."

"Do not pretend ignorance. When I see a broadsword appear from thin air before my eyes, I know that magic is in use. You brought none with you, I'm sure; the Forgotten King would not make free with his own, and everyone knows that overmen use no sorcery. So you must have taken it from that fool bandit I entrusted it to. Undoubtedly he told you how to work it, fearing your sword more than he feared my vengeance."

"Undoubtedly, save that dead men do not often trouble to explain such matters to their slayers."

"Indeed. Well, nonetheless, here you are, and you would appear to be without the Jewel. You also lack your sword, and your dagger appears damaged, which makes it rather useless. This leaves only the axe slung on your back. Would you care to match it against my magic, or will you go peacefully, giving me your word that you will not serve him whom you call the Forgotten King?"

"This axe is not my only weapon."

"No?"

"No. Permit me to show you" He stepped forward, trying to look natural as he struggled to pull the basilisk from the tunnel. To his consternation, the monster hissed in annoyance.

Shang froze. Garth grinned and gave up all pretense, struggling to drag the basilisk out into the cellar.

The wizard closed his eyes and spoke. "I trust, overman, that you have that beast under control?"

"I do, wizard."

"I assume that you turn yet another of my devices to your own ends."

"Perhaps."

"You waylaid Dansin, no doubt. I have been overconfident. When next I meet a representative of that yellow-clad demon, I will be more cautious."

"I think it unlikely you will ever meet another."

"It will not concern you in any case. You will recall that I told you I would kill you if you captured the basilisk."

"We all make foolish remarks on occasion." Garth thought that the scrabbling, scratching sounds of the basilisk's progress had changed, indicating that it was past the doorway. He did not care to look to verify the fact. He moved another foot or two, then stopped.

"Before I dispose of you, I must compliment you on your success. I was not sure that the Sealing Rod would hold such a creature."

"It works quite well, thank you."

"Have you any final words, a message for your family, perhaps?"

"I think not; I have no intention of dying." Garth wondered what Shang planned to do; he was rather limited in his actions by the need to keep from meeting the basilisk's gaze. As the overman watched, Shang reached up for the torch beside his head.

"It is a shame that your intentions will not alter the fact."

Some instinct of caution told Garth that even with his eyes shut, Shang could be deadly. He suddenly decided that a retreat would be in order.

Shang held the torch now, having found it by touch. He turned back toward the cellar and spoke three words that Garth could not understand. The words echoed unnaturally, ringing from wall to wall – magic of some kind. Closing his eyes, Garth dove for the door to the crypts, flinging the basilisk, hissing in protest, back down the stairs. He turned and looked again just in time to see Shang fling the torch amidst the wine-racks, where it exploded with a blinding flash and a wave of heat in a burst of supernatural flame that ignited the racks on all sides. They blazed up brightly, and the flames spread rapidly. Struggling with the reluctant lizard, Garth forced his way hurriedly back into the tunnel. Even there the heat was like a blast furnace. From the corner of his eye, Garth could see Shang leaving the cellar, his sleeve shielding his eyes from the painfully bright firelight. It was quite possible that he had not seen Garth flee and believed him to be trapped in the inferno that now filled the cellar. Had the torch struck nearer, or between himself and the door, he would most likely be trapped.

He found it necessary to retreat further down the stairs. This time the basilisk did not resist. It was feeling the heat as well. For his own part, Garth noticed that his breastplate bore a new mark where its finish had scorched and blackened, and that his hair was singed and crumbling. Only his leathery hide had saved him from incineration. A human would probably have died almost instantly. Shang's ignorance of the strengths of overmen might well be his undoing.

Seeing no reason to bake himself any more than necessary, Garth retreated further, stopping only when he reached the point where the basilisk was almost in sight of the bottom. Even here, he felt the heat of the flames; despite the curves in the staircase, the tunnel was lit a vivid orange around him. The flame was not magic merely in its origin, but in its nature, burning far hotter than any natural flame could, given such fuel and such a location. Garth was impressed. He wondered if those three incomprehensible words were the entire spell, or whether Shang had prepared things in advance and the words were merely a trigger. The latter would speak more highly for Shang's foresight, but the former for his magical prowess.

When the fire still burned unabated after perhaps half an hour, Garth relaxed and settled down for a long wait. It occurred to him that he might in fact be trapped permanently, but he thought it highly unlikely. Curiously, he found himself thinking more clearly and breathing more easily than he had before; the fire was apparently absorbing or consuming the basilisk's vapors somehow, while it drew cool, clear air up from the depths.

After due consideration, he decided there was nothing to be done until either the fire burned itself out or it became clear that it wasn't going to. Therefore he ate a little of his dwindling store of provisions, took a sip of water from his half-empty canteen, and went to sleep. His last waking thoughts were worried, though; the basilisk had no food or water. He had no idea whether it needed such things or not; he had seen no trace of them in the crypts. And somewhere above ground, Koros would be getting very hungry. It had been at least a day, probably much longer, since he had left the warbeast.

Chapter Eight

Although Garth had no way of keeping track of time, he was sure that at least a day, and possibly as much as three days, passed before the heat subsided sufficiently for him to risk venturing back up to the head of the stairs. His food and water were exhausted, though he had been as sparing of his meager supplies as he could tolerate in his enfeebled and overheated condition. The basilisk, as an occasional glance in the mirror revealed, showed no signs of hunger or fatigue.

He had slept only twice during this period, as his slumbers were haunted by confused dreams in which he saw again the basilisk's unspeakable gaze. On both occasions he awoke trembling, unsure of anything except that he feared those baleful eyes as he had never before feared anything.

The orange glow had died down to invisibility within the first few hours, but when Garth had mounted part way up the stairs he was stopped by the unbearable heat that remained. He retreated, but ventured up again every so often, each time going a few steps further, as the wine cellar cooled. Finally, on one such attempt he came in sight of the door-or at least where the door should be. The dull red light of the embers beyond showed him that the oaken door had burned, its iron hinges hanging limp, partially melted, from their bolts; the bolts themselves sagged. The wooden doorframe was gone, as if it had never been. The hinge-bolts protruded from bare, blackened stone.

A few attempts later, Garth was able to approach closely enough to see the black lumps of metal that dotted the uppermost steps where the spikes had fallen from the burning door. The spikes had melted into hard little puddles, still hot to the touch and half buried in fine grey ash. The red glow beyond had waned considerably.

Despite the presence of that glow, Garth decided to risk a dash across the cellar. If Shang had seen him retreat to the crypts, which seemed unlikely, he would not expect an escape attempt so soon. Furthermore, thirst was becoming a real problem.

Looking through the burnt-out doorway Garth saw, in the hellish light, that the wine cellar was evenly covered to a depth of almost a foot with fine grey ash and lumps of melted glass. Looking toward the stairs to the kitchen, he saw that the iron rail had melted away and been lost in the ash below. The red glow itself came from beneath the ash, in rows that marked where wine-racks had once stood. It gave the cellar floor the appearance of an immense grill, and lit the stone walls and arched stone ceiling eerily. By staying between the glowing areas, Garth hoped to avoid serious burns. However, he realized that his boots, scorched and shredded by basilisk venom, would give little protection. He removed his scarlet cloak and tore it in half, then used each piece to wrap one of his feet. He rather regretted the necessity of such an action; the cloak had been a gift from one of his wives, and had proven useful in the past.

He considered the basilisk, and decided he had no means of protecting it; he would just have to hope that it could survive the brief roasting. He would be slowed down by its weight, at least until he had gone far enough to force it out into the ash. From that point on it should move quickly enough. The monster had already demonstrated that, though stubborn, it was far from stupid.

When his feet were as well protected as he could manage, he nerved himself, took a deep breath, and set out.

The ash was finer than he had thought; his every step stirred up a grey cloud. The air was too hot to breathe. His feet were baking, his entire body was baking in his armor; his eyes were dry, the hot air distorted everything, and flakes of ash were blinding him. The basilisk was a two-hundred-pound drag; he could barely move it. A misstep, and his foot touched a live coal. The cloth covering flared up briefly, then died again as ash smothered the flame, though it still felt as if it were on fire.

Finally, when he knew that he could not go much further, he was at the stairs. He clambered up the first three, out of the carpet of hot ash, and leaned against the wall. It, too, was hot; he removed his hand quickly. His burnt foot was agonizing. The first thing he saw when his eyes were clear of cinders was smoke rising from the blackened cloth. A closer investigation showed that the bottom of the wrapping was still on fire, a smoldering line of sparks in an irregular and expanding circle revealing the scorched layer beneath. As quickly as he could manage, Garth untied the binding cords and stripped away the smoking rags; underneath, his boot was also black and smoldering, the sole gone completely. He tore it off, then turned to the other foot. It was better, but not much; that boot, too, had to go, tossed into the hot ash below.

His bare feet were uncomfortable on the hot stone of the steps; he moved further up the staircase. As he did, he heard a violent hissing from the far side of the cellar. Remembering at the last minute not to look, he backed down again. Apparently the basilisk had not yet been forced out of the tunnel.

For the first time since he had trapped the monster, he drew out the wooden rod that controlled the invisible barrier and placed it on the third step from the bottom, sweeping away the thin layer of ash. That freed him to move about, while the basilisk remained confined. When he had scouted out the kitchen, he would return and retrieve the talisman.

Limping, favoring his badly scorched left foot, he climbed the stairs. The door at the top was closed.

It had not burned, however; it was lined with steel, and the heat had apparently been insufficient to melt it this far from the main blaze. It was still too hot to touch. Further, the padlock on the other side was apparently in place.

With a growl of annoyance, Garth unslung his axe; there was little room to swing on the railless steps, but he had no alternative.

It took several swings to break through the steel and the wood beyond, but in the end it was done, though the axe's edge was dulled. Once he had a small opening, it was a matter of a few seconds to shatter the rest of the door to kindling and scrap. Unfortunately, as Garth well knew, the noise would undoubtedly bring Shang.

As the last chunk of door flew from the twisted hinges, Garth observed several things simultaneously: The kitchen was flooded with morning sunlight, a bright, cheerful room much as he remembered it; his sword lay on a nearby table; several mirrors had been set up, so that anything emerging from the wine-cellar was confronted with its own image repeated perhaps a dozen times; Shang stood in an open doorway; and the wizard held a cloudy amber disk in his upraised right hand.

Acting instinctively, Garth flung his axe and dove for his sword. His wounded foot betrayed him, and he fell awkwardly to the floor, halfway beneath the table he had meant to reach, while his axe missed the wizard by several inches. Shang ducked as the axe flew by, a matter of reflex; he had been in no danger. As the weapon fell rattling to the floor, the wizard laughed.

"A poor throw, overman." He raised the disk again.

Although Garth had no idea what the thing was, it was plainly a weapon of some sort; in desperation, he drew and flung his broken dagger, momentarily forgetting its blunted tip. Luck was with him; despite its altered balance, the knife flew truly and struck the disk broadside. Had the disk been solid there would have been no result, but it was thin crystal and shattered spectacularly as the flat of the blade hit. Shang screamed as a yellow cloud of something between liquid and vapor settled seething over his hand. Garth caught the now-familiar odor of the basilisk.

Since Shang was plainly incapacitated for the moment, Garth clambered to his feet, leaning heavily on the table, and snatched up his sword; armed, he faced the wizard again.

Garth had hoped that the poison would kill the wizard, but it had not;

instead, Shang clutched a blackened stump where his right hand and forearm had been. He glared at Garth, his eyes glittering. Garth guessed that glitter to be pain and hatred made manifest.

"Overman," Shang said, his voice hoarse with agony, "I had meant your death to be quick and painless, a simple transformation; but now you will die slowly."

Garth saw no point in answering a dead man; he knew that, if he were to live, Shang had to die. He made no reply, but approached the crippled and unarmed wizard with raised sword.

He never reached him. Shang made a curious gesture with his remaining hand, and the overman froze in midstride; his muscles would not respond. Despite his mental struggle, his sword began to descend, his limbs to sag; he drooped forward, then fell numbly to the flagstone floor. There was no sensation at all, no pain, no shock as he hit the stone, only the crash of his armor and the rattle of his dropped sword.

"The Cold Death is slow, overman, but it is not excessively painful. I trust that, should we chance to meet in Hell, you will not hold my actions against me. Do not bother to struggle; nothing can break the spell while I live and will it. You will only hasten the end by tiring yourself."

Garth heard these words faintly, as though from a great distance. He was losing touch with the outside world, and even with his own body. The pain in his foot was gone; he could no longer feel the heat of his armor; his vision was dimming.

His sense of time faded with the rest, and he had no idea how long he lay motionless on the kitchen floor, staring at the leg of a table; he knew only that his flesh was growing colder, that he was dying. It did not hurt; Shang had been right about that. Garth would have preferred pain, however, to the gradual cessation of feeling that he was experiencing. He had a profound sense of his impotence in the face of this sorcerous death at first, but then this, too, began to fade. His physical sensations were utterly gone, leaving him adrift in total void, where his memories and emotions were also beginning to fade.

Something happened; the spell was disturbed. His sight flickered briefly back into existence, and with it the strength to turn his head. He did, and saw Shang turning away. Hearing returned, and he could make out Shang's worried muttering and a distant crashing.

Something was happening, something that had seriously distracted the enchanter.

Then something huge and black flashed through the open door behind Shang, and abruptly the wizard was gone, lost in a ferocious assault of claws and teeth and fur; his screams were swallowed in the hungry growls of the warbeast that had attacked him. Before Garth's dulled eyes, the huge wizard was torn into pieces and devoured.

Although Garth was too far-gone in the depths of the Cold Death to feel any surprise, his first conscious thought was that he might have anticipated such a thing. It had clearly been days since Koros was fed.

Shang had left one loose end too many; typically careless human behavior.

Then his thoughts were interrupted by the first twinge as sensation began to return, and for several long minutes he was unaware of anything except pain.

The return to life was hideously painful, infinitely more so than the slow approach to death had been. His entire body burned with a sensation akin to the stinging felt when a frostbitten member is thawed too quickly, save that it was everywhere in his flesh, and a thousand times more intense. He imagined that even his bones were aching, and whenever he thought the agony was diminishing it would suddenly return, worse than ever.

It was extremely fortunate that Shang had been so large and so plump; a smaller, more typical human would have been insufficient to satisfy the warbeast's hunger, and Garth was hardly in any condition to resist should his mount decide to devour the overman in addition to its first victim.

When at last the after-effects of the Cold Death had subsided to occasional fits of trembling and a generalized weakness and nausea, Garth opened his eyes to see Koros standing calmly a few feet away, contentedly licking the marrow from a broken thighbone. The light seemed dim. He struggled to his feet and rubbed his eyes; the light *was* dim. The kitchen was lit from the east, and the sun was now well past its zenith, so that the chamber was grey and shadowed. That alone told Garth how long he had lain fighting off Shang's final spell. Judging by the altered light and a glance at the shadows visible through the window, the experience had taken the better part of a day, at least six or seven hours.

Which, he realized, meant that the basilisk had been unattended in the burnt-out, stifling-hot cellar for half a day. He started for the shattered cellar door, then stopped, uncertain; how was he to keep Koros from petrifaction?

He looked at the immense beast, and his uncertainty grew. He was not even sure he dared to approach the animal. However, it was plain that he would have to. Cautiously, he retrieved his sword from where it lay and neared the creature. It turned from its morsel and studied him. He could read nothing in its eyes; its catlike gaze, though it held none of the hypnotic horror of the basilisk's, was equally inscrutable, less interpretable even than human emotions, though Garth assumed the warbeast to be a simple and straightforward creature in its behavior when compared with the twisted motivations of men and women.

It did not growl, which encouraged him. Not wanting to antagonize it, he sheathed his sword; the weapon would have been little use against so powerful an adversary in any case, and it was surely intelligent enough to know a weapon when it saw one.

Something in its manner changed, becoming more familiar and reassuring; it seemed less tense.

He said, "Koros . . . beast . . ." then stopped; it understood only commands, and he did not know what command to give. Finally, he arrived at the obvious. "Come here, beast."

Obediently, the monster stretched itself, a leg at a time, and trotted the pace or two necessary to bring its black-furred muzzle a few inches from Garth's face. It blinked and made a low noise in its throat that the overman knew to be an expression of satisfaction or pleasure.

Greatly reassured, Garth patted the huge head and told it, "We go." He pointed to the door through which it had entered, and Koros promptly turned and led the way. Which was, Garth told himself, just as well, since he had no idea of the best route out of the palace.

Looking monstrous and out of place, like a kitten in a doll-house, the warbeast led its master back through a series of dim rooms, tapestried and ornate chambers, until they emerged blinking into the light of the setting sun, which shone pinkly on the white marble walls and the empty marketplace. Descending the three steps to street level, Garth looked about. There were no signs of life. Silence reigned; not so much as a gust of wind could be heard. Regret brought a sigh to Garth's lips; he had hoped that Shang's death would revive the people of Mormoreth, but it had plainly failed to do so. Perhaps, since it was the basilisk's venom that had powered his magic, the spell could be broken by the slaying of the basilisk, but quite aside from the fact that he had agreed to bring it back alive, he had no idea how to go about killing the monster, nor even if it was possible at all. But then again, perhaps some magicks were permanent, deriving from external energies rather than their wielders' personal force.

It suddenly occurred to him that the wooden rod had better have a source of power other than its creator, or else he had not captured the basilisk but merely brought it up and freed it.

Turning, he ordered Koros, "Wait." He remounted the palace steps and retraced his path to the kitchen. He noticed in the entry hall, as he had not before, the ruined remains of the great golden door that Koros had battered down in its pursuit of fresh meat; the gems had been scattered about the floor, the beaten gold torn from its frame in broad, twisted segments, the solid oaken frame clawed to splinters, as if an entire army had set out to destroy it rather than a single underfed animal. Garth imagined the fury of the warbeast's attack, and shuddered. How, he wondered, could so much raw strength belong to a single animal? And why did such an animal submit to the control of an overman it could kill with a single blow?

Such questions were worrisome and irrelevant; he forgot them, and limped back to the cellar entrance.

It was curious. The warbeast had not harmed anything in the intervening rooms; not a single chair or table was upset, not a single tapestry or ornament damaged. Yet there was the door, and in the kitchen there was Shang. Or rather, there were a few tattered scraps of his gold-embroidered robe, and a few broken bones, as well as smears and spatters of dried blood. Little more remained. A few slivers of glass and a venom-coated broken dagger marked the spot where the wizard had stood when Garth shattered his crystal device, and an upset table was evidence that Koros had not brought him down instantly, but had had a brief struggle. It was a poor end for a man who had thought himself powerful. There was not even enough for any sort of ritual interment; even Shang's skull had been shattered. The largest fragment remaining was half a jawbone.

It was, Garth supposed, rather ghastly; he had heard the term, and it seemed to apply. The scene had very little emotional impact on him, however, in its physical detail. He had been confronted with gorier events in the past, involving his own kind. Rather, it was the symbolic significance which affected him. Shang had been a man seeking power and glory who had achieved a measure of both, apparently; yet he was now just as dead as any creature that died, and just as powerless. Garth had little doubt that Shang would be forgotten in a few years.

That was the fate he had made his bargain to avoid.

Chapter Nine

Pausing at the cellar doorway, Garth reached in his pack for his mirror. He didn't find it; instead he cut a thumb on a razor-sharp shard of glass. The mirror had been shattered by one of the falls he had taken that morning.

Turning back to the kitchen, he once again observed the array of mirrors Shang had set up; they were, as yet, an unexplained mystery. Perhaps they had been somehow intended as a defense against the basilisk. That seemed unreasonable to Garth; surely, if he could tolerate the reflection of the monster's gaze, such a reflection couldn't bother the basilisk itself. Still, Shang must have had something in mind.

Therefore, Garth collected the mirrors and stacked them face down in a corner, taking the smallest to replace his own shattered glass. This done, he made his way cautiously down the cellar stairs, keeping his eyes fixed on the mirror. He wished that the iron railing were still there; he was decidedly unsteady on his scorched bare feet.

The vast chamber was still unbearably hot, but the red glow had died. Garth found himself in gloom alleviated only by the dim grey light that trickled in through the broken doorway. He had to grope to find the talisman. His hand fell upon it at last, and he picked it up, moving back up a step or two, further from the hot ashes that still covered the bottom treads.

The basilisk hissed in annoyance; it was still alive and still confined. Garth breathed a sigh of relief. He considered leaving the creature where it was while he devised a cover for its magical enclosure, but decided that it would be better to remove it from the heat. He had not seen it, and its hissing sounded as healthy as ever, but he doubted it could be happy where it was.

Thus decided, he began hauling the resisting talisman up the steps, struggling to keep his footing. His progress was slow, and he found it necessary to drop his mirror so that his hands were free to use in steadying himself. He closed his eyes and inched upward, dropping to his hands and knees as his tortured soles protested.

The basilisk hissed again, more loudly; in fact, it kept up a steady racket for several minutes, until he was clambering out into the kitchen once more, when it abruptly ceased. He feared that the creature had succumbed, but dared not look back to see. Instead he proceeded on through the open door to the next room, and was immensely relieved when the resistance on the wooden rod suddenly vanished, indicating that the basilisk was again moving under its own power. Once he had that confirmation of its survival, he put down the talisman and shut the door, so that he would not accidentally meet the monster's gaze.

Now he needed something to cover the invisible cage with, or at the very least to rig an opaque barrier of some sort to keep between the warbeast and the basilisk. A large piece of fabric, or several such pieces sewn together, would be perfect. He looked at the tapestries that hung on every wall, but rejected them; they were heavy, and would add too much weight to Koros' burden. A better supply of fabric was available.

He found his way to the entry hall again, and out into the square. The sun had set, and the long shadows were blending into the gathering twilight. Koros was waiting, obediently. It growled slightly upon seeing its master emerge. Garth heard the sound and recognized it as a growl of hunger rather than greeting; already it had digested much of its most recent victim, and had yet to fully make up for its prolonged fast. It was, Garth decided, warning him.

He approached it, patted its muzzle, and stroked its triangular, catlike ears. It made no sound, but merely flattened its ears back against its broad skull. It was not in a mood to properly appreciate such gestures. Garth removed his hand and told it, "Hunt."

Immediately it pricked up its ears again, turned, and trotted away down the avenue that led to the city gate. It would be a long time before it returned, Garth was certain; there was no game to be found in Mormoreth Valley. It would have to find its way to the mountains, track and kill sufficient wildlife to satisfy its vast appetite, then return. Such an enterprise would give him more than enough time to sew a covering from the canopies and curtains of the market's abandoned merchants' stalls.

It was, he discovered, very pleasant to sit and rest, to get off his mistreated feet. He reposed briefly on the palace steps, watching the crimson sunset fade from the western sky, as he considered what he needed. He was unsure of the exact dimensions of the enclosure, most particularly of its height; it seemed to extend for perhaps thirty feet, and could be assumed to be circular. It was at least seven feet high, as he recalled from the occasion in the Annamar Pass when he had been the one enclosed. He would assume that such was its size. If it were less, the extra fabric could drag, or be trimmed away; if it were more, additional cloth could be sewn on. It would take several of the canopies, most of which were less than ten feet across.

He would need needle and thread, of course, but those could doubtless be found in the chambers formerly occupied by the palace women.

The journey back to Skelleth would need provisions, as well; the thought reminded him that he was ravenously hungry. It had been so long since he last ate that he had grown used to the aching in his belly and come to ignore it – particularly since he had been kept busy by other concerns.

One of which had led him to leave the basilisk in the kitchen. A nuisance, that. Still, upon consideration, he decided that food was his first priority. There was no longer any need for haste.

It proved, upon mirrored investigation, that the basilisk was asleep in a corner. Garth did not disturb it by moving the barrier, but crept in as quietly as he could and ransacked those cabinets not cut off by the invisible enclosure. The selection was somewhat limited, since the wall made perhaps a fourth of the cupboards inaccessible, but the overman found several shelves of wine, a large quantity of salted beef sewn in linen to prevent insects from contaminating it, several baskets of reasonably fresh fruit, and other viands sufficient to provide him with a feast such as he had rarely enjoyed. He lost track of time sometime after he had moved his booty into the next room, shut the kitchen door, and lit several candles. He was aware at one point that he had drunk more wine than was wise, and at another that he was extraordinarily sleepy, but most of the evening was simply a blur. He awoke the next day wrapped comfortably in a thick woolen tapestry depicting several nude women dancing about a fountain, with a pain in his belly, a dry throat, and vague memories of unpleasant dreams full of evil, reptilian eyes. The sun was pouring through the courtyard windows, and a glance at the angle told him that it was almost noon. The candles he had lit had all burned down to puddles of congealed wax.

He started to rise, then abruptly changed his mind; the burns on his feet had developed into an oozing, peeling mass of blisters.

Ruefully considering this, it struck him how little life resembled the tales told of past heroes. In the stories, when a quest had attained its goal and those opposing the hero had been slain, the story was at an end. There was never any mention made of difficulties in getting the object of the quest back home.

Wincing, he managed to struggle to his feet. A nearby table held the remains of the preceding night's banquet, and he scraped together a satisfactory breakfast from the leftovers. After he had eaten the ache in his belly was less, though still there – undoubtedly the result of gorging himself after a fast, stretching the stomach unmercifully. Half a bottle of some unfamiliar golden wine removed the dryness from his throat. He began to feel somewhat better, despite the mess his feet were in. His head seemed remarkably clear now that he was no longer suffering from exhaustion and the peripheral vapors of the basilisk. He rather dreaded the necessity of opening the kitchen door eventually; the atmosphere in there must be quite unhealthy by now.

Fortunately, it could still be put off. He had not yet made a cover for the invisible cage, and that would take a good bit of time. Reluctantly he rose from his breakfast and, tottering on his blisters, set out in search of a needle and thread strong enough for his purpose.

After an hour's search he located a needle and supply of heavy thread in a back storeroom, apparently intended for the repair of saddles; it seemed perfect. He limped back across the courtyard and out into the market, blinking in the noon sun, and began collecting fallen canopies.

Koros returned from its hunt when the shadows were of a length equal with their sources, the hour of midafternoon. Garth had sewn together a dozen large pieces of fabric into a gaily patterned circle a good fifty feet across, and was debating with himself as to whether it would be sufficient. Koros' return decided him; he would risk it, and maybe get a start on his journey to Skelleth.

He wondered what the warbeast had found to eat. It seemed well fed, though there was little or none of the usual blood on its mouth. It didn't matter, of course, as long as the animal was satisfied.

It would be necessary to get Koros out of sight of the market temporarily while the cover was put on the cage. Garth had already decided that it would be impractical to try and cover the enclosure while it was still in the palace, where it would become entangled at every doorway. The barrier seemed to pass through walls as if they weren't there, but the cover, being ordinary cloth, would not be so cooperative.

He led the warbeast to a convenient alley and instructed it to wait. Then it was a matter of mere minutes to fetch the basilisk out and drape the covering over the enclosure. It fit admirably; the cage proved to be about thirty feet in diameter and ten feet high, as he had guessed, so that the skirts of the cover were easily made to touch ground on all sides but did not drag more than a few inches. They did tend to flap somewhat in the breeze, so Garth took the time to lash the chains he had carried in his pack throughout the entire adventure in place at the bottom edges, gratified to be getting some use from them after having gone to the trouble of dragging them about for so long. The added weight acted to keep the cover exactly in place. Standing back a few paces, Garth admired his handiwork; the basilisk could not be seen, and Koros was safe—and so was he. He could look around without worrying about mirrors and such. All there was to be seen was a large cylindrical tent. The basilisk apparently didn't much like its new habitat; it was hissing angrily in protest. He ignored its complaints; he had only agreed to bring it back alive, not to bring it back happy and contented.

It was a matter of minutes to summon Koros, tuck the wooden talisman securely into the warbeast's harness, and mount, removing at long last the weight on his feet. He had become so used to walking on them that the lessening of that pain resulted in a burst of euphoria, as if he were pleasantly drunk. He felt like singing; unfortunately, he knew no songs, and doubted he could carry a tune if he did. Overmen were notoriously unmusical. Instead he chanted, reciting an elaborately bloodthirsty historical saga that he had learned as a child. As Koros strode through the streets of Mormoreth toward the ruined city gate, Garth lost himself in chanting the tale of one of his own ancestors who had single-handedly held a city in the long-ago Racial Wars between men and overmen, the wars that had driven the outnumbered overmen into the Northern Waste.

He had done it, he told himself between stanzas; he had captured the basilisk, and was now riding comfortably with his quarry dragging behind him, its tentlike covering apparently moving of its own power as it followed Koros without any visible attachment. He was safe from the wizard Shang; though he had not truly defeated him, nonetheless the wizard was dead and no longer a threat. He was well fed, his wounds were minor and healing. Life seemed very pleasant.

This happy mood could not last; it was ruined when he reached the city gates and realized that the basilisk's carefully prepared enclosure would not fit through them. Garth broke off his chant in annoyance. It proved necessary to lead Koros well away along the curvature of the city walls, then to drag the cloth covering off and out the gate, then to move the enclosure out and reassemble the whole affair. After the brief respite, the pain in his feet was worse than ever; he limped badly as he struggled with the recalcitrant basilisk and its uncooperative cage. When he was again mounted and moving, he turned sidesaddle and did what he could to clean and bandage the ruined soles, which were now oozing blood and pus in equal and copious amounts. The sun was well down the western sky, and the shadows did nothing to aid him. In all, when he at last turned his face forward once more, he had little inclination to resume his chant. Instead he began to wonder blackly what the Forgotten King could want with a basilisk.

It seemed quite plain that the old man had known all along what Garth would encounter. Why else would he have sent the overman on such an errand? There was no point in wondering *how* he had known that the only living thing in the crypts was a basilisk; he had known, most likely through magic. Further, he had not told Garth. Why? To avoid frightening him into abandoning the bargain? It seemed unlikely that the Forgotten King had so badly misjudged his new servant. No, the old man had wanted Garth to be ill prepared. Two possibilities came of that conclusion: either the King had wanted Garth to fail, to die attempting the almost-impossible task, or he had wanted to provide a severe test of Garth's resourcefulness. Perhaps it was a combination; perhaps the task was intended to end in either success or death. The former would prove Garth to the King, and the latter would remove a nuisance.

But there must be thousands of possible quests that would serve such an end; it would have been much simpler to order him to duel to the death with some formidable antagonist. The King must have some use for the basilisk, then, or maybe he considered Shang to be an enemy. No, in that case he would have sent Garth to kill Shang. He had some use for the basilisk.

What possible use is a basilisk?

It provided an unlimited supply of poison, of course, and could be used to turn people to stone; that was why Shang had wanted it. Could the Forgotten King be planning to do to Skelleth what Shang did to Mormoreth? If so, Garth wanted no part of it. Or perhaps he intended to use the basilisk against someone else; the High King at Kholis, perhaps, or worst of all, against Garth's own people, to finish what the Racial Wars started three hundred years ago.

Whatever the old man had in mind, Garth had little doubt it was something evil; it was hard to imagine how the basilisk could be used for anything that was not in essence evil. It was a creature of death. As he had told himself in the crypts, if there were gods, the basilisk served the god of death, the being humans called the Final God. He tried to recall everything he knew of that god; there was very little. There was a myth that any being who spoke the true name of the Death-God would die instantly, unless he had already sold himself to an evil power. Also, the Final God had brothers and sisters. Garth had no idea what the forbidden name might be, nor which of the thousands of gods were kin to Death.

If the basilisk were in truth a creature of the Death-God, then did the Forgotten King serve him as well? If so, Garth thought, he might well come to regret his bargain. He wanted no truck with the forces of evil; they were already far too strong for his liking. If he had to sell his life for the immortality of his name, he might settle for a lesser degree of fame.

He would have to discuss matters more thoroughly with the Forgotten King.

The sun was down before he had covered a third of the distance to the foothills of the Annamar Pass, but Garth ignored the darkness and kept Koros moving, dragging the huge cloth cage down the highway. Even in the darkness it was hard to lose one's way, since the road was bounded on either side by high grass. An occasional glance backward in the gathering gloom showed that the vegetation in the unkept roadway and for a few feet on either side withered and died as the basilisk's cage passed over it, further proof, were any needed, of the virulence of the monster's poison.

It was some time around midnight that Garth reached the spot where he had camped before entering Mormoreth, where he had separated from Elmil. It seemed as good a place as any to spend the remainder of the night, he decided. It took perhaps five minutes to unburden the warbeast and secure the Sealing Rod, and five seconds to fall asleep. His last waking thought was to wonder what use the Forgotten King had in mind for the basilisk.

His sleep was uneasy, troubled once again by dreams in which his eyes met the basilisk's gaze, dreams of feeling once again the numbness of the Cold Death as the monster and the Forgotten King watched him perish. Finally, he awoke, to find Elmil standing over him, propped on a rude crutch, with a sword naked in his hand.

He started to rise, but stopped when the bandit made a threatening motion with his sword. Reluctantly, he lay back.

"Greetings, overman."

Garth said nothing.

"You broke your word. I thought the word of an overman was good."

Astonished, Garth said nothing. His eyes widened slightly, but Elmil, having as little experience with overmen as Garth had with humans, noticed nothing.

"Have you an explanation?"

"I am unaware as to how I broke my word."

"You swore that you would not slay Dansin."

"I did not slay Dansin."

"You swore your beast would not slay Dansin."

Garth started to speak, then halted. He had not foreseen such a possibility. He would have to be more careful when setting Koros free to hunt – assuming he lived long enough to do anything. Choosing his words carefully, he said, "I did not order it to slay Dansin."

"Yet it did so."

"I was not aware of this"

Elmil's voice was controlled and steady. Garth could not tell if the bandit was suppressing fear, or rage, or hatred, or was merely tensing in preparation for the kill. "Your beast devoured Dansin without provocation, though you swore it would not."

"It was hungry."

"So you let it feed on my comrade?"

"I did not know what it ate. I was in Mormoreth. I had been trapped in the crypts beneath the palace for several days, and Koros had not been fed. It killed and ate Shang, but was still hungry. I set it free to hunt. I did not know that it would kill Dansin, nor even that he was in the area. Had I not let it hunt, it might have turned on me."

The point of Elmil's sword moved slightly away from Garth's throat. "Shang is dead?"

"Yes."

"You killed him?"

"Koros killed him."

"What is in that tent?" He nodded toward the magic cage.

"The basilisk."

"Basilisk?"

"The monster I was sent to capture."

"What kind of monster?"

"A very poisonous one. Its gaze will turn one to stone."

Elmil said nothing.

"It was the basilisk that permitted Shang to turn the people of Mormoreth to stone. He collected its venom."

"I don't believe it."

"Then look for yourself."

Elmil managed a feeble grin. "Maybe I do believe you, after all."

"Good. May I get up?"

Elmil hobbled back and permitted Garth to sit up. Remembering the sorry condition of his feet, the overman declined to stand.

"You still broke your word."

"True, though it was unintentional. My apologies, though I realize they can do little to comfort you or Dansin."

"It is the custom among my people to pay for a man's death."

"I have little to give for blood-money." An idea struck him. "Except, that is, for the city of Mormoreth, which I took from Shang. Will you accept the city as weregild?"

It was Elmil's turn to be astonished.

"As you know, the people of Mormoreth are no more and, now that Shang is dead, the city is empty. It's a good city, though there are a few broken doors and rather a lot of statues."

"It is a farmer's city." The barbarian's tone was uncertain, belying his words of rejection.

"Cannot bandits learn farming? Surely it's a more profitable trade, and it is definitely safer."

Elmil grinned. "Very well, Garth Oath-Breaker, we will accept your payment for Dansin's life."

"Good."

"The sun is well up. Will you be riding soon?"

"I suppose I shall."

"Perhaps I will accompany you as far as the South Road."

"If you wish."

"It will be a great surprise to my tribe to hear that we now own the Valley of Mormoreth."

"You paid heavily for it; eleven of your tribesmen are dead."

"True. Those of us who survive will have to take extra wives to compensate."

Garth was unsure whether this was a joke, a fact to be regretted or a pleasurable circumstance, so he said nothing. Human sexuality was utterly incomprehensible to him.

The conversation ceased, and Garth rose, limping, to saddle Koros.

Chapter Ten

Nine days later Garth halted his warbeast as Skelleth came into sight in the distance; he did not care to ride boldly into the village dragging the basilisk's enclosure. For one thing, he doubted it would fit through the narrow, winding streets. For another, such a spectacle would undoubtedly stir up all manner of gossip, and he doubted very much that the Forgotten King would appreciate that. There was also the possibility that some fool would peer under the cloth cover, which was becoming somewhat bedraggled. It had rained twice on the journey home, a foretaste of the spring rains that were due any day now, and the cloth had stretched and sagged while wet. Mud had spattered all along its lower edge, and the constant friction where the chains dragged on the ground had worn away small patches here and there, though fortunately not enough to provide a view of the interior. In all, the thing looked a mess, though it was still serviceable, and Garth's esthetic pride also contributed somewhat to his disinclination to parade through the streets with such a thing trailing behind him.

Recalling his first entry into Skelleth, he decided that it would not even do to ride Koros; if he wanted to avoid being the cause of a crowd of onlookers, he would have to sneak into town on foot, looking as small and human as he could manage. Therefore he would have to leave Koros and the basilisk somewhere where he could find them again but passers-by would not. He knew Koros would keep anyone who happened along at a distance no matter where he left it, even right where it was in the middle of the highway. He wanted not merely to keep the basilisk safe, but to keep it undetected. Glancing about, he made out a rather scraggly copse off to his left, and decided it would provide the best cover of anything on the muddy, lightly farmed plain surrounding Skelleth.

Ten minutes later he was glad that the cloth had been muddied, as the mud provided some degree of camouflage; the weather-beaten little trees of the copse could hardly hide so large an object by themselves. Having ordered Koros to guard the spot, he turned and headed again toward the village, wearing a rough grey cloak he had pieced together from his bolt of cloth to hide his armor and weapons, and with rags tied around his otherwise bare feet to protect them from pebbles and to hide the coarse black fur that covered them. Fortunately, his burns had healed almost completely on the trek from Mormoreth.

This arrangement had another advantage, he realized; he would be able to inquire as to why the Forgotten King wanted the basilisk. Should he be planning some great evil, Garth could withhold his knowledge of the monster's whereabouts, which he could not have done had he simply hauled the creature directly into town.

It was an hour's walk to the East Gate, and Garth spent the time considering the most tactful way to coax the Forgotten King into explaining what he wanted with what was undoubtedly the most deadly creature in the world. It did little good; his mind did not readily lend itself to verbal subtlety in such matters.

There was no guard at the gate; there had been none when he left, either. Garth was not surprised. There had been very few wars in his lifetime or that of his father, save for minor squabbles and pirate raids, and there was nothing in Skelleth worth fighting for in any case. Such a village, in such a desolate region, had little need for guards. However, when he had passed the ruins into the part of the town that was still inhabited, he was surprised to see the streets empty. It was midafternoon, and he would have expected to find women on their way to market, farmers trading with villagers, and dogs and children playing in the street. Instead the streets were deserted.

But they were not quite silent. Garth could hear, coming from somewhere ahead, the sound of a good-sized crowd. It grew louder as he proceeded, and was apparently coming from the market-square in front of the Baron's mansion. Although it would be possible to reach the King's Inn without crossing the square, Garth's curiosity was aroused; he continued toward the sound. As he neared, when the next corner would bring him in sight of the market, the sound suddenly changed from the muttering of a milling, waiting crowd to an expectant hush. The event, whatever it was, was beginning.

He turned the corner and found himself looking at the backs of a dozen people. The whole village had apparently turned out. As unobtrusively as possible, he joined them, and peered over the heads in front of him.

There was a platform in the center of the square, perhaps six feet off the ground and ten feet wide. Three men were on it, two of them standing and the third kneeling before a block of wood. The kneeling man wore the mail shirt and leather breeches of the town's men-at-arms, and was very young and very pale. He seemed upset about something, though Garth's limited understanding of human emotions and expressions prevented him from recognizing the lad's abject terror. The standing men were very different. One was rather fat, wore a black robe, carried a double-bladed axe that Garth assumed to be ceremonial, as it was not sturdy enough in construction to use in battle, and had a rather blank look to his face, while the other, who was decidedly thin and somewhat shorter than average, wore a gaudy tunic of red and gold and an expression that Garth guessed to be resentment. The latter had his hands clasped behind his back and, Garth noticed, a gold circlet on his head. It was he who spoke.

"By virtue of the hereditary grant given my father by Seremir, third of that name, High King at Kholis of Eramma, and by my accession to my father's lands, properties, and titles as enacted in law upon his death, I, Doran of Skelleth, son of Talenn, am rightful Baron of the village and lands of Skelleth and the Northern Waste. As such I am charged with the keeping of the law, with the protection of my realm and the realm of Eramma under the High King, and with the maintenance and promotion of the public welfare." This speech was recited in a sing-song tone; obviously, it was a ritual to be recited before taking an official action, though Garth had no idea what action was about to take place.

"It has been established that Arner, son of Karlen, has disobeyed my laws and orders given for the good of the state, in that he deserted his assigned post without permission. Therefore, as is my right and duty, I hereby decree that he suffer the punishment I have deemed fitting for such an offense and be put to death." He hesitated, briefly, as if unsure of what he wanted to say next. An angry mutter ran through the crowd. Garth, shocked by the realization that he was watching a public execution, stood utterly motionless. Part of his mind was telling him that he should have known all along. What else could such an axe be for? A headsman's axe did not need to cut armor nor parry weapons, so it could be lighter and more fragile than a battle-axe and still serve its purpose.

The Baron's speech was continuing. "Furthermore, inasmuch as the condemned did flee from lawful imprisonment, it is my right and duty to levy further penalties, which in such a case can only be made manifest in the manner of death. However, I have declined to have the condemned put to torture or death by slow fire, but have instead decreed that his death be swift and painless." The Baron's expression was very curious as he said this. Garth could make no sense of it at all. "Further, as is customary, I grant the condemned the right to speak here before the townspeople, though ordinarily this privilege is not granted to a recaptured fugitive. I am being as merciful as the law allows. In exchange, I hope that the condemned will reveal the names of those who assisted his escape, and that he shall forgive me for his death." These last few words seemed strained, as if the man were making a great effort in speaking them. Garth found himself wondering why the Baron was making such a speech; surely it was more than the law required.

"The condemned may speak," announced the black-robed executioner.

Arner, his expression still panic-stricken, though Garth did not recognize it as such, looked desperately out over the crowd. He licked his lips and tried to speak.

"I . . . I . . . I wish to apologize for whatever wrongs I have done. I beg to live, my lord; but I will not . . . I will not say who aided my escape, for they acted from mercy." The Baron was standing totally motionless, his face frozen, his jaw clenched. The crowd was utterly silent. Garth began to suspect that they were not happy with Arner's imminent death. But desertion, he knew, was ordinarily punished with death. He was puzzled. Why should Arner be an exception? Or rather, why should the villagers want Arner to be an exception?

Arner was speaking again, more strongly this time; his fear had apparently lessened. "The Baron has asked my forgiveness. I will grant it." The Baron looked surprised, an expression much the same in humans and overmen. Arner was addressing the crowd now, rather than the two men beside him on the platform. "It makes no difference in any case, for what can the forgiveness of a single soul avail when our Baron has sold himself to the Dark Gods?" A murmur arose. A suspicion appeared in Garth's mind; was Arner trying to incite a riot, an attempt to free him by the population of the entire town? "The Baron who rules our village is in the service of the Lords of Evil! He has brought madness upon himself and woe upon our village! Does he not kill someone every spring, whether they deserve it or not? It is a sacrifice! Why does our trade lessen, and our people starve? Because the evil gods will it, and the Baron allows it! He will execute me, yet he allows overmen to walk our streets unmolested!"

Arner's speech was suddenly cut short. In response to a gesture from the Baron, the executioner had clapped a hand across the prisoner's mouth. Beside him, the lord of Skelleth was visibly trembling.

Bringing himself under control, the Baron announced, "The right of the condemned to speak does not allow him to commit further crimes. I will allow Arner to speak further if he will refrain from seditious slander. Although it is not my place to debate with criminals, I must insist that I am not in league with evil gods, and I will not permit it to be said that I am. Furthermore, it was not *I* who permitted an overman to enter Skelleth unescorted, but Arner himself. Otherwise he would not be here. Arner, you may continue."

Arner ceased struggling, and the executioner removed his hand. The condemned man looked around, across the crowd, and seemed to sag. "I have nothing more to say."

"Then let the sentence be carried out." The Baron turned and left the platform. Garth watched, appalled, as Arner was bent over the block. The axe fell.

The executioner knew his job; there was but a single stroke, and a single gout of blood, and it was done.

The overman, meanwhile, was mulling over the Baron's final remarks. How was he involved in Arner's death? Had the post Arner deserted been at the North Gate? If so, it was bad luck on Arner's part that he had happened along when he did. Still, the man had deserted his post, and such a crime was punished by death among humans.

The crowd was beginning to disperse. Garth paid little attention, but stood where he was, waiting for the square to empty sufficiently to allow him to cross, bent over to hide his height and with his face and armor hidden beneath his makeshift cloak as best he could manage in the shadows.

A man cast him a suspicious glance, then moved on. Another paused and looked at the large figure crouched in the gutter. His eyes were sharper than those of the first man, apparently, for he raised a cry.

"The overman is here! The overman is skulking about our streets again!"

The crowd, which had been quiet, began to mutter as the townspeople turned toward this new attraction.

"Silence, man, or you die." Garth hissed his words through his teeth as his hand fell to his sword hilt.

"What do you want here, monster?" It was someone new who spoke. Already a dozen men had ringed Garth in.

"Why do you pollute our village?"

"Are you a creature of the Baron?"

"Why did you want Arner dead?"

Garth realized he had no chance of dispersing this gathering quietly. He stood straight and flung aside his hood and cloak, making sure his sword and armor were visible.

"I meant no harm. It was no doing of mine that Arner died. I did not know of his existence until today, when I heard the noise here and came to investigate. As for my business in Skelleth, it is my own; it has nothing to do with the Baron nor with any of you. Now, let me pass."

"You're not welcome here, monster."

"Go back where you belong."

A lump of mud was flung from somewhere; it flew past Garth's ear and splattered against a wall. This was a bad sign, the overman knew. Words would not harm him, but once the step was taken from words to action it became very easy for matters to get entirely out of hand.

"I want no trouble. Let me go about my business in peace."

A voice came from several rows back. Most of the crowd were now watching the overman. "I've heard it said that overmen have no gods, but I think that's a lie. You serve the Lords of Dûs, don't you?"

"I serve no gods."

A second mudball flew by, missing Garth's shoulder by inches; a third splattered messily against his breastplate. He drew his sword. The front row of hecklers tried to step back but was unable to; the crowd pressed too close.

"If you will not let me pass in peace, I go in war. Would you start again the Racial Wars?" Garth spoke in his most booming and impressive tones.

"You make empty threats. Who are you that your death will start a war? Your life for Arner's!" A rock bounced harmlessly from his armor, and he began to wonder who it was who wished him so ill; the same voice had accused him of evil-worship and, he thought, of wanting Arner dead.

"I am Garth of Ordunin, and mighty among overmen. Who are you that taunts from behind others?"

There was no answer except another rock; this one ricocheted ringingly from his helmet. Another dollop of mud stained his armor, then another.

"If you wish my death, I would know your name, so that your fellows will know who to blame when Skelleth is smoking ruin in vengeance for this harassment."

"Monster, you will not be avenged. There are not enough overmen left to harm Skelleth. Perhaps you are the last of your race; is that why you have fled your homeland?"

"You know nothing of what you speak. Come and face me." Garth thought he had spotted the speaker, a dour old man wearing dark red. His answer brought nothing but more mudballs, however, this time a veritable shower of them. Reluctantly, he prepared to hack his way to safety. Shielding his eyes with his left arm, he raised his sword.

"I give you a final warning, humans. Let me go, or many of you will die." There was a movement in the crowd. Garth thought he saw helmets. Had the men-at-arms joined the mob?

"Put up your sword, overman! And you people, go home!" The shout came from a man in a steel helmet. Garth recognized him as the captain of the guard who had confronted him on his first arrival. He did not obey, however; the man was still well back in the crowd, and Garth had no desire to get killed before assistance could reach him.

"Go on, go home!" It was a new voice, and Garth saw that a dozen guards were attempting to break up the mob, pulling people away and sending them off.

"With your permission, Captain, I will retain my sword at ready for the moment. But I will use the flat if it becomes necessary to strike."

"Very well. Come on, you, move along!" Garth could see that the guardsmen were also making use of their swords to swat reluctant villagers. In a moment the crowd had diminished by half, and the guards were gathering in a ring around the overman.

"I thank you for your protection, men."

"Don't thank us yet. The Baron sent us to fetch you when he heard the disturbance."

"Oh."

"I trust you have no objections."

"I am not in a position to object."

"Good. Come on." The captain led the way toward the Baron's mansion. The remnants of the crowd parted reluctantly before the dozen swords that ringed the overman. They had crossed perhaps half the square when a clod of mud struck Garth's helmet.

"Monster!" The crowd had not been cowed for long.

"Stop that!" The captain sounded genuinely angry.

"Herrenmer, don't you care that that monster is responsible for Arner's death?"

"Arner deserted his post, Darsen. The overman didn't kill him." The captain's voice was cold as he answered the red-garbed old man. The taunter wasn't easily stopped, however.

"What about you, Tarl? Why are you protecting the monster?"

"To get my pay, Darsen." That got a laugh from the crowd. Garth was glad that the mood seemed to be lightened somewhat. No more mud flew, and he and his escort reached the elegantly carved door of the mansion without further incident. The captain opened it, and Garth stepped in. The captain and two others followed, while the remainder stayed on guard outside.

The antechamber was pleasant enough, though small; it was hung with woolen tapestries done in very few colors, with no gold or silver, and floor, ceiling, and walls were all of wood. Skelleth was not wealthy enough to have numerous dyes, nor to waste rare metals on ornaments, nor to import marble or other stones. Granite and basalt suitable for building could be found in the hills to the north, however, and Garth was slightly startled that none had been used for the floor.

He had little time to consider such matters; rather more quickly than he had expected, and with a complete lack of ceremony, he was ushered into the Baron's audience chamber. His three-man escort remained with him.

The chamber was perhaps twenty feet wide and twice as long, with an acceptably high ceiling. Once again, tapestry covered the walls, save where three windows, rather above eye level, admitted greyish daylight. A little brief consideration told Garth that those windows faced north, which explained the poor light, and opened onto the alley where the King's Inn lay, which explained why they were so high off the floor. Who wanted a view of that mess?

Below the middle window stood a large, unadorned oaken chair. The Baron, still wearing the elaborately embroidered red and gold he had worn at Arner's execution, sat sprawled sideways thereon.

"Greetings, overman."

Garth was unsure of the proper ceremonial for the occasion, but since the guards were not kneeling or bowing, he decided that any such sign of respect on his part might be construed as obsequiousness. He merely stood as he said, "Greetings, my lord Baron." He was glad he had thought to sheathe his sword in the antechamber; though he might want to attempt an escape out the windows, the sword would do less good than having both hands free, and could easily have offended the Baron. At the very least it would have put him on guard.

Considering the possibility of escape, he began gauging the distance to the windows with his eye. It would take several steps and a leap, and then he would have to break the glass and frame – naturally, considering the alleyway's odor, the windows were not designed to open. There were only six men in the room: his three guards, the Baron, and two courtiers, probably the only two the town had. Escape would be possible if this audience went badly.

The Baron had been considering him silently.

"Who are you?"

"I am Garth of Ordunin."

"Ordunin being the overmen's city on the northeast coast, I believe."

"That is quite correct."

"What brings you to Skelleth?"

"I was just passing through."

"I find that highly unlikely. Where were you bound, that it was necessary to pass through Skelleth?"

"I passed through before en route to Mormoreth, and was able to obtain provisions here for the journey. I had hoped to do the same for my return to Ordunin."

"What did you want in Mormoreth?"

"I had been sent to find something."

"Oh? Did you?"

"Find it?"

"Yes."

"No."

"How unfortunate. What was it?"

"A gem."

"What gem?"

"We had heard that there was a gem in Mormoreth that could turn an overman invisible."

"Oh? But you couldn't find it?"

"No."

"Who sent you after it?"

"The Wise Women of Ordunin."

"Who are they?"

"Oracles that live near Ordunin."

"Why did they send you for this gem?"

"I should think that would be obvious; such a gem would be extremely valuable."

"Why did they send you, rather than someone else?"

"I am reputed among my people to be fairly competent."

"I see. So you went to Mormoreth seeking this gem. On foot?"

"No."

"Then where is your mount?"

"My warbeast was slain by bandits on the Plain of Derbarok."

"Yet you escaped?"

"I surrendered my gold, and they let me go."

"While you still had your sword?"

"Yes." Garth realized he had made a mistake, but it was too late to correct it.

"Curious."

"I had slain several, and they did not wish to fight further."

"Ah, of course. Bandits are a cowardly lot."

Garth shrugged.

"So you made the journey to Mormoreth and back in four weeks. I take it you encountered the bandits on your return trip?"

"Yes."

"How did you avoid them on the journey thither?"

"Luck."

"Ah. And how long were you in Mormoreth, searching for this gem?"

"I don't recall, exactly."

"Oh."

There was a pause, then the Baron continued, "And now you're passing through again, on the way to Ordunin."

"That's right."

"You are in Skelleth only to obtain provisions."

"Yes."

"It took two days at the King's Inn to gather supplies for the journey to Mormoreth?"

"Yes." Garth did not like the direction the questions were taking.

"And for this quest after a magic jewel, you needed chains, rope, a cage for pigeons though you had none with you, and a bolt of good cloth."

"I hoped to trade for the gem."

"With such worthless items you hoped to buy an enchanted gem? You are an optimist, aren't you?"

Garth shrugged again; he hoped the gesture seemed natural.

"What of your gold?"

"I had little with me."

"Then with what did you buy your freedom from the bandits in Derbarok?"

"What little I had, which I had gotten for my goods in Mormoreth."

"And, poverty-stricken though you were, you spent a good bit of gold here in Skelleth feeding an old man? And I have heard that the stable boy who tended your warbeast mysteriously acquired enough gold to buy a share in the last ice-caravan, as well. Could that gold have been yours?"

"I . . ." Garth stopped. He could not think of a reasonable answer.

"And how is it that these 'Wise Women' sent you south with little gold? That, my friend, was not wise."

"Very well. I did have a great deal of gold. The ropes and chains were to take hostages, should my offer of gold for the gem be refused."

"Ah, that's better. And the cage?"

"I bought no cage."

"The carpenter Findalan says you did."

"He is mistaken."

"That seems unlikely."

Garth shrugged again.

"And what of the old man you spoke with?"

"He seemed congenial, and I needed to learn the route to Mormoreth."

"I see. He must have been very congenial indeed."

Another shrug.

"However, I have heard otherwise from every other person who has spoken with this old man."

"Oh?"

"He is well known in Skelleth as the surliest, most unfriendly creature in Eramma."

"Perhaps he likes overmen."

"Perhaps." The Baron shifted position, so that he was sitting up. He leaned forward to rest his elbows on his knees, and put his hands together, resting his chin on his fingers. "Do you know his name?"

"No."

"You didn't ask?"

"It seemed unimportant."

"I would be interested in learning his name."

"Why?"

"That man has lived in the King's Inn since before I was born, yet no one seems to know his name. He is referred to simply as 'the old man,' which seems lacking in respect. I would like to call him by his right name."

"I am sorry; I did not ask."

"It has been said that the old man is a wizard of some sort."

"I wouldn't know."

"Tell me about Mormoreth. I have never been there."

Garth was caught by surprise by the sudden change of subject. "Well, it's . . . it's a city of white marble, in the middle of a fertile valley-"

"I know all that. What of the Baron of Mormoreth?"

"There is no Baron of Mormoreth. The city is ruled by a wizard named Shang." It did not seem wise to admit that Garth had left the city in the hands of bandits.

"Oh. Did you meet this wizard?"

"No."

"Why not? I should think he would be the obvious owner of this magical gem you sought."

"Perhaps; but he does not allow visitors."

"But surely, a . . . a *person* as resourceful as yourself would not let a mere detail like that stop him!"

"I did not care to start any trouble."

"Oh. Yet you started trouble here."

"Not intentionally. I wished no trouble. Your villagers wished otherwise."

"Ah, yes, I understand they blame you for today's execution."

"Some of them, yes."

"Just as well that they blame you and not me. They liked Arner far too well to blame *him,* but *somebody* must be responsible." The Baron smiled. Garth did not like the expression.

"Tell me, Garth, how did the bandits manage to kill your warbeast?"

"A sword through its eye."

"Do you expect me to believe any of this?"

There was no change in tone or expression, and Garth groped awkwardly for an answer.

"It's true!" was all he could manage.

"Some of it may be."

"Believe what you will, I have spoken the truth." On occasion, Garth added mentally.

"Why did you not obtain ropes and chains in Ordunin?"

"I knew I could get them here, and I did not wish to burden my mount unnecessarily."

"Are you aware it is no further from the port of Lagur to Mormoreth than it is from Ordunin to Skelleth? There are no bandits if one goes by sea."

"There are pirates. And I was not aware that Mormoreth was near Lagur. As I mentioned before, I had to ask the old man for directions."

"The Wise Women did not know?"

"No."

"You have no old maps in Ordunin? Mormoreth is a thousand years old."

"Our maps are untrustworthy."

"Less trustworthy than directions obtained from a senile old fool in a tavern?"

"It seemed so at the time."

"So you went a dozen leagues or more out of your way to visit Skelleth."

"Yes."

"I will tell you, Garth of Ordunin, what I believe of your tale. I believe you went to Mormoreth. That is all; the rest is all lies."

"Believe what you will."

"I do not believe that a bandit in Derbarok killed your warbeast but let you live. When did this take place?"

"Five days ago." That was, in fact, when he had passed the site of his first battle with the bandits.

"You made the journey from Derbarok to Skelleth on foot in five days?"

Garth realized he had made another mistake, and made no answer.

"I understand that, when the crowd was threatening you, you warned them that your fellow overmen would avenge your death."

"I did."

"But what if I send a messenger demanding ransom for you, and hold you prisoner here?"

"By what law?"

"As a trespassing enemy. As you must be aware, Eramma never concluded peace with your people. We are still nominally at war with all overmen. Why else must all your trade be by sea? Why else have no overmen visited Skelleth in three centuries?"

"Holding me could make the war an actuality again."

"I think that unlikely. Surely a modest ransom is preferable to slaughter."

Garth had no answer. The Baron was quite correct.

"Do you still claim that you return empty-handed from Mormoreth, that your visits to Skelleth are merely for provisions?"

"No. My visits to Skelleth are what I say, but I have lied as to the rest. Should you imprison me, my warbeast will come seeking me and undoubtedly kill a good many of your people before it can be stopped."

"Ah! And where is this beast?"

"I left it in hiding near the city wall."

"And why, pray, did you not ride into town as before?"

"I did not wish to create a disturbance."

"That could be the reason, but I doubt it; no, I think you left the beast to guard something. I think your quest to Mormoreth was successful."

"Why would I leave the beast and the magic gem elsewhere? I could easily hide such a gem on my person. And for that matter, if I had a gem that renders one invisible, would I have been seen, assaulted, and captured?"

"Perhaps you do not know how to use such a gem. However, I prefer to believe that that, too, is lies. You went to Mormoreth for something too large to conceal, if in truth it was Mormoreth you visited. No, I believe that you hold a prisoner. Why else the chains and ropes? Or perhaps some valuable beast, which you keep caged. You came to Skelleth because the old man had made his interest known. You agreed on the price, perhaps, and now return to arrange delivery."

Garth was dumbfounded by how close the Baron's guess came to the truth. Could the man be a seer of some sort?

"Now, surely, this would make more sense than a futile search for an untrustworthy trinket like an invisible jewel? The only question is the nature of your captive."

"You seem very apt at deluding yourself."

"Oh? I do not think I delude myself. You yourself say that your warbeast waits somewhere nearby. Why not escort me to it, and we will see whether or not it guards some worthy prize?"

"Why should I do that?"

"To purchase your freedom."

"But you cannot hold me for long in any case. Koros will free me or die in the attempt, and I doubt you want that."

"Koros being your warbeast? Well, even should the beast be loyal enough to do as you say, it would be slain before it could reach you in the dungeon. I care little for the villagers it may kill; Skelleth is overcrowded and starving.

Further, such an attack would permit me to reverse your earlier threat. The High King at Kholis might welcome an excuse to send his troublesome and warlike barons to a far-off invasion of the Northern Waste. No, Garth, why not avoid all such difficulties and complications? I will make it a wager, of sorts, a bargain you can ill refuse; lead me and an armed escort to your warbeast, and I will let you go free. However, any captives, man or beast, that your mount guards will become my property. Surely that's equitable? If you're telling the truth, you lose nothing at all; if you're lying, you will still be free." The man grinned.

Garth could find no legitimate reason to reject such an offer. It would get the basilisk into Skelleth safely, yet keep it out of the Forgotten King's hands for the moment. Or perhaps it would rid him of the Baron, if he could coax the man into glancing under the covering. And there was a better chance of escape out amid the surrounding farms than here in the Baron's mansion . . . though perhaps escape would be appropriate now. He glanced casually up at the windows again, as if considering the Baron's proposal.

"Oh, by the way, should you escape, we will post a guard at the King's Inn – with crossbows." Garth looked down again, startled and annoyed. Had his thoughts been that obvious? This human apparently had none of the difficulty in interpreting overman expressions that Garth had in reading human ones. He wondered again if the Baron were a seer or wizard. Perhaps he really had sold himself to the gods of evil. That, Garth told himself, was silly; in all likelihood there were no such gods.

"Well, overman, will you lead us to your warbeast?"

"Yes. If I have your oath before these witnesses that you will free me immediately thereafter."

"I will even return your weapons, which I am afraid will have to be confiscated during the journey. To render escape less tempting."

"Very well; your oath."

"How would you have me swear?"

"I know little of human oaths. As you please."

"Very well; I swear by the Seven, by the Seven, and by the One that I will abide by the agreement made and free you if you lead us truly."

As this oath was spoken, Garth watched the face, not of the Baron, but of one of the courtiers listening. The man remained impassive at the first "by the Seven," blanched at the second, and looked confused at "by the One," throwing a quick glance at his lord. Garth guessed that the apparently meaningless numbers did indeed have some theological significance, though he could not imagine what it might be. Pretending comprehension, he nodded. "That will do."

"Good. But it's late. You will be my guest for the night, and we will go in the morning."

Chapter Eleven

The next morning Garth awoke at the first light of dawn. He had been given a room in the east end of the mansion, and sunlight seeped through the curtained windows, though the sky was still mostly dark, making patches of gold on the yellow walls.

He was in a comfortable bed and had eaten well as the Baron's dinner guest the night before, but he was not happy. He had had bad dreams again, and furthermore, he did not really like the bargain he had struck with the Baron. He would almost certainly have to hand over the basilisk, and it would be a considerable nuisance recapturing it should the Forgotten King insist he do so.

He rose and dressed. Scarcely had he donned his armor – he had no other garments with him, and the mansion staff had nothing available large enough for his use – when there was a rap at the door. He growled acknowledgement, and the Baron entered, accompanied, as always in Garth's presence, by a pair of guards.

"I see you are up. I trust you slept well?" The Baron appeared slightly irritated, Garth noticed; perhaps his own rest had been uneasy.

"Well enough." Remembering the courtesies due a baron, he added, "Thank you, my lord."

"Then let us be gone."

"As you wish." He watched silently as one of the guards picked up his sword and axe. His broken dagger he had left in Mormoreth, coated with basilisk venom. Although he had no desire to rush matters, he could think of no legitimate reason for delay; he followed as the Baron led the way down the stairs and past the sentries into the town square. There the party paused as a further contingent of half a dozen men-at-arms joined them. Thus reinforced, the Baron bowed infinitesimally and said, "Now, my dear Garth, if you would lead the way." His manner struck the overman as slightly odd, and the sardonic smile that had been present the day before was lacking. Garth wondered what had caused the transformation as he led the way to the East Gate, a drawn sword inches from his back.

Somewhat over an hour later, the entourage arrived at the copse. Koros stood there, waiting placidly. It growled a greeting to its master, while keeping a wary eye on the nine men with him. The party came to a halt a few yards from the cloth-covered enclosure.

The Baron said nothing, but merely looked sourly at the tentlike object. He seemed to sag curiously. When the silence had begun to become oppressive, Herrenmer, the captain of the guard, said, "You made no mention of a camp, overman."

"I had no reason to mention it."

"Your tent is very peculiar. Is such a structure usual for travelers among your people?"

Garth shrugged.

Herrenmer turned to the Baron. "My lord, shall we search the tent?"

The Baron said nothing. Garth interposed, "My lord, can you trust your men? It might be best if you searched for yourself, if I did indeed bring some great treasure from Mormoreth."

The Baron's slight frown turned into a baleful glare. He picked one of his men, one Garth had not seen before that morning, and demanded, "How much money have you got?"

The man looked startled, and pulled out a purse. It held four silver coins.

"You search."

The man selected bowed and said, "Yes, my lord."

Resignedly, Garth watched as the soldier circled the cage looking for a door-flap. He had made it too obvious that there was some sort of trap. Although the Baron had somehow changed his entire manner from loquacious good humor to gloomy silence overnight, he was still no fool.

The man sent to search announced, "There is no opening. Shall I lift the edge and crawl in?"

The Baron shouted, "Of course, idiot!" The man promptly fell to his knees and began to lift the chain-weighted border. Garth tensed himself to make a sudden move, and closed his eyes. To cover his actions, he yawned; but that failed to fool the Baron.

"Wait!" He looked at Garth, who opened his eyes and looked back. "Around the far side." He glanced at the men behind the overman, and Garth felt the tip of a sword at his back.

Herrenmer said, "Overman, if there is some danger within, I suggest you tell us. The agreement made no allowance for traps, and my men would feel little remorse for killing you if one of their comrades is harmed."

The Baron nodded agreement. Herrenmer called for the searcher to wait. "Is there danger, overman?"

"I believe so," Garth admitted reluctantly.

"Explain," Herrenmer demanded.

"This is not exactly a tent, but a cage. It holds the monster I was sent to capture and bring back alive."

"The monster would tear my man to pieces, I suppose? Then why hasn't it torn the tent?"

"The monster will not harm your man with either teeth or claws. It is enclosed in a magical protective circle."

"Then what danger is there?"

"It is said that the monster's gaze can turn one to stone."

Herrenmer looked utterly disbelieving. The Baron interjected, "What kind of monster?"

"It is called a basilisk."

The Baron nodded gloomily. Herrenmer looked, from the overman to his master and back again.

"What," he asked loudly, "is a basilisk?"

"A sort of poisonous lizard," Garth explained.

The Baron muttered, "Your bargain."

"The basilisk is yours, if you want it; that was the agreement. When I am properly armed and safely astride my mount, I will tell you how the enclosure can be moved. I will not tell you how it may be removed, as that was not included in the agreement. It was said only that I would give any spoils to you, not that I would show you how to use them." Garth was rather proud of himself for thinking of this loophole. It had occurred to him on the walk out from the village. "If you do not want the basilisk, I will be glad to take it with me and be on my way."

The Baron snorted. "I daresay. How is the cage worked? I said I would free you and arm you, but a dead overman is as free as a live one."

In response to the Baron's words the sword point at Garth's back jabbed slightly. Koros growled warningly.

"If you kill me, not all of you will live to return to Skelleth."

The Baron had apparently said all he cared to say. Wearily, he motioned to Herrenmer, who said, "What about a revision of the original agreement, or rather an addition to it? Your life in exchange for the workings of the protective circle."

"If you kill me, you will not only not know how to use the enclosure, you will be unable to move it, assuming any of you survive Koros' assault. You will have to kill the warbeast to survive, and I doubt any of you can."

"We have a stalemate, then. You have not turned over your captive as agreed. Therefore, we will take you back to Skelleth and kill you there."

"I will tell you how to move it; freeing it would be far too dangerous. Is that not sufficient?" Garth wished he could reach his sword or his axe; the man carrying them stood off to one side, just a little too far to reach in a single lunge. If he were armed, he was sure he and Koros could easily handle eight soldiers and an unarmed baron.

Herrenmer was obviously unsure of how to respond to Garth's answer. He turned to the Baron, who nodded.

Turning back, he said, "Very well, overman. You may live, and we will free you, in exchange for the basilisk, caged as it is. However, henceforth, you or any other overman passing through these lands must pay tribute to the Baron, as is his right to demand."

Garth considered briefly, then nodded. "The cage may be moved by moving a talisman; I left it over there, partially buried." He pointed, and the soldier sent to search the "tent," who had wandered back to the party, went to find the object indicated. A few seconds later he held up the wooden rod.

Herrenmer asked, "How does it work?"

"Move the rod beyond a certain distance and the cage will follow it. It may require some strength to move."

The man holding the talisman tried to rejoin the group, but stumbled and fell awkwardly backward when the rod he clutched suddenly refused to move beyond a certain point. Turning, he hauled on it with his full strength. Slowly, inch-by-inch, the rod yielded, and as it did the cage followed, the cloth cover flapping loudly. A loud hissing came from within.

One of the guards said, "Vala, what's that sound?"

"The basilisk," Garth answered. After a pause, he added, "I have fulfilled my end of the agreement. Give me my sword."

The man holding his weapons looked questioningly at his captain, who looked at the Baron. The Baron did nothing. He stood motionless, frowning at the basilisk's enclosure. Shrugging, Herrenmer waved for the man to approach. He obeyed promptly, and began to offer the sword to its owner. Herrenmer interrupted, "Wait. Overman, your word that you will not harm any of us, nor take back the monster."

"I have given my word that my captive would be surrendered."

"It has been; we ask only a reasonable reassurance before returning your weapons."

"You may have my word that I will leave this place in peace."

Herrenmer glanced at the Baron, who was still frowning detachedly. Seeing no indication that he was even conscious of the conversation taking place, Herrenmer said, "That is sufficient." Garth reached out and received his sword; it felt good to hold it once again. Strapping it on, he glanced at the cage as the basilisk hissed again. It was quite probable that he would have to recapture the damnable monster, and that the sword would be necessary to such an endeavor. He did not look forward to it. With the scabbard secure at his waist, he accepted the proffered hilt of his axe, and slung it on his back in its accustomed place. Thus equipped, he crossed to where Koros waited and hauled saddle and pack into place on the warbeast's back. A moment later the straps were secured, and Garth swung up onto the saddle. The men-at-arms had watched these proceedings with casual interest; they made no comment as Garth turned his mount and rode off northward across the muddy farmland.

It appeared, of course, that Garth was taking the fastest route back to his homeland. This was not the case. Once he was sure he was well out of sight he turned Koros westward, and proceeded around the northern edge of Skelleth. Since he now knew, from Arner's execution, that a guard was maintained on the North Gate, he avoided that entrance to the town, giving it a wide berth, and instead rode on to the West Gate. It seemed unlikely that any guard would be kept there; no one had any reason to expect any traffic from the west. Garth's rather limited knowledge of geography led him to the conclusion that a road leading west from Skelleth could only lead to the Yprian Coast, which he believed to be inhabited only by a few starving barbarians.

It would have taken three or four hours to reach the West Gate on foot, but the warbeast's steady glide, seemingly unhampered by the mud, covered the distance in an hour and a half. It was still well before noon when Garth dismounted and led Koros cautiously up to the crumbling remains of the town wall.

Three hundred years of neglect, decay, and declining population following the loss of Skelleth's original purpose as a military base and her consequent lack of trade had, as Garth had observed when he first arrived, left the outer limits of Skelleth a desolate ring of ruins, inhabited only by thieves, rats, and outcasts – until such vermin starved to death, as large numbers invariably did every winter, leaving room for a new crop each summer. Some public-spirited official, a century past, had had several of the uninhabited houses pulled down, but the industry of the townspeople had extended no further than that; the roofless, tottering ruins were left where they were. Though they provided very little shelter, it was not shelter Garth sought, but cover. When he had passed the West Gate into this no-man's-land, he turned from the street that led into the village and made his way carefully through the rubble-strewn, overgrown maze of avenues and alleys.

It took him perhaps twenty minutes to find what he sought – a cellar, hidden by two walls that still stood shoulder-high on the side toward the main road, which appeared relatively safe and not unduly difficult to climb out of. It took a moment's coaxing to get Koros to leap down into such an uninviting pit, but Garth had decided that it was necessary to hide the beast somewhere; he plainly could not ride boldly into the village, nor did he care to leave Koros outside the walls advertising its master's presence to anyone who passed – such as the Baron's guards, who might well be set to patrolling the area, in case more overmen approached. This basement would serve admirably as a base of operations, and Garth cared very little whether Koros liked it or not.

It would, however, be a good idea to make sure the warbeast was fed. There was no urgency; it had eaten a day and a half ago, leaving at least twenty-four hours before there was cause to worry.

That left him with nothing to do. He did not dare enter Skelleth proper by daylight, but planned on sneaking to the King's Inn under cover of darkness to speak with the Forgotten King. He could make no further plans until he had discussed the situation. That left him rather at loose ends until sunset, still a good seven hours off.

He polished his sword until it shone; with a suitable stone, he sharpened both sword and axe to a razor edge; he took inventory of his supplies; he brushed down the warbeast; he polished his breastplate; he brushed off his makeshift cloak; he cleared half the cellar so that Koros could move about. By sunset he had exhausted his ingenuity. He spent the last half hour before the skies seemed sufficiently dark in watching the clouds drift and thicken. When he did finally clamber out of the ruins, it was with a better knowledge of the ways of clouds and a suspicion that it would be raining by midnight.

Chapter Twelve

Crouched awkwardly, Garth stood under an overhanging upper story, dripping wet, his slit nostrils filled with the reek of decaying sewage. The smell, as much as his memory of the route, told him that he had at last found the right alleyway. Unfamiliar as he was with Skelleth, and not daring to use the main thoroughfares, he had wound his way cautiously inward from the ruins, only to become quite lost. His prediction had been fulfilled sooner than he had expected. It was pouring rain two hours after sunset, while he was still attempting to convince himself that he was not lost. The attempt had failed; it was pure luck that finally brought him to the malodorous alleyway behind the baronial mansion, and Garth knew it. The rain had proven a blessing in disguise, in that it had driven everyone indoors, making his detection less likely; but it was a mixed blessing at best, as he was cold, wet, and miserable, and the crowd at the King's Inn was staying late rather than walk home in such a storm. He dared not enter until the mob inside thinned out enough to allow him to walk across the room without bumping elbows on every side. He wished once again that he knew how to curse as he wondered how a tavern in such an appalling neighborhood could attract such a large clientele.

From his refuge, Garth could see up the alley to the back of the Baron's mansion. Lights shone in several windows. From snatches of conversation picked up from passers-by, Garth knew that the Baron had made a triumphal procession out of bringing the basilisk into Skelleth; the cage had been paraded, safely covered, through the streets to the market square, where it had remained, heavily guarded, until sunset, when onlookers had been chased from the area. It had disappeared when they were allowed to return, and no one knew where it had gone, nor what it was, nor where it came from, nor anything else about the mysterious tentlike object. In short, the knowledge available to the public was no more than Garth would expect, and much less than he had feared. It would not do to have it known that a basilisk was around; some fool would be certain to test its legendary powers of petrifaction.

A movement from the direction of the King's Inn caught his attention. He turned and watched motionlessly as half a dozen drunken farmers reeled and staggered through the puddles toward their homes – or where they drunkenly assumed their homes to lie. Garth was doubtful that they would all make it out of the alley, let alone to their various places of residence. Sure enough, one stumbled and fell headlong in a stinking pool of rainwater and sewage. His companions helped him up, and the whole party was soon out of sight.

The overman guessed it to be about midnight. Abandoning his bit of shelter, he made his way slowly, bent and shuffling, toward the inn. A glance through the window confirmed that, though the crowd had thinned, there were still too many people. A closer look showed that the Forgotten King, invisible in his ragged saffron cloak and hood, was seated in his customary place, as though he had not moved since Garth's departure a month before. It also showed that a good many of the patrons were unconscious, which, combined with the fact that the rain showed no sign of lessening, caused Garth to reconsider risking entry. He was still arguing with himself when a movement off to his left caught his eye.

A man was approaching from the far end of the alley. Even at that distance and despite the rain and darkness, Garth could see that he wore a sword and helmet. The Baron must have set the guards to patrolling the streets.

Without further thought, Garth shuffled through the tavern door and stood, dripping wet, just inside. No one paid him any attention at all; they were all too busy with ale, wine, and conversation. Remembering to retain his stooped posture, he shook himself to dry his garments, then began to inch his way through and around the crowd toward the table where, despite the throng, the Forgotten King sat alone. Behind him he heard the door slam shut. He had left it slightly ajar, and assumed one of the patrons, disliking the cool outside air, had closed it. He did not turn to look for fear of showing his face.

A sudden silence descended over the room, and his curiosity got the better of him. He craned about, as he had seen stiff-jointed old men do, and caught a glimpse of the soldier he had seen on the street and sought to avoid. The man was shaking water from his hair, paying no mind to the wet, cloaked figure halfway across the room. Relieved to see that the guard was not pursuing him, Garth proceeded on to the Forgotten King's table and eased himself into an empty chair. Carefully keeping his face shadowed, he peered around the edge of his hood to see what the soldier would do when he had dried himself somewhat.

He did exactly what anyone would expect a man to do in a tavern on a cold, wet night; he shoved his way to where the innkeeper was dispensing spirits and loudly demanded a pint of warm red wine. The fat, harried fellow ignored other importunities to fetch the beverage requested, and gratefully accepted the coin proffered in exchange before returning to his regular customers.

The soldier downed half the wine at a gulp, then turned and seemed to notice the crowd for the first time.

"What are all you scum doing here?" he demanded. "You know the Baron disapproves of such frivolity."

A voice in the crowd called, "He doesn't approve of his guards drinking, either." That caused a good bit of laughter. The soldier himself grinned broadly.

"As often as not he doesn't approve of anything at all, 'tis true; but then again, he has spells where he's as merry as any, and in his fits he couldn't care less either way. So, as we don't know his mood just now, if you don't say anything, neither will I, and we'll all be the better for it. The gods know a man needs something to warm his belly on a night like this. But there's another man due in fifteen minutes who may not be so agreeable. The Baron thinks the overman will be trying to sneak back here." That called forth a burst of derision and treasonous remarks about Skelleth's lord, and Garth could make out no more conversation.

He turned to the yellow-robed figure across the table and whispered, "Is there somewhere we can speak privately?"

He was unsure whether the cowled head nodded slightly or not, but a moment later the old man rose and turned as if to go. Garth did likewise, only to find himself following as the Forgotten King led the way upstairs. At the head of the stairs a corridor led toward the front of the building, with four doors opening off either side. It was utterly bare and smelled of dust, a dry, ancient smell despite the rain which rattled on the roof above it. There was no ceiling; the naked rafters and planks of the inn's roof were dimly visible some fifteen feet overhead, and the ridgepole ran along the center of the passage.

Behind them, Garth heard the sound of chairs pushed back and departing feet. The soldier's warning had apparently had some effect, and he wondered if it had been necessary to abandon the cheery tavern for this dark musty corridor that somehow reminded him of the crypts beneath Mormoreth.

Heedless of the darkness, the Forgotten King led the way directly to the farthest door and brought an ornate key out from under his tatters. It clicked loudly, and the door swung open, revealing a large, low-ceilinged room with a broad, many-paned window overlooking the street, whence a dim glow trickled in to provide the only illumination. As Garth stepped across the threshold, the old man reached up to an ornate wrought-iron candelabrum, and the huge tallow cylinder that topped it sprang alight, though Garth had seen no splint, spark, or match. The candle cast a dull, smoky light whereby Garth could make out something of the furnishings.

The room was a bedchamber. A velvet-canopied bed stood against the far wall, with elaborate candelabra on either side, both freestanding and on tables. The light was too dim to distinguish colors, but the velvet coverings reminded Garth of dried blood.

A gust of wind slapped rain against the glass, and Garth looked toward the window. Two low chairs, richly upholstered and resembling none he had ever seen before, stood on either side of a low table that glittered oddly, as though it were made of mica-bearing stone.

The old man motioned toward these chairs. Cautiously, Garth settled his weight on one, and found it surprisingly comfortable, though too low to sit straight in. He adjusted himself as best he could and peered through the gloom at the King.

The silence was finally broken when Garth announced, without preamble, "I have returned from Mormoreth."

The Forgotten King did not deign to reply to so obvious a statement, and after a pause Garth went on, "I brought forth that which I found in the crypts, and it is now in Skelleth."

"Indeed?" The dry, hideous voice startled the overman, though he had heard it before. He had forgotten while traveling just how harsh it was. Likewise, noticing the hands that clutched the arms of the Forgotten King's chair, he saw all over again how old and withered the man was. His fingers were little more than bone bound in a thin layer of wrinkled skin. His face was hidden, as always, and Garth wondered again what his eyes looked like.

"Yes."

"Then deliver it to me, and we may resolve further the terms of our bargain."

"There are matters to be settled first."

"Indeed?"

"I believe you know what it was I found."

The King made no answer.

"I do not believe you would have set me such a task had you not known its nature."

Again there was no reply.

"Therefore, I believe that you have some use for this creature. When we spoke before, you made mention of certain desires of your own, which required things you do not yet possess. This creature is one of those things, is it not?"

"I have a use for the basilisk."

"What use?"

"That is not your concern."

"Perhaps not; still, I would know what it is."

"That was no part of our agreement."

"True. But when we framed our bargain, I had no idea that I was being sent for so venomous a creature."

"Ah. How does that alter the agreement?"

"I want no part of unleashing so potent a force of death as the basilisk. I can see no use or need for such a creature unless you plan to use it as Shang did, to destroy large numbers of people."

"Nonetheless, I have a use for it, and you have agreed to bring it to me as the first part of our bargain.

"As I told you at our first meeting, I am weary of the omnipresence of death and decay. I do not wish to contribute to the spread of death."

The yellow-clad figure stirred slightly. "Garth, do you know what year this is?"

Garth was puzzled by the apparent change of subject. "It is the year three hundred and forty-four of Ordunin."

"Do you know no other reckoning?"

"The men of Lagur call it the Year of the Dolphin, I believe."

"This is the year two hundred and ninety-nine of the Thirteenth Age, the age in which the goddess P'hul is ascendant over all the world."

"I do not see the significance of this."

"P'hul is the goddess of decay, the handmaiden of death, one of the greatest of the Lords of Dûs."

"I still fail to see why this is of any concern to me."

"This is the Age of Decay, Garth. There is nothing you nor anyone can do to prevent the continuance of universal decline, so long as P'hul remains dominant."

"Such fatalism is irrelevant. I do not believe in your gods. And even if I cannot prevent death and decay, at the very least I can avoid contributing to it."

"Perhaps. Yet perhaps not. How many deaths have you caused already upon this errand?"

"A dozen men died that I might bring you the monster."

"One, undoubtedly, was Shang, the wizard responsible for the depopulation of Mormoreth. The rest, I take it, were bandits?"

"Yes."

"You mourn the loss of these twelve?"

"Any death is unfortunate."

"Yet you killed them."

"I acted in self-defense."

"Still, you killed them. Can you really avoid contributing to decay and death?"

Garth was silent for a moment, then answered, "I killed in self-defense. You are under no threat so dire that you need the basilisk to defend you."

"So you will not deliver it?"

"Not unless you first satisfy me that you will not use it to slaughter."

"But I can do that without revealing my purpose."

There was another moment of silence, or rather, a moment in which the only sound was the steady patter of rain at the window. The glow of the single candle flickered. Finally, Garth said, "How?"

"I swear, by my heart and all the gods, that I have no intention of using the basilisk's gaze or venom to slay others. That oath satisfied you once."

Garth said nothing, considering.

"If that is not sufficient, then I will swear further by the God Whose Name Is Not Spoken."

Garth hesitantly said, "I have been warned that you are an evil being."

"Ah. Shang thus warned you?"

"Yes."

"What is evil? Perhaps I merely opposed Shang, who destroyed an innocent city. In any case, even evil beings are not lightly foresworn, and you have heard my oath."

Garth made no answer. He felt slightly ashamed, though he was unsure why.

"Will you fetch now the basilisk?"

Garth cleared his throat. "Yes."

"Good. Deliver it to the stable here at the inn. I will have a place readied."

"There are still things I wish to know," Garth said hesitantly.

"Indeed?"

"I have heard that you have lived here for decades, yet no one knows your name."

"This is true."

"Why?"

"That is not your concern"

"Are you in truth evil, as Shang alleged?"

There was a pause before the old man replied, "I do not know what evil is."

"What is your name, that you have told no one?"

"I was once called Yhtill, a name which surely means nothing to you."

It was indeed meaningless to the overman.

"You have sworn not to misuse the basilisk." Garth was still confused, seeking further reassurance. The Forgotten King's answer was little comfort.

"I am certainly less likely to do harm with it than the Baron of Skelleth, to whom you gave it."

Garth started, wondering how he had known that, then told himself angrily that the old man had undoubtedly heard about the mysterious tent in the market-square and put three and three together when Garth said that the basilisk was in Skelleth. In any case, the remark was undoubtedly true. The overman rose awkwardly from the too-low chair, wrapping his wet, tattered grey cloak about him, and announced, "I will bring it."

The old man said nothing, but merely rose, with an ease and silence surprising in one so aged.

Garth turned to go, then paused. It had occurred to him that there might be soldiers in the tavern, and he did not care to venture boldly past them. Also, he had been away from Koros longer than he had planned, due to losing his way in the rain and winding streets, and, ever insecure, he wished to be sure the warbeast was fed and reasonably comfortable.

He stood, feeling awkward, a few feet from the door.

"You hesitate," the Forgotten King said.

"Yes. I would know if there is a back way. I do not care to go through the tavern again. Your townspeople dislike me, and the guardsmen serve a Baron who has banned overmen from the village."

"Ah."

"Also, I would attend to my warbeast before undertaking the recapture of the basilisk."

"As you wish. I have waited this long; such a delay can mean little. Unfortunately, there is no exit from this place save through the common room. Perhaps you would care to wait while I secure a goat to feed the beast and make sure your route is clear."

"I would be most grateful." Garth might have continued with a remark on how much he appreciated such consideration from one he had agreed to serve, but he no longer had an audience; the old man – whose unpronounceable name Garth could not bring himself to use – had already left. The overman called after him, hoping he would be heard only by the right ears, "Could you make it two goats?"

There was no answer; silence descended upon the dim room, save for the steady drumming of the rain.

Chapter Thirteen

Garth's wait was not long; perhaps fifteen minutes had elapsed when the Forgotten King appeared in the doorway, motioning for the overman to follow. He obeyed promptly, springing up from the chair he had waited in. In truth, he was glad to leave the room, which in its dusty dimness had an atmosphere that unsettled him. During his wait he had studied the furnishings more closely, and noticed that they were stranger than he had at first thought. Beneath a universal layer of dust, the woods and upholsteries could be seen and felt not to be any common substance that the overman was familiar with, but rather unnaturally smooth and somehow alien. What he had at first taken for walnut and ebony had grains unlike any wood Garth knew. What he had taken for leather and velvet had a strange wrongness of texture, and he was certain that no ordinary animal had produced these substances. The whole room was somehow unnatural, as if it were a sorcerous illusion, and he was relieved to be out of it and in the bare but reassuringly normal corridor.

The Forgotten King led the way to the head of the stair, then turned and rasped, "The way is clear. The inn is closed, and the two goats are tied by the stable door."

Garth nodded. "Thank you," he said, as he groped at his belt for his purse. "How much did the goats cost?"

"They are paid for."

Garth paused, and looked closely at the old man.

Almost immediately he regretted doing so, as the man's mummylike hands and hidden face rather unsettled his nerves. He shrugged and left his money where it was. No doubt the King had more than enough gold to pay for such things, even if he hadn't seen fit to use it when last Garth was in Skelleth.

"I thank you again," he said.

"You pamper that animal," the old man replied.

"Better to pamper it than risk letting it become uncontrollably hungry."

"Perhaps."

Without further ado Garth turned and strode down the stairs. As the Forgotten King had promised, the common room was empty and dark. The brass fittings of the liquor casks gleamed dully in the dim light that trickled in through the spotless windows, a light that did little to alleviate the blackness. Carefully, Garth crossed the tavern, managing to reach the door with only a single bumped shin. As quietly as he could contrive he slipped the latch, opened the door, and slid through into the noisome damp of the alleyway. There was a narrow overhang above him, so that the rain, which had lightened to a steady drizzle, did not immediately reach him. With that momentary respite, he straightened his cloak, pushed his sword out of sight, and stooped, so that when he stepped from the threshold he seemed once more a bent old man, albeit an exceptionally tall one, with hood pulled well forward to keep the rain from his eyes.

A few paces to his left was the stable door. He headed that way, only to step ankle-deep in a foul-smelling puddle that he had not seen in the dark. The cold water thoroughly soaked the rags he had bound on in lieu of boots, and he wished again he knew some appropriate curse for such occasions. He started to step back out of the water, then changed his mind and strode on; what more could happen?

He promptly cut his newly healed left foot on some sharp object under the even black surface of the water. Growling angrily, he marched on, and emerged without further hurt on the stable threshold. Peering inside, he could see nothing at all, but his hand on the doorframe encountered a tether. He pulled at it, and was answered with the bleating of a goat.

Now it merely remained to get the goats to Koros, then to find and retrieve the basilisk. Dragging the reluctant goats, he marched off westward.

It was well after midnight, and the streets were, as far as the overman could see, utterly deserted. He maintained his stoop and the concealment of his hood, which in any case kept off some of the rain, but decided against struggling through the murky side streets, risking losing himself again. He had just concluded that even the high road west from the village square would be safe, and clearly the best and fastest route, as he passed the dark doorway of the King's Inn, when someone stepped from the middle alley of the three that met the one he was in, scarcely a dozen yards away. The dim glow from the few remaining illuminated windows glinted yellowly from his shoulder, and Garth realized the man wore mail – it was one of the Baron's men-at-arms.

It was only common sense, after all, for the Baron to post a guard on the inn. Garth silently reprimanded himself for not expecting it. It was too late to hide; the soldier had seen him. He kept on walking, dragging the goats, as if the man's presence were of no importance to him.

"Ho, there!"

Garth stopped short. He paused a second before replying, glancing about as if to be certain he was the one addressed.

"Yes?" He pitched his voice an octave above its natural range.

"What are you doing here?"

"I'm going home."

"Where's that?"

"West of town."

"Where did you get those goats?"

"Bought them."

"At midnight?"

"This afternoon. I stopped for a drink or two, that's all."

"Well, old man, I know they're stolen as well as you do. But I have orders to stay here and guard this pesthole of an inn. Maybe I could forget I saw you."

As the conversation had proceeded both parties had kept moving, so that they were now only a few feet apart from one another, Garth keeping his head low so that all he could see of the soldier was his feet. He didn't see the guard's outstretched palm, but he caught the meaning of his remarks. The man wanted a bribe.

"I have no money, sir, else I'd pay you for your kindness." He tried to make his voice shake as he said that, but the attempt sounded unnatural at best.

The soldier peered at the bent, cloaked figure that still stood as tall as himself, and decided that he wasn't going to get any money without a fight. Annoyed, he ordered, "Well, be off with you, you and your damned goats. And take the rain with you." He turned, disgruntled, and splashed off to his lurking-place in the middle alley.

Trying to sound like any fawning peasant, Garth said, "Yes, sir, and thank you, thank you very much, and bless you, and may the gods keep you safe." He sloshed onward through the puddles, dragging his reluctant goats but being careful not to display too plainly his superhuman strength. It was only when he was well past the center alley, in fact at the corner of the westernmost alley near where he had waited before entering the tavern, that he dared to halt and abandon his role of an elderly human. Growling, he peered through the rain but could see nothing. He doubted that the small, pale eyes of humans were as good as his own blood red ones, and therefore concluded that if he could see no one, no one could see him. He stood straight long enough to ease a little of the ache in his mistreated back, gave a jerk that sent the goats tumbling and bleating, then resumed his crouch more to keep his face dry than to maintain his façade and marched off through the black and dripping streets.

He made the rest of his journey without incident, looping through the noisome side streets until at last he emerged onto the west road, then making excellent time on that relatively wide, straight and well-drained street. The goats gave up fighting his superior strength, and in fact hurried on willingly, apparently hoping that the overman would get them in out of the rain.

Even though there were no further delays other than the poor footing and visibility caused by the rain, Garth knew that only three hours remained before dawn when he finally found himself looking at the distinctive ruined wall that surrounded his chosen cellar. Since he hoped to slip into the baronial mansion before sunrise, he was hurried and impatient. He called out for Koros while still a dozen yards away.

There was no response.

Oh, well, Garth told himself, the beast must be asleep. He trudged on, leading the goats, which were beginning to show some signs of reluctance. Perhaps they had caught the scent of warbeast.

Splashing through a puddle, Garth rounded a broken wall and peered into the darkness of the basement where he had left Koros. He was unable to distinguish a thing. Here he had no scattered light from the village windows, and the moon and stars were hidden by the clouds. The only light was a dim luminescence that seemed to come from the clouds themselves.

It was hardly surprising that he could not see a black animal, no matter how large, in a pitch-dark hole. He wished he had some means of making a light, but there was nothing around not far too wet to catch a spark from his flint.

He called again, to be answered only by the very faintest of echoes. As he continued to look downward, away from the pale glimmer of the sky, he had the impression that his eyes were adjusting to this more absolute darkness, yet the cellar continued to appear a smooth black. It seemed somehow unnatural; suddenly apprehensive, Garth groped for a chip of rubble and tossed it into the cellar, listening for the click of the pebble on the stone floor he had cleared that afternoon.

Instead, he heard a small "ploosh" as the shard struck smooth water, and he realized why he had been apprehensive. His senses, either sight or sound, had detected the fall of rain on water rather than pavement, though he had not immediately realized it. Though the storm had trailed off to little more than a drizzling mist, it was still there. However, Koros wasn't.

The warbeast was more tolerant of water than its feline ancestors, and fully as obedient as one could reasonably expect, but it would scarcely stay in a hole flooded well over a foot deep. Garth crouched thoughtfully as he tried to guess where the creature would have gone upon deciding to abandon the place it had been ordered to stay.

It seemed to him that it would do one of four things: it would seek out its master for further instructions; it would go hunting, as it had not been fed for a day or two; it would go home, either to Ordunin or, if its memory was long enough, to Kirpa; or it would merely seek shelter, a dry place where it could wait out the storm. And in any of those four cases, it might eventually return to await Garth.

If it had gone seeking Garth it might even now be lost in the village, wandering the empty streets in search of him. That could be very bad, but there was nothing Garth could do about it. If it had gone home, well, it was gone. Likewise, if it was hunting, it would come back in its own time and not before, and there was no way Garth could find it. He might search the area on the chance that it merely sought shelter and found some nearby, but the overman did not feel that it would be wise to waste the time. Instead he would leave the goats here, and hurry back to Skelleth after the basilisk. When he had delivered the monster to the Forgotten King there would be time enough to find Koros. The only thing he regretted was that he had left his supplies in the cellar, where they undoubtedly remained somewhere under the dark rainwater. He did not care to venture down there after them.

His decision reached, he looped the goats' tether around a narrow stone that protruded from the ruin and hurried back toward the high road. Without the goats to impede him he made much better time. Though the rain continued, the thin trickle made little difference. He still had better than two hours until dawn when he reached the empty village square.

It bothered him somewhat that Koros had vanished, and also that he had no supplies except his sword and axe, both hidden under his grey patchwork cloak. His feet were both chilled through and thoroughly uncomfortable in their sopping rags, and the cut on his left sole, which had seemed insignificant at first, was becoming painful enough that he found himself limping. He wished that he had found himself a cobbler and gotten new boots before undertaking any further adventures. It was too late to turn back now; Koros might be found by the Baron's men at any time, revealing its master's continued presence in Skelleth. Also, the longer the Baron retained the basilisk the more likely harm would be done.

The square was deserted, but the Baron's mansion plainly wasn't. There were lights visible in several of its windows. Still, Garth doubted that there were many people within awake enough to oppose him; most likely the Baron and a few chosen men were doing something, perhaps studying the basilisk.

Though there were lit windows, there were fully as many that were dark. Garth chose a convenient one of these and carefully pried open the casement. The lock gave little resistance, and Garth decided it must not have been properly set. His choice of window had been lucky, he told himself. Then the hinges squealed, and he realized why the lock hadn't held; the casement didn't fit its frame correctly, which both loosened the lock and twisted the hinges. He froze momentarily, but there was no sign of activity in response to the sound.

More cautiously than before, he inched the window open a little further until the could squeeze himself through. Slowly he slid himself past the frame, easing his battered feet onto the floor inside gently, lest the floor squeak as the window had.

The room he found himself in was at least as dark as the square outside; darker, in truth, since there was no glow from the illuminated windows here. He could make out no detail at all, though he had a vague idea of the chamber's size. It was medium large, perhaps twenty feet square, with a ceiling that seemed uncomfortably low to the seven-foot overman. There was no sign of life. Garth thought he could see a large dark table in the center of the room, and there was a dim glow under one door as if a torch were lit, not in the next chamber, but in the one beyond. That was the only door he could see in the darkness; others, if there were others, blended invisibly with the walls.

His bare toes, protruding from their wrappings, felt the edge of a lush carpet. Almost without thinking, he reached down, tore off the drenched tatters, and let his bare feet enjoy the feel of the thick, soft pile. He stripped away his dripping cloak as well. He wanted to leave no watery trail through the mansion. Gathering up the wet cloth, he dumped it all unceremoniously out the window, then drew the casement shut, being careful not to let it squeak as it had when opened. He could retrieve the garments in case he wanted to disguise himself again for a leisurely departure, but he would not be encumbered if fast action were necessary. Nor would the wet rags prove that he had entered the mansion, since they were outside. The only evidence inside was the damp spot at the edge of the carpet, which, with luck, would dry out before it was noticed. It had certainly been a considerably neater entrance than that he had contrived in Mormoreth; there was no fallen canopy nor dangling rope this time.

He considered his next move. He had no idea where to find the basilisk. The house was not overlarge. It could be searched in less than an hour, ordinarily; the necessity of stealth would not more than double that. He would begin, optimistically, by exploring those rooms he could reach which were unlit and presumably unoccupied.

Feeling his way along the wall, he stumbled slightly against a chair and caught himself with his hand on what felt very much like a doorframe rather than an ordinary wall panel. Detouring around the chair, he investigated further and found the latch-handle. It opened readily, and he entered the next room, as dark as the first.

There was no evidence of what he sought; most especially, he could detect no scent of the monster. He groped onward, through another door that admitted him to the entry hall he had seen when first escorted into the house; he could recognize it, even in the dark, by its dimensions, its relative location, and its odor of polished wood. The door to the audience chamber was closed, and a bright line of light showed over the top. Interestingly, the bottom met its sill so closely that the overman could not detect as much as a flicker from beneath the heavy doors, but the glow at the top was more than enough to keep him away. Instead he crossed to the far side, where another dark doorway led to the east wing, where he had spent the preceding night.

His nostrils caught a faint whiff of basilisk, and he decided that, wherever it was now, the monster must have been brought in this way. Pausing, he tried to locate the faint scent more exactly, but could not. With a shrug, he crept on through the east doorway. The door itself was wide open.

He was in a hallway. Ahead on his left was the stairway leading to the bedrooms, while ahead on his right a paneled gallery led to the room where he had dined as the Baron's guest. He recalled that there was a door leading under the stairs just before the entrance to the dining hall. It had been closed when he had passed it before.

Peering into the gloom at the head of the stairs he thought he could detect light, and possibly voices. Furthermore, it seemed very unlikely that the Baron would haul the creature up there. He decided to leave any searching of the upper floor for last, and proceeded cautiously down the right-hand gallery. The entrance to the refectory was dark; the door under the stairs wasn't quite. A very faint glimmer could be seen under it, as of a light around at least one corner.

Although the dining hall seemed almost as unlikely as the bedrooms, for the sake of thoroughness Garth decided to investigate it, rather than the illuminated and therefore dangerous doorway. He reached for the latch-handle, only to find it locked. His immediate reaction was to consider this evidence that the basilisk was indeed within; but, recalling his several similar premature guesses in Mormoreth, he paused to consider the matter further. He had the advantage this time of having seen the room, a large and richly furnished chamber. It occurred to him that those furnishings, which included gold candlesticks, were worthy of protection. The door was undoubtedly locked to prevent light-fingered servants from making off with what were probably the most valuable items in the house.

Not that that meant that the basilisk *wasn't* there; it would make sense to put it in a place that had good, solid locks. However, it did mean that, for the moment at least, Garth wouldn't seek it there. He knew almost nothing about picking locks, and forcing them, which he was rather better at, was often a noisy, messy job, and always left traces. Should he not find the monster elsewhere he could always return.

Turning from the locked door he was confronted with a choice; he could ignore the faint light and try the door under the stairs, he could move on to the upper floor, or he could retrace his steps to the west wing and check for other doors in the first two rooms he had explored. He sniffed the air, hoping it would yield a clue.

There was a trace of basilisk odor, as there had been in the entrance hall. The basilisk had been brought into the east wing, though once again, he could not tell exactly where.

With a shrug, he turned to the door beneath the stairs; it was closest. It opened readily, admitting the overman to a tiny roomlet, scarcely bigger than a closet, with doors on three of its four sides. He had entered by one of these. Both the others showed light at the bottom, though one was bright and the other dim. The dim one was on his left, and could only lead to stairs going down, parallel to the stairs that ended somewhere over his head. After a brief consideration, Garth was sure that the other led into the kitchens; the door through which the servants had entered during his meal as the Baron's guest was only a few feet away, and it would be logical for the kitchens to be convenient to both dining hall and cellars. It would also be logical to put the basilisk in the cellars, where there would be no need to shutter windows to prevent casual passers-by from glancing in and being petrified. The light under that door was quite faint. Garth decided to risk the stairs. The door opened easily, though with a faint squeak, as if it were not used often.

The stairs were crude blocks of stone descending between rough stone walls. At their foot Garth could see a rectangle of dimly lit whitewashed stone wall and a few feet of flagstone flooring, apparently forming a sort of T with the stairs.

For once Garth was grateful for his bare feet, which permitted him to move silently as he crept down the stairs. He had almost reached the bottom – in fact his foot had just touched the last step – when he heard the rattle of a latch and a door opening, somewhere to his right. He froze. The door closed again. He relaxed slightly, letting out his held breath, then tensed again. There were footsteps approaching, moving at a brisk pace with no attempt at stealth. Too heavy for the Baron or either of the courtiers Garth had seen, they were undoubtedly those of a guardsman. Silently, Garth's hand fell to his sword hilt. The steps were very near now, and he heard the clink of chain mail. He drew the sword from its sheath.

The steps halted abruptly, and Garth realized that the man must have heard the hiss of steel against leather. He flattened himself against the right-hand wall, sword held ready. A moment of silence, then the steps began again; this time they advanced slowly and cautiously. At the fourth step Garth judged that his unknown visitor must be well within reach of his sword. At the fifth he tensed, and at the sixth he sprang out to confront the newcomer.

Unfortunately, he had misjudged the distances. He collided awkwardly with the guardsman, and his injured left foot gave way and folded under, so that both of them fell sprawling on the floor with a loud clatter of arms and armor.

Garth was first to recover, and within seconds he was standing over the man, who had not yet risen beyond all fours, with his broadsword at the man's throat. The soldier's own sword lay a yard from his hand, where he had dropped it when he fell. Neither moved for a long moment. Garth was unsure what to do next, while his captive did not dare do anything for fear the overman would slaughter him. Garth studied the situation, keeping his sword where it was.

They stood in a narrow, whitewashed corridor, lit by a pair of torches clamped to the wall a few yards along in the direction the man had come from. Just past the torches, the corridor ended in a heavy wooden door; another, similar door was midway along the right-hand wall. Both were tightly shut. In the opposite direction the corridor opened into a storeroom, its walls lined with wooden casks, which extended back along the wall beside the staircase. It was unlit.

It seemed to Garth that interrogation was in order; he was deciding upon the phrasing of his first question when, with a loud rattle, the door at the end of the corridor swung open.

Chapter Fourteen

The newcomer was, of course, another man-at-arms. He took one look at the scene before him and shouted, "The overman!" before slamming the door.

Wasting no time, Garth started his questioning and demanded, "Where is the basilisk?"

His captive promptly pointed to the door that had just slammed, and answered, "In the dungeon."

"How many men are there?"

"Uh . . . about ten, I guess."

"And the Baron?"

Garth could scarcely hear the affirmative reply because, with much foot stomping and sword rattling, the door was again flung wide, to reveal half a dozen men-at-arms.

"Surrender, overman!"

Garth merely glared at the soldiers and twitched his sword so that its tip flashed in the torchlight, less than an inch from his captive's throat. The man who had demanded his surrender fell silent, and for a moment no one moved. Then the guards were rudely shouldered aside, and the Baron strode a pace or two into the corridor.

"Surrender, overman," he said.

Garth said, "And if I do not?"

The Baron merely nodded toward his men's drawn swords.

"If I am attacked, this man dies."

The Baron shrugged. "What of it?"

Garth hesitated; he had not expected such open indifference. "I doubt your handful of farmers can take me," he said at last.

"If they cannot, I have others."

"You misunderstand. Should you set your men on me, I would consider your death a matter of self-defense."

The Baron considered this, frowning.

"I have come to retrieve the basilisk. Let me take it and I will go in peace."

"No."

"Why not? What use have you for the monster?" Garth was trying his best to be reasonable.

The Baron studied him contemplatively for a long moment, then said, "Why should I tell you?"

"To prevent bloodshed. Perhaps we can reach a compromise."

The Baron said nothing; the silence grew. Garth shifted uneasily, unsure what to do next. His decision was made suddenly when he heard movement above and to his right. There were more guards at the top of the stairs, sent around by another route while the Baron delayed the overman. Enraged at himself for allowing such a ruse, he kicked his captive so that the man rolled awkwardly onto his back. Garth fell back against the corridor wall, his sword ready to meet an onslaught while his left hand freed the axe slung on his back. The stairway door opened and a handful of men burst through, rushing down the first few steps only to freeze when they found the overman alert and ready.

Garth placed a furry foot on the chest of his prisoner to prevent the loss of what little bargaining power the man might provide, then repeated, loudly, his earlier question. "What use do you have for the monster?"

The Baron took his time, studying the overman's face, before replying. "War."

"War against whom? My people?"

"I had not yet decided."

"I do not understand. If you have no enemy, why do you want the basilisk?"

"Let me tell you a little family history, Garth. My father, damn him, was the commander of the armies of the High King at Kholis; he served long and well, and when he retired from active duty, the king offered him a barony; he was permitted to choose any barony, anywhere in Eramma, that was not currently held.

"Eramma is a large country, overman, the largest in the world; there were a dozen empty thrones available, from Sland to Skelleth. My father, may P'hul devour his soul, chose Skelleth. He had had his fill of court politics and petty border disputes, and so chose a barony so poor, so unpleasant, that no one would ever bother him with such matters. Little did he care what his son might think of ruling such a frozen wasteland!"

The Baron was working himself up into a towering rage, totally unlike either the frowning gloom or the smiling urbanity that Garth had seen heretofore, and the overman began to wonder if the man was sane. Surely such disparate moods were not quite normal in a single man!

"Well, I *have* ruled over this little trash-heap of the gods. I have endured two dozen ten-month winters and as many muddy, malodorous summers, and I have had enough, more than enough! Other barons sneer at me. None have deigned to visit this pesthole for fear of contracting pneumonia, and when I have visited them I am seated at the foot of the table, like a commoner! Nor can I hope to improve my status by improving Skelleth, for there is nothing here to improve! The town was built as a frontier citadel for the Racial Wars, and has declined ever since. There is no money to be had here. I can afford no castle, no court; every cent of taxes is spent to maintain my three dozen guards, who are the laughingstock of every army in Eramma!"

The Baron had worked himself up into shouting, almost screaming. Now his voice dropped to a low and ominous tone.

"Listen, Garth, I have had enough. One way or another, I will change Skelleth or leave it. The next caravan will carry a letter from me to the High King, offering the services of myself and certain magicks in any war he chooses. If he ignores this, I will find my own use; with the basilisk I can take what I will. I can make myself King of Eramma if I want. If I give you the basilisk, I remain nothing, a worthless lord of an even more worthless land. Now, what compromise can you possibly suggest?" He glowered almost as balefully with his ice-blue eyes as Garth with his huge red ones.

The overman could think of no answer.

The Baron's anger subsided, and he seemed to collapse into himself, withdrawing into his gloomy silence again. It seemed to require an effort for him to order his men, "Take him."

The men behind the Baron surged forward and around him, but stopped just out of reach of Garth's sword; likewise, the men on the stair advanced, but did not attack, apparently unwilling to approach in such confined quarters.

Garth laughed, partly from genuine amusement at their timidity and partly to cow them further. He shifted his foot to his captive's neck, and announced, "I will slay this man after I have disposed of the rest of you, not before."

One of the men on the stairs gathered his courage and charged, yelling. Garth smashed at the attacker's hand with the flat of his broadsword, and sent the man's own weapon flying. The man, finding himself suddenly disarmed, turned his assault into a diving tackle. Garth caught him a blow on the head with the flat of the axe as he hit, so that the overman fell back against the wall while his assailant lay on the floor, stunned. Garth struggled for a few seconds to retain his balance and succeeded, stepping forward to straddle both the men on the floor, the one fully conscious and the other dazed. As soon as he did he found himself in combat, two short swords chopping at him. He dodged one and parried the other, and with a quick riposte ran the point of his blade through one man's shoulder. The guard gasped in agony and fell, writhing, as Garth withdrew the weapon just in time to counter another blow at his side. Holding the attacker's sword on his own, he brought up the axe in his left hand and hacked at the wrist behind the hilt. The soldier dropped his sword and fell back.

There was a momentary lull as others moved to replace their defeated comrades, and Garth took the opportunity to shout, "So far I have been merciful. The next man dies!"

The warning had an immediate effect, as the advancing men paused, uncertain.

"I do not wish to slay anyone, but neither do I wish to be defeated. Stand away!" As he spoke, Garth mentally congratulated himself upon having met his foes at a corner, where they could not approach en masse nor surround him. "Baron, this will avail you nothing except slaughter. Your men cannot take me!"

"Nor can you escape." The Baron's voice was quiet, barely audible, in contrast to Garth's shout, but its import more than made up for that, as the overman knew it was true. He could butcher anyone who approached him where he was, but if he moved out of the corner he would be surrounded and killed. Stalemate.

There was a sudden flurry of movement at the end of the corridor near the Baron. Someone had entered, and was whispering to his lord. Garth could make out nothing but the word "beast." He wondered what message could be arriving at such an hour and in such circumstances, but could do nothing to satisfy his curiosity. Instead he took the opportunity to kick away swords that had fallen within reach of the men he stood over, lest they retrieve and use them.

That done, he looked over the heads of the guards at the Baron's face. Whatever the news was, it seemed unwelcome, as the customary frown was deeper than ever. Then, with a curious shrug that seemed to leave him smaller than before and with an audible sigh, the frown vanished, to be replaced with an expression of utter despair such as Garth had seen heretofore only on caged animals – the expression that meant the animal would soon waste away and die. The Baron sagged, as if it took all his will merely to stand upright; he leaned heavily on the corridor wall.

One of the men-at-arms nearest the Baron asked solicitously, "Is there anything we can do, my lord?" His voice was sympathetic, but Garth thought he detected a note of contempt where he would have expected surprise or confusion. Surely this sort of collapse could not be a common occurrence?

The soldier had sheathed his sword and was helping the Baron to stand. He looked toward the overman, standing at the foot of the stairs on what would have been the natural route to the Baron's bedchamber, then glanced back toward the door to the dungeons, unsure which way to go. The messenger also looked about, apparently noticing Garth for the first time, and asked, "What should we do, my lord?"

The Baron shook his head and managed to croak, "Doesn't matter." Garth was appalled. The man was clearly suffering some sort of seizure, displaying the symptoms of a person in deep shock or sorely wounded. The entire party was now watching the Baron rather than the overman; swords were lowered, crouches abandoned. Seeing the easing of tension, the man escorting the Baron led him through the cluster of soldiers, past the motionless overman, and up the stairs, where the remaining men fell back to make room.

When he was past and out of sight around the corner at the top of the stairs, a man remarked casually, "It's a bad one this time."

A companion nodded, as heads began to turn in Garth's direction again. The overman, for his part, was utterly astonished by this turn of events, and glanced about in confusion. Could this anticlimax be the end of the battle? He was about to ask what the messenger had told the Baron when he received an even greater surprise. The guardsmen on the stairs moved abruptly downward, retreating from something, and there appeared at the top a huge black catlike head, with golden eyes and gleaming fangs, peering down at the torch lit corridor.

"Koros!" Garth's greeting burst forth involuntarily. He was almost as amazed by how happy he was to see the beast as he was by its presence. It growled pleasantly in response, but made no effort to move closer. It apparently didn't care to try squeezing around the corner onto the narrow staircase. Seeing this, Garth ordered it, "Wait," and turned to the nearest guard, one of those he had wounded in the brief melee.

"Where is the basilisk?"

"In the dungeon."

"Show me."

The man glanced around at his companions, who merely shrugged or looked away. One ventured to comment, "The Baron said it didn't matter." He did not look as if he meant it.

Resignedly, the wounded man turned and led the way to the door at the end of the corridor. Beyond it was a small room holding a rough wooden table, with several rings of keys hung on the wall and a statue standing in the center. The statue was of a wretched underfed youth. Garth stared at it in dismay.

His guide, feeling some explanation was in order, said, "The Baron wanted to test the legend. He promised the boy his freedom if he lived."

"His freedom?"

"He was awaiting sentencing for theft."

"Oh." Garth paused as the man took a set of keys from the wall and opened an iron-bound door at right angles to the one by which they had entered. As it swung wide to reveal a dreary stone passage, lit by a single torch, he said, "Tell me about the Baron. What is wrong with him, that he acted as he did just now?"

The man shrugged. "No one knows for sure. He's always been that way. He has these moods every few days where he refuses to do anything, he can't stand, can't speak. Once or twice he has slashed his wrists, but then bandaged them before the blood loss was serious. He's usually at his best, full of wit and charm, just a day or two before, which makes it seem all the worse. When he's well, he's a very clever man, there's no doubt, as methinks you've seen. But of late his fits have been getting worse. Some say he's under a curse, or that he deals with evil forces and suffers thus as payment."

Garth suggested, to see the man's reaction, "Perhaps he's mad."

"Oh, there's little doubt that he's mad! The only question is why."

This served only to confuse the overman. "If he's mad, why is he permitted to remain in power?"

The man gaped at Garth in astonishment. "He's the Baron! The High King gave Skelleth to his father! How could that be changed?"

Garth was on shaky ground, since he knew very little of Eramman politics, but ventured, "Could you not petition the High King to replace him?"

The man was slow in replying, "Well, I suppose we could, but why? He's not that bad, and he is our rightful lord. Better a madman like our own than one like the Baron of Sland!"

Since Garth had no idea who the Baron of Sland was nor what he was like, he could make no cogent reply. Instead he fell silent and permitted his escort to lead him into the passageway, a corridor about twenty feet long ending in another door identical to that he had just passed, with another corridor opening off the middle of the right-hand side and with several metal doors in the left wall, apparently leading to cells for imprisoning criminals. The smell of basilisk was readily noticeable.

The pair turned down the side corridor, which extended about thirty feet, with five doors on each side and a blank grey wall at the end, where another torch served to lessen the gloom. The guide stopped and pointed. "It's in the second cell on the left."

Garth nodded. "Where is the Sealing Rod?"

The man looked blank.

"The talisman that keeps it imprisoned. Where is it?"

He shrugged. "I don't know what you're talking about."

Garth, though annoyed, saw no reason for the man to lie. "Were you present when it was brought here?" he demanded.

"No."

"Well, fetch me someone who was."

The guard turned to go, and Garth suddenly realized what an incredibly stupid thing he was doing. It would be a very simple matter for the fellow to just close and lock the dungeon door and post guards with crossbows, in case Garth should hack down the door with his axe. Koros would be no problem; it had been told to wait, and as long as it was fed it would do just that. It might be a bit inconvenient having a warbeast in the front hall, but it could be lived with. And when Garth had starved to death, a way could be found to dispose of it.

"Wait!" Preferring safety to dignity, Garth ran to catch up.

Chapter Fifteen

The gathering at the foot of the stairs had broken up. There was no sign of the recent abortive battle except one or two small spatters of blood on the stone floor. A lone guardsman sat on the bottom step, cleaning his sword. It was the man Garth had disarmed and knocked unconscious. His hand bore a few scratches where the rough hilt had been torn from his grasp. The sword was also scratched, apparently having suffered when so rudely flung about. As Garth and his escort approached the man picked it up to sight along the blade, and muttered, "Aghad and Bheleu!" The blade was bent.

The escort interrupted. "Saram, the overman is looking for someone who saw the basilisk put away."

The man addressed as Saram looked up and growled, "So what?"

"I don't know who was there. I thought you might."

"I was there myself. Why?" He looked from his fellow soldier to his recent adversary.

Garth spoke on his own behalf. "I want to know where the Sealing Rod is."

Saram squinted up at him, which Garth was sure could only be an affectation in the dim torchlight, and asked, "The what?"

"The wooden rod that keeps the basilisk caged."

"Is that what it is? A carved stick about thus?" He held up his hands to indicate the length, having laid his ruined sword on the step beside him.

"Yes."

"Why?"

"I want the basilisk."

"But why should I tell you?"

Garth had no ready answer.

"You're worried you won't get the monster out of here before the Baron comes out of it, eh? Probably right, unless you can make it worth my while to help."

Comprehension dawned on Garth. He dug out his purse and handed Saram a coin. Saram studied it, acknowledged it to be gold and of sufficient size, and stood up.

"I'll show you. Come along."

Garth hesitated, then ordered his original guide, "You too." Together they followed Saram as he stalked down the corridor, clutching his naked sword.

Having appropriated a ring of keys in the wardroom, Saram promptly went, not to the cell that held the basilisk, but to the last door on that side. Unlocking it at last after trying half a dozen different keys, he swung the heavy metal door open to reveal a tiny cell containing nothing but a mound of straw. He indicated the pile and said, "Under there."

Garth started to step into the cell, then thought better of it. That would be even stupider than merely getting himself locked in the dungeon. Grabbing the other soldier, he said, "You get it."

The man obeyed. Apparently no trickery had been planned. The rod was indeed under the straw, and was handed promptly to the overman.

"Good. Now unlock the cell with the basilisk in it"

Saram handed the keys to his comrade and said, "Here. Your turn." He then attempted a hasty departure, to be discouraged by the overman's hand on his shoulder.

"Wait. Don't look at it and you'll be safe." He motioned to the other, who reluctantly approached the cell he had earlier indicated, wrinkling his nose at the smell. The key turned in the lock, and the door swung out an inch.

Suddenly noticing that he was on the wrong side of the basilisk, Garth said, "Enough," and began walking up the corridor. The rod in his hand began to resist when he had gone a few paces, and he found it necessary to push it over toward the wall opposite the creature's cell; even then it required considerable force to move it, and he wondered how the Baron had ever gotten it there in the first place. Had the cell door not already been unlocked he might have dissolved the barrier, but as it was he did not dare, nor did he care to take the time to lock the door again for the few minutes necessary. Instead he merely pressed on, and heard a ferocious and familiar hissing in response. The two men-at-arms were rather visibly taken aback. It was only the fact that Garth had not yet sheathed his sword that kept the one whose name he didn't know from running.

Then suddenly he was past the crucial point, and the abrupt cessation of resistance almost sent him sprawling. Saram, his composure at least partly recovered, ventured, "'Twas easier getting it in here."

Garth growled as he steadied himself, carefully looking away from that ominous inch-wide opening; his displeasure was caused as much by the dry, deathly stench that was filling the passage as by the man's irritating remark. The venomous vapor had had half a day to accumulate in the tiny room, and the air of that cell was undoubtedly lethal by now. Well, at least its next occupant need not worry about vermin.

He motioned for the guards to precede him out. He did not care to speak aloud and give that poisonous atmosphere greater access to his lungs. They obeyed promptly, both of them beginning to gag on the fumes. They had not developed the tolerance Garth had from his prolonged exposure in Mormoreth, and would probably have been more sensitive in any case, being merely human. They seemed too busy choking to try trapping Garth in the dungeon, but nonetheless he kept his sword ready and made sure both remained within easy reach until they were all in the wardroom. His left hand kept a secure hold on the rod, which he thrust into his belt.

There was a hiss from behind as the basilisk objected to being moved, and the nameless guard started to turn, thoughtlessly. Garth slapped him, hard, with the flat of the sword, leaving a small slash in the sleeve of his mail shirt where the edge had not been angled away sufficiently. Startled, the man looked at the overman rather than the basilisk. Without a word, Garth pointed at the petrified prisoner who stood a yard away. The guard shuddered and looked faint. Saram tried to grin, but he, too, was pale.

Since there were no further doors between him and the outside that could stand up to more than a few quick blows of his axe, he decided there was no reason to keep his two-man escort any longer. With a motion he indicated that they could go. The first promptly ran for the stairs; Saram started to depart at a more leisurely pace.

"Wait!" Garth called, remembering something. Saram stopped, but did not look back. Although, from where he was, the monster was around a corner and therefore invisible, he was not taking chances.

"Where is the cover for the enclosure?" Garth demanded.

Saram shrugged. "Don't know."

"Find it. You were there when the basilisk was delivered. You must have seen what became of it."

"It was dragged off toward the other stairs."

"Find it and bring it here."

Obviously none too pleased, Saram shrugged again, then nodded. He strolled off for the stairs again. Garth choked back an order to hurry; such a command would do no good when the man was out of sight. Besides, he was already beginning to regret opening his mouth at all. Though the vapors in the wardroom were not concentrated enough to really bother him, they seemed to have put a foul taste on his tongue that he would have greatly preferred to do without. He wondered whether the monster's trail would do any harm to his bare feet; it seemed unlikely, since it had only passed along this route once. In any case, he felt nothing but the ordinary cool stone against his soles.

Having sent Saram off, Garth now had to wait where he was, for fear of petrifying the guard on his return should he move any further; this meant he had nothing to do but contemplate his surroundings and avoid looking behind himself.

There being little else in the room worthy of study, he found himself inspecting the remains of the unfortunate youth used to test the basilisk's legendary power. He was interested to notice the expression, which meant little to him, but was plainly not the look of abject terror he would have expected. He had seen human panic on Arner's face when that youth, somewhat older and a good bit healthier than the current specimen, awaited his execution, and the aspect of the alleged thief bore no resemblance to that distorted countenance. Instead, Garth decided, there was something resolved about it; the mouth was shut, even compressed, so that those hideous oversize human lips scarcely showed; the jaw was set and the eyes open, but not unnaturally wide. The overman found himself wondering what peculiar combination of emotions could produce such a look on the face of one facing certain death. No, not certain death; he had been told that he might die, or that he might go free. It suddenly struck Garth that the young thief had been inordinately brave to take such a risk. Theft was not a capital crime in Skelleth, he was sure. He did not know what the customary penalty was, but to gamble one's life, one's very existence, on an unknown chance for freedom, with no chance to defend oneself . . .

He shuddered slightly. It was not a thing he would care to do in such a situation. Though he thought highly of himself, Garth admitted that he probably would not have such courage. Perhaps the humans placed a higher value on freedom than overmen did, or a lower value on survival. The latter was certainly possible from what little he had seen of human society. Perhaps their beliefs in supernatural powers, gods and the like, had something to do with it; he had heard that most believed in some sort of existence after death, where the essence, the personality of the individual – they had a special word for it, the soul – lived on, in some other world. The idea seemed very nebulous and unlikely to Garth, but such a concept would undoubtedly account for the disregard for life some humans seemed to display – such as the dead thief he was studying.

But then, the boy had been very thin. Garth imagined he could make out the bones in his arms and legs, and ribs made visible ridges in his ragged tunic. Perhaps he had gone mad from hunger, like an unfed warbeast, and taken the first opportunity to leave his cell, despite the possible consequences. That did not explain what Garth was now fairly certain was the determined expression on the stone face, though; a starving warbeast appeared to be angry, enraged rather than determined.

Overmen, he knew, did not go mad from hunger – he had seen too many of his people starve to death in bad winters to doubt that – but perhaps humans did. He was musing on the Baron's apparent insanity, wondering if it were diet-related, when Saram called from the foot of the stairs. The villagers seemed to take their lord's insanity for granted. Such afflictions were plainly far more common among humans than among overmen.

It did not occur to Garth that his own behavior, leaving his home and family for an idiot quest after fame, might well be considered mad by his fellow overmen.

Turning his attention from such theoretical musings back to immediate concerns, he saw that Saram stood well down the corridor, facing the opposite direction and clutching a huge bundle of dirty cloth.

"Bring it here!" Garth called.

"Get it yourself," Saram retorted, dropping his burden to the floor with a rattle of chains.

Garth glanced down at the wooden rod at his belt, then pulled it out and placed it carefully on the floor; he didn't care to haul the basilisk out into the passageway yet. Leaving the rod there, he strode down the corridor to where Saram stood, one foot on the bundle.

"It was in the armory," the guardsman said as Garth drew near. The overman suddenly realized that the man held a sword, not his ruined short sword, but a long, thin rapier that glinted where it caught the torchlight. Sometime during his wait, Garth had sheathed his own blade, and his hand now fell instinctively to its hilt.

"Oh?" Garth tried to sound noncommittal as he stopped a few paces from Saram's back. He had no idea what the soldier had in mind. Surely he could not plan to tackle an overman single-handed!

"It's a long trip to the armory."

Suddenly remembering Saram's earlier actions, Garth thought he understood part of the man's behavior, though the sword remained a mystery. He said "Oh" again, and pulled out a gold coin. An open palm appeared to accept it, apparently in response to the clink of metal when Garth reached into his purse. The overman put the coin on the palm, and both promptly disappeared. So did the sword, which was sheathed in the same flurry of motion.

"Anything else I can get you?" Saram still kept his back to the overman.

"No."

Saram shrugged, and strolled back up the stairs, leaving the cover where it lay on the floor. Garth watched him go, more than a little confused by the man's behavior. Had the sword been entirely to keep him from snatching up the cover without paying? It began to appear that all the humans he met were insane; the Forgotten King demanding delivery of a basilisk while swearing not to use it in the only way Garth could imagine, the Baron collapsing into a near catatonic depression as he watched, the boy-thief risking his life for freedom, Saram's irrational behavior . . . it was all more than Garth could understand.

Finally, shrugging, he turned and walked back to the wardroom, being careful not to look toward the basilisk. He untangled the cover as best he could in the limited space, then lifted it up to shield his eyes as he proceeded back into the dungeon. There was no room to drape it properly around the enclosure, so he made do with hanging it across the leading edge. There was barely room above the barrier to squeeze through enough chain and cloth to keep the battered shroud in place. Once that was done, it was a matter of a few minutes to drag the whole mess to the stairs and to start up them. There was some difficulty in getting the leading edge of the cover up the steps, and Garth found it necessary to feel his way back down, eyes closed, to untangle things three times.

A trace of venom had apparently found its way into the cut on his left foot and was stinging abominably, but Garth refused to let that slow him. Upon first reaching the top of the stairs, he saw bright morning sun pouring through a nearby window, plainly showing that it was full day out. He could ill afford to waste further time. The Baron might recover at any moment, or Herrenmer, the captain of the guard, might take charge and decide to stop the overman. Garth considered it fortunate that Herrenmer had not been present at the predawn encounter, Judging by his performance at the confiscation of the basilisk, he would not have allowed Garth to simply go on about his business as had the other guards.

As well as the sunlight, Koros was waiting at the top of the stairs. Garth greeted it affectionately, if rather hurriedly, and hooked the Sealing Rod into its halter before leading it out to the entry hall, carefully keeping the warbeast's golden eyes facing forward, away from the imperfectly hidden basilisk.

They met no one in the hallway. Undoubtedly the residents of the mansion didn't care to come too close to Koros' fangs.

In the entry hall two men-at-arms were guarding the front door, which stood slightly ajar. Garth could see splintered wood where lock and latch had been ripped out, presumably by the warbeast's entrance in pursuit of its master. The doors were still on their hinges, though, and reasonably intact. It was just as well. Garth had no wish to further antagonize the Baron, though he doubted that the mad nobleman would ever forgive what he had already done.

Upon seeing the overman and warbeast appear, the guards stepped back, and one drew his sword.

Garth said, "Don't worry; we're leaving. Shield your eyes; we are taking the basilisk."

The guards said nothing, but merely looked at one another, nodded, and stepped further back – through the door to the audience chamber. Garth continued forward and swung open the front door.

Immediately he regretted doing so. He reprimanded himself for not noticing the mutter of noise outside.

It was market-day, apparently; the square outside the mansion was thronged with people milling about, merchants hawking their wares, farmers selling their produce, and children running underfoot. Several turned and stared in astonishment at the armored apparition standing in the door of the Baronial mansion, and Garth stared back.

Offensive action seemed called for, before the crowd could remember its earlier aggression; Garth had no desire to be pelted with mud and stones again. He drew his sword and stepped forward into the sunlight, roaring at the crowd.

Immediately those nearest him fell back, terrified.

Koros, in response to its master's bellowing, appeared at his shoulder. The crowd's murmur died away for a long moment, then returned to a higher pitch. It occurred to the overman that he would have to empty the square completely before he could safely bring the basilisk out, since only in the square itself was there room to straighten the covering. Therefore he strode boldly forward with sword raised, his left hand unslinging his axe, the warbeast growling along a few paces behind him. When he had reached what seemed a good point, where Koros could join him without hauling the basilisk's enclosure past the open door of the mansion, he stepped up on a merchant's box and bellowed, "Go! This place is mine!"

Like magic, most of the mob evaporated. It had already cleared a wide path from the mansion door to his speaking-box, and that path quickly widened to include the whole square. Guards posted around the edge, whom Garth had not noticed before in the crowd, hesitated, but gave way before the rush of villagers and also retreated. A few die-hards remained, but another bellow and a swing of his sword sent them scurrying. A short charge and a feint in the direction of a straggler sent even the stubbornest fleeing. To be certain, Garth circled the market, bellowing and making threatening gestures up each street. The market square was indeed empty.

Well satisfied with his achievement, Garth hurried to the basilisk's enclosure as Koros dragged it forth, and rapidly spread the covering around it properly. He knew that any second people would begin drifting back to watch whatever happened. He only hoped that they would remain intimidated, and not work up a raging mob over his supposed responsibility for Arner's execution. He also hoped that the guards would not rally.

When the cloth-and-chain covering was securely in place Garth tried to rush to Koros' side, but found himself limping badly on his injured and poisoned left foot, so that his progress across the square was more of a stagger than a run and his mounting more of a scramble than a leap. Once safely astride, he directed the warbeast toward the best route around the mansion toward the King's Inn, and looked at his foot.

The cut itself was insignificant, as he had thought all along, but the venom had caused massive swelling and discoloration. He comforted himself with the thought that there couldn't have been much of the poison or he would be dead already. As it was, he once again regretted the loss of his supplies; the medicinal herbs that now lay under a foot of rainwater could have treated the wound.

Also, of course, the warbeast's saddle, now drowned, was somewhat more comfortable than its bare back. That could be endured, however, though Garth would have preferred to have the guide-handle rather than merely the halter he had left on the beast.

To Garth's delight, the villagers fled before his advance. He had been rather worried that they might stand their ground. His extended contemplation of the petrified youth had given him a higher opinion of human courage than he had previously held.

Were it not for the pain in his foot, he would have enjoyed the ride; the sun was bright and warm, though clouds were gathering, and he was at long last about to deliver the basilisk to the Forgotten King. Unfortunately, the aching wound served to remind him of less pleasant matters: that he had lost all his supplies save a part of his gold, his sword, and his axe; that he had no boots nor cloak to his name; that he was surrounded by enemies; that the injury might well become gangrenous and therefore fatal; that he didn't know if the warbeast had found and eaten the goats. All in all, his situation struck him as unenviable, and he was very glad indeed that this ridiculous quest was nearing its conclusion. He had little patience left.

So little patience, in fact, that after installing Koros and the basilisk in the stable beside the tavern – and frightening away the new stable-boy – he marched boldly if somewhat limpingly into the King's Inn with drawn sword, ready to deal with whatever he might find there, up to and including the entire village guard. All he found, however, was half a dozen morning drinkers guzzling ale, the innkeeper polishing brass, and the Forgotten King sitting motionless at his usual table.

The overman stopped in the center of the taproom and looked around at the silent, terrified customers. A sudden feeling of anticlimax, like that following the Baron's collapse, washed over him as he realized that this peaceful tavern was the end of his adventure. It seemed inappropriate. But then, he reminded himself, was this really the end? He had yet to deal with the Baron, and it might be some time before he could return again to his home and family. Also, there was still the mystery of what the Forgotten King wanted with the basilisk. He sheathed his sword, crossed to the old man's table, and seated himself.

The Forgotten King, as usual, did nothing to acknowledge his existence.

"I have brought the basilisk."

"Where?" The hideous voice was a shock, as always.

"In the stable, as you suggested."

"Good." The old man began to rise, but Garth caught his arm. He immediately regretted it; even through the voluminous yellow sleeve he could distinctly feel every bone and tendon, as hard and tense as wire. The arm had none of the natural warmth Garth had expected. He snatched his fingers back, as if burnt.

"Wait."

The old man seated himself again, his head raised, apparently looking at Garth, though his eyes were invisible under his hood.

"Will you tell me why you want the basilisk?"

"No." The voice seemed even drier than usual, and was definitely lower in pitch.

Garth thought better of further argument. After a brief pause, the Forgotten King rose, and this time the overman made no move to stop him. Instead he started to rise himself, only to sit down abruptly after attempting to put weight on his left foot. The old man gave no obvious sign that he had seen the movement, but he paused, standing beside the table, and hissed something in a language Garth had never heard before, totally unlike either the speech used throughout the northern lands or the ancient dead tongues the overman had seen in books. Then he turned and moved silently across to the door as Garth, somewhat taken aback, sat and watched him go.

It was only when the door had swung shut behind the tattered figure that Garth realized the pain in his foot was gone.

Chapter Sixteen

By midafternoon Garth had given up wondering about the Forgotten King's purpose, and turned his thoughts instead to such practical matters as footwear. He did not care to go barefoot any longer than necessary; life without boots was proving thoroughly unpleasant. If his feet weren't being burned or stabbed, they were cold, or wet, or both, making his life miserable in any number of small ways. As the sunlight inched its way across the tavern floor, from early morning to noon, he had expected the old man's return at any moment and put off any real thought. As the bands of light beneath the windows swung past the vertical and began to lengthen, he had alternately worried lest the Forgotten King had accidentally perished and hoped that the old fool had indeed done so, all the while asking himself what use a basilisk could be. And now, as the light began to dim and the early diners arrived, he had turned to more worthwhile musings.

He had just decided that it would be perfectly reasonable to ask the innkeeper to recommend a good cobbler when the King at last reentered the taproom, as silent as ever but perhaps more stooped, as if dejected. Garth immediately surmised that whatever his goal might be, the old man had failed to attain it.

The yellow-robed figure sank quietly into his usual chair, his head bent low. Garth waited a polite moment before speaking, noticing that the ragged cloak the old man wore smelled faintly of basilisk venom.

"Greetings, O King."

The old man said nothing.

"What of the basilisk?"

"It lives." The dry voice was faint.

"What is to become of it now?"

"I care not."

"Has it served your purpose?"

There was a long pause, then what might have been a sigh. "No. No, it has not."

Before Garth could continue, something registered suddenly. For the past few seconds he had heard footsteps approaching the tavern, but had not paid any attention. A sudden realization catapulted that information to the conscious level and the center of his attention. The footsteps were those of several men, marching in step.

Soldiers!

There was a sudden blur of motion as the tavern door burst in, revealing a small crowd of the Baron's guards. Almost simultaneously, Garth jumped up and snatched up the heavy oaken table one-handed, to serve as a shield until he could draw his weapons. Two heavy crossbow quarrels thudded into the ancient tabletop, their barbed heads projecting from the solid wood in a direct line with Garth's chest.

Then, in shocking contrast to the flurry of activity, there was a long moment in which everything seemed frozen, suspended in time. Garth stood, his makeshift shield clutched in his left hand, his sword ready in his right, facing a dozen men-at-arms across half the width of the taproom. The crossbowmen seemed startled; they made no move to reload. The other guards were armed with swords – not their customary shortswords, but proper three-foot broadswords. The customers seemed paralyzed with astonishment, gaping at the battle tableau of a lone monster at bay holding off a dozen warriors.

And behind him, where the overman could not see him, the Forgotten King was grinning as he had not for centuries, his eye-sockets alight.

The silence was broken by a discordant screech from behind the soldiers, barely recognizable as the Baron's voice.

"Kill him, you fools!"

Hesitantly, the foremost trio of guards advanced, only to fall back again as Garth crouched, sword raised. Again, all movement ceased, save for the maniacal dancing and yelling of the Baron, who stood in the doorway haranguing his men. The tension in the room mounted, as each side awaited a move from the other. Garth knew that his best move would be a sudden assault followed by a quick retreat, but he also knew that that would kill at least one of his foes, and he had hopes, even now, of avoiding bloodshed. He could see familiar faces among the guards. Herrenmer stood in the second rank, his steel helmet freshly polished; Saram held a crossbow and stood to one side, unmoving; the young man who had led him to the dungeon stood behind his captain; and other faces were also recognizable, men he had encountered upon his arrival in Skelleth, men who had saved him from the mob, men who had helped to confiscate the basilisk, men he had fought in the mansion basement. Now they all stood facing him, with orders to kill.

Behind them the Baron continued to rave, his words all but unintelligible. Then one phrase suddenly rang out clearly in the tension-filled room.

"Remember Arner!"

Garth could see that those two words affected the guards, though he was not sure how. Expressions changed, stances shifted. Saram turned toward his master, his face showing surprise. Garth was too busy watching the swordsmen to pay much attention, until there came a sudden clatter.

Saram had flung down his crossbow. Even the Baron fell silent. Garth waited for the man to draw his sword, but instead he announced loudly, "This is stupid. Innkeeper!"

The other men forgot their opponent, and turned to gape in astonishment as Saram crossed to where the terrified tavern keeper stood beside the huge casks.

"Pour me an ale, you old fool," said Saram in a normal voice that seemed like a bellow in the sudden stillness. The innkeeper hurried to comply, as Saram lounged comfortably against the wall and declared, "You people can get yourselves slaughtered if you want to, but I don't intend to die on behalf of a mad baron. Luck to you all!" With this last he raised his just-delivered mug in sarcastic salute, then gulped down a large mouthful of the foaming brew.

The guards looked at one another, dumbfounded. Then, abruptly, a man flung down his sword, saying, "Bheleu take it!" He, too, crossed to the liquor barrels and poured himself a drink, ignoring the protests of the innkeeper. That ended the tension, and in moments the entire party of soldiers was at ease, drinking, joking, and laughing. Only the Baron remained in the doorway, screaming imprecations at his men.

Garth relaxed, righted the table, and sat again, looking amusedly at the two shafts protruding from the wood. He was startled when Saram appeared, pulling up a chair.

"Mind if I join you?"

"Whatever you please. I am at your service." Garth was not given to polite exaggeration; he meant it. It was quite likely that Saram's disgusted revolt had saved his life, and he felt indebted to the man.

The guard casually took a long draught from his mug, and seated himself.

There came the noise of a commotion near the door, and all but the Forgotten King turned to see what was happening. The Baron, finally tiring of his ineffectual yelling, had snatched up a dropped sword, apparently planning to attack the overman single-handed. Several of his men had jumped him and were now struggling to get the weapon away from him before anyone was hurt. Garth could hear muffled curses from the writhing mass of men, and saw one man roll apart, his hand bleeding from a long, shallow scratch.

The man's voice rose above the hubbub. "Oh, Death, that hurts! Aghad and Pria!" Several men not involved in the struggle rushed to his aid.

Then the knot around the Baron broke up. The sword had been flung safely out of reach, and the Baron lay on the floor, crying like an infant. With a low curse and a glance at his wounded companion, one man launched a vicious kick at the fallen noble's midsection. The Baron crumpled into a ball and lay, sobbing.

Someone gently reprimanded the kicker. "You shouldn't have done that."

Herrenmer appeared from somewhere and knelt over his lord. Looking up, he called, "Someone help me; we'll get him safely in bed in the mansion." Willing hands reached out, and in a few moments Herrenmer and another guard were assisting the Baron, still weeping, out into the sunlit alley. The guard captain paused in the doorway to announce, "We'll be back soon."

The episode over, Garth and Saram turned back toward their table.

They sat silently for a moment as Saram poured his remaining ale down his throat. Then, thumping his mug on the table, he said, "I've been wondering about you."

Garth looked politely blank. "Oh?"

"Whatever under the gods brought you to Skelleth?"

The overman considered the question; ordinarily he would have refused to answer it, but in the present state of gratitude he felt unusually open and willing to talk.

"I was on a quest, of sorts."

"A quest?"

"Yes."

"A quest for what? I don't mean the basilisk; I mean why did you go off questing?"

"I wanted to do something of true significance."

"Go on."

"I wanted to change things, to have a lasting influence on the world. I went to an oracle near Ordunin, but was told that no mortal could change the way things are."

"Ah, so you asked to be immortal?"

Neither Saram nor Garth noticed the Forgotten King's reaction to this question; he looked up, light glinting in his eyes like two lonely stars in two black pits. Neither noticed, because Saram was too startled by Garth's reaction, and Garth was not noticing anything. Instead he was staring at Saram, his expression a baleful glare that appalled the man. For several seconds neither spoke. Then Garth muttered, "I never thought of that," and dropped his gaze to contemplate the tabletop.

There was another moment of silence, ending when Saram said, "Then what did you ask for?"

"I asked for fame – that my name be known forever."

"One of those!" Saram leaned back, studying the overman. "Why do you want fame? I never saw much point in it."

Garth looked up. "I wanted something to survive. I had never considered the possibility of living forever myself, but it seemed that having my name live on would be better than nothing."

Saram nodded sagely. "I see. Never thought that, myself, but I can see how one could. So you set out to become famous?"

"I asked the oracle how I might achieve everlasting fame."

"Oh?"

"Yes. I was told to come to Skelleth, find the Forgotten King, and serve him without fail."

"Find who?"

"The Forgotten King." Garth pointed a thumb at the old man, whose head had sunk back to its usual droop.

Saram's surprise was evident. "The old man?"

"Yes."

"Forgotten King? King of what?"

Garth shrugged.

Saram turned to the yellow-robed figure and demanded, "King of what?"

"Of Carcosa. In exile." The dry voice was quieter than usual, but still shockingly harsh.

"I never heard of it."

The old man said nothing, and Saram turned back toward the overman.

"Serving him was supposed to ensure eternal fame?"

"Yes."

"It seems unlikely."

Garth shrugged. "It was the word of the oracle."

"It still seems unlikely."

"I have reason to trust the wisdom and truth of the oracle."

"Well, I know nothing of that, but it doesn't seem possible. Nothing lasts forever, certainly not fame."

Garth shrugged.

"But think, Garth, can you name a single person who lived more than a thousand years ago?"

The Forgotten King's cowl rustled as his head turned at this question, but he said nothing as Garth admitted, "No, but I have made no study of human history. Overmen have not existed that long."

"Well, can you name the first overman, or the wizard who created him?"

"No."

"Llarimuir the Great." Startled, both Garth and Saram turned toward the Forgotten King, who continued, "Llarimuir created a dozen overmen and overwomen simultaneously; there was no first."

Saram demanded, "How do you know that, old man?"

"I remember."

"But it was a thousand years ago!"

The Forgotten King said nothing, and after a moment Saram turned away again.

"Most people know nothing of that, and no one can say with certainty that this old fool is correct."

Garth said nothing. He was remembering the Forgotten King's eerie room upstairs and the casually miraculous cure worked on his wounded foot, and wondering who and what the King really was.

Undaunted, Saram continued, "How do you expect to achieve this fame? Do you expect the old man to tell you how? Or do you think he can do it for you?"

Garth remarked, quietly, "He is a wizard."

Saram snorted. "Then why does he live in a tavern in Skelleth? Why does he not have a place in the warm south?"

Garth shrugged again.

"So you intend to continue to blindly serve him?"

"I am not sure."

"Oh?"

"I am not sure I still want the fame I sought."

"Oh. But you still believe the old man could make it happen?"

"Yes."

Saram abruptly rose. "I'm going to get some more ale." He strode away, mail clinking faintly. Garth watched him go, then turned to the Forgotten King.

"You still will not say why you wanted the basilisk?"

The old man said nothing.

"Then what of my goal?"

"I have not yet decided upon your next task."

"Nor have I decided that I wish to accept it."

"What of your bargain?"

"I begin to doubt it."

"You doubt I can grant your desire?"

"No; I doubt whether I truly desire it, and at the price asked."

"Is the price too high?"

"It may be. It may be that I asked the Wise Women of Ordunin the wrong questions; it may also be that the deaths of a dozen men are more than I wish to pay."

"Yet, already, from this first errand, your name is known in Mormoreth and throughout Skelleth."

"Known as the name of a murderer."

"Nonetheless, it is known. You made no provision as to how you wished to be remembered. You merely wished that your name be known until the end of the world, and I can promise that if you serve me successfully, you shall have that."

"I wanted fame, not notoriety!"

"You made no such specification."

Garth could feel a cold rage growing inside him. He felt betrayed, both by the Forgotten King and by the Wise Women who had sent him to Skelleth. He had trusted them; most particularly, he had trusted the King solely because the Wise Women had said he should, and trusted him to the point of killing for him. He said nothing, but merely glared at the ragged yellow cowl. Then, abruptly, he rose.

"Sit down."

The hideous voice could not be ignored; Garth hesitated, then sat, silent with fury.

"You would wish, then, not merely to have your name known, but to have it honored?"

Garth could not bring himself to speak; he nodded.

"I have no objection to altering our bargain to that effect."

His rage subsided in sudden confusion. "What?"

"You are from Ordunin."

"Yes." Garth was now completely bewildered.

"It is a poor city."

"Yes."

"Yet you have wealth. There is gold to be mined, fish in abundance, rich furs to be trapped. Why, then, are you poor?"

The overman made no reply at first. When the old man said nothing and the silence began to grow, Garth said, "Because we must trade away our wealth for food. An overman cannot live on fish alone, nor can every overman spend his time fishing, for someone must work the mines."

"Where do you trade?"

"At Lagur, ten days sail southeast."

"Why?"

Comprehension was seeping in as Garth replied, "Because trade overland was impossible, we thought. The Racial Wars made it so. And we know of no other ports."

As he spoke, Saram resumed his seat, a full mug sloshing in his hand. "What's due to the Racial Wars, did you say?"

Garth looked at the yellow-robed figure to see if he wished to explain and, seeing only a faint trace of a smile, said himself, "The impossibility of trade between Skelleth and Ordunin – and in fact, between all Eramma and all the Northern Waste."

"Well, the Racial Wars are long ended, it seems, yet there's still no trade, is there?" Saram gulped his ale. "I don't suppose Skelleth has anything you'd want up there. You've got ice and hay of your own."

"But you, here in Skelleth, can trade with the south."

"So?" Saram did not yet see Garth's point.

The Forgotten King interrupted before Garth could speak. "Saram, why is Skelleth dying?"

"Because we haven't got anything to eat or trade."

"And what if you had gold, and furs, and other valuable goods to trade with the south?"

Saram looked at the old man, then turned to Garth. "You mine gold up there?"

Garth nodded. For a moment the oddly assorted trio sat silently. Then the overman remarked, "There may be difficulties. They hate me here; I am blamed for Arner's death, and overmen are still mistrusted of old."

Saram waved that away. "No one will care once they see gold."

Garth made no reply.

The old man smiled sardonically, making his face even more horrifying than usual.

"Thus, O Garth, will you be known as the one to bring wealth and prosperity to Ordunin and Skelleth. Is this more pleasing to you?"

The Forgotten King's question needed no answer, but Garth had a question of his own.

"Why do you suggest this scheme? I have not fulfilled your purpose, you say, yet you offer this advice. Why?"

"Is it not to my benefit that Skelleth prosper? It seems that I must live here for a time yet. I have no wish to inconvenience myself with either starvation or fleeing south, should Skelleth continue to decline."

There was a pause, then Garth replied, "Earlier you spoke of this being the age of decay, and told me that there was no way for mortals to defy the will of the gods and reverse that decay."

"Perhaps I was pessimistic."

The overman remained unconvinced. Ha said, after another moment's silence, "Whatever your reasons, the idea has merit."

"Indeed. So you will return to Skelleth with gold and furs, and become the hero and benefactor of its people. When you do, mayhap we will speak again."

"Perchance we will." Garth rose. "Though never again will I blindly obey you, O King. Saram, come. We have unfinished business."

Startled, Saram rose; not caring to argue, he followed as Garth led the way to the tavern door, pausing only to scoop up one of the two crossbows that lay where they had been dropped, motioning for Saram to get the other. He did, and followed Garth out into the alley, blinking in the slanting light of the setting sun as it peeped through the clouds. Though a few eyes glanced up curiously as the pair departed, the buzz of conversation did not lessen and no man moved to halt them.

Outside, the overman leaned his crossbow against the wall of the Inn and ordered, "Load them." He strode on and vanished into the stable. Saram shrugged and wound back the string of his weapon. He still wore a quiver holding eleven quarrels, not having bothered to remove it after the abortive battle in the tavern.

Inside the stable it was dim and cool, the pleasant smell of fresh hay and the stink of manure mingling weirdly with the stench of the basilisk. Garth crossed to where Koros stood waiting placidly, the Sealing Rod still securely tucked into its harness. A pace from the warbeast's side he stumbled over a small object.

Pausing, he looked down and saw he had trod on a stone, a curiously smooth and symmetrical stone. He picked it up, and found it was a stone rat; his foot had snapped off its tail, which lay in fragments amid the straw on the floor. He immediately turned his gaze to the other side of the stable, where the basilisk lurked silently within its enclosure. There was no opening in the cloth cover. The rat had not, then, chewed its way in; nor could it have crawled under the cloth, for how would it get back out, once petrified? No, the cover must have been lifted and replaced in the course of whatever the Forgotten King had done, and the unfortunate rat had been in line with the creature's gaze. Nothing else was disturbed. Odd that the King had taken such a risk as looking at the monster, Garth thought. Then he thought again, remembering certain things the old man had said, and a possible understanding dawned.

Then he dismissed the matter from his mind and returned his attention to Koros.

When Garth emerged from the stable leading the warbeast, both crossbows were loaded and cocked, leaning against the wall. The overman picked up one in passing and Saram retrieved the other, following Garth at a distance of a few yards. They continued up the alley until the basilisk's enclosure appeared in the stable door and slid into the street. When it was clear of the doorframe and the cloth cover free of all snags, Garth stopped and pulled the Sealing Rod from its place in Koros' harness. Saram watched in some confusion as Garth proceeded to tap several of the carved facets, one after the other.

When he tapped the final spot there was a soft sigh from the basilisk's direction, and Saram turned in time to see the cloth covering sinking to the ground, like a tent with its supports suddenly removed. It did not come to rest flat on the ground, but instead revealed the outline of an immense lizard, thrashing about angrily under the entangling fabric. Saram raised his crossbow.

Garth fired first; the bolt struck the basilisk in the neck, and the thrashing momentarily heightened as a gout of yellowish ichor stained the dirty cloth. Saram fired; his missile struck somewhere in the body, drawing another spurt of the basilisk's pale blood. The thrashing ceased as Garth calmly cranked back the bowstring for another shot.

He continued to wind, load, and shoot until all eleven quarrels protruded from the motionless form, and the alleyway reeked with the smell of basilisk more than it ever had with common ordure. A pool of reddish-gold, watery blood covered most of the fallen expanse of rough cloth, and a single green-scaled claw showed through a small tear. His last bolt shot, Garth thrust the now-useless crossbow at Saram, who accepted it while still clutching his own in his other hand.

The overman swung gracefully up onto the warbeast's back and announced, "You can tell the Baron that the basilisk is his, if he wants it. He can thank me when I return." Then, with a word to Koros, he rode off, turning north at the first corner and vanishing amid the first drops of a light rain.

Book Two: The Seven Altars of Dûsarra

Chapter One

The rider paused at the top of the low ridge; the plain that lay just beyond was spread out before him under the pale stars of late summer. Directly before him there was an interruption of the flat earth; jagged silhouettes rose in black humps, huddled together within an uneven stone ring. The circle was broken at the point nearest him, and a single shattered wall rose to mark what had once been a substantial gatehouse; beside that wall flickered an orange flame, as warm as the stars were cold.

Although he was still too far away to discern any details, he knew that this was the town of Skelleth, and that the single light was the watch fire of the guardsman at the ruins of the North Gate. He had been here before, and knew that of the five gates in the crumbling city wall only this one was guarded. It was guarded against him and his kind.

There was no sign of life other than the lonely fire, and even had the man posted there been fully alert – as he undoubtedly was not at this hour – he could not have seen the rider or his party at such a distance in the dark. Their approach was undetected.

The mounted figure sat for a moment, his face invisible in the darkness and the shade of his trader's hat, studying the panorama; he glanced up as a nightbird flew overhead, and his eyes shone a baleful red with reflected starlight. His hollow-cheeked face had no nose, but only close-set slit nostrils; ragged black hair hung almost to his shoulders, but there was no trace of a beard on the leathery brown hide of his jaw. He was inhumanly tall and correspondingly broad. He was, in short, not human, but overman.

His long-fingered hand, with its oddly-jointed thumb and opposable fifth finger, grasped the guidehandle of his mount's harness, an unnecessary precaution; his warbeast was trained to obey verbal commands or the pressure of its rider's feet, and moved with such feline smoothness that there was no danger of dislodging its master. The creature was blacker than the night sky, and as silent; its golden eyes and polished fangs were the only discernable features. It stood the height of a man and, from its stubby whiskers to lashing pantherlike tail, measured a good eighteen feet. Its triangular ears were up and alert, but it gave no warning growl.

Accordingly, the overman raised his arm in the signal to advance and led his companions over the final ridge and down onto the plain. His warbeast moved with silent catlike grace, its great padded paws disturbing not a single stone; the rest of the party was not so circumspect.

There were four in the party, all grown overmen, but only the leader rode a warbeast; his three followers made do with yackers, the universal beast of burden of the Northern Waste. Each rode upon one of the ugly creatures and led another heavily laden with the goods they hoped to trade in Skelleth. There was something slightly ludicrous in the stately dignity of the overmen as they perched stiffly upright upon the broad backs covered with ropy, matted brown hair, and guided their beasts with finely tooled silver bits in slobbering black-lipped mouths full of uneven yellow teeth. The yackers' hooves rattled on every pebble, it seemed, and there was a constant snorting and rumbling from the six shaggy, drooping heads.

They were traveling the ancient Wasteland Road, which led straight to Skelleth's North Gate; as the last yacker reached the foot of the ridge, the leader turned his warbeast off the road, heading west instead of south.

"Hold, Garth!" called the second in the procession.

The leader tapped a signal with his heel and the warbeast halted. "What is it?"

His companion drew up beside him and asked,

"Where are we heading? Is that not Skelleth?" He pointed to the flickering watch fire.

The third overman pulled up beside them as well as Garth replied, "Yes, of course that is Skelleth, and that is where we're going."

"Then why have we left the road? These yackers are quite slow enough as it is."

It was the third overman who replied, "Larth, did not Garth explain our situation to you?"

"I remember nothing that explains our turning away from our destination."

"Then you remember nothing. We are to enter the town in secrecy."

"It was not you I asked, Galt."

"Galt, however, speaks correctly," Garth said. "The Baron of Skelleth does not want overmen in his town; most especially, he does not want me there. When last I saw him he ordered his guards to kill me on the spot. Fortunately, they did not cooperate. However, if we can present the Baron with a peaceful trading caravan in the market square, not as a possibility but as an accomplished fact, I think he can be made to see reason and accept us."

"So we are to sneak in like thieves?"

"Why else are we traveling by night?" Galt's tone was sweetly reasonable.

"It is not dignified!"

"And what would be dignified?" Garth inquired.

"To ride directly in by daylight, and demand as our due that we be allowed to trade."

Galt snorted. "That might be dignified, but it would also be stupid, perhaps fatally so. Garth says there are more than thirty guardsmen in Skelleth; true, they are mere humans, and none too well equipped by his account, but there are only four of us, and we are not exactly well-armed either."

Garth added, before Larth could reply, "It would not do for friendly traders to be bristling with weapons; we cannot risk incidents involving bloodshed.

That is why I required that you three be unarmed, and I will conceal my own weapons before we begin our dealings with the people of Skelleth."

"Quite correct." Galt nodded in agreement. Larth continued to look unconvinced.

"Still," he demanded, "why have we left the road?"

His answer came from the fourth and youngest overman, who had not yet spoken, showing the proper deference to his elders; he could not, however, refrain from replying, "Because there's a guard on the road, stupid!"

Larth's voice was emotionless as he said, "Galt, restrain your apprentice."

As all knew quite well, that flat tone was indicative of building rage; Galt did not hesitate to order his underling to shut up.

When Larth had calmed somewhat, he asked, "How do you know that we can find another entrance unguarded?"

"I don't know for certain," Garth said. "But when I was here before, they guarded only the north; the West Gate opens on a road that leads only to the Yprian Coast, which has reputedly been deserted for centuries, so what need to guard it? Therefore, we will enter through the West Gate. We will reach it by circling wide around, well out of sight and sound of the guard at the North Gate. Now, if we are to reach the market square before dawn we must move onward, so let there be no further debate." His warbeast, in response to a signal undetectable to the others, strode onward.

"Very well," Larth said. It took rather more to get his yackers moving once again, but a moment's prodding eventually registered with their dim brains and they resumed their plodding and snuffling. Galt and his apprentice were not far behind.

There was still an hour remaining before first light when the little caravan reached the West Gate – which was, as Garth had expected, unguarded. It was also in such a state of total ruin that only the fading trace of an ancient road leading through the rubble showed where it had been, and it was only under protest that the yackers could be compelled to make their way across the jagged bits of broken stone. Garth's warbeast paid this minor inconvenience no heed whatsoever.

Once inside the wall there was little immediate improvement in their surroundings. On either side of the road stood nothing but ruins. Gaping holes half-filled with rubble showed where cellars had been of old, sometimes rimmed with uneven remnants of walls of stone or wood or plaster, and between these pits were the broken pieces of buildings that had had no cellars and now lay in heaps upon bare earth.

Galt commented, in a careful whisper, "Hardly the awesome fortress that our ancestors described."

Larth, in a rather less cautious mutter, replied, "Who can tell in this darkness? It looks deserted; Garth, are you sure this is Skelleth?"

"Yes, I'm sure; only the central portion is still inhabited. When the wars ended so did the town's reason for existence, and so did the supply trains from the south that kept it going. It's been slowly dying ever since. That's why I think the people will welcome trade, even if it's with overmen."

"I hope so." Larth's voice sank into an incoherent mumble.

The party moved on, and around them the buildings became less ruinous;

on either side stood sagging, abandoned houses and shops – derelict, but still upright. Rotting shutters hung from bent hinges; broken doors stood open, revealing only blackness. Then, as they approached the surviving center, more and more doors were closed, even barred, and fewer shutters missing or broken. Before too long the only openings on either side were other streets, rather than empty lots where buildings had been razed or had fallen in. Everything was dark, however; the people of Skelleth were clearly all still abed.

Finally the street debouched into the market square that occupied the town's exact center; it, too, was dark, silent, and empty. Garth was pleased to see that the Baron's mansion, which occupied the entire north side of the square, was as dark as any other building. He stopped his warbeast in the center of the market and motioned for Galt to join him. When Galt obeyed, he whispered. "This is the place, trader; that is the seat of the local government. Where would you suggest we set up?"

Galt studied the square carefully, and finally pointed to the southeast corner. "That looks good."

Garth nodded. "Then you three set up there. It occurs to me that a warbeast will not be a welcome sight in Skelleth, and I am going to put Koros and my weapons somewhere out of sight. I would suggest that you do the same with the yackers; just tie them up in an alley somewhere, where they won't upset the merchants. Koros, I think, had best go somewhere further out; I'll find a ruin somewhere on the West Road."

"As you wish."

"I'll be right back. Just remember, keep it peaceful."

Galt nodded. Garth turned and rode back along the route they had just come, while the others made their way to the southeast corner of the market and dismounted, stiff from their long ride.

Galt studied the location with a practiced eye, then indicated a spot in front of a tightly shuttered shop, just beside the mouth of a narrow street. His apprentice immediately hauled a bundle off one of the yackers and began spreading blankets on the ground designated. Larth stood nearby, peering apprehensively about in the gloom, and Galt found himself grateful that Garth had made sure the party was unarmed; Larth was plainly nervous enough to have drawn sword at the slightest sound, which would simply not do.

Of course, that was Larth. He himself was not so easily bothered, nor so easily commanded. The dagger in his boot was simply a sensible precaution, and none of Garth's business.

Leaving Larth to his anxiety, he began hauling bundles off yackers. In a matter of moments the ugly beasts were unburdened. Galt whispered to his apprentice, "Tand, you start spreading out our wares. Get Larth to help you if you can, but don't start an argument. I'll be back in a moment."

He gathered up the lead ropes from the six harnesses and began coaxing the yackers down the narrow street, out of the market. The beasts were not actively uncooperative, but it was still difficult to manage all six of them, so that he was several minutes at the task.

Finally he managed to get them arranged in a circle, their lead ropes tied together. Although they could still move about, they were far too stupid to move all in the same direction; this arrangement should keep them more or less in the same place for quite some time. It did block the street, but Galt hoped that wouldn't matter much. It didn't look like a major thoroughfare. Besides, that meant that the overmen could not be taken from behind by enemies coming up this street; even if they got past the yackers, the inevitable noise would serve as a warning.

The yackers were a new problem for him. Though he was a master trader, all his previous experience had been gained on expeditions to Lagur, since that was the only place the overmen of the Northern Waste currently traded. There were no yackers used on such expeditions, since all trade with Lagur went by sea.

Once the beasts were taken care of, he returned to the square. He could hear the sounds of furs being unpacked; either Tand was working incredibly fast, or he had gotten Larth to help him, judging by the noise.

Then, just as he was about to turn the corner into the market, the sounds stopped abruptly. So did he. Something was happening, obviously. Peaceful, peaceful, he reminded himself; he fixed his most nearly human smile upon his face and strolled forward as casually as he could.

Larth and Tand knelt motionless amid heaps of furs and carved whalebone, staring off to their right. Following their gaze he saw a ragged human farmer, pulling a rickety cart half-full of squash, standing motionless in a street opening into the eastern end of the market. The farmer's mouth hung open and his eyes were wide, the whites palely visible in the first light of morning – light which had crept up while Galt was securing the yackers without his noticing it. It appeared very much as if this man had never seen an overman before, and quite possibly he hadn't. Larth and Tand were also staring, and it occurred to Galt that it might well be that neither of them had ever seen a human being before.

This, Galt knew, was the decisive moment. Secrecy was gone. Now, if their mission was to succeed, they needed to convince the humans that there was nothing out of the ordinary about overmen trading in their marketplace. Garth had hired him as an expert on dealing with humans, and he knew that humans could be convinced of anything if only approached properly.

He waved gaily, broadened his smile, and called, "Greetings, good sir! Would you care to see our wares?"

The man turned his gaze from the others to Galt, but his mouth remained open and his eyes wide.

Galt gestured at the heaps of trade goods. "We have fine furs, such as are rarely seen in these lands; we have fine carved implements of use in any home. Come and look, friend!"

The man's mouth slowly closed. He swallowed, and looked back and forth between the overmen. His eyes roved around the market square and found no one else and nothing out of the ordinary – except the party of overmen. Galt judged him to be recovered from his shock and considering the situation. He would not turn and run, because that would mean abandoning his cart; it had been a stroke of luck that the first human to find them had been so encumbered. He had two sensible options; he could behave as if the overmen belonged there, or he could raise an alarm. It was Galt's job to convince him the former was the better course.

Still smiling, he called, "It costs nothing to look, sir, and should something catch your eye, our prices are reasonable." They certainly were! This trip was not expected to make a profit, nor break even, but only to establish an opening; accordingly, he and Garth had agreed that they would refuse no serious offer – though they would haggle, of course; that was expected, and suspicion would be aroused if they did not – and would even give away goods free if it seemed advisable. "If you haven't brought any money, we might trade for those fine vegetables."

That decided him. The man found his voice and called, "Wait a moment, and I'll come look." He began moving again, wheeling his creaking cart into the square.

As he did, a shuttered window in the second story of the building the overmen had chosen to set up in front of opened, and a head was thrust out. "What's all the yelling? It's not yet dawn!"

Galt doffed his hat politely and called up, "My apologies, good lady; it was thoughtless of me to bellow so."

The head, which was indeed female – Galt hadn't been completely certain – turned to look at him. There was a moment of silence save for the creaking of cart wheels as the farmer positioned his wares. Then the woman asked, conversationally but in an unsteady voice, "You're an overman, aren't you?"

"Yes, good lady, my companions and myself are overmen, come to trade peacefully. We have fine furs and jewelry that would surely please one as lovely as yourself; Tand, hold up that white fox for the lady."

Tand was still motionless with surprise, but picked up his cue with only the briefest hesitation and stood, displaying an excellent fur.

The woman noticed Larth and Tand for the first time but paid them little heed, looking instead at the stacks of furs. There was a pause, and then she said, "I'll be right down." Her head vanished from the window, and Galt's false smile relaxed into a genuine one. The danger was past. They had been accepted.

When Garth returned several minutes later he found a small crowd clustered around his companions, bickering cheerfully over quality and price.

Chapter Two

Garth glanced apprehensively at the door to the Baron's mansion as it swung open for the first time that morning. So far whatever gods there might be had smiled upon his little caravan; they had had no trouble on the road from Ordunin, nor with the merchants and farmers who had so far entered the market. The reactions of the villagers to a quartet of overmen sitting calmly in their midst amid displays of furs and carved whalebone had varied from simple acceptance to astonishment and horror – which could usually be soothed by a few quiet words and perhaps a gold coin or two. The fact that those already there appeared unconcerned had been a major factor in preventing general alarm or even a riot.

Unfortunately, Garth knew the Baron of Skelleth and his guards would not be so easily swayed. His previous visit to this northernmost outpost of humanity had ended messily, and the Baron had ordered his death, more for being an overman and uncooperative than for any specific crime.

Of course none of Skelleth's pitiful guardsmen were likely to try and tackle four overmen; Garth thought it unlikely that the village's full complement of three dozen would have been a match for his party if he hadn't insisted his companions be unarmed. They were on a peaceful trading mission, and he was determined to see that it stayed peaceful. For far too long had the overmen of the Northern Waste been dependent upon the sea traders of Lagur, who missed no opportunity to exploit their monopoly; if Garth succeeded in opening a land trade route through Skelleth the monopoly would be broken, and his people would have their first chance at a decent life since the bitter Racial Wars of three centuries earlier – and incidentally Garth would be honored and wealthy, which would be enjoyable.

The door was open now, and three guardsmen stepped through, blinking in the bright summer sunlight; Garth recognized one of them. The tall one in the steel helmet was Herrenmer, captain of the guard.

The unknown pair took up their posts, one on either side of the door. Herrenmer, having stationed his men, took a casual glance around, his duty done for the moment. His gaze fell on the overmen and Garth saw him tense. He spoke to his men, but Garth could hear nothing over the noise of the market; then all three started across the square toward the outlanders, Herrenmer in the lead, all three with hands near their swords.

Garth put down the wolfskin he had been showing to an overweight woman and said, "Larth, keep an eye on my goods while I speak to these men." He stood and stepped forward to meet the soldiers.

The trio stopped a dozen paces from the displays; Garth stood halfway between. There was a moment's pause, then Herrenmer demanded, "What are you doing here?"

"We have come to trade."

"You know that the Baron wants no overmen in Skelleth."

"I was aware that he wanted no armed overmen adventurers, an attitude I can fully understand, since such would tend to disturb the peace of your town; but surely he can have no objection to four unarmed traders, whatever their race or nation!" Garth had carefully thought out this little speech in advance, and was pleased to see that it had the desired effect, leaving Herrenmer momentarily confused and speechless. He pressed his advantage.

"I have heard the Baron himself express dismay at Skelleth's poverty and lack of trade; surely, then, he will be glad to have a whole new people eager to deal with Skelleth. We have gold and furs and other goods to trade for our needs, which will make Skelleth's merchants wealthy when sold in the south, where we dare not venture. Surely the Baron cannot object to that, for where the merchants are wealthy the government cannot fail to profit thereby."

"I know nothing of that; it is not my concern." Herrenmer paused, considering, then went on, "I will speak with my lord further about this." He turned and strode angrily back to the mansion; his two men followed, and when Herrenmer vanished through the still-open door, slamming it behind him, they took up their posts once more.

Garth watched them go, then turned back toward his companions. Before he could take a step, however, he heard his name called. He stopped and looked about for the source.

A waving hand caught his eye, and he recognized a man approaching across the market. "Greetings, Saram," he called.

"Greetings, Garth," the man replied.

Saram was heavily built, of medium height; he wore his hair short and kept his full black beard neatly trimmed, though he claimed it was not from vanity but practicality. When last Garth had seen him, he had worn the mail shirt and short sword of the Baron's guards, with iron studs in his leather helmet marking him as a lieutenant; now he wore a ragged but clean tunic of gray homespun and went bareheaded. Only the leather pants and heavy boots remained the same.

He drew up within convenient speaking distance and remarked, "So you have returned as you promised." His tone was casual, but his green eyes flicked warily about, missing nothing.

"I have," Garth answered politely. Saram had done him considerable good when last he was in Skelleth by refusing to attempt to kill him.

"The old man said you would." Saram's eyes focused on Garth's face as he spoke.

The overman shrugged, his face impassive, and said nothing.

"I had my doubts, but here you are. Where is your warbeast? I was sure you'd bring it if you came." Saram glanced idly about.

"It's hidden nearby. I saw no need to frighten your townspeople."

"Wise of you, no doubt. And you brought friends with you this time."

"Companions, rather; I am not myself adept at the ways of buyer and seller, so I brought the master trader Galt, his apprentice Tand, and my double-cousin Larth." He pointed out each of the other overmen as he named them; young Tand and stolid Larth did not notice, but Galt nodded in acknowledgment.

"Pleased to meet them all, I'm sure. Gods, what are those?" This last was in response to glimpsing the yackers, just visible from where he stood.

Garth was startled. "Yackers. Don't you know them?" He glanced down the alley at the great beasts of burden, which stood quietly meditating, safely out of the bustle of business.

"No. I never heard of them." Saram stared at them momentarily, then turned back to the overman and said, "Garth, I have a message for you. The old man wants to talk to you."

Garth replied, "I don't want to talk to him."

"No? He claims to have a proposition for you."

"I am not interested; when last I made a bargain with him it resulted in nothing but deaths and difficulties."

"Just as your agreement with the Baron did him little good," Saram said smiling crookedly. "Yet you expect him to listen to your explanations about your renewed presence in his domain."

There was a moment of silence. Then Garth said, "Your point is made. I will hear the King out. Where is he?"

"Need you ask?"

"No. A moment, then." He turned and called to his companions, "I have an errand; Galt, you take charge here." Then to Saram he said, "Come on," and the pair ambled off across the market square.

Their goal was an ancient tavern called the King's Inn, though no one knew of any connection between the inn and any recognized monarch; it stood on an alley that had once been but a few steps from the village market, but which had been cut off and left to die when the first Baron of Skelleth erected his mansion across the north side of the square, leaving no opening to the streets beyond. The alley, now accessible only by a winding route through the maze of byways that made up most of Skelleth, had sunk into a state of decay and filth unequaled throughout the known lands; yet the King's Inn remained an island of comfort amid the surrounding squalor and retained a steady clientele. Among its regular patrons, so regular in fact that he had never been seen outside its walls, was a strange old man, so very old that none remembered a time when he had not been there daily, crouched silently over his corner table. This man Garth knew as the Forgotten King, having been given this title for him by the Wise Women of Ordunin, but the townspeople had no name for him at all. Until the overman first came, some three months earlier, few ever spoke to him, fewer received an answer, and none sought him out; but in recent days, since being expelled from the Baron's guards for insubordination, Saram had spent many hours sitting at his table, trying to coax him into conversation and receiving only a few cryptic words for his trouble. Among those few words were instructions that when – not if, but when – Garth returned, Saram should bring him immediately to speak with the mysterious ancient.

Saram led the way through the stinking streets, fortunately dry from the recent lack of rain, and Garth followed, his reluctance concealed by the casual stroll he affected. The slanting sunlight had not yet made its way past the upper story of the inn in its slow daily crawl down the building's sagging half-timbered façade; the ordure that lined the alley was still hidden by shadow, but its smell was not so easily to be concealed, and not for the first time Garth marveled that humans could live with it. He held his breath as he and Saram picked their way to the door and wiped their feet on the stone step before entering.

The tavern's interior was a welcome change from the filth of the alley; not so much as a speck of dust marred the ancient floor, worn by centuries of shuffling feet into a subtle wooden landscape of low hills and gentle valleys that showed clearly that its furnishings had not shifted nor its patrons changed their habits in many a long year. Each table crowned a hillock, each chair rested in wide grooves cut by the dragging of its legs. The great barrels of ale and wine that lined the western wall loomed above flooring so stained and worn that Garth wondered how it still held – he had no way of seeing the thickness of wood beneath, but only that this most popular part of the room had a good two inches less floor remaining than elsewhere. The slate hearth that stretched along half the eastern wall before the vast cavernous fireplace showed little wear, being harder stuff than the soft floorboards; curiously, the ancient stair that crossed the back wall had only the slightest indentation in each tread. Plainly, it was as a tavern rather than an inn that the establishment survived, since those stairs were the only access to the rooms upstairs.

Though every inch of the room was clearly old, worn, and well-used, none could ever think it deserted for it was spotlessly clean, save for the oft-scrubbed stains left by centuries of spilled wine. The morning sun had not yet climbed high enough to pour unchecked through the polished and age-purpled windows, yet the brass fittings on the barrels gleamed dully, the stacked mugs of pewter and china and glass glistened on their shelves, the blackened hearth shone dimly. The only spots of uncleanliness were two drunken farmers adorning opposite sides of a small table near the door, clad in dirty gray homespun, with greasy hair and smudged faces, who slouched forward muttering to one another. The innkeeper, though a plump middle-aged man wearing a well-stained apron, gave the impression not of disarray, but like his tavern, of well-worn comfort. The room's only other occupant, sitting alone in the corner between chimneypiece and stair, seemed somehow beyond such mundane concerns as cleanliness.

It was this lone figure that Garth and Saram were interested in. The innkeeper watched apprehensively as the pair entered and crossed the room, and twice opened his mouth to protest their presence, but each time lost his nerve and remained silent. When they had seated themselves across from the old man, he gradually relaxed and returned to his task of polishing mugs that already showed a flawless silken sheen; but he polished the same mug for a good fifteen minutes with short, nervous strokes, and cast frequent glances at the overman who had intruded upon the peace of his place of business.

For a moment after they had settled in their chairs neither Garth nor Saram spoke; they considered the strange figure across from them, who sat motionlessly, seemingly oblivious of their presence.

The old man whom Ordunin's oracles had called the Forgotten King wore tattered yellow rags from head to foot, and despite the summer warmth he kept them wrapped tightly about him, his cloak closed and his hood up, so that its shadows hid much of his face. A long, scraggly white beard reached down across his sunken chest, and what could be seen of his hands and face was skin as dry and wrinkled as that of a mummy, with as little evidence of anything between skin and bone. His eyes were lost in darkness; in all their conversations with him neither Garth nor Saram had ever seen his eyes, and only on the rarest occasions had either so much as caught a glimmer of light from them. The shadows gave the illusion that he had no eyes, but only empty sockets; perhaps that, more than anything else, was why generations of taverngoers had seen fit to leave him sitting alone and unmolested.

Garth studied him, but saw nothing he had not seen before. Garth was a typical member of his species in most respects, and as such he was not particularly good at recognizing human faces or reading emotion in them; still, there was something about the Forgotten King's face that made him uneasy.

He shifted in his chair, which creaked beneath his weight. He was out of proportion with his surroundings in a tavern designed for mere men; he towered above the others, his natural height of near seven feet augmented by a woolen trader's hat that not only shaded his red-eyed, sunken-cheeked horror of a face, but hid a steel half-helmet. Peaceful mission or no, Garth was given to caution; despite his orders to his companions and hiding most of his armor and weaponry with his warbeast, his flowing brown cloak concealed a sturdy mail shirt, and a stiletto lurked in his right boot-top – the latter a precaution that was incidentally rather uncomfortable, as its hilt, though safely hidden by his leggings and the sparse black fur that adorned his leathery hide, chafed when he walked.

He studied the old man, but said nothing.

Beside him Saram glanced from the overman to the King and back again, his finger poking idly at a small circle of mismatched wood in the table-top – a circle that was the sawn-off shaft of a crossbow bolt Saram had fired at Garth, on the Baron's orders, during Garth's previous stay in Skelleth. The overman had used the table as a makeshift shield, and the barbed quarrel had proven impossible to remove, so that the innkeeper had cut it off and sanded it down to blend with the oak.

After a moment, when it appeared that neither Garth nor the old man was willing to speak first, the ex-soldier cleared his throat and said, "I have brought Garth here, as you asked."

The old man nodded very slightly, but gave no other sign that he was aware of the presence of others at his table.

There was another pause, this one briefer than the first. It was broken when the overman finally announced, "I am here at your request. Speak, then, and tell me what you want of me. I have business to attend to."

The old man spoke, in a voice like the rustling of long-dead leaves. "Garth, I would have you serve me further."

The overman suppressed the shudder that ran through him at the sound of that voice; he had heard it before, but it was something that one could not truly remember – or want to remember. He replied, "I have no desire to serve you, nor any person other than myself."

The Forgotten King raised his head slightly and spoke again. "There are very few in these waning years of the Thirteenth Age who are fit to serve me. I do not care to wait for another."

"That may be; I do not deny that you may have uses for me. But why should I serve you? You offer me nothing, and I have little cause to trust you after the outcome of my last venture in your service."

"What would you have?"

"I would have nothing of you but to be left alone. When you promised me fame, my service yielded nothing but a dozen deaths and much trouble to no purpose."

"I did not slight you."

"Is my fame then so great? I see little evidence of it, old man."

"Did you then fulfill your service to me with a single trial?"

"No. I saw my folly after the single trial and went home."

"Yet you have returned, upon my advice."

Garth paused. That much was true; it had been the Forgotten King who pointed out the possibility of trade through Skelleth and its potential benefits.

"What of it? I did you a service, and you paid me with a simple suggestion I should have thought of for myself – but did not, I admit. We are even, then. I have no wish to serve you further. Hire Saram, here!"

Saram was startled out of his silence. "I? Oh, no; I am no adventurer."

The Forgotten King ignored Saram and said, "Is there then nothing that you seek, Garth? Are you content with your lot?"

There was a moment of silence; Garth contemplated the shadowed face while Saram looked back and forth, and neither could see where the old man's gaze fell. Finally the overman admitted slowly, "No, I am not content. I still seek what in truth I sought before; I want to know that I am not insignificant, not merely a meaningless mote in an uncaring cosmos. I sought eternal fame because it seemed to me that that was as close as I could come to making a real difference, and my nearest approach to immortality. I see little point in wealth or power or glory that will last only so long as I live. What, then, can you offer me? I no longer feel that the promise of undying fame will suffice to comfort me; can you offer more?"

"Under the proper circumstances I can give you whatever you want. If you fear death, I can promise you life to the end of time. If you seek to give your life a significance beyond the norm, then we are at one, for it is to work a fundamental change in the nature of our world that I seek your aid."

There was another moment of silence; then Garth asked, "What is this change you seek? You speak around your purpose. When I served you before you had me fetch you the basilisk and would not say why you wanted it; was it for this same mysterious goal?"

"My goal is unchanged." The harsh monotone of the old man's voice was likewise unchanged, but his head sank slightly, deepening the shadows that hid his face.

Garth sat back, considering. He had concluded, after much thought, that the Forgotten King's use for the basilisk – a use for which it had proven inadequate – included the old man's own death. He had no idea why the ancient would want to die; had he perhaps wearied of his long life? Nor had he any idea why a single old man should have difficulty in dying should he choose to do so, yet it was indisputable that he had survived whatever he had done with the basilisk. Perhaps, Garth thought, he had somehow misinterpreted previous events, for how could one lonely old man's suicide have cosmic repercussions?

That assumed, of course, that the old man spoke the truth. It was possible that he was indeed under some sort of curse of immortality which he hoped to break with Garth's aid – and dead men are under no obligation to fulfill their promises, so that he would offer whatever the overman wanted, knowing that he would never have to pay.

Then again, it was possible that the old man – who was very probably a wizard of some sort – really was attempting some world-shaking magic. That did not mean that his purposes were anything Garth sympathized with.

"What is this goal? Why will you not tell me? It could be some monstrous evil, some affront against nature and the gods."

"I seek only to fulfill that purpose the gods have given me, Garth; I swear this to be true."

"You still do not say what it is."

"Nor will I."

"And yet you ask me to serve you in this, without knowing?"

The old man said nothing, but nodded very slightly, once.

"I must consider this carefully. I will speak with you again when I have decided." Garth rose and strode from the table; Saram stirred, but reseated himself, and when the overman had left the tavern and the door had closed behind him, he turned back to the Forgotten King.

"It seems you offer a bargain only a fool would accept, full of vague terms and mysteries."

The Forgotten King said nothing, but Saram detected a faint shrug of his sagging shoulders.

Chapter Three

As Garth rounded the last corner and came in sight of the marketplace, he saw Galt standing talking to someone. His fellow overman towered over the surrounding crowd, readily distinguishable, but at first Garth could not see who it was he was speaking with; then, as he began threading his way into the throng, he caught the glint of sunlight on a steel helmet and realized that Herrenmer had returned, presumably bearing the Baron's decision. He hastened his pace; the villagers, awed by his size and terrified by his face, parted before him, so that a brief moment later he was at Galt's side.

"Ah, Garth, it would seem that the local government wishes to speak with you and you alone. I offered myself as your representative, but was refused." Galt spoke smoothly and quickly, in a light tone, but Garth recognized a note of tension in his voice and saw that Herrenmer's hand was on his sword hilt. Behind their captain stood a full dozen guardsmen and, though no weapons were actually drawn, it was plain that a confrontation had been brewing.

"Oh? I apologize for my absence, Captain Herrenmer, but one of your townsmen wished to speak with me in private."

"The Baron also wishes to speak with you, overman; immediately." The man's voice shook slightly.

"I will oblige him momentarily. Larth, I leave you in charge. Galt, you come with me, in case we need to discuss business." The other overmen nodded; Garth took a step toward the mansion, but was halted by Herrenmer's hand raised in restraint.

"Wait a minute; I was told to bring you, not this other monster."

"But Galt is the business manager for our party. Should we need to discuss exact terms I will want his advice."

"If it will ease your mind, Captain, I will promise not to speak unless spoken to." Galt's voice was honey-smooth.

Herrenmer looked from one hideous face to the other, from Garth's crimson eyes to Galt's golden ones, and at last shrugged and led the way across the square.

The Baron's audience chamber was much as Garth remembered it, a fairly spacious room hung with old tapestries, with three small windows high in the northern wall behind the Baron's seat providing the only light. The Baron's seat was a simple oaken chair, and the Baron himself sat slouching in it, a small, slender man wearing a richly embroidered scarlet robe, with a circlet of gold on his brow. He fingered his thin black beard for a moment, then spoke.

"So it's true; you have returned."

This being self-evident, no reply seemed necessary, but Garth did not care to antagonize the Baron further with insolent silence; he replied simply, "Yes."

"I had not thought you would have had the gall to do so, despite your boast to that scum Saram, yet here you are. You have even brought others of your filthy race."

"We have come on a peaceful trading mission."

"So I am told. Are you aware that you are under sentence of death here, on charges of trespass, espionage, and crimes against the state? And that all your stinking species are enemy aliens?"

"I was aware that you were not eager to have us here. I hope to convince you that it would be to your advantage to welcome us."

"And how do you plan to do that?"

"In two stages: firstly, I will convince you that a regular trade between Skelleth and the Northern Waste will be very much in your own interests; and secondly, that killing me or otherwise thwarting me would make that trade impossible."

"Very well, then, I will listen. Why should I allow you monsters to trade on my lands?"

"Because we have much gold, from hidden mines in the northern mountains, with which to pay for what we want. Surely, much of this gold will find its way to you, in the form of taxes and tariffs. You told me once that you were not happy with your inheritance and hoped to improve your lot by war and plunder; would it not be equally satisfying to make yourself rich by peaceful means? Or even if it is the blood and glory of war you seek, will not our gold help to finance such an ambition? The terms of our former agreement, which you apparently feel I violated but which I feel I merely interpreted differently from yourself, included a statement that all overmen crossing your lands would pay what tribute you might rightfully demand; we will honor that, so long as such tribute does not make our trade prohibitively expensive. Surely you cannot refuse such an opportunity!"

"Dare not tell me what I can or cannot refuse, overman! Still, you make it sound very tempting. If your gold is as plentiful as you imply, I could indeed find uses for it." The Baron mused for a moment and then went on, "But then, to your second point, your own life; why should I not accept trade arrangements with your people, but still put you to death? I could easily demand your life as the necessary tribute; would not overmen give up a single life for a new trade route?"

"Perhaps they would under certain circumstances, but they will not give up my life, for I am the hereditary Prince of Ordunin, and the life of a reigning prince is not within your rights to demand." Garth was relying on the Baron's ignorance of the culture of the overmen of the Northern Waste in this, for in fact the title he claimed, though genuine, was strictly a ceremonial honor with no real significance beyond the privilege of speaking first in the City Council, a privilege it was customary to waive.

There was a moment of silence as the Baron considered this. Then he shifted his gaze to Galt and demanded, "You! Who are you?"

"I am Galt, my lord, a trader out of Ordunin."

"And who is this?" He pointed at Garth.

"That is Garth, Prince of Ordunin, a lord of the Overmen of the Northern Waste." Galt spoke casually, his pale blue cloak draped across one arm, his wide-brimmed hat shading his yellow eyes, looking completely at ease and unconcerned. Long years of experience had taught him that such a pose was most desirable in almost every sort of dealings with humans, be it trade, diplomacy, or less formal activities.

"You will swear to that?"

Galt blinked, and smiled a lipless smile. "If you wish."

"I do."

"I swear by my head that this overman is Garth, hereditary Prince of Ordunin, son of Karth and Tarith, known to me as such for many years and so recognized by all my people."

"There were more of you, were there not?"

"Yes."

"Will they so swear?"

"Undoubtedly. Larth is Garth's double-cousin, and Tand has known him since childhood."

The Baron turned back to Garth. "Why did you not let me know this before, that I might have treated you as your rank deserved?"

"Why should I tempt you with a prince's ransom?"

"Are you not doing so now?"

"No, for I am not alone this time, and furthermore my people are now aware that Skelleth is no longer the mighty fortress that repelled our ancestors' attacks. Even should you take all four of us captive, there would be no ransom but fire and sword. As you surely realize, paying out ransoms sets a bad precedent."

The Baron scowled and slumped back in his chair. After a thoughtful pause he said, "It seems that you have the better of me in this matter; to indulge my whims would be far too costly, so I must let you live and go free. However, if you are in truth the reigning Prince of Ordunin, then there are other demands I may make. You seek for your people the free use of roads and rights of way that I happen to have proprietary rights upon. Our two nations are technically still at war, however, so that I cannot under ordinary circumstances grant such permissions as you seek without being untrue to my own oaths as vassal to the High King at Kholis; this is true though it would obviously be of great advantage to me personally and to my realm, and though our war has been unfought these three hundred years. Had you considered this?"

"Not in detail," Garth replied; he hesitated, and then continued, "I am not fully conversant with the laws of Eramma and I assumed that reasonable beings such as ourselves could find some way around such an obstacle."

"And I think we shall, Garth, I think we shall." The Baron grinned. "There are conditions under which I may make a separate peace, without the intervention of the High King; specifically, I can accept your surrender and your oath of fealty to me as a vassal prince."

"What?" Garth's reply was startled from him.

"Yes. You see, that would finish off the war very neatly, and remove any obstacles it might create. Under the terms of my own commitment to the High King I cannot surrender myself to you unless defeated in battle, but there are no such constraints upon you. Were you my vassal and loyal servant, our two peoples would no longer be at war." The grin widened. "Furthermore, as my vassal, your underlings would of course have full access, free of tariff, to all my lands. They would of course be required to pay the customary taxes, and tolls for the use of some highways, but only at the same rates as my human subjects. In short, your goal of establishing open trade would be achieved."

Garth was too shocked to speak. After a pause, the Baron said, "Come, now, overman, is this so unreasonable? You offered any reasonable tribute; is a simple oath of fealty and the consequent obligation unreasonable? The hundred barons of Eramma do not think so."

Garth stammered, then fell silent. He gathered his wits and replied, "I cannot give you an immediate answer. I cannot make such a commitment without consulting my City Council." His initial astonishment was fading, to be replaced with a growing outrage; how dare this mere human even consider making himself lord over overmen? Still, it would be well to remain diplomatic; perhaps some lip service could be paid to such an arrangement briefly, until a more sensible agreement could be worked out. It was a matter that did, indeed, warrant the consideration of the City Council.

"Oh? Your Council? Very well. I had hoped to conclude this matter here and now, but I suppose I can tolerate some delay. Where is this Council?"

"In Ordunin." Garth stopped himself from adding, "Of course."

"Of course. In that case, it seems to me that the sooner you are on the way back to Ordunin, the better. I will give you twenty-four hours to be out of Skelleth on the Wasteland Road, and I will have you swear, here and now, that you will present my proposal to this Council as soon as you reach Ordunin, and that you will present it fairly and reasonably, as I have presented it to you. Agree to these terms, and your companions may remain and trade in peace."

Garth suppressed an impulse to lash out in rage. His expression, as always, remained blank and calm. It required an effort, though, for him to say, "I do so swear that I will present your proposal fairly to the City Council immediately upon my return to Ordunin."

"Good! I think our business is done then; begone! I would talk to this trader." The Baron waved him away peremptorily.

Garth bowed, giving no sign of his fury, and departed, the Baron's guards stepping quickly out of his way.

The Baron watched him go and smiled to himself. The overman would meet his terms, he was sure; he would swear the oath of fealty, thinking that he was committing himself to a few demeaning ceremonies and light taxation, service in name more than fact. It would be thoroughly delightful then to spring upon him the actual reason for his oath – an oath that included the obligation to provide his lord with all the military force at his disposal. It would be a simpler matter to pick a fight with that half-wit lord of Ur-Dormulk, who would march his army to Skelleth expecting an easy victory only to be met, not by three dozen half-trained farmers, but by warbeasts and overmen. Never again would that fat fool laugh at Doran of Skelleth! Never again would he be ignored and ridiculed, seated at the foot of the High King's table at the decennial meetings in Kholis!

A hundred overmen in full armor, a hundred warbeasts, would make him the most powerful baron in Eramma. *That* was the tribute he intended to exact from this absurd commerce!

When the door had closed Garth away from sight, he bestirred himself from his daydreams of power and glory and waved Herrenmer up to his side. He whispered a few words in his captain's ear, then turned his attention to Galt.

"So, trader, you seek to bring wealth to our two lands. What would you consider a fair tax upon your receipts?"

As Galt roused himself to begin negotiations, Herrenmer slipped from the room; the overman paid him no heed.

A moment later Garth was halfway across the market square, returning to his two companions, when he heard the clink of mail and the thudding of booted feet running behind him. He turned to see Herrenmer hurrying after him.

"Did you seek me?"

The guardsman caught his breath, then replied, "Yes. I am to accompany you until you are outside the walls."

"I have twenty-four hours."

"I know; nonetheless, I am not to let you out of my sight until you leave Skelleth."

Overmen do not show anger in their facial expressions, a natural concealment that is ordinarily an aid to survival, since it permits them to utilize the element of surprise more readily even in a state of unreasoning fury. Perhaps the only drawback is that it leaves them inexperienced in reading the faces of other species, such as humans. It was definitely for the best at this particular moment that Herrenmer took Garth's impassive expression for a mild contemplation of the situation; had he known the seething rage that was building he would have had his sword drawn and been calling for reinforcements. Instead he shrugged, and looked away from the overman's hideous face, preferring to watch the ragged farmers and peasants rather than gaze at that leather-hided skull.

Garth had been annoyed by the Baron's apparent ingratitude in response to the promise of vast wealth he had done nothing to earn; he had been further irritated by his lack of trust in demanding that Galt – Galt, and not Garth – swear to Garth's identity and title; he had been appalled and infuriated at the suggestion that he swear fealty to this petty human tyrant, and disgusted that the Baron was so insistent upon haste. He had stood for it all and resisted the temptation to fling the dagger in his boot through the man's heart, or simply to tear him limb from limb, only to have this final insult thrust upon him. He was to be escorted from the town like an outlaw or some other undesirable!

It robbed him of all privacy and dignity, and as such it was the pebble that sank the barge. He could not quietly accept this!

He would not go slinking back to Ordunin like this, cast out of Skelleth until he declared himself servant to a scurvy madman, sworn to beg the City Council for permission to degrade himself and his people! He would defy the Baron, somehow.

Unfortunately, it would not do for him to do so openly; the Baron was essential to the development of peaceful trade. If Garth killed him or otherwise seriously harmed him, it might well bring down the wrath of all Eramma upon not just himself, but all overmen, as untrustworthy brigands. It might even be enough of an incident to start up the long-dead Racial Wars again. A subtle poisoning might escape detection and do no harm to the prospects of peaceful trade – but it would also be thoroughly unsatisfying. He wanted the Baron to know what his effrontery had done.

Was there perhaps some way he could exploit the Baron's madness? As he had seen on his previous venture, and as all Skelleth knew, the Baron periodically lapsed into fits of depression so intense that he was unable to move himself at all, even to eat, so that he had to be carefully tended, like an infant, until the spell passed. Between these depressions his moods ranged from the alert intelligence he had displayed today to surly silence or screaming rage; Garth had seen all these moods, though not enough to see whether there was any pattern to them. He had also heard it said that there was an annual cycle, and that the Baron was at his worst in the spring.

He considered all this as he continued across the square to where Larth and Tand sat; Herrenmer stayed at his side, but said nothing. He stood over his seated companions, who were engaged in quiet conversation, having no customers at the moment.

"I have been ordered to return to Ordunin; there are matters I am to present to the Council there."

The two looked up, startled. After a second's pause Larth asked, "Should we pack up, then?"

"No; the Baron requires no departure save my own. You two and Galt will stay until you have completed the disposal of these goods and the arrangements for future caravans. I leave Galt in charge; Larth, you will handle my share of the goods and proceeds and deliver it to Kyrith."

"Kyrith? Your wife? Will you not be in Ordunin?"

Garth glanced at Herrenmer, standing well within earshot. "Do not concern yourself with my whereabouts."

"Are you to leave immediately?" Larth asked.

"I have until tomorrow, but there are other matters I must attend to, and I will be home by year's end, most likely."

He actually had no idea when he would be home, but as it was still summer and the year was reckoned to end with the vernal equinox, it would almost certainly be before that. He had as yet no idea where he was going; he only knew that it would not be Ordunin. The Baron had required him to leave Skelleth, and to swear that he would speak to the Council immediately upon reaching Ordunin – but neglected to make sure that he would in fact go to Ordunin.

Garth had no intention of going back to Ordunin under the present circumstances; another annoyance to be credited to the Baron. He would have said as much, and explained the entire situation to his companions, had Herrenmer not been so close at hand, spying for his master.

He stood for a moment longer but thought of nothing more worth saying, and neither Larth nor Tand volunteered any more questions; then he spun on his heel and strode off toward the King's Inn at a pace that left Herrenmer half-running after him.

At first he did not seek out the Forgotten King's table, but merely sat alone near the front window, gazing out at the garbage that lined the alley and the back wall of the Baron's mansion while he poured mug after mug of good cold ale down his throat. Herrenmer attempted to sit at the same table, but Garth picked him up by the neck with one hand and forcibly seated him elsewhere, despite his protests. The captain did not care to argue further, and instead sat where he had been placed, glowering at the overman. He was joined by Saram, who had still been at the shadowy table in the back corner, and the two men discussed that morning's events, Herrenmer providing the facts of the overman's audience with the Baron while Saram embellished them with comments on the Baron's crafty nature and underlying insanity, and the probable benefits of allowing northern gold into the village.

It was well after noon when Garth finally made his decision; he would not undertake to swear his allegiance to any master, but he had no doubt that the Forgotten King's service would be less galling than that of the Baron. He would, accordingly, arrange a new bargain with the old man, the fulfillment of which would undoubtedly take him off to some foreign realm and provide him with something to do other than return to Ordunin. Something might come up that would show him a satisfactory solution to his current quandary.

As time had slipped past, sunlight had crept across the floor and slanted into the depths of the fireplace in the eastern wall, and several other patrons had drifted in, to find themselves congenial company and comfortable seats or merely to drink a pint and drift out once again. Garth paid none of them any heed as he rose and made his way to the corner where the old man still sat, unmoving, as if mere seconds had passed since the overman had departed, and not half a day.

Herrenmer saw his charge rise, and rose himself to follow. He found, to his astonishment, that his feet refused to obey him; he could stand, and move freely to either side, but when he attempted to take a step toward the overman's retreating form, it was as if his boots were glued to the floor's ancient planking.

He stared at Garth's back, then looked beyond to the yellow-cowled figure that sat, still unmoving, in the corner. A tattered edge of the old man's hood flapped, though there was no wind in the tavern, nor any open door or window that might admit a breeze; Herrenmer caught a glimpse of light glinting from a hidden eye. He could not see the eye itself, but only that single fleeting sparkle in the shadowed socket; he felt a chill sweep him from head to toe, and he told himself that he really had no interest in approaching the strange old fellow. He reseated himself at his table; after all, he reassured himself, there was only the one door. He could keep an eye on Garth perfectly well from where he was, and need not worry about him slipping out another way.

An involuntary shudder ran through him, and he decided that he would just as soon not even watch the overman's conversation; he would watch the door. He turned his attention back to Saram, who had watched the whole brief byplay with intense interest, but now resumed regaling his former superior with the unlikely tale about his current mistress that Garth's move had interrupted.

Neither Saram nor Herrenmer noticed that someone else had also observed the captain's curious hesitation, and now watched with interest the overman's conversation with the mysterious yellow-clad figure. A dour old man wearing clothes the color of drying blood, this observer sat near the fireplace, ostensibly drinking his luncheon; his eyes, however, flicked swiftly about, missing nothing that happened in the taproom, but always returning to the mismatched pair in the back corner, their conversation just within range of his hearing.

Garth himself was oblivious to the whole thing; he had been facing the wrong direction. He seated himself across from the Forgotten King and gazed for a moment at the ragged hood that shaded the ancient face; its color was scarcely visible in the sheltered gloom, and the overman wondered how yellow could look so dark. From where he sat he saw no motion, no glint of light, but only shadows and the old man's wispy beard trailing from his withered chin.

"Greetings, O King," he said.

"Greetings, Garth." As always, the hideous voice was an unpleasant surprise.

"I have considered your proposed bargain."

The old man made no reply, but Garth thought he might have nodded slightly.

"I would know more about what services you would require of me."

There was a contemplative silence for a few seconds, then the old man replied, "I require certain items. I do not at present recall exactly which."

Garth, not yet over his anger at the Baron, felt a twinge of annoyance at the old man's vague reply. "Listen, I do not care to waste my time prying words from you. I will not bind myself to your service, but at present I seek a way to divert myself while I consider what manner of reply to make to your Baron of Skelleth. What are these items, and where are they to be found? Would you have me fetch them?"

The King was again silent for a moment, and Garth's irritation grew; finally, the old man said, "You are to bring me whatsoever you find upon the seven high altars of the seven temples in Dûsarra."

"Dûsarra?" The name was unfamiliar.

"A city in Nekutta, far to the west."

"And will I find upon these altars that which you need for your mysterious cosmic purpose?"

"You will find the solution to your problems with Doran of Skelleth; let that suffice for the present."

"What? Will one of these altar objects provide some magical means of dealing with that madman? You are being deliberately vague."

The old man shrugged.

Garth sat for a long moment, thinking. It was plain that he would coax no further explanation out of the Forgotten King, and the task set was exasperatingly cryptic. Still, such a quest would undoubtedly be an interesting diversion, and the old man had said it would provide a solution to his problems – presumably some means of coercing the Baron into behaving reasonably, or else a means of carrying out a satisfactory vengeance without destroying the fledgling trade. He had never caught the old man in an actual lie, and there could be no doubt he had knowledge beyond what was natural.

And what else was he to do? He could not return to Ordunin under the present circumstances. Until he could come up with some way out of his oath to the Baron he had nothing better to do and nowhere better to go. Running some fool errand halfway across the world would be a welcome distraction. That was all he had expected until the King had made his final statement, and he had thought it sufficient; the old man's words, curious as they were, could only make it more tempting.

However, they also somehow made Garth uneasy.

"I will do it," he said. "I will find this city you speak of, and rob these seven altars, and we will see whether my problems are solved thereby."

The Forgotten King smiled behind his beard.

Beside the fireplace, the old man wearing dark red nodded to himself.

Three days later, in a windowless chamber bright with golden tapestries and gleaming lamps somewhere in the black-walled city of Dûsarra, the high priest of Aghad sat, sipping bitter red wine and studying an ancient text. With a rustle of draperies and robes one of his subordinates entered, and stood waiting until such time as her exalted master should deign to notice her.

The wait was brief; the high priest lowered his book and demanded, "Yes, child?"

"Darsen of Skelleth sends a message." The underling held up a narrow strip of parchment such as could be wrapped on the leg of a carrier pigeon.

The high priest held out his hand, and the acolyte surrendered the note. He read it, then crushed it in one great brown hand.

"We must see this prospective visitor. Go tell Haggat to ready his scrying glass."

The acolyte bowed and vanished through the curtains with another swift rustle; the high priest picked up his book once again, glanced at the page, placed a thin strip of embroidered velvet upon it to serve as a bookmark, then closed it and slid it onto a shelf beside a dozen others.

Fifteen minutes later the priest strode into another windowless room; this one was draped in black and deep red, its somber gloom scarcely softened by the light of a single immense candle. A plump middle-aged man in a loose black robe stood within, holding a great crystal sphere in his hands; the acolyte knelt beside him, her face hidden in the shadow of her hood.

"She has told you what I wish to see?"

The man nodded, and held out the sphere.

The high priest reached out and took it; he cradled it in his hands and gazed into it. The other two maintained a complete silence.

Deep within the globe's interior, the flickering reflection of the single candle's flame twisted and shaped itself into the form of a sunlit path, a narrow road through grassy countryside; as the high priest watched a figure appeared, riding down this golden strip of light. Mounted on a huge catlike black beast, clad in helmet, breastplate, and flowing brown cloak, the figure was that of a red-eyed overman.

The priest studied this vision for long minutes, then handed the sphere back to its master.

"This overman may be useful, perhaps very useful indeed. You, Haggat, will inform me of everything you can learn relating to him. You may have this acolyte as your personal property, to aid you in this and as your reward. Understood?"

The man nodded; one hand fell and pulled aside the acolyte's hood, then stroked her night-black hair possessively. The other hand balanced the crystal sphere, which flashed and glittered strangely. Despite the dim and uneven light, fear was plain on the girl's face as she looked up at her new master.

The high priest turned and left, thinking intently; although not the focus of his contemplation, he found himself aware that he considered Haggat to be very pleasant company. A man with his tongue cut out could not chatter on aimlessly as so many did.

He pulled his mind away from such distractions, and considered seriously what would be done with this thieving impertinent overman.

Chapter Four

The sun was sailing low in the western sky, as vividly red as Garth's eyes, turning the narrow wisps of cloud into a ruddy web of light and shadow. The overman admired the uncanny beauty of the scene; the colors seemed brighter, more fiery, than the sunsets of the Northern Waste. He mused as to why this should be so.

His mount seemed unimpressed. It kept its head low, its catlike ears spread, clearly displeased with its surroundings. Garth could hear, very faintly, the crunching of volcanic cinders beneath the warbeast's huge soft paws, a rather remarkable circumstance. Ordinarily the beast moved as quietly as any lesser feline, its padded feet as silent as the moon.

No wonder, then, that it disliked this strange new country! The sound of its own footsteps was alien, a constant reminder that it was far from home and all things familiar.

Ahead of them, dead black against the crimson-flushed western sky, there reared up yet another mountain range. Already in the fortnight's journey from Skelleth they had crossed one chain, the highest and most rugged Garth had ever seen, through a narrow pass, and made a detour around the southern end of another, lesser range. Now they were approaching a third such barrier, this one actively volcanic, as evidenced by the red-lit smoke that twined across the sunset clouds, and by the thin coating of fresh ash and cinder that lay across the countryside, clear proof that there had recently been a minor eruption.

According to the rough map the Forgotten King had provided, his goal, the city of Dûsarra, lay somewhere in the foothills of this range, but as yet he saw no sign of it. He wondered that people would live in such a land, with the shadow of fiery destruction looming over them, but there was no question that they did; for some time now the road he traveled had wound through farmland, elaborately irrigated and lush with unfamiliar crops. He had noticed that the farmers' houses were all roofed with tile or tin, rather than the more customary thatch; plainly, straw was too easily set ablaze by vagrant sparks drifting on the breeze that blew steadily down from the mountains, a warm, dry wind that brought with it strange new odors, scents he had never known before.

He had come this far without incident, which pleased him. After agreeing to undertake this journey it had been a matter of an hour or so to obtain an assortment of bags and pouches, to carry whatever he might find, and a week's supply of food and water, which he had augmented on the road by hunting and minor thefts from untended fields and wells. Thus equipped, he had allowed himself to be escorted out the North Gate, whereupon he circled around to the West Gate, where he had retrieved Koros and his weapons and other supplies. He had then circled further, to the southwestern highway, a branch of which he was still following. Unlike his previous quest in the Forgotten King's service, which had led across barren, deserted lands inhabited only by barbaric little tribes, this journey had wound through league after league of settled, civilized countryside, more than he had known to exist upon the face of the world; he had dodged a double dozen of villages, and given a wide berth to a huge walled city indicated on the old man's map as Ur-Dormulk, all before even crossing the first mountains that marked the border between Eramma and Nekutta. Five times now he had set Koros free at night so that the warbeast could hunt its own food, and each time he had worried that it might not be able to find any meat to its liking except human flesh in the form of sleeping farmers, as there was not much wildlife to be found in such thickly-settled regions. Fortunately, Koros seemed to have managed, preying on stray goats and sheep when nothing else was available; Garth was grateful that it remained true to its training and avoided killing anything humanoid – when it could be avoided. It had, on occasion, eaten people when nothing else edible could be found, and it had eaten those it happened to kill in self-defense, but as a rule it knew not to.

It was an extremely useful animal, the finest product of a thousand years of selective breeding and magical shaping, but its voracious appetite could be very inconvenient. Ordinarily it was supremely obedient, but its loyalty decreased as its hunger increased, and Garth knew that five days without food, as opposed to the usual three days it went between meals, would render it willing to devour anything that moved, including its master.

It had fed last night on a pair of plump goats, and usually when recently fed it was as placid as a pampered housecat; today, though, the harsh landscape and crunching cinders seemed to upset it, and it growled softly, low in its throat, as a new twist of smoke drifted up the western sky.

Garth watched the smoke, and suddenly realized it had risen from a point between peaks; he stared at the jagged black shapes and thought he made out the curve of a dome amid the irregular constructions of nature. The shadows still obscured all color and detail, but the longer he looked the more convinced he became that there was, in fact, at least one man-made structure in these somber hills. He called the word that Koros recognized as a command to halt, as even the smooth grace of the warbeast's stride jogged him sufficiently to make it difficult to focus at so great a distance.

Yes, there was something there. He could not be sure what, as the sun was now slipping below the highest peaks, making it harder than ever to distinguish anything. He looked about, to rest his eyes, and noticed a farmer, a hundred yards away, leaning on a hoe and studying the overman and warbeast.

"Ho! Farmer!" he called.

The man did not move.

"Come here! I would speak with you!" He motioned.

The farmer looked about, as if to see if the overman meant someone else, though there was no other living being in sight, only the man's own twenty acres and the empty road stretching away in either direction. Then he shrugged and came, dragging his hoe casually, to stand a dozen yards away.

"Farmer, is that Dûsarra?" Garth pointed at the spot where he had seen the dome.

The farmer followed the direction of the pointing finger and said, "I suppose it is." His accent was strange to Garth, harsh and guttural, but his words were plain enough.

"How far is it?"

The farmer shrugged. "Couldn't say. You're an overman, I know, but what is that you're riding?" He studied Koros closely, from the glittering three-inch fangs in its jaw to the tip of its lashing tail, and from its glossy black-furred shoulder to its huge padded paws. A good eighteen feet long, the monster resembled nothing so much as an overgrown panther, though proportioned differently in order to support its greater bulk. It had a cat's golden slit eyes and triangular ears, stubby black whiskers on its muzzle, and a long slender tail. No panther had such fangs, though, and both legs and face seemed oddly elongated; it stood nearly as tall as the farmer himself. Pure black throughout, with no touch of color nor single gray hair, its muscles rippled smoothly under its fur; it clearly had no trouble at all in carrying the full weight of the armored overman and his supplies.

"It is a warbeast."

Koros growled.

The farmer suddenly seemed less sure of himself. He had assumed that any animal that served as a beast of burden, however formidable it might appear, must be docile and harmless – but no peaceful ox nor temperamental cart-goat ever made a noise like that. He thought better of previous actions, and said, "Dûsarra is ten leagues distant, my lord, along this same road, three leagues past the crossroads at Weideth."

"Crossroads?"

"Yes. It's of no importance, though; for Dûsarra you ride straight through on this same road, making no turn."

"What is Weideth?"

"The village at the crossroads; a small town, with no wall. You'll have no trouble there."

Garth was less certain of that than his informant seemed to be. This man seemed to accept an overman and warbeast calmly enough, but would an entire village?

"Is there no way around it? I do not wish to be seen."

"Around? No, my lord, not that I know of; the terrain thereabouts is very rough, and Weideth lies in a narrow pass, astride the road. It's a wonder they don't charge a toll, in truth."

"I see. My thanks, man."

The man bowed and stepped back, and when Garth made no further comment nor move to stop him, he turned and departed at a brisk pace.

This village, Garth thought as he urged Koros forward once again, was a nuisance. He did not dare risk losing his way at this point; he would have to ride through and hope he did not create too much of a commotion. Ten leagues to Dûsarra, and that three leagues past Weideth, the man had said; that meant he was seven leagues from the village. Seven leagues was two or three hours ride, perhaps a trifle more if the terrain was bad; if he kept riding he would pass through the village well after full dark, and reach Dûsarra in the middle of the night, while if he stopped and made camp he would arrive at midday tomorrow. Midday was scarcely a good time to try and slip unobtrusively through a village, nor was it a good time for reconnaissance in Dûsarra. He was not tired, and Koros was well-fed; he should have no trouble in completing his journey without further delay. If he were to be a thief, then he would arrive as a thief in the night; he spoke the command for a trot and the warbeast strode on, the only sound the soft crunching of cinders.

The moon was near full, making it easy to follow the road even after the sun was well down, though it was not actually necessary to see it since straying to either side would mean passing through the tall grass of late summer, easily two feet in height, that flanked the way. Besides the pale light of the moon, Garth noticed as well a dim red glow flickering about the mountaintops that grew as he approached – volcanic fires, of course. He began to share Koros' dislike for this country; such eerie lights seemed threatening. A volcano active enough to light the clouds at night could well be active enough to bury its surroundings in ash and lava, yet here he was riding ever closer.

It was more than two hours after he spoke to the farmer, well after the last trace of daylight had faded in the west, with only the white moonlight and the red glow of the volcano to see by, that he was first spotted by one of the sentries. Garth did not see the young woman, nor would he have paid her much heed if he had, but she saw him, and studied him closely before slipping from her hilltop post and running back to Weideth with her report.

The Seer of Weideth was finishing his final cup of wine and seriously considering retiring for the night when the sentry burst into the village's single nameless inn – which also served as the public meeting house and in rainy weather as a makeshift marketplace – with her news. She looked about wildly for someone to report her discovery to, but the village elders were all long abed; for want of a better audience, she directed her shout at the Seer.

"There is an overman on the East Road, riding upon a creature like none I have ever seen!"

The Seer smiled at her melodramatics. "Have you, then, seen every sort of beast there is? There are frequently overmen on the north and west roads, and they do not all make do with horses and oxen."

"Yes, but this one is on the East Road, and wearing armor!"

The Seer started to dismiss her with a wave. "Overmen do not use the East Road," he began.

"This one does! If you will not listen to me, I'll find someone who will!"

His hand fell, and for the first time the Seer looked directly at the girl's face. He realized that she spoke the truth; a part of his talent was knowing the truth when it was spoken, and this young woman – she could have seen no more than eighteen years – was not merely excited or mistaken. There was an overman on the East Road, which no overman had ridden in three hundred years; an overman had come out of the east.

"The prophecies say that death and destruction lie in the east," he said.

"So I have heard," replied the girl sarcastically, her hands on her hips.

"We must wake the elders."

The sentry nodded. "They will know what to do."

"Yes. We cannot let an eastern overman reach Dûsarra."

It was several minutes later when Garth turned a corner in the winding road, which for the last three leagues had twisted its way through the foothills and now led along the bottom of a narrow defile, and caught a glimpse of Weideth. It was only a very brief glimpse, however, for the village he had thought he saw vanished almost instantly, leaving only another few hundred yards of highway that stretched out from his warbeast's feet and turned right out of sight behind a hill up ahead.

He blinked. There was no village. There was no sign of a village; there was only the road.

He stopped his mount with a word and studied the road. There was nothing there. After a moment's consideration, he arrived at a few possible explanations for what he thought he'd seen – a neat row of cottages on either side of the highway, a widening of the gorge into a respectable valley. It could have been a trick of the moonlight, though it had seemed too detailed for that. It could have been a mirage caused by some unknown effect of the volcano, letting him see a village that in fact lay somewhere else. It could have been a hallucination caused by volcanic gases; he had heard of such things. It could be that he was more tired than he had known, and his mind or his eyes were playing tricks in consequence.

Or it could have been magic.

This last possibility seemed actually the most likely, and it did not bode well; still, there was nothing he could do about it sitting where he was. He signaled to Koros, and the warbeast strode forward. Nothing unusual happened; the barren hills continued on either side. When they had traversed halfway to the next turn without incident, Garth relaxed. There seemed to be no danger.

If it were magic, Garth mused, what sort of magic had it been? Had an entire village been transported away in an instant? That seemed unlikely. Perhaps the village had been a mere illusion. If so, had it been intended for him, or for someone else?

As it neared the bend in the road, Koros hesitated; it seemed unsure whether to follow the road around to the right, or to proceed straight ahead up the side of the defile. Garth turned its head right, and it resumed its steady forward progress.

This served to distract Garth momentarily; it was not typical of the beast's behavior. It usually knew to follow the road unless directed otherwise. Ah, he told himself, it meant nothing; the creature was tired. Perhaps he *had* just imagined the village in his own fatigue. As he had just been thinking, perhaps the village had been an illusion.

Or perhaps this deserted gorge was an illusion, and it was the village that was real.

That thought had a disturbing plausibility, and Garth stopped his mount. The village of Weideth was supposed to be around here somewhere, yet he had seen no trace of it except perhaps that single fleeting glimpse. It was at a crossroads, and Koros had hesitated as if uncertain of the correct path – as if at a fork or crossroads.

But why, assuming that he was in fact in the middle of Weideth, was such an illusion created? He looked down at his mount, and at himself; the warbeast's fangs gleamed in the moonlight, and his sword slapped his thigh as he moved.

He was not, he admitted to himself, the sort of character whose appearance inspired confidence in strangers. No doubt the villagers had some sort of magician amongst them who used illusions of this sort to render the town invisible to any travelers who looked dangerous.

If it were an illusion, he reminded himself.

That could be tested, he decided; he ordered Koros to stand and guard, and dismounted cautiously.

He still seemed to be in a rocky, empty passage through the hills, not a village – but there was no reason the illusion should be less effective on an unmounted overman than upon one riding a warbeast. He stepped carefully off the road; and reached out to touch a convenient boulder.

It was there, all right, and felt very much like stone. He ran his fingers across it. Yes, it was smooth stone. He flattened his palm against it, and slid it downward a few inches.

One of his thumbs slipped into a crack; he looked more closely. Yes, there was a crack visible; he must have missed noticing it in the moonlight, if it had actually been there all along. What was under his thumb felt very much like mortar. He ran his hand sideways; the crack was dead straight and perfectly horizontal. He reached over further, where there appeared to be nothing but open air.

His hand struck something; he felt it carefully.

It was glass. It was a small square pane of glass held in lead, and beside it was another, and another. He blinked.

He was standing before a small house built of cut stone, his hand touching a casement window; other houses stood to either side. Behind him Koros growled uneasily.

He whirled. He stood near the middle of a village, just as he had seen it. What had appeared to be a turn in the highway was indeed a crossroads. That meant that he had been diverted from his route; he had turned north instead of continuing westward.

He growled in annoyance. He did not like this. He did not like magic. He did not like the necessary conclusion that there was somebody with unknown preternatural abilities actively trying to deceive him. His hand fell to his sword hilt as he looked about, and he mentally commended himself upon traveling well-armed since leaving Skelleth – armor was uncomfortable, but prudent.

The village was still and silent; the only sound was his own footsteps. The houses were all shuttered and dark – except for one. At the crossroads stood a building rather larger than the average cottage, with a signboard hung above its door; whatever message the sign might bear was invisible in the darkness, but the place was probably an inn or public house, and light showed through its curtained windows.

His magical antagonist might be working at some distance, or might be hidden in darkness somewhere – but it seemed more likely he or she was in that single illuminated room.

What, then, was he to do about it?

He had two choices; he could ignore the incident and be on his way, or he could confront whoever lurked behind those curtains. If he ignored it he would be leaving a potential danger behind him, able to attack from the rear, and sitting on his route home. That would not do.

He reminded Koros to stay where it was, loosened his sword in its scabbard, and marched to the inn. The door stood slightly ajar; he kicked it open and stood aside, lest an ambush be prepared for him. Nothing happened; he stepped forward again and looked within. A sudden wave of vertigo swept over him; he blinked, and looked through the door.

He was looking into his own home in Ordunin, the rambling stone and wood house that he had built with his own hands. For a moment he froze in astonishment, but the incongruity suddenly seemed unimportant. He was home!

He stepped inside and looked about. Through the large window to his right he saw the wide plank terrace and the spectacular view of the bay beyond; sunlight sparkled from the waves and poured warmly into the room. He listened, and could hear the ocean's roar very faintly; nearer at hand a bird sang somewhere.

He noticed that he still wore his helmet and breastplate, his sword on his belt and axe on his back; such precautions were surely unnecessary here in his own domain! He reached up to remove the helmet, but paused; how had he come home? He had no memory of the journey, and he had not intended to come here; returning home meant that he would have to speak to the Council, in accordance with his oath to the Baron. Something was peculiar about this, and until he recollected what it was, it would do no harm to keep his armor and weapons on. He was not particularly uncomfortable – though a trifle overwarm – and he could bear to take such a simple precaution.

There was a sound somewhere further inside the house; that would be one of his family, of course. It would be a pleasure to see them all once again. He wondered what the date was; he seemed to have forgotten, yet he always kept track of such things, to know when to expect his wives to be in heat. He would have to ask. He called out, "Ho! Who goes?"

A door opened and an overwoman entered; Kyrith, his favorite wife. Her scent reached him, and warmth spread through him; she would be ready any time.

By human standards she was far from beautiful; she was as tall and flat-chested as any overman, and her face as inhuman; to Garth, she was a fine, handsome creature. Her golden eyes were warm and inviting; her black hair was long, for an overwoman, and Garth reached out to run his fingers through it. Her scent was entrancing.

She smiled, and caught his fingers; he smiled back.

He felt his body reacting to her odor; that smell was the only sexual stimulus that affected an overman, and it was irresistible. He reached out both arms for her; she smiled, and poked at his breastplate.

"Shouldn't you remove your armor?" she asked.

He growled playfully, reached up to remove his helmet, and stopped. Something was wrong. Something was very, very wrong.

Kyrith was mute. The *real* Kyrith was mute, at any rate; she had fallen years ago while skiing, a fall that sent slivers of ice through her throat. She had lived, with only a slight scar, but her voice was gone forever. This was not her: The whole thing was an illusion.

He thrust the false Kyrith away and drew his sword; the illusionist had made a fatal error in giving Kyrith a voice, but there was no doubt that his or her magic was effective. Not only had the image of his home been perfect, but the sounds and smells, and his memory had been befuddled as well. Garth dared not take any further chances.

"Show yourself, magician, or I will lay about with this blade until I find you!"

His home vanished, and he was in a small village tavern; a fire burned low on the hearth, and a chandelier held a dozen stubby candles, casting their wan light across a dozen empty tables and five human beings.

One was an old woman who lay sprawled on the floor where he had flung the false Kyrith; she wore a hood and cloak of pale blue that spread about her in disarray, revealing her bony blue-veined legs and wrinkled face. Her hair was long and silvery-white. She made no move to rise, but lay where she was, watching Garth with terror in her expression.

The other four sat clustered about a table. There was a young woman in brown leather helmet and tunic and black skirt, a bow leaning against the back of her chair and a quiver of white-fletched arrows slung on her shoulder. Beside her sat a man of indeterminate age, his face hidden beneath a gray hood, his gray cloak hiding all but his hands – muscular hands, one of which clutched the handle of a pewter mug.

The remaining pair wore pale blue robes that matched that of the woman on the floor, and both were likewise old; one was a man with steel-gray hair and gray-streaked black beard, the other was another white-haired woman, shorter and thinner than her fallen comrade.

There was a moment of silent consideration, and then Garth demanded, "Why have you beset me?"

There was an uneasy silence; no one answered him.

"Is this the way you treat all travelers? Or is it because I am an overman? Because I wear armor? What do you want of me?"

The old woman at the table said, in a high and broken voice, "We meant you no harm."

"Then what did you mean? You have twice attacked me with your illusions; why?"

"We did not attack you; we sought only to have you pass through our village without seeing it."

"You diverted me from my path; I am not bound northward."

"We did not know that; we thought you must be, for it is to the north that overmen are said to dwell."

Garth considered that for a few seconds; it did have a logical ring to it. "You attempted to deceive me when I entered this tavern."

"We sought only to remove your weapons, so that we could deal with you more easily."

That accorded with the facts. Garth relaxed slightly. This handful of humans was no threat to him, save for their magic, and he seemed to have beaten that; only one even bore arms, and that one a mere girl.

"Which of you conjured those illusions?"

The man in the gray hood, silent heretofore, spoke up. "It is a joint effort; no one of us is essential."

Garth considered this, and chose to doubt it; such a claim was good tactics, and more likely tactics than truth. "Who are you all, then?"

"I am the Seer of Weideth, and these three are the village elders." He indicated the other man and the two old women.

"Who is she?" He pointed at the girl with his sword.

"She is just the one who saw you coming in time to warn us. She is no one of importance."

"You call yourself a seer?"

"Yes."

"Can you read the future, then?" Garth had heard of such talents, and had in fact dealt with an oracle, the Wise Women of Ordunin, who seemed to know something of events yet to come; he could see many uses for such an ability.

"On occasion. I'm afraid I'm not much of a seer, if the truth be known. I do have knowledge and talent beyond the ordinary, but I have little control over it. I am the last and least in a long line of Seers in Weideth, and I spend more time studying the prophecies of my predecessors than making my own."

That explained why he had failed to foresee that Garth would not be deceived by the illusions, and therefore Garth decided to believe it. He had the impression that the man was being reasonably forthright. Perhaps a similar frankness on his own part would enable him to resolve this episode in short order and get on his way once more. He wanted to reach Dûsarra before morning; before midnight would be nice.

"Listen, then; I mean no harm to you or your village. I intend no evil toward any person or community outside the village of Skelleth. I bear no ill will for your mistaken attempts at self-defense. Let us end our dispute peaceably; I will not harm you, but will go about my business. In exchange you will refrain from bothering me further with your petty magic. Is this not fair to all, and a desirable conclusion?"

The Seer said to his comrades, "He speaks the truth as he knows it."

There was a moment of silent consideration as the elders looked at one another; the larger woman clambered to her feet, then found a chair and seated herself. Garth lowered his sword, but did not sheathe it.

It was the sentry who first spoke, saying, "But what about the prophecies?"

The male elder nodded. "There is that."

"What prophecies?" Garth said. "I am not an unreasonable person. Explain your meaning, and perhaps I can accommodate you."

The humans all turned toward the Seer, making plain that they felt it was his place, as Seer, to explain. He obliged.

"There are two prophecies that led us to be especially wary of your coming, overman. The first, made long, long ago, said merely that death and destruction lie in wait in the east, and shall come out of the east in their time. The second, made by my immediate predecessor – who unlike myself, was one of our greatest Seers and prophets; there seems to be an alternation – well, his was an elaboration upon the first, and says that when an overman from the east comes to Dûsarra he will unleash chaos and catastrophe upon the world. You see, therefore, that we do not wish to see you proceed westward from our village, since that road leads only to Dûsarra."

Garth considered this. It sounded vague to him, and he was reluctant to pay it much heed; he had business in Dûsarra.

"Does the prophecy give my name, or a more exact description?"

"No."

"Does it say that any overman from the east will bring disaster, or that there will be one specific one?"

"It implies one specific overman, but we prefer not to take chances; you are the first overman to come up the East Road in a very long time, the first since the prophecy was made."

"I have come from the Northern Waste, though, not from the eastern lands. I have no intention of unleashing anything."

"I never heard of the Northern Waste; still, it must lie to the east, or you would not have come on the East Road. Your intentions may prove to have very little to do with what actually occurs."

"Still, I do not think I am the overman prophesied, and I intend to go to Dûsarra. I would advise you not to try to stop me, nor to obstruct me when I return on my way home."

"We will not bother you once you have reached Dûsarra; it will be too late by then. Anything we might do after that would be pointless revenge, and we are not so foolish as to attempt it. However, I beg you to reconsider. Do not go to Dûsarra! You may not be the overman we were warned of, but why risk it? You are a good man . . . Ah, I mean a good person. Do not chance bringing destruction upon yourself and others!"

"I regret that I cannot oblige you. It seems that we will not be able to part as friends after all, and in that case I must ask this young woman to surrender her bow to me; I have no desire to be shot in the back. I will leave it, undamaged, on the road west of the village. I must also insist that no further distracting illusions be used; I know where and who you are, now, and would take it very ill should you attempt to divert me."

He reached out for the bow; reluctantly, her eye on the sword in his other hand, the girl gave it to him.

"My thanks. I take leave of you now, and wish you all well. I truly hope and believe that I am not the overman your prophets spoke of." He nodded politely, and backed out of the inn, sword in hand. No one made any unfriendly move, nor any move at all; all five sat in silent dismay.

Once outside, he turned and ran toward where he had left Koros; he had little doubt that despite his warning, some other attempt would be made to stop him, and he wanted to put as much distance between himself and the village as he could before the humans could reorganize sufficiently to launch their attack.

His eyes were no longer accustomed to the darkness after his conversation in the lit tavern, and he stumbled on the rough roadway; annoyed, he called his warbeast's name.

There was an answering growl and the beast appeared in the darkness before him, its golden eyes gleaming in the moonlight. He sheathed his sword and reached out; Koros obediently stalked up to him. He grabbed the harness and swung himself into the saddle, then gave the signal for a trot – not the warbeast's fastest pace by any means, but Garth thought it would be sufficient and did not care to risk more in the darkness.

He directed the beast toward the west road, and then paused; how could he be sure it was the true west road, and that the humans had not used another illusion to confuse him? The moon's position was correct, and the red glow of the volcano lay in the right part of the sky, but he already knew that their illusions were good enough to encompass such details. He carefully reviewed his movements after leaving the inn, and determined that they had not in fact turned anything around – unless they had once again twisted his memories. He doubted that they had had time to do anything of the sort, though of course they could have distorted his time sense as well.

He could not in fact be certain, but after consideration it seemed that it was unlikely the road was illusory, and he had no way of proving whether it was or not. Accordingly, he would assume that no illusions were being perpetrated, and if it later developed that they were, he would come back here and demonstrate to the Seer and the village elders the folly of angering Garth, Prince of Ordunin.

He signaled for a trot again, and rode swiftly out of the village, away from the crossroads and the dimly-lit inn.

Chapter Five

The farmer had told him that it was three leagues from Weideth to Dûsarra; that was over an hour's ride, but a glance at the sky and some calculation indicated that he could still make it by midnight, with luck. It depended in large part upon how tired Koros was. So far, the creature showed no signs of fatigue at all.

They were leaving the village, passing the last few houses that straggled out along the road, when Garth glimpsed movement from the corner of his eye; he ducked, instinctively, and the shadowy batlike form that swooped at him swept silently by, its glittering black talons inches from his face.

The girl's bow was still clutched in one hand; he flung it aside, wishing he had taken her arrows as well, and dove from the warbeast's back, drawing his sword as he landed rolling on the rocky highway. Ahead and above, the bat-thing wheeled and came at him again.

He got a good look at it as it attacked; it was not a true bat at all. Its wingspread was a good ten feet, and though its wings were stretched leathery hide like a bat's, its body and head were those of a bird of prey, round black eyes and hooked black beak making up the face, outstretched talons gleaming. He ducked under its lunge again and brought his sword up to meet it.

The sword passed through it unhindered, leaving no mark, meeting no resistance.

The tension left Garth's body; he grinned and stood upright. The thing was another illusion, of course, not even a particularly clever one. Did they expect him to cower away from the thing without fighting?

Apparently they did, or they wouldn't have sent it. He turned back toward

Koros, preparing to remount, ignoring the bat-thing that wheeled and dove.

Its claws ripped his helmet from him and raked bloody furrows across the back of his head.

He swung around again, sword ready, growling in pain and anger; his sudden turn sent spatters of blood flying from his wounds. They were real, no doubt about it, and painful, but not deep. The elders of Weideth had more magic than mere illusion at their disposal.

The thing was coming in for another pass; he dodged and swung at it with his sword. As before, the blade passed through the monster as if it were a mere shadow. Garth growled.

On the next pass he dodged again, and lashed out not with his sword, but with his free hand, clutching at the thing's leg. His hand closed on nothing but air, and the claws raked his wrist.

This began to be serious; although not too bright, the thing was persistent and would eventually tire him out and claw him to pieces. It seemed to possess a curious one-way tangibility like nothing Garth had ever encountered. He had thought it might have some protection against cold steel when the sword had no effect, but his hand had been equally incapable of touching it. Hand and sword had passed through its body without touching it, yet its claws had made themselves felt twice.

Its claws had been felt – but only the claws! Even when Garth had left himself completely undefended in the mistaken belief he was dealing with an illusion, it had not used its great evil beak, nor struck him with its wings – wings that made no sound and created no wind.

As it turned for another assault, Garth studied its talons; they glinted in the moonlight unlike any claws he had ever seen, a glassy black sheen rather than the sparkling highlights of polished bone or nail. They were not smoothly curved, nor scaled and jointed, but twisted and jagged. They looked very much like some sort of glass or crystal rather than part of a living creature.

It swept down upon him again, those strange black talons outstretched, and Garth's sword came up to meet it, not sweeping through its intangible belly this time, but striking at the talons themselves.

He was rewarded with a tinkling crash as his blade struck and reduced one great spiked claw to a shower of glittering splinters.

The creature's mouth opened, as though to cry in pain, but no sound emerged; it swept up and away from him and circled briefly.

He took a moment to stoop and pick up a shard of the shattered claw; now that he held it in his hand, he could readily identify it. It was obsidian – black volcanic glass. It was quite tangible and ordinary.

Overhead the thing seemed to recover itself, and dove at him again.

This time he made no effort to dodge, but simply held up his blade horizontally before his face and kept it steady with both hands as the full force of the creature's claws smashed into it. The obsidian talons shattered spectacularly, sending glassy needles spraying in every direction; a few slivers stitched tiny cuts across his hands or spattered from his breastplate. His face was protected by the blade, but his eyes closed instinctively.

When he opened them again the creature was gone, the only trace of its existence the splinters of volcanic glass that lay scattered about, glistening in the moonlight.

He brushed himself off, sheathed his sword, retrieved his helmet, and looked about. No new threat was apparent, Koros was unharmed, and his own injuries were minor. He mounted the warbeast, then turned, and bellowed back toward Weideth.

"Seer, if you can hear me, be warned! If you send anything else against me, destruction will indeed be unleashed, as I will wipe your village from the earth! Hear me, and be warned!"

There was a faint echo of his shout from the hills on either side, but no other reply. He turned westward once more and rode on.

Chapter Six

Something over an hour later he emerged from between two hills to find himself with a clear view of Dûsarra crowning the long, smooth slope that rose in front of him. Moonlight glimmered from the city's domes and towers, a soft silver that seemed to give no light at all; comparing the silhouetted buildings with the smoky red sky behind them, Garth realized that they were all dead black in color, and that therefore even the brightest moonlight could not illumine them. The city was walled, though Garth thought it unlikely any wars were ever fought in such rugged land; the wall, too, appeared to be built of the same black stone. In the poor light Garth could not see where the wall ended and the ground below began; the slope before him appeared to be a smooth sheet of darkness that blended into the city without break. Peering closely, Garth realized that the hillside was, in fact, an ancient lava flow; it was a single vast slab of stone, where nothing grew. The road he followed ended at its foot, leaving the traveler to follow whatever route he chose across that rocky expanse.

He urged his mount forward onto the stone; Koros obeyed without protest. They had come to the end of the fresh cinders a league or so back, where the road had curved toward the north; whichever volcano had thrown them up, it was apparently not the one that towered above Dûsarra, lighting the sky before them a murky red.

As they made their way up the slope, something caught Garth's eye; there was something about the city wall that didn't look right. He stared harder, and saw it again; there was a glimmer of light directly in front of them, apparently in the middle of the wall. Could someone be camped in front of the gate? It was possible, but the light somehow didn't look like a campfire, nor did it look to be on the slope outside the walls. A window in the wall, perhaps, with a lighted guardroom beyond? That might be, except that it must be an inordinately large window to be so visible at this distance; although difficult to judge exactly at night, Garth was sure there was still another mile or so of this rocky slope to be climbed.

A few moments later he realized what it was; the city gates were open, and the square just inside was lit all around with torches.

It was very nearly midnight, yet Dûsarra's gates were wide open, as if it were noon of market day. Garth wondered what kind of strange city he was approaching; could this be some sort of religious festival? Were they so trusting of strangers that they left the gates open at all times? If that was it, then why were the walls maintained, and why was the market lit? No, that could not be the reason, for he could make out vague shapes moving about; there were people there, just exactly as if the city's inhabitants were going about their ordinary business in the dead of night. He began to hope that it was, in fact, some kind of holiday or religious event; that at least would be understandable.

It suddenly struck him that his stealthy nighttime approach wasn't going to make much difference after all. Well, he thought, at least by torchlight it would be less obvious that he was an overman than it would be at noon. But then again, a city that lived by night might well sleep by day, and he might have done better to approach by daylight.

No, that was absurd; there had to be some sane reason for this nocturnal activity. He could not imagine what it could be, but there must be one. He'd know soon enough; he gave up wondering and rode on.

Dûsarra, he decided as he rode through the gate, was a very strange city, at least by his standards; but then, he had not actually traveled that much. Outside his own land he had seen only Skelleth, Weideth, and Mormoreth, and from a distance Ur-Dormulk; Mormoreth was a dead city, Skelleth might as well be, Weideth was only a village, and Ur-Dormulk he had not gone within a mile of. Perhaps Dûsarra was normal, and the others strange. He halted his mount, and looked about the square he found himself in.

It was a fairly conventional marketplace; merchants, stalls lined every side, each with torches illuminating it, one or two torches per stall. The market was busy; men and women strolled about or rushed, haggled over prices, gossiped with friends, and generally did whatever people ordinarily did in a city market. Only the stars overhead and the flickering torchlight made the scene seem unnatural.

Garth noticed with interest that the natives dressed differently from the people of Skelleth; where the men of Skelleth wore tunic and trousers and the women wore blouse and skirt, here both sexes wore long, shapeless robes. The poverty-stricken people of Skelleth could afford only the drabbest of dyes, but here Garth saw many attired in blood-red as well as the more usual browns, grays, white and black. The majority seemed to be wearing a dark blue shade; the current fashion, no doubt, or perhaps representative of some social class. Many had hoods pulled up over their heads.

Well, he should be able to blend in reasonably well; although for most of the journey he had worn openly his breastplate, helmet, and mail, with his sword on his belt – a welcome change from the scratching hilt of his stiletto, which was packed away in his bundle of supplies – he had had the foresight to throw his rough brown cloak on before approaching the city. The trader's hat he had worn in Skelleth was not appropriate here; none of the natives wore any headgear but the loose hood. His cloak naturally included a hood, though he had never had occasion to wear it. He pulled it up, then paused; he would already stand out as remarkably tall, and should do nothing to exaggerate his height. He removed his helmet, then pulled the hood into place before stuffing the headpiece into the pack behind him.

As yet, he had seen no sign that anyone had noticed his presence, which was all to the good; they were all too busy with their own concerns. It was odd that there was no guard on the gate, though.

He dismounted and ambled casually forward, stooping to disguise his height, hoping that in the uneven torchlight no one would notice that he wasn't human. They would, of course, notice Koros; there was no disguising a warbeast. But there was also no cause to object strenuously to a warbeast, most particularly since these people probably had no idea what one was.

Of course, he wouldn't want to take the beast along when he went temple-robbing; he would have to find an inn with a good stable. Besides needing a place to leave Koros, he was hungry and thirsty, and a tavern would undoubtedly be a good place to pick up information about the temples, as well. It seemed reasonable that there would be an inn facing on the square, convenient to the gate but, studying the shadowy stone façades behind the merchants' stalls, he could see no signboards indicating one, nor other evidence of one's existence. With a mental shrug, he stepped up to the nearest stall, where a silk dealer debated the value of a bolt of his best bleached fabric with a would-be buyer.

He waited politely until the two arrived at a mutually satisfactory price; then, while the customer carefully counted out his hoarded coins, he inquired of the merchant, "Is there a good inn to be found near here? I have traveled far."

The merchant, eagerly watching the small pile of silver grow, said, "There's the Inn of the Seven Stars."

"Could you direct me there, then?"

Pointing without looking up, he said, "Take the first street on the left."

"My thanks." There had certainly been no danger there of being spotted as an overman; neither man had looked at him at all. He returned to where Koros stood, just inside the gate, and told the warbeast to follow him; finding the break in the ring of booths and buildings that marked a street, first one on the left, he led the warbeast through the crowd into the darkness of what proved little more than an alleyway. No one took undue notice of him or his beast; he decided that Dûsarra must be more cosmopolitan than he had thought, if its people were so blasé about such creatures in their midst.

The alley was unlit and almost uninhabited; after the relative glare of the market it took his eyes a few seconds to adjust. Like their countrymen in the market, the few people who strolled the byway paid Garth and Koros no heed. Here all wore their hoods up and pulled well forward, unlike the market where the bare-headed predominated.

He made his way carefully through the gloom; the shadows of the buildings on either side kept the moonlight from lighting the way adequately, but the narrow street was clear of obstructions. At least this inn stood on a cleaner street than the King's Inn, Garth thought.

He rounded a slight curve, and found the way brighter; light poured from around a second turn, which brought the street back to its original direction. He turned the second corner, and had found the inn; the light poured from its broad front window, and he could hear voices within. The door stood open, not surprising on a warm summer night, and above it hung a sign; the light from the window let him make out seven stars arranged in an oval, white paint on blue. A wide arch just beyond led, he hoped, to an attached stable. He crossed the field of light, and found a boy asleep in the archway. The distinctive odors of horse and ox reached his slit nostrils, convincing him that his hopes were correct. He prodded the boy gently with a booted toe.

The lad woke up immediately and sprang to his feet, but said nothing.

"I need stabling for my mount."

"One mark the night, sir, and feed is extra."

"I have no local currency; will this do?" He produced his smallest gold coin, and dropped it in the boy's hand. The lad looked at it, then carried it over to the light that spilled from the tavern door.

He studied it for a long minute, then asked, "What is it?"

"A northern gold piece."

"Gold?" The boy looked at it again, then tested it with his teeth.

"Of course it's gold."

"Yes, sir; but we see little gold here. Most pay in silver. My apologies for the delay; the third stall is yours, my lord." He bowed.

Garth ignored the stable-boy's obsequiousness and led Koros to the indicated stall, which proved spacious enough and well lined with straw, though not particularly clean. A bucket of passably clear water hung from one side, and in view of its recent feeding Garth saw no need to provide the warbeast with any other sustenance. He removed pack and saddle and placed them to one side, then told Koros to stay and headed for the tavern door. He had no worries that anyone might disturb his supplies; anybody fool enough to try would be ripped to pieces immediately. A warbeast was a very useful thing to have.

Although from the street the tavern had seemed brightly lit, once inside Garth found it otherwise; the light came from a row of lanterns hung across the window and from two low-burning hearthfires, one at either end of the main room, and from nowhere else, so that most of the room remained dim and shadowed. The chimneys did not seem to draw well either; a haze of smoke seemed to hang over everything.

A dozen assorted locals adorned the various tables that were scattered about, and there was not a lone innkeeper, as Garth had expected, but two serving-maids and a boy, all adolescent, distinguishable from their patrons by virtue of gray aprons worn over their robes. Probably the innkeeper's offspring, he decided, and their father must be in the kitchen or ending to rooms upstairs.

He beckoned to the nearer girl; she scurried over, leaving the spit she had been turning, which held a shapeless lump of meat a foot or so above one of the fires. "Yes, sir?" she said.

"Bring me ale and meat; and have you any fruit? I could use something sweet." Garth spoke in a voice well above his natural range and stood stooping to disguise his inhuman height, his hood pulled well forward.

"Yes, sir." She hurried off, and he seated himself at a convenient table.

As he waited for his food and drink he studied his surroundings; he wanted someone to talk to, someone who would tell him about the city and the temples. What he saw were a dozen robed, hooded figures huddled over their tables, speaking little to each other, let alone to a stranger who would not allow his face to be seen. The universal Dûsarran garb made him wonder momentarily if the Forgotten King hailed from this strange city, but on consideration he decided it was unlikely. The King wore yellow, a color he had not seen displayed anywhere in this country, and went in rags despite his claim of royalty, while here, dark colors predominated and most wore clothing in far better shape than his own travel-worn cloak. Further, the King was pale-skinned, while the Dûsarrans, from what he could see, were of a middling shade, lighter than his own hide but browner than the men of Skelleth; and finally, the Dûsarran robes tended to be loose and flowing, while the King kept his garments wrapped tightly about him.

But of course, Garth suddenly realized, not everyone in the room wore the standard robe and hood; the two serving-maids and their brother; if such he was, wore shorter, low-necked robes with no hoods, dark blue in color. All three were barefoot, with long brown hair tied back in single braids down their backs. The similarity in hair color further convinced Garth that they were siblings, as the shade and texture were almost identical.

These three might be more willing to converse than their customers; filling an eager ear would surely be more pleasant to such young folk than carting mugs and plates about. He paid them more attention than he had.

The boy was the youngest, probably well short of his full height, and still totally innocent of any beard; Garth was no judge of human ages, but the lad was plainly far from maturity. As such, he would probably be limited in his knowledge; among overmen, at least, religion and philosophy were not the concerns of children, so Garth guessed that the boy would know nothing of the temples.

Of the two girls there seemed little to choose, from the overman's point of view; they were of about the same size, and presumably therefore near the same age. They were as tall as many adult human women; Garth wondered again at the quirk of nature that made men and women so different in size, unlike overman and overwomen. Women seemed such small, fragile things, and oddly proportioned, at that.

One girl seemed slightly the more active of the two; Garth decided she must be the younger. It was her older sister he had spoken to when he arrived, and it would presumably be the older who would bring his food. In that case, he would simply speak to her when his meal was ready.

Even as he decided this, the girl emerged from a door at the rear carrying a heaping plate and full mug, which she balanced easily as she crossed the room to set them on the table before him.

"My thanks." He kept his face hidden and his voice high as he looked at his meal; beside the expected slices of red meat were three chunks of some pasty yellowish substance, and a curious red fruit, like none he was familiar with, adorned one edge. "What are these?" he asked, indicating these strangers.

"Roast potato, sir. And our last good apple; we have no other fruit in store at present."

Both names were meaningless to the overman; he could not even be sure of their spelling, through the girl's thick Dûsarran accent. At least Nekutta spoke the same language as Eramma and the other northern lands, even if they spoke it strangely. Still, the "apple" was plainly a local fruit; the potato was another matter.

"What is potato?"

"Ah? Oh, you're joking!"

"No; I have traveled far."

"It's . . . it's a root, a vegetable. Eat it, and see." The girl was flustered; Garth was not sure if that was desirable or not. He did have her talking.

"Here, sit down; I will try this root of yours, but I have some questions about your city. Perhaps you can answer them."

"But . . ."

"I am a paying customer, am I not? You can spare a few minutes." He tapped the table with a gold coin, then suddenly realized that it was a mistake to draw attention to his inhuman hands; he dropped the coin, and drew his hand back out of sight. The girl apparently hadn't noticed anything out of the ordinary; she stared at the coin for a moment, then snatched it up and dropped it down the neckline of her robe. Garth was amused. He had never before seen a human keep anything there, but it seemed a logical place for a woman to put a pocket. The coin had been a fullsized gold piece, not one of the little bits such as he had given the stable-boy, and he remarked, "That will cover the meal as well, will it not?"

"Oh, yes!" The girl dropped herself into the chair opposite him, smiling.

"Good. Tell me of your city; I am a wanderer from far to the east."

"What is there to say?"

"Ah . . ." Garth had not expected that response. He was not experienced in dealing with humans. "Why is the marketplace so busy in the middle of the night? And the gate wide open?"

"It always is."

That demolished the religious festival theory once and for all. "But why? In most cities business is a matter for daylight, and the night is given to sleep."

"But this is Dûsarra!" Her tone implied, even to the untrained ear of an overman, that he was being purposely dense. He picked up a chunk of potato on his knife and ate it, while considering this; the stuff seemed edible, but not particularly tasty.

"And what is so special about Dûsarra?"

"You do not know?"

"No."

"The very name tells you."

Garth had paid little attention to the name, assuming it nothing but a noise that represented this particular place; he considered it a bit more carefully, and still saw nothing significant in it. The ending was a standard designation for a gathering place, and the root, *Dûs,* was completely unknown to him.

"I do not understand."

"'Dûsarra' means 'the place of the Dark Gods' Here we worship the gods shunned by the outside world; mostly Tema, the goddess of night. Perhaps, stranger, you have made a mistake in coming here if you did not know that."

"Perhaps I have." He sat silently for a moment, thinking.

He should have expected something like this from the Forgotten King. He knew very little about human religions, beyond the fact that no two seemed to agree about anything, but he had heard of the Dark Gods; they were supposed to demand human sacrifices, and to be wholly evil in nature. It had been rumored that the Baron of Skelleth was a secret devotee of theirs, and that had been considered sufficient grounds for immediate execution if proven; it remained only a vague rumor. It was said that, unlike most gods, they still interfered directly in mortal affairs, and would grant their followers special powers and abilities in exchange for gruesome payments of blood, death, and torture. Evil wizards were said to have sold themselves – their souls, to use the human term that overmen did not use – to the Dark Gods.

And the entire city of Dûsarra worshipped these deities? It seemed incredible. How could a thinking being worship evil?

"Tell me, then, about these gods." At least the conversation had taken a turn toward the temples without obviously being steered there.

"There are seven of them, the seven Lords of Dûs, the counterparts to the seven Lords of Eir worshipped elsewhere. I know very little about most of them; I am a follower of Tema, like the rest of my family."

"How did you come to be such?"

"I was brought up in the faith, of course."

"How did the city come to worship these gods?"

"I don't know; it always has. My father told me once that it was part of a cosmic balance that these misunderstood and maligned gods should have one city of their own."

"Are they not evil?"

"Tema is not!" Her face was suddenly animated, and Garth was taken aback by her ferocity. "Tema is beautiful! The night is wonderful, cool and calm; I would never be a day worshipper! How can people live with all that glaring light? And all the sweaty heat? And all the beasts roam by day, and insects. The sun is so bright you cannot look at it, and it drowns out all the beauty of the flames. There are no stars in the daytime! I . . ." She subsided suddenly. "Forgive me."

"No, forgive me; I did not mean to offend you. In other lands I have visited, the Dark Gods are thought to be the gods of evil."

She shrugged. "They are obviously ignorant heathens. There are no evil gods, really; evil is just misunderstandings between people, or between people and the gods. That's what the priests say."

"I see. You worship the night-goddess. What of the other six?"

"They have their followers, too, but I do not heed them. I sometimes think that some of them *are* evil, despite what the priests say. Aghad, for example; his followers make my skin crawl, and his priests frighten me. I have seen them gathering at his temple. And of course, no one worships The God Whose Name Is Not Spoken, though he has a temple."

Garth began to have a rather unsettled feeling; he had heard of The God Whose Name Is Not Spoken. That was the god of death, known throughout the world; it was said that to speak his true name was to die instantly. And they worshipped him here?

No, the girl had just said that they did not, but that there was a temple dedicated to him. Was it one of the seven he would have to rob?

It must be; everyone seemed to agree that there were only seven temples in Dûsarra. Although he would not admit to being in any way superstitious, and although his own people insisted that either there were no gods or they did not meddle in the affairs of mortals, he did not care to rob the temple of Death.

On the other hand, his practical sense told him, if there were no worshippers, it would be unguarded and the easiest of the lot.

"Tell me who the seven gods are."

"You mean the seven who have temples?"

"Are there others?"

"Oh, yes; there's Tema's daughter Mei, the lady of the moon, and any number of others."

"Just tell me the seven."

"Bheleu, P'hul, Sai, Aghad, Andhur Regvos, and Tema."

"That's only six, if I heard you rightly."

"Well and there's the Unnamed God. You know."

"Oh, of course." It was apparently considered bad luck to mention the death-god too often even by circumlocution. "I know him, and P'hul, and you have told me Tema is the goddess of the night; who are the others?"

"Bheleu is god of destruction and war, I think. Andhur Regvos is the god of darkness."

"Why has he got two names?"

"I don't know."

"Oh. Go on; what about the other two?"

"I don't know; Aghad and Sai are secret. Their temples admit no outsiders. They both . . . well, that's just a rumor. Never mind."

"And all the city lives by night, to accord with their religion?"

"Oh, no! Not all! Only the worshippers of night and darkness. But we're most of the city. I don't know anyone who lives by day, but of course that's partly because I'm asleep all day."

"I am interested in this; could I visit the temples?"

"I don't know about the others, but I can take you to the temple of Tema."

"Good. But first," he said, realizing that he had been talking while his food grew cold and that he was ravenously hungry, "I will eat."

He did so, and found the food and drink good; the girl laughed gaily when he tried to eat the apple core and all.

Chapter Seven

The temple of Tema was a massive, imposing structure; most of its area was covered by a looming black dome, which Garth thought was probably the one he had first seen from ten leagues' distance, and the entrance was through the base of a tower that stood a good hundred feet in height. The entire building was constructed of huge blocks of black stone, finely polished, and with elaborate carvings on either side of the wide, open doorway. The door was reached by climbing a flight of thirteen black stone steps, flanked by balustrades carved into a maze of intertwined black serpents. Garth did not particularly care for the place; although undeniably impressive, he did not like the impression it gave of looming over one, black in the moonlight, and the way its size served to diminish its inhabitants. The robed and hooded figures entering the dark portal looked like little children, out of proportion with their surroundings.

He also didn't like the darkness within; not the slightest glimmer of light showed through the door. That was appropriate for the temple of the goddess of night, but he still didn't like it.

The tavern girl was beside him as he mounted the steps; it occurred to him suddenly that he didn't know her name. Of course, she didn't know his name, either. Ahead of them three other worshippers, robed in midnight blue, vanished into the darkness of the doorway.

A moment later, he and the girl also stepped into the gloom of the interior. Garth paused for a moment, to let his eyes adjust, and realized he could detect no trace of the three who had entered just ahead of them; no sound of rustling clothing, no footsteps, no odor. His psychic discomfort increased.

The girl had not hesitated, as he had, and was across the room, an antechamber about forty feet square; he heard her whisper, "Come on!" He came, and rejoined her, standing a pace or two from the inner wall. He had expected a draped doorway, or some other opening into the temple proper, but could make out no sign of one; there seemed to be merely a blank stone wall. Then, with startling abruptness, a portion of the stone wall swung inward; the heavy scent of incense drifted out to him. He made out a figure in the opening, darkly clad, but with pale skin and white hair that gleamed in the faint moonlight that reached it. The darkness within that opening seemed no more absolute than in the antechamber; that was some comfort, anyway. The girl stepped through the opening, and he followed, to find himself in the main temple.

The odor of incense was almost overpowering; its smoke swirled in great clouds, almost invisible in the darkness. Moonlight filtered in from somewhere, though he could see no windows; the walls were blank and dark behind him, and he could not see the far side. The room he found himself in was obviously huge; all about him were constant indefinable whisperings and rustlings, which were distorted by distance and echoes and which seemed to drift in the smoke. He could not make out either the far wall or the roof; his eyes had not yet had time to adjust.

A change in the movement of the air prompted him to turn, and discover that the opening he had entered through had vanished; the wall seemed solid once more. The white-haired apparition had also disappeared. He turned to face the interior again, and was relieved to see, dimly, the figure of the tavern-girl, still only a few paces in front of him.

She motioned for him to follow, and led the way across the chamber; he obeyed, carefully maintaining his stooped posture, and noticed that where she moved silently, his boot heels tapped loudly on the stone floor.

They went perhaps a hundred feet, then stopped; the girl turned slightly, and knelt in a curious submissive position, head lowered, hands in front of her. Garth imitated her, and waited for his eyes to adapt themselves.

He was kneeling at the back of a crowd of humans, all in a similar devotional posture; the chamber, he saw, filled the entire interior of the great dome, easily two hundred feet across and sixty or seventy feet high at the center. The moonlight came from hundreds, perhaps thousands of tiny holes that pierced the dome, and which he realized after a moment's study were intended to resemble stars, arranged in the constellations that could be seen in the middle of a winter night.

The great circular floor was cluttered with people, both kneeling and prostrate, but none were speaking, not even in a whisper; the constant sounds that echoed and re-echoed from the dome were the inevitable rustlings of the worshippers' clothing, no more. Or at least, nothing more he was sure of; some of the sounds seemed too strange to be so readily explained.

All these people, whether prostrate or upright, faced in the same direction; as his eyes continued to adjust, he gradually made out the object of their adoration.

The figure of a human female was carved from the same black stone as wall and dome; it was thirty feet or so in height, and a masterpiece of sculpture. She stood against the wall, upright, but not stiffly erect; her arms were upraised, spreading her stony cloak above the worshipping throng. The cloak itself blended into the wall and dome indistinguishably, and Garth saw, looking around, that its folds were continued indefinitely, so that the entire chamber was contained within it, "stars" and all. The figure itself was depicted as clad in a loose robe such as all Dûsarrans seemed to wear, but arranged so that the graceful curves of the woman's body could be seen. The face was oval, smooth and serene, and surrounded by a halo of drifting hair that blended into the dome in the same manner as the cloak. The overall impression, to the overman, was one of grace and soothing calm; he was not equipped to appreciate the goddess' sensual nature, and although the symbolism of the goddess spreading her cloak of night across her followers was plain to him, he did not fully comprehend the comforting motherliness that the worshippers of Tema found in that image. Still, he understood, in an intellectual way, that humans would have little trouble in putting their faith in such a deity. No wonder the girl had been upset when he called the goddess evil.

He was so involved in his study of the magnificent idol that it was several minutes before he even noticed the altar that stood at her feet.

It was a great chunk of meteoric iron, its sides still burned and twisted from its fall, but with the top sheared off and polished to a gleaming metallic shine perceptible even in the darkness of the temple. There was no mistaking that this was the altar that Garth had come to rob, and there upon it was what he must steal; he could make out only a vague round shape, a foot or so in diameter.

There was a spot of light on its surface, he noticed; one of the pinholes in the dome was directly in line with the moon, and a beam of its light was now falling directly upon that thing upon the altar. He wondered whether it was intentional.

Then, so suddenly that he almost lost his balance in his startlement, the room was filled with chanting; the incense swirled more thickly than ever, billowing forth from a dozen niches spaced around the wall. Priests appeared behind the altar, completely hidden in black robes that exaggerated the usual looseness to near parody; one reached forward, and what Garth suddenly realized was a cloth cover vanished from the thing on the altar.

It immediately blazed up into scintillating light, so bright in the darkness as to seem almost blinding; it was a great crystal, a sphere with a million facets, which trapped the thin beam of moonlight and reflected and refracted it into a glittering display of pure white light. Garth thought for a moment that it was a diamond, but dismissed that as absurd; no diamond could be so large, and he doubted that even diamond could catch the light like that. This was some sort of gem or crystal that was totally unfamiliar to him.

It was also a gem he would have to steal, if he were to perform his errand in Dûsarra.

He knelt, listening to the priests chant, and wondered how he was ever going to manage it.

Chapter Eight

There were words to the chant, and the ceremony undoubtedly had some specific significance, but Garth made out none of it; he was too lost in his own thoughts to listen, and the echoing dome distorted the singsong enough to make it difficult to discern its meaning. It sounded to the overman like nothing more than a randomly shifting drone.

He paid little attention as the dark-robed priests lifted the great crystal and moved it ceremoniously through elaborate patterns in the air, alternately sprinkling the crowd with sparkles of reflected moonlight and plunging them into darkness; he was planning out his actions. There were questions he would have asked the tavern-girl, but she was lost in the chanting, her lips moving silently, her face enraptured. He saw instantly, when a stray glint of moonlight lit her features, that she would be of no use to him for a while.

Since this was the temple of night, it seemed a safe assumption that all prayers and worship were nocturnal; by day the place should be almost deserted, though probably there would be a few priests about. It was already well after midnight; he had merely to wait until dawn, grab the crystal, and depart. If possible he would wait until no priests were about, but if necessary he could force his way through them. There was no sign that they carried weapons of any sort; a drawn sword should awe them into letting him pass, most particularly since most humans had an almost superstitious fear of overmen, who were, after all, a good bit larger and stronger than humans, and by human standards hideous monsters.

It would be advisable to find some quiet hiding place where he could wait until daybreak; if he merely stayed where he was he might draw unwanted attention. He considered leaving and then returning at sunrise, but rejected it immediately. He had no idea how to open that swinging wall, or even whether it could be opened from the outside at all. Even if it could be, it might be kept locked by day.

The ritual ended with a simple chant that the worshippers repeated along with the priests; every other word was the name of the goddess, and it was just six words, but Garth could not make out the other three. It was recited three times; then the priest lifted the crystal one last time, placed it on the altar, and lifted its cloth cover back over it. Its final gleam lit the priest's eyes, despite his overhanging cowl, and Garth started with surprise; the priest's eyes were as red as his own! For an instant he thought that perhaps the robed figure was another overman, but dismissed it; he was too small, by far, and like the person who had admitted him to the chamber, his hair was gleaming white, while all overmen had coal-black hair. Besides, that quick glimpse had shown him eyes with pupil, iris, and white, while overmen had only pupil and iris. No, the priest was just a freak of some sort.

The ceremony was over, and the tavern-girl rose and motioned for him to follow her out; he shook his head. She frowned at him, and then shrugged and left. Almost all the worshippers, kneeling or prostrate, were getting to their feet and heading toward the entrance, but Garth remained where he was, to await the dawn.

It was a long, weary wait; he had not realized how tired he was, but the effects of a long day's ride were catching up to him well before the night was over.

When the crowd had departed he was left alone in the middle of the stone floor, but the cowled priests, who moved with quiet rustlings but no words along the wall behind the altar, paid him no heed. Moments after the last of Tema's devoted had departed, new ones began to trickle in; by the time a half hour had passed the chamber was becoming crowded once again with people kneeling with hands clasped before them, or flat on their bellies, all facing the magnificent black stone idol.

The scattered bits of moonlight that found their way through the holes in the dome shifted as the moon crawled across the heavens outside, and an hour or so after the tavern-girl's departure a spot of light appeared on the cloth-covered sphere atop the altar. A priest withdrew the covering, and the chanting began anew.

This time it was not his planning that kept Garth from hearing the words; it was his efforts to stay awake. His knees hurt from kneeling so long without moving on hard stone, his eyes ached from the strain of seeing through the unchanging dark, and his whole body was weary from his long ride. He knew that to close his eyes would be to fall asleep. He had arisen early, before dawn, which meant that when the new day arrived he would have gone better than twenty-four hours without sleep; that was no remarkable feat, ordinarily, but after a day spent riding and now passing long, dull hours crouching in the dark, it began to seem impossible.

The second ceremony ended, the crowd dispersed, and newcomers trickled in; still he knelt there, and still no one paid any attention to him. The priests shuffled about at the goddess' feet; all seemed to have long, pure-white hair, and at least two had the same strange red eyes. All were pale-skinned, unlike the other Dûsarrans Garth had seen; even those whose faces remained completely hidden showed their hands on occasion, and those hands were uniformly white and apparently hairless. There were few other similarities amongst them; some were tall, some short, some fat, some thin. There seemed to be at least one priestess among them, judging by what little could be distinguished through the flowing robes. Garth had once seen a white wolf, a beast with snow-white fur and blood-red eyes; a Kirpan scholar had referred to it as "albino." These priests must be albino humans. He had not known such existed. And why should all the priests be such? It seemed a peculiar requirement, if such it was; why were albinos especially suited to serve the goddess of the night?

Wondering about such trivia managed to keep him awake through a third and final ceremony; this time, when the final simple chant ended and the gem was covered, the crowd moved more slowly, and for the first time Garth heard worshippers speaking amongst themselves. Likewise, the priests ended their apparently aimless wanderings; all but three of the half dozen or more he had seen vanished, though Garth could not see where they had gone. The remaining trio stood motionless behind the altar, the center one with his hands resting one on either side of the shrouded crystal.

Garth estimated it to be two hours before dawn still. Since this new behavior seemed to demonstrate that the temple's services were through for the night, he got to his feet; his knees stung as circulation returned to the areas where it had been cut off. He gazed up at the idol, as if in adoration, so that no one would question his failing to depart.

His eyes had long since become adjusted to the faint illumination, but now he found himself unable to distinguish details of carving that had been clear before; he blinked, but it made no difference. The scattered moonlight was not evenly distributed; had it merely shifted? No, it was growing uniformly darker. He had a moment of irrational fear that he was going blind before he realized what was happening.

The moon was setting.

That, of course, was why there were to be no more ceremonies, and why everyone was departing; with the moon down, the temple would be far too dark for use. People would run into one another, face the wrong way, and generally be unable to behave appropriately; even night-worshippers recognized that. He wondered what they did on moonless nights; were there no services at all? The starlight was plainly inadequate. Or what of overcast nights? Would torchlight from the streets or the glow of the volcanoes reflected off the clouds be enough? There would be no beam of moonlight falling on the great crystal.

Well, interesting as they might be, such considerations were irrelevant, since this night had been clear and moonlit. The spreading darkness would actually work to his benefit, since no one would be able to see him steal the gem; he studied the altar, measuring the distance between it and himself, so as to reach it quickly in the dark.

The three priests still stood behind it; the last worshippers had drifted out, and Garth realized they were looking at him, noticing this last straggler. That was not what he wanted. He turned and headed for the door, but stopped a foot from it, and turned to look again, hoping that anyone who saw him would not think that unusual.

Apparently the priests didn't, if they were able to see at all in the deepening gloom; Garth doubted they could see him any more, as he could no longer see them. Although he did not know for sure, it seemed unlikely that those squinty little human eyes could be as good as an overman's – though of course the priests' eyes were not quite normal.

A gong sounded somewhere, and the stone door swung slowly shut; whoever worked it thought Garth had left. He stepped away from it and lost himself in the darkness.

There were rustlings and whisperings in the blackness, which was now almost total; the moon was down. Although the dome made it very hard to locate sounds, Garth judged that the three priests were moving away from the altar.

In a moment the sounds were cut off as if a curtain had dropped across a doorway; straining, Garth could hear faint footsteps departing. The priests were gone.

Moving with all the stealth he could contrive, Garth inched across the broad stone expanse that lay between him and the altar; he could not see more than a few inches in front of him, and the quiet shuffling of his boots seemed magnified into a low roar by the echoes.

After what seemed hours, his outstretched hand touched something; he studied it with his fingertips, and decided it was a fold in the idol's cloak; he had missed the altar and hit the wall, off to the left. Cautiously, he felt his way along the fold until it swooped up out of reach, then moved on along the wall until he came to the idol's slippered feet, which he knew to be immediately behind the altar. He turned until he faced directly away from the wall, and peered into the darkness; he thought he could see the dim outline of the altar. He took a step forward and felt in front of him, reaching down to the height he estimated the altar to be; his hand brushed against a polished surface. Using both hands he groped about the altar-top and found the cloth-covered stone. He picked it up, cover and all, and tucked it under his cloak. Now he had only to get out of the temple undetected.

He knew that the concealed door to the antechamber was directly opposite the altar. He considered feeling his way along the wall until he found it, but rejected that idea; he might walk right into priests reentering the chamber, or at the very least be heard through whatever doorways they had departed by. Instead, he aimed himself by dead reckoning and set out across the floor.

Again, it seemed to take hours to cross, but at last an outstretched hand touched stone. He came up within inches of the wall, but could see only blackness; he felt along it with his hand, seeking a latch or seam or hinge. His left hand was occupied in holding the pilfered altar-stone under his cloak; it took a long time to cover an area with only his unencumbered right. He worked his way along, first three paces to the right, then twice that distance to the left, then back to the right once more; a feeling of desperation crept into him as his fingers found nothing but yard after yard of smooth stone.

Suddenly there was a sound behind him; he whirled, his right hand dropping automatically under his cloak to the hilt of his sword, but could see nothing in the darkness.

"If you return the stone you may go in peace, thief." He recognized the voice as one of the priests. He made no reply.

"You cannot open the door; only the priests of Tema know its secret."

Garth wondered how many were there, and how they had gotten so close to him without being heard; he judged the voice – for so far only one had spoken – to be ten, perhaps fifteen, not more than twenty feet away.

"Return the gem."

He needed time to devise an escape. "And if I do not?" he asked.

"Then you will die here."

Garth adjusted his grip, hugging the crystal closer to him, and drew his sword. "I have a counterproposal. You will open the door for me, or you will die, not I."

There could be no doubt that the priest or priests had heard and recognized the scrape of steel on leather as the blade left its sheath; there was a pause before the voice spoke again.

"It is possible that you may kill one or two of us before you yourself perish; if so, we will die in the sure knowledge that we have served our goddess and will be admitted to her realm for all eternity. You, on the other hand, will die damned forever for your sacrilege. I ask again, return the stone; it is not too late. Return it, and we will yet let you depart peacefully, even though you have drawn a weapon in our sanctuary."

Garth made no answer for a long moment, and the priest said nothing, apparently granting the thief time to consider the hopelessness of his position. The overman, however, was not considering options or the lack thereof, but rather was noticing that he could distinguish, very faintly, the outline of a lone figure a dozen feet in front of him. This was not the result of any adjustment; his eyes had long been at their extreme of sensivity. No, there was new light filtering in, the first dim gray of approaching dawn. That reminded him how long it had been since he last slept, and he suddenly felt weary even as he considered how the growing light would work to his advantage. The priests were undoubtedly accustomed to living almost entirely in darkness; they would not do well outside their temple in daylight, if he could once get out into the streets.

He wondered if the priest could see him at all; the light was not evenly distributed. Further, was he aware that he, himself, was visible? And it was now apparent that the priest was alone. Probably the lone man had been making a final inspection round of some sort, and tried to bluff out the intruder; unfortunately for him, his bluff was now ruined.

Knowing that he faced a single opponent, Garth finally struck upon a scheme.

"If I hand you the crystal, will you then open the door and let me go, unpursued?"

"Yes."

"Will you swear it, by your goddess?"

"I swear it, by Tema."

"Very well." With a great show of reluctance, Garth held out the gem with his left hand, purposely extending his arm not directly toward the priest but a little to one side, as if he still could not see where the man was. His sword remained ready in his right hand.

The priest stepped forward, and carefully lifted the stone, using both hands. He stood for a moment, and Garth demanded, "Now open the door."

"Let me return the stone to the altar first."

"No! You said you would open the door when I returned the stone." He lifted his sword as if to slash blindly in front of him; although the light was actually growing steadily, and already permitted him to distinguish such details as the cracks in the floor and the folds of the priest's robe, he hoped to continue his ruse of blindness a few moments longer. He had no specific reason for it; he was merely snatching every advantage he could, as his training in war and statecraft had taught him.

"If you insist." The priest tucked the crystal under one arm and crossed to the wall; his free hand brushed across the black stone surface and caught something Garth could not make out. With a considerable effort, the priest pulled; the section of wall swung open, and gray light poured in. Garth had forgotten that the great portal faced east, but such was the case; and although the sun was still below the horizon, the sky above it was already warmly pink. The spacious antechamber was much less ominous in the cold morning light than it had been by moonlight, merely a large, bare room, with half one wall opening onto a stair to the street.

Garth smiled with satisfaction. Moving with superhuman speed, he leapt across the few feet separating him from the priest; in scarcely a second from the opening of the door, his sword was at the man's throat.

"Now, O priest, you will give me back the stone. I have handed it to you, and you have opened the door; now I will take it again and go, unpursued,"

"No!"

"Yes."

"You cannot take it!"

"You will die if you do not give it to me."

"My brothers will find you."

"What of your oath? You swore I would not be pursued."

"No! I swore you would leave unpursued, not that there would be no pursuit after your departure. If you take the altar-stone, the followers of Tema will seek you out, wherever you go."

"Perhaps. I will risk it. Now give me the stone, and I will go."

"No!"

"Listen, fool, if you give me the stone I will leave you alive, and you may lead the pursuit; if you force me to kill you, there will be no one who knows who took the stone. It would be to my advantage to slaughter you out of hand, but that is not my wish. Give me the stone and live."

"You could kill me anyway."

"Why should I wait? Give me the stone!"

"No! Help! Brothers! Thief, murderer!" The priest began shouting at the top of his lungs. Disgusted, Garth grabbed for the crystal, and got a tenuous hold with the long fingers of his left hand; his superior reach had caught the human by surprise, and the priest's own grip slipped for an instant. That was all the time Garth needed; he snatched his hand back, the stone clutched as tightly as he could manage. With a scream that echoed and re-echoed from the dome, the priest lunged for it, and automatically, without thinking, without meaning to, Garth reacted as a warrior reacts; he ran the man through, impaling him on his broadsword. Blood spattered the wall behind the priest, and Garth exclaimed in disgust, a wordless noise in his throat.

There was no doubt that the man was dead, or as good as dead; Garth's reflexes were as reliable as ever, and if he had not put his blade straight through the heart it had been a very near miss indeed. He had the stone, though. Now he had only to get away with it; the other priests must have heard the shouting, especially that final scream.

He yanked his sword out of the priest's body; a good foot of the blade had protruded through the back of the robe, and it took a second pull before it came completely free, allowing the unfortunate man to fall to the floor. His hood fell aside, and for the first time Garth saw his face; a thin, pale face, red eyes wide and glazed in death, mouth gaping and filling with sluggishly flowing blood. Long white hair was flung across his features, tangling with a skimpy white beard; he had been a young man, perhaps only a novice rather than a full priest. Garth was not at all pleased. He had hoped to avoid killing anyone on this errand. He wiped his sword on the hem of the man's robe and stepped across the corpse into the antechamber, carefully avoiding the spreading pool of blood, then paused for a moment to sheathe his sword.

There was a cry from behind him; he glanced back and saw nothing but darkness. Nonetheless, he sprinted for the steps.

More shouts sounded, and something whistled through the air by his ear; disdaining dignity he dove forward, curling into a ball around the stolen altar-stone and rolling down the thirteen steps to the street, where he sprang up and ran, paying little heed at first to direction but merely dodging at random from alley to street to alley. His hood flew back, revealing his inhuman visage, but none of the startled passersby attempted to stop him.

At last, well after the shouting was lost in the distance, he slowed; he paused in an unoccupied alleyway to restore his obscuring cowl and height-disguising crouch, and hobbled out, doing his best to appear a harmless old man. The altar-stone was under his cloak, hidden by his crouch.

It took him half an hour to find himself on a street he recognized; from there he made his way to the market place, and thence to the Inn of the Seven Stars. He dared not enter the tavern, as the followers of Tema might find him there; instead he went to Koros' stall in the adjacent stable. There he decided to take a look at his booty, and pulled the great crystal from under his cloak.

It sparkled eerily in the morning light; he gazed at it in fascination. It was very beautiful, an intense, cold beauty. He found himself studying its depths raptly, searching for something he could feel there; he had a sensation of being observed, and of unearthly power, as if the night-goddess herself were watching him from within the gem. He was unaware of anything but the gem, and the deep cold gleaming light within; he lost his sense of time, and felt as if he had been looking into the crystalline glow for all eternity, trying to meet the gaze of Tema. A cool stillness, like the air of a clear night, absorbed him, and he knelt utterly motionless.

With the abruptness of a lightning bolt he felt a warm touch on his face, like a flame on ice; he turned away from it involuntarily, and the spell was broken as the gem ceased to be the center of his direct gaze.

He blinked, and realized he was kneeling foolishly in the straw of the stall holding the stone while Koros nuzzled him curiously, wondering why he did not move.

He had survived hypnotic spells before, and had a healthy respect for them; he covered the great crystal with straw, being very careful not to look directly at it. The straw would also hide it adequately; no one would be able to come close enough to find it without first disposing of the warbeast. Garth pitied anyone who might attempt such a feat.

His booty secured, he paused for a moment to decide his next action; he seated himself comfortably on a pile of straw, his mount standing placidly over him. Long before he could reach any decision his fatigue caught up with him, and he slept.

Chapter Nine

He awoke slowly, his mind fuzzy; there were voices somewhere nearby. It took him several seconds before he recognized his surroundings as Koros' stall in the inn's stable; more seconds passed before he remembered that he had fallen asleep there unintentionally. His neck ached; he had slept with his head propped awkwardly against the side of the stall. He rubbed it absently and listened to the voices.

There were two of them, both young human males; they were arguing about something, apparently the ownership of some item. A small item, it seemed, since the one who possessed it apparently carried it on his person.

Garth sat up and looked around; it was daylight, and judging by the shadows either very early or very late. He thought for a moment, calculating the orientation of the stable, and decided that it was late afternoon. He had slept most of the day away, which was probably just as well. He had needed the rest.

He recalled the events of the night before, and checked to be sure his loot was still secure; it was. He had thought that the crystal was clear, but looking at it in the sunlight – being very careful not to let it trap his attention once again – he saw that it was milky white. Not that it made any difference, he thought; he had no use for the thing. He covered it over with straw again.

The argument outside was winding down; some sort of compromise had apparently been reached.

It was none of his concern. He clambered to his feet, promising himself that never again would he sleep wearing mail; every link seemed to have left a permanent impression on his back, despite the quilting underneath and the breastplate on top. Reminded of the breastplate's presence, he removed it; mail alone should certainly be sufficient for anything he was likely to encounter in the city. He was still wearing his sword as well, he realized when he almost tripped over it.

Koros growled a greeting, and the voices outside suddenly stopped. Then one asked, "What was that?"

The other replied, "I don't know. Dugger said there was some kind of foreign monster in number three, but I figured he was lying as usual."

There was a pause. Garth patted the warbeast's nose, and reached down to his pack for the wire brush he used for cleaning the monster's ears, which had a habit of picking up burrs and other such unpleasant little items. The first voice spoke again.

"Should we check?"

"I don't know."

"I'm going to look. Come on."

"Go look yourself."

"Oh, come on."

"Well, all right. If you want." There was the sound of footsteps approaching; light footsteps. Definitely young humans, Garth thought, as he stood with brush in hand.

A moment later two adolescent faces peered over the stall door, and almost immediately vanished again. Garth grinned to himself. Then, slowly, first one face and then the other inched back into sight.

"Greetings," Garth said.

"Uh . . . greetings," said the taller of the two boys.

"I hope my beast didn't upset you."

"No." Then, after some hesitation, the lad went on, "You're an overman, aren't you?"

"Yes." There was no point in denying the obvious, since his cloak and hood were lying in disarray on the straw, leaving his noseless, leathery face and black mail in plain sight.

"Oh."

The other boy asked, "What's that?" pointing timidly at Koros.

"A warbeast."

"Oh."

"How'd you get in here? I've been here all day."

Garth shrugged. "I got in."

The boy decided further questions were not in order; instead, he explained, "But I'm supposed to watch the stable and make sure everyone pays their bills."

"You needn't worry; I will pay. I paid the other boy for the first day."

"Dugger? Oh." There was silence for a moment; the two had apparently exhausted their questions for the moment. Garth began cleaning the warbeast's ears with the brush; there were no burrs or thorns visible, but the creature seemed to enjoy it anyway.

When the silence seemed to be becoming uncomfortable, he asked, "What's the news today? I have been busy since dawn."

"Oh! Then you haven't heard! Someone murdered a priest in Tema's temple, and half the city is hunting for him."

"Who did it?"

"No one knows. Mernalla says she took a stranger to the temple last night, an old man with a funny accent, so they're looking for him, but the priest was killed with a single sword-thrust, so it probably wasn't anyone old. It must have been a warrior."

"Why would anyone kill a priest?"

"I don't know; I think there's some kind of secret about it." Garth noticed from the corner of his eye that the boy who hadn't spoken as much was looking at him strangely, paying altogether too much attention to the sword on his belt. The youth suddenly fell back out of sight, and a moment later, apparently in response to a tug, the other followed.

Inevitable, Garth thought to himself as he put the brush away. Still, there was no proof of any sort against him. No one had seen him clearly. It was interesting that the temple priests had not revealed the loss of the altar-stone.

Perhaps it would be wise to remove himself from the premises, at least for the present; perhaps he should move Koros, too. He was unfamiliar with the city, though, and hiding places might be hard to come by. This stable was convenient, and as yet there was no real evidence against him; with luck he would not be bothered. He reminded himself to do a proper job of cleaning his sword at the first opportunity.

He also reminded himself that he had six more temples to rob. Furthermore, since as a stranger he would automatically be under suspicion, the sooner he finished his task and departed the better. Therefore, he should get on with it.

First, however, he would get himself a meal; he had not eaten since the preceding midnight, more or less, and the sun was now well down the western sky.

He debated whether or not he should wear his cloak; the boys had not reacted negatively to the presence of an overman, but that said nothing about the reaction of adults. He picked up the garment, and saw to his disgust that there were bloodstains on it; he had not seen them in the dim morning light, as they blended with the brown fabric. There was the evidence to convict him of murder and sacrilege. The cloak would have to be promptly disposed of; he rolled it up and tucked it under his arm, making sure the stains were not in any way visible. He would have to do without it; he hoped that overmen were not utterly abhorred in Dûsarra. To the best of his recollection Nekutta had not fought in the Racial Wars, but of course history had never been his favorite subject of conversation. And even if it had, no word of anything significant had reached the Northern Waste for three centuries; anything could have happened in that time. Still, so far as he knew, no overman had been seen in this part of the world since the wars; the humans would probably be too surprised to do anything much about him.

Besides, he had no choice. He had only brought the one cloak, since he had planned on a trading journey to Skelleth, not a long adventure. With a word of praise to Koros, he opened the stall door and stepped out into the stableyard.

The sun was even lower than he had realized, and the western sky a smoke-streaked expanse of crimson. He could hear the clatter and conversation in the Inn of the Seven Stars, and faintly, in the distance, the sounds of the marketplace; through the archway that was the only connection between the stable and the outside world he glimpsed occasional passersby, hurrying or strolling, striding, ambling, or strutting about their business.

He had seen little of the stable the night before, for want of proper illumination; he looked about him, hoping to see some convenient place to dispose of the incriminating cloak.

The yard was a long, narrow strip of bare dirt, with half a dozen large box stalls on either side, built of rough unpainted wood and roofed with red tile. One end was the archway to the street; the other end was a blank gray stone wall. Against the stone wall was a trough, itself carved from the same gray rock, presumably intended for watering whatever beasts of burden used the stable.

Garth strolled along the yard, peering into the stalls; most were empty, but three contained horses, the creatures that the overmen of the Northern Waste had long considered merely a legend. Garth had encountered such animals once before, far to the east; he had not expected to see them here.

He considered burying the cloak in the straw that lined the stalls, and rejected it; it was too likely to be found, drawing suspicion on the patrons of the inn, and possibly resulting in the conviction and death of whatever innocent happened to be renting the stall he chose.

He reached the end of the row of stalls without striking on any better solution, and saw that the stone trough was empty and apparently had been for quite some time; a spider had spun its web across one corner.

It occurred to him that probably no one had even noticed that the trough was here for years; people became accustomed to their surroundings and forgot the parts that did not concern them. He dropped the bundled cloak into the trough.

There was still a fair chance that some person – perhaps one of the stable-boys – would find it; but the trough was deep, and the cloak was material that would burn, but not too brightly. The flames would not show, and with luck no one would notice another wisp of smoke in this smoke-shrouded city. He had tinder, flint, and steel in a pouch on his belt, as always; it was a moment's work to set the garment afire.

Whatever ashes might remain would not be particularly noticeable in the accumulation of dust and debris in the bottom of the trough, and the blood-stains would certainly not be recognizable; the matter was dealt with. He rose, and started toward the arch.

Before he was halfway down the yard he heard voices approaching; before he was more than a pace or two past Koros' stall four figures appeared, not merely passing by on the street but coming through the arch toward him. He stopped.

Two of the four were the two boys; a third was the girl who had taken him to Tema's temple, and the fourth was a large man, clad in the usual Dûsarran robe, black in this instance, but belted about the waist and with a long, straight sword and sheath hanging from that belt.

"Greetings." Garth spoke politely.

"Greetings, stranger." The foursome stopped, a few feet into the yard. Garth nodded, then started walking again, as if to pass them by and depart.

"Wait, stranger." The man's hand fell to the hilt of his sword. Garth stopped again. The man kept his gaze on the overman as he asked his companions, "Is he the one?"

Both boys replied, "Yes." The girl said nothing.

"Mernalla?"

"I don't know. I don't think so."

"Could it have been he?"

"No . . . no, it couldn't. The man was shorter, with a higher voice, and he wore a dirty brown robe."

"You said he was tall."

"For a man, yes."

Garth interrupted, "Might I ask, sir, why you are interested in me?"

"We're looking for a murderer."

"What has that to do with me?"

"You are an armed stranger; naturally, that makes you suspect."

"I suppose it does. When was this murder done? I only arrived in Dûsarra last night."

"A priest was slain early this morning."

"A priest? Could it not have been an internal matter?"

"The priests of Tema do not kill their own."

"Then perhaps some rival cult is responsible?"

The man started to reply, then stopped himself. The girl looked at him as he considered the suggestion, while the two boys continued to stare at Garth. At last, after a long pause, he said, "You have a good point. It could have been them. It could well have been."

Garth was pleased to see that the man was accepting his decoy so readily. "After all," he said, "what cause could a stranger have to commit such a sacrilege? I am in Dûsarra to obtain some goods for my employer; what have I to do with temples, or with murders?"

"Nothing, I am sure." The man smiled. "My apologies for detaining you." He stepped aside, making room for Garth to pass.

One of the boys demanded belligerently, "What have you got that sword for, if you're a trader?"

"What?" Garth looked at his waist in feigned surprise. "Oh. Just habit, I assure you; an adventurer such as myself is accustomed to traveling armed."

The man swatted the boy on the shoulder and said, "Come now, there's no law against wearing a sword, else I'd be a criminal myself. From what I hear, traveling the Yprian Coast without a good blade is akin to suicide." He smiled at Garth again.

Garth smiled back, unenthusiastically, and moved on past the foursome. He turned into the adjacent tavern and found himself an unoccupied table. The swordsman's final comment was bothering him. Why should the fellow assume that Garth had come by way of the Yprian Coast? Why was no one particularly surprised at the presence of an overman in Dûsarra?

Could it be that other overmen came to this city? Could there be an established trade route through the Yprian Coast?

A middle-aged man took his order for a meal and a drink.

If any overmen had come here from the Northern Waste, he should have heard of it; he was, after all, high in the councils at Ordunin, to which all his people swore allegiance. Perhaps there were renegades, along the western shores of the Waste?

His ale arrived, and the innkeeper assured him that his food would soon follow.

Another possibility finally struck him; could there be overmen living *outside* the Waste? On the Yprian Coast itself, perhaps? That explanation worked quite well; should such overmen exist, Dûsarra would be a natural place for them to trade with Nekutta and the other southern lands. The map showed the coastal plain lying just the other side of this volcanic mountain range; although the road across the mountains would most likely be rougher traveling than the routes east into Eramma, the Yprians, if they existed, would probably not dare to venture into Eramma. The overmen of the Northern Waste had not dared to do so for three centuries; the bitter memories of the Racial Wars had kept them out as effectively as any physical barrier.

Likewise, the northerners had never ventured to the west, across the Gulf of Ypri; their histories taught that the western lands were empty and desolate. Undoubtedly, the Yprians were taught that the Northern Waste was an uninhabited wasteland, as it actually had been until three hundred and fifty years ago.

This was a matter that would bear investigation when he returned home; he considered abandoning his quest and leaving Dûsarra immediately. He could drop off his one piece of booty with the Forgotten King in Skelleth on the way . . .

No, he couldn't. He could not return to Ordunin yet; he was still bound by his oath. Nor could he reenter Skelleth without first going to Ordunin; the Baron would not tolerate that. He could perhaps sneak into the village, but to skulk about thus, and to bring only one of the items he had been sent for . . .

No, his pride would not allow that. He would complete his task here in Dûsarra first.

The innkeeper was at his elbow, setting a plate heaped with steaming mutton and those vegetables – potatoes? – before him. He pulled a gold coin from the pouch on his belt and said, "Is there a room available?"

"Oh, yes; my lord. I'll fetch the key." He took the proffered coin and vanished again.

There were six temples remaining; if he recalled the girl's words correctly, one of them was as nocturnal as Tema's, and inasmuch as it would be dark by the time he finished his meal, that would be his next target. The worshippers of darkness, of course; the god with two names. Andhur something. That was the one.

Time enough to find it later; he turned his attention to the food. The mutton was excellent.

Chapter Ten

The temple of darkness was a huge black pyramid, topped by a small dome that replaced the apex, and surrounded by a wide, empty plaza paved with basalt. Upon receiving directions from a passing Dûsarran, he had had no trouble at all in finding it; it stood near the center of the city, and several broad streets ended at the stone plaza.

Unlike the temple of Tema, this structure had no imposing tower, no vast open doorway; it was stark and simple, completely unornamented, and the only entry Garth could see was a single small door in the center of one side of the broad base. There were no steps; it opened directly onto the plaza.

The whole area seemed deserted; only a very few pedestrians made their way around the perimeter of the pavement, moving from one street to the next. None approached the temple. Perhaps, Garth thought, it was because the twilight still lingered; the western sky was still rosy, though overhead the sky was dark indigo, and in the east it was almost black and sprinkled with stars.

He still couldn't recall the god's second name; he had merely inquired after the temple of darkness, which had been sufficient.

Even if the god's devotees thought it too early, Garth was impatient; he crossed to the door, and found it open. Inside he could see nothing but darkness; that was to be expected. Cautiously, he stepped inside.

He was in a small antechamber, scarcely ten feet across; enough light trickled in from the door behind him to show him that. Another door was in the center of the opposite wall; there was no other opening in the bare stone. With a shrug, he crossed the room and tried the inner door.

It was unlocked, but held with a simple latch; he pressed the latch button, but before he could pull on the handle a sound behind him startled him into releasing it.

The door to the outside had slammed shut when he squeezed the latch, which perhaps wasn't as simple as he had thought; apparently there were mechanisms to make sure no light was permitted beyond this chamber. He was now surrounded by total blackness, a darkness so complete that his eyes could not adjust no matter how long he waited. He could not see his hand in front of his face, he discovered. By feel, he found the handle of the inner door once more, and swung the portal open.

The darkness beyond was just as total; cautiously, he stepped through.

With arms outstretched before him, he took a second step; his fingers struck stone. He turned right; another step, and again he hit stone. Turning full about, he tried the one remaining direction, and again encountered a wall.

He stopped. Had he walked into a closet?

There was a rustle of garments; he could not identify the exact direction from which the sound came. He listened more closely, and made out the faint sound of breathing. Someone was in this tiny room with him.

"Is someone there?" he asked.

"Who are you?" The voice was soft and hissing.

"I am but a curious stranger. What is this place?"

"This is the central shrine of Andhur Regvos, Lord of Darkness and Master of the Blind. Why have you come here?"

"I was curious, good sir."

"Is it the custom in your land to enter holy places unhidden?"

"I was unaware of your temple's nature; I meant no harm."

"Very well; then you may depart in peace."

"Sir, are you a priest of this temple?"

"I am."

"Could you, perhaps, permit me to stay? I am as yet uncommitted to the worship of any god, and I would learn more of your cult, for I may want to pursue your creed."

The priest said nothing for a long moment, and Garth wished he could see the man's face. Finally, the priest replied, "I know no reason this should not be; though I doubt very much if you will choose to follow the path of Regvos, I have no desire to turn away a seeker of truth, even one as casual as yourself. Give me your hand."

Garth held out his hand, and almost immediately felt a bony grip upon it; he wondered if the priest had some magical means of seeing in the dark. He said nothing as he was led through a door he would have sworn was not there a moment ago when he felt the wall. Beyond, he judged that he and the priest were passing through a narrow corridor; it turned and twisted unmercifully, doubling back on itself, turning at unexpected angles, and generally giving the impression of being designed to confuse. Garth held out his free hand to avoid collisions with walls and pillars, and discovered by so doing that they were passing by several branching corridors; they were winding their way through a maze, there could be little doubt. Garth became disoriented, despite his best efforts, and was astonished when a final turn left them standing in a room he judged to be quite sizable, from the echoes and the feel of the air, where he would have expected the blank outer wall of the temple to be.

The priest released something, and Garth felt a heavy velvet curtain fall upon him; he stepped forward and it slid behind him, closing off the winding passages from the chamber he now stood in.

"Have you a tinderbox, or other agent of light?"

The priest's voice distracted Garth from his attempt to estimate the size of the chamber; he admitted, "Yes, I do."

"Such are not permitted here; surrender it, please."

Reluctantly, Garth took the pouch containing flint, steel, and tinder from his belt and handed it over.

"Thank you. Now, I must return to my duties; I leave you to contemplate the darkness. Another will be with you, in time." The priest's hands were gone; Garth heard three footsteps, and then, without so much as a rustle of garments, the priest was gone. Garth could hear nothing of him; no breathing, no heartbeat, no movement.

Unsettled, he took a few tentative steps forward; gauging the echoes of his boots on the stone floor, he judged the room he was in to be very large indeed, though not as immense as that under the dome of Tema's shrine. The air was chilly; he could feel that even through his armor and padding.

This was, then, most likely the temple sanctuary. Altar and idol would be in this chamber, somewhere – if they existed. It occurred to him that there was no need of an idol, to the god of darkness when this chamber was full of the presence of the god himself. Even an altar might be thought unnecessary; how would he explain that eventuality to the Forgotten King?

Before he started worrying about that, he told himself, he should be sure it was the case. Arms outstretched, he took another few steps. Nothing there.

A voice suddenly spoke, not a dozen feet away.

"Greetings, stranger. Welcome to the shrine of Andhur Regvos. I am told you seek instruction; the best instruction is the darkness itself."

"What?" Garth realized his response was scarcely diplomatic, but it escaped him before he could control it.

"The best proof of our faith is felt in the darkness; do you not feel it? In this absolute darkness, do you not feel the sensation of supernatural presence? Does not a subtle fear, a certain respect, find its way into your heart?"

"I . . . I am not sure."

"That very uncertainty is a sign of the awe that our lord inspires; you, an unbeliever, feel only the lightest touch of his power. You have known only Andhur, the darkness that passes; before entering this shrine, you have most likely never even known what full darkness was like, for in the outside world the light creeps in everywhere, continuing the eternal battle. Here, though, is the fortress of Andhur, where the darkness does *not* pass, but endures forever. The darkness goes on, though you and others like you may leave and return once again to the light."

"You speak of Andhur; I thought your god's name was Andhur Regvos?"

"The two names identify the two aspects of the deity; Andhur, the lesser of the two, is that darkness which may be penetrated by light, the darkness that is external. Regvos is internal darkness, that darkness of body and soul which does not pass; you would call it blindness. As darkness comes in many forms – night, shadow, and shade – so does blindness. We, the priests of Andhur Regvos, are seekers after the totality of blindness, as we have, in this temple, achieved the totality of darkness."

Garth was becoming confused; this bizarre philosophy was distracting him from his purpose. He suppressed the urge to say he did not understand, for fear of triggering a long explanation. Instead, he said, "And what of your rituals?"

"Our ceremonies are of no concern to outsiders."

"Have you an idol, as do most shrines?"

"No; what need we with some stone image when the palpable presence of our divinity is all around us?"

"An altar, then, where the rites are performed?"

"Yes, we have an altar, only a dozen paces away from you. Fortunately, our god keeps it safe from your defiling gaze. I see that you have not the makings of a worshipper of darkness; you are too concerned with mundanities."

"Perhaps you are right. Pardon me, then." Garth strode on recklessly in the same direction he had headed before, which he believed to be directly toward the center of the chamber; he hoped to locate the altar and remove whatever it held before the priests could do anything to stop him. After all, would not the darkness hinder them, too? True, they lived in it much or all of the time and were fully familiar with the temple, as he was not; still, finding and stopping a thief in utter blackness would not be easy.

He had gone only eight paces, rather than the dozen the priest had suggested, when his leg struck a low obstruction. He felt about, and decided it was indeed the altar, about three feet high, ten feet long, and perhaps five in width. In its center his groping hands found an object, vaguely spherical and covered with cloth, perhaps a foot in diameter. Another stone, no doubt, like the one he had taken from the temple of Tema. Curious.

"Hold! What are you doing?"

"I merely wished to touch the altar." He picked up the stone; having no cloak to hide it under, he tucked it under his left arm. It wouldn't matter that it was visible until he was out of the temple, and in the open streets he would rely on his superior speed to escape.

He had what he came for, and in the darkness no one would even know it was gone until the ceremonies began. He returned the eight paces to where he had stood before, and said, "My apologies if I startled you."

There were rustlings behind him; a new voice spoke. "The stone is gone! He has the stone!"

Garth growled, wishing he knew an appropriate curse; his people, being atheistic, used none.

Suddenly there were rustlings on all sides; there were priests all around him. Had they been there all along?

"Return the stone to its place, defiler." The voice was that of his instructor, but lower, more authoritative in tone.

Garth ignored it; if he spoke it would only help them to locate him. He crept toward the entrance.

A dozen hands clutched at him; fingers curled around his wrist.

With a bellow, Garth leapt back and drew his sword, keeping his left arm firmly around his prize.

"Away!" he shouted.

"No, desecrator; you must return the stone."

"I have no wish to harm you, but I will if I must."

"Yes, thief, we heard you draw your sword; but can you use your blade in the dark? There are many of us and but one of you. We can find you, for we have lived all our lives in darkness, but how can you find us? Here, of all the world, the blind rule and the sighted serve."

Garth slashed out blindly with his sword, but hit nothing. Again, unseen hands clutched at him; he tore free, and slashed again. He wished he had not so willingly surrendered the flint and steel that had been his only means of making light; if he could see, he would have the advantage.

At least, he so assumed; so far he had detected no weapons. Certainly none had been used against him, and how could the priests risk them in the dark? It would be far too likely that they would hit their companions instead of them opponent. And if the priests were blind, as the voice had implied, light would give him a truly immeasurable advantage.

"Give up, defiler. You cannot get away from us; even should you somehow slay us all, you will never escape. The only exit is through the maze, and without a guide you will never find the true path."

Garth made no answer, but swung the sword again, and again struck nothing. Fingertips brushed his arm, and he moved instinctively away. He was no longer sure of his location relative to altar and entrance; escaping the priests' attempts to capture him had distracted him and moved him he knew not where.

"Do you know what will happen, defiler, if you do not surrender? You will tire eventually; you will fall, and sleep, and when you do we will capture and bind you."

Garth slashed again, and thought he nicked something; perhaps a sleeve. Not flesh, unfortunately.

"Then, when you are securely bound, you will make a sacrifice. Not to Andhur, the darkness that passes, but to everlasting Regvos; you will become one of us."

Instead of a sweeping slash, Garth tried a lunging jab; he was lucky, and a yelp of pain answered him. He doubted he had inflicted a serious wound; there was as much of surprise as pain in that cry. He had probably pinked someone's arm.

"Blasphemer! Do you know how the sacrifice is performed, in cases such as yours? A rope, a thick rope knotted twice, is placed around your head, with the knots resting upon your closed eyelids."

Garth attempted another jab, this time aiming for where he judged the voice to be coming from; the speaker paused as steel whistled near him, but the blade did not connect. When next the voice spoke it had moved well to one side, although Garth had heard no footsteps or rustling garments.

"Then we will begin the Great Ritual, and with each chant the rope will be twisted a half-turn tighter, until the knots crush . . ."

A particularly fast, vicious lunge tore cloth audibly, and the voice cut off abruptly; Garth heard two quick steps away from him. He was heartened; he was beginning to think that nothing could faze the man.

The voice did not speak again; instead, he felt fingers groping. He whirled abruptly and slashed close in and was gratified to feel the blade cut into flesh and scrape on bone; he had caught a wrist before it could be withdrawn. There was not so much as a whimper of pain, though; Garth marveled at the fortitude that implied.

Even in the dark, the sword gave him quite an advantage; all about him were his enemies, so he could strike freely. That would not get him out of the temple, necessarily, but it might drive away his tormentors, at least temporarily. He charged, swinging wildly.

The sword whistled and cut through cloth, but struck nothing more substantial. He charged again, in a different direction, and struck nothing at all. He stopped and listened.

He could hear nothing; had the priests retreated? He knew they were exceptionally good at being silent, but he was fairly sure that none stood within reach. He wished he could feel about him, but his left hand was occupied with the stone and he dared not lower the sword in his right. He stood for a moment, trying to decide on his next move.

He had not planned on this fight; he had not expected these annoying priests to notice the loss of the altar-stone so promptly.

A hand closed on his right forearm; he yanked free and slashed. The blade bit into something; there was a gasp, and when he raised the weapon back to the guard position something wet ran down over the quillons onto his hand. He felt a grim satisfaction at that; a blow that drew so much blood so quickly might well be mortal. He almost wished that the priest would taunt him again; the silence was making him nervous, and surely the others must have some comment to make about the man he had struck?

There were retreating footsteps, two sets moving together, as if carrying something between them; he heard something drag. There had been no sound of a body falling, however; his victim was still upright, merely being helped away.

In hopes of surprising and further discouraging his antagonists, he leapt forward without warning and laid about him with the bloody sword; there were short, sharp cries, but he did not feel the blade connect with anything. He recalled that he was dealing with humans, much shorter than himself; were they ducking under his blows? He went down on one knee and made a long, horizontal sweep with his blade, scarcely two feet from the floor; it ended abruptly when his steel struck something much harder than flesh or bone, and he almost lost his grip as the blade rebounded, ringing, from what he realized must be the stone altar.

Two hands grasped at his shoulder; he twisted away and struck without thinking, swinging the sword in a downward arc. It struck the altar again, rather than his assailant, scraping across stone, and for the first time since entering the temple Garth's eyes responded; there was a blue-white flash, almost painful after such a long time in absolute darkness, and Garth stood motionless for an instant, dazed, wondering what he had just seen.

At last, he realized what had happened; his sword had struck sparks. The altar, whatever stone it was made of, had served as flint to his weapon's steel.

A hand closed on his right ankle; he guessed that the priest who had grabbed his shoulder had ducked, and was now aiming lower. Remembering the direction the grip on his shoulder had had, Garth guessed where on the floor his attacker would have fallen and chopped downward; the blade bit into cloth and flesh, and a high-pitched scream echoed through the chamber. Garth stepped away, without attempting to finish the human off; he had another idea.

The altar, he realized, could provide the light he needed, if he could find something to use as tinder. He mentally reviewed everything he had with him. A purse, containing a dozen gold coins; a dagger in his belt; the belt itself; a leather pouch that held dried beef, dried fruit, an awl, and other useful items – such as the map the Forgotten King had given him, showing the route to Dûsarra. It was old, dry parchment; it should burn readily.

Unfortunately, he had both his hands full at present.

It was also necessary not to let the priests know that he was up to something; he made a few feints and jabs with his sword, not seriously expecting to hit anything, just to keep up appearances. Then, carefully, he bent down and placed the stone firmly between his knees; he dared not put it down anywhere for fear a priest would snatch it away. His now-free left hand plunged into the pouch and pulled out the map; he placed it in his right hand, held tightly against the hilt of his sword by his outer thumb and two fingers, then returned the stone to its place under his left arm.

He made a trial pass at the altar with the sword, and with a long, diagonal blow scraped up a shower of sparks. This time he was ready, and saw them plainly; the altar was rough stone, his sword was smeared with blood that was black in the faint light. He watched where the sparks fell and placed the map accordingly, still neatly rolled.

It occurred to him that the map would not burn for very long once lit, but he had nothing else readily combustible; he would have to make do.

As he withdrew after placing the map, a hand pressed against his back; he whirled and slashed, and was rewarded with a yell and the hiss of steel cutting cloth. Thinking quickly, he dropped the altar-stone, and simultaneously clamped a foot atop it and reached out with his left hand.

He caught something; he held a handful of cloth, and yanked. There was loud ripping, and a long piece of fabric came away in his grip.

"What are you doing, blasphemer?"

He ignored the voice as he drew his dagger with his left hand and awkwardly twisted the cloth around the blade, securing it as best he could one-handed; with his right hand he took a few aimless swings with his sword, to make the priests maintain their distance. The dagger-torch thus produced wouldn't burn well, he knew; it wanted grease or fat or oil on the cloth.

He placed it on the altar beside the map, feeling carefully to be sure the roll of parchment was still there.

Again the voice asked, "What are you doing?" Garth thought he detected a worried tone; undoubtedly the priests could hear everything he did, making it plain that he was up to something.

"Why do you draw your dagger, thief? Is not your sword sufficient to deal with unarmed priests? Is that cloth a bandage? Have we wounded you so severely?"

Garth was relieved that his scheme had not been deciphered. He pulled his largest piece of dried meat from his pouch and smeared it along the blade of his sword, letting it soak up what remained of the blood; for the first time in his life he was grateful that his provisions were of less than premier quality, for there was a significant amount of fat in the meat, and he hoped the blood would serve to soften it up somewhat.

There were rustlings all around him; the priests were also up to something. Something was being dragged toward him.

He smeared the bloody meat against the cloth wrapped on the blade of his dagger, then flung it aside.

He had prepared as well as he could; he struck at the altar again with his sword.

The angle was wrong; only a very few sparks glimmered briefly. He swung again, and a more encouraging shower of blue-white pinpoints spattered across the altar and parchment, but they vanished without igniting anything.

"Do you seek to enrage us further by smashing our altar? Fool! You cannot damage it, no matter how strong your arm; no man can!"

Garth was amused that they thought him a man; he resisted the temptation to correct their mistake, as it would hinder his identification once he was gone. He struck at the altar again, and sparks flew; again, and again, his blade grating on stone. He was ruining the edge, he knew.

He paused to catch his breath, and the darkness swallowed him up again, seeming more complete than ever after the brief respite the sparks had provided; but was it complete? From the corner of his eye he caught a faint flicker; he bent near the altar.

Yes! A dull orange glow tinged the edge of the rolled map; a spark had caught!

Holding his breath, ignoring the rustling movements behind him and the dragging which was scarcely ten feet away, he gently fanned the ruddy glow; his efforts were rewarded with a tiny tongue of flame that leapt up suddenly.

Exulting silently, he carefully lifted the burning parchment and held it high, turning to take his first good look at his surroundings.

As he turned, a heavy net was flung across him; that, of course, was what the priests had been dragging. He managed to hang onto his sword and the burning map, but his foot slipped from atop the altar-stone. Fortunately, it, too, was tangled in the net, where the priests could not get at it readily even if they were to locate it.

He struggled to remain upright, and succeeded; the priests, thinking him human, had underestimated his strength.

For a moment he was too busy studying his newly visible environment to pay the net much heed. He was in the middle of a large room, perhaps a hundred feet across, totally devoid of furniture save for the altar itself, which was a single block of rough stone. The walls were bare, unfinished stone; here and there were hung heavy draperies, presumably concealing doorways. The dim light of his small flame was not sufficient to make out color or detail.

The heat of the flame began to reach his fingers, and he recalled himself to his immediate situation; he set to methodically cutting his way out of the net with his sword, which was fairly easy. In only a moment, he had cut a hole large enough to let the net slide down across his body onto the floor.

The priests formed a ring around the net, tugging at it, trying to force their captive down; they were unaware that their actions actually made Garth's escape much easier, providing the tension necessary to cut the strands, and pulling the severed net down off him.

Once mostly free, he wasted no time in snatching up his prepared dagger and setting the greased cloth ablaze; it produced a dim, smoky, malodorous flame, but it burned. He dropped the flaming remnant of his map and again looked about.

This time he studied the priests; all wore black, or at least colors dark enough to be indistinguishable in the available light. They were babbling excitedly, aware that their captive had somehow eluded the net and set something on fire; the odor was unmistakably that of something burning. Garth regretted that, as it removed much of the element of surprise.

There were about two dozen of them; they covered a wide range of sizes and shapes and, judged by their faces, varied in age from scarcely adult to positively ancient. Their garments were uniformly dirty and ragged, and their faces filthy, but after all, who would care in the eternal darkness of the temple? Or even outside, who expected the blind to be concerned with appearances? That thought drew Garth's attention to their eyes, which he immediately regretted; some were not bad, being merely permanently closed or open and staring sightlessly, but others were glazed, whited over with cataracts, flooded with blood and scar tissue, or simply gone, leaving bloody sockets.

He noticed that one had a long, jagged tear in his robe, revealing a cut across his chest; it seemed singularly clean and bloodless until Garth lifted his makeshift torch for a better look. When the dim light shone full on the man's chest the cut suddenly began oozing blood thickly, and the priest hissed in pain.

Another had a makeshift bandage tight, around his wrist; as the light hit it blood seeped through, staining it a dark red.

A man, an old man, lay on the floor not far from him; a trail of blood showed that this was the priest who had grabbed Garth's shoulder and ankle, only to be wounded at the base of the altar. Whatever dark magic had stanched the wounds of his companions until light hit them had apparently been overtaxed by the severity of his injuries, as his blood seemed to have flowed freely enough. The old man was still breathing, faintly, and Garth wondered if he would live.

Looking across the floor beneath the net Garth saw another trail of blood, where two priests had dragged away the first one he had seriously wounded. His eyes followed the trail to where it vanished under one of the curtains; that, he supposed, would be sleeping quarters, or some similar place where they could tend their wounded.

"So, thief, you lied to us, and brought in some way to make fire. We dare not attack you, thus, when you have your sword and we are unarmed; but still, you cannot find your way out. The maze will stop you."

For the first time Garth could see who spoke; it was a tall, elderly man, his hair gray with age. One sleeve was slashed where Garth's sword had cut it. He had no eyes, but merely empty sockets, long since healed from whatever injury had destroyed his sight.

It seemed unlikely to Garth that the maze could actually be all that impossible; with a wary eye on the priests, he put down his sword for a moment, transferred the dagger-torch to his right hand, picked up the cloth-covered stone with his left, tucked it back in its former position under his arm, put the torch back in his left hand – which could still hold it, although it was not free to make large motions – and picked up the sword. This operation took a minute or more before he was comfortable again, but the priests kept their distance; they knew they were no match for him except in the darkness.

Thus organized, with sword in his right hand, torch in his left, and stone under his left arm, he crossed the dirty stone floor to the drapery through which he had entered; he identified it by its position relative to the altar.

The curtain was wine-colored velvet, he saw when the torch came near enough to make colors distinguishable; it was stained and dusty. It was also, he thought, a good place for an ambush; he slashed at it with his sword, rather than marching through.

There was a piercing scream, and a body fell forward, dragging the drapery down beneath it; he had cut the man's throat. A long, serpentine-bladed dagger rattled on the flagstones as a new, darker stain spread across the ruined velvet.

The bulky stone under his arm kept him from thrusting the torch forward to illuminate what lay beyond the now-open doorway, so he proceeded with deliberate caution, in short steps, looking both ways and always aware of the double-dozen enemies behind him.

There were no further attacks; he stepped through the doorway into the maze.

No fewer than five corridors branched away from where he stood; he studied them all, and then, without hesitation, marched up the one second from the left. He could not hope to remember the twisting route he had followed coming in, let alone reverse it, but he had no need to; in four of the corridors dust lay thick on the floor. Only one route was actually used.

This same method served him well at every intersection, and there were a good many of them; no doubt it would be a great mystery for the surviving dark-worshippers to ponder.

At last, when he was beginning to wonder if he had somehow managed a wrong turn after all, the corridor he followed ended, not in a blank wall, but in a heavy iron door, bolted on his side. He sheathed his sword; surely, no enemy would be able to reach him here! He slid the bolt, and the door swung inward silently with only a gentle tug, revealing the closet-like compartment he had entered from the antechamber.

"Who's there?" The black-robed figure whirled to face him, though the man's eyes were blank and sightless; it was the priest who had led him through the maze, he was sure. "Why did you not signal?"

Annoyed, Garth drew his sword again, and held it to the man's throat. "Silence," he commanded. The priest obeyed admirably. Garth pulled him back into the maze, then stepped past him into the closet space and let the iron door swing shut; it apparently had springs to keep it closed. The side he now saw was not iron at all, but stone; a thin panel of cut stone had been riveted to the metal framework.

He was pleased the man had not put up a fight; he had killed at least one of the priests here, perhaps two or three, and wanted no more bloodshed.

He had no difficulty in opening the door to the antechamber; however, when it swung open, the gust of wind caught his already-dimming torch, which flickered and almost died. He stood where he was for a moment, hoping it would recover; instead, it faded to a dull glow. Most of the cloth was ash.

It mattered little; he was almost out. He crossed the room, and pulled at the door to the outside.

It refused to yield. He bent to look at the handle, as the last flicker of his torch waned and died. He felt for a latch, but found none.

A possibility occurred to him; he groped his way back across the room and closed the door to the maze entrance, making certain it latched securely.

That done, he returned to the exterior door; this time it opened easily and he stepped out into the plaza, to stand blinking in the bright moonlight.

Chapter Eleven

There was no sign of pursuit; perhaps the priests of Andhur Regvos thought him lost somewhere in their labyrinth.

The plaza was still mostly empty. A few humans wandered about, ignoring him, though he was sure he must be a rather strange sight: an overman emerging from the temple with a bloody sword in one hand and a scorched and blackened dagger in the other, and a great black stone – the cover had twisted out of position, and he could see that the altar-stone was of some material resembling obsidian – under one arm.

Of course, he was still mostly in the temple's shadow; or perhaps the Dûsarrans assumed him a participant in some secret ritual best left uninvestigated.

It would not do, he knew, to walk the streets of the city like this; he shrank back into the doorway, and seated himself on the paving, letting his three burdens fall.

He took the cloth cover from the stone, and carefully wiped his weapons clean before sheathing them; now the only problem was to conceal the stone itself.

Or was that, in fact, a problem? After all, he realized, no one had ever seen the thing. To the uninitiated, it would appear merely a large chunk of obsidian, a substance that he had seen sold freely in the marketplace the night before.

He knew it was still somewhat risky, but could think of no way to conceal his booty; so, once his blades were cleaned and sheathed and he had removed what soot and blood he could from his hands and mail shirt, he tucked the stone casually under his arm and strolled away unmolested.

It was still relatively early; he had to some extent lost track of time while in the temple but, judging by the position of the moon, he estimated it to be well before midnight. He would have to decide whether or not to tackle another of the remaining altars immediately, or whether it would be better to delay. The decision, however, could wait until he had disposed of his prize.

He found his way back to the Inn of the Seven Stars and headed for the stable, to deposit this new stone with his earlier prize. There was a boy sitting in the arch; Garth recognized him as the boy he had paid for Koros' keep when he first arrived. If he had understood the conversation of the other two boys correctly, his name was Dugger.

It occurred to Garth that the lad could be a loose end; he would identify the warbeast-riding overman with the brown-cloaked old man who had expressed a suspicious interest in Tema's temple. That was not something Garth wanted known.

He stepped into the arch; the boy clambered to his feet and said, "Greetings, sir. How may I serve you?"

A rather more polite greeting than he had given the night before, Garth thought; gold had a truly salutary effect on human manners. "In two ways, boy. Firstly, you will see that my mount is fed tomorrow night; it is to be given as much fresh raw meat as you can carry, or a live goat or two if you prefer, and a bucket of water. Secondly, you will make no mention of me to anyone unless asked, and if you are asked, you will deny seeing me in any guise other than my present one. Is that clear?" As he spoke this last phrase a large gold coin appeared in his hand, held up so that it sparkled in the moonlight.

The boy nodded eagerly. "Oh, yes, sir!"

"Good. Excuse me; I would tend my beast." The coin dropped into the boy's hand, whence it promptly vanished to some hidden pocket, and Garth passed into the stableyard.

Koros growled a greeting as its master opened the stall door; Garth ignored it while he dug out two sacks from his bundled supplies. He stuffed the obsidianlike stone down into one, then dug up the now-clear white crystal he had hidden beneath the straw and packed it on top, with straw around the edges to keep the sharp facets from cutting the rough fabric. That done, he tied the sack shut and stashed it under his other supplies. The other sack he folded into a small bundle and stuffed under his belt; it would, he hoped, carry whatever he found in the next temple.

Five temples remained. There was no point in wasting time, he decided; he would immediately pursue his quest and loot a third shrine. Things had not gone well in the first two; he had killed at least two people so far, possibly as many as four. That was not good. He would try to be more careful henceforth. If he kept on killing people at that rate . . .

He did not like killing people. A major reason he had been reluctant to serve the Forgotten King was that his first errand had resulted in a dozen deaths, perhaps more. However, whenever he found himself in a combat situation, his reflexes took over; he acted first and regretted it later. He was not proud of that, but recognized it as a part of his nature; all he could do was try to avoid combat situations.

Five temples remained, including the temple of Death; he would leave that for last. What were the other four? P'hul, the goddess of decay, was one. There was one that the tavern-girl had said frightened her; Agha? No, Aghad. That was it. He recalled hearing the name spoken back in Skelleth, as an oath; that sounded promising.

He considered visiting the tavern again, but decided against it; he was not hungry, nor even particularly thirsty, and could just as easily get directions on the street.

That in mind, he left the stable, nodding to the stable-boy who winked in reply, and headed for the marketplace.

As it had been the night before, it was bustling, crowded and torchlit. He strolled about a bit first, watching the reactions of the Dûsarran populace to an overman in their midst.

There were none; they accepted him as a matter of course. There must indeed be established communications between Dûsarra and a population of overmen somewhere.

Casually, he struck up a conversation with a merchant, pretending an interest in his display of stone carvings; when he learned that the carvings represented the Dûsarran gods, his feigned interest became quite genuine.

"Who is this, then?" he asked, indicating a six-inch carving of truly astonishing ugliness; it had a fanged, twisted, sneering face, with exaggerated masculine characteristics, and was done in a rough, primitive style.

"Aghad, of course."

"And this?" He indicated a skull-faced, helmeted statuette that held a miniature sword almost the length of its body.

"Bheleu, god of destruction. One of your kind, so it is said."

"What?" Garth looked more closely, and saw that the face was not a skull; the statuette had ragged, straight hair, two thumbs on either hand, and eyes rather than sockets. In short, it was a carving of an overman.

How very odd, Garth thought, that humans should worship a god in the form of an overman. After all, overmen had nothing to do with the gods, being atheists; and weren't gods supposed to have existed throughout time, while overmen had only come into being a thousand years earlier? He looked over the whole display. He recognized the slender, graceful Tema, though these little idols did not have cloaks that spread out above them; a god with two eyeless faces he readily guessed to be Andhur Regvos. There were more of those two, in various sizes and with some variation of detail, than any others; there were a dozen or so of the fanged horror depicting Aghad, and perhaps half that number of the overmanlike Bheleu. There were two other recurring forms, both female; one held dagger and whip and wore a cruel smile, while the other was robed and cowled. He took a closer look at one of these; under the cowl the artisan had carved the face of a mummy, wrinkled skin stretched over bone. It had a nose, however, so it was not intended to be an overwoman; Garth guessed it must be P'hul.

That was only six, however.

"I only see six of the gods here."

"Naturally." The merchant looked surprised. Garth realized his mistake; the seventh god was Death, and even were there a market, it would probably not be considered safe to try representing him.

He tried to cover his foolishness. "Of course. Who is this?" He indicated the woman with whip and dagger.

"Sai."

Garth looked blank.

"The goddess of pain and suffering."

"Oh, yes." He contemplated the display again. "And each has a temple here in Dûsarra?"

"The name says as much."

"Where are the temples? I might want to visit them."

The merchant looked at him strangely. "Very few foreigners visit the temples."

"I was just curious."

"Oh. Well, the temple of Tema is back that way," he said, indicating the direction, "and most of the others are on the Street of the Temples, over that way." He pointed toward the northeastern part of the city.

"My thanks." Garth took a final look at the array of idols, then turned away, heading northeast.

The Street of the Temples was not hard to find; it was a broad, straight avenue, paved with stone and obviously intended for ceremonial processions. Most of its length was lined not with temples, but with houses and palaces; it was obviously one of the more desirable neighborhoods. There were a few shops, all closed for the night; this part of the city belonged to the day-people, not the night-worshippers.

One end of the street was the gate to a palace, the largest and most elegant Garth had yet seen; that, presumably, belonged to the city's overlord. The other end, which was much further from where he had happened onto the avenue, appeared to be nothing but the blank stone face of the volcano on whose slopes the city was built; the street was cut into the stone for a few yards, keeping it at a negotiable slope, and then abruptly stopped.

Along the considerable distance between palace and mountainside, Garth saw four temples; they were readily distinguished from the adjoining residences because each was built entirely of black stone and surmounted by a dome of some sort, while the palaces and other buildings were flat-roofed and built of various materials. The temples were arranged two to each side, spaced along the street, dividing it into five equal lengths.

Garth had arrived on the street directly across from the temple second from the overlord's palace; it made little difference to him which he visited next, so he chose the nearest and strode across the pavement.

The temple was mostly hidden by a high wall, built of the ubiquitous black stone; only the dome, a relatively modest one, could be seen. The wall had no windows, no eaves overhanging, nor any other architectural features suggesting it was part of the temple proper; Garth assumed it enclosed a yard, and that the temple lay within the yard.

The only visible entrance was a pair of gates, perhaps ten feet high and eight feet wide, made of some metal that gleamed an eerie silver in the moonlight; they were not simple flat surfaces, but shaped into ornate curves and ridges. With a start, Garth realized that the ridges formed recognizable runes, two to each gate, spelling out AGHAD.

As he approached the gates he noticed another surprising feature; the wall was built of carefully cut stones, all exactly the same size, and every stone block had carved upon it those same four runes: AGHAD. The name of the god was repeated a thousand times over on the wall of the temple.

Well, Garth thought, at least he need not wonder which temple it was. He reached out to try the gates, but before his hand touched the gleaming surface it parted and swung open before him, revealing the courtyard beyond.

He did not much care for such trickery; he looked carefully in all directions before cautiously stepping through, but could see no sign of how the gates had been opened. He tried to peer through the crack at the hinges, only to discover there was none; each valve hung from a single intricate hinge that extended for its full height.

The courtyard beyond seemed innocent enough: a broad expanse paved with loose gravel, with a fountain playing in its center. A long colonnade surrounded it on three sides; behind the far colonnade there stood the temple itself, an elegant building of black stone, with many windows and much ornamentation.

On every column, on all three sides, was a bracket holding a blazing torch, a welcome change from the darkness of the first two temples.

It should have been beautiful, with the soft hiss of the fountain, the dancing firelight, the columns and arcades. It wasn't. There was something dim and menacing about it, and its proportions seemed somehow wrong, as if the architect had calculated the perfect dimensions and then maliciously distorted them.

Garth stepped past the gates and noticed for the first time that there were curious faint brown stains on the silvery metal. He had no time to study them, however, for as soon as he was clear the gates swung shut behind him, as mysteriously as they had opened.

He was debating whether to try to reopen them or simply to proceed when a long, lingering scream sounded from somewhere inside the temple; Garth tensed, his hand on his sword hilt. The scream cut off abruptly, to be replaced by soft, mocking laughter that echoed eerily along the colonnades.

His curiosity was piqued, and the matter of the self-closing gates was forgotten. He started forward.

"Greetings, overman." The voice was deep and somber. It came from somewhere behind him, he thought; he whirled, sword drawn, but saw nothing except the closed gates. He noticed that they were now barred. He had not heard the bar falling in place; he reprimanded himself for not being sufficiently alert. "Welcome to the temple of Aghad." The voice now sounded somewhere to his right; he turned more slowly, wishing that these Dûsarrans weren't all so fond of trickery. He still saw no one.

"We do not receive many visitors here." Again, the voice had shifted; he decided to ignore its movements, since they were obviously some sort of trick. "Aghad is not a popular god, I fear. The masses prefer harmless, impotent little Tema." The voice laughed, softly.

Garth announced petulantly; "I don't like speaking to someone I cannot see."

"It is not intended that you should like it."

"Why not?"

"Dear infant, you are ignorant, aren't you?"

"In some areas, yes. Religion and its mystical trappings are not popular in my homeland."

"Oh, dear, not popular! Aghad is not popular anywhere, fool. Aghad is fear, hatred, loathing, all the things men – and though you will not accept it, overmen – feel for the unknown, for the different, for what they cannot understand."

"I can understand why such a deity holds little appeal."

"Oh, yes, I'm sure! Why have you come here, then?"

"I wish to visit all the seven temples."

"You lie with half-truths."

"What would you have me say, then?"

"You come to steal, scum. The altar-stones of Tema and Regvos are hidden at your warbeast's feet, at the Inn of the Seven Stars."

Garth did not answer, but merely tightened his grip on his sword.

The voice laughed again.

"Oh, witling, put down your silly knife. We serve Aghad here, and Aghad alone, not Tema nor Regvos, nor Sai, P'hul, or Bheleu. Aghad is hate, thief, hate, envy, and every emotion that turns fellow against fellow. We who serve Aghad have no reason to aid or sympathize with our brother priests of the other temples. Sack all Dûsarra if you will, burn the city to the ground! We will not stop you."

"Do you not care for your own temple? You have said I came here to steal."

"Idiot, self-hatred is most basic of all; if one does not hate himself, how is he to despise others so like him? You may take what lies on our altar, for it is no unique thing, but a common substance, replaced at each ceremony. We do, however, demand payment."

Garth did not lower his blade. "What payment?"

"You must make a proper sacrifice to Aghad."

"What sort of sacrifice?"

"Ordinarily a supplicant must betray a friend, deceive a lover, or in some other way spread dissent; but in view of your foreign origin, filth, something else is in order. A service to our god: Slay us six priests or more, one from each of the other temples. You slew the one at the door of Tema's temple, and a priest and priestess both of Regvos, though a third you let live. You have made a good beginning. Now, you must slay four more, from each of the four remaining temples, or the devotees of Aghad will make certain you do not leave the city alive."

Garth made no attempt to conceal his astonishment "Are you serious?"

"We are."

"Why?"

"Because our agents in each cult will blame your actions upon another, and discord will spread. You have already begun our task for us, you know."

The reference to his conversation with the swordsman in the stableyard did not escape his notice. It was obvious that the cult of Aghad had some truly superb means of gathering information, whether it was by magical methods or merely an efficient system of spies and informers. He still found it almost incredible that these people wanted him to kill their countrymen.

"You serve a strange master, priests of Aghad."

"No stranger than yours, Garth of Ordunin, late of Skelleth."

Garth hid his surprise; after all, whatever their methods, there was no reason to believe they were limited to this one city. The cult of Aghad could easily extend throughout all the human kingdoms, for all Garth knew.

"What if I decline to pay your price?"

"You are free to do as you please, dolt; we merely present you with the following options, for you to choose from as you will. You may take what you find upon our altar, and fulfill our demand, and go in peace. You may take what you find upon our altar, refuse to do as we ask, and die before you leave Dûsarra. Or, lastly, you may decline our offer entirely and live, but with the knowledge that your cowardice has offended our god and our cult."

"None of these options is particularly appealing."

"That does not concern us. Now, if you would see our altar, slave, pass the fountain, and before you will be the door to the sanctuary."

Garth considered for a moment. He had no wish to kill anyone; however, it might prove necessary, as it had in the first two temples, in which case he might as well take whatever there was here. He had no intention of wantonly slaying priests just to please these abominable Aghadites, though. If it did not become necessary to dispose of the required four priests, he would simply rely on his own strength and wit to elude the Aghadites and escape the city.

He moved cautiously past the fountain toward the temple itself, only to halt abruptly. Lying on the gravel behind the fountain was a human corpse, face down, an empty tin cup near its hand.

"What is this?"

"Note the odor of the fountain, wizard-spawn."

He was beginning to resent the constant supply of insults the hidden priest provided. He obeyed, though, and sniffed the crystal-clear spray. The scent of bitter almonds stung his nostrils; had he had a nose, he would have wrinkled it in disgust.

"Very pretty."

"The poor fool came seeking a cool drink; we could not refuse so simple a request, could we?" The priest burst out laughing, a roaring laughter tinged with hysteria. Garth began to suspect the man was mad. It would seem reasonable; would a sane man serve such a god? Unsettled, he walked on, keeping his sword ready in his hand.

The colonnade was perhaps ten feet across, a distance sufficient to put the wall of the temple in darkness; the columns which held the torches blocked out the light, since the flames were all on the courtyard side. Garth hesitated to step into that shadow, particularly since he could not see the door the priest had said was there. Then part of the shadow opened inward, and light the color of blood poured out.

Garth stepped forward through the double doors into a room hung with tapestries and lit by flames behind sheets of dark red glass set in the walls between the hangings. The room was not overlarge, and Garth wondered if it were, in fact, the sanctuary, or merely an antechamber; it was scarcely twenty feet square. He saw no altar, but there were no doors other than that by which he had entered, either.

He moved to the center of the chamber, and the doors promptly closed behind him. He was getting used to this sort of thing.

The ruddy light made it hard to distinguish details; he could not say what any of the tapestries depicted. He stood, waiting, to see what would happen next.

A curious thrashing noise came from somewhere above and ahead of him, and a muffled voice, too high for a man or overman, made a wordless noise. Harsh laughter rang out, growing louder and higher; the thrashing ceased, or perhaps was merely drowned out by the laughing, and the tapestry directly before him suddenly slid upward into the ceiling, revealing a large alcove. A more normal light shone from this opening; hundreds of candles were arranged in tiers on its three walls, every one burning brightly, illuminating an elaborate golden altar. The top of the altar was a panel of red-enameled wood, almost completely covered by a flood of coins, gold and red.

As he approached and cautiously reached for the coins, Garth wondered what the red ones were made of; he had never seen a metal so brightly crimson in hue, and stone coins were rare, being too brittle for everyday use.

He scooped up a handful and realized they were all ordinary gold; the red was fresh arterial blood, blood that ran down his wrist and dripped from his fingers. Revolted, he flung down the coins and turned away.

The tapestry plunged back into place, trapping him in the alcove, but not before he had seen the outer wall of the room to be blank, with no trace of the door he had entered by except a space of bare stone between hangings.

The laughter rang out louder than ever.

Chapter Twelve

He stood frozen with surprise for an instant; a soft sound behind him brought him whirling around to face the altar again, only to discover that it was gone. In its place was a crouching panther; Garth raised his sword, ready to meet its attack, and stepped back against the tapestry, so that the big cat would have further to leap and therefore less momentum when it hit.

No attack came. Instead, a heavy velvet curtain fell between him and the beast, leaving him enclosed in a space scarcely three feet wide. A few of the myriad candles were included in his compartment, so that at least he could see.

He pushed at the velvet barrier; it did not yield. Something held it taut. It was apparently secured to very solid retainers all around. He leaned his full weight against it with no result.

He shrugged, and turned to the tapestry that separated him from the main part of the room. It was anchored just as firmly. He looked about.

His enclosure was perhaps eight feet long; he stood in the center. At either end a dozen candles stood on black iron brackets bolted to the walls. Below him, the floor was a single slab of stone, a dark gray stone, probably slate. Looking up, he saw that the ceiling was covered with gold leaf, worked into elaborate swirls and floral designs. At one end, partly obscured by shadows, hung what appeared to be a cord; its lower end was above his line of sight, which explained how he had failed to notice its presence before.

He took a step and reached for it, hoping it was the draw-cord for one of the hangings; it raised a serpent's head and hissed angrily at his approaching hand.

Things were happening too fast; he bisected the serpent-rope with a sweep of his sword, and then slashed at the velvet curtain.

The blade penetrated with no difficulty, and Garth peered through the rent in the fabric; the panther was gone, if in fact it had ever truly been there, and the altar restored, the gold exactly as he had left it, the blood beginning to dry. He wondered how much of this was illusion, how much magic, and how much simple mechanical tricks.

"Very good, Garth." The laughter had stopped, and now the familiar taunting voice spoke. "You have slain a harmless rock-snake and destroyed a thousand-year-old Yeshitic hanging. Take your gold and begone. Ignore the blood; it came from an Orûnian virgin, just turned sixteen, but she was none of your kind. You need not regret her death." The priest tittered obscenely, and Garth's growing anger crystallized into hatred. At the back of his mind he knew that the priest wanted this, that he, like his foul god, thrived on hatred, but that only served to strengthen the emotion. Growling, he stepped through the ruined curtain, sheathing his sword as he did so, then pulled the sack from his belt and scooped the golden coins into it, ignoring the clotted blood.

"Oh, fine, underling; we might hire you as a parlormaid, should you have the courage to apply. Now go and slay us four priests, if you can; or priestesses, if that is more to your taste, though Bheleu and the Final God are served only by men. Go, and bother us no further, scum."

There was a click behind him; he turned to see that the tapestry had vanished again, and that the double door stood open once more. A sudden gust of wind brushed him, coming from nowhere that he could detect, and the candles flickered and died, leaving only the crimson glow of the torchlit panels.

He took a step toward the exit, then paused. In a final act of defiance, he drew his sword, set aside the sack of gold, gripped the hilt in both hands, then turned and chopped at the altar, sending the enameled top flying to either side, hewn in half. Another blow, and the golden filigree splintered and crumpled. He sheathed his weapon, spat at the broken remains of the altar, then picked up his booty and strode out the doorway. No laughter followed him.

The tapestry fell into place behind him, and the doors slammed shut. He marched through the colonnade and across the courtyard, noting that the corpse was gone from beside the fountain; then he stopped, as his gaze fell on the silvery gates.

The body of an old, old man, withered and emaciated, was nailed to the gates, the feet on one valve, the outstretched arms on the other; horrified, Garth saw that the narrow chest was still rising and falling, slowly and irregularly. The man's face was twisted in agony, his eyes tightly shut. Garth shivered in revulsion as he saw that strips of the man's skin had been cut loose from his flanks and nailed to the gates as well.

Sickened, Garth bellowed, "You filth! Why is this man here?"

There was silence for a moment as his cry echoed and was lost among the columns; then, very softly, that hideously familiar voice spoke, in a smiling, insinuating, smirking tone.

"You seem to enjoy wielding that sword of yours, child; use it to open the gate."

Garth stood motionless for a long moment. Then he dropped the sack of coins and strode to the gate; with all the care he could manage, he began pulling out the nails that held the old man. It was a delicate, difficult job; they had been driven in firmly and required all his strength to pry loose, while the slightest twist or tug might wrench the torn flesh and cause the victim new agony. Garth was very glad that the man was unconscious before the first nail came free.

Fortunately, the metal of the gates was soft, and did not hold the nails as well as wood would have; the superhuman strength of Garth's fingers was sufficient, with some slight aid from his dagger in prying at the larger spikes that held the feet.

At last, Garth had the man free, and lowered him gently to the gravel; the gates opened to only a slight tug. He picked up his sack and stepped through to be sure the way was clear; he intended to carry the old man back to the Inn of the Seven Stars and see that he received the best possible care, but it would not do to be seen carrying him about the Street of the Temples.

The street was empty; he turned to see the gates swinging shut. Desperately, he reached out, flinging himself forward to try and stop them, seeing the old man lying on the gravel through the narrowing gap, but he was not fast enough; the portal slammed shut, forcing him out into the avenue.

With a bellow of rage, Garth flung himself at the gates again; they did not yield. The shock of his impact bruised his shoulder, despite the padding and mail that protected it.

He whipped out his sword and hacked at the metal; the weapon had served him well but suffered in consequence, and this was too much. It broke, leaving him clutching a hilt and a half-foot of blade, and sending slivers of steel in a dozen directions. The gates remained firm, though the top of the GH rune was scratched and battered out of shape.

Once again, he heard laughter; something was flung over the wall, to fall heavily on the pavement at his feet. It was the old man's corpse, hacked messily in two, as it would have been had he used his sword to open the gate as the priest of Aghad suggested.

Speechless, Garth stood staring at the bloody remains for a long moment, then turned and left, as that final hysterical laugh trailed after him.

Chapter Thirteen

The moon was still well above the horizon; Garth estimated he had three hours or more until dawn. Although ordinarily he might have called it a night and returned to the Inn of the Seven Stars, the events in the temple of Aghad had enraged him, and he was too full of fury and adrenaline to go quietly back to the inn. Instead, he swung the sack of gold over his shoulder and marched down the avenue toward the overlord's palace, and toward the temple that stood nearest it. He was aware, with part of his mind, that he was being slightly reckless, since he no longer had a sword and was encumbered by the Aghadite gold; he was, however, too mad to care. He would have preferred to devote himself to destroying the temple of Aghad, and hunting out and killing the owner of that taunting voice, but knew that he wouldn't have a chance of succeeding; the priests would undoubtedly be expecting an attack. Instead he would take out his anger on whoever might be guarding this other temple. Even armed only with a dagger and a broken hilt, he knew he could handle any two humans. He regretted that he had left his battle-axe in Koros' stall with his other supplies, as an inappropriate item to be carrying about the city streets.

This next temple, he saw, was the most bizarre he had yet approached; where the others had been built of black basalt or marble or similar stones, this one was constructed of gleaming obsidian, arranged with sharp, broken edges projecting wherever possible. It was a high, narrow building, surmounted by a pointed dome, and fronted with a small forecourt. The court was perhaps twenty feet square, with obsidian walls eight or nine feet high around it, and a pair of large openwork steel gates at the front.

Garth wondered where, even in this volcanic country, they had found so much obsidian. Further, how had they constructed a building from it? Obsidian was not suited for construction purposes. It must be a façade, he decided, covering up a more ordinary structure.

The gates did not spell out the name of the deity here, nor was it carved in the walls. Instead, the gates were made of twisted, jagged spikes welded together into portals resembling a wall of thorns. There were no handles, and from each of the large spikes projected dozens of needlelike smaller spikes. Where there was no room for these, the metal had sawtoothed edges.

Even in his anger, these gates gave Garth pause; there was nowhere that he could touch them without risking injury. The points appeared razor-sharp. Appropriate, he thought, for the god of sharpness, should there be one. He wondered what sort of insane cult would build such a thing.

He ran the broken stump of his sword through one of the gaps in the glittering tangle of sharpened steel, and pulled; to his surprise, the gate opened readily. He had expected it to be locked for the night.

He stepped through, and noticed for the first time that the courtyard was paved, or perhaps lined, with obsidian, arranged with all possible points and sharp edges projecting upwards, and left thoroughly uneven. Walking on it was difficult, and even through the thick soles of his boots he could feel the knife-edged volcanic glass cutting into his feet.

He made his way gingerly across the broken expanse to the door of the temple building; it, like the gates, was a web of steel spikes. He shoved at it with the broken sword; a long needle-pointed projection caught his finger and gashed it painfully, but the door swung open. It, like the gate, was unlocked. As it began to move, Garth suddenly realized that the night was not silent; somewhere, several voices were wailing, as if in great pain or abject despair. As the door opened wider, he knew it was coming from inside this temple; it swept out over him.

Light also assaulted him, a sharp white light totally unlike the yellow of torchlight or the red of a fire. This glare was tinged with blue, like the flash of lightning. He ignored it. He was in no mood for caution. When the door stopped swinging, he stepped through.

He was at the bottom of a set of uneven steps, steep even for an overman, and all crooked; he clambered up them into the temple proper.

It was a single vast room, twenty feet wide, a hundred long, and at least fifty feet high, not counting the interior of the dome. The walls were jagged, rough stone, and seemed to lean inward; Garth was not sure if this were some illusion, or whether the room actually narrowed toward the top. The floor was broken, uneven flagstones, but far more negotiable than the obsidian courtyard. The light came from dozens of flares that blazed on one wall, burning with a vivid, painfully bright light and casting sharp-edged black shadows of the score or so of worshippers who knelt before the altar. The shadows did not move; the flares had none of the comforting flicker of more ordinary flames.

The altar itself was a single chunk of granite; behind it stood three black-robed priests, faces hidden by hoods, and on it lay a naked young woman – perhaps only a girl. Garth was a poor judge of human age or maturity.

The central priest held a long narrow-bladed dirk clutched in his fist; the man to his right held a coiled whip, and the third priest held a loop of ordinary rope.

The wailing came from the worshippers; the priests and the girl on the altar were making no sound that Garth could detect.

Behind the priests, carved on the end wall of the temple, Garth glimpsed the image of a smiling naked woman, hands outstretched toward the altar; the shadows of the priests made it hard to distinguish details. Although the image he had seen in the marketplace had been robed and held weapons, he recognized the face and evil smile of the idol; this was Sai, goddess of pain and suffering.

No one was paying any attention to him. He put down his sack of blood-stained Aghadite gold, and strode forward across the shattered floor. As he drew nearer, he saw that the priest's dirk had blood upon its tip, and that the naked girl's body was laced with narrow, shallow cuts. He wondered whether the ceremony was to have ended with her death as a human sacrifice, or whether she would merely have been tortured and released; it was clear from her face that she was not a willing participant. He grinned at the prospect of frustrating these sadists. It would be almost as satisfying as killing Aghadites. Still, he hoped he could avoid killing any, not only because he disliked causing unnecessary deaths, but because he did not want the Aghadites to have the satisfaction.

He was even with the back of the small crowd of worshippers, now; he bellowed as the priest lowered the dagger for another cut. He did not want the girl injured further. After all, she was what he had found upon the altar, and therefore what he was to take back to the Forgotten King. He wondered what the old man would make of her.

Startled, the priest stopped his motion; the crowd's wailing wavered.

"Drop that knife or die, priest!" He kicked aside a kneeling figure that blocked his path and stepped up to the altar; his broken sword was still in his hand and, although scarcely the weapon it once was, it could still cut. It should, he thought, be adequate for dealing with this bunch.

The priest backed away, but the dirk remained in his hand.

Garth drew his own dagger, which was now longer than his sword, and also longer than the priest's blade, having been made for an overman rather than a mere human. He saw that the sacrificial victim was tied to the altar and cut away the ropes.

Immediately she rolled off the altar, sprang up, and started toward the door; Garth caught her before she had gone more than a single step, dropping the stump of his sword but keeping the dagger ready in case a priest or worshipper should attack. His hand gripped her arm, none too gently, as he said, "Wait. You go with me." She winced, and nodded.

The wailing had ceased altogether; the worshippers knelt in shocked silence. The man who held the dirk, presumably the high priest, cried out, "Blasphemer! The girl is our sacrifice!"

Garth grinned broadly. "No longer, priest." It occurred to him that, had he come at a different time, he might have found something entirely different on the altar, something more to the Forgotten King's liking, and added, "I was sent to fetch what lay upon this stone."

He was actually quite pleased he had arrived when he did; the girl was obviously an unwilling victim.

"You have made a mistake! She is nothing but a sacrifice!"

"What else was upon your altar?"

"Who sent you? Some wizard?"

"I come from the temple of Aghad." Garth was perfectly willing to stir up discord as long as it was directed properly, and in fact he spoke the literal truth.

"What do they want with our ceremonial weapons?"

"No one said anything about any weapons."

"There is no need for subterfuge; you came for the whip and dagger. What . . ." The priest's question was cut off abruptly as Garth, releasing the girl, leapt over the altar and grabbed the man by the throat.

"Priest, you talk too much. Give me the dagger." Garth marveled at the man's stupidity; it had been remarkably cooperative of him to reveal so quickly what was ordinarily kept on the altar.

The priest made a desperate and futile stab at Garth's side with the dirk; it was turned by the overman's mail. Garth's own dagger was not turned. He ran it through the priest's wrist, and the fingers sprang open. The dirk clattered to the floor.

The priest who held the whip suddenly came to life; like everyone else in the temple, he had been watching motionlessly, too confused and surprised to do anything about this intrusion, but now he lunged forward and came up holding the dropped dagger.

He stabbed at Garth; the thrust was parried, and the man retreated. Meanwhile, the high priest struggled in Garth's unbreakable grip. His hands clutched at Garth's arm, impeding his movement as his fellow made another thrust, and the dirk missed Garth by mere inches. Annoyed, Garth flung the high priest aside; he struck the wall at the feet of his idol, fell limply to the floor, and lay still. With one disposed of, Garth turned to face the other, who had assumed a proper knife-fighting stance despite his hampering robe.

The third priest leapt upon Garth from behind and swung a loop of rope around his neck.

To the priests, this seemed to give them an advantage; to the overman, it was a petty annoyance. Keeping his dagger in his left hand, he reached up with his right, and closed it on the would-be strangler's throat. As the man tried to pull his rope taut, Garth's grip tightened, digging in with both the thumbs on his right hand.

He misjudged the strength of the man's neck; there was a loud crack, and the priest tumbled from his back, eyes already glazing over. As he fell, his head struck the edge of the granite altar with another, similar crack of breaking bone. There could be no doubt that he was dead.

The remaining priest froze; he was facing the wall of flares, so that the lower half of his face was visible despite his overhanging cowl, and as Garth watched his mouth fell open and the blood drained from his jaw. The dagger and whip dropped from shaking fingers.

"Girl! Get them!" Garth's voice was sharp, and the girl hastened to obey; she had been watching the fight, and any thought of failing to cooperate with her saviour – or new captor; she was as yet unsure which Garth actually was – had vanished. She hurried around the end of the altar, ignoring the effect of the rough floor on her bare feet, and snatched up the weapons. The lone conscious priest stepped back out of her way without protest.

"Go wait on the steps. And," he added in a bellow, "any who hinders her will die!" Again the girl obeyed immediately, and the worshippers made no move to stop her. Garth followed her at a more leisurely pace, pausing to pick up his sword hilt from in front of the altar.

At the top of the steps he sheathed his dagger and picked up the sack of coins he had deposited there upon entering; he paused, considering, and glanced at the girl's feet. They were bleeding, and the obsidian courtyard was far worse than the shattered flagstones of the temple. He handed her the sack, telling her to hold it; she accepted it and nearly dropped it, astonished at its weight. He then put his arm around her middle and picked her up, dagger, whip, gold and all. After some adjustment he found a position that was fairly comfortable for both of them, though he suspected his mail was scratching her bare skin more than she cared to admit, and strode down the steps out of sight of the worshippers of Sai, who had silently watched the entire proceeding, without making a move in his direction.

Chapter Fourteen

The door and gates were still open, which was gratifying; he was heartily tired of portals that closed themselves. With the added weight of the girl on his shoulder, the jagged obsidian cut even deeper into the soles of his boots. When he finally stepped out onto the pavement of the Street of the Temples, he could feel that one puncture had gone clear through and, although his foot was not bleeding, the boot was plainly ruined. He sighed. The whole escapade in the temple of Sai had been a satisfactory way of working off his rage, leaving him reasonably calm, but it was sure to have unpleasant repercussions and results, of which ruined boots were only the first and least.

Adventuring seemed to be hard on feet and footwear; his first errand for the Forgotten King had destroyed a good pair of boots and various makeshift replacements and given him an assortment of burns, cuts, and blisters.

He found the street he had followed before and turned off the Street of the Temples, heading for the Inn of the Seven Stars. When he was out of sight of the avenue and presumably reasonably safe from immediate pursuit, he sheathed the stump of his sword and lifted the girl down off his shoulder. There was no reason to wear himself out carrying her; she should be able to walk well enough. Besides, it would be difficult to converse while carrying her, and he had several questions.

She seemed glad enough to be on her feet again; she brushed herself off slightly, making small yelps of pain whenever her hands accidentally disturbed the blood clotting on the dozens of cuts that crisscrossed her belly and breasts. She looked with dismay at the wounds, and at the reddish smudges left by Garth's hands, which were still damp with the blood of the various victims of the cult of Aghad. Garth guessed that the cuts must be very painful, though she did not whimper or complain, but stood, waiting for him to speak.

"Follow me; we are going to my inn."

She nodded, but hesitated.

"What's the matter?" he asked.

"My lord, I am naked." This was obvious, of course, but Garth had given it no thought.

"Is that bad?"

"It . . . it is not proper. I cannot walk the streets naked."

Garth sighed. "You will have to; I have no spare garments with me."

"But everyone will stare!"

Although not out of any concern for her modesty, he found that argument was the most effective she could have used; Garth did not want to draw attention to himself. Although he had thought he was safe from recognition by the followers of Tema or Andhur Regvos, the Aghadites knew that he was responsible for the desecrations of both those temples as well as their own, and he had made a public display of himself just now in the temple of Sai. If he maintained a casual manner and walked the streets openly, he doubted that most Dûsarrans would pay any attention to him; they hadn't done so previously. However, if an unclothed female was sufficiently unusual to attract stares, he could not afford to be seen with one. Someone might well point him out to Aghadites or followers of Sai who might otherwise have missed him.

Accordingly, he removed his belt, peeled off his suit of mail, and began untying the gambeson underneath. He stopped abruptly when he noticed the girl backing away apprehensively.

"What's wrong with you? I'm just going to give you this to wear; I have nothing else available."

"Oh!" The girl calmed visibly; Garth stripped off the quilted garment and handed it to her, standing uncomfortably in little but his soft leather breeches and natural coat of thin black fur. She accepted it, but then stood motionless, watching Garth don his armor once more.

He looked at her, wondering why she was just standing there.

She burst out, "You're furry!"

"You're not," he replied. "Put on the gambeson; this night air is cool."

"Oh!" she exclaimed again. Flushing slightly, she managed to pull the oversized padded shirt over her head; Garth noticed that she winced in pain as she worked it down over her body, and realized that it must be rubbing against the cuts inflicted by the sacrificial dagger. It must be horribly painful and irritating, yet she gave only a single quiet squeak, then began struggling with the ties at either side intended to keep the garment tight on the wearer's body. The lower hem, which came to slightly below Garth's waist, reached her knees; it not only covered her nakedness, but completely hid the cuts, which was doubtless all to the good if it didn't hurt her too much.

When she had the gambeson arranged as best she could manage, she asked, "Are all overmen furry?"

Garth, still struggling to get the mail settled comfortably, took his time about answering and limited his reply to, "Yes."

When he had the iron links arranged so that they did not scratch or chafe intolerably, he turned his attention to the girl. It was fortunate, he thought, that he had had his armor and accoutrements dyed or painted black, to decrease visibility. The gambeson's quilting did not show in the dim light, where it might have in a lighter-hued fabric. From a distance one might well mistake it for more ordinary attire – if not for the fact that it only reached the girl's knees. Still, it was better than nothing. He picked up the dagger and whip, stuffed them in the sack with the gold, and swung it over his shoulder.

"Good. Come on."

The girl obeyed, as he led the way back toward the Inn of the Seven Stars. He kept to the shadows and back alleys as much as possible and looped around the marketplace, giving it a wide berth. These tactics were fairly successful; the few passersby they encountered gave them no more than a passing glance.

This journey was hard on Garth's nerves; he kept expecting to hear someone shouting out the presence of the wanted thief and committer of sacrilege. Eventually, however, the pair reached the inn without being accosted, and crept through the archway into the stable. Dugger the stable-boy was still on duty; Garth motioned for him to be silent, and he assented with a grin and a nod.

Koros was curled up asleep but still occupied most of his stall, which had been designed with smaller animals in mind. Garth stepped in and settled comfortably on the straw on the other side, beside his supplies and the concealed loot from his first two thefts; with only a slight hesitation the girl obeyed his gesture and sat down beside him. He found a sponge in his pack, wetted it with water from one of his canteens – he would have to fill them soon – and said, "Get that thing off so I can clean your wounds."

She obeyed, untying the gambeson and pulling it over her head; despite the delicacy she displayed in this, Garth saw that several of the cuts beneath had been rubbed raw by the garment and were bleeding anew. He began washing away the blood and dirt as gently as he could but she still twitched away occasionally when the contact of water or the pressure of his hand stung her.

As he attended to this task he asked, "Now, girl, who are you?"

"My name is Frima." The girl's voice was high, but not unpleasant; she spoke timidly.

"Are you Dûsarran?"

"Yes, of course!"

"How did you come to be a sacrifice to Sai? Are you one of her devotees?"

"Oh, no! I worship Tema. The priests of Sai kidnapped me from my father's shop last night."

"How is it that the ceremony was being held at that hour? I had heard that only the cults of Tema and Andhur Regvos lived by night."

"That's right; that's why the sacrifices to Sai are – ow! – always at night."

"I do not understand."

"The cult of Sai is secret; its members do not – ooh! – do not admit their allegiance. Therefore, they hold all their ceremonies at night, when – ooh! – when the darkness provides cover, and when they will not be missed from their daytime occupations."

"Are the other cults equally secretive?"

"The day-dwelling cults are, yes. Ouch. That's part of why the night-dwellers avoid them; would you want to associate with someone who worships pain – ow! Damn them! – or disease? It is said that many of the day-dwellers worship no gods at all, but that's not much better, and there is no way of knowing which are which."

Garth finished his cleaning, and rummaged in his pack for the pouch of healing herbs he carried. "Your city has a very complicated way of life. Are kidnappings such as yours common?" He located the herbs, and worked some into the sponge.

"Oh, yes; people disappear all the time."

"Your overlord allows this?" He began rubbing the herbs gently along each cut; the girl cooperated by remaining as still as she could while she answered.

"There is nothing he can do. The bodies are never found, and there is no way of knowing which cult is responsible."

"Then why does he not destroy all those cults that practice human sacrifice?"

"Oh, that must never happen! The gods themselves have chosen Dûsarra; the Dark Gods must have temples here, or there would be a great disaster! Besides, nobody knows which cults have human sacrifices and which don't."

"It would seem obvious," Garth said as he finished spreading on the healing compound, "that the cult of The God Whose Name Is Not Spoken must practice human sacrifice; cannot the overlord at least destroy that one? I have noticed that even in Dûsarra most people want nothing to do with that god."

"There is no cult to destroy; no one worships the Final God but a single old priest. The god himself calls sacrifices to his temple, and no one who has entered the shrine has ever been seen again, except the priest. No one knows what is inside; no traces are ever found. No clothing, no bodies. Whenever a Dûsarran wishes to die, for whatever reason, he merely goes to the god's temple, and when the god is not satisfied with the number of suicides, he turns men mad, so they go to the temple without knowing what they are doing. The overlord would not dare to harm the priest or the temple, for then he himself might be called."

Garth made no further comment on the subject; instead, he said, "I am afraid I cannot properly bandage your wounds; they are too many, and I have not the necessary cloth. I hope they will not trouble you." He sat back to consider his situation, and the information Frima had just given him.

Frima, hesitantly, asked a question of her own. "Who are you? Why did you rescue me?"

"I am Garth of Ordunin, and I came to Dûsarra to steal whatever I found on the seven altars. You were on the altar of Sai, so I am stealing you, and will take you back to Skelleth with me."

"Are you going to ravish me?"

Garth looked at her in surprise. The question explained her behavior when he had stripped off his gambeson for her use, but the ignorance it implied was startling. "I couldn't if I wanted to. We are different species, as different as Koros, here, and an alley cat. Overmen take no interest in anything but overwomen."

"Oh." He was unable to see her blush in the darkness, and would not have understood its significance if he had.

"I am taking you to Skelleth because you were on the altar of Sai; I have no other interest in you." He wondered if her sexual expectations were justified by her appearance; she seemed fairly clean and healthy, with little excess fat but no bones showing, but beyond that he had no more idea of whether she was attractive than a bull would have. Overwomen were as noseless, flat-chested and furry as himself; they relied on scent for stimulation, not appearance, and Frima held no more interest for him than any other animal. He supposed men would like her, although her chest seemed rather overdone even for a human.

She was silent for a few seconds, and then burst out, "I don't want to go to Skelleth! Besides, if you're from Ordunin, why are you taking me somewhere else? And where is Ordunin, anyway? And Skelleth?"

"Ordunin is in the Northern Waste. Skelleth is in Eramma. I have undertaken this task for someone who dwells in Skelleth. I care very little whether you want to go or not, and I suggest you not argue. It was not specified that I bring you back alive." Garth was not seriously annoyed, but merely wanted quiet to think in and spoke harshly to silence the girl. His ploy succeeded; Frima shut up and shrank back into the straw. He had not intended to kill any of the followers of Sai, though he was repulsed by the use of torture and human sacrifice; he hoped the high priest, scum that he was, survived. He regretted snapping the other priest's neck, not so much out of respect for the life lost as because it would undoubtedly please the cult of Aghad. It had been inevitable, though; he had been attacked, and had responded appropriately. Besides, the man's death had cowed the others very nicely.

He had plundered four of the seven altars; three remained, two of them on the Street of the Temples. The robberies of the temples of Tema and Andhur Regvos had not gone particularly well, but would produce no definite identifications; on the other hand, several devotees of Sai and Aghad now knew him on sight, and the Aghadites knew his name as well. Frima claimed that both cults were secret societies, and presumably would not therefore spread their information about, but on the other hand might well try to dispose of him themselves.

This whole affair was getting very complicated.

He had intended to use his room in the inn in the normal manner and sleep in a comfortable bed; he had not done so previously only because he had collapsed from fatigue before he made it that far. However, now that he was definitely a hunted fugitive, even if not readily identifiable to all his pursuers, he decided that that would be a mistake. He would remain here in this stable. It was uncomfortable and uncivilized, but it was where Koros was, and where his loot and his weapons were. No one would be able to sneak up on him while he was guarded by the warbeast. Furthermore, although a siege might be effective, no frontal assault here would be able to defeat both him and his beast; it would be impossible to pour men into the stall in large enough numbers. He knew, with neither false modesty nor overconfidence, that he was capable of handling at least three human warriors at once, and that Koros could deal with twice that number. In a room at the inn, half a dozen men might slip in and kill him; in the stable, with the warbeast beside him, those same men wouldn't have a chance.

Not only that, but by keeping Frima here he avoided any inconvenient questions as to what a human female was doing with an overman – quite aside from her attire.

That reminded him of her current state of undress; he recalled that somewhere in his bundle of supplies he had a spare tunic, intended for social occasions, that would doubtless serve her better than his gambeson. Even should she fail to appreciate it, at the very least he would have padding for his mail once more; it was digging ferociously into his back where he leaned against the wall of the stall.

He reached for his bundle of supplies, and discovered that he could no longer see it; the moon was down, having sunk beneath the horizon while he mused, and the dawn was still an hour or two away. He reached for his flint and steel, only to be reminded by their absence that he had surrendered them to the priests of Andhur Regvos.

Well, the inn would have lanterns, or torches, or some form of portable illumination. "Wait here," he ordered the girl, as he stepped out of the stall.

There was very slightly more light in the stableyard than in the stall, a peculiar reddish light. He looked up, wondering why starlight should be such a color, and discovered that no stars were visible. Clouds had blown up out of the east, and most of the sky was overcast; the reddish glow was the reflected fires of the active volcanoes and the city's torchlit market. The strip of clear sky to the west narrowed as he watched, a vanishing black gap between the stable wall and the encroaching red-gray clouds.

He shrugged. A little rain never hurt anyone. He strode out the arch to the tavern adjoining.

The taproom was not crowded; half a dozen dark-robed customers sat scattered about among the tables. There was no sign of the two serving maids or their brother, but only a middle-aged woman of unhealthy appearance, carrying away empty mugs and replacing them with full ones.

"Ho, there."

She glanced his way, but did not pause until she had dealt with her current batch of ale; that properly distributed, she wound her way through the chairs, shoving them under appropriate tables as she went, until she stood in front of the overman.

"And how may I aid you, sir?"

"Have you a lantern? I would tend to my mount, but the light is inadequate."

"A lantern? Not for sale."

"Could I borrow one, then? I can pay."

She shrugged. "As you please." She departed, winding her way across the room again to vanish through a door at the back. A moment later she emerged again, a shuttered lantern in her hand. Garth took it, thanked her, dropped a coin in her palm and left; he failed to notice the steady gaze of one of the patrons studying him, and was out of sight through the stable's arch when the same man also departed, walking quickly in the direction of the temple of Tema.

Chapter Fifteen

Frima didn't think much of the tunic. It was scarcely longer than the gambeson, and she insisted there was a cold draft on her shins despite the fact that Garth could not feel a breath of air. Further, it was embroidered in red and gold, as was appropriate for a Prince of Ordunin on formal occasions, and she seemed to consider such adornment a sign of decadence. She pointed out that no Dûsarran wore any garment with more than a single color to it, and although the midnight-blue of the tunic was perfectly acceptable, she found the bright trimmings utterly appalling.

Garth let her complain, so long as she wore the thing and returned his padding. He pointed out that he preferred to have her look like a foreigner; she replied that she hadn't known foreigners were so tasteless.

Despite her complaints, Frima donned the tunic. Garth, meanwhile, returned his gambeson to its proper place beneath his mail, tossed aside the hilt of his sword and its now-useless scabbard, and tied his battle-axe to his back. He wished he had thought to bring a second cloak. It was something he would do on any future adventures; that, and a spare pair of boots. He felt very exposed wandering the streets wearing armor openly, as if he were inviting attack; it seemed though that he had no choice. He also thought that carrying the axe was inviting trouble, but it was undoubtedly safer than going unarmed.

Besides, he relied on the fact that the humans would not expect a fugitive to walk openly in their midst.

He had no real plans at this point; he still had three temples to rob, but he was tired and hungry and had a captive to take care of. It occurred to him that he should have gotten food while in the tavern getting the lantern. He stood, and leaned over the door of the stall, peering through the arch at the street.

A pedestrian passed by, and a second later an oxcart followed. There was a hint of dawn in the eastern sky, visible only as a slightly paler shade of gray in the cloud-cover, but present nonetheless. Dugger the stable-boy was gone, and presumably one of his daytime compatriots would show up at any minute; Garth had no desire to waste more money bribing them to silence as he had Dugger. He decided he did not care to venture forth just now, and instead found his meager remaining supply of provisions, left over from his journey.

Frima looked dubiously at the strips of dried meat and the handful of berries he offered her, but took them and ate them; he ate his fill likewise, and washed the unappetizing fare down with the metallic-tasting water from his one remaining canteen, leaving enough for his prisoner to do the same. He was surprised when she made no complaint; it was just as well, though, as she would probably be eating more of the same throughout the long ride back to Skelleth.

His hunger assuaged, he sat back and contemplated whether he would do better to tackle the remaining shrines by daylight or at night; after some thought, he decided he simply didn't have enough information, and asked Frima her opinion.

"Would it be safer to rob the altars of P'hul and Bheleu by night or day, girl?"

Frima, who had said nothing since she stopped complaining about her new garb, answered, "I don't know."

"The worshippers live by day, but their ceremonies are held at night, correct?"

"Yes."

"What of the priests? When do they sleep?"

"I don't know. Perhaps they have no need to sleep at all."

"Everyone, human or overman, needs to sleep."

It seemed plain the girl was to be of no use in deciding. It appeared to him that the priests must sleep during the day, and that therefore that would be the optimum time to make his attempt, but if he were seen abroad in daylight he would be inviting retaliation from the cult of Sai.

Of course, at night he was risking the revenge of Tema and Andhur Regvos.

It was no use; he was unable to decide on such a basis. He considered instead what he would do if he did not choose to rob another temple immediately.

Obviously, he would sleep.

Did he want to sleep?

Well, yes, now that the subject came up, he realized he was quite weary and could use a nap. He would take one, and when he woke up he would go rob the next temple.

The matter finally decided, he announced, "We will sleep now." Without waiting to see what Frima thought of this, he stretched himself out as best he could on the straw and fell soundly asleep.

Frima did not immediately follow his example, but instead sat and reviewed the events of the night just ending and the one before it. She had been tending her father's shop while he attended the regular moonlight ceremony at the temple when three large men had entered, claiming a pot they had bought there had a faulty seam; she had known that they were lying, for her father was undoubtedly the best tinker in Dûsarra, but had looked at the pot anyway, and found herself gagged, then grabbed, then bound, and carried off in a sack over one man's shoulder. She had spent the following day in a small, cramped cell somewhere, but had been too frightened to sleep for a long time, even though it was obviously after dawn; when at last she had dozed off, it was to be rudely awakened by the same three men, who removed not merely her bonds but her clothes as well, before dragging her, struggling all the way, to the altar of Sai.

She had known, from the instant that the gag was pressed into her mouth, that she was being kidnapped by one of the day-dweller cults; it was a familiar concept, a traditional childhood fear, suddenly become much too real. She had had no real hope of escape; nobody ever escaped from the temples. Instead she had tried to behave properly, as befit a true follower of the night-goddess and the daughter of the city's best tinker. And then, when the ceremony was well under way and she was paying attention to nothing but the pain from the cutting of the priest's knife, this great red-eyed, bloody-handed monster had appeared and freed her.

She was familiar with overmen; every so often one would come to the shop, to buy a belt-buckle or have a harness repaired, never to buy the pots and kettles that were her father's pride. They spoke rudely and carried swords, and had faces like Death himself – or at least like Bheleu, as represented in the little idols she had seen in the marketplace. She did not like overmen; they were big and dangerous and mysterious, and it was said that they laughed at the gods yet were not struck down, which implied some sorcerous might, although she had never heard of an overman magician.

But then an overman had rescued her, and she suddenly owed her life to an inhuman monster. This creature casually snapped a man's neck with one hand and spoke of killing her as if she were no more than one of the dogs that prowled the alleys, but then fed and clothed her and bathed her wounds. He even declined to rape her; she didn't seriously believe his statement that he couldn't. She was, in fact, still virgin; the high priest of Sai was to have ravished her as part of the sacrificial ceremony, a part that had not yet been reached when she was rescued. Her three captors had not dared to usurp the priest's privilege.

Further, Garth spoke to her in a perfectly civil manner, more so than any overman she had met before, and did not strike her, but merely threatened. Then when he spoke, he claimed to be from some semi-mythical wasteland and said that he planned to take her to someplace in the forbidden land of Eramma, whether she wanted to go or not. It was all very confusing. Overmen came from the Yprian Coast, and rode oxen or great horses, not huge black panthers.

She found the whole affair incomprehensible and was unsure of her feelings toward Garth. He had kidnapped her, but saved her from death; he had threatened her life, but now lay sleeping peacefully a few feet away, trusting her with his own life. What was to prevent her from escaping, or even killing him with his own weapons? She stood.

A low growl reached her, and she sat down again very quickly. She had thought that the huge black beast was asleep, but it was watching her now, its golden eyes gleaming in the pale morning light that filtered dimly in. She stared back.

It blinked, then casually lowered its head and appeared to go to sleep once again.

She stared for a moment longer, then relaxed. There was no point in arguing with the monster. Still thoroughly confused, she settled back, realized that she was in fact exhausted, and fell asleep.

She slept uneasily, and when Garth had rested enough to take the edge off his fatigue, he was awakened by her thrashing about. At first he did not remember his situation very clearly and his hand instinctively went to his axe, but he recalled himself in time to avoid smashing the girl's skull.

It was midmorning; he had slept four or five hours. Frima had not, having kept herself awake until after dawn, and he saw no reason to wake her. Unsettled though she might be, her troubled sleep was probably better for her than no rest at all. Garth suspected it was the discomfort of the dozens of unbandaged slashes that kept her from resting easily; he regretted that he had not been able to bandage them properly – assuming, of course, that she would have allowed it – but at least he had done what he could.

Although he could have used more rest himself, he decided against going back to sleep. Instead he got to his feet and brushed off the straw that stuck to his mail; then he slung his axe on his back, stuffed a sack under his belt and, with a calming word to Koros, left the stall.

Heretofore, all his crimes had been committed at night; he hoped that undertaking his next in broad daylight would make it that much more unexpected. It is to a fugitive's advantage to be unpredictable.

One of the two stable-boys he had spoken with the preceding day sat in the archway, whittling carelessly at a scrap of wood with an old table knife; he showed no sign that he was aware of Garth's presence. That was fine with Garth; for the first time, he gave serious consideration to finding some other way out of the stableyard.

The sun was faintly visible, well up in the eastern sky, but obscured by a layer of cloud. Elsewhere the clouds were thicker, and nowhere was the sky any color but gray. Any lingering glow from the volcanoes was submerged in the more powerful drabness of the daylight. It was not raining, but puddles on the packed dirt showed that it had been while Garth slept.

He looked about, studying anew the double row of stalls, the blank wall, the open arch. There was no exit at ground level except the arch. There was no truly compelling reason not to use it. The stable-boy was certainly no threat in and of himself.

Garth looked at the lad again, who was still intent on his lackadaisical carving; it was the boy who had been the more belligerent of the two, who had demanded he explain why he carried a sword. It occurred to him that the boy might think it strange that he no longer carried the blade.

Garth decided he did not want the boy to see him. He did not want anyone to see him leaving the stable; he did not want to make his connection with this place any better known than it already was. Quite aside from logic, he was emotionally and intuitively displeased by the idea. His position had become so complicated that its logic was beyond him, and he resolved instead to rely on his instincts. Accordingly, he found himself another way of leaving the stable.

There was no alternative at ground level unless he wanted to knock out a wall; he had not the time to burrow his way out. That left one direction – up. He swung open the broad door of Koros' stall until it stood out perpendicular to its closed position; it projected out from beneath the roof of the stable. He tested its strength; although it was not as solid as he might have desired, it was adequate. Using the door as a steppingstone, he vaulted upward so that his head, arms, and chest were above the level of the roof's edge; he caught himself, then crawled upward until his full weight rested on the wet red tiles.

He was very pleased to note that he had made the ascent with a minimum of clatter; the lack of his scabbarded sword was an advantage in that respect. He drew himself carefully upright, being sure not to put his full weight upon any part of the roof until he had tested it sufficiently, then surveyed his position.

The roof he was standing on was about ten feet wide and fifty long, sloping toward the stableyard; on the far side of the yard was another virtually identical to it, and the two were connected at either end by a narrow wall, which looked wide and strong enough to walk on if it became necessary – but not if it remained unnecessary. Beyond the other roof was the wall of the upper story or stories of the Inn of the Seven Stars; along the upper edge of the roof he stood on was a blank wall of gray stone, extending upward at least twenty feet. He wondered what it was; he had not noticed from the street what building occupied that position, and the featureless expanse gave no clue. There was no exit in that direction. The wall was too high to leap, and he was not a very good climber.

On the opposite side the stone wall of the inn was spotted with windows, half a dozen of them, but all, he was happy to see, shuttered; there was no danger of being noticed by the occupants of those rooms, and having his presence on the roof questioned. That wall was lower; the windows were all in a single tier, and he judged the distance between the roof of the stable and the roof of the inn to be no more than a dozen feet, probably less. The inn's roof was constructed of the same tile as that on which he stood, but was much, much steeper, and there were at least two skylights visible between the chimneypots. There was no exit by that route, either. At the one end, beyond the wall, lay the open street. That left only one direction unexplored; he could not see what lay beyond the blank wall at the stable's inner end. Though the upper stories of other buildings were visible beyond, there was a definite gap immediately behind that wall.

He made his way carefully along the sloping surface, trying to avoid dislodging any of the battered tiles, until he stood within a pace of the edge. He peered over and found himself looking into a small enclosed yard, strewn with garbage and half-flooded by the morning's rain. An unpleasant odor drifted faintly to his slit nostrils.

The far side of the yard was filled by a simple two-story structure, apparently an ordinary house; on either hand walls five or six feet high separated it from similar patches of earth, though due to the angle of his vision he could not see much of either, despite the height of his perch. The left-hand yard was, as far as he could see, cleaner than the central one; of the right-hand yard he could not even see that much.

He paused to consider, and glanced back at the stableyard; from his elevated position he could see that the abandoned trough where he had burned his cloak now held an inch or so of murky rainwater, black with the ashes of his garment.

There was no reason to bother crossing over to the right-hand yard; of the other two, both were accessible from the roof he was on. The central yard spanned the stable yard and perhaps half of each of the roofed-over stables; the left-hand yard extended across the remaining four or five feet.

The left-hand yard would be a longer drop, being below the higher portion of the roof; therefore, he made his way to the bottom corner, where the gray stone of the wall extended out from beneath the red tiles, lowered himself over the outer edge, and let himself drop.

He landed with a splash, and immediately felt water seeping into his right boot through the puncture made by the obsidian in the forecourt of Sai's temple; it was cold and sluggish, probably made up of filthy mud as much as water. He wished he knew how to curse, as humans did; he tried muttering the names of a few gods but it provided no relief, and he growled instead.

It was hard to judge accurately the depth of the water, because his boots sank into the mud beneath the weight of his armored body; there was at least an inch, though.

He slogged across the little court, his boots thrusting aside decaying fruit peels and muck-coated old bones, and climbed onto a stone doorstep that rose above the water; he could feel the water draining slowly from his ruined boot, leaving a slimy residue and a wet lining.

The door was centered in the wall. There were two narrow windows on either side, all dark and curtained, but with their shutters open. That implied that there was someone somewhere within, but most likely not in these rearmost rooms. He tried the latch. It yielded, and he leaned on the door. It did not yield.

A wordless noise of annoyance burst from him. He leaned harder, letting his left foot fall back into the befouled water the better to brace himself.

The door still did not yield, and in a burst of anger Garth lifted his axe over his head and swung it at the recalcitrant barrier. Splinters flew. He struck again, and felt the blade slice through into the space beyond. The door was not unreasonably thick.

He pulled the axe free and let it dangle loosely in his right fist as he leaned to peer through the crack he had made.

The room beyond was dark, and he could see nothing. He stood back, and swung the axe again; the wood of the door gave, bursting inward, leaving two wide gaps. He slung the axe on his back once again and ripped out the broken wood between the two slits, giving him an opening wide enough to get his hand through. He reached in and, as he had expected, found that the door was barred; the bar lay only a few inches below the opening, and it was no great feat of dexterity to lift it free and let it drop to the floor inside.

It occurred to him that he was making a great deal of noise, yet so far no one had appeared to question him; luck was apparently with him. It did not occur to him that he might have made less noise going in through one of the windows. He worked the latch and pushed on the door again.

It still did not open. He pressed harder, and it bowed inward but remained closed. There were other bars; judging by the way the door bent, one near the top and one near the bottom.

His patience, which had been in very short supply since his embarrassing display of ineffectuality in the temple of Aghad, ran out, and with a roar he freed his axe again and swung it horizontally into the wood. Splinters sprayed, and a large chunk of one of the boards that made up the door snapped off and fell with a loud splash into the murky water. He struck again, with no thought or care as to the effects of his blow, and the blade wedged itself into the wood, scattering more shards. He ripped it free, bringing most of a plank with it, and let it hang from one hand again while the other reached through the greatly enlarged hole.

He could feel the upper bar, but his forearm was not long enough to allow him to dislodge it; he withdrew, then thrust the other hand in, and used the axe to knock the bar away. It fell with even more noise than the first. He felt for the third bar, and hooked it upward with the corner of his weapon; its fall could scarcely be heard. Then, still angry, and with his hand and axe still thrust within, he tried the latch again.

The door opened a few inches.

He withdrew his hand and slammed the door aside; its shaken frame gave way when it struck the wall behind it, and collapsed, twisting out of shape and leaving a disarrayed mass of tangled wood, rather than a door, hanging from the bent hinges.

Ignoring it, Garth stepped inside.

He was in a small kitchen; a stone sink stood against one wall, and tables and cabinets abounded. There was no sign of life, but it was reasonably clean, with no accumulation of dust; the house was not abandoned. Perhaps the owner was deaf; Garth could not imagine any other reason not to investigate such noise as he had just made, if the occupant were there at all and capable of movement.

Perhaps he or she had gone out and not bothered to close the shutters; perhaps he was bedridden. In any case, Garth was not particularly concerned; he had merely wanted some other route out of the stable. He crossed the kitchen, and strode through the open archway that led to a large front room. Unlike the kitchen, this room was the full width of the house, about twenty feet; it was slightly longer than that from front to back, and the low ceiling made it appear even broader. Garth found that he had to stoop. The kitchen had allowed him to stand upright so long as he avoided the beams that supported the upper floor, but this larger room had a plank ceiling.

There was a door in the wall behind him, which he guessed led to a storeroom of some sort beside the kitchen, and along the left-hand wall a stairway led to the upper level. Assorted chairs, rugs, and tables were scattered about; a broad hearth and massive fireplace occupied the right wall. The far side had two wide bow windows, with curtains drawn across them, and a heavy oaken door between.

He crossed to the door, drew the lockbolt, and opened it slightly, peering out; it appeared to be a residential neighborhood, with no shops or public buildings visible. He opened the door and stepped out.

The sun had broken through the clouds; the street was deserted. He closed the door behind him but left it unlocked, and headed to his right, the direction he judged would best bring him to the Street of the Temples.

Chapter Sixteen

He had been very fortunate in emerging on an empty street; he found few others as he made his way across Dûsarra, but somehow he reached his goal without being accosted. Several people had cast curious gazes in his direction and a mutter of conversation had frequently followed him, but no one had dared to stop him. Now, he strode openly along the Street of the Temples, hoping his luck would hold.

He was approaching a temple, the third from the overlord's palace; it loomed before him, a huge cube of black stone, dotted with dark windows and topped by a broad dome. Seven shallow steps led to its open portals; there were no gates, no courtyard, no indication which deity was worshipped here. He was only a few paces from the bottom step when someone behind him cried, "Hold, overman!"

He hastened his pace, hurrying up the steps; he heard running feet somewhere behind him as he stepped through the doorway into an antechamber.

The room was small, with a wooden floor that gave dangerously beneath his feet, and walls hung with moldering, faded tapestries. He wondered briefly if the place was abandoned; since the daylight cults were secret, one might have died out without anyone knowing it.

There was a door in the inner wall with a rusty iron handle; Garth grabbed it, only to have it crumble in his grasp. He raised a fist to pound on the door, in hope that someone would admit him; to his astonishment, the door burst inward at his first blow, its hinges screaming in protest. Dust flew up in clouds, and a paroxysm of coughing overtook him, but he managed to stumble through. As he did, he realized there were no further sounds of pursuit behind him; instead, a voice exclaimed in dismay, "We can't go in there!"

He stopped. If he were not pursued, there as no need for haste. He wiped the dust from his stinging eyes and looked about.

The door he had entered through stood beside him, and it was immediately obvious why it had yielded so quickly; it had been eaten away from within by termites and rot, so that his blow had merely finished their work. The latch that had held it remained where it was, rusted to the frame, and the wood had turned to powder around it, so that the door's edge now had a gaping hole in it.

He was in a room perhaps fifteen feet across and twenty feet long; like the antechamber, and unlike any of the other temples he had yet visited, it was floored in wood, wood which sagged visibly at the center beneath the weight of a thick carpet. The walls, too, were wooden, except for one end; that was stone and obviously one of the temple's outer walls, since three narrow windows pierced it, providing the chamber with light.

The room's ceiling was upholstered in silk, silk that was discolored with half a hundred old and new stains, that was black with rot in spots. Like the floor, it sagged in the center. Cobwebs hung from every corner.

There were furnishings; two ornate tables adorned the far wall, flanking a doorway, and an assortment of faded, dusty chairs were strewn about.

Over everything hung the smell, the stench of rot, mold, and decay; Garth suddenly felt quite certain he knew which temple he had entered.

He took a cautious step forward into the room; the floor creaked ominously, and new odors of corruption assailed his nostrils. He put a hand on a wood-paneled wall, only to snatch it away quickly when he felt the wood start to give; like the door, it was riddled by worms and rot. There could be no doubt that this was the shrine of P'hul, goddess of decay.

"Greetings, stranger." The soft voice came from somewhere to his right; the usual guttural Dûsarran accent was modified by a curious lisp. He turned, to see that a gray-robed figure had entered the room.

He started to speak, but stopped as the figure threw back its hood, revealing the reason for the lisp.

"Is something wrong?" The priestess' voice was solicitous.

"No. I was just startled."

The woman's lower lip was a twisted mass of oozing, festering flesh, and much of her face and neck was swollen and shapeless; one of her hands lacked a finger. Garth recognized the human disease of leprosy and shuddered slightly. His pursuers had had reasons other than religious respect for declining to enter this place.

The priestess smiled, the friendly expression made hideous by her affliction. "Of course. It is customary that the servants of P'hul bear her handiwork upon their flesh, but I suppose it might well startle those not accustomed to such sights. Why have you come? What brings a healthy overman to the temple of decay?" Garth noticed that she was aware of her lisp, and struggled particularly hard to be sure she pronounced the name of her goddess correctly. He felt a twinge of pity.

"I was merely curious."

"I am surprised. We see few strangers here. How may I help to satisfy your curiosity?"

"Tell me of your goddess, if you would." Garth was not particularly interested in learning about P'hul, but he wanted time to think, and guessed that the priestess, absorbed as she was with her beliefs, would be quite willing to talk for hours about them with only minimal encouragement. Where he would have raised suspicion by questioning her on more mundane matters, he was sure that in the enthusiasm of the true believer she would not find anything strange in his willingness to listen to endless blather about her religion.

"If you wish, gladly! I am sure you know the basic nature of P'hul; she is the cause and essence of all disease and decay throughout our world. She ages us all, she makes us easy prey for death, so that the old will make way for the young. She turns the leaves from green to brown, pulls them from the trees, and makes them rot, so that they will feed the earth. She eats away fruit, that the seeds within may flourish. By plague and disease, she removes the unfit and unworthy. The worms of the earth and the lowly insects serve her, devouring all that she gives them, and in turn they feed the birds of the sky and the beasts of the field. She is the handmaiden of death."

As the priestess spoke, her words distorted by her lisp, Garth thought back over recent events; it struck him suddenly that he had been behaving recklessly, almost idiotically, since leaving the temple of Aghad. Marching openly into the temple of Sai had been foolish, even if it had allowed him to save an innocent life. He had not planned well there; even his fight with the priests had been mismanaged, as he should have been able to overpower all three without killing any.

"There are those who say that death is the great evil of our world," the priestess went on, "and that if P'hul serves him, then she must likewise be evil. That is not so; death would exist regardless of P'hul. The goddess readies us for his touch; is it not better to die old and weary, than to be cut down while still healthy and vigorous?"

His behavior this morning had been even more erratic. There had been no reason to go leaping about on the roof, smashing down the doors of unsuspecting citizens, and so forth. He had merely been responding to the repressed anger that still seethed within him, using up as much energy as possible and finding excuses to destroy anything handy.

"Knowing that one must die after a set number of years, is it not better to know that death will come as the end of a decline, a surcease from decay, than to see it strike abruptly while one is still strong? Our lives are thus in balance, with the ascent from infancy countered by the descent into senescence. Aal, the Eir-Lord of growth, is P'hul's twin and counter; neither could exist without the other. Aal dominates our youth, P'hul our age."

Obviously, he was still resentful of the helplessness he had felt in the temple of Aghad.

"In order that there be growth, there must be decay; for there to be new, the old must make way, else the world would be buried beneath growing things."

It was plain that his effective exile from his homeland at the hands of the Baron of Skelleth, through that stupid oath he had so foolishly taken, still rankled.

"Yet still, even granting the necessity of decay, why should we worship the goddess?"

Buried still deeper, he knew, was anger at the Forgotten King, who treated him like a foolish child and manipulated him like a marionette, and at the

Wise Women of Ordunin, the trusted oracle that had first sent him to Skelleth.

"Because we see the underlying beauty in her works; because we perceive that decay brings peace, and that contentment can be found therein. She provides an end to struggling against our inevitable fate, and a surcease from care."

All, of course, were symptoms of his anger at his own helplessness, his resentment of his insignificance in the cosmos; it was his inability to reshape the world as he chose that underlay his rage at all these manifestations of his lack of omnipotence.

"Every farmer prays to Aal; every parent of growing children worships him. He has no need of the service of such lowly creatures as ourselves amid this flood of adulation. Yet without his sister he would be nothing, and we choose to give her the recognition she deserves, as best we can, in response to her marks upon us."

Early in the priestess' lisping dissertation, she and Garth had both seated themselves upon the nearest chairs; the priestess had ignored the cloud of dust that rose from the cushions, and Garth had tried to do the same even as he hoped that the moldering seat would support his weight. Now the servant of P'hul leaned forward, her chair creaking beneath her, and asked, "Do you have any questions?"

"I . . ." Garth had not yet given any thought to the matter on hand, that being how he was to rob the altar; he stalled, asking a question he was only vaguely interested in. "I have heard that this is the Thirteenth Age of the world, the Age of Decay, and as such it is ruled by P'hul. Could you explain this? Do not all the gods prevail over their own concerns in every age?"

"Yes, of course they do. The ages of the world are little more than a theory worked out by the theologians, philosophers, and astrologers, yet they seem to apply in some ways. I do not understand how they are determined, but it is said that certain signs mark each era. Our own age has been one of declining population, fading wealth, and loss of knowledge, and thus is credited as the Age of P'hul, since these are the symptoms of a decay of mankind – and overmankind – as a whole, just as P'hul's diseases cause the decay of individuals. The theologians say that this is because during this age P'hul is at the height of her power, while those gods equal to or greater than herself are resting, or somehow weakened. Decay progresses faster than growth; but there is still growth, and when this age ends the balance between P'hul and Aal will be restored, and some other deity will temporarily rise above the cosmic balance.

"The astrologers say that the age is ending even now; that the Fourteenth Age may in fact have already begun, or if not it will soon arrive."

That caught Garth's attention; months earlier, the Forgotten King had told him that it was hopeless to try and halt the spread of death and decline while the Age of P'hul lasted. If it were in truth ending, perhaps there were better times ahead, an era in which great things could be accomplished.

"What will the Fourteenth Age be? What god will predominate?"

"I do not know. The Twelfth Age was the Age of Aghad, marked by great wars and great betrayals, and much of the world's history was lost in that period, which lasted much longer than the three centuries of P'hul's dominance, so that although scholars may know something of the Eleventh Age, I do not.

Thus I cannot see any pattern. Perhaps it is time for one of the Eir, the Lords of Life, to flourish; although I serve a Lady of the Dûs, I would not regret such a change."

"Might not any god rule? I have heard of gods who were not of the Dûs, nor, I believe, of the Eir."

"Such gods, if they exist, are but lesser beings – except for Dagha, of course. There are the seven Dûs, the seven Eir, and the God of Time who created them all; these are the fifteen great gods, and you may be sure that one of these will represent the world's new age."

"This is the Thirteenth Age; the Fourteenth is soon to begin; but there are only fifteen of these higher gods. What will happen when each has ruled for an age?"

"Perhaps they will start over."

Garth sat back and considered that. The whole system sounded rather haphazard; ages of varying length, in no known order? Only fifteen possible rulers? Interesting as it might be, and despite the seeming appropriateness of describing the last three centuries as an age of decay and the period ending in the Racial Wars as an age of hatred, he decided the whole system was just another human exercise in meaningless theorizing. After all, men could not even prove the existence of a single one of their myriad deities; how, then, could any trust be put in a system based on those gods? Besides, if this was currently the Thirteenth Age, then long ago there must have been a First Age; what came before that? He shook his head.

"I am confused. Perhaps you could show me your temple while I digest this new knowledge."

"If you wish." The priestess rose; Garth followed her example, pleased that she was being so cooperative. Any tour of the temple must surely include its altar.

The gray-robed woman led him through a creaking, cobwebbed door into a dim wood-floored passage hung with ragged, decaying tapestries; he was surprised to see several doors opening to either side. This temple was much more elaborate than some.

"These are the study chambers of our scholars," his guide explained. She opened a door, apparently at random, revealing a small room, little more than a cell, lined with shelves that sagged beneath the weight of hundreds of books, scrolls, and papers, and illuminated by a single miniscule window. A narrow desk stood in the center, with a single rickety chair behind it; more papers were spread out upon it, held in place by a human skull that served as a paperweight.

"The skull is just a reminder of the mortality of mankind," the priestess explained.

"How is it that your . . . that you maintain such scholars? I have seen no sign of such learning elsewhere in Dûsarra."

"It is the way of our faith. The more we know of the world, the more we know of the gods who created it; and the more we know of the gods, the better we are able to serve our goddess. I have heard that there are many scholars among the followers of Aghad, though perhaps that is more from a wish to harm mankind than to serve the gods; and there is a splendid library in the temple of Tema. The priests of Regvos, of course, are unable to read. The priests of Bheleu have not the patience for study. Of the cults of Sai and the Final God I know nothing."

As she spoke the priestess led her guest away from the uninhabited scholar's cubicle, closing the door behind her. At the end of the passage, ignoring another corridor that ran perpendicularly to the first, she started up a narrow spiral staircase of rusty iron that swayed unsteadily beneath the weight of the two. Garth inquired where the bypassed corridor went.

"The dormitory," she replied.

"Have you some reason not to show me that?"

"I did not think it would interest you; our accommodations are simple. Besides, most of my fellow servants of P'hul are asleep at present, and I did not wish to disturb them. Are we not entitled to our rest and privacy, as much as ordinary people? Our diseases make us outcasts, but we are still human."

"Of course; I meant no offense. Your ceremonies are at night, then?"

"Oh, yes. The Lords of Dûs are, after all, the dark gods; all are nocturnal, whatever the habits of their worshippers." As she said this she emerged from the shaky spiral and waited for the overman to join her.

They stood in a fair-sized antechamber, its far wall dominated by a vast double door; either end was of wood, hung with rotting remnants of cloth so far gone in decay that Garth was unsure whether they had originally been banners, tapestries, or something else. The staircase was in a curved niche in the rear wall, which was of unadorned black basalt, pierced by three narrow lancet windows. The priestess crossed the room with an assured, easy stride, which Garth took note of. The woman might be diseased, but as yet the sickness had not seriously weakened her; she moved as well as most humans. Garth could not guess her age; she was well out of adolescence, beyond doubt, and had not yet acquired the white hair and stooped posture of extreme age, but beyond that he could not see any indication of her years. The ruination of her countenance erased any wrinkles that might otherwise have provided a clue.

She swung open the great doors and the pair stepped into the chamber beyond.

Garth found it necessary to hold his breath until the dust had subsided somewhat.

The chamber seemed vast, larger than it actually was; it extended up the full remaining height of the temple and included the entire inside of the dome. It was approximately square, about forty feet on a side, but its dimensions were distorted by smoke and dust swimming thick in the stagnant air. Dim colored light seeped through dirt-caked stained glass, painting murky patterns on the worn wooden floor and on the intricately carved railings that adorned three tiers of balconies. These extended completely around all sides. A brighter patch of untinted light flooded the center of the room, pouring from a ring of windows at the base of the dome; in the middle of this circle stood the altar, Garth saw hazily. The brilliant sunlight lit it in a blaze of splendor, but simultaneously obscured it behind a wall of equally well-lit cobwebs, incense smoke, and drifting dust.

The altar was a broad, square platform, raised two or three feet off the floor, built of carven wood, its sides upholstered in silk, its edges clad in corroded copper thick with verdigris; the top had strips of faded, moldering carpeting along each side, and a square of plain mahogany in the center.

There was nothing upon it except a thick layer of dust.

Garth stared at it resentfully.

"This, of course, is the temple sanctuary. It is here that we perform our rituals, affirming our devotion to the goddess, asking her to remember us and deal mercifully with us."

She paused, expecting Garth to comment; the room was beautiful, or had been once, and she seemed sure the overman would appreciate this. He, however, was not paying complete attention, and said nothing. Unsure whether this was rudeness, or whether he was too taken by the room to respond, she added, "Many of us like to come here often, aside from the ceremonies, and simply enjoy it."

Garth recovered himself. "Forgive me. I was distracted." He looked at the rest of the room: the webstrewn galleries, the cracked and dirtied colored windows, the smoke-softened column of sunlight. Despite the universal decay, the room was lovely, warm and inviting; perhaps the decay even helped, softening harsh colors, rounding sharp edges, blurring the flaws. It struck him that there was something very strange about such beauty in such a place. Should not the temple of decay be foul and malodorous? Should it not be slimy and rotting?

"It is not what I had expected," he said truthfully, when he saw that the priestess was still awaiting some comment.

"Oh?"

"No. I . . . I had thought there would be an idol."

"Perhaps there was, once; much of the original interior fell to dust long ago. As is inevitable for our faith, every part of the temple has been refurbished at least once; since we are required to use only perishable materials and to do what we can to promote their decay, eventually they fall away completely and must be replaced if the temple's usefulness is to continue. Save for the stone and some of the glass, I doubt any of the present structure is more than four or five centuries old."

"Four or five . . ." Garth was dumbfounded; his native city of Ordunin was less than three hundred and fifty years old, the most ancient surviving overman community. "How old is the temple?"

"Oh, it's only about two or three thousand years old, but of course it's not the original either; there has been a temple of P'hul ever since Dûsarra was founded."

"When was that?"

"Nobody really knows."

"Oh." It had not occurred to Garth that the city, or any city, could be more than two thousand years old. He struggled to accept such a concept.

"In any case, there has been no idol in my lifetime."

"Oh." Garth had hoped to somehow bring the conversation to the empty altar unobtrusively, but seemed to be meeting with no success – although these digressions were informative. He decided that a more direct approach was in order.

"I see your altar is empty, while the other temples in the city keep precious objects or ceremonial devices there."

"I know nothing of what the others do. We keep nothing upon the altar. It serves merely as a centerpiece for our rituals. Supplicants sometimes pray atop it; it is said such prayers are especially heeded."

"Has there ever been anything kept upon it, then?"

"Not that I know of, save for the dust; that, of course, is everywhere. Why do you ask?"

Garth saw no reason to deny the truth. "I was asked – by a philosopher of sorts – to see if I could obtain what stood upon your altar."

"Oh, I see." She smiled, the expression all the more horrible in the wash of green light that fell across her from a nearby window. "It must have been a surprise to see it empty."

"Yes, it was."

"You are welcome to take the dust, if you wish."

"Thank you; I appreciate this courtesy."

"It makes no difference to us; we sweep off the altar every few months anyway."

"Oh." Garth pulled the bag from his belt and looked at it dubiously; it was of a moderately coarse weave. It was quite likely it wouldn't hold dust very well.

But then, how much could that matter? It was, all in all, only dust. He knew nothing of magicks, but surely dust was dust. Feeling foolish, he scraped up a heap of dust from the altar, gray fluff of no distinction whatsoever, and stuffed it into the bag. That done, he knotted it shut and shoved it back under his belt.

"Thank you," he said again.

"Is that all you came for, then?"

"Yes."

"So I have spoken to no purpose?"

Garth did not like the tone of the priestess' voice. "I have found your words very interesting, woman. Do not feel that you have wasted your time."

"Have I not?"

"No. This visit has been most informative, truly."

"It may be more than that, of course." Her smile had returned.

"How mean you?"

"You have been in our temple for some time; perhaps the hand of the goddess is already upon you."

"What do you mean?"

"All those who serve P'hul here bear her signs; her priests are the senile, the diseased, those with leprosy and cancer and tuberculosis and all the other wasting sicknesses. The very air of this shrine is rich in disease. You have spoken at length with a leper, where most men flee from my slightest touch. It is very likely that you already carry some illness within you; if not my own, then one of the others."

Garth said nothing; he felt a brief instant of panic, but suppressed it immediately, reminding himself that, despite what this creature might believe, no overman had ever contracted leprosy. Nor were most other diseases worth his concern; very few human diseases could affect overmen, and those that could were either not contagious, or of the more virulent and fast-acting sort, not wasting sicknesses. Overmen had their own ills.

"Shall I escort you out, then? You have what you came for."

"I am in no hurry. I do not wish to offend your goddess by so quickly shunning her shrine."

"Truly? Perhaps I have wronged you in my thoughts."

Garth shrugged.

There was a sound behind them; both turned to see a bent, shuffling figure at the head of the stair, on the far side of the antechamber beyond the still-open doors.

It was a man, clad in the soft gray robes of a priest of P'hul; he was shriveled with age and moved slowly, as if in pain. His hair was white and unkempt, straggling down about his face, tangling indistinguishably with his beard. He blinked at the overman and the priestess.

"Greetings, Tiris. This overman is a visitor to our temple." The priestess spoke loudly, slowly, enunciating every word as carefully as she could with her deformed lip. The old man shuffled nearer; she said softly to Garth, "His hearing is poor. Tiris is the oldest of our priests; he is said to have the special favor of the goddess, to see things that others do not."

Garth was not impressed. He had seen enough of humanity to suspect that men and women were far more gullible than his own people; age and a mysterious manner could be sufficient to create the reputation of a so – called wizard. He could not deny that true wizards existed and that magic was abroad in the world; he had been confronted with the real thing on several occasions. That did not mean that he was willing to bow before every crazed old man with a trick or two on hand. He said politely, "Greetings, Tiris."

The old man stopped and studied Garth thoroughly with squinting blue eyes. Suddenly, in a voice that did not shake, a voice that was far stronger than the man's withered form seemed capable of holding, he announced, "Greetings, Bheleu."

Chapter Seventeen

For a moment no one moved; Garth and the priestess were too startled, and the old man had apparently exhausted himself. Then Garth said, "I am not Bheleu; I am called Garth of Ordunin."

Tiris shrugged and said, "As you please."

Garth was irritated, but tried not to show it. It seemed plain to him that the old man had confused him with the idols of Bheleu that were sold in the market; perhaps the senile old fool was not even aware that he was an overman, but assumed the idols depicted a unique being, in which case his bizarre error seemed almost reasonable. He considered pointing out that, quite aside from the absurdity of casually meeting a god in a temple not his own, he carried no sword and wore no helmet, but it would do no good, he decided.

The priestess was edging away from him. He found that amusing; a leper, the most shunned creature in all the world, avoiding an ordinary overman because an old man called him by a god's name.

"I assure you, I am no god."

"As you please. Whatever you are, you are beloved of our goddess; if you are not her brother lord, you are his representative. The Age of Bheleu begins tonight, you know; you have come just in time."

"In time? In time for what?"

"To receive P'hul's service. Her power wanes as her age ends, yet she owes her elder brother fealty; before she withdraws from our mortal realm she will do her duty and serve you, to aid the cause of the Lord of Destruction."

The priestess was now openly backing away from the overman. Garth muttered, "This is absurd. I have no connection with any god." He was uneasily reminded of the prophecies cited by the Seer of Weideth; people seemed determined to see him as a bringer of destruction.

"Perhaps you are not aware of your role. We all serve the gods, and you more than any other."

Garth was unsure whether the reputedly deaf old priest had heard his remark, or merely guessed his thoughts. Whichever it was, he was not pleased. He wanted to retort that he served no one, but could not do so, since he was in fact serving the Forgotten King. Strange as the old man was, he was no god.

Was he?

What was a god like? Could the mysterious old creature be some sort of divinity? It seemed unlikely.

"I serve no god," Garth said.

Tiris shrugged, but said nothing further; instead, he turned and shuffled away, along one side of the sanctuary.

Garth turned to his guide, who was now almost cowering against the wall. There could be no doubt that she, at least, believed completely in the old man's mystical powers of discernment.

Disgusted, he marched past her and made his way down the rusted spiral stair; he had what he came for.

He strode down the passage, ignoring the creaking of the floor. The door at the end still stood open; he passed through that, then through the one he had burst in with his fist. Across the outermost chamber and out onto the sun-drenched steps he went.

Only at the last minute did he recall that he had been pursued to the temple's entrance, and that his pursuers might well be waiting for him.

They weren't. Luck was with him.

It was early afternoon; the avenue was spattered with strolling citizens, enjoying the warm sun that had long since erased all trace of the morning's rain. Several noticed him emerging from the brooding darkness of P'hul's temple, but raised no outcry, preferring instead simply to give him the widest possible berth. Remembering the leper-priestess' face he understood their attitude, and was grateful for it. He would not be bothered for a few moments, at least, not so long as it was known where he had just been.

He was slightly hungry but not at all tired. There were but two temples remaining. He thrust aside thoughts of food and joined the northbound traffic, heading for his next target.

He glimpsed the temple of Aghad to the southeast, and recalled with pleasure that he had not harmed anyone in the temple of P'hul.

Ahead of him loomed the fourth temple on the street, and presumably the last, unless the city's final shrine was concealed somewhere further along; he saw at once that it was a ruin. He had not noticed it at night, when the black of the sky blended with the black temple, but it was unmistakable in the golden daylight. The great dome was a skeleton, a metal framework, bent and sagging, with only a few broken fragments of its original stone sheathing left, clinging forlornly to its lower limits. It sat atop a broad, low structure, mostly hidden by the surrounding buildings, but with wide cracks and gaping holes visible.

This was either the temple of destruction or the temple of death; in either case, a ruin was appropriate. Therefore he did not assume it to be abandoned.

He suspected it to be the temple of Bheleu; it seemed more fitting. That would make the temple he had not yet located the temple of The God Whose Name Is Not Spoken, which was also reasonable. A god whose very name was secret would not have his shrine openly upon a major avenue.

As he approached more closely he saw that the temple had a courtyard in front, similar to those of Sai or Aghad; a pair of steel gates stood open, blasted from their frame and hanging, twisted metal remnants, from bent hinges. Garth wondered what force load ripped them apart; he knew why it was done, if this was indeed the temple of Bheleu, but he could not imagine what means had been employed.

Inside the gates the court was a rubble-strewn expanse of stone, tall grass growing unchecked between crooked flagstones. The temple itself was closed off by a pile of wood, stacked across a shattered doorframe. No trace of the original doors remained; only the rough planks and logs. They looked like nothing so much as firewood; Garth wondered what in the world they were doing there. He had never before seen firewood stored in someone's front door.

He paused before the gate, and suddenly realized he was becoming a center of attention. Several passersby had noticed him approaching and studying the temple, and were in turn studying him – though none dared approach more closely.

He decided that it would be advisable to wait until nightfall before entering the temple. For the present, he would get himself a meal.

He turned away from the blasted temple and headed back down the avenue. He thought he remembered seeing food shops somewhere near the overlord's palace.

His memory had not failed him; he found a butcher shop, a bakery, and a vintner. A slice of good beef, fried in the baker's best dough, and washed down with a sweet red wine did much to ease his hunger.

Thus fortified, he decided to return to the Inn of the Seven Stars until nightfall. It should be fairly easy to get into the temple of Bheleu under cover of darkness, particularly since it stood in a diurnal part of the city. There was always the possibility that he would once again be interrupting a ceremony of some sort, of course; he would have to be cautious in his approach. He hoped to get there shortly after sundown, when the night's festivities, if any, would not yet have begun.

Had it been later in the day he might have chosen to wait closer at hand; but it was little more than an hour past noon, and he was slightly apprehensive about leaving Frima untended all day. Furthermore, it was about time Koros was fed, and he didn't entirely trust Dugger to see to it.

Accordingly, as he left the vintner's shop he turned his steps southwestward; he had gone scarcely a block when he heard a commotion behind him. He started to turn, to see what was happening, when he heard a voice shouting, "Overman! Hold!"

Instantly he began running, dodging into a narrow alley; behind him he could hear disorganized pursuit.

It was no great feat for him to outrun even the fastest humans on a clear field, but he was unsure how he would fare amid the winding streets of Dûsarra; therefore he kept running and dodging long after he had ceased to hear his pursuers, leaving a trail of startled citizens. Overmen in and of themselves were no strange sight to the city's hooded inhabitants, but an overman running full-tilt through the streets, mail clinking and battle-axe slapping his back, was something else; they stared after him in astonishment.

At last he found himself in an uninhabited byway, with no sign that anyone was still after him; he stopped, caught his breath, and tried to figure out where he was.

He had not seen this street before. He was lost.

His flight, he knew, had led him primarily southward; therefore, since the sun was now past its zenith, he need only head toward it to make up for the westward progress he had missed. He moved on, following the sun, proceeding with stealth and caution; carefully peering around each corner before crossing intersections.

He had apparently found his way, somehow, into a nocturnal quarter; there were no people about, and he passed at least one street-corner shrine holding a black onyx idol of Tema. He was slightly surprised that such a costly item was not stolen; either it had some protection he could not see, or even the daydwelling Dûsarrans did not care to offend the city's most popular goddess.

The streets narrowed, and their twists and turns sometimes forced him off his intended course until he reached the next corner; he made a full circuit of one particularly crooked three-sided block without meaning to, and had to head further southward to find another street that ran to the west.

The continued emptiness of the streets lulled him, and his caution decreased as corner after corner revealed nothing but closed shops, shuttered windows, and drying mud. Thus, he almost walked openly into the marketplace when it appeared unexpectedly before him. Recovering, he backtracked into still-unoccupied alleys, and looped around to the north, giving the square a wide berth. This took him through areas not wholly asleep, and he found himself peering around corners and furtively scurrying from one alleyway to the next.

Finally, he emerged into the street where the house he had broken through stood; it was still apparently empty. Cautiously, he tried the door, and found it just as he had left it. He guessed that the owner had not yet returned home.

He made his way through the house into the yard, where the rainwater had subsided to a few small puddles and a broad expanse of mud; it was a simple matter for him to vault onto the wall separating this yard from the next, and from there to clamber onto the roof of the stable.

It was midafternoon; the sun's angle was about the same as it had been when he left, save that it stood now in the west instead of the east. He eased himself over the edge of the tiles, and dropped into the stableyard.

The stall was as he had left it, save that Koros was awake and standing quietly; Frima still slept. Garth tucked the bag of dust into the larger sack that now held the two stones, the bloodstained gold, and the whip and dagger from the other temples, then sat, considering what to do until nightfall.

Nothing suggested itself; he closed his eyes for a brief nap, and was quickly asleep.

Chapter Eighteen

He awoke to moonlight in his face; it washed the stableyard in silver, fading to gray the hard yellow dirt, and blurring the several shades of gray wood and gray stone to a single paler hue outlined in black shadows.

With a growl, he climbed to his feet; he had overslept. It was obviously two or three hours past sunset.

Something moved in the dimness of the stall. He peered into the gloom, and realized it was Frima shying away from him. His growl had frightened her.

With a start, he noticed where she was; she stood beside Koros, her tiny hand on the warbeast's great black head, petting it. She had apparently gotten on friendly terms with the monster. Her other hand held the wire brush Garth kept for grooming his mount, and the beast's eyelids drooped in an expression of feline contentment; obviously the two were getting along very well indeed. Garth felt slightly sorry he had interrupted such a pleasant scene.

"Excuse me," he said, "I overslept. I meant to wake at sundown."

"Oh! I didn't know; I would have wakened you if I had." Frima sounded genuinely contrite, although she had not been at fault, and Garth felt a twinge of annoyance. This girl thoroughly confused him with her abrupt emotional changes that seemed to have no perceptible logic to them. He forbore to comment further, and instead readied himself for his assault on the temple of Bheleu, straightening his mail – which was really quite uncomfortable to sleep in; once again he was stiff and sore – and checking his dagger and axe, wishing his sword were still intact.

He also wished his boots were still intact; he discovered that the mud in his right boot had dried to an abrasive grit. He removed it, and wiped it out as best he could with a spare sack. That reminded him to tuck one in his belt, which he did immediately after re-donning the boot.

His feet had gotten rather unsavory, he noticed; that came from sleeping shod, no doubt. He decided he owed himself a long, luxurious hot bath as soon as he could manage one.

Frima watched all this silently, her hand absentmindedly stroking the warbeast's neck. At last, she asked, "Where are you going?"

"To the temple of Bheleu."

"To rob its altar?"

"Yes."

"Is that the last one?"

"No; I still have to rob the temple of death."

"But you can't! No one has ever come out of there alive!"

"Except the old priest, and what he can do, I can do."

She was plainly unconvinced. "What am I to do when you are killed?"

"Whatever you please."

"But the beast won't let me leave!"

"You need not worry about that; if I do not return within a day or so, Koros will go hunting. It's due for a feeding, and when it's hungry enough it will hunt, regardless of anything else. I would suggest you find a weapon; there is a stiletto among my supplies, and of course the dagger from the temple of Sai. You may be able to convince it that other food would be more easily obtained than you, particularly since it knows I don't want you harmed."

"He eats people?" She snatched her hand from the warbeast's neck.

"It; it's a neuter, not a male. And yes, it eats people. It even ate a wizard once."

"Oh." Her voice was tiny.

"I wouldn't worry; it seems to like you."

She made a small wordless noise, as Garth looked himself over. Finally satisfied with his preparations, he ordered Frima and Koros, "Wait here," and marched out of the stall.

Dugger was on duty, as he had expected. There was, therefore, no reason to go clambering around the roof; besides, he was pretty well over the anger that had made him so reckless earlier. Simply recognizing its existence had helped considerably, and he was better rested now – though he was slightly annoyed at having overslept.

He strode to the archway and asked the drowsing stable-boy, "Have you arranged to feed my mount?"

The boy awoke with a start, and said, "It's you!"

"Yes."

"You're the temple-robber!"

"Am I?"

"Aren't you? I . . . they said it was an overman, and you're the only overman I've seen around in weeks."

"You don't see every stranger that comes to Dûsarra, though, do you?"

"No."

"So you can't be sure I'm the one who robbed the temple."

The boy hesitated, and admitted, "I guess not."

"And that being the case, I think you should give me the benefit of the doubt. Now, I told you last night that I wanted you to feed my beast; have you done anything about that?"

"I forgot."

"It's just as well." It had occurred to Garth that anyone taking the beast its meal would see, and wonder about, Frima. An overman had no business with a human female, especially not keeping her penned in a stable. Dugger had seen her enter, but there was no point in reminding him and letting him see she was still there. "Is the street clear? Others might mistake me for the temple thief, and I'd prefer not to be delayed."

"Oh." The boy leaned out and looked both ways. "I don't see anyone."

"Good." He stepped past the lad, looking about for himself, and set out toward the Street of the Temples.

He encountered no difficulty; he was becoming familiar with the city, and knew which streets were diurnal, which nocturnal, and which seemed to have traffic around the clock.

As it had been the night before, the Street of the Temples was as silent as death, not a single thing moving on its moonlit pavement. He made his way quickly to the ruined temple, only to halt abruptly as he approached; a faint murmur disturbed the silence, coming from the shattered dome.

He hissed in annoyance. Another ceremony; it seemed as if no matter what he did, he was fated to arrive during some silly ritual or other.

At any rate, he could approach this one cautiously and watch, and then decide what to do; whether to wait until it ended or interrupt it or simply go away and try again later. He crept onward, slipping stealthily through the blasted gates, into the littered courtyard beyond.

The firewood was gone from the doorway, which now gaped at him like a toothless mouth; orange light shone from within. He stepped to one side, and peered cautiously around the broken frame.

The interior of the ruin was a single vast space; if there had ever been any internal walls, they were nothing now but part of the dust that served as a floor. The black stone walls and the tattered metal frame of the demolished dome were lit by a great bonfire that blazed in the center of the temple, and around this conflagration danced a score or more of red-robed figures, prancing about and chanting eerily, casting long black shadows that writhed across red-lit walls and the deeper blackness of the cracks in the stone.

The scene had an odd fascination to it. Garth stared.

There was no sign of an altar, unless the bonfire could be considered that; it was certainly the focus of the worshippers' attention. Garth blinked, and studied the leaping flames more carefully. That was undoubtedly where the wood that had earlier blocked the entrance had gone. Logs of all sizes were heaped crudely together; in the center, a single slim, straight rod stood straight up, almost invisible through the flames.

He blinked again; the chant seemed louder. There was something about that single upright object that bothered him. It was not wood; it gleamed, it shone too bright a shade of red. There was a crosspiece near the top.

A dull rumble reached him, penetrating the chant that seemed to fill his head; distant thunder, he told himself. He glanced up, and saw that the stars had vanished, covered over by clouds. The brewing storm had blown up extraordinarily quickly, he thought, or else he had been watching the dance longer than he had realized. The moon was hidden, while it had been bright and clear when he entered the court; he had not noticed its loss in the brighter light of the fire. He looked back at the ceremony, if such it could be called; it was lacking in the pomp and dignity of more familiar rites, though it certainly had a power of its own. The chanting filled his ears again, and his gaze was absorbed in the flames. As he watched, there came a second low rumble; as if in response, the central portion of the bonfire fell inward, leaving a ring of flame where there had been a cone, and revealing that strange upright object, which now stood dimly glowing behind the flickering curtain.

It was a sword. An immense two-handed broadsword was thrust through the center of the pile of burning wood. A great red gem blazed in its pommel. It was straight and strong, a good yard of bare metal showing between the quillons and where the blade vanished into the flaring coals; the hilt was black, and long enough to give even an overman's hands plenty of room. Assuming it to be properly proportioned, Garth estimated its full length at six feet or more.

A truly magnificent weapon; it made the sword he had shattered appear little better than a pocketknife. He stepped into the doorway to see it better.

The devotees of Bheleu paid no heed, but whirled on in their dance; it grew more manic now, and the chanting rose in pitch, split into two antiphonal voices pursuing one another in hypnotic rhythm.

Altar or no, Garth knew that this sword was what he had come for. This was what he wanted, of all Dûsarra. A sword like that would make him invincible. His gaze was fixed upon it in fascination.

The steel gleamed in the firelight and the chant merged with renewed rumbling, washing over him in a wave of close-packed sound. He saw nothing now but the bonfire and the glowing sword; the dancers flicked across his field of vision with no more meaning than the flickering of the flames. He would take that sword; he would wait until the dance had ended and the fire died, and tear it free.

No! Why wait? He would burst into the chamber while the dancers remained lost in their chanting gyrations and snatch it out red-hot from where it stood! Then he would flee, he thought at first, but instantly other thoughts crushed that out; he would not flee! Flee? An overman flee before humans? He would not flee; he would wield that splendid blade among the worshippers until it shone as red with blood as it did now with heat.

Somewhere a part of him knew this was insane, this uncontrollable craving for the possession of the sword; that part struggled vainly to restore calm. It revolted at the thought of wanton and unnecessary bloodshed.

It was brutally suppressed by the unearthly power that now dominated him, erasing his conscious self; his rationality was drowned in a flood of unreasoning blood-lust, like nothing he had ever felt. He had known the wild and involuntary passion that consumes an overman when he scents an overwoman in heat; he had known the roaring blind fury of battle rage that made a mortal warrior a berserker; this new lust was so strong as to make those mere shadows, trivial wisps of emotion, though it partook of both in flavor. He could contain it no longer.

An instant later the reeling, semi-hypnotized dancers were delighted to see the great dark form of an armored overman stride roaring into their midst, red eyes ablaze; they knew at once, with the absolute conviction of the fanatic, that this was their god who confronted them. They screamed with ecstasy, the chant collapsing into chaotic raving; the earth rumbled beneath them, and lightning forked across the sky.

Boldly, unhesitatingly, as if unaware of the flames and heat, the apparition marched up onto the verge of the holy pyre and wrenched the sacred sword from its place; his hands smoked with the heat of the hilt, and the stench of burning skin filled the temple. The overman paid no heed, but, raised the blade above his head and whirled it about, so that it blazed and flickered in the firelight.

"I am Bheleu!" cried the monster in Garth's body; he thrust the blade upward at the heavens, to be answered by a crash of thunder and a blinding flash of lightning. The bolt struck, spattered, and sizzled across the spiderweb metal frame of the ruined dome; sparks showered upon the worshippers, who danced maniacally, screaming their devotion. A second bolt came on the heels of the first, leaping from the clouds to the peak of the dome, and thence to the point of the sword; it poured through Garth's body and blasted the bonfire apart at his feet, scattering burning wood.

The thunder was now a steady pounding as other bolts showered across the city; Garth's hands fell, the sword still clutched in them, and his eyes blazed crimson as the blade chopped through the skull of the high priest of Bheleu.

The worshippers screamed in frenzy, crying the name of their god.

The blade swung up, red with blood and gleaming gold in the firelight; lightning flashed, silver steel shone for an instant, and the sword came down, hacking through a man's neck, spraying blood into the scattered fire where it sizzled and stank.

"I am destruction!"

The worshippers cried hoarse approval, and surged toward him, forgetting their dance. The blade blazed upward, flashed down; blood showered unnoticed across fire, earth, and flesh. There was no trace of resistance; the eager worshippers flung themselves in the weapon's path as the earth shook and the sky raged, and the monster wielding it merely laughed.

For half an hour their god walked among his people, slashing aside all who approached him; for one insane half-hour he brought the total destruction their creed proclaimed holy. The priests of Bheleu had been warriors, for their faith required it. None shrank from the sight of blood, nor cringed away from the dismembered and disemboweled corpses of their comrades; instead they fought amongst themselves for the right to approach and be slain, their religious fervor blended with the old fighting fury, the death-wish of those who slay made manifest.

Throughout, the thunder rolled and roared, crashing arrhythmically about the ruins, and lightning blazed again and again across the open dome. Every so often a bolt would strike the exposed steel, and the temple walls would shake. With the agility of the warriors they once were, the worshippers kept their feet and pressed forward to the slaughter.

At last, as the dripping blade swung flashing upward for the final stroke, there came a crash of thunder like none before; the last devotee fell to his knees before his god, deafened and blinded, as the sword blazed red and silver against the sky, whirling about the head of the crazed overman-monster. It swooped down, like a hawk upon its prey, and struck the man through, entering the front of his throat and protruding between his shoulder-blades; no more metal showed, but only blood, red, brown, and black, coating the blade and spattered liberally across the temple floor.

The final lightning bolt's pealing echoed among the shattered walls, covering the sudden silence that fell with the death of the last screaming priest; overhead, the blasted dome sagged, twisted, and broke. Snapping sparks were strewn amid the dying remnants of the pyre, and drops of molten metal flew hissing downward. The framework continued to crumple, collapsing slowly, as the storm finally broke, whipping fat raindrops across the prostrate corpses and the upturned face of their slayer.

For long moments the overman stood motionless; rain filled his eyes and ran in cool streams across his face. The sword was still clutched in his hands, its hilt slimed with gore, its blade still thrust through his final victim. The madness was passing, fading, shrinking into itself somewhere within him; he blinked away the rain, and lowered his gaze from the storm.

He looked at the sagging, slack-jawed figure impaled on his sword, at the score of slaughtered men, at the scattered remains of the bonfire dying in the rain. His hands fell from the hilt, and sword and cadaver tumbled forward at his feet. He stepped back, appalled, and sank to his knees; then, for the first time in a hundred and forty years, Garth wept, as the shattered metal of the dome crashed to the ground around him.

Chapter Nineteen

He came to as the first glimmer of dawn broke through the clouds; he was lying sprawled on the dirt floor of the temple, surrounded by tortured scraps of metal and ragged, red-clothed corpses. Ashes and charred wood were scattered at his feet.

Before him, the elongated hilt of the great broadsword protruded from the throat of his final victim; the gem set in the pommel gleamed as red as blood, but the blade had been washed clean by the rain. In the dim light the metal was dull gray.

He got slowly to his feet, and the events of the night seeped back into his mind; he grimaced in disgust.

Here was the destruction the Seers of Weideth had foreseen. What had come over him?

He found himself unwilling to admit that he had in truth been possessed by some higher power, acting as no more than a puppet; but then, the thought that he had within him such berserk savagery, so easily roused, was almost equally unacceptable. True, his rage and hatred of the Aghadites still smouldered, and his anger at the Baron of Skelleth likewise. Had the babblings of that senile old P'hulite suggested to his suppressed darker side that he take out his aggressions thus? Perhaps the dance of Bheleu had hypnotic properties designed to release a watcher's pent-up emotions; perhaps some mystic fumes, invisible and unnoticed, had affected him. He had heard that volcanoes produced such gasses, and Dûsarra was built on the slopes of a great volcano.

It really mattered very little; what was done was done, and could in no way be altered.

He recalled the roaring storm, of which nothing remained but, puddles and dispersing clouds; the dome had been blasted away. He remembered the fiery lightning – had it actually struck him? That could not be. He looked at his hands; the palms were burnt black. He shuddered. Had he really pulled the sword red-hot from the fire?

No. He rejected that. The whole thing could not have been as he remembered; he must have been under some magical influence, whether hypnosis or hallucinogen or even actual possession he did not know. He had slain the entire cult of Bheleu, yes; there had been a storm, and lightning had destroyed the ruins of the dome; but beyond that, he refused to accept any of it. He had no idea how he had burned his hands, or how the bonfire had been spread about, but he rejected his memories of those events.

His hands were numb, he realized; the nerves might well have been destroyed. At the very least they had been temporarily overloaded. If they were intact, at any minute sensation might begin to return, and he was quite sure that the result would be pain like nothing he had ever suffered before – except possibly once, when he had recovered slowly from a wizard's death-spell. He cringed at the thought. That experience was not something he could bear to think about.

He still had one more temple to rob, and his escape to make good; he was a wanted fugitive. He could not afford to waste any time. If he waited for his hands to heal, he might be hiding and running about the city for weeks. On the other hand, if he moved quickly, perhaps he could finish his task before the pain began, and before any infection set in – if such were to happen. It might be that his hands were permanently ruined.

He did not care to consider that; instead, he snatched the sword of Bheleu from the final corpse and wiped the remaining blood off on the man's robe. He had not seen the temple of The God Whose Name Is Not Spoken, but he somehow thought he knew where it must be. The dead have returned to the earth, humans were wont to say; death is a part of the world. It was appropriate, then, for the god of death to have his temple in the earth itself.

Garth marched from the ruined shrine, across the rubble-strewn courtyard, and through the shattered gates into the street; it was still early, and none of the day-dwellers were yet about, so it stretched bare and empty from the overlord's palace to the blank stone of the volcano.

Garth turned right, toward the bare stone.

As he approached he made out what he had expected to find at the end of the avenue; amid black shadows and black stone was a deeper shadow. There was an opening into the mountainside that he knew to be the temple of the Final God.

It did not occur to him to wonder how he could now know, with such certainty, things that he had not even guessed at prior to the carnage in the temple of Bheleu.

The great broadsword was naked in his unfeeling hands; there was no way he could sheathe it, no other way he could carry it. Even had he still worn his old sword's scabbard, it would never have held the five-foot blade of this monstrous weapon.

He paused at the brink of the cave; it seemed very odd that such a cave would exist here within the city walls, but it undeniably did. He peered into the gloom, but could see nothing. He recalled what Frima had said of it, but paid it no heed; mere myths, to impress gullible humans.

A voice spoke from behind him, saying, "You broke your word, Garth."

He turned, but could see no one; the speaker was hiding somewhere. Garth made no attempt to locate him; he recognized the voice. It was the same one that had taunted him in the temple of Aghad.

"I gave no word."

"You gave assent by silence to our bargain, thief, yet you harmed no one in the temple of P'hul."

Garth marveled at the perversity of this creature, criticizing him for not killing enough people when the Aghadite had surely seen the bloody havoc he had wreaked during the night. "Do not the many deaths in Bheleu's shrine more than compensate?"

"No. You were to slay a priest of P'hul."

"Who? The leper girl? The senile old seer? I gave no word, skulking liar; if I have failed of the terms you set me, what of it? Annoy me no further."

"You were to slay a priest of P'hul. Now you enter the temple of the Final God, yet the cult's priest is nowhere within. You scorn our agreement, and be sure that if you come alive from this cavern, you shall die nonetheless."

"In time, no doubt, I shall; but it will be none of your doing! When I emerge from this place I will depart this city, and I suggest that you not get in my way."

"Say what you will, but be aware that we can suppress information as well as disseminate it, and it is by our grace that the angry mobs gathered by the temple of Tema have not yet beset the stable at the Inn of the Seven Stars. Their agent who spied upon you and the owner of the house you so cavalierly broke open were kept from spreading the word by the followers of Aghad, but even now we are withdrawing our aid; the boy Dugger is being punished for his silence, and the good people of the city are no longer being held in check."

This speech caused Garth genuine concern for a moment; then he shrugged it aside. He had faith in the invincibility of his warbeast.

Still, there was no time to spare. Ignoring the further comments of the Aghadite, he plunged into the gloom of the cave, finding some slight gratification in the knowledge that the other would fear to follow.

There was no gate, door, nor guard; the reputation of the Final God was quite sufficient to keep out the unwelcome.

The gray light of early morning faded behind him as he marched down the smooth, sloping floor, but somewhere ahead of him he detected a faint, ruddy glow. He would not have to contend with complete darkness.

The entry passage gradually widened and the glow became more pronounced, until at last he found himself in a large chamber, where the natural cave had been artificially enlarged. The floor was smooth and level, the walls straight, but the central portion of the ceiling was the rough and broken surface of a cave, showing where the original opening had been, while the sides were lower and shaped into smooth vaulting, obviously the work of human hands.

It was impossible to distinguish any colors, for here the only light was the pure red of that mysterious glow that came from somewhere beyond the far side of the chamber; it seeped up from the continuation of the natural tunnel, which Garth could see sloped sharply downward. A dry warmth seemed to come with it. Shapes were plainly discernable, and Garth saw that the walls were carved into high-relief friezes of a grotesque and hideous nature, depicting twisted, semi-human creatures, cavorting obscenely, butchering one another while simultaneously engaged in a wide variety of perverse couplings. Garth wondered what manner of imagination had created such things.

In the center of the chamber stood the altar, high and narrow; it was scarcely a yard wide, but almost five feet in height, its sides smooth stone that blended seamlessly into the floor. Apparently, Garth thought, it had been carved from a column or stalagmite. The top was ornate and slanting; it was tilted up to resemble a reading stand, such as could be found in the best libraries, with elaborate decorative carving along either side and surmounted by a strange semi-human skull. The space where an open book would have stood, were it in fact a reading stand, was bare, smooth polished stone.

That meant the skull was what he had come for. He crossed to the altar and looked at it.

It was somewhere between human and overman in size and shape, save that it was impossibly tall and narrow, and two twisting horns thrust up from its temples; its teeth were gone, and its jaws leered open.

He put aside his sword and reached for it, and discovered that it was somehow anchored to the stone altar; furthermore, it was coated with some sort of slime, so that his senseless fingers slid from their hold.

Probably just drippings from the roof, he decided, though there was no discernable moisture in the warm air. He grasped and tugged at the skull, but it refused to yield.

A faint rumbling sounded, and he felt a vibration in the stone beneath his feet; he thought vaguely that it was unusual for a second thunderstorm to blow up so suddenly, and ran his fingers over the sides of the skull, wishing they weren't still numb.

They came away coated with slime; he peered at it closely, and realized that this was no dripping cave-water. The red glow dimmed slightly; he glanced up, then returned to his study of the skull.

The coating seemed to be some sort of ichor, though he had seen no sign of life in the cave-temple. The skull appeared to be firmly secured to the altar by a heavy rivet through the base of the cranium.

There was a faint tingling in his hands; the nerves were not wholly destroyed. He glanced down at them, and the red glow seemed to dim still further. There were blisters forming. He looked up in time to see the thing coming at him before its shadow covered him in darkness, shutting out the faint crimson light.

Chapter Twenty

The thing was huge; its eyeless head seemed to fill half the chamber, and its gaping lipless maw appeared capable of swallowing an overman, armor and all, in a single gulp. It had no neck, nor in truth a distinct head, but only a long, segmented body reaching back into the farther tunnel and filling it so completely that the red glow, whatever it was, could no longer pass.

It was, in short, a monstrous worm.

Garth retreated instinctively, and feeling the weight of his axe upon his shoulder he reached up and freed the familiar weapon, forgetting for the moment about the more formidable sword he had left beside the altar.

He was in darkness, having been allowed only that single glimpse of his attacker; now he judged its location by sound and the feel of the moving air on his face. It was swinging its head about blindly in the area of the altar, where he had stood instants earlier, presumably groping for its usual sacrifice.

Cautiously, wary that the slightest sound might alert it – there was no knowing what senses guided such a creature – he inched backward toward the entryway.

Some part of his mind undoubtedly noticed the totality of the surrounding blackness; it was with only mild surprise that he found the entrance blocked by a solid metal barrier, which must have slid silently into place while he investigated the altar. He wasted no effort in battering at it; undoubtedly other victims had tried that, though perhaps none as powerful as himself, and it would leave him with his beck exposed and inviting. Instead he turned at bay, and waited for the monster's attack.

The creature was not slow in obliging with an awkward lunge; he heard a slithering as it poised, and felt the rush of air toward him, giving him time to spring aside, hacking with the axe as he did so.

The blade bit into something with a sick, squashing sound, but there was no blood or ichor sprayed onto his hands, nor any sign of pain or injury from the monster worm. He wrenched the axe free and backed away, his left flank to the wall.

He wished his hands were capable of normal sensation; he wanted to test the edge of his blade, to see if anything had come away upon it, or if perhaps it was coated with the same slime as the altar. He was fairly sure this creature was the source of that substance, and somewhere beneath his wary attention to his situation he wondered whether it was an exterior lubrication or a saliva of some sort.

His palms stung, not from the impact the axe had made on the monster, but with the first twinges from his burns.

The head swung toward him again, and there was a brief flash of murky red as the creature's swooping lunge allowed a trace of light to pass; he saw the horny rim of its toothless mouth sweeping toward him and dove from its path, flailing with the axe. It sank into the thing's flesh, and was wrenched from his grasp.

He felt a brief second of panic as he realized he was virtually unarmed against this hideous pet of the god of death, then remembered the great sword that presumably still lay somewhere near the center of the chamber. He clambered to his feet, his twitching, stinging fingers clutching at the carvings that lined the wall without feeling them; when the worm reared back for another lunge, he took three running steps under its raised head and dove headlong, hands outflung.

The rattle of steel on stone told him that his hand had struck the sacred weapon. The pain in his palms was becoming a distraction, but he forced himself to ignore it as he groped for the sword.

Above him the worm's body twitched as it thrust forward, and a solid fist of air knocked him flat to the stones; it was scarcely a foot above him, writhing about in frustration, unable to detect him.

He forced his hands to close on the sword, though the motion of bending his palms sent a shudder of agony up his arms. The blade scraped across stone and the monster turned, twisting back upon itself, only to find the space within the chamber insufficient for such a maneuver.

There was a scraping sound followed by a rattling, as the axe he had left embedded in the creature was dragged along the wall and dislodged.

His unwilling hands arranged themselves upon the hilt of the sword, and a surge of renewed strength swept through him. Adrenalin, he told himself.

The worm was dragging much of its length back down into the tunnel; there was another brief flash of ruddy light. It was giving itself room, the room to move its head and get its hungry maw onto the reluctant morsel it knew was there.

He rolled aside, and felt the rush of air as it lunged; it missed, and he swung the great broadsword as he lay on his back inches from its flank. The blade cut deeply into the monster, but there was still no perceptible effect. Slime ran sluggishly over the quillons and across the back of his hands.

He struck again, before the thing could move far – vast and powerful as it was, it was also ponderous and, except for the swift lunges that used its own weight to drive its head forward, not capable of fast movement – and again the blade sliced messily into the yielding substance of the creature.

It was like cutting at mud.

He hewed again as it reversed direction, pulling back for another attack; with a ghastly sucking sound a sliver of its cold, damp flesh came free where this new cut met an earlier one.

An idea came to him as he rolled onto his belly and pushed himself further toward the wall. The thing's vitals were not within reach of his blade, it appeared, but he could cut the monster. If he could hack away enough of its insensitive outer layer in one spot, sooner or later he would injure it, perhaps inflicting enough damage to drive it back down into its tunnel, leaving him to deal with the metal door. No animal in Garth's experience, of whatever kind, could long survive having chunks cut away.

It would all be much easier if he could see what he was doing.

He flung himself sideways as the rush of air warned him of another lunge, chopping with the sword as he did so. The monster withdrew, a little more slowly than before; Garth wondered if he had already made himself felt. It paused; Garth knew from the sudden cessation of the slithering noise of its movement. He judged the head to be somewhere in the center of the chamber, perhaps hovering above the altar.

It was, he decided, time he took the offensive; with a bellow of simulated rage, intended to get his blood flowing more hotly, he lurched to his feet and charged the thing, the heavy sword swinging in front of him.

The blade struck the thing's horny jaws with a grating, scratching sound, without penetrating; the monster reared away nonetheless, and Garth flung himself beneath it. He found himself crouched beside the altar, and it occurred to him that that was a good place to be; obviously, the creature could not destroy the altar, or it would have done so years ago. It would be unable to come at him from above or behind if he kept his back to the stone column.

The head swooped down again, only to stop short as it struck the altar-top; Garth took the opportunity to strike two quick blows, at converging angles, and was gratified when the second blow left a chunk of pasty worm-flesh hanging by a thread.

The monster did not retreat this time but pressed forward unheeding, mindlessly trying to force its way past the stone altar. Garth had no intention of passing up such a chance, and followed up his first pair of blows with a series of chopping cuts, hacking more deeply into the wound he had made.

Slivers of flesh pulled away to hang loosely or fall at the overman's feet. The slime that coated the monster drooled sluggishly across Garth's hands and wrists, seeming to soothe the stinging agony of his burns – which he was ignoring anyway in the heat of battle.

He was striking from a crouch beside the altar, and was unable to get the full force of which he was capable into his blows from such a stance; since the head was swaying back and forth he dared not stand up, as he knew that apparently gentle motion could knock him away like a leaf in a windstorm. Still, he knew that he could inflict more damage more quickly if he could get into a position where he could swing his blade freely, and where gravity was working with him rather than against him. If he were *atop* the worm . . .

His hacking had cut a ragged, oozing hole in the thing's side, a break in its smooth, slick surface; it served him as a foothold as he launched himself upward, scrambling madly with the great sword clutched in one stinging hand while the other hand and both feet scrabbled for holds on the thing's smooth wet flesh.

He realized he was not going to make it; he felt himself beginning to slide back, when the worm suddenly changed its direction, swinging toward him, apparently in response to his weight. For an instant he feared he would be smashed against a wall before he had time to leap clear, and he clung desperately, attempting to claw his way upward.

To his surprise, this panicky action was successful; the monster's motion had given him the additional traction he needed, and he was able to pull himself up astride the thing's "neck," using the sword as an anchor.

Now he only had to worry about being smashed against the ceiling; there was no way the thing could get at him here. He pulled his dagger from his belt and thrust it into the yielding flesh, to serve as a handhold, then set to the messy business of cutting his way through the monster with the great broadsword. He used both hands, pausing now and then to catch himself on the hilt of his dagger when he felt himself slipping.

Spraddled across the vast back as he was, he still was not striking with much power; it seemed to be sufficient, though. In moments he had carved out a trench, which he crawled into, ignoring the oozing discomforts of the omnipresent slime that seeped from every inch of the thing's flesh. Here he was much more secure, and could kneel while he wielded the sword, cutting his way deeper into the worm.

The monster was apparently unwilling to give up its prey; it did not retreat down its passage, but instead flung itself about the temple chamber, as if seeking the little pest that was now slicing deeper and deeper into its back; several times Garth thought that the violence of its movements might dislodge him, or that he might lose his grip on his sword.

Then, finally, he felt the blade bite into something more substantial than the creature's flaccid flesh; he pulled it free, releasing a spurt of viscous ichor and a ghastly stink. He had found the thing's vitals.

He had little time to appreciate his accomplishment; the thing went into wild convulsions that made its earlier movements seem like nothing, and he was flung aside like a bothersome insect. His head struck the stone wall; the sword flew from his hands, and the darkness that filled his eyes enfolded him completely. His last sensation was an eerie awareness of distant, barely audible laughter; something was pleased with him.

Chapter Twenty-One

Frima was not happy with her situation. Still, while being penned up in a stable with a man-eating monster at the whim of an overman was scarcely a pleasant thing, she had to admit it was better than being sacrificed to Sai.

It had been some time now since Garth had marched off to rob the last two temples, and Frima was reasonably certain that he would not be coming back. All her life she had been told that nobody ever returned from the temple of death, and although Garth was plainly not the Unnamed God's ordinary victim, she did not think he could manage to defy one of the basic facts of Dûsarran existence. She was, therefore, stuck here until such time as Koros should give up waiting. The overman had said it would be a day or so; she had waited a night and a morning and half the afternoon, but the beast showed no signs of departing. It had allowed her to go through Garth's belongings, and she had found the stiletto he had mentioned; the knife did little for her self-confidence, however, as she had no idea of the proper way to use one, and found it completely inconceivable that such a puny little thing could deter a creature as magnificently powerful as the warbeast.

The monster was undeniably beautiful, and friendly enough; she found herself alternately petting it, and then cowering away from it as she recalled what Garth had said. It had once eaten a wizard! Wizards were the most powerful beings she had imagined prior to her abduction, yet this thing *ate* one as if he were no more than a mere mortal!

It did not occur to her to doubt Garth's words; his delivery had been entirely convincing, and she was a fairly trusting sort anyway.

She got up and walked toward the door of the stall, to try her luck at leaving once more; as always, Koros made no protest until her hand actually reached over toward the latch, whereupon it growled warningly. She withdrew her hand, sighed, and looked out at the empty stableyard. She was about to turn away when a movement caught her eye.

There was someone just beyond the arch; several people, in fact. She leaned out a bit to get a better view, and Koros growled again; she ignored it and continued to peer through the arch.

There was a great mass of people out there; not passing by, but gathering together. She wondered what they could want.

It occurred to her that perhaps they might rescue her; she considered calling out. After some thought she decided not to. Koros would undoubtedly take it amiss, and there might be bloodshed. She was not desperate yet.

There was a curious snuffling at her side, and she realized that the warbeast had come up beside her and was also watching the people outside the arch.

There was much discussion and shouting going on, but she could make out no words. A robe fell open for a moment, revealing that its owner wore a shirt of mail and had a sword on his belt. Thus alerted, she looked more closely and saw that several – perhaps all – of the men gathering wore swords, making curious bulges beneath their robes. Furthermore, all of the gathering crowd were men, as far as she could make out; nowhere did she see a beardless face.

Someone in a dark red robe had made his way to the center of the arch; now he turned and addressed the crowd, a fist raised above his head. She still could not make out much, over the shuffling and rustling of the crowd, but she caught the words' "overman" and "defiler."

Beside her, Koros growled.

The man in red turned, and pointed into the stable – pointed directly at her, it seemed. The crowd surged, and with this apparent leader in the van marched into the stableyard.

Koros leapt from the stall in a single fluid motion and landed, feet braced apart, in the center of the yard. It roared a challenge that seemed the loudest sound Frima had ever heard, and the crowd's forward movement suddenly ceased.

Frima watched in astonishment; quite aside from the confusing events unfolding before her, she found herself wondering how a beast as large as Koros had managed to leap through the relatively narrow opening between the stall door and the overhanging roof. More of its height must be in its legs than she had realized.

Koros roared again and took a single step forward, toward the crowd of men; Frima saw that several had drawn swords, yet none dared approach any closer to the warbeast. In fact, they were gradually falling back.

Another roar and another step, and Koros sank into a crouch, like a cat preparing to pounce. The crowd's backward movement accelerated, and in a brief moment all were once again on the other side of the arch. Koros rose again, stretched itself, yawned, and stood calmly awaiting whatever might happen next.

The man in red stood out from the crowd once again and spoke; this time Frima could distinguish his words, as Koros had frightened the crowd into relative stillness.

"Fellow Dûsarrans, we are not cowed by this unholy monster, but merely cautious! It is not with this beast that we quarrel, but with its blasphemous master! Let us then wait here for his return, when we shall strike him down in our righteous anger, slaughter his monstrous pet, and return the sacrifice he has stolen to her rightful place! We will cleanse our city of this filth!"

This speech was greeted with rousing applause. Frima, hearing the line about restoring the sacrifice, found herself very glad that she had not called out for aid. She suddenly saw Koros not as her jailer but as her protector, and found herself waiting eagerly for Garth's return – while simultaneously dreading it, lest he be butchered or prove in the end as bad as the cult of Sai – and still suspecting that he might not return at all.

Chapter Twenty-Two

Garth had no idea how long he was unconscious. When he awoke he lay sprawled on the stone floor, the sword of Bheleu at his side. The red glow shone unobstructed from the tunnel, lighting the gem in the sword's pommel with a murky crimson fire. Pools of gelid slime were scattered about, and his mail was thick with the stuff. He lay still for a moment, gathering his thoughts.

He reached out and grasped the sword; as his fingers closed around the hilt, he realized that they no longer hurt. He sat up, released the sword, and looked at his palms.

There was a slight puckering of the flesh, as of wounds almost fully healed, but no other trace of burns or blisters. Horrified, he wondered how long he had lain senseless.

He tested his sensitivity, pressing his fingers to various surfaces, and knew a moment of panic when his first trial, feeling the texture of his chain armor, seemed dull and blunted; it was with great relief he realized it was the coating of slime that deadened his sense of touch. Running his fingers across the carved walls he could detect no lessening of his tactile sense. He was fit, then.

But how long had he been here? What had become of Koros, who had been due for a feeding? Or Frima, who had been left with the hungry warbeast? Of the booty taken from the first five temples? Had anything come of the threats of the Aghadite priest?

He clambered to his feet.

As if on cue, as he turned his gaze toward the metal door that sealed the entrance, the barrier slid silently into the wall, and a stooped figure entered, garbed in a robe of such a dull black that it reflected none of the red light whatsoever. The man's face was hidden by his hood, as was customary for Dûsarran priests, so that in his almost invisible garments he appeared to be an animated shadow, deeper and darker than the others that lay about the cave.

No light entered with this apparition, and at first Garth assumed this to mean that it was night outside; he did not immediately recall that the passage was long and winding enough to admit virtually none of the sun's light whatever the time of day.

The robed figure was small and frail in appearance, despite the complete lack of visible detail. Garth thought at first that it might be a girl or young boy, despite the slowness and caution of age in its movements; but when the priest spoke, although his voice was high and broken, there was no doubt that he was an old man, despite his childish stature.

"I hear you breathing," he said.

Garth made no reply.

"Can you not speak? I know you are there, and alive."

"Yes, I am here. What would you have me say?" Garth picked up the sword as he spoke; the little old man appeared harmless, but he did not care to take any unnecessary chances.

"Whatever you care to say."

"There is nothing I care to say to you."

"Would you answer a few questions, from courtesy?"

"Perhaps. Ask what you will." Garth noticed that the priest had turned his head toward him only when he had spoken; that, and the man's words, made it seem fairly definite that, like the priests of Andhur Regvos, this feeble old man was blind. It seemed curious that such a decrepit and harmless person should be the sole servant of the most feared of deities – assuming that there was, as he had been told, only one priest of the Final God. Feeling that the priest need not occupy his full attention, he looked over the chamber, noting the already-rotting chunks and slices he had cut from the monster, the still-wet slime stains, the great pool of ichor where he had finally reached the thing's viscera, and the skull-topped altar that stood undamaged and unplundered.

"Have you seen what takes most who enter here, leaving no trace?"

"Yes."

"It did not take you."

"It tried hard enough."

"What happened?"

"It came up from the tunnel; I dodged. We fought, and I managed to injure it. I was struck unconscious, but its wound was severe enough that it preferred retreat to finishing me." That, he thought, was a succinct and accurate summary of his desperate battle; he guessed that such a simple account would serve him better than any elaborate boasting, at least until her fully understood the priest's attitude toward the monster. It might well be considered blasphemous to have defended himself at all.

"What is it?"

"You don't know?" Garth's astonishment got the better of him and was plainly revealed in his tone.

"No. I am but the caretaker of the temple; I know nothing of the god's mysteries. The true servant of the Final God has not yet returned. What was it you fought?"

Garth was suddenly reluctant to speak, though he knew no logical reason not to tell the man the nature of the temple's inhabitant. "Tell me first more of your cult. Are you not the high priest of The God Whose Name Is Not Spoken?"

"No. I am a lesser priest. The books of prophecy say that the one true high priest of death has not been in Dûsarra in four ages or more, and will not return until the dawn of the Fifteenth Age."

An uneasiness filtered into Garth's mind at this new mention of the human system of numbering the ages. "This is the dawn of the Fourteenth Age, I was told."

"Yes. When this new age grows old, the high priest will return."

"If he has been gone for four ages . . . the Thirteenth Age lasted three hundred years. Your high priest must have died centuries ago. Is it his heir you await?"

"Oh, no! It is the one true high priest of the god of death. It is in the nature of his service that he himself cannot die."

There was a pause as Garth digested this information. He recalled mention made of immortality in the King's Inn of Skelleth. An unpleasant theory crept into his thoughts.

The Forgotten King had assured him that he sought to fulfill the purpose that the gods had given him, but which gods were they he spoke of?

He looked again at the unnatural skull that grinned atop the altar. "What else do you know of your high priest?"

"Oh, there are many legends! He was a king of old, in a land so ancient that its existence is forgotten; he made a bargain with the gods of life and death, whereby he shall live until the end of time, but he came to regret this and abandoned the service of his kingdom and his gods to wander the earth clad in rags. He will return when the Fifteenth Age, the Age of Death, begins, to complete his agreement. He alone has spoken to the Final God and lived; it is part of his task to be certain that The Name That Is Not Spoken is not lost. He commands all the world's ancient magic, but has no use for it. There is much more in the sacred texts – his name, which I cannot pronounce truly, and the records of his doings."

"Do your sacred books speak of the Sixteenth Age?"

"No, they cover only the current cycle, which ends with the Fifteenth."

"What do they say of the Fourteenth, then?"

"The Age of Destruction? It shall begin with the decimation and defilement of Dûsarra, and be an age of fire and sword. There is mention of a mighty servant of Bheleu who shall do the bidding of the Forgotten King."

"The Forgotten King?"

"Another name for the high priest of Death."

"The high priest of Death." Garth stared at the skull as he resolved that the prophecies would not come true.

"Yes." The old priest's voice sounded less certain.

"The thing from the tunnel was just a worm." Garth marched out, shoving the blind priest aside, leaving the horned skull on its perch.

The priest ran after him, calling for him to wait; Garth stopped and allowed the old man to catch up, as he had thought of another question he wanted to ask. He saw that the man's hood had fallen back, but took no notice.

"How long was I in there?" he demanded.

"The priest of Aghad said you entered at dawn; the sun is now almost setting."

"Only one day?"

"Yes." The priest's voice was now timid.

Garth stared at his hands. How had they healed so quickly? The sword of Bheleu was still clutched in his right fist; he had a momentary impulse to fling it away, but stopped himself. His dagger had stayed stuck in the monster worm; his axe was lost somewhere within; his old sword had shattered on the gates of

Aghad. This infernal blade was his only weapon, and he had no intention of attempting to escape Dûsarra unarmed; after all, the priests of Aghad had promised to kill him.

He continued up toward the mouth of the cave, slowly enough that the priest could keep up with him; as the ruddy volcanic light faded behind him, a faint glow of a paler pink grew ahead.

The priest was babbling at him, asking question after question about the worm; he did not bother to answer most of them, but replied that yes, the slime on the altar came from the worm; no, he had not been able to see all of it; no, it had not all fit into the chamber; no, he did not think he had killed it; yes, it ate people, probably swallowing them whole.

At last the mismatched pair emerged into the gray light of gathering dusk; Garth kept the sword at ready as he stepped out onto the pavement of the Street of the Temples. He glanced at the priest, and saw the man's face for the first time.

His hair was pure white; one eye was gone, the other was pink under a frosting of cataracts; some sort of growth covered one side of the face. From one of the dead-black sleeves protruded the smooth stump of an arm, the loss of the hand long since healed over. He was the most repulsive human being Garth had ever seen.

That, of course, was appropriate for a priest of something as repulsive as death.

As Garth noticed these details the priest talked on, marveling at the idea of a monster worm, speaking of all the people it had devoured, unmindful of the overman's scrutiny. Garth interrupted him.

"Old man, how were you able to read your books?"

"What? Oh. I was not always blind, and I have an acolyte, who reads to me when I wish to be reminded."

"You have no powers of second sight?"

"No. I am just a caretaker."

That was, Garth thought, unfortunate; it would have been very convenient had the old fool been able to foresee the actions of the Aghadites. He had encountered enough seers on this quest that another would scarcely have been surprising; but as it was he would have to rely on his own abilities. He started to speak a farewell, to take his leave of the man, but was interrupted by a familiar voice from somewhere in the rocks behind him.

"We offer a final chance, traitor. Kill the old idiot and you may yet be allowed to live."

Chapter Twenty-Three

For an instant, Garth considered his position. His primary goal was to get out of Dûsarra alive; a secondary goal was to get Frima, Koros, and his loot out with him. It would be pleasant if he could also kill some Aghadites, both because it would discourage pursuit and because it would be enjoyable; he had no moral compunctions about that, since the cult was responsible for any number of murders. However, he was at a disadvantage here; the Aghadite was concealed, presumably in a good defensive position that he had had plenty of time to establish, and Garth had no idea of the number of his foes. There might be the single priest, or the entire cult, or even several cults. Direct battle was therefore inadvisable. Returning to his primary objective, he considered the best way to achieve it; the Aghadites could not have known when he would emerge from the temple of death, unless they had oracles or seers available, and even then they'd want confirmation. At this instant, messengers of some sort were most likely carrying word across the city; the Aghadites wouldn't rely on a single ambush. There were probably people waiting for him at the stable and at the city gates.

If he could reach them before the messengers did, surprise would be on his side. Accordingly, he made no answer to the taunting voice, and paid no further heed to the ancient priest of the Final God, but took to his heels, running full speed straight down the Street of the Temples, ignoring the few startled pedestrians who scattered before him.

He had reached his decision in far less time than required to explain it; by the time the Aghadite had finished his second sentence, Garth was a dozen yards down the avenue, the great broadsword still in his right fist. The long blade was awkward, and slowed him as he ran, but it was his only weapon.

It occurred to him that there might be enemies lurking in the temples along the way; at the first opportunity he turned right and dashed down a side street. He had not forgotten his experience of being lost in the maze of narrow streets that made up most of the city, but considered the risk less important than being unpredictable. A person could not be ambushed or apprehended unless his path was known in advance.

There was one very definite problem that he foresaw; the city had only the single gate, and he knew of no other way past the wall. Also, of course, he wanted to get Frima and his other booty. Koros could take care of itself.

He turned left after he had put two blocks between himself and the Street of the Temples, and found himself in a relatively straight lane paralleling the avenue; he followed it as far as he could, and found himself in a familiar alleyway, one he had traversed before. He slipped from a full run into an easy jog, and headed for the Inn of the Seven Stars.

Dûsarrans who happened to be out on the streets gave him a wide berth; an overman with naked sword in hand was nothing to argue with, particularly when he seemed to be in such a hurry.

The long run across the city tired him rather more than he had hoped; he had apparently not fully recovered from the battle with the worm and the blow on the head. His pace had slowed perceptibly when he turned onto the street where the house he had broken through faced.

He was not entirely sure why he had chosen to approach from this direction; the Aghadites would undoubtedly have it guarded. But they would also have the archway entrance to the stable guarded, and the route through the house would offer more cover and less opportunity for his foes to overcome him by sheer numbers. That it would also offer more cover for an ambuscade had not escaped him; still, he chose to risk it.

The street was not empty as it had been on previous occasions; a handful of men and women, in the usual dark robes and hoods, stopped and stared as he broke again into a full-speed charge toward the door midway in the block.

There was a hiss, and an arrow embedded itself in the hard-packed dirt of the street; it had not come anywhere near him. There was an ambush – but he had taken them by surprise.

He did not bother to try the door when he reached it; only fools would have neglected to lock it. He took the sword in both hands and hewed mightily, hoping the blade would prove sturdy enough.

Another arrow swished past his ear to shatter on the stone of the house's façade.

The sword struck the heavy wooden door and cut into it like a knife into cheese; the hilt suddenly felt hot in Garth's hands. He dismissed it as a trick of his imperfectly healed palms. He ripped the blade free and struck again.

The door exploded inward in shattered fragments, and Garth stepped through; he knew that something beyond his understanding was at work, as he had not the strength to so destroy the door with just two blows, but he had no time to worry about it. Two more arrows flew somewhere behind him.

The room inside was much as he remembered it – the stairway along one side, the archway to the kitchen at the back, the ceiling so low he was forced to stoop. There were details that were different, however; primarily a corpse that lay sprawled before the door, its skull split by a chunk of oak from the demolished door. It had been a man clad in helmet, mail, and breastplate, armed with sword and short spear.

The sword in Garth's hands twisted sideways, and he found himself chopping horizontally; there was a short scream as the blade cut through the belly of a second man who had lurked beside the door, a rattle as he dropped his sword, and a dull thud as he fell forward into a pool of his own blood.

The red gem in the sword's pommel blazed up as bright as a lantern in the dim room. Garth could no longer pretend that the weapon was nothing but simple steel; he had neglected to consider another ambusher at the door, and the sword had disposed of that possibility for him. The thing was not to be trusted. It was still his only weapon, though, and he still had no time for such considerations.

An arrow came in through the door and stuck in the leg of the corpse; Garth moved rapidly across the room. More cautious this time, he wielded the sword with his own will in sweeping around the corners of the kitchen arch and succeeded in wounding another man, who gasped and dropped his weapons as the blade cut his arm open.

Other men responded with attacks of their own; three men with drawn swords faced him, abandoning any attempts at stealth or surprise.

Behind him he heard steps descending the staircase; there was no time to waste. As his right-hand foe made a slashing feint, Garth brought the sword of Bheleu up from beneath; the man's sword was driven back sideways into his own forehead. The curving quillon snapped, leaving a ragged gash, and there was the crack of snapping bone as the thumb that gripped the hilt was crushed against the harder bone of the skull.

A second opponent's blade scraped across Garth's mail as he continued the upward sweep of the great broadsword, freeing it from the shorter sword of the man who was even now collapsing in agony; the tip of the weapon scratched a line in the wooden ceiling as it swept over the head of the central swordsman, its upward momentum too great to be checked immediately. Then it came sweeping down, and cut halfway through the left-hand man, entering his neck and chopping down into his chest.

The central opponent, seeing his comrades defeated in a matter of a very few seconds, made a wild lunge at Garth's unarmored throat; the overman dodged aside, yanking his blade free from the new-made corpse. Seeing his lunge unsuccessful, the man simply released his grip and let his sword fall, raising his hands in surrender; Garth checked his swing as best he could, but the sword cut deep into the man's side anyway, slicing through mail as if it were cloth. The Dûsarran's breastplate stopped it before the blade struck bone, and Garth hoped the wound would not prove fatal. The man slumped to the floor, and Garth stepped over him.

Ahead of him the doorway to the little yard was open; nothing had been done to replace the door he had ruined earlier. There might, he knew, be more men outside, waiting in a third ambush. Hoping to take them by surprise, he charged out, sword thrust out ahead of him, and whirled about when he reached the center of the tiny yard.

The little court was empty; unfortunately, the ones on either side were not. Men armed with crossbows peered up over the six-foot walls. Garth saw them in time to keep moving, to provide as poor a target as possible.

Bolts whirred and clattered against the walls as he stooped and dashed back into the kitchen, to find himself facing the men who had been upstairs. Two were archers, armed only with short bows, bent and strung but with no arrows nocked; they presented no immediate threat, and he ignored them. The others, three of them, were armed with swords. All five were bent over their fallen comrades, unready for combat; none made any threatening move when confronted with an angry overman holding a six-foot broadsword.

Taking no chances, Garth bellowed, "Drop your weapons!"

With varying amounts of reluctance, the five complied.

"Now, out of the house! Take your wounded and go! Hesitantly, they obeyed. Of the six men Garth had defeated, three were dead; the one who had been made to gash his own forehead was unconscious, but not seriously injured; the one who had been last to fall was alive but in bad shape, still bleeding despite makeshift bandaging; and the one who had had his arm cut while lurking in ambush was ambulatory but unarmed, the muscles of his right hand slack under rough bandages. The newcomers carried out the wounded, two to a man, with the man still on his feet aided by his remaining comrade. Garth watched them go.

He had lost the element of surprise; instead, he now had a defensible position.

There was a loud roar behind him; he whirled, sword ready, then recognized the sound.

Koros! The warbeast was fighting. Its battle cry was loud enough to be heard for half a mile, but by the volume Garth judged it to be much nearer; probably in the stableyard, defending Frima and Garth's supplies.

The roar sounded again, mingled with a human scream. Garth wished he were able to see what was happening, but he dared not venture out into the waiting crossfire again.

The roaring continued, and other sounds mixed with it: the clatter of weapons, hoarse shouts, piercing screams. With a start, Garth recognized the snapping of crossbow strings.

That could be serious; thick as the warbeast's hide was, at close range a crossbow bolt might pierce it. If a marksman got lucky and put a quarrel in the beast's eye or mouth it could do real damage. Garth did not want to let his faithful beast face danger alone. He peered out the door to the little yard, just to verify the continued presence of the crossbowmen on either side.

There was no sign of them. No faces or weapons showed above the walls. Startled, he took a cautious step outside, expecting the crossbowmen to reappear at any instant.

They didn't. The warbeast's roaring had died to a low growl, and the sounds of resistance had ceased; whoever it had been fighting, it had apparently won. Garth listened, and realized the sound was coming not from directly ahead, beyond the wall of the stable, but from his right. He turned and took a few steps, so that he could look over the stone wall that came to about the level of his mouth.

Koros was in the next yard, its head lowered out of sight; the warbeast's back was low enough that he had not noticed it before. Two crossbow bolts were lodged in its fur, but Garth saw no sign that it was seriously injured.

That explained what had happened to half the crossbowmen; the other half must have fled in terror, he surmised. It left the whereabouts of Frima and his supplies a mystery, though. He kept a cautious watch as he crossed the yard and leaned against the wall, watching his mount.

Koros was eating ravenously, and Garth remembered, with a trace of chagrin, that he had neglected the beast's feeding since arriving in Dûsarra. There were corpses or fragments of five or six men scattered at the monster's feet; Garth judged that that would be plenty, as it had not been all that long since it was fed. Ordinarily it would not have disobeyed his orders so soon. It must have been irritable with hunger, and became annoyed enough with the Dûsarran soldiery to forget its order to stay and guard.

It was quite likely still irritable, and Garth had no intention of bothering it until it had eaten its fill of its victims. He watched as it ripped apart sturdy mail with its fangs to get at the soft flesh beneath, and marveled anew at the sheer power of the beast.

The sound of clanking armor from beyond the stableyard wall suddenly reminded him that his goods and captive were still unaccounted for; he vaulted up onto the lower wall between the private courts, the sword of Bheleu in his hand, giving himself a good view of the red-tiled roof of the stable and some sight of the stableyard.

Men were marching; he could see little more than their helmets, but it seemed clear they were heading for the stall where he had left Frima. As if in confirmation of his conclusion, his captive's voice called out, "Koros!"

Wasting no further time, Garth launched himself up onto the roof and ran clattering across the tiles. The helmeted men looked up at the sound to see a bellowing overman, spattered with blood, swinging a huge broadsword around his head.

It provided an excellent distraction; they stopped short, the leader a pace or two from the door of the stall. That foremost man even obligingly took two steps back, the better to view this newcomer.

A cry went up. "The overman! The overman!" There was a commotion in the street and more men poured through the arch in response. Garth bellowed again, shouting, *"I'a bheluye!* I am destruction!" He knew that the psychologically correct action at this moment would be to leap down into the men before him, slashing about with the sword; such an assault would almost certainly drive them all back out through the archway. Unfortunately, he could not bring himself to cause such unprovoked bloodshed, and instead merely whirled the blade about his head again, so that it flashed redly as it caught the last light of the setting sun.

The men stared up at him open-mouthed; none advanced – but none retreated, either, though there were some who shuffled uneasily. He was not going to awe them into flight unless he attacked, but he could not bring himself to do so. Quite aside from his aversion to such wanton aggression, it was a long leap down from the roof; even if he made it without injuring himself, which shouldn't prove too difficult, he would most likely stumble or fall upon landing, which would destroy his dignity and ruin the effect of his entrance by revealing him as merely mortal, leaving him open to a concerted counterattack.

The solution to his quandary arrived suddenly, just as the perfect moment passed and the men began to recover their nerve; in a single silent bound, Koros cleared the stable wall, rebounded from the roof with a spray of shards of tile shattered by its weight, and landed atop three of the Dûsarrans. They died without knowing what had hit them, as the warbeast's claws shredded robes, armor, and flesh; the crunching of bone was audible throughout the stableyard over the triumphant roar that Koros released as it struck. The swords the three men had held flew from their hands and clattered on the armor of their companions behind them; one laid open a man's scalp before falling aside.

Not satisfied with the single attack, Koros leapt again, a short, powerful pounce that smashed another man to the ground so suddenly that the man behind him went down as well, his leg trapped beneath the falling body even as he turned to flee. The first man was ripped open from forehead to groin by a slash of the warbeast's fangs as the second lay screaming, pinned beneath the weight of the monster's forepaws on his companion's corpse. As an afterthought, one of those great velvet-padded paws licked out, in a motion identical with that of a kitten batting a ball of yarn, and the beast's curving claws snatched the screamer's head off, spraying blood across the heels of his fleeing comrades.

Garth stood on the rooftop, virtually forgotten, and watched as the crowd of warriors vanished back through the arch into the street. The huge broadsword hung loosely in his hands as Koros, with a brief gaze at the fleeing Dûsarrans, declined to pursue and settled down to feast on the five it had slain. It licked its claws daintily, cast a glance of its slit-pupilled eyes at its overman master, and began eating.

When a moment had passed with no further attention paid him and no sign of a renewed assault from without, Garth tossed the sword to the ground, then cautiously lowered himself over the eaves and dropped down into the yard.

The gathering dusk had shrouded the stables in semi-darkness, and he had no way of making a light; he peered through the gray gloom at the familiar stall, and made out the pale oval of Frima's face above the door. He strode up to her, and found she was staring fixedly, mouth gaping, at Koros as it chewed contentedly on a human thighbone.

"We must get out of the city," he said.

She said nothing, but continued to stare. Her mouth closed; her throat worked, making no sound, and her jaw fell open again.

"Our best hope is to ride Koros. It can probably carry both of us faster than we could move on foot, and we need not worry about separation."

She was silent for a second longer, then blinked and turned toward the overman. "Ride *that?*" Her voice was hoarse.

"Yes. It is the same animal you petted yesterday, and now that it has eaten, it should give us no trouble."

Her gaze turned back to Koros who, having eaten its fill, was licking its paws clean, then traveled across the fragmentary remains of its victims, to rest at last on the severed head that had rolled, unwanted and unnoticed, across the yard, to lie against the wall beside the arch. Her mouth twitched, and she turned away to vomit on the dirty straw that floored the stall.

Garth waited patiently until she had finished, then said, "It would be helpful if you would aid in loading the supplies."

Chapter Twenty-Four

Although it was plain from the rattle of armor, the mutter of voices, and an occasional quick glimpse through the arch that a considerable body of armed men lurked in the street in front of the inn, there were no further attacks nor attempts to enter the stableyard. Koros was completely docile once he had eaten his fill, and Garth had no trouble in loading and tying down all his remaining supplies and the sack containing the assorted loot from the first five temples – excluding Frima, who remained nervous and reluctant to approach the warbeast. When that was done, he found a place for the great sword, slipping it into the harness in such a way that its oversized blade ran along the beast's right flank, with the hilt at its neck. It would not be very accessible, but it would be secure; Garth was much more willing to trust their defense to Koros than he was to try and hang onto the awkward weapon while riding at high speed. When that was in place, he lifted Frima onto the back of the saddle, and swung himself up into position in front of her.

His current plan was simplicity itself; he and Frima would hang on as best they could while Koros made a dash for the city gate. The Dûsarrans had not yet had much opportunity to see the warbeast in action, and it was Garth's hope that they would be unable to do anything to stop such a dash. There was always the chance that a lucky archer would put an arrow through the beast's eye, or through his own throat, or through some part of the unarmored girl behind him, but he could see no way to avoid that risk.

He made a final check of the knots and buckles securing everything, adjusted his own seat, and reminded Frima to hold on well; then he leaned forward and spoke in the warbeast's triangular ear the single word that meant, "Take us home."

It snorted, and padded silently out into the yard; it circled once, studying its surroundings, and then, with no warning, launched itself upward.

It landed on the now-familiar roof with a crunching of broken tiles, continued forward with a shorter leap to the brink overlooking the street, then dove over the edge into the street, ignoring the crowd of humans.

Garth had expected the warbeast to take that route, but the actual fact was nothing like the expectation; never before had he been subjected to such sudden changes in velocity and direction, such abrupt rising and falling, and his firm grip on the harness seemed suddenly very precarious. His stomach churned with the movement; he had once been in a storm at sea – or at any rate while aboard a ship, though technically it had been in a sheltered bay and not on the high seas – and the seasickness that had briefly overcome him on that occasion was the only comparison he could think of for this new and thoroughly unpleasant sensation. The seasickness had developed slowly and gradually; this motion sickness was as sudden and instantaneous as the motion that caused it. He leaned forward, eyes closed, clutching at the beast's neck, fighting the need to vomit.

Frima, behind him, was equally affected; her head snapped back and forth with each leap, as she fought to retain her hold on Garth's waist. Her just-emptied stomach rebelled painfully, but was unable to expel what was no longer there. Her eyes watered with the pain.

Thus neither could see what was happening, which was probably just as well. Unmindful of the puny humans, Koros had landed full in their midst, flattening several, then bounded forward again, leaving half a dozen dead or maimed. A shower of crossbow bolts, fired far too late, tore through the spot where it had first appeared on the stable roof, and a random spatter of crossbow fire continued to follow in its wake as it made its way through the crowd toward the marketplace. At first its path was strewn with bloodied corpses and new-made cripples, but very quickly the mob vanished from in front of this unstoppable juggernaut, and it moved forward in its normal smooth glide instead of a series of violent assaults.

Garth recovered himself enough to marvel at the number of men his enemies had mustered, and at the incredible power and speed of his mount. He had seen the beast in action before and admired its fluid might and blurring quickness, but watching that velocity and being carried along were two entirely different things. When Koros moved at its full fighting speed, the wind in the faces of its riders was like a solid wall pressing them back; it was impossible to keep his stinging eyes open for more than a second at a time.

Koros had displayed more strategy than could be expected of a mere beast; instead of taking the shortest and most direct route to the marketplace it had looped northward around several blocks, and now entered the square from a totally unexpected direction. It had moved faster than the news of its approach, and burst unheralded into the broad plaza; for the first time since leaving the stable, it roared.

The market was still much as usual; the merchants' stalls ranged around the sides, lit by an abundance of torches, and surrounded a crowd of people. The crowd, however, was distributed in a most unusual manner, with squads guarding each entrance and a large mob on the street that led to the Inn of the Seven Stars. Someone was shouting, haranguing the mob.

There was another unusual feature, far more important: the city gates were closed.

The warbeast's roar echoed from the stone of the city wall and the wood and metal of the gates, and for a moment the murmur of the crowd ceased; the speaker broke off in mid-sentence and a brief silence swept the square, to be swallowed in renewed shouting and jabbering.

No one moved as Koros stalked across the marketplace to the gates. It stopped a few yards away and looked up at the barrier, its golden eyes gleaming in the torchlight. Garth, still dazed from the wild ride – which had taken less than a minute – did the same.

The gates were iron-bound oak, towering up into the darkness, black against the stars; they were at least thirty feet high. Garth was unsure whether Koros could leap such a height, and apparently it was unsure itself; he was quite certain, however, that it could not do so while carrying two passengers and assorted baggage. He would have to dismount and get the portal open.

His head was clearing rapidly, but he did not feel himself capable of walking yet; instead, he spoke a soothing word to his mount and peered at the gate to see how they were secured.

A heavy bar lay across a row of brackets; in the shadows and flickering torchlight he could not see what the bar was made of, but he supposed it would be some sturdy wood, perhaps tarred to resist weathering. Above and below it were masses of knotted rope, apparently lashings around cleats on the two valves; these, too, were dark.

A sound distracted him; he turned and saw that the mob was approaching, apparently planning to overpower overman and warbeast by sheer numbers. He saw an assortment of swords, maces, axes, clubs, and other weapons brandished amongst the robes, and the glint of torchlight on steel armor here and there where robes had fallen open or hoods been pushed back. He wondered why so many seemingly ordinary Dûsarrans had such accoutrements available; did the city rely on militia in times of war?

He recalled that he was unarmed at the moment, and reminded himself that he did not want to be on Koros' back during any fighting that might occur. Accordingly, before the foremost attackers could reach him, he slid from his beast's back and pulled the sword of Bheleu from its place in the harness.

It came free just in time; seeing his actions, the Dûsarrans had broken into a run, hoping to kill him before he could defend himself. Instead, the foremost attackers, too busy running to properly defend themselves, had their bellies slashed open. The sword of Bheleu cut through robes, armor, and flesh with equal ease, and the overman's greater reach, combined with the length of the great blade, meant that the first Dûsarrans were dead before they could strike a single blow.

Behind them their comrades halted, momentarily deterred, and Garth grasped the opportunity for psychological combat.

"Scum! Is this the way of Dûsarra, to send hundreds against a lone warrior? Cowards all! Has any among you the courage to face me in single combat? True, I am more than a mere man, but I have already fought long and hard. I slew the abomination in the temple of death! I destroyed the cult of Bheleu!"

There was renewed muttering in the crowd; none approached. After a few seconds, a voice cried out, "You have defiled our temple!"

"I have defeated a monster that ate human flesh; I have slaughtered those who worshipped slaughter; and I have freed an innocent victim from a vile sacrifice! Does this defile your temple?"

"You slew the priest of Tema!" There was a rumble of response. There was no doubt that most of the mob were worshippers of the goddess of night.

"Who says this? I have fought in the temple of death; I have killed in the temple of Bheleu, and in the temple of Sai, and I have mocked and defiled the temple of Aghad, but who is it that says I have harmed a priest of Tema?"

"You defiled the temple of darkness!"

"Who says this thing of me? Let me face my accuser!"

There was an uneasy stirring but no further shout; a few took a hesitating step forward, only to retreat once again. Then a tall figure appeared at the edge of the crowd, pushing its way forward.

Garth stared at the approaching person; whoever it was, he stood head and shoulders above the majority of the crowd, his face hidden by a hood the color of drying blood. A path opened before him, and the last third of his journey across the market to face Garth was made in bold strides.

"Who is this that comes to meet me?"

"It is I, defiler; it is I who say that you slew the priest of Tema and robbed her altar, that you slew priest and priestess of Regvos. And I am he who will face you in single combat!" With that the hood was flung back, revealing the noseless brown face of an overman, yellow eyes gleaming in the torchlight.

It took Garth a moment to realize he faced one of his own species; he recognized that voice, and for several seconds was aware only that he was face to face with the high priest of Aghad. His enemy had delivered himself; here was the opportunity for a part of the revenge he craved. He raised the sword of Bheleu.

"Priest of Aghad! People of Dûsarra, you have believed the ruler of the cult of treachery, the high priest of lies and deceit, whose altar I desecrated in righteous anger! Let our duel decide my fate!"

The Aghadite grinned and flung aside his robe, standing upright; for the first time it occurred to Garth that he might not win this fight. After all, he was tired, while the overman priest was still fresh. Furthermore, when he abandoned his concealing crouch, the Aghadite was almost eight feet in height, a monstrous size even among overmen. He was curiously lopsided, his right shoulder much higher than his left; such deformities were common among the infants of the Northern Waste, but their victims were customarily killed at birth. That had been a reason for the slow rate of increase in the Waste's population, but necessary, due to the very limited food supply.

Silvery mail gleamed on the monster overman's arms and legs; his chest was adorned with a gleaming red-enameled breastplate. A sturdy steel skullcap with chain-link earflaps protected his head, and blued-steel gauntlets covered his hands. Garth wondered for an instant where he had obtained the gauntlets, which were made to accommodate the peculiarities of an overman's double-thumbed, long-fingered hands; his own hands were unprotected.

Still grinning, the Aghadite reached up and slid his sword from a sheath on his back; its hilt was blood-red and its blade dull black – save for the edges, which gleamed silvery-red in the firelight. It was a magnificent weapon, a two-handed, double-edged broadsword. It was in fact, to all appearances, the equal of the sword of Bheleu.

The creature was a priest, Garth told himself; he could have little real battle experience. His own greater skill should give him the advantage despite the monster's longer reach and presumably greater strength.

The black blade whistled; Garth parried the attack, only to find his enemy's weapon ducking downward unexpectedly, under his own silver blade. He dodged, and escaped injury.

The priest's grin remained, and Garth knew that the maneuver had not been the luck of a beginner. He made a feeble riposte, which was easily parried.

He felt a thin seep of despair as he reflexively met and countered the reply to his blow. This was not what he wanted. He was weary, his stomach hurt from his wild ride, his hands seemed weak and unfamiliar with scar tissue; this was not how he had wanted to face the priest of Aghad.

Of course, he had not known that the priest was an overman. One of his own kind! One of his people, serving – heading! – that loathsome cult! Despite his weariness, his despair turned suddenly to anger, and his next blow was faster, more aggressive than before.

He would not despair, he told himself; despair was the province of Sai, sister to Aghad. Of course, anger was the work of Aghad himself, and that realization angered him further. He would show this grinning monster his mistake, make plain to him his poor taste in employers! The sword of Bheleu flashed up, knocking aside the Aghadite's next blow, and whipped around and over, scratching enamel from the scarlet breastplate. The Aghadite's grin wavered.

Aghad! Aghad was nothing! His time had ended centuries ago; this was the Age of Bheleu! The red gem in the sword's pommel blazed.

"I am Bheleu!" Garth screamed.

The grin vanished. The black sword swung up into a parry, and with a long swooping blow the sword of Bheleu came down upon it, shattering it; splinters of black metal sprayed, ripping the silver mail, scoring the red breastplate.

The priest's face went blank with shock as he stared at the remaining foot of blade that protruded from the long hilt he clutched; instinctively, he brought the stump up to meet another blow that came sweeping toward his skull.

The sword of Bheleu went diagonally through blade, hilt, and hands; bones snapped and blood spurted, but the high priest of Aghad had no time to react. The blade traveled on, shearing through helmet and bone, and the brain that had devised so many taunts and trials was spattered in gory bits across the front of the crowd surrounding the battle.

The force of the blow was such that the corpse did not crumple, but was instead stretched out at full length upon the dirt of the marketplace, surrounded by gleaming shards of the black sword, a red-and-gray spray of blood and brain making an elongated halo about the ruined head.

The victor raised his sword in triumph, ignoring the baleful red glow of the gem in its pommel, and bellowed, "I am destruction!"

Koros roared in answer.

Then, abruptly, the spell vanished; Garth staggered and stared in horror at the dead form of his foe. He lowered the sword and looked about.

With the death of the Aghadite, much of the crowd had decided Garth had proved his point; the mob was shrinking steadily. The portion remaining, however, was the most militant group; when the berserk monster that had butchered their leader reverted to an exhausted overman, they began to advance toward him. Garth lifted the sword again.

The warbeast roared again, and stepped up beside its master; the advance halted. From the corner of his eye Garth noticed that Frima was no longer astride the beast's broad back, but he dared not divert his attention from the angry crowd to worry about her.

The sword felt unbearably heavy. Although the mob was reduced to a fraction of its former size, it was still more than Koros could handle unaided; not that the warbeast was likely to be killed, but it would be too bogged down by the enemy's numbers to defend Garth. He would have to defend himself, and he knew he couldn't unless the trance came over him again – and he didn't want that. He could never be sure it would pass.

And of course, he had no way of knowing what would bring it on; it had come twice now, once in the temple of Bheleu and once here in the market, but it had not touched him in the temple of death, so it was not anger or physical danger that triggered it.

Perhaps the sword itself would save him, as it had in the house behind the stable; he glanced at the pommel and saw that the glow of the gem had died away to a faint glimmer, which was not encouraging.

Perhaps he could talk the mob out of attacking; with sword and warbeast and strong words he might be able to deter them. He raised the blade above his head, with an effort he hoped was not visible, but before he could speak a low rumble sounded, as it had in the temple of Bheleu.

Recovering from his startlement more quickly than the Dûsarrans, Garth realized that the sound had come at the perfect moment for him; he took advantage of it by speaking in his deepest, most resonant tones, lower than any human throat could produce.

"Hold, scum! I have slain your champion in fair fight; would you still dare defy me?"

A tall young man in dark red robes answered him.

"You are still a blasphemer and defiler, a murderer and committee of sacrilege; the gods demand your death!"

"Fool! Which of your gods would dare? I am the servant of Dûs, Bheleu, the bringer of destruction; death and desolation follow me as hounds. What are you, to stand against me?" Even as he spoke, Garth wondered how he chose these words; although he knew his best hope lay in convincing his foes he was more than mortal, he felt that this eloquence was not entirely of his own making.

"You are Garth, an overman from the Northern Waste, sent here to steal by a third-rate wizard!"

This man was obviously another Aghadite, since he knew so much. Garth prepared to denounce him as such, but before he could speak a new voice sounded.

"This is Bheleu incarnate, come to herald the new age, whatever he may have been before! Let those who defy him know that P'hul and her servants recognize this her brother and serve his ends!"

The speaker of this proclamation stood behind the remaining mob and to one side, with a dozen gray-robed figures ranged behind him, all with hoods pulled forward and faces hidden. As he looked at them, it seemed to Garth that the light changed and the square became brighter.

Then it became brighter still, and he realized it was no illusion; some new flame had appeared behind him, but he dared not turn to see what it was.

There was a moment of near-silence as those who still stood against Garth muttered amongst themselves; the overman noticed that more had drifted away and vanished into the streets and alleys.

"The Lady P'hul your sister gives you greetings, my lord; what would you have of her?" The gray-robed speaker raised a staff toward Garth,

Before he could consciously decide upon a reply, Garth found himself shouting, "I am destruction!"

In a chorus, the priests and priestesses of P'hul replied, "Destruction!" Hands flew up, and a fine gray powder was scattered on the air, to be spread across the market by a sudden gust of wind.

"No!" cried the Aghadite. "The overman is a fraud and a thief! Slay him!" He drew a sword from beneath his robe and charged forward, a dozen others with him.

A black blur filled Garth's vision for an instant, followed by a flash of bone-white claws and gleaming fangs, and a spurt of rich red; but as Garth had anticipated, there were too many attackers for Koros to handle; even as half a dozen died screaming, others surged around and past the warbeast. Garth met them with a long sweep of the sword of Bheleu, disemboweling one, hacking open the side of another; a third came within reach and sent his own sword at Garth's flank. The overman twisted, and the blade scraped across his breastplate, bruising his flesh beneath despite his padding.

The sword of Bheleu came free. As Garth brought it around to run the point through the neck of his near-successful assailant, he saw that a new fire was kindling in the red gem. That threat disposed of, he turned to meet the next, and saw that the P'hulites were leaving, walking calmly away, without any opposition; he had hoped that they would aid him. A dozen allies, no matter how ill, might have turned this battle in his favor. What had been the meaning of their speeches, then?

His blade demolished a man's face. Blood now covered half its length, starting at the tip.

Where, he asked himself, was this Bheleu when he was needed? Garth's arms ached as he heaved his unyielding weapon about.

A face appeared before him, and he tried to bring his blade to meet it; before the blow fell, however, the face seemed to dissolve. The mouth fell open; skin cracked like dry mud, oozing pus; white gum filled the eyes, and the man fell mewling at Garth's feet.

The sweep of the sword of Bheleu met no resistance, the man having fallen from its path; Garth struggled to regain control and defend himself even as the shock of what he had just seen filtered through him.

New screams ripped through the square, added to those of the men Koros was slaughtering; a blade lightly grazed Garth's throat, the dying effort of a man whose skin was peeling in blistered strips from his flesh. Gazing around, looking for new attacks, Garth saw none; instead, men lay dying on the ground, their wounds seeping white ooze rather than the natural red of blood. Those still on their feet were fleeing in terror; as Garth watched, more fell as they ran, to lie whimpering in the streets for their last few seconds of life.

The sword of Bheleu fell unheeded from his hands. He had brought chaos and catastrophe to Dûsarra, despite his protestations.

A cry distracted him. "Lord Garth! Help!"

Recovering himself somewhat, Garth picked up the sword again and turned in the direction of Frima's voice.

She was at the gates, struggling to lift the heavy bar, a task obviously beyond her strength; the rope bindings were gone, leaving smouldering ash, and a torch lay on the ground near her feet. As he started toward her, he saw that the merchants' canopies on the eastern side of the square were ablaze; that had been the new light that had appeared behind him as he faced westward confronting the mob. He had no idea who had set them afire, or why; it was something he meant to ask Frima at the first opportunity.

He had intended to add his own waning strength to her attempt to lift the bar from its brackets; but as he approached, the sword hilt in his hands seemed to move of its own volition, and he found himself hacking at the center of the bar as he would hack firewood with an axe.

The sword, or whatever agency controlled it, seemed to know what it was doing; at the second blow the central span shattered, the wood reducing itself to splinters in a thoroughly unnatural way. The ends remained intact, but did not prevent the gates from being opened far enough to permit first Frima, then Garth, and finally Koros to slip through into the empty night beyond.

Chapter Twenty-Five

The air was dry and warm as the trio moved down the stone hillside in an automatic effort to put some distance between themselves and the chaos of the Dûsarran marketplace; the orange glow that leaked through the gates paled until it was lost in the cloud-filtered moonlight. Somewhere behind them a faint rumbling sounded.

A few hundred yards from the city walls, Garth stopped and gathered Frima and Koros to him. He set about checking the straps and knots that had held his supplies and loot in place on the warbeast's back throughout the fighting as he asked, "How did the fires start?"

"I did it. With a torch from one of the posts."

"Why?"

"As a distraction; there were men sneaking around behind you."

"Oh." That was disconcerting; he had been totally unaware of any such maneuver. "Thank you. And the ropes on the gate?"

"They were tarred, to keep them from stretching in the rain; the tar burns well. That's why I had the torch when I saw the men coming."

"Thank you. You have been most helpful."

There was silence for a moment as he pulled tight a loosened buckle. A faint crackling came from the city; the fire must be spreading. Garth glanced up, but saw no sign of pursuit.

"I don't know *why* I helped you!" Frima burst out suddenly. "You're kidnapping me!"

"That's true," Garth replied. "But would you want to stay in Dûsarra at present? With fire, panic, and disease loose in the streets?"

"No." Her voice was fiat and definite, all defiance gone.

"That disease – have you ever seen it before?"

"No, but I have heard of it. It is the White Death, which P'hul uses to dispose of those who have displeased her. She must favor you, as her priest said."

A few days earlier Garth would have dismissed that as mere human superstition; now, he was less certain. The events of the last few days and nights definitely seemed to have involved powers beyond any he was familiar with. He slid the sword of Bheleu into the place in the harness it had occupied before, wishing he had some other more convenient and more trustworthy weapon.

"It may be," he said, "that the Forgotten King will have no use for you. In that case, you shall be free to go as you please; you may return to Dûsarra and to your family if you choose. I make no promises, however."

"I may just escape before that." Her tone had lightened.

"I hope to prevent that. Recall that you are unarmed and half-clad, and that the city is a most unhealthy place just now."

"Oh, don't worry, silly." She petted Koros, who was licking blood from its claws.

Garth smiled. No one had ever called him silly before. At least, not for a century or so.

A blaze of red light lit the sky; Garth and Frima turned to see that one of the volcanic peaks was brightly aglow. A moment later the now-familiar rumbling shook the slope beneath their feet.

"I think it would be wise to depart," Garth remarked. He lifted the girl onto the warbeast's back, then swung himself up in front of her. He was weary and would have preferred to sleep, but it seemed quite clear that he would not be safe anywhere near the city.

When both were astride, Koros started forward in its customary swift glide, apparently unbothered by its recent exertions. As Dûsarra and the fiery volcano receded behind them, Garth contemplated recent events.

His life-long atheism he now suspected to be incorrect; there was something that had directed his actions since his acquisition of the sword of Bheleu. No other explanation was adequate. Whether it was in fact the god of destruction he did not know, nor did he understand the relationship between this power, himself, and the sword. Whatever it was, it had gained him powerful allies in the cult of P'hul, and it might therefore have made him enemies as well – something he would have to be watchful for henceforth. The enmity of the cult of Aghad he had earned himself, and it was plain that the cult had power in lands besides its own; that, too, he must be watchful for.

The sword itself he did not trust; were it not his only weapon, he would have sworn never to touch it again. As it was, he was eager to deliver it to the

Forgotten King and be done with it.

The Forgotten King – there was another matter for consideration. The old man was the high priest of death; it was not desirable, therefore, to serve him any further. Garth would deliver the loot from the various altars to him and then go his own way.

The vague promises of fame, of possible immortality, and of some great cosmic significance were, at present, of little interest; his recent dealings with cosmic powers had left him far less enthusiastic about such matters. There were mundane matters enough to occupy his time. There was the possibility of trade with the overmen of the Yprian Coast, should they actually exist; there might well be repercussions from the events just past to be dealt with; there was his vengeance to be taken upon the Baron of Skelleth. Trade or no, he was determined to have his revenge.

He rode on through the night, Frima hanging on forlornly behind him as she left the only home she had ever known, Koros padding smoothly along. His mind seethed with schemes to humble the Baron, with schemes to seek out and destroy the cult of Aghad, with thoughts of great deeds to be done. None of the three noticed the great red gem set in the pommel of the sword of Bheleu, protruding from the warbeast's harness alongside its furry chest, where it burned with a murky flame the color of blood.

Book Three: The Sword of Bheleu

Chapter One

Galt, the overman trader, shifted uncomfortably, sending a rivulet of cold rain down the back of his neck and under his mail; it soaked into his quilted gambeson and trickled slowly down his furry back, chilly and damp and thoroughly unpleasant. He suppressed a growl. The itching of the armor was quite bad enough without this added discomfort. He wondered how warriors could stand to wear the stuff day after day. Despite the padded undergarment, he was quite sure that he had acquired several scrapes and scratches from the metal links, and nothing he had tried had alleviated the itching. He suspected that he was allergic to the quilting.

Wearing the mail was bad enough; the added annoyance of drenching rain during his watch had him ready to give up the whole venture. And what was he, the co-commander, doing standing watch in the first place?

Packing up and going home would undoubtedly be the sensible thing to do, he told himself; Kyrith, however, didn't see it that way. She had insisted on this ridiculous siege, and that meant he was stuck here. The City Council would never forgive him if he left her here unsupervised, in sole command.

In truth, though, he knew he didn't provide much supervision; there was no doubt that, whatever their nominal status, Kyrith was in charge and he was not. She was all fire and drive and fury, despite her handicap, while he had been restrained and reasonable. It was no wonder at all that anyone fool enough to have volunteered for this all-volunteer force would prefer to follow an aggressive idiot, a warrior and the wife of a warrior prince, rather than a quiet, calm trader.

He blinked rainwater out of his great golden eyes and pulled his cloak more closely about him; with his free hand he removed his broad-brimmed hat, shook off what he could of the accumulated rain, then jammed it back on his head. He glanced behind him at the dark shapes of the camp tents, black humps against the gray-black sky. The rain had put out the last trace of the campfires, and the last lantern had been extinguished hours ago. The old Wasteland Road was invisible in the darkness and the northern hills too distant to see through the falling rain. A gust of wind swept water into his face, and he snorted, blowing the moisture out of his slit nostrils. Those ugly noses the humans had apparently had some use after all; they kept out the rain. There were plenty of advantages to being an overman, though, and on balance he felt his species came out ahead. The very word for his kind implied as much, of course. He looked about, peering through the rain and the darkness.

Immediately to his right waited the warbeast he had been assigned, its flank less than a yard away; its eyes were closed, either in sleep or to keep out the rain, he was unsure which. Its glossy black fur blended with the night sky and the darkened plain, so that it seemed almost a phantom, its edges indistinct, as if it were only a vague outline of an animal. Its triangular ears were laid back against its skull, smoothing its already sleek shape still further; its pantherlike tail lashed silently from side to side. Galt knew that most cats disliked water – very few overmen kept pets, but he had seen them aboard the trading vessels out of Lagur – and he wondered if the creature was as miserable as its feline forebears would have been if forced to stand in pouring rain for hours on end. He was not familiar with warbeasts, and could not tell from its face or its actions; to him it seemed as calm and impassive as ever, save for the motion of its tail.

To his left was empty plain; several yards away a dark shape rose up against the night sky where some human farmer had built his home. Somewhere beyond that, lost in the gloom, he knew there was another overman standing watch with a warbeast ready at his side.

Ahead of him, perhaps a hundred yards away, stood the ruined wall of the town of Skelleth, and the fallen towers that marked its North Gate. A pale flicker of light reminded him that some unfortunate human was also stuck with watch duty, but that man, whoever he was, at least had the comfort of a fire and whatever shelter was provided by the one tower wall that still stood.

Galt envied the man his fire. Even if he had had enough dry fuel to keep a fire going, he would not have dared to light one; it went against policy and good sense in so underequipped a siege as this one. The enemy forces could use such fires to locate the sentries, making it that much easier to send spies out between them, and to smuggle supplies in.

The firelight flickered oddly, and Galt's attention was drawn to it briefly, but he dismissed it as unimportant. The guard had probably walked in front of it, stretching his legs, no doubt.

The light flickered again, and then seemed to brighten. Galt blinked rain away and peered at it more closely.

It was brighter; in fact, there were now two lights, and one was moving. The watch fire remained where it was; the increase in brightness had been the addition of this new light, whatever it was. He watched and listened carefully.

The new, smaller light was slowly approaching. Galt stirred uneasily, sending another trickle down his back, and his right hand closed on his sword hilt. The light was definitely coming closer. Although it was hard to be sure through the hissing rain, he thought he heard boots sloshing through mud. He patted the warbeast's side, then returned his hand to his sword and loosened the blade in its scabbard. The warbeast's eyes opened, gleaming a ghostly pale green in the dimness as they caught the faint light; its tail stopped lashing. Galt took a step forward.

He had forgotten the added weight of his armor and that he had been standing in mud for several long minutes without moving his feet; there was a soft sucking sound as his boot came free, though the motion required little more effort than it would have ordinarily.

The light suddenly stopped moving, still at least a dozen yards away; there was an instant of silence, save for the pattering of the rain, and then a voice called softly, "Overman?"

Galt made no reply, but slapped the warbeast's neck in the signal meaning "separate and surround"; the monster obediently slipped silently away in the darkness. Galt spared a second to wonder how anything that large could move so quietly in the rain and mud.

"Overman? Please, if you're there, I come in peace. I want to talk to your leader." The voice was speaking in little more than a loud whisper, but Galt had no trouble in making out the words. Aware that the warbeast was circling around and that a shouted command would bring it leaping upon the intruder, Galt decided he could risk replying.

"Who are you?" he asked.

There was a pause; the light swung, and slogging footsteps approached a few paces. Galt could see that the glow came from a lantern held by a human, but could make out no details.

"My name is Saram. I used to be a lieutenant in the Baron's guard. I want to speak with your leader."

"Saram?" Galt was startled; he knew the man very slightly, having met him in the course of the trading expedition that had started this whole silly mess. Garth, the leader of that expedition, had spoken with Saram at length. Since Garth's disappearance was more or less the cause of the siege, conversation with the man might prove worthwhile.

"Where are you?" the human asked.

"Never mind where I am. Hold the lantern up so I can see your face."

The man obeyed; although he was still too far away for Galt to be certain, his face could well have been Saram's.

"What do you want?" Galt asked.

"I want to talk to the leader of your expedition."

"About what?"

"About Garth."

"Speak to me, then. I will decide whether what you say is worth bringing to the attention of our commanders."

"But . . . who are you? I can't even be sure you're an overman. Come where I can see you."

Galt considered. The man was merely human, and it was plain that he was alone; unskilled as he was in fighting, Galt was sure he could handle a lone human-particularly with the warbeast lurking somewhere close by.

"As you wish." He walked carefully forward until he stood at the outer edge of the lantern's circle of light. His left hand dropped from holding his cloak closed and fell instead upon the hilt of his dagger; his sword was drawn and ready in his right. "Speak," he commanded.

Saram hesitated. "Who are you? You look familiar."

"I was unaware that humans could tell one overman from another."

"I may be mistaken."

There was no harm in admitting his identity. "No; we've met before. I am Galt."

"Oh, of course; the trader."

"The master trader, yes." There was a moment of silence as each considered the other; then Galt demanded, "Speak. What have you to say regarding Garth?"

"I know where he is."

"Do you know when he will return?"

"No. But what difference does that make? He is not in Skelleth. I will swear to that."

Galt smiled humorlessly. "I am afraid it will take more than the word of a single human to convince our leaders of that. If he is not in Skelleth, then where is he? As a matter of fact, Saram, I know as well as you that the Baron of Skelleth banished Garth; I was there, after all. Unfortunately, there are those who prefer to view that entire scene as a fraud, a drama to convince me that Garth was not in Skelleth while the Baron laid subtle plans for his capture."

Saram snorted, a sound barely audible above the drumming rain. "That's absurd."

"To you, it may seem so. To overmen and overwomen who know nothing of humankind, it seems perfectly plausible. The treachery of mankind is legendary among my people."

"But if I say where Garth has gone?"

"Merely another lie. However, I admit to a certain curiosity; where *has* he gone? He told me only that he would be back before the start of the new year."

"I had hoped to have some assurance of peace before revealing what I know."

"I'm afraid that we'll just have to forget about it, then. A pity. I would very much like to know."

Saram considered for a moment, looking up at Galt's inhuman face, and then said, "He has gone to Dûsarra on an errand for the Forgotten King."

Galt did not reply immediately; this brief answer raised so many further questions that he preferred to tally them up in his head before asking any.

When he had thought it over, he asked, "Who is the Forgotten King?"

"An old man who lives in a tavern in Skelleth; more than that is hard to say. He claims that his kingdom is also forgotten and that he has lived here in Skelleth for centuries. There is good reason to believe him a wizard of some sort."

"Why would Garth be running errands for him?"

Saram shrugged, and the lantern bobbed, its light dancing and spattering. "Garth is not, perhaps, the least gullible of beings. Apparently, some oracle told him that the old man could grant him wishes, and he believes it. I think that his current quest is supposed to be rewarded with immortality."

"An oracle, you say?"

"I believe he mentioned one."

"The Wise Women of Ordunin, perhaps?"

"I don't know; it could be."

This began to make sense. Garth was one of the privileged few the Wise Women would speak to, and he had consulted them on several occasions. No one had ever yet known the Wise Women to be wrong, or actually to lie; however, they took a perverse delight in misleading their questioners. Undoubtedly Garth had misinterpreted some deliberately vague answer and betaken himself to this mysterious old man on the basis of that misinterpretation.

"Why, then, did this so-called King send Garth to Dûsarra?"

"I'm not sure. He has some complicated magic he's planning, but he lacks some of the necessary ingredients, it seems, and I think Garth was supposed to bring back something he needed."

"Where and what is Dûsarra?"

"I believe it is a city far to the west, in Nekutta."

"How far?"

"I don't know."

Galt contemplated this. "Could it be so far that he has not yet had time to return? It was a month or more ago that he vanished."

"Certainly it could. The world is a very big place."

"We overmen wouldn't know. These past three centuries we have had little opportunity to see it."

Saram ignored the sarcasm. "I haven't seen much of it, either, but I've heard that the land extends for hundreds of leagues to the west and south."

"So it is your belief that Garth is off adventuring in this Dûsarra and will return in due time?"

"Unless he gets himself killed, yes."

"Why have you told me this? Why come here, alone, in the middle of the night, in the pouring rain, to tell us that our missing comrade is running some fool's errand for a crazy old man?"

Saram was momentarily taken aback. "It's the truth."

"Quite possibly it is, but why have you told me?"

"To end the siege!"

"You think this information will end the siege?"

"Why not? You came to rescue Garth; Garth isn't here."

"It would be more pleasant for all of us if things were that simple. Unfortunately, they are not. Garth is not the *reason* for our presence so much as the *excuse.* We are here at the behest of his wife Kyrith – who has come seeking her husband, true. But do you think sixty of Ordunin's warriors and a dozen of the best and most valuable warbeasts would be out here solely to please a lone overwoman who prefers not to believe that Garth would rather go off adventuring than come home to her? I was there when the Baron sentenced Garth to exile and I do not think the man was dissembling. Further, I know Garth reasonably well, and I am well aware that in his resentment of his exile he would be disinclined to go meekly home to his wives and children. I know that he might well be impulsive enough to undertake this mission you mention, yet here I am, wearing armor in this miserable rain, watching the North Gate of your stinking village in the middle of the night.

"No, I will be frank. Garth's disappearance was only an excuse. This expedition was intended as a show of force. Our intent was to ride into the market square, confront the Baron, and renegotiate the terms of our existence. For three hundred years overmen have lived a lean and bitter life in a harsh wasteland because your ancestors defeated ours in the Racial Wars and drove us into the barren north. We believed that the defeat was final and irreversible. Our legends taught us that Skelleth stood at the border, a mighty fortress, ready to oppose any attempt on our part to renew our acquaintance with the rest of the world. Your people were reputed to be our implacable and deadly foes.

Rather than confront you, we sailed the full width of the Sea of Mori and traded with the smugglers of Lagur for the necessities our land could not provide, paying whatever they asked because we had no choice and knew no better.

"Then Garth came south on some quest of his own invention and discovered that Skelleth was a pitiful ruin, three-fourths abandoned and on the edge of starvation, worse off than we were ourselves. He returned with me and two others to establish trade and, in accordance with our long tradition of bowing to human demands, we allowed your Baron to set the terms of that trade, including Garth's banishment and a dishonorable oath.

"However, this is not just. We saw, we four, just how low Skelleth had sunk. There is no longer any reason for us to cower. It is not fitting for us to do so. Therefore, we shall not. The time has come when the overmen of the Northern Waste are going to assert themselves once again."

"Have you then decided to start the Racial Wars anew?" The harsh sarcasm in Saram's tone was unmistakable.

Galt chose to ignore it. "No. We have no wish to commit mass suicide, either slowly by starvation or quickly by a disastrous war. We had planned to ride into the market and confront your Baron; we would present our demands, and he would have no choice but to agree as completely as possible. He would, of course, be unable to produce Garth. His failure to do so would allow us to maintain a position of moral superiority in what would otherwise be a case of outright aggression, and from that position we would dictate terms – the revocation of Garth's exile, the elimination of all tariffs and restrictions on trade, and free passage throughout his domain."

"It's a lovely theory."

"Yes, it is. It would have worked, too, had your Baron done his part and met us in the marketplace yesterday morning. He is no fool; he would have given in rather than risk a war he could not win."

Saram paused before replying. "It's hard to know," he said, "just what the Baron would do. He is mad, after all. You have only seen him during a lucid period. It's his madness that fouled up your whole plan."

"Is it?"

"Of course!"

"Your captain swore by all the gods that the Baron was ill in bed and could not move or speak. That put us in a very awkward position; we had no choice but to leave the town and begin our siege. Was he lying?"

"No, he spoke truly, but this is a regular occurrence. Every fortnight or so the Baron's madness overtakes him, and he sinks into a state of depression so intense that he cannot speak, cannot stand, cannot feed himself. Such an attack occurred when word arrived that your company was approaching Skelleth."

Galt digested this information. "How long will this last?"

"Who knows? It varies. This looks like a bad one; it could be days."

There was a moment of silence, save for the pattering rain, as each considered his position. Saram was the first to break it.

"Then you will stay until the Baron recovers and meets your demands?"

"Yes. For myself, I was tempted to abandon the whole thing and try again later, but Kyrith would have none of that. She is quite convinced that her mate is somewhere within your walls and she has no intention of departing without him. Most of the warriors are over-eager young hotheads who did not care to give up their chance for glory so easily, and they supported her. This is the first time in more than three hundred years that the warriors of Ordunin have been on the offensive, and they like the feel of it."

"I am . . ." Saram paused, as if reconsidering what he had to say, then went on, "I am surprised that you have merely besieged us. Why not take Skelleth by storm?"

Galt snorted. "And start the Racial Wars again? I know little of human politics, but while I doubt the High King at Kholis will interfere with trade negotiations no matter how we carry them out, he can scarcely be expected to ignore the capture of one of his baronies."

"It would seem we have a stalemate then."

"Only temporarily; sooner or later your Baron will recover and face us. It should be a simple matter to resolve everything when that happens."

"I hope you're right."

"In the meanwhile, of course, I must stand watch in this miserable rain. There is no need for you to be here, though; go home and dry off. I appreciate your efforts at peacemaking, but there's little you can do."

"So it would seem. Farewell, then, Galt, and I wish you luck." He turned, and began slogging back toward the ruined gate. The overman watched as the lantern light receded and finally merged once again with the light of the flickering watch fire.

Chapter Two

The rain stopped shortly after dawn. Garth mounted his warbeast – which had been named Koros after the Arkhein god of war by a captured bandit a few months earlier – for the last leg of his long journey back to Skelleth from the black-walled city of Dûsarra. The clouds lingered in the sky, hiding the sun, making the day gray and gloomy, allowing the road to remain a soggy, muddy mess. Garth's supplies and clothing and the clothing of his human captive had all been thoroughly drenched when Garth had found no shelter from the downpour the evening before, and they remained uncomfortably damp for hours. Even Koros' fur was soaked, and the captive, a Dûsarran girl who called herself Frima, complained about the smell.

It didn't bother Garth particularly, though he couldn't deny its presence. He ignored her monologue; in the last two weeks, spent mostly in the saddle, he had grown accustomed to Frima's fondness for complaining.

When she had exhausted her first topic, the smell of wet warbeast fur, she went on to others – her own sopping garments, the unsuitability of her attire for a respectable person, the length of the journey, and all the other things that displeased her about the world and her place in it.

The overman didn't really blame her. He wasn't particularly happy about being caught in the rain; the water had soaked into the garments he wore under his mail, and the armor was holding the moisture in. His own fur was as wet as the warbeast's, though not as odorous.

Even Koros seemed to be irritated, and it was usually the most tranquil of beasts as long as it was properly and promptly fed and not attacked. The mud of the highway stuck to its great padded paws, slightly impeding its usual smooth, silent, gliding walk, so that its footsteps were audible as faint splashings.

Frima was still complaining when Garth first caught sight of Skelleth, a low line of sagging rooftops and jagged broken ramparts along the horizon.

He pointed it out to her, and she immediately forgot her complaints. "You mean we're finally there?"

"Almost."

"I can't see any domes or towers."

"There aren't any."

"There aren't?"

"No." Garth had long ago gotten over his annoyance at the girl's habit of asking questions over again and simply answered each one however many times it might be asked. They had been together more than a fortnight, and he had grown accustomed to queries, and complaints. She was only human, after all; he couldn't expect much from her.

"What are their temples like, then?" she asked.

"To the best of my knowledge, there are no temples in Skelleth," he replied.

"There aren't?"

"No."

"Really?"

"Really."

"Are they all atheists, then?"

"No. At least, I think not."

"Are you an atheist?"

"I used to be; I am no longer certain."

"Why aren't you certain?"

"Because I saw and felt and did things in Dûsarra that have convinced me that at least some of your seven gods exist – though I am not certain they are truly gods, rather than some lesser sort of magical being."

"They're not my seven gods; I worship only Tema!"

Garth did not bother to answer. Instead, he studied the horizon carefully. Skelleth looked different from this angle; he had never approached from this direction before. Even when he had left on this expedition, he had done so by way of the West Gate, and then circled southward onto the highway he now rode.

He wondered briefly if it might be wise to enter by another gate. After all, he was still an exile by order of the Baron of Skelleth. It might well be advisable to use caution until such time as a proper opportunity for vengeance presented itself.

But no, that was not what he wanted; he would ride directly into town, defying the Baron to stop him. He had previously acquiesced to his banishment to avoid damaging the prospects for trade, but his trip to Dûsarra had proven very educational indeed; besides learning more about the gods humans worshipped, he had become convinced that Skelleth was by no means the only possible overland trade route between the Northern Waste and the rich lands of the south. It should be possible, he thought, to circle around Skelleth and trade directly with southern cities; he no longer believed that the old hatred between men and overmen would be strong enough to prevent commerce from flourishing once the southerners saw the gold his people mined in the Waste. Furthermore, he had learned that the Northern Waste was not the only surviving colony of overmen; Dûsarra traded with overmen who lived on the Yprian Coast, and though he knew nothing about these people beyond the simple fact of their existence, he saw no reason that his own people couldn't trade with them as well.

With all these opportunities, he had no intention of being pushed around by the mad baron of a filthy little border town.

He had no intention of cowering before the Baron of Skelleth; he would ride straight into town, straight into the market square. If the Baron objected, then Garth would laugh at him. Better still, Garth would kill him! He would take the great sword he had brought from Dûsarra, hack the Baron into pieces, and spill his blood across the dirt of his village . . .

"The ruby's glowing again," Frima said, interrupting his chain of thought.

Garth looked down at the hilt of the immense two-handed broadsword that was strapped along the warbeast's side. Sure enough, the large red jewel that was set in its pommel sparkled with more light than the morning sun could account for.

The thing had been at him again, he realized; it was the sword's influence that had made him think of killing the Baron. He forced thoughts of blood and destruction out of his mind, concentrating instead on his knowledge that the sword he had taken from the burning altar of Bheleu, god of destruction, was trying to warp his personality again. It had tried to do so several times on the journey from Dûsarra to Skelleth, but so far he had been successful in resisting its influence. He had avoided killing Frima several times, and kept himself from killing three farmers, two innkeepers, a drunkard, four travelers, and a blacksmith encountered along the way. The fact that both Frima and Koros remained calm and sensible had helped, and the glowing of the red stone served as a warning signal, allowing him to become aware of the insidious effects before they became irresistible.

He would be glad when he got rid of the thing. Along with the rest of his loot, including Frima, it was to be turned over to the Forgotten King. He would be reluctant to turn the sword over to anyone else; he knew how dangerous it could be. The Forgotten King, however, was a feeble old man and a wizard, presumably well able to resist such spells.

Of course, he was also the lost high priest of The God Whose Name Is Not Spoken, the god of death, according to the caretaker of that god's temple in Dûsarra. And it was a magnificent weapon, beautiful and deadly; it was a sword a warrior could be proud of indeed! With a blade like that he could slaughter any foe . . .

The red glow caught his eye, and he fought the bloodlust down again. He would have to discuss various matters with the King before he turned over the sword – or the other loot, for that matter; just because none of it had affected him significantly didn't mean it didn't have magical power – but one way or another he was going to have to get rid of the thing. He could not keep fighting off its domination forever.

The warbeast growled faintly, a noise he couldn't interpret; it was not the growl that meant danger ahead, nor was it a growl, of displeasure. He looked away from the stone, but could tell nothing more from the back of the great beast's head than from its growl.

"Are you all right?" Frima asked.

"I think so," he replied. "It hadn't gotten a good hold on me yet."

"That's good. I think there's someone on the road ahead."

Garth peered into the distance; the girl was right. That, then, must have been what Koros was growling about. There was a mounted figure ahead in the middle of the highway, perhaps a hundred yards from Skelleth's ruined gate.

Had the Baron posted guards on this road, too? Previously only the North Gate had been guarded. The figure was quite large for a human. Garth tried to identify the mount; it did not appear to be an ox, a yacker, or even a horse. He had never seen any of the Baron's soldiers mounted.

Koros growled again and this time was answered by a roar from ahead. The animal was another warbeast, which meant that its rider was almost certainly an overman.

What, Garth asked himself, was an overman doing on the highway southwest of Skelleth? And with a warbeast? There was something very strange going on.

Koros was making a hissing whine that was its noise to express frustration; Garth told it, "Go ahead."

The warbeast let loose with a roar in answer to its fellow and quickened its pace slightly.

Frima shifted behind him. He looked back to see that she had clapped her hands over her ears. He had not, and regretted it; Koros' friendly greeting left his ears ringing.

The other warbeast was moving now, approaching them. When Garth judged that he was within earshot, he called, "Ho, there! Who are you?"

The reply was faint, but distinct. "I am Thord of Ordunin! Who are you?"

"I am Garth, also of Ordunin!" He began to call another question, but thought better of it; he could wait until they were closer and save his breath.

A moment later the two came together; their warbeasts began to snuffle and growl at each other in the ritual greetings of their kind. Koros was by far the larger of the two, clean and sleek from nose to tail, every inch of its hide glossy black, while the other beast was slightly scruffy about the lower jaw, with its left fang broken off short and a patch of tawny brown fur on its belly. Both had great golden eyes.

Thord was the larger of the two overmen by about an inch in height and perhaps twenty pounds in weight; his black hair was hacked off just below the ear, while Garth's reached his shoulders. Other than that, the two were quite similar. Both had the noseless, sunken-cheeked, lipless faces of typical overmen, and the leathery brown hide, beardless, but with a thin coat of fur from the neck down. Each had eyes of a baleful red. Thord wore full armor: mail coat, breastplate, helmet, gauntlets, greaves, and metal-clad boots. Garth wore a wide-brimmed trader's hat, battered mail shirt, soft leather breeches, and ragged, worn-out boots. Thord bore a sword and dagger on his belt and had a battle-axe slung on his back. Garth's only weapons were a stiletto in one boot and the two-handed broadsword thrust through the warbeast's harness.

Thord was alone; Garth had Frima perched behind him on Koros' back. The Dûsarran girl was in her late teens, with black, curling hair and brown eyes; her skin was a shade or two darker than that of the pale people of Skelleth, though lighter than any overman's. She was barefoot and clad only in an embroidered tunic that would have reached her knees were it not bunched up higher as she sat astride the warbeast – hardly respectable garb for a human female, as she had told her captor repeatedly. Though she was fully grown, particularly in the bust, and not especially thin, it was a safe wager that she weighed less than half as much as either of the overmen.

Thord spoke first. "So it really is you, Garth! Where have you been?"

"I have been traveling in Nekutta, on business of my own. What are you doing here on human land with this warbeast?"

"We have Skelleth under siege; I am assigned to guard this road." There was a note of pride in his tone.

"Siege?" Garth looked out across the empty plain stretching away in all directions, broken only in the northeast where Skelleth stood. There was no sign of an army, siege engines, or even other guards.

"Oh, yes. We have insufficient numbers to surround the town completely, so we are using sentries such as myself in a ring around the walls, with orders to summon others wherever they might be needed. The humans are so weak that they haven't even attempted to break out yet."

Garth suppressed a derisive smile; he did not care to insult a fellow overman, but the absurd inadequacy of such a "siege" was very obvious to him. If the humans had not yet broken out, it was not due to weakness, but either because they had not yet gotten around to it – probably because of poor organization – or did not choose to do so. He wondered what fool had contrived such a strategy even more than he wondered why his people had suddenly seen fit to take military action. "Who devised this scheme?" he asked.

Thord smiled. "Your wife, Kyrith."

"What? Kyrith?" All mockery was forgotten in Garth's astonishment.

"Yes. She and Galt the master trader are our co-commanders, appointed by the City Council."

Garth was momentarily dumbfounded. When he could speak coherently again, ignoring the plaintive questions Frima was asking, he demanded, "What is going on here? Explain this!"

Thord was taken aback at Garth's flat and dangerous tone, but replied,

"Kyrith was concerned about your safety, Garth. She thought that the Baron of Skelleth must have abducted you when you did not return with the others from your trading mission. Galt told her that you had been exiled and had gone off on your own rather than return home ignominiously, but she didn't believe it. She petitioned the Council for permission to raise a company of volunteers to march down here, confront this Baron, and demand your safe return. The Council agreed; the story is that, though they believed what Galt said, they thought such a threat might frighten the Baron of Skelleth and the other humans into treating us better in the future. They insisted, though, that Galt share the command, since Kyrith knew nothing of Skelleth or of human ways and might behave rashly in her anger."

Garth interrupted. "They might have done well to include a commander who knew something of military matters. This so-called siege cannot possibly have cut off communication between Skelleth and the rest of Eramma, and we can only hope that no one in town has seen fit to summon reinforcements from the south as yet."

It was Thord's turn to be struck dumb. "Reinforcements?" he asked at last.

"Yes, reinforcements! Decayed as it may be, Skelleth is still an outpost of the Kingdom of Eramma, the nation that defeated ours in the last of the Racial Wars. They could probably have ten thousand men here within a week, to flay us all alive." He had no real idea how large a force Eramma's High King could muster, or how quickly it could reach Skelleth; his figures were sheer guesswork. He had no doubt at all, however, that the Erammans would have no trouble in obliterating a force of overmen too small to lay a proper siege.

"Oh." Thord's face remained impassive, but his discomfiture was plain in his stiff silence. Garth heard Frima suppress a giggle. He hoped that Thord hadn't noticed. He would undoubtedly be mortally offended to know that a human was laughing at him. Garth himself was slightly irritated at the girl's lack of respect and was equally annoyed at the stupidity of Thord and his comrades who had volunteered for so asinine and dangerous a scheme.

"Go on, then; you just explained how the Council came to grant their permission for this venture."

"Oh, yes. Well, Kyrith had no trouble in finding sixty volunteers, and was allowed a dozen warbeasts as well. We marched down and arrived yesterday morning, but the Baron refused to see us; one of his guards told us he was sick in bed. Galt thought that we should just set up camp somewhere to the north, in the hills, and wait, but Kyrith didn't want to do that; she was afraid that the Baron might slip out unnoticed, I think. There was a vote, and Kyrith won, and we laid siege to the town yesterday afternoon."

That was a relief, Garth thought; it was too soon for any messages to have reached the cities of Eramma. It was possible that Skelleth's people had not yet even noticed that they were besieged; things could still be handled peacefully.

"All right," he said, "you've done your duty, but I'm relieving you now. You go back and tell my wife to call off this ridiculous siege. I'm safe and well and I'll come and find her as soon as I've finished a little business of my own in town. Where is she camped?"

"The main encampment is on the Wasteland Road to the north, but I can't leave my post yet."

"Nonsense. You go tell her I'm here." Garth was in no mood to argue; if he left Thord standing guard here on the main highway, the fool might attack a caravan or an innocent traveler, should one happen along.

"I have my orders, my lord."

"Forget your orders. I outrank whoever gave them and I'm countermanding them. This siege will end immediately; as a member of the City Council, the Prince of Ordunin, and a lord of the overmen of the Northern Waste, I am assuming command. Now, go tell that to Kyrith and tell her to wait for me and do nothing hostile toward the humans until I arrive. Is that clear?" Without his intending it, his right hand crept down toward the hilt of the great two-handed broadsword; the gem in the pommel gleamed blood-red.

Thord hesitated a moment longer, trying to decide whether Garth did in fact have the authority to overrule a commander appointed by a quorum of the City Council. Garth was here and annoyed; the Council was not. That decided him. "As you wish," he said, as he turned his warbeast's head northward.

Garth watched him go; he was growing angrier as he thought about the stupidity of the overmen who could plan and execute such an inept maneuver – his own chief wife among them. A siege was a delicate and sometimes dangerous operation, not a casual lark. It would serve the lot of them right if someone did happen along and take them in the rear. It would be only just and fitting if the entire sixty were slaughtered. For half a silver bit he'd go up there himself and teach them all something about war – teach them at swordpoint!

"Garth?" Frima's voice was not entirely steady.

The human had interrupted his chain of thought – the insolent creature! He almost snarled as he asked, "What do you want?"

"The jewel's glowing again." She pointed.

It was, indeed, and glowing relatively brightly. He looked at it and told himself that the anger he felt was not his own. There was no reason to be angry with the girl, who had acted as she thought best. There was no reason to be angry with Kyrith and her volunteers – at least, not reason enough for him to take action. They didn't know any better.

It took several minutes of effort to force himself back to a state of comparative calm. When he had managed it, he told himself that he would really have to get rid of the sword as soon as he possibly could.

Well, that was part of the personal business he wanted to attend to here in Skelleth; he intended either to deliver the loot he had brought from Dûsarra to the Forgotten King or dispose of it someplace where it wouldn't endanger anyone in the future.

With that in mind, he urged Koros forward toward the town's southwestern gate.

There was no guard; had the townspeople realized they were besieged, there almost certainly would have been, he told himself. Therefore, they apparently hadn't noticed. That was good; it meant that no act of war had yet taken place as far as the humans were concerned.

It struck him as curious that the only gate the Baron saw fit to guard was the one leading north. True, the other four all faced nominally friendly territory, and there was no real threat in any direction – except perhaps from his own people. Duty at the North Gate was a convenient punishment for guardsmen who had displeased the Baron; Saram had told him that, months ago. The other gates were less suitable, since they were more sheltered from the cold winds and more likely to have traffic disrupting the boredom.

Whatever the reasoning behind it, he was glad that the Baron did guard only the north. It meant he could enter the town unseen.

The gate before him was actually merely a gap in the wall where the road wound its way through the rubble of long-fallen towers; there was no trace left of the actual gate that had once been there. Koros had no trouble in making his way through it. The road through the West Gate was partially blocked by debris, but this one was not; it was kept clear for the caravans that provided Skelleth's only real contact with civilization.

Inside the wall, Garth found himself surrounded by ruins. The town had once been a fair-sized city, in the days when it was humanity's main bulwark against the overmen in the final years of the Racial Wars three centuries earlier, but when the fighting stopped, so did the flow of supplies and men from the south. Skelleth had withered, shrinking inward, until now it was mostly abandoned. The remaining village was clustered about the market square and the Baron's mansion, surrounded by acres of crumbling, empty buildings.

His goal was the King's Inn, the tavern where the Forgotten King lived. It stood on a narrow, filthy alley behind the Baron's mansion, right near the center of town, so there was no way he could hope to reach it undetected. That being the case, he saw little point in trying; skulking about through the ruins would just slow him down, and he wanted to get to Kyrith's encampment before she had time to do anything else stupid.

Therefore he rode straight onward, ignoring the astonished pedestrians and householders who stared as he passed.

It was quite likely that word would reach the Baron, which was unfortunate; Garth was still, after all, under sentence of exile, forbidden to enter Skelleth without the Baron's express permission. He might have to kill a few guardsmen in order to convince the humans that he would come and go as he pleased, with or without their permission.

It might be fun to kill a few guardsmen; he would use the sword, of course, and hack at them until . . .

He caught himself and glanced down at the glowing ruby before Frima had time to say anything.

It would not be fun to kill anyone. Humans had just as much right to live as he himself did. If he were forced into a confrontation with the Baron's soldiers, he would just have to hope that he could bluff them out of attacking, as he had done once before. He would not kill anyone if he could help it.

He didn't want to harm anyone, he told himself.

He had to repeat it over and over as he rode through the streets, watching the townspeople scatter at his approach. He had to resist the temptation to order Koros to charge, to ride them down like so many goats, to snatch the great sword from the warbeast's harness and swing it among them.

By the time he reached the King's Inn he was muttering aloud, "I mustn't harm them. I mustn't kill anyone."

Far to the west, in the city of Dûsarra, in a room draped in black and deep red and lit by a single huge candle, a pudgy, balding man in a flowing black robe held a clear crystal globe and stared into its depths. Constant use of the scrying glass was tiring and it seemed to age him, but it was one of his greatest pleasures. His abilities grew stronger with practice, and of late he had practiced much.

He had not, however, practiced as much as he might have liked; he had other duties now, many of them. A month ago he had been under orders that severely limited his use of the glass, but when his special abilities were not needed his time had been entirely his own. Now he had no restraints upon him, no one who could tell him what to do or not to do, but with this freedom had come responsibility for all the affairs of his sect. He, Haggat, was the new high priest of Aghad, god of fear and hatred, and it was his job to keep the cult healthy and active. He could not do that merely by studying his glass; he had to sit in judgment on disputes, choose what course the cult would take, and sift through and consider all the information gathered by means both magical and mundane.

He had delegated many tasks, as many as he thought he could without weakening his authority, but he still found much of his time being spent on administrative trivia. It was a relief and a joy when he could return to his first love, spying.

Unfortunately, his time was running out; he had to go and tend to business, choosing a candidate for the night's sacrifice. He could not put it off if the victim was to be readied in time.

That was a great pity; he had been watching his favorite subject, the overman who had made him high priest by slaying his predecessor. Garth's image had been hard to summon of late, and Haggat did not think it was entirely due to increasing distance. Something was interfering, some magical force of great power. It was probably the Sword of Bheleu that was responsible.

The overman was not doing anything of great interest at the moment; he had apparently arrived in Skelleth and was making his way through the streets. Now he seemed to be stopping at a small tavern. He was muttering something, but the glass showed images only, without sound, and the scene was not sufficiently clear for lip-reading.

Haggat had better ways to spend his time than watching an overman take his noon meal, which was undoubtedly Garth's intent. The image was blurring, and the sacrifice had to be chosen. He lowered the sphere, letting the vision within fade out of existence.

He would return, however, when time allowed. Garth had defied and defiled the cult of Aghad, and it was Haggat's duty to make sure that he suffered for that.

The cult of Aghad was quite expert in such matters.

Chapter Three

"Where are we?" Frima asked.

"This," Garth answered, "is the King's Inn, where the Forgotten King may be found."

"Does he own it? Is that why it's called the King's?"

"I don't know; it doesn't matter."

"Are you really going to give me to him?" Her tone was wistful; Garth could not precisely identify the emotion, wistfulness being more or less alien to overmen, but he realized she was not pleased.

"Yes, I am; that is why I took you from the altar of Sai and brought you to Skelleth. I have no other use for you. It may well be that he will have no more need for you than I do, though, in which case you will most likely be free to go your way."

"Oh." That single syllable carried many mingled emotions; Garth was aware of none, and even Frima herself did not fully understand her feelings at that moment. There was trepidation as she faced an unknown fate, mingled with anticipation of meeting a wizard, hope that she might be freed, regret that her association with Garth was apparently about to end – a maze of confused and confusing sentiments.

They were in the alley behind the Baron's mansion, surrounded by filthy mire and an appalling stench. A few paces ahead, on their left, was the open door of a tavern, and its broad, many-paned window of ancient purpling glass was just beyond. The day was still gray and cloudy, so that the alleyway was full of shadows and the lanterns gleaming inside the King's Inn made the door and window into welcoming oblongs of light.

No one had dared interfere with the warbeast's smooth, silent progress through the town, but any number of villagers had seen it pass, and it was possible that some had recognized which overman it was carrying. Word had probably already reached the Baron of Garth's arrival; he could not afford to waste any time. He hoped that he would be able to speak with the old man and be gone before any opposition could be sent to stop him.

There was a stable just past the inn, but he ignored it and left Koros standing in the alley while he gathered together the booty he had brought from Dûsarra in fulfillment of the Forgotten King's task.

Most of it was contained in a single good-sized sack, which he slung over his shoulder. Frima was another part; he lifted her to the ground and ordered her to accompany him and remain silent. Finally, there was the bewitched sword; he was hesitant to handle it directly, since he well knew that, even when he was not actually touching it, it was able to exert considerable control over his emotions and actions. There seemed no good alternative, however, so at last he pulled it from the warbeast's harness, using only one hand and keeping a layer of cloth wrapped about the hilt so that his flesh was never in direct contact with the metal or the black covering of the grip.

At Garth's command, Frima led the way into the bright, clean interior of the tavern; she was less able to run away with him immediately behind her. He carried the sack in his left hand and the sword in his right, but had she made any suspicious move, he could have dropped them quickly and grabbed her.

The inn's main room was a pleasant contrast to the noisome alley; it was just as Garth remembered it, warm and clean and worn. The walls were paneled in dark woods, and light came from several oil lamps on tables and overhead beams, as well as from an immense fireplace that occupied much of the right-hand wall. Glassware and pewter sparkled faintly on shelves. The wall to the left was lined with great barrels of ale and wine, bound and tapped with shining, polished brass. At the rear a wooden stair led to an upper floor. To the right lay the broad slate hearth that spread before the gaping stone fireplace.

The oaken floor was worn into strange, smooth shapes that showed that the furniture had not been rearranged in centuries. Shallow troughs led between and around the tables, where the feet of countless patrons had scuffed along; slight grooves marked where each chair had been dragged to and from its table over and over again. The tables themselves stood atop low hills, their legs perched on the only parts of the floor that had not been worn down.

Half a dozen humans were present. There was the portly, middle-aged innkeeper, a trayful of ale-filled mugs in his hands. There were two unkempt villagers in dirty tunics who had been calling for their ale when the girl and the overman entered; they fell suddenly silent as they caught sight of the newcomers. There was a guardsman in mail shirt and leather helmet, speaking to a black-haired man with a neatly trimmed beard; Garth recognized the civilian as Saram, formerly a lieutenant in the Baron's service, and a man who had sometimes been of service to both Garth and the Forgotten King.

And finally, there was the King himself. He was an old man wrapped tightly in his tattered yellow cloak and cowl, sitting at a small table in the back corner beneath the stairs. He might once have been tall, by human standards, but was now ancient, bent, and withered. The cowl hid much of his face, so that all that could be seen was the tip of his bony nose and the wispy white beard that trailed from his chin.

Garth pointed him out to Frima; she stared in open astonishment. *"That's* the king you want to deliver me to?"

"Yes," Garth replied. He fought down annoyance at the girl's surprise; he was very much aware of the sword he held in his right hand and the faintly glowing red gem set in its pommel.

The innkeeper and the other four patrons watched silently as the pair made their way to the corner table. The innkeeper stood still, not daring to move, lest he block their path accidentally, until they had passed him; then he hurried to deliver the ale he carried, before his customers had a chance to react to the overman's presence by leaving without paying.

The pair of civilians muttered quietly to one another. The guardsman, with no pretense of stealth, told Saram, "I think I had better go and tell the captain."

"You do that," Saram answered. "I'll stay here and watch." His eyes followed Frima across the room.

The soldier nodded, rose, and departed, as Garth seated himself across from the yellow-garbed figure. Frima nervously sat at the nearest unoccupied table; there was something about the old man she found disturbing. She realized that even when she looked directly at him – or as nearly as she could – she could not see his eyes, but only darkness. His face was dry and wrinkled, drawn tight across the bone, and no matter how much she adjusted her position or her gaze, she could not make out his forehead or his eyes through the shadows of the overhanging cowl. They must, she decided, be sunken back into his head; he did not seem to be blind. There must be more there than empty sockets.

Garth paid no attention to the shadows; he had seen the old man before and knew that he always appeared thus. He was not certain why the King's eyes could not be seen or how the trick was managed, but it had become familiar. He knew that the old man could see, and that sometimes a glint of light could be seen, as if reflected from an eye, so he was sure it was just a trick of some kind.

"I have brought you what I found upon six of the altars in Dûsarra," he said without preamble.

The old man shifted slightly and placed his thin mummylike hand atop the table. "Show me," he said.

His voice was a dry, croaking whisper. Frima shuddered. The voice sounded of age and imminent death. It reminded her of the stories she had heard of P'hul, the goddess of decay. It was said that where the goddess walked, the ground turned to dust, plants fell to powder, pools dried up, and trees withered and died; the Forgotten King's voice would have fitted such a deity to perfection.

Garth dropped the sack he still held to the floor beside him and gripped the sword with both hands. "First," he said, "there are matters to be settled."

"What matters?"

The voice was the same; somehow Frima had thought that it would change, that the old man's throat would moisten.

"I want to know why you want these things. I want to know why you have refused to tell me what you plan to do. I want you to explain who and what you are and what you are doing in this run-down tavern in a stinking, half-deserted border town."

"Why?"

Garth made an inarticulate noise of surprise and frustration. "Why?" he said, "You ask why? I have reasons, old man. If you want these things you sent me after, you will have to answer me."

The yellow-draped shoulders lifted slightly, then dropped.

"Don't shrug it off! I want to know what you think you're doing." Garth lifted the sword, and Frima saw that the red stone was glowing brightly, a fiery blood-hued light.

The old man lifted his hand from the table and made a gesture with one long, bony finger; abruptly; the glow was gone. The red stone had turned black and now resembled obsidian more than ruby.

Garth and Frima both stared at it in silent amazement. The overman had half-risen; now he sank slowly back into his chair. There was a moment of silence.

It seemed to Garth that a fog had lifted from his mind. He felt curiously empty, as if a moment before his skull had been packed with cotton that had just now vanished, leaving it darkly hollow. His vision seemed preternaturally clear and pure, as if it had somehow been washed clean of an obscuring haze of blood and red light. The anger he had felt was gone, wiped away in an instant, taking with it the irritability and confusion that had seemed to color his every thought for the last two weeks.

Perhaps oddest of all was that, though he was still among the same people as he had been among before, he felt alone for the first time since he had seen the sword glowing red-hot in the ruined temple.

He knew with crystalline clarity and utter certainty that he was himself again – and only himself – where he had been something else minutes earlier. He felt clean, and it was a very good feeling indeed.

He wondered how long it could last. The sword was supposed to be a link to the god Bheleu; whatever the Forgotten King might be, could he defy a god? Was it truly the god of destruction who had influenced Garth? If so, how long would it be before he reasserted his authority? Garth looked apprehensively at the sword's pommel.

The stone remained dead black. At last, somewhat reassured, Garth said, "I want to know how you are able to do such things. I apologize for the anger; as you obviously are aware, the sword has – had – a hold on me, and has caused me to behave irrationally at times. However, it is not the sword, but my own will that forces me to insist upon an explanation before I give you these things I stole. What are you? What is it you hope to achieve?"

"You are troubled," the old man said, "because you have been told that I am the high priest of The God Whose Name Is Not Spoken and you do not want to aid one who serves Death."

"You do not deny it, then?"

The Forgotten King did not answer.

"You understand, then, why I am reluctant. I know that at least one of these objects has magical power – I would have said very great power, had I not seen you deal with it just now. I suspect that some of the others are also magical, though subtler. I know that you sent me on this errand in the hope of acquiring items necessary for some great feat you hope to perform, but you have consistently refused to tell me anything of the nature of this feat. Is it any surprise that, when I learned your identity, I feared that this purpose must be dire indeed? The tasks you have set me are hardly comforting; you asked me to bring you the basilisk from Mormoreth, the deadliest creature I have ever encountered in fact or legend, and to rob for you the altars of the dark gods. Everything would seem to indicate that you plan some truly ghastly act of mass death in the service of your god."

The old man sat silently for a moment, apparently considering this; as he did, Frima was distracted momentarily. Saram had crossed the room and now stood beside her.

"Do you mind if I join you?" he asked softly, indicating one of the other chairs at her table.

"No," she replied without thinking; then she added, "Garth might object, though."

"Oh, I don't think he will," Saram whispered. "Those two are too involved with each other to pay any attention to us." He seated himself across from the girl, and together they watched and listened as the Forgotten King answered.

"I care nothing for any god's service. I seek only to die."

After a brief pause, Garth answered, "I had suspected as much. I could see no use for a basilisk except to kill. When you swore you meant to harm no other, I guessed that you wanted it to slay yourself. Later, though, I doubted my conclusions, for you said that what you sought would have some great significance to the rest of the world, and the death of one old man did not seem to fit. I thought that you might perhaps be lying, that in fact you did want only to die, and that all your other claims were merely to entice me to aid you – but the Wise Women of Ordunin told me that if I served you, my name could live until the end of time, which did not fit such a hypothesis.

"Now, you say that you seek simply your own death; how can this have such mighty repercussions? How can my aiding you ensure my eternal fame? I do not understand. Further, you say that you care nothing for the gods, yet there was no mistaking the Dûsarran priest's description; you *are* the one he described as the high priest of the Final God."

"I was," the Forgotten King answered.

"Were? Have you forsaken the service of the death-god?"

The old man did not answer.

Garth sat silently for a moment, then said slowly, "I think I begin to see. The Dûsarran said that it was in the nature of your service to the god of death that you, yourself, cannot die. You wish to die, though; you have lived more than four ages, he said, and now you grow weary. Yet you cannot die so long as you serve The God Whose Name Is Not Spoken. You have therefore forsaken your service – or sought to. You did not die when you met the gaze of the basilisk; your immortality is still strong. Death has not accepted you, the god has not accepted your renunciation of him."

The old man nodded very slightly.

"Then is it that you mean to force the gods to acknowledge your resignation, so that you may die? Do you intend to invoke the gods themselves?"

The Forgotten King did not answer.

"That must be it; you will bring The God Whose Name Is Not Spoken into our own world, so that you may end your pact with him. Such a conjuring would indeed be a feat worthy of eternal fame, a thing unequalled in history."

The yellow-robed figure shifted slightly. "Not 'unequalled in history,' Garth. I did it once, when I first made my pact."

"I can see, too, how you could offer me immortality; I could be presented to the god as your replacement. Such an eternal life does not appeal to me."

The King shrugged.

"This conjuring – how is it to be done?"

"I have not said that I plan any such thing," the old man answered.

"You keep up your air of mystery, but what else can you intend? You do not deny it, do you?"

Again, the sagging shoulders rose and dropped.

Garth sat back and considered. His chair creaked beneath his weight. The Forgotten King would not confirm it, but his theory made sense; it hung together neatly and fit all the known facts, as well as the old man's previous statements. Why, then, did the King not admit it? There must be possible consequences that he thought would displease Garth and discourage any further aid. Such consequences must be fairly easy to discover, too; if they were in the least esoteric, it would be simple enough to keep Garth from learning of them.

He thought the matter over. Bringing The God Whose Name Is Not Spoken into the mortal realm – what would that entail? The god sometimes demanded human sacrifices; could that be it? It could, indeed. Further, the invocation itself surely would involve the speaking aloud of the unspeakable name, whatever it was – that was supposed to mean certain death. Obviously, it would not kill the Forgotten King, but what of those around him? What of Garth himself? What would the presence of personified Death do to the surrounding area?

He had no way of knowing what would be involved. Probably no one knew except the Forgotten King.

"What will happen to those around you, if you are successful in whatever magic you intend to perform in order that you may die?"

The old man shrugged once again.

"Do you mean that you do not know, or is it merely a matter of indifference to you?"

"I do not know exactly."

Garth paused, phrasing his next question carefully.

"Have you reason to believe that the magic which will permit you to die will also bring about other deaths?"

After a moment of silence, the King replied, "Yes."

"How many other deaths?"

"I don't know."

"One? A few? Many?"

"Many."

That was it, then; that was why the old man had been so reluctant to say what he was after. Furthermore, it was the reason Garth would not serve him any longer and would not turn over the booty he had brought from Dûsarra.

At least, that was what Garth told himself. Then he reconsidered and asked, "Is it possible that there might be some other way in which you could die, some way that would harm no one else?"

The old man answered, "I do not know of any such possibility; I have sought one for centuries without success. The basilisk was very nearly my last hope for such a death."

Very nearly his last hope, Garth thought – not absolutely. There was a chance, then. He would not aid in the Forgotten King's scheme to loose The God Whose Name Is Not Spoken, but he might be willing to help out in other ways. He might not win eternal glory by helping the old man to die, but it would be something worth doing. He would not assist in bringing the gods down from the heavens, but he would put an end to an immortal and kill the high priest of Death. That was something that would be noteworthy and significant. He did not feel that he owed the King anything, but there was no reason he shouldn't take pity on him.

That being the case, he did not wish to antagonize the ancient wizard-priest. However, he also was hesitant to turn over the Dûsarran loot. He sat, debating with himself what he should do next.

"You said you had brought me things; let me see them." The dry, deathly voice cut through his meditating.

"Forgive me, O King, but I am reluctant to give you what I brought, lest you perform your magic and cause these many deaths we spoke of."

"I asked only to see them."

He could hardly refuse such a request, under the circumstances. Perhaps the old wizard could tell him what some of the items were, what magic they possessed.

"First," he said, "there is the sword. I pulled it from a burning altar in a ruined temple, apparently dedicated to Bheleu, god of destruction. It appears to have great power – or at least, some power." He remembered the seeming ease with which the King had turned the blood-red gem black and decided to forego guesses as to relative magical might.

"It is the Sword of Bheleu, true token of the god," the Forgotten King said.

Garth was startled; the old man rarely volunteered information. He looked at the shadowed eyes and thought he might have seen a glint. Was the ancient actually showing signs of excitement?

Interested now himself, the overman reached down and lifted the sack onto the table, then thrust a hand into it.

The first item he brought out was wrapped in cloth. "This is the gem from the altar of Tema, the goddess of the night," he explained. "I keep it concealed because it has hypnotic properties that can snare the unwary." He placed the head-sized bundle on the table beside the sword.

At the other table, Frima sucked in her breath.

"What is it?" Saram whispered.

"He robbed Tema! That's sacrilege!"

"It is?"

"Of course it is!"

Saram would have said something further, but Garth was bringing a second stone out of the bag. This one was unwrapped and gleaming black, apparently a faceted and polished chunk of obsidian.

"This," the overman said, "came from the altar of the god of darkness and of the blind; I don't recall his names offhand." He plunged his hand in again and pulled out a small pouch.

"The altar of P'hul was empty, save for dust; I brought you some of the dust." He tossed the pouch beside the two stones, and dragged out a larger and obviously much heavier pouch. He opened it and poured coins out on the table top. They were all gold, but encrusted with something dark brown and powdery.

"This is what I found on the altar of Aghad; the stains are dried blood." A bitter note crept into his voice as he added, "At least two people died while I visited that temple, for no reason but to amuse the Aghadites."

Firma interjected, "You slew their high priest, though."

He turned, reminded of her presence. "I would prefer that I had slain the entire cult, as I did Bheleu's. Come here, girl." He beckoned.

Hesitantly, Frima got to her feet and stepped up beside the Forgotten King's table. Garth placed a hand on her shoulder. "This," he said, "is what I found on the altar of Sai, goddess of pain. However, lest she not be what you had in mind, I also took what I was told the pain-worshippers customarily kept on their altar." He dumped the almost-empty sack out, revealing a coiled whip and a narrow-bladed dagger.

"Was there nothing else?" the King asked.

"I am afraid I didn't think to bring the ropes they used to bind their sacrifice."

"That is not what I meant. This is junk for the most part, Garth. The stones are the true pieces, but their power was largely spent long ago. The sword – that is worthwhile. The rest is nothing, mere trash. This whip is a false imitation; the true token of Sai is shod with silver. The token of Aghad is a golden dagger. P'hul's tool is a ring, now in the possession of a council of wizards."

"This is what I found on the altars," Garth replied. He was amazed at the King's loquaciousness.

"What of the seventh altar?"

Garth hesitated. "I took nothing from the altar of Death," he replied.

"Why?"

"I did not trust you; I feared what you might do should it prove as powerful a force for death as the sword is a force for destruction."

"The book was there, though?"

Startled, Garth stared at the King. "What book?" he asked.

"There was no book?"

"No."

"Then what was on the altar?"

He could see no harm in telling the truth. "There was a horned skull, from no species I have ever heard of."

There was a moment of silence. Then the King said, "Did you move it?"

"No, I left it there. It was attached to the altar, and I thought better of separating it."

"Of course it was attached, you idiot! It's part of the altar! Was there nothing else?"

It was the first time Garth had ever heard the old man raise his voice; it was not a pleasant experience. Though still not loud, the sound seemed to bite through him.

"No, nothing else. The top of the altar was empty. Oh, there was slime all over it, from the monster . . ."

"I care nothing about slime! I need that book!"

"There was no book there, I am quite certain."

"Begone with you, then! Keep your trinkets and leave me in peace; I must consider this." With that, the old man rose, wrapped his cloak more tightly about him, and moved around the table and up the stairs.

Garth watched him go in open-mouthed astonishment; then a glimmer of light caught his eye, and he turned to see that the stone in the pommel of the Sword of Bheleu was red once more and flickering with a fitful, uneven glow. He felt a moment of horror as the familiar suffocating blur of anger and confusion closed on him; the horror faded with the death of the mental clarity sufficient to recall what he had lost.

Chapter Four

Saram was the first to speak after the Forgotten King's abrupt departure. "What was that all about?" he asked.

"I don't know," Garth replied. His thoughts seemed muddy and vague and laced with a lingering annoyance.

"What happens now?" Frima asked.

The overman had been staring at the steps the old man had just ascended; at the sound of the girl's voice he turned to face her.

"It would seem," he said, "that you're free now. As I told you, I have no use for you; I brought you here only because the old man told me to bring whatever I found on the altars, and you were on Sai's altar. I thought that my taking him literally might convince him to be less cryptic in the future. It appears it hasn't quite worked – but that's not your concern. I delivered you to him, and he rejected you, so I have no further need for you. You're free to do as you please."

"Will you take me back to Dûsarra, then?"

"I hadn't planned to."

"Oh, but you have to! I can't go back myself; it's not safe, and I don't know the way!"

"Do you really want to go back? When we left, there was a plague loose in the city."

"Oh." She was immediately less enthusiastic. "That's right, the White Death was in the marketplace, and the city was on fire. Maybe I don't want to go back. What should I do, then?"

"That's up to you." Garth rose. "I have affairs of my own to attend to, and I want to get out of here before the Baron sends his soldiers after me – if he hasn't done so already."

"You can't leave me all alone in a strange town!"

Garth hesitated. "I can't very well take you to a military camp, either. How would I explain a human's presence? Besides, I can't keep looking after you forever. At least here in Skelleth you're among your own species."

Saram interjected, "I could look after her for a while, I suppose."

The overman was startled. "It is not necessary; she's not your concern."

"I don't mind."

Garth looked from Saram to Frima and back. Was he missing something here? Had the former guardsman taken some sort of interest in the girl? He had noticed them speaking to each other, though he had not heard what had been said.

What sort of an interest could it be, though? He knew that he didn't understand humans very well, but what sort of attachment could have been formed so quickly? No, more likely the man was just curious about the Dûsarran, or wanted to do Garth a favor, doubtless expecting the debt to be repaid later. There was nothing wrong with that; Garth already felt he owed Saram something, as the man had been of assistance in the past.

"Very well, then. Perhaps you can find her some more suitable clothing; she's been complaining about what I gave her, and I would like to have my tunic back."

"Don't worry; I'll take good care of her." There was something odd about the man's smile, Garth thought, but he dismissed it.

The sword and other items were still strewn across the table; though he was eager to be on his way to straighten out the mess Kyrith and Galt seemed to have gotten themselves into, Garth paused to gather them up. It would not do to leave magical objects lying around where any casual tavern patron might pick them up. He knew from personal experience that the white stone and the sword were dangerous, and the black stone might be as well. The rest the King had dismissed as junk, but gold was gold, and not to be thrown away, while the whip and dagger were decent enough weapons. The pouch of dust he almost left, but an instinct for tidiness overcame him, and he threw it into the sack with the rest.

The sword, of course, didn't fit in the sack; he kept it clutched in his right hand while his left hefted the bag up onto his shoulder. The gem flickered dimly.

A final glance assured him that he had left nothing behind except Frima. The Baron's guards could appear at any moment, he knew. He turned and strode out the door.

Saram and Frima watched him go. When he was out of sight, the former guardsman turned and looked his new companion over carefully, then said, "Sit down, girl, and tell me about yourself."

Frima saw the obvious appreciation in Saram's eyes and noticed that the man's hair and beard were as dark as any Dûsarran's, and they neatly framed a strong, attractive face. With a shy smile she sat and said, "My name is Frima. What would you like to know?"

Outside the King's Inn, Garth slid the Sword of Bheleu back into his warbeast's harness, then climbed onto the creature's back. Koros stood placidly, apparently paying no attention, until the command came to go; then, instantly, it surged forward in its customary smooth, steady glide.

If guardsmen were coming, they had not yet arrived; there was no opposition as overman and warbeast made their way northward through the twisting streets. The ground had finally dried somewhat, though it was still soft underfoot, and the warbeast's great padded paws were able to move with catlike silence, no longer hampered by clinging mud.

As he rode, Garth found himself wondering at the Forgotten King's behavior. What had the old man expected him to bring back? He had spoken of a book; what book did he mean? There had been no book in the temple of Death. The temple had been a cave in the side of the volcano that towered above the black walls of Dûsarra, a cave that had been enlarged artificially, with elaborately carved walls. The altar had looked as if it were carved from a stalagmite; it was tall and narrow, he recalled, with a sloping top, rather like a lectern or reading stand, with the eerie horned skull where a candle or lamp would go on a reading stand. Other than the skull, it had been completely empty. There had been no book. There had been nowhere in the cave that a book could have been hidden where it would not have risked being consumed by the monstrous thing that lived in the depths below and behind the temple.

The altar was, he had to agree, the right shape to hold a book. Could the doddering old priest who tended the temple have taken the book and hidden it somewhere outside?

Why would the caretaker do such a thing? To protect it from the thing within, perhaps? That might be it. He would suggest such a possibility to the Forgotten King should he ever care to return to the old man's service.

What made this book so precious?

That, actually, was fairly easy to guess from what the King had said. The book must be necessary for the magic he intended to perform. Perhaps it was a book of spells, containing the needed instructions and incantations, or perhaps the book itself had some magic to it.

Whatever the exact situation, it didn't really matter. What mattered was that he had performed the errand he said he would perform for the King, keeping his word, and that the King was not able to perform his death-causing magic. That put his dealings with the old man at an end. Now he was free to do as he pleased with the loot from Dûsarra, to deal with the upstart Baron of Skelleth as he saw fit, and to straighten out the actions of Galt and Kyrith. When the Baron and his wife's war party had been taken care of, his time would be his own once again, and he could relax and figure out what to do with the magical sword and gem at his leisure.

He was approaching the North Gate now; as he had expected, there was a guard posted in the ruined watchtower beside the road. He expected no difficulty there; the man was supposed to keep enemies out, not to prevent them from leaving.

Beyond the gate lay open plain, and perhaps two hundred yards along the Wasteland Road stood the encampment he was headed for. He could see warbeasts standing calmly in a group at one side and overmen milling about amid the tents. They appeared to be moving in an aimless muddle; he hoped they weren't as disorganized as they looked. How could the City Council have been so stupid as to send them out without a competent warrior in command?

The human guard had noticed him now, alerted by the jingling of armor and harness; Koros' soft footfalls were inaudible. The man rose to his feet, short sword drawn; even Garth, inhuman as he was, could read the confusion and nervousness on the young human's face.

"Halt!" the guardsman cried.

It was too soon for trouble; Garth spoke a word to his mount, and Koros halted a few feet from the soldier.

The man was obviously unsure what to do next, so Garth took the initiative. "I think you are making a mistake in stopping me, man," he said. "I am leaving peacefully. You are here to warn of approaching enemies; I am not approaching, but departing."

The soldier was still plainly uncertain.

When no response seemed forthcoming, Garth continued, "Besides, you cannot very well stop me. You are a lone man on foot, while I am an overman with a warbeast and with many more of my kind within earshot." He motioned toward the camp. "I suggest you tell me I can go, before I become impatient."

The logic of this was irrefutable. The guard sheathed his sword and waved Garth on. "You . . . you can go."

"Thank you," Garth replied politely. He tapped a signal to Koros, and the warbeast moved onward. He didn't bother to look back.

Behind him, the guard considered for a long moment. He faced a difficult decision; should he leave his post to inform his superiors of this occurrence, or should he wait until his relief arrived?

His relief was due at sunrise the following morning, and it was now scarcely past midday. Anything could happen in so long a time. If he stayed where he was, the overman might have time to work some dreadful plan. He would be of little use where he was; his only purpose, really, was to run ahead of any attack that might come and give a warning, since a single man couldn't be expected to delay even a lone overman for more than a few minutes. For that purpose the two scouts Captain Herrenmer had posted in hiding on either side of the gate should be plenty; the gate had remained openly guarded only so that the overmen would not be certain that the men of Skelleth had taken any action at all.

Of course, if he left his post, the overmen would see that and know that action *had* been taken.

A third solution occurred to him, finally, one that was wholly satisfactory. He left his post for a few moments, as if answering a call of nature somewhere in the rubble of the crumbling walls, and found one of the hidden scouts. After informing the other man of what had happened, he returned to the gate and resumed his watch.

Meanwhile, the scout was on his way back into the center of town, staying always out of sight amid the ruins.

Chapter Five

The encampment was fully as disorganized as Garth had feared. He was halfway from the wall to the camp before anyone even noticed his presence, and no effort was made to stop or slow him before he reached the cleared area in front of the tents, though he was obviously out of place in his battered mail and drooping trader's hat, his warbeast laden with bundles, so unlike the clean, sleek, new appearance of the other overmen.

There was no sign of Galt or Thord, but there were various overmen standing, sitting, or walking about, and Kyrith stood in front of one tent, listening to a young warrior Garth did not recognize. The two turned when someone called out a warning of Garth's approach.

The young overman started to demand an explanation, but Kyrith's hand on his arm stopped him. She scribbled something on the wax-coated tablet she carried. He glanced at it, then looked back at the new arrival.

"You're Garth?" he asked.

"I am Garth, Prince of Ordunin. Who are you?"

The warrior blinked his red eyes and replied, "I am Thant, son of Sart and Shenit."

"I never heard of you. Are you helping to run things here?"

"Yes."

"Have the sentries been called back, as I told Thord to do?"

"Well, no. You see, we could not be certain . . ."

"I don't care why. If you want to make yourself useful, Thant, son of Sart and Shenit, then you can go run around the village and fetch back all the sentries that you fools have posted. I'm putting an end to this absurd siege before it brings the wrath of all humanity down on us.

Thant blinked again, then looked at Kyrith. She nodded. He hesitated a moment longer, until Garth bellowed, "Move!"

He moved. Garth called after him, "And when you get back here with the sentries, we'll break camp! I want us out of here before sunset!"

When the warrior was well on his way, Garth dismounted, swinging himself easily to the ground, and strode toward Kyrith. She met him halfway, and they embraced briefly. There was no passion in their embrace, and they did not kiss; for overmen and overwomen, marriage was a matter of convenience and companionship; sex was an involuntary function that occurred when an overwoman was in heat. Their mouths were virtually lipless and hardly suited to kissing. Had Kyrith been in heat, Garth's attentions would not have been so perfunctory.

When they released each other Garth asked, "Where are Myrith and Lurith and the children?"

Kyrith pointed northward. Garth asked, to be sure he was not misinterpreting her gesture, "You left them to take care of the house?"

She nodded.

"That's all right, then. Why did *you* come here, though? What did you want to stir up trouble for? Didn't Galt tell you that I'd be back by the end of the year?"

She reached for her tablet. Garth stopped her. "Never mind. We'll discuss it later." Communicating with Kyrith was annoyingly slow and inconvenient ever since the accident that had put shards of ice through her throat and destroyed her voice. He knew that she found it as frustrating as he did, and she resented it when he let his irritation interfere with their conversations; ordinarily he would have been more tactful about declining to let her write out her answer, but he did not want any unnecessary delays now. The people of Skelleth might well have been stirred up by the siege or his own ride through town. He said, as a partial explanation, "We have to straighten out the situation in Skelleth. Thord told me that Galt is your co-commander. Where is he?"

She pointed to one of the tents and made a sign indicating sleep.

"He's asleep? It's after noon!"

She scribbled on her tablet and showed him the words: "Night watch."

"I need to talk to him."

Kyrith signed for him to wait and headed for the tent.

Garth waited and looked about. There was no organization to the camp at all, it seemed. The warbeasts were off to one side, in a rope enclosure that obviously wouldn't stop them for more than five seconds should they decide to leave; there was no sign of any food supply for them, and a hungry warbeast was as dangerous to friend as to foe. Had the overmen been letting them hunt their own food? That was fine for one, two, or maybe even three, but there were half a dozen in the pen, and more still out on sentry duty. A dozen warbeasts hunting in the same territory could strip it clean in a matter of days and might well start fighting amongst themselves over the game they found. Furthermore, most warbeasts weren't picky about what they ate so long as it was sufficiently large and fresh; they would hunt humans as readily as anything else, and that would hardly be good for interspecies relations.

He couldn't judge just how hungry the penned beasts were, but they did not look as if they had been fed in the last day or two; that was good, as it implied they had last hunted somewhere to the north, where humans were rare and uncivilized and wouldn't be missed by the people of Skelleth. It was also bad, however, because it meant they would demand feeding soon.

The tents were apparently placed at random, wherever their owners' whims had chosen; most were clustered loosely about a large, square-framed one that Garth assumed must serve as a command post. Some were not set up properly; pegs were left hanging or lying on the ground.

There was no sign of any central supply; it appeared that each tent held its own stocks of food and water and its owner's own weapons and armor.

In short, the camp displayed all that was worst in the behavior of overmen. Garth knew from his studies of the history of the Racial Wars that the humans had not won solely because they had never outnumbered his kind by less than five to one; they had had superior organization, as well. Humans were naturally social animals; though they tended to be careless, sloppy, and stupid, they were able to function well in groups. A single competent military commander could organize a thousand humans and get them to fight with some semblance of efficient cooperation.

Overmen, unfortunately, were less gregarious. Each, when pressed, would invariably put his own well-being before that of anyone or anything else, including the very survival of the species. They resented taking orders, and, in fact, usually wouldn't obey even direct commands without an explanation of why they should. An army of overmen didn't function as a single unit, but as a collection of individual warriors, each ferocious enough in his own right, but with no sense of loyalty to his comrades, and prone to go off on solo adventures at the first opportunity.

What little cooperation overmen did display had been forced upon them by events, and its forms had usually been learned from the humans they despised. Marriage was a human invention that overmen had adopted because it simplified family responsibilities and inheritances. Cities facilitated trade and government – but even so, the overmen had only one in all the Northern Waste, and it sprawled over several square miles of coastline and hill with a population of less than five thousand, the houses strewn randomly about the countryside rather than laid out along streets.

For that matter, nobody actually knew what the population of Ordunin or of the Waste was, as there had never been sufficient cooperation to conduct a census.

This camp, then, seemed typical of overmen when there was no strong organization and leader forcing them to behave. He knew, from his own military experiences in battling the pirates who occasionally raided Ordunin, that overmen could be made to form a coherent fighting unit – but it was extraordinarily difficult. Where one human officer might reasonably hope to manage a hundred soldiers in an emergency, each overman had commanded no more than ten, at the very most; three was better. Every two or three officers then needed a commander.

And here, sixty overmen were under two co-commanders with no intermediate organization apparent.

Had the expedition been set up properly, there would have been a supply train accompanying it, including a herd of goats to feed the warbeasts and a good stock of replacement armor and weaponry. There would be three captains, he thought, each with two lieutenants, each with two sergeants, each with three or four soldiers. The tents would have been set up in some pattern and the warbeasts tethered in a ring around the camp, to serve as the first line of defense.

Kyrith and Galt emerged from the tent, and he put aside his thoughts. Galt blinked at the daylight; the sky was finally beginning to clear. "Greetings, Garth," he said.

"Greetings, Galt. What are you doing here? What is this so-called siege supposed to do?"

"Don't blame me for the siege; that was Kyrith's idea, and I was overruled."

"What are you doing here in the first place?"

"We came to speak with the Baron of Skelleth. Kyrith didn't believe that you had gone off on your own willingly; she thought that the Baron had you prisoner somewhere in Skelleth or had killed you, and she gathered these volunteers to come find you. The City Council sent me along. We had intended to ride into the village, confront the Baron, present our demands, and settle the matter on the spot, preferably by gracefully accepting his capitulation."

"You needed sixty armed overmen for that?"

"As we both know, Garth, the Baron of Skelleth takes a great interest in military matters. Your disappearance gave us sufficient excuse for a show of force, which, it was felt, might serve to convince him where simple negotiation would not."

Galt's smooth manner irritated Garth. He snapped, "It didn't work?"

"It might have succeeded had the Baron met with us. Unfortunately, we were told, with much sincere regret, that he was sick in bed and could not see us. We did not care to force the issue then and there, but Kyrith was unwilling to do nothing; hence the siege."

"The Baron refused to see you, and you simply left town?"

"We set up the siege."

"Siege! You call this farce a siege?"

Galt shrugged, and Garth's annoyance grew.

"You accepted the word of the humans that the Baron was ill? You did not insist upon seeing him?"

"No. The captain of the guard swore by half a dozen gods I never heard of and by various parts of his anatomy that the Baron was ill in bed. I spoke last night with the man called Saram, whom you know and whom I believe you trust, and he told me that the Baron's illness is legitimate – a side-effect of his madness."

"Did it not occur to any of you that it would be far more effective to camp in the marketplace, where you could not be so easily ignored or put off, rather than to establish a siege you cannot possibly maintain? Furthermore, a single message slipped past your pitiful line of sentries could bring the wrath of the entire Kingdom of Eramma down on you and on the Northern Waste, since a siege is undeniably an act of war. Had you camped peacefully in the square, you would have been honest petitioners, breaking no laws."

Galt was slow to reply. "Such an audacious action did not occur to me."

"Audacious? The Baron of Skelleth is the audacious one! He dares to dictate terms to overmen as if we were mere peasants? To refuse your embassy an audience? It is time that we showed him the error of his ways. I propose that we march back into town; if he will still not speak with us, we will camp in the market until he does."

"I am not sure that would be wise. I did not approve of the siege, but I think that your plan faces the same objections. We dare not push the Baron too far; we need this trade with Skelleth."

"No, we don't. We can trade anywhere we please. The Racial Wars are over, Galt, whatever we may have believed while isolated in the Northern Waste, and regardless of what the Baron of Skelleth may have told us. I have just returned from a city called Dûsarra, where overmen are an everyday sight. The humans have forgotten their fear and hatred; remember how short their lives are! To them, three centuries are a dozen generations, almost five lifetimes."

"How can overmen be a common sight anywhere outside the Northern Waste?"

"Ah, this is the best news of all! There are overmen living on the Yprian Coast. We are not the only survivors."

"The Yprian Coast? That barren wasteland?"

"Is the Northern Waste any better?"

Galt did not answer that. Instead, he asked, "Are you sure we could trade elsewhere?"

"At the very least, we could trade with the Yprians and with Dûsarra. I think we could probably go anywhere we pleased without interference; humans care more for gold than for ancient hatreds."

"Still, any overland trade route would have to go through the Barony of Skelleth; it extends from the Yprian Gulf to the Sea of Mori."

"What of it? Do you think the Baron's thirty-odd guardsmen can patrol the entire border?"

"It would still be preferable to have the Baron's permission."

"Yes, it would be preferable, but it is not necessary, and it would also be preferable to make plain to all that overmen are not to be treated with the disrespect the Baron of Skelleth has displayed."

While Galt digested this, Kyrith scribbled on her tablet, then handed it to Garth. It read, "What disrespect? Why not go home?"

He handed it back. "No, Kyrith, I can't go home yet. I can't go back to Ordunin until the Baron releases me from my oath."

She made a questioning gesture.

Garth said, "What are you asking?"

She wrote and handed him the tablet. It read: "What oath?"

"Galt should have told you," Garth replied. "He was there. I swore an oath to the Baron of Skelleth when last I saw him. He proposed that in order to remove all legal impediments to trade between Skelleth and the Waste and to put a formal end to the war with Eramma, I, as Prince of Ordunin, should surrender and swear fealty to him, thereby making Ordunin and its territory – which is to say, the entire eastern half of the Northern Waste – part of the Barony of Skelleth. He called this a simple and reasonable thing, but we both knew he devised it to humiliate me, as I had humiliated him once before. He insisted that I swear to present this proposal to the City Council as soon as I returned to Ordunin. I was unarmed, on a peaceful trading mission, and caught off-guard; I swore the oath he demanded. I will not present any such disgraceful scheme to the City Council, however. Therefore, if I am not to break my sworn word, I cannot return to Ordunin until the Baron releases me from my vow. This is one reason we must confront him, quite aside from trading concessions or my exile from Skelleth; he must release me. He *will* release me. He will release me, or I will kill him."

Garth's voice had gone flat and toneless during this speech, which was a sign of mounting anger among overmen. Galt and Kyrith both noted it, and Kyrith put a hand on her husband's arm, attempting to calm him.

Galt noticed the gesture, and something else caught his eye as well. Koros stood behind its master, and an immense two-handed broadsword, easily six feet in length, was thrust horizontally through the warbeast's harness, along the creature's right flank. A huge red jewel was mounted in the weapon's pommel, and the gem was glowing with an eerie, bloody light of its own.

"Garth," he said, "that's an interesting sword there. Where did you get it?"

Garth turned to glance at the sword and froze when he saw the crimson glow. He had been working up to a murderous fury, imagining himself using the sword to impale a cowering, whimpering Baron of Skelleth; visions of blood and fire had been flashing through his mind. Now, he struggled to suppress those urges.

For a moment he regretted leaving Frima in Saram's care; had she been there, she would probably have warned him sooner.

When he thought he had himself more or less under control, he said, "I found it in Dûsarra, in a ruined temple. It appears to have some sort of enchantment to it." He found himself curiously reluctant to speak of it, and therefore did not explain the nature of its power over him and did not mention Bheleu or any other deities.

"It's magical? Is that why it's glowing?" Galt was fascinated; he had heard of magic, but had never before seen any at first hand. He looked more closely. The glow seemed to have dimmed somewhat, but it was still clearly visible.

"Yes."

Galt stepped around the other two, to get a better view of the strange gem.

"Don't touch it!" Garth roared.

Startled, Galt stepped back. "I wasn't going to."

Garth was annoyed with himself; there had been no need to bellow at Galt. He was unreasonably touchy about anything having to do with the sword, it seemed; he told himself that he would have to keep that in check. He would also have to get rid of the sword, and quickly; its hold on his emotions seemed to be getting stronger and had been quite dangerous enough before. It would not do to go into a killing frenzy while negotiating with the Baron of Skelleth.

On the other hand, it was a beautiful weapon, a magnificent blade; it would be a very impressive thing to have along during negotiations. He would take it, he decided, and keep himself under careful control. After all, he could not safely leave it lying around untended and he would not trust it in the hands of any of these idiotic volunteers. He would worry about disposing of it after he had settled with the Baron.

He had turned away as he reached this decision and therefore did not see the glow flare up brightly once more. Galt saw the increased brightness, but did not realize it had any significance and said nothing. His attention was distracted from the sword when Garth announced, "I want the entire company packed up within an hour, so that we will have time to reach the market square and set up camp there before full dark." Galt turned away to help in breaking camp and paid no more attention to the great sword or the shining jewel.

He had a curious feeling, however, that he was being watched.

Garth had lived with that feeling almost constantly for more than a fortnight and no longer noticed it, but he, too, was slightly troubled. He seemed to sense mingled amusement and triumph without actually feeling either emotion himself.

Chapter Six

Herrenmer, captain of the guard, had wasted no time; within five minutes of hearing from the scout that an overman had ridden openly *out* of Skelleth to the encampment on the Wasteland Road, he had summoned his five lieutenants and told them to put every man on active duty immediately. He didn't know exactly what was going on, but he intended to take as few chances as possible. He was sure that the overman was Garth. Earlier, Shallen had reported that the self-proclaimed Prince of Ordunin had turned up at the King's Inn, and no other overman had been seen inside the walls since the whole company had been turned away the preceding morning.

When he had heard that, Herrenmer had immediately sent someone to see if the Baron was able to take charge of affairs once again. The report had been negative; he was stirring, but not yet coherent.

Herrenmer had not dared to take action against Garth on his own authority; he was nervous about the overman's claims to nobility, since he didn't understand just what that might entail. Therefore he had just waited.

Now, however, Garth had gone to join his fellows. With their leader back it was unclear just what action the overmen might take, but it seemed likely that they would do something. Garth's absence had been one of the things that had been mentioned by the leaders of the main group when Herrenmer had spoken with them yesterday.

They might be satisfied now that he was back and just go home peacefully – but Herrenmer didn't expect it. He thought that they would now probably march back into town and cause more trouble.

He intended to see that it was not that simple.

Once his lieutenants had gone to find and bring back all the men, he gave orders to those men who were already available that they were to proceed immediately to the north wall, with crossbows, moving under cover of the ruins and staying out of sight of the overmen. This time the overmen would not be able just to walk in unhindered.

When reports began arriving that the ring of sentries that the overmen had set up around the town was being removed, he was sure that something was planned, and soon. It was still possible that they were simply going home, but he would be shirking his duty if he took no action because he made that assumption.

When he had sent twenty men northward, he gave orders that the rest of the guards were to serve as a second line of defense here in the village, in case the overmen did march in despite his efforts. That done, he himself headed toward the North Gate.

He had not yet reached it when the overmen began moving south.

When Garth had announced his intentions to the gathered volunteers, there had been no dissent; all present seemed to take it for granted that he had assumed command and had the right to do so. Many of the warriors cheered when he spoke of showing the Baron that overmen would not be pushed around any longer. They were obviously glad to be taking action, any action, rather than standing guard or sitting around doing nothing.

Camp had been broken quickly and with reasonable efficiency; while that was being done, someone had found Garth an over-the-shoulder sheath for a two-handed broadsword, so that he was able to carry the Sword of Bheleu slung on his back, rather than strapped inaccessibly in his warbeast's harness.

When everything was packed away and stored on the back of warbeasts and overmen – Garth regretted again that no one had thought to bring a supply train; even a handful of wagons or yackers would have helped – the company was formed up into something resembling a military formation, rather than a mob. He placed himself front and center, with Kyrith on his right and Galt on his left, all mounted on warbeasts. Behind them came a second row of five warbeasts carrying the overmen Garth thought showed potential. The main body of troops followed, arranged in ten rows five abreast, and the remaining five warbeasts and overmen brought up the rear.

It would have pleased Garth to have the overmen march in step, perhaps to some rhythmic marching chant such as he had been taught by one of his great-grandfathers, but he decided it would take more time and effort than it was worth. If he had time, he thought, he would also have liked to set up a proper military organization with a command structure that might actually work, rather than the current loose arrangement. He hoped that such organization would not be needed. With luck, the troops would not be required to do anything but stand there looking formidable, and that they could do.

When he was satisfied with the formation he took his place at the head and gave the order to advance.

Movement was ragged and uneven at first, but the warriors got the hang of it fairly quickly. By the time they were within fifty yards of the North Gate, they were moving more or less in unison, staying more or less in their places in the formation.

Ahead of them, Garth saw the guard at the North Gate turn and run as they approached. He smiled; it felt good to inspire such obvious fright. Of course, the guard was just doing his duty, running to alert the village, since one man could not possibly hope to stop more than sixty overmen, but it was still pleasant to see.

He glanced back and saw that other overmen were smiling as well.

Then he heard the slap of a bowstring and ducked instinctively. A crossbow quarrel whirred past his head.

He knew, in a vague and detached way, that he should get down, order his troops to do the same, and appraise the exact situation before taking any direct action, but a blinding wave of fury drowned all such logic. He reached up and grabbed the hilt of the great sword and pulled it from its sheath.

"Human scum!" he bellowed. "You dare defy me?" The sword came free, and he swung it over his head.

The sun, low in the western sky, vanished behind a cloud at that moment, and the glow of the jewel was visible to friend and foe alike.

"I am Bheleu, bringer of destruction!" Garth cried. "Who dares stand against me?"

Two dull snaps sounded, and two more bolts sped toward him; he spun the sword and somehow met both in mid-air, striking sparks as their barbed heads hit the steel of the sword's blade. The quarrels flew harmlessly aside; one left a trail of smoke in the air.

As it moved the sword shone silver, then white, as if the blade were now glowing as well as the gem. Garth laughed. "Flee, humans! Flee before the wrath of a god!"

Clouds had gathered overhead with incredible speed, and a distant roll of thunder answered him.

No more crossbows were fired. The guardsmen, already terrified at facing three times their number in overmen, did as they were told and fled. None of them cared to face this supernatural being who could knock arrows out of the air with his glowing sword. The cover provided by the crumbling wall and heaped rubble suddenly seemed hopelessly inadequate; when the last to arrive, who had not yet had time to conceal himself, turned and ran, the others were quick to follow.

The overmen watched in amazed confusion as their foe, who had appeared from nowhere, vanished with equal speed, while Garth raved and did mysterious things with his strange sword.

As suddenly as it had come, the spell departed, and Garth found himself holding the sword awkwardly above his head while men newly visible were running southward into the town. That was not what he wanted; he wanted to negotiate peacefully. The show of force was to have been just that, a show; he had no desire to risk starting the Racial Wars anew. "No!" he called, "they mustn't flee!"

Behind him, someone overheard him and misinterpreted his intent. "After them!" he called.

Before Garth could recover sufficiently to countermand, his troops were surging forward, yelling and cheering. They poured over the broken remnants of the wall and into the town, pursuing the running guardsmen.

Galt and Garth were both shouting, trying to stop the forward rush, but neither could be heard above the clamor. The warriors of Ordunin were on the offensive for the first time in three hundred years, and enjoying it.

Garth quickly realized that he could accomplish nothing where he was. The other overmen were getting further away and more scattered with each passing second; he would have to head them off. He ordered Koros forward, along the roadway and through the gate. Galt followed his lead; Kyrith trailed behind.

Garth reached one of his warriors, grabbed the overman by the shoulder, and bellowed in his ear, "Let them go! Form up on the road!" Before the warrior could acknowledge the command, Garth was on to the next.

Moving in a straight line and mounted as he was, he quickly passed all the infantry; the warbeasts, fortunately, had not joined in the headlong dash after the fleeing humans. He had collared half a dozen of his troops, and they were now gathering on the road as he had ordered, but looking none too pleased about it. He turned and bellowed, "Hold! Let them go!"

Another half-dozen overmen stopped and looked at him.

"Get back in formation on the road!"

Reluctantly, those who heard him obeyed; the clump of warriors on the road grew. Galt, too, was gathering them in.

A few moments later Garth had to turn and head off a few who had wandered well off to one side. When he came back with them in tow, he found that Galt had managed to gather more than half the company into position. The rest, seeing what was happening, were now drifting back, one or two at a time.

It took perhaps fifteen minutes before they were all together, and Garth found himself again at the head of sixty overmen.

He was also, he discovered, apparently in command of four human soldiers who had been captured. He ordered their captors to release them and had them come to the front of the column where he could address them.

"Men," he said, "I wish to apologize for our part in this unfortunate incident. However, you brought it upon yourselves by firing on us. We are here as a peaceful embassy, whatever the appearances may be, and do not wish harm to anyone. Our people remember the Racial Wars, though, and remember that your ancestors stole our lands and goods and drove us into the wastes; thus their eagerness in pursuing you. We know that our best hopes lie in peaceful trade, but the desire for vengeance is strong. Do not provoke us in the future, and both sides will benefit. I am sending you back to your captain and to your lord, the Baron of Skelleth, and I want you to convey to them our intention to come and treat with them. We want only to speak peacefully with them, but we come prepared for whatever eventualities may arise. I will not be responsible for anything that may occur if we are again attacked without cause. Do you understand?"

The four heads bobbed up and down.

"Good. You may go then." He waved a hand in dismissal.

The four men, hesitantly at first, moved down the road. With each step they moved a little faster; by the time they were lost to sight amid the ruins along the winding road, they were almost running.

When they were gone, Garth turned to look over his troops. They were slightly less impressive than before, as their armor was no longer spotless and shiny; the scramble across the rubble had left them spattered with mud.

There were fewer smiles in evidence than previously. A speech was probably needed, Garth decided. To give himself time to devise one, he called, "Was anyone injured?"

The overmen shifted about, but no one answered.

"Did anybody injure any of the humans?"

Again, there was no reply.

"Good. Now, warriors of Ordunin, I have a few words to say. We are here on a peaceful mission, not to start a war. I am not sure whether you are all aware of it, but the Racial Wars are finished and we do not want to start them all over again. We cannot afford to. The humans outnumber us probably a hundred to one in the world as a whole and have every logistical advantage; that has not changed in the past three centuries. Therefore, whatever the temptations or provocations, we must not take any aggressive action unless driven to it. In the incident that just occurred, I know we were fired upon from ambush without warning or justification, but remember that the humans were probably terrified at the sight of us and acted without thinking, in defense of their home. You saw that the display I put on frightened them away almost immediately. I did not call for their pursuit; what I said was simply in surprise at the ease with which they were driven back, as I had wanted to speak to them. Someone among you – I did not recognize the voice – then called for pursuit and you obeyed. I ask that, in the future, you obey only orders given by your three commanders: Galt, Kyrith, and me. Is that understood?"

There was a reluctant chorus of assent.

"Good. Then take a moment to brush yourselves off, so that we will look suitably impressive when we confront the Baron, and get back into formation."

A moment later, again impressive in shining armor and neat formation, the company renewed its advance down the street toward the center of Skelleth. Garth regretted once again that he did not have time to teach the overmen to march in step and hold a properly tight formation; that, he thought, would really have provided a show!

Ahead of them, Herrenmer met his fleeing soldiers halfway between the wall and the square and gathered them together and brought them back into some semblance of discipline. He had to knock a few heads to do it, but he managed. Once that was done, he made his plans. He knew that his little force could not stop the overmen in open combat, and there wasn't time to set up a decent ambush along the road; therefore, the best course of action would be to withdraw to the marketplace and meet them there. Accordingly, he formed his men up in a column and marched them back to the square.

Along the way he wondered just what magic the overmen actually possessed. The old legends of the Racial Wars made no mention of overmen using magic. The wizards had fought almost invariably on the human side; at least, so he had heard.

It wasn't really his concern; he was a simple soldier. Magic was for others to worry about; he could only do the best he could with what he had.

As Garth passed the first houses that still had roofs, he was considering what he would say to the Baron. He glanced back over his shoulder at the hilt of the Sword of Bheleu; it would not do to go into a berserk rage while trying to negotiate trade concessions or have his oath renounced. The Baron of Skelleth seemed to have a special talent for annoying Garth, who had found the man difficult enough to deal with in the past without any supernatural interference. He hoped that he would be able to keep his anger down. Perhaps, he thought, the little display he had put on at the North Gate had used up the sword's power for a while; he had felt no particular anger since.

Its magical power aside, the sword was truly a beautiful and impressive weapon, and he would regret parting with it. The blade was six feet of gleaming steel; the hilt was made of some black, polished substance he couldn't identify, the pommel was a silver claw clutching that immense red jewel. It looked like a ruby, though it was hard to believe a ruby could be that large. Whatever it was, it was the color of fresh blood, and he was relieved to see, glancing back, that though it sparkled in the afternoon sun at the moment, it did not appear to be glowing.

He would definitely have to get rid of the thing. It might even have been wise to dispose of it before speaking with the Baron, but he could not bring himself to do so. That would have left him virtually unarmed, and he wanted every advantage when confronting Doran of Skelleth.

His first sight of the Baron had been as the man presided over the execution of the guardsman whose negligence had allowed Garth to enter Skelleth unannounced the first time he came south; the townspeople had blamed Garth for the man's death. The Baron had demanded at swordpoint that Garth turn over to him the basilisk that he had just gone to great trouble to fetch. Garth had come out ahead in that encounter by stealing the basilisk back and later killing it before the Baron could recover it – but that had so annoyed the Baron that, when Garth returned as a trader, he was systematically insulted, humiliated, and forced to swear the oath he now hoped to have revoked.

They were well into the inhabited area now, but there were no people to be seen; Garth guessed that they had been warned by the guards and had taken shelter. He caught sight of someone on the street ahead, making hand signals to someone else Garth could not see before the signaler vanished around a corner. Whatever other advantages the overmen might have, they would not have the element of surprise.

They didn't need it, Garth told himself. An overman could easily handle any two humans, and a warbeast half a dozen; and Skelleth's entire military was comprised of about three dozen guards – perhaps not quite that many, since the Baron had executed Arner and dismissed Saram as a result of Garth's earlier visits and might not have replaced them yet. Garth's company could deal with the guards easily, should it become necessary.

If the civilian population were to attack them, though, there might be a real problem. Garth had no idea what Skelleth's population was; he doubted anyone knew. It didn't matter, he assured himself. This was to be a peaceful demonstration, not a battle.

The streets remained deserted, save for occasional figures ahead who vanished as soon as they signaled that the overmen were approaching. Garth spotted three of these before he led his party into the northwest corner of the marketplace.

The square was not deserted. There were no merchants, no farmers, none of the ordinary villagers going about their business; instead, there were two dozen guardsmen lined up neatly in front of the Baron's mansion, along the north side of the market. They were divided into two equal groups, one on either side of the central door, with each group arranged three deep and four abreast. Every man wore a shoddy mail tunic and held a drawn short sword; every head wore a leather helmet, and every belt bore a dagger. Four of the helmets were studded with iron, indicating that their wearers were lieutenants; these men were located in the center of each block.

This pitiful squad, Garth realized, represented the armed might of Skelleth, the once-great fortress from which his people had cowered in fear for three hundred years. He suppressed an urge to laugh in their faces as he marched his own force into the center of the square, swinging around to the south to come to a halt in some semblance of formation, directly facing the human soldiers. In this half-circuit of the market he and his troops got their first good look at the civilian population of Skelleth; the people were crowded into every street that entered the square, except for the one the overmen had marched on. They watched with varied emotions the arrival of their traditional foes. None stepped across the invisible line dividing the market from the rest of the village.

Whispers, rustles, and shuffling feet were audible, but no one spoke aloud until Garth bellowed, "We have come to speak with the Baron of Skelleth!"

The sounds shifted subtly; fewer feet scraped the dirt, more voices whispered. From the corners of his eyes Garth could see the mouths of two streets; both were full of people, all ragged and dirty, and almost all thin and unhealthy. These were the invincible warriors his ancestors had feared. A surge of fury fountained up within him; how could he and his people have taken so long to discover their foe's weakness? It was not fitting that overmen should have feared such creatures.

The door of the Baron's mansion opened, and the whisperings faded in anticipation.

It was not the Baron who emerged; the whispering flourished anew as Garth recognized the man who stepped out into the square and stood between the two groups of guardsmen. Tall for a human, dark of hair and eye, wearing the steel helmet that was his badge of rank, Herrenmer, captain of the Baron's guard and Skelleth's military commander, faced the overmen.

"The Baron is not well," Herrenmer said. "I have just come from his bedside. Perhaps I can serve in his place."

Only the Baron could free Garth from his oath, so Garth's reply was immediate. "We have come to see the Baron on matters that cannot be left to underlings. We have come peacefully seeking an audience, despite the assault upon us by your men, and we will remain here in this square until that audience is granted."

"Very well; I will inform the Baron of what you have said and see if he feels well enough to deal with you himself." Herrenmer turned and re-entered the mansion.

Garth and the overmen waited, sitting astride their warbeasts or standing where they were. Garth remained as motionless as he could; the sinking sun was hot on his left cheek, and there was an unpleasant itch below his left arm. Even had he been able to scratch it through his armor, to do so would have ruined the dignity of his appearance. Instead he sat, waiting for Herrenmer's return or the Baron's emergence, growing steadily more irritated as the whispering in the watching crowd ebbed and flowed.

Beside him, Galt and Kyrith also sat still; but behind them, the other overmen were less restrained. They were in unfamiliar territory and looked about themselves with interest.

The poverty and decay of the town were plain on all sides; the only building not in obvious need of repair was the Baron's mansion. Shutters were missing or broken, roofs sagged, doors failed to fit their twisted frames. It appeared that little had been done to maintain the town in the three centuries since overmen had last seen it. For the most part, the warriors thought very little of the place.

The mansion's door opened again, and again the whispers hushed; this time Herrenmer pushed the doors wide and latched them open, then stood to one side. A moment later the Baron of Skelleth emerged, shuffling forward uncertainly. He was clad in a black robe embroidered with red and wore a circlet of gold on his brow; his hair and sparse beard were black. He was small and thin and seemed even smaller as he was hunched over slightly; his right hand appeared to tremble slightly as he raised it and said, "Greetings, overmen."

"Greetings, Doran of Skelleth," Garth replied.

"So you have come to torment me further? Is not the life the gods have cursed me with torment enough to please you?" His face twisted in a ghastly smile; he raised his head, struggling to stand upright, and looked directly at Garth. The overman met his gaze and was taken aback by the abject despair he saw there, the liquid sorrow of a dying animal.

He was slow in replying, "We have come to ask you to reconsider some of your previous decisions. My people are not pleased by your actions in response to our attempts to establish peaceful and profitable trade between our two nations."

"You have forced me to rise from my sickbed because I have allowed you insufficient opportunity to swindle my subjects?" The parody of a smile remained, perhaps broadened. Garth, already annoyed, felt his anger piling up within him; he began to wonder whether the Baron was exaggerating his illness. The question was not that of a man sunk in unbearable woe; it smacked rather of the cleverness that Garth had seen the Baron display when at the peak of his cycle.

"We do not swindle anyone. You have compelled me to swear an oath that is intended to humiliate me. You have exiled me from your realm for no reason other than your personal dislike for me. The trader Galt tells me that the tariffs and regulations you propose, should my people refuse to acknowledge you as our overlord, are prohibitive, making peaceful trade impossible, although we all know it would benefit Skelleth as much as Ordunin. We have come here to ask you to correct these injustices, to benefit the people of your village as well as ourselves."

"What injustices? I ask nothing unreasonable!" The mocking smile was gone; the slouch and the trembling had lessened until they were almost imperceptible. The eyes were still desolate, though; Garth found that disturbing.

He did not understand this man at all. His failure to understand enraged him further. His answer was shouted, not spoken. "Nothing unreasonable? Is it reasonable to prevent the enrichment of us all merely to feed your own bloated ego? Do you seriously think that any overman could swear fealty to a human?"

Beside him, Galt's red eyes shifted back and forth, scanning the crowd. He was not happy with what he saw; Garth's outburst was provoking fear and resentment in both soldiers and civilians; this was plainly visible in their faces. He upbraided himself mentally for allowing Garth to act as sole spokesman;

Garth was not as stupid as some overmen, nor as ignorant or careless, but he did have a nasty temper at times, and was not trained at restraining it. Galt, on the other hand, had spent most of his apprenticeship learning to take in his stride the asinine behavior a trader was likely to encounter among humans; he was sure that he could have handled this affair with greater tact.

It would have been difficult, he thought, to have shown less tact. He debated breaking into the conversation himself, trying to calm everyone. He was quite sure that, if Garth was not careful, this debate could lead to bloodshed and disaster. He cast a glance sideways at Garth, but could read nothing in his face; before he could reach a decision his gaze was caught by the hilt of the strange broadsword that Garth had acquired. The red gem set in it was gleaming brightly.

The Baron, too, seemed to notice the sword as he replied to Garth's outburst. "Do your people need this trade so desperately? You come here armed, with a force twice the number Skelleth can muster, the least of you carrying weapons and armor better than I can afford for myself. Your leader has a sword set with gems. Every one of you is well-fed and healthy, as far as I can see. Yet you protest mightily that I have demanded more than you can give. My people are starving, overmen. Look around you; my people are dying of cold and hunger. Is it unfair that I ask tariffs of you before allowing you to come and frighten them into giving you what little they have in exchange for the worthless trinkets you bring them? Is it unfair that I have hoped to collect taxes from you, that I might relieve their suffering? Is it unfair that I have tried to keep away from them those of you known to have committed murder, such as you? Is it unfair that I have asked your people to come only in groups small enough to pose no threat to the safety and well-being of Skelleth? Our two nations have been at war for half a millennium, Garth; now you come here, defying the laws and edicts of this realm, and demand that you be treated as an honored friend and neighbor. Can you think that I will give in willingly?"

Garth's right hand had crept across his chest toward his left shoulder and the hilt of the great sword during this speech; his fingers touched the weapon as Galt replied quickly, "You are twisting the truth and playing with words, Baron. We would not protest reasonable tariffs, though they would go, not to your starving people, but into your own pocket. We have no wish to cheat or deceive your people. If you do not want what we can trade, we will pay in gold for what we need. We can abide by restrictions on our travel in your lands, but you have ordered that no party of more than three may come; how can we form caravans to pass the dangers of the road in safety? Your claimed reasons for distrusting us are nonsense; Garth has killed in self-defense, but is no wanton murderer, and the war between our peoples ended three hundred years ago. You have asked us to give up our independence as a nation simply to obtain the right to trade; would you be willing to surrender your barony to us were the situation reversed?"

Galt's intrusion into the conversation had come as a surprise to everyone present; Garth had thrown him a startled glance, but let him speak. The Baron continued to stare directly at Garth.

"I do not parley with servants," the Baron said.

Galt fought back a reply; it was Garth's turn again.

"He speaks the truth, Baron, perhaps more eloquently than I could, while you lie. You say that you do not parley with servants, yet you seem willing enough to speak to one you call a murderer; where is the logic in that? Galt is no servant, as you well know; you seek to insult and enrage us. Why?"

There was a moment of silence; then the Baron turned and began walking back toward his home. "I do not answer to murderers," he said.

"Hold, man!" Garth bellowed; his right hand closed on the sword and snatched it out of its sheath. With a flourish, he swung it about and hoisted it crosswise above his head.

The Baron stopped on the threshold and turned back to face the overmen again. "I have called your bluff, Garth," he said. "I hold all power here, save what you take by strength of arms. You have that strength; we both know that. You could kill me, and destroy Skelleth – but to do so would start the Racial Wars anew, and this time humanity would not be satisfied to drive you filthy monsters into the wilderness. This time, Garth, they would wipe you out, to the last stinking freak. You have no other choice; accept my terms, or fight and die. I will not change my terms. I am neither fool nor coward to be impressed by this handful of would-be warriors. If your people want to trade here, then you, Garth, are exiled, and sworn to offer your City Council the opportunity to surrender to me. Any trade in Skelleth will be by *my* rules. I will forgive you this one intrusion, but the next time armed overmen come here, I will send word to the High King at Kholis. Now, put away that ridiculous sword and go, all of you; leave me in peace!"

Garth's mounting fury could no longer be contained; he spun the Sword of Bheleu over his head, screaming, and then hurled it at the Baron's back as the man stepped through the doorway.

With a roar, the sword burst into flame in mid-air, and plunged burning into the Baron's back; his embroidered robe blazed up immediately as two feet of fiery, bloodstained blade protruded from his chest.

Despite the obvious force of the blow which had so easily pierced him, the Baron staggered and remained upright. He turned one last time, to face out toward the marketplace; his clothes and hair were lost in red flame. For an instant it seemed to Garth that his eyes, too, were afire.

"Fool!" he said; then he toppled forward onto his face. The sharp impact with the threshold drove the blade backward through his chest and out his back; as he twitched one final time it came free and fell forward across one shoulder, its hilt pointed directly at Garth.

Chapter Seven

There was a frozen moment of near-silence; the only sound was the crackling of the flames. For long seconds, no one moved.

Garth thought he heard soft, mocking laughter; he turned, but could not locate its source. The fury still boiled within him, but when he had thrown the sword its hold had loosened, and he was able to think again.

As he looked around, he saw shock and astonishment on every face; humans and overmen alike were staring at the burning corpse. No one was laughing; no one smiled; no one spoke. Then one of the guardsmen broke the silence, speaking in a harsh whisper that carried to every corner of the square. "Black magic!"

Another voice, this one from one of the crowded streets, shouted, "Kill them! Kill the overmen!" Garth spun about and thought he saw the shouter, an old man wearing dark red who stood in the forefront of the crowd in the street that led to the West Gate. He had no chance to reply or to make certain of his identification before he heard the snap of a bowstring. Instinctively, he ducked.

For the second time that day, an arrow whistled over his head; it continued on, to scrape against Galt's breastplate before falling to the clear ground between the soldiers of Skelleth and the first row of warbeasts.

"Down! Get down!" Garth called; following his own advice, he slid from the saddle. As he reached the ground, a ragged volley of arrows followed, coming from all directions.

Immediately, he understood the entire situation and berated himself for not anticipating it. He had seen the twenty-five guardsmen in front of the mansion and considered them to be the entire force, even though he knew there were more than thirty men in the Baron's service. The others had been stationed in windows and on rooftops all around the square. The Baron had been a clever man, even in his madness. It was possible there were other dangers hidden in the crowds – and the crowds were themselves a problem, blocking every avenue of retreat save one, keeping the overmen bottled up in the market where they were easy targets.

More arrows flew, whistling and buzzing; the thumping of bowstrings was now coming in a steady, uneven rhythm. Around him, the overmen were shouting; he heard a cry of pain and the growling of a warbeast.

It was far too late now to prevent bloodshed; despite his good intentions, the sword had overcome him, and this peaceful mission had become a battle.

That being so, Garth told himself, it was a battle he intended to win. The anger still seethed in him; it had been far too long since the overmen of the Northern Waste had won a battle, and this seemed a good place to start.

He looked around; the situation was bad. His troops, completely untrained, were milling about in confusion as arrows rained down on them from every side; half the mounted overmen had followed his example and dismounted, but the others were still on their warbeasts, looking about in dazed confusion. The villagers, soldiers and civilians alike, were staying well back, letting their archers deal with the invaders. None of the overmen had yet taken any action to remedy their vulnerable position.

"Ho, overmen of Ordunin!" Garth bellowed at the top of his lungs. "The battle is begun, whether we want it or no! Advance, then, and kill the guardsmen!" He gave this order, not because he considered the soldiers a threat, but because the archers would be reluctant to shoot into a melee involving their own comrades. It was the simplest order he could think of that would serve a useful purpose at this point. Once he had his overmen acting together again and responding to his commands, he could worry about better tactics.

Confused and angry, the overmen were glad to obey; now that they had a direction, they charged forward around the warbeasts that blocked their way. The mounted warriors did not seem to hear Garth's order; they continued to look about in confusion. As Garth watched, an arrow caught one young overman in the throat; soundlessly, he slid sideways out of the saddle, blood welling in his mouth, his red eyes wide with shock.

The overmen who had dismounted joined their companions in the charge, leaving their beasts behind. Garth suddenly realized that none of them really knew how to control the great animals.

The best thing for morale, Garth knew, would be to join the charge himself; there were tactical considerations, however, that were more important. As he had hoped, the archers were slackening their fire for fear of hitting their townsmen; but when the overmen had wiped out the humans – as they inevitably would do – the archers would again have a clear field of fire. The bowmen remained, therefore, the biggest threat, and Garth knew his best weapon was the warbeasts. It was time to pit the two against each other. When the first overmen reached the human soldiers, Garth spotted the location of one archer as the man leaned out from behind a chimney to release another arrow. With a wordless growl, Garth pointed this out to Koros, then ordered the warbeast, "Kill!"

The monstrous animal roared in response, a sound that drowned out the growing clamor of the battle for a moment, then turned and leaped onto the back of its neighboring kin. From there it sprang upward in a magnificent jump that landed it on the roof where the bowman lurked. Shards of splintered slate flew in every direction at the impact of the warbeast's weight; the man had time for one short scream before Koros smashed the chimney out of the way and ripped him apart.

Garth did not wait to watch the archer's death; he was already pointing out another to Kyrith's warbeast. When that animal had leaped for its target he turned back to Galt's, and then started on the first row of five.

Not all the warbeasts were as successful as Koros; one missed the roof it was aiming for and tried to scramble up the wall, its claws tearing out chunks of wood and plaster. Another made its leap perfectly, but landed on a thatched roof that was unable to support its weight; the beast and the archer it pursued both vanished into the building's upper floor, amid growls and screams.

Not all the bowmen were on rooftops; some were behind upper-floor windows too small for the huge animals to fit through. The warbeasts, direct and simple creatures, dealt with this by ripping out the wall around each window.

When he had sent warbeasts after every archer he could locate, leaving four of the animals in the middle of the square, Garth turned his attention back to the fighting in front of the mansion. His troops appeared to have the situation in hand. Outnumbering the humans two to one even after the casualties inflicted by the archers, the overmen seemed to have their main problem in avoiding their own fellows. The twenty-five guards had been reduced to a knot of half a dozen, clustered in front of the open doors around the burning body of their lord.

The civilian population of the town had done nothing yet except to produce a great deal of noise; no one had ventured into the square. The crowds seemed smaller; probably, Garth thought, many had fled and taken shelter wherever they could. Those who remained merely watched, yelling.

Garth dismissed them from consideration for the moment and strode forward to aid his warriors in dealing with the surviving guardsmen.

"Hold!" he called. "Stand back!"

Reluctantly, the overmen obeyed. The remaining humans stood, swords bristling, and waited.

"There is no need to continue the fight! Surrender and we will allow you to live."

Herrenmer was one of the survivors. It was he who answered, "Never, monster! We saw how well we could trust you when you slew the Baron!"

Garth fought down a surge of anger. "Have not enough of your men died, Herrenmer? We outnumber you now by almost ten to one and we have our warbeasts as well. You have fought bravely and well on behalf of your dead lord, but you have lost; give up and we will let you live. I swear it."

"Hah! This for your sworn word!" He flung his short sword at Garth, much as Garth had flung the Sword of Bheleu at the Baron.

Garth, however, ducked; the sword flew over his head and landed rattling on the hard ground beyond.

Several of the overmen growled, but made no aggressive move; this was between Garth and the human.

"Herrenmer, don't be a fool. Now you've even lost your sword; you can't fight anymore. Say that you surrender, and no harm will come to you."

Herrenmer did not answer; instead he looked about in desperation for a weapon to replace the one he had lost. He found one; whirling, he dove for the hilt of the Sword of Bheleu.

Garth could not allow that. He knew how dangerous the great sword could be. He could not let a human, particularly one already almost berserk, get hold of it. He dove after Herrenmer.

The guardsman was much closer; before Garth had covered half the intervening distance, the man's hands closed on the hilt. He screamed and immediately released it again, his palms smoking; the stench of burning flesh reached Garth's nostrils. It was too late to halt his own lunge, however, and he, too, grabbed the hilt.

He felt no pain, though the hilt was hot in his grasp. Instead, a wave of strength surged through him, filling him with fiery exultation. The red gem glowed more brightly than the dying flames of the Baron's garments, more vividly red than the blood that was pooled on the mansion's threshold.

Garth stood, the sword clutched in both hands; around him were the five remaining guardsmen, while Herrenmer lay crying at Garth's feet, the man's scorched hands held out before him. A foot or two away lay the smoking remains of the Baron. The sight of the dead enemy seemed a very good thing to Garth at that moment. He laughed in triumph. He had conquered! He was master of the village and could do with it whatever he pleased. He could destroy it all if he chose – and that was exactly what he chose!

Still laughing, he whirled, sword held out before him, and cut down the remaining humans. The blade sheared through armor and flesh and bone as easily as through air, leaving a trail of sparks behind. When he had completed the circuit, slicing open all five bellies before anyone could react, he plunged the point through Herrenmer's chest.

The captain gasped and twitched, then lay still; the other five took a few seconds longer to die. Garth pulled the sword free and looked about him.

The overmen – *his* overmen – were staring at him open-mouthed with surprise. They did not understand who led them, he realized. He cried out to them, "I am Bheleu, god of destruction! Death and desolation are my companions, woe and hatred my tools! Follow me now to glory such as you have never imagined!"

Some of the overmen still seemed uncertain; he lifted the sword above his head, blood dripping from the blade, so that the light of the jewel could shine on them. "Skelleth is ours," he cried. "Ours to destroy! These humans have fought us, defied us; let us teach them the consequences of their defiance!"

The uncertainties were fading; enthusiasm flickered in the circle of the overmen's red eyes.

"Burn the village!" Bheleu called through Garth's mouth.

"Burn the village!" a few of the warriors answered.

"Slaughter the humans!"

"Kill the humans!"

They were with him now; the overman-god laughed, and the sword flamed over his head. He plunged it down, slamming the point into the threshold of the Baron's mansion; the stone step exploded into red-hot splinters, spraying up around him, but leaving him unscathed. The shards that landed inside the building set a dozen small fires on the wooden floor.

"Go, then! Kill and burn!"

The answering shout was wordless; the overmen turned away and ran with drawn weapons at the dwindling crowds in the surrounding streets. Garth laughed again, raised the sword, and swept it in an arc through the air; wherever it pointed, flame erupted. In seconds every building around the marketplace was ablaze. He strode forward into the square; behind him, the mansion flared up suddenly. He turned and gestured with the sword; the Baron's home was lost in a roaring curtain of flame. In moments it collapsed inward, falling into its own cellars; behind it, through the flames, Garth could see the King's Inn, where the so-called Forgotten King dwelt. He flung the fiery might of the sword outward toward it, as he had toward the other structures, but nothing happened. Again he tried, calling aloud, "I am Bheleu!"

The inn remained unharmed. He made a third and final attempt, willing all the god's available power to flow along the blade and strike at this resistance.

The tavern still remained untouched. Reluctantly, Garth gave up. He turned back to the buildings around the square; those, at least, behaved properly, flaring up like lit torches at his slightest whim. He laughed and marched out into the village, spreading fire and destruction, but his dark joy was marred by his strange failure with the King's Inn.

The villagers scattered and hid before the onslaught of the overmen. Most took refuge in their homes or in the ruins that ringed the village. A few fled into the wilderness beyond the walls. None managed to put up an organized defense. Some found weapons; many barricaded their doors and windows. None had the foresight and ability to gather the townsmen so that their greater numbers could be of use against the overmen.

The overmen marched in small parties from door to door, smashing in barricades and butchering those who resisted. Where the resistance was too strong to be dealt with easily, warbeasts were called in. In all of Skelleth the only weapons that might have been effective against the great hybrids were buried in the burning ruins of the Baron's mansion. The animals served the overmen as battering rams, as armor, and as instruments of terror.

The humans who surrendered were spared, in most cases, and taken prisoner; the prisoners were gathered in the market square, guarded by four overmen and four warbeasts. A few overmen were too full of bloodlust and fury to restrain themselves, and some villagers were slain whether they surrendered or not, but generally even those individuals calmed down after a single such incident apiece.

Garth was the exception. As darkness descended, he strode laughing and screaming through Skelleth, killing every human he saw, burning every building he passed with the unnatural flames from the sword. Even the other overmen kept well away from him. He needed no warbeast to batter down barricades; a single blow from the sword shattered any defense set up against him. He seemed to take delight in killing those who could not fight back; he left the burning, dismembered corpses of women and children behind him.

It was full night when he came to one house where the door and shutters had been reinforced with steel. He was unable to carry through his first intention of burning his way in; when the wood had crumbled to ash, the metal still held. With a cry of *"I'a bheluye!"* he struck at the steel with the sword. Sparks showered, but the blade did not penetrate. He struck again, and this time the door exploded inward in a shower of twisted fragments.

There was no one in the room beyond; he stepped in and looked about. Even to his hazy, berserk mind, it was obvious that someone had locked and barred the door he had just destroyed. That meant that there was a prospective victim somewhere in the house. He decided to find this person.

The kitchen was empty; the back door and rear windows were locked and bolted. That left the upper floors. Garth found no stairs, but a ladder led through a trap in the ceiling.

The second floor was a single large chamber, furnished in a style that was luxurious by the standards of Skelleth, if ordinary enough in more fortunate places. A single bed stood against one wall; furs covered part of the floor, and hangings were on each wall. Tables and chairs were scattered about. Like the rooms below, it was unoccupied. Another ladder led upward.

With a snort, Garth climbed the second ladder, awkward with the great sword in his hand, and found himself in an unfurnished garret. There was a window at each end. The window at the back stood wide open; on either side of the window were stacked cages that held cooing birds. In front of the window stood a dour old man garbed in dark red.

With an exclamation of delight, Garth recognized him. This was Darsen, the rabble rouser, the troublemaker. This was the old man who had blamed Garth for the death of Arner the guardsman months ago and almost incited a riot; this was the man who had begun the battle by shouting, "Kill the overmen!"

This would be fun, the overman thought; this man would die slowly. Garth advanced upon him, the sword held ready in his hands.

Darsen had been facing the window, clutching something in his hands; now, as he turned to face the approaching overman, he flung the object out the window. Garth saw the bird flapping wildly, catching itself in midair. He paid it no attention; pigeons had nothing to do with him. If the old man chose to spend his last pain-free moments playing with birds, that was his privilege.

The human tried to duck under the sword and slip past Garth, but did not make it; the overman's left hand released the hilt and grabbed the collar of the red robe. The last thing Darsen saw before pain forced his eyes shut was Garth's face, grinning broadly, teeth gleaming red in the light of the glowing jewel.

Outside the window, the bird was flying westward, toward Dûsarra.

Chapter Eight

The nightly sacrifice was done; this had been a sunset ritual, simpler and quicker than the midnight ceremonies used on special days. The victim's death had been relatively easy, and there had been no elaboration.

Haggat wondered whether such sacrifices were actually worth doing; did Aghad take pleasure in *every* murder? There was little real hatred in such slayings, little of the pure, dark emotion the god fed upon. Some stranger dragged from his bed had been killed; how did that help the cause of fear, of hatred, and of loathing? It did not truly increase the worshippers' hatred of their fellow Dûsarrans; if anything, he suspected it helped assuage their anger. It probably did little to increase the city's fear; the people had long since become accustomed to such random deaths and were much more frightened at present by the White Death, the plague that was loose in the city.

The sacrifices were traditional, though, and there was no real reason to stop them. They were no great drain upon the cult's resources, and the worshippers did enjoy them. His personal acolyte certainly did; she had been quite enthusiastic tonight, he thought. It was amusing to see the change that had taken place in her over the recent weeks. She had been a timid little thing at first, awed by her close contact with the then high priest, frightened at being given to Haggat, the temple's seer.

She had had reason to be frightened, since tales of Haggat's idea of pleasure were common among the cultists. But she had discovered that she could survive his amusements and even enjoy some of them. With the death of his former master and Haggat's elevation to high priest, she suddenly found herself second in the cult's hierarchy. That position she enjoyed completely.

Now, as he had expected, she had prepared his special chamber; the scrying glass was gleaming, freshly polished, and the candle was lit. She knelt by the doorway, awaiting his appraisal of what she had done.

He saw nothing wrong and made a sign of dismissal; she prostrated herself, then backed stiffly out of the room, closing the door behind her. He knew she would be waiting in his bedchamber when he was done with the glass.

There was no hurry, however; he enjoyed using the glass as much as he enjoyed his less savory pursuits. He picked up the crystal globe and held it so that the image of the candle flame distorted within it.

When last he had used the glass, he had seen the overman Garth entering a tavern in Skelleth. It would be interesting to see what had become of him in the hours since. He concentrated on the globe.

The image of the flame grew and twisted, and then reddened.

That was unexpected; Haggat knew of no reason the image should be red. He wondered if the interference he had become familiar with was taking some new form. He tried to clear and strengthen the contact.

The crystal sphere was flooded with blood-red light. Two faces appeared, both etched in black and crimson. One was inhuman, eyes gleaming brightly; the other was a man, his face twisted in pain and terror. Haggat recognized them both, Garth and Darsen.

The high priest was surprised and confused. What was going on in Skelleth? Why was Darsen frightened? Why were the two of them anywhere near each other? Darsen was one of the more competent agents of the cult of Aghad and he certainly knew better than to confront so dangerous an opponent directly. He had been instructed to observe the overman and to do what he could to annoy and inconvenience him, to stir up fear, anger, and hatred. Had he gotten careless and provoked the overman openly?

A moment later it was plain that Darsen's terror had been justified; Haggat could still see nothing but the two faces, but he knew death when he saw it. Darsen was dead. The cult had lost its only agent in Skelleth.

Garth dropped the corpse, and Darsen's dead face vanished from the image in the globe. Haggat could not make out the overman's surroundings even now, but only his face, hellishly red.

Garth looked up, and it seemed as if those baleful eyes, almost glowing in the red light, met Haggat's. The Aghadite knew that was impossible; only the greatest of sorcerers could detect a scrying spell. Still, those crimson eyes seemed to be watching him. Disconcerted, he let his concentration slip and lost the image of the rest of Garth's hideous face. He saw only the eyes.

Then a third red glow joined them, and Haggat drew back in shock and horror. What was *that?* He seemed to sense something dark and brooding in it, something beyond his comprehension. The new glow grew, and Garth's eyes faded. The crystal was suddenly hot in Haggat's hands, intensely hot; he dropped it.

It did not merely shatter when it hit the floor; it exploded, showering sparks and red-hot gobbets of glass in every direction. Miraculously, nothing caught fire, but Haggat would not have noticed if it had; he was staring at the burns on his palms.

This was powerful magic indeed! Could the so-called Sword of Bheleu truly be linked to the god of destruction himself? He had not seriously considered that possibility before. He knew of no device linking its user to Aghad, and had seen no reason to think other gods would provide what his own did not. He had dismissed such claims as superstition, or boasting, or an intimidating bluff.

This overman, however, seemed to have power of an order only divine intervention could explain. In that case, it would not be safe to use ordinary measures against him. Garth had defied the cult of Aghad and slain its high priest. For that he must die horribly; that could not be altered. Methods could be changed, however, and where Haggat had previously planned to use the cult's own elaborate system of spies and assassins to torment and eventually kill Garth, he now thought that might be unwise. It would be better to turn another enemy against the overman and let the two destroy each other, allowing the Aghadites to assess their power, and leaving the survivor weakened so that the cult might then handle him directly.

Furthermore, he knew exactly the right enemy to use for this purpose; an enemy of his own, an enemy he had long sought vengeance upon.

The priesthood had not been his first choice for a career; as a youth he had set out to become a sorcerer and had served several years as a wizard's apprentice. His master, a very great magician, had mistreated him, insulted him, abused him, and withheld secrets from him. His frustration and anger had fed upon each other and grown in him until finally, one night, he had demonstrated decisively how well he had learned his lessons and how much his master had underestimated him. The demons he conjured took more than an hour to finish pulling the old wizard to pieces.

It was only after the demons had done their work and been sent away that he learned one of the facts his master had concealed from him – the existence of the Council of the Most High, a secret society of magicians of every kind that sought to limit and control the knowledge and use of the arcane arts. His late master had been a member and had carried a spell that alerted his fellow councilors the instant he died.

The killing of one of their number was something the Council did not condone under any circumstances. They destroyed or confiscated all Haggat's belongings, placed a geas upon him that severely limited his magical abilities, cut out his tongue to prevent him from revealing any of his forbidden knowledge or reciting incantations, and then dumped him before a temple of Aghad, the god of treachery and ingratitude, among other things.

Aghad was also, as Haggat had known even then, a vengeful god, and he had willingly entered the priesthood in the hope of eventually gaining the revenge he had sworn. Though he rose steadily in the cult's hierarchy, due largely to the little magic he still retained, vengeance had eluded him; he had been unable to convince the cult to take action against the Council. Even now, when he had become absolute ruler of the Aghadites, he had not yet attempted anything. He knew that the Council was too powerful and too well-informed to be attacked without much careful planning and preparation. Its members included virtually all the most powerful wizards of the northern lands, and to defeat such a confederation would require great stealth and skill – or equal power.

He had assumed that no equal power existed in the world, but now, he thought, this enchanted sword that the overman called Garth carried might be just such a power. It angered him to think that the weapon had lain unused in Dûsarra, a few hundred yards from his own temple, without his knowledge. It could well have been there, offering countless opportunities for theft, since he first came to the city. He had been unaware of it until this overman came along and blithely stole it, wiping out Bheleu's cult in the process, defiling Aghad's temple, and spreading the White Death in the marketplace.

Now, though, Garth and the Council of the Most High would both pay for their temerity in defying him. He needed merely to turn one against the other. Certainly one or the other would be destroyed, and he could then deal with the survivor.

How, then, could this be accomplished? How could he convince the Council that Garth was a menace, or convince Garth to attack the Council?

There was a hesitant knock on the chamber's door; the voice of his chief acolyte called, "Is all well, master?"

He turned, his chain of thought broken by this distraction, and noticed for the first time the damage done by the exploding glass. Glittering chips were strewn everywhere, and the draperies that lined the walls were spattered with smoking scorched spots where bits of hot debris had struck them. His own robe was similarly damaged, with several smoldering patches and half a dozen holes where the flying shards had penetrated. None had struck his flesh, though; the protective charms he carried, feeble as they were, had at least done that much.

His hands were another matter; when he snapped his fingers to summon the acolyte into the room he discovered that his fingertips were burned, as well as his palms. He winced with pain; when the acolyte limped into the chamber, he had his fingers in his mouth, a pose most unbecoming the dignity of his position as high priest.

The acolyte was not stupid enough to remark on it or to acknowledge in any way that anything was out of the ordinary. She said, "Forgive me, master, but I heard a strange noise, and feared for you. How may I serve you?"

Haggat considered for a moment. He would want her back in his bed shortly, but wished to have a few minutes to think first, and he knew he might as well put her to use. He made a sweeping gesture, indicating the broken glass on the floor.

"Your scrying glass?" The girl tried to keep her voice emotionless, but it was clear that she was puzzled.

He did not deign to nod; the fact that he did not hit her was acknowledgment enough that she was correct.

"I'll have it cleaned up immediately." She noticed the damaged hangings and added, "I'll have the draperies replaced as well, and inquiries will be made toward acquiring a new crystal. Is there anything else, master?"

It was not worth explaining by sign or note what he was considering; he would think it out himself first, before consulting with the other priests. He dismissed her with a wave, then caught himself. He did not want her to think that her duties would be done for the night after the clean-up. He pointed in the direction of his bedchamber.

"Of course, master; I am yours to do with as you will." She bowed low and backed out, favoring the leg and foot he had injured a few nights earlier.

He looked about at the scattered chips of glass. How could he turn the Council and the overman against each other?

When Darsen's carrier pigeon arrived three days later with the old man's report describing the destruction of Skelleth and the murder of the Baron, Haggat had his answer.

Chapter Nine

Garth awoke to find himself lying in the middle of a narrow alleyway; to one side was an old ruin, to the other side a burning building. Directly before him the Sword of Bheleu lay in the dirt, the gem in its pommel dark.

It was night; his only light came from the fire. Stiff and sore, he clambered to his feet and looked about.

He recognized the burning building; it was the house where he had found and killed that old man. He vaguely remembered the actual killing; he had spent a long time at it. There was blood on his hands, he noticed, but he could not be sure that it came from the old man; he had killed several people. It might even have come from a wound of his own, though he hadn't noticed any.

He tried to remember what he had done after the man in red had finally died, to explain why he had found himself unconscious in an alleyway, but it was all very hazy. There had been something watching him, and he had done something with the sword – not cut, nor set afire, but something very difficult, something that had tired him. He couldn't recall exactly what. After that he had staggered out, setting the house ablaze behind him, and that was all he could remember. He must have collapsed immediately afterward.

Whatever he had done, it might have drained the sword of its power temporarily, he thought. He could detect not the tiniest spark of light in the jewel; it hardly even had the glitter of a normal gemstone. That was well; it meant that, at least for the moment, he was in control of himself.

That being the case, he knew he should get rid of the sword while he could. He had offered it to the Forgotten King, and it had been refused – or at least, it had not been accepted. That certainly discharged any obligation he might have had to the old man, so he was free to dispose of the weapon as he saw fit. He did not want to keep it. He wanted nothing further to do with it; it had made him do insane things, incredible things. It was the sword that had been responsible for the Baron's death and the burning of the village, and if he kept it, he knew he could not control the sword indefinitely; sooner or later the gem would glow anew, and he would again spread destruction and death.

What, then, was he to do with it? The simplest solution would be to let it lie where it was and leave, but that would not do; some passing human would doubtlessly find it and pick it up, and there was no telling what would happen then. It was true that Herrenmer had been unable to handle it, but he could not rely on such a thing happening again. He did not understand the nature of its magic, and it seemed wholly untrustworthy, one moment burning with supernatural power, the next seeming nothing but an ordinary blade.

He could not give it to anybody else; anyone but the Forgotten King would probably be overcome by it as he had been. The King seemed able to control it, but he did not trust the old man; besides, the King had rejected it.

He would have to find a safe place for it, someplace where no one could get at it – either that, or destroy it.

Could he destroy it? That would put an end to the problem once and for all.

It would be a shame to destroy such a beautiful weapon, but it was probably the only final solution. There was no hiding place in the world where it could not eventually be recovered. He would make the attempt.

He coughed; smoke from the burning building was beginning to reach him, though so far flames were only visible through the windows. He realized he was warm, almost hot, though the night was cool. It was time he moved away from the fire.

He reached down and reluctantly picked up the sword, keeping a wary eye on the gem. It remained dark.

He found his way out of the alley and debated briefly which way to turn. He wanted privacy for his attempt to destroy the sword. He turned left, which he was fairly certain would take him out of the inhabited portion of Skelleth and into the surrounding ruins.

Though it was a moonless night, he had no trouble at all seeing his way; burning buildings lighted the sky behind him a smoky, lurid orange. The breeze was following him, carrying smoke and ash with it; his eyes stung, and he had to blink often.

He wondered what was happening around the marketplace. Had the overmen suffered many casualties? Had they butchered the villagers? How many survived on each side? Had any of the humans fled south, to gain the aid of their kin and bring the wrath of the High King at Kholis down upon the invaders?

Had he started the Racial Wars all over again?

Whatever happened, it would take time before any human reinforcements could arrive. He wanted to use that time to destroy the sword, so that he could deal with any new threats rationally.

He came to a place where a wall of heavy blocks of cut stone had been tumbled into the street, to lie in scattered chunks. For the first time it occurred to him to wonder what could have brought down such a wall; was Skelleth prone to earthquakes?

There were too many questions, far too many questions.

Whatever had knocked down the wall, the blocks of stone were well suited to his purpose. He laid the sword across a large slab, its quillons and hilt extending to one side, the last foot or so of its blade on the other. He placed another stone atop it, so that it was held firmly between the two smooth, solid surfaces. That done, he located another large, heavy block – one that he could lift, though it strained his inhuman strength near to its limit. He was not in the best of condition, after waking up in an alley after a messy battle, but he could still haul about three hundred pounds of stone up to chest level.

He then climbed atop the other two stones, so that his own weight was added to that on the sword, holding it motionless. Taking careful aim, he then dropped the stone he carried onto the sword's hilt, planning to snap it off the blade at the edge of the bottom stone.

He had gone to this amount of trouble because he was quite sure that this sword could not be broken simply by slamming it against a rock or bending it over his knee. Even a magic sword, though, could hardly survive his arrangement of stone, he thought. The finest sword ever forged could not withstand the shearing force of a three hundred-pound stone block dropped on its hilt while it was held motionless.

The block fell, struck the hilt and shattered. Garth could not see in detail what had happened, because he was too busy trying to keep his balance; the stone on which he stood had cracked, its two halves sliding to either side. He found himself falling, and dove off the stone, landing on his hands and knees. Slightly dazed, he got to his feet and turned to look at the blocks.

The sword lay gleaming, unharmed, on the stone he had used as a base; the block he had used as a cover lay in two jagged fragments on either side. The stone he had dropped had been reduced to scattered pebbles.

That approach obviously wouldn't work.

He thought he heard mocking laughter. He whirled, trying to locate it, but saw nothing. He turned back and saw that the gem was now glowing brightly.

He resolved not to touch the thing. If he did, he was sure he would be possessed once more by whatever malign force the sword served.

It shone, red and beautiful, before him.

He would not touch it.

It seemed to beckon; the blade gleamed red, as if washed in blood, and the stone beneath was lighted as well. His hands suddenly itched. He knew that the itching would stop if he held the sword, which seemed to be drawing him. He wanted to pick it up, to hold it before him, to wield it in berserk fury.

He fought down the urge and stepped back.

The movement seemed to lessen the pull slightly, and he remembered that the spell of the basilisk and of Tema's gem was broken if the victim could look away in time. He forced himself to turn his head and look away.

The pull was still there, but not as strong. He heard laughter again. Anger surged through him. Who dared laugh at him? He would skewer whoever it was! He took a step toward the sword, then stopped.

The anger was not his; it was the sword's influence. The laughter was familiar, and he remembered that he had heard it before. He had heard it when he slew the Baron; he had heard it in Dûsarra, when the sword had used him there. He listened closely, then shuddered.

It was his own voice, his own laughter, the same maniacal sound he had made when possessed by the sword's power. Now, however, it came from somewhere outside him.

This was beyond him; he knew he was dealing here with forces he could not comprehend. The lure of the sword still drew him, but a stronger, more basic urge was also at work. He was afraid.

With a final brief glance at the glowing gem, he turned and ran.

A hundred yards from the fallen stones, he slowed; fifty yards further along the street, he stopped. His sudden fear had subsided, and the compulsion drawing him to the sword had faded with each step, until it was now no harder to handle than a mild hunger in the presence of poisoned food.

He had to consider all this rationally, he told himself. He had to think it all through logically and follow the logical course of action.

The sword had some unholy power to it. It could steal control of his mind and body and turn him into a berserk monster. It could burn without taking harm, and set fire to anything in sight – or almost anything; he remembered the King's Inn. That had probably been protected by the Forgotten King's spells.

The sword could shatter stone and cut its way through solid metal as well. It resisted his attempt to destroy it and tried to draw him to it, as if it wanted him to carry and use it – but when Herrenmer tried to touch it, it had burned him. Was there some mystic link between the sword and himself?

He remembered how he had pulled it from the burning altar of Bheleu. Had that created a connection somehow? But even then, he had been drawn to it as if hypnotized, though he had not yet touched it. None of the worshippers of Bheleu had been affected by any such compulsion, so far as he could recall. Perhaps it had an affinity for overmen; he knew that the idols of Bheleu always took the form of an overman, though the god's worshippers had all been human.

That connection could explain a great deal. It made clear how the sword had existed before his arrival without having captured anyone until he came to rob the ruined temple. He had no idea when the blade had been forged, but he was sure it was not new.

But then, could he be sure? The blade had no nicks or scratches and bore no sign of ever having been used. The hilt was not worn. On the other hand, the blade showed no smithing marks, and the hilt did not have the rough feel of new work not yet smoothed by use.

The age of the sword was a mystery, he admitted.

Still, it seemed unlikely that it had been newly forged just in time to be placed in the altar the night he arrived to steal it. It had almost certainly been in the cult's possession for some time previous to his acquisition of it, and there was no evidence that it had ever before usurped anyone's will or caused widespread destruction.

Perhaps it was indeed attuned to overmen, and could not be used by humans. There were overmen in Dûsarra on occasion, he knew, traders from the Yprian Coast, but none of them would have any reason to visit the Street of the Temples. It was possible that none before himself had ever come within range of the sword's spell.

Its call did seem to be limited by distance.

Was there, perhaps, another explanation? Was he constructing his theory on insufficient evidence?

He felt that he could be sure that no one before him had wielded the sword to any great effect in Dûsarra, at least not within the past several years. If any such event had occurred, it would almost certainly have been mentioned to him by Frima or by Mernalla, the tavern wench he spoke with – or perhaps by the high priest of Aghad or the caretaker of the temple of The God Whose Name Is Not Spoken. None of them had made any significant comment about the temple or cult of Bheleu.

The god of destruction had been mentioned, however. Tiris, the ancient priest of P'hul, had told him that he, Garth, was either Bheleu himself or his representative. Garth had dismissed that as the babblings of a senile old man, but perhaps it had not been entirely that. Tiris might have known something of the magic sword and somehow recognized Garth as the one who would wield it. There was nothing particularly distinctive about Garth, except the fact that he was an overman.

That was evidence, then.

No other theory seemed to fit very well. Therefore, he would act on the assumption that the sword's magic was somehow geared so that only overmen could use it – or more accurately, it could use only overmen.

If that was in fact correct, then he need not worry about leaving it where it was. Wandering humans might come across it, but they would not be able to handle it. He would order the overmen to stay away from it, or perhaps even post guards around it.

Whatever became of it, he did not want to touch it again. He wanted to retain his own mind and will. The sword was insidious and unpredictable; he had managed to restrain it on the journey back from Dûsarra, when violence would have been nothing but an unfortunate incident, but had completely lost control here in Skelleth, where the resulting battle might have been the opening engagement of a new Racial War. Its magic had seemed to fluctuate randomly in strength, but Garth was beginning to suspect that it was not random at all.

Perhaps he could wall off this part of the village to keep out the curious. Some way to destroy or control the sword might eventually be found, or perhaps he could persuade the Forgotten King to do something with it, since the old wizard was plainly able to handle it.

That could all wait. He was rid of it for the moment and could turn his attention to other matters.

He and his troops had sacked and burned Skelleth with little or no justification. He had personally murdered the Baron, stabbing him dishonorably from behind. The people of Eramma would have to find out eventually; so major an event could not be kept secret. There would be much careful negotiating to be done if full-scale war was to be prevented, and only a near-miracle could restore the possibility of the peaceful trade he had hoped to establish.

Other trade routes were possible, though. There were overmen on the Yprian Coast, and a route might be found to Dûsarra or other cities in Nekutta. So far, the overmen of the Northern Waste had acted only against the people of Eramma; the other human nations would have no grievance. If overland routes could not be found, the sea trade need no longer be limited to Lagur; there were other seaports in Orûn, he was sure, though he knew no names. There might well be other lands of which his people knew nothing, lying beyond Orûn to the east and south, or beyond the Gulf of Ypri to the west. Expeditions would have to be sent out.

There was so very much to do!

The first thing to do was to gather together the survivors of both sides of the battle and set up some sort of organization. That could best be done from the marketplace; it was the one gathering place in town, the place where anyone seeking aid or leadership would go.

Garth knew he should return there immediately. He headed in that general direction, following the glow of the fires that were centered on the square. There was enough light for him to find his way, and within a few moments he found himself on a street he recognized. He followed it in the direction of the market.

He had been certain of the street's identity; but as he approached the market, he thought for a moment that he had made a wrong turn and become lost. The square and its surrounding buildings were unrecognizable; not a single one of the surrounding structures still stood. The smoldering ruins were more thoroughly destroyed than those on Skelleth's fringe. Only the fact that he knew there was no other large clear space in the center of town reassured him that it was indeed the familiar square.

The market was thronged with people and animals, sitting, standing, or lying, clumped together at random. There were several overmen in sight, and a few warbeasts, but most of the crowd was made up of ragged humans and their pets and livestock. The majority were bunched tightly together in a mass that occupied most of the square, avoiding the hot and sooty rubble that surrounded it.

The overmen seemed to be distributed around the perimeter, Garth realized, acting as guards. It was obvious, though, that they were too few to have halted any concerted effort by the humans to leave. The warbeasts were posted in various streets, but the buildings had been so completely leveled that anyone with footwear adequate to protect him from heat and sharp edges could easily have walked out over the rubble between the streets. The humans stayed where they were because they had nowhere else to go.

He looked at the mob of sooty, filthy, ragged humans, at the sooty and bloodstained overmen, and at the smoldering ruins. This desolation was his own doing. He was appalled. How could he have done this?

No, he told himself, *he* hadn't done this. The Sword of Bheleu, or whatever power controlled it, was responsible. Garth's only fault had been over-confidence in believing that he could resist the weapon's magic. He was a reasonable being, with only good intentions; he would not willingly have contributed to such devastation. The sword's power had warped his thoughts and clouded his mind, subtly feeding the honest anger he had felt toward the Baron of Skelleth and using it to overcome his resistance.

He was rid of the thing now, and it was time to start making amends.

"Ho, there!" he called to the nearest overman. "Who's in charge?"

The warrior had been facing away from him, watching the milling humans; now he turned, and Garth recognized him as Tand, Galt's apprentice. His face was black with soot, but that did not quite conceal a line of blood on one sunken cheek. His breastplate was dented near the left shoulder, and a sword was ready in his hand.

When Tand saw who had spoken he lowered the sword. "Oh, it's you," he said. "Galt and Kyrith are over there, talking to some of the humans."

"Thank you." Garth's gaze followed the younger overman's pointing finger, but he could not make out the two named with any certainty. He started to walk in the direction indicated.

"Garth?" Tand's voice was uncertain.

He stopped and turned back toward the apprentice. "Yes?"

"What happened? I thought this was to be a peaceful expedition, but you slew that human, the Baron, and then everyone was fighting. How did it start? Why did you kill him?"

Garth did not reply immediately. After a moment's consideration, he said, "It was as one of the guardsmen said; it was black magic. I was not myself. There was a spell upon me. I am sorry that it happened and I assure you I won't let it happen again."

"Can you prevent it? How can you stop magic? If it could control you once, why not again?"

"I know what caused it and I have removed the cause."

"Are you sure?"

Garth felt a moment of anger that the youth doubted him, and began a harsh reply. He stopped abruptly. The sword used and magnified anger, until his will was swallowed by his rage; could he be sure it was not still affecting him? He had left the sword in an empty street half a mile away, but he did not know how far its influence might extend. He could not give it any chance to gain control and lure him back. He suppressed his annoyance, fighting it down inside him. He did not answer the trader's apprentice, but turned and marched away.

Galt and Kyrith were in the northwestern corner of the square; Frima and Saram stood facing them. Koros stood, unattended, a few paces to one side. Garth noticed that Saram's arm was around Frima's waist, and hers was on his shoulder; the two of them, alone of all in sight, were clean, not smeared with dirt and soot.

Galt looked up as Garth approached and called, "Ah, Garth! We missed you!"

"Greetings, Galt. Greetings to you all."

"We were just discussing matters with these two humans. We're told you brought the female here from the city of Dûsarra."

"I did." Garth was not interested in talking about Frima.

"She tells us that you rescued her from a sacrificial altar in order to deliver her to the old man who lives in the tavern here."

Garth did not want to discuss the Forgotten King either. "Galt, you ask questions that do not concern you."

"I ask on behalf of your wife, since she cannot speak for herself; she wishes to understand her husband's actions. I, too, am curious."

"It seems foolish to me to waste time on such trivia when there are far more important concerns to be dealt with. We may have just started the Racial Wars again; surely you realize that."

Galt's voice lost its normal lilt and turned flat as he replied, "Of course I realize that. You and your temper may have consigned our entire species to extinction, and we must do everything we can to prevent this war from spreading. I saw no need to discuss that immediately, however, since there appears to be little we ourselves can do at present. Your behavior is something else entirely. You must guess, Garth, that all those who know you are curious about how you have acted these past few months. I had hoped that we might come to understand your motives and perhaps learn what has brought about our present catastrophe, the better to prevent its recurrence. You are now inextricably involved in affairs of consequence, and your actions are therefore a matter of importance. Thus, we were attempting to understand them."

"It was not my temper that did this," Garth replied, gesturing to indicate the smoking ruins and ragged crowd. "It was that enchanted sword I brought back from Dûsarra."

Kyrith made a sign to Galt, who said, "That was another subject that concerned us. Where did you get that sword? Why did the gem seem to glow? What sort of an enchantment does it bear? And where is it now? You were very vague about it before. And how did you make it burst into flame and spread fire about the way it did?"

"I didn't make it do anything. The sword has a will of its own, a very ferocious and destructive one, and it got out of control. It acted on its own."

Galt was silent for a moment before replying, "Are you serious?"

Garth suppressed his annoyance. "Yes, I am serious. The sword is very powerfully enchanted and is either itself an independent entity or is magically linked to a spirit or wizard of some sort."

"You said before that you found it in a temple someplace?"

"I pulled it from the altar in the temple of Bheleu, the god of destruction, in the city of Dûsarra."

"The god of destruction? Is that what you were shouting about?"

"That was more of the sword's doing. The entity that controls it claims to be or represent Bheleu. It might be telling the truth. Enough of this, though; we have to straighten out the mess here and make peace with Eramma before the High King at Kholis sends an army to destroy us."

"A few moments will make no difference. Garth, you have been acting strangely for these past few months. You have gone off on mysterious expeditions with little or no notice, vanishing completely for weeks with no explanation, leaving your wives and family to worry. You have undertaken single-handedly to establish trade with the humans of Eramma. You have now returned unexpectedly from your latest venture and immediately started a disastrous battle . . ."

Garth interrupted, saying, "The battle was not disastrous; we won easily. It's the consequences of the victory that may be disastrous."

"I stand corrected. Let me finish, though. You started, then, a battle that could have disastrous consequences. You have acquired a sword with which you are able to perform destructive magic and you claim it has a mind and will of its own; after the battle the sword has mysteriously vanished. You have brought back with you a human female of no particular value, and then abandoned her. You have behaved oddly, perhaps even insanely, screaming a lot of nonsense about gods and death, while setting fires on all sides. I am told by this human, Saram, that you have made some sort of pact with a local wizard who has promised you immortality.

"Garth, surely you see that to all appearances you have become completely irrational, madder than the Baron you slew. We have all deferred to you, and let you go your way, so far as was practical, because you are a respected overman, an honored member of the City Council, an experienced military commander, the hereditary Prince of Ordunin, and generally as highly placed and well-considered as it is possible to be among our people. A great deal of eccentricity can be tolerated under such circumstances. There are limits, however, and until Kyrith and I, the legally appointed co-commanders of this force, have received some acceptable explanation of your behavior, we cannot allow you to go on as you have. The consequences could be too severe. If you refuse to explain yourself, we will be forced to consider you deranged – dangerously so, but perhaps only temporarily – and to exclude you from all authority. If you cause any further difficulty, we may have to disarm you and confiscate your goods and weapons, perhaps even place you under provisional arrest. Do you see our position?"

Garth listened to this speech with shifting emotions. At first he was annoyed, then astonished that Galt and Kyrith could think him to be mad. He was silent for a moment, considering.

He *had* behaved irrationally, he knew that. He had been under the sword's influence. He might even now be less than fully under his own control; he knew that the spell could be subtle and that he need not be touching the weapon to be affected, though he thought it must weaken with distance. He could not be trusted, either by himself or by others. Unpleasant as that conclusion was, he knew he had to accept it.

Hesitantly, he said, "You are correct, Galt and Kyrith. You are entitled to an explanation. I am not mad; I have reasons, reasons I think good and sufficient, for everything I have done. I can see, though, that from your viewpoint my behavior has been strange indeed. I will be glad to explain myself and let you decide for yourselves how to deal with me."

Saram broke into the conversation. "If I might make a suggestion," he said, "there is no need to stand about out here while explaining. The King's Inn, over there beyond the ruins of the mansion, was not damaged by the fighting. Frima and I were inside it the whole time, which is why we're unharmed. I suggest that we go there, where we can sit and speak more comfortably, and get some ale to keep tempers from fraying."

Garth realized that he was, in fact, quite thirsty, his throat full of smoke. He nodded consent.

"An excellent idea," Galt agreed.

Though the Baron's mansion was gone, the cellars remained, half-filled with rubble and not readily passable in the darkness, forcing the party to take a roundabout route to reach the street where the King's Inn stood. As they passed the ruins, Garth glanced down and noticed something pale in the wreckage. He looked more closely and saw that it was a statue. It had once been a human being, Garth knew; the Baron had used him as a test subject for the basilisk's legendary power. The overman suddenly no longer regretted killing the Baron, whatever the repercussions might be.

The street that ran behind the destroyed manor had been the town's filthiest alleyway, dark and forbidding; now, though, the destruction of the surrounding buildings had let in fresh air and firelight, so that it was no longer much worse than any other debris-strewn byway. Its most outstanding feature was the presence of an unburnt building, the King's Inn.

The three overpeople and two humans picked their way through the gloom, past broken stones and fallen timbers that littered their path, while Koros padded silently along a few paces behind, following its master.

Galt remarked, "It's curious that this tavern should have survived unscathed, so close to the square."

"It is more curious than you know," Garth said. "It alone, of all the buildings in Skelleth, withstood the power of the sword when I tried to set it ablaze."

"I think that you and I, Garth, both suspect why this is," Saram remarked.

"Tell me, then," Galt said. "Or is this some great secret that you two share?"

"No, hardly that," Garth replied. "This inn is the home of the Forgotten King, the wizard I first came to Skelleth to find. He seems to be capable of many amazing things; saving his home from the flames is simply the latest example of his power."

"From what I know of the old man," Saram added, "he could probably have saved the entire village, but preferred not to take the trouble."

Galt snorted in derision. "If this man is such a mighty wizard, what is he doing in a pesthole like Skelleth?"

"That's one of the mysteries about him," Saram answered.

They had reached the door of the tavern; it was closed, despite the relatively warm weather, the only sign that there was anything out of the ordinary. The broad front window was clean and unbroken, the half-timbered walls clean and smooth, with no sign of smoke or soot anywhere.

Saram opened the door and led the party inside; Koros, at a word from Garth, waited in the alleyway.

Chapter Ten

The interior of the tavern was crowded with people, all human. As the three overpeople entered a sudden quiet spread before them. Three dozen pairs of eyes watched them intently. In the silence Garth could hear the sound of a knife sliding from its sheath.

Saram muttered, "I think you had better say something."

"People of Skelleth!" Garth said. "We have come in peace. The battle is over. We mean you no harm; we have come here to drink and to talk, nothing more."

The silence and tension remained; the crowd still watched.

"Innkeeper," Galt called, "five mugs of your best ale!" He sauntered into the room, found an empty chair, and seated himself. The table he had chosen was occupied by two grubby, middle-aged men in stained tunics. "I hope you don't mind if we join you," he said casually, "but there don't appear to be any vacant tables."

One of the men muttered a vague reply; the other sat and stared.

Galt waved to Garth and the others. "Come and sit down!"

Hesitantly Garth obeyed, taking the remaining empty chair at the table. Kyrith followed, and stood awkwardly for a moment until Saram brought her a chair from a neighboring table.

"Uh . . . we were just going," one of the villagers said. He rose and backed cautiously away. His companion sat and stared.

Saram escorted Frima into the vacated place, then tapped the lingering human on the shoulder. "Excuse me, friend, but would you mind moving to another table?"

The man looked up, startled. "Hah? Oh . . . no, no, of course not." He got awkwardly to his feet and followed his companion, backing away from the table and finding an empty chair elsewhere.

Saram seated himself and remarked, "That's better." He raised an arm and called, "Innkeeper, where's that ale?"

Galt remarked, "Garth, you really don't know much about dealing with humans. You don't want to make speeches to a crowd like this; just convince them that you belong. Actions are far more convincing than words."

"A truth I had forgotten momentarily," Saram agreed.

The other patrons were beginning to lose interest and turn away. The innkeeper was approaching with a tray bearing ale. Garth glanced around the room, realized the crisis was over, and allowed himself to relax. He also noted in passing that the Forgotten King was at his customary table, as if nothing had happened.

"Now, Garth," Galt said, "we would like to hear your explanation for your behavior."

"One moment." The ale had arrived, and Garth downed his in a few quick gulps. He handed back the empty mug and said, "Keep refilling this until I tell you to stop."

The innkeeper nodded. "Yes, my lord."

The other four were not hasty in their drinking; the man departed with Garth's mug while they sipped their ale.

"Where shall I begin?" Garth asked.

"Wherever you please," Galt replied.

"At the beginning," Saram said.

Kyrith nodded in agreement.

"What beginning?" Garth asked.

"We thought your behavior odd when you first ventured south from the Northern Waste," Galt replied. "Why not begin by explaining how that came to pass?"

"I am not certain where the beginning of that was," Garth said. "Last winter, I suppose, though I cannot name a date; it seemed to grow gradually."

"Start with that," Galt told him.

"Very well. You all know how the winters in our lands can wear on one – save perhaps Frima, who is not from these northern realms. The shortness of the days, the paleness of the light, the cold, the snow, the ice – all oppress the mind and the senses. This past winter seemed to affect me more than usual, though it was not an especially harsh one. I found myself depressed and bored; each day I told myself that it would pass, but each day I seemed to sink further into gloom. I could think of nothing but death and despair, and the futility of our lives, struggling to live in the Waste, able to do little more than survive. Every event seemed to contribute to my melancholy; when the hundred and forty-fourth anniversary of my birth arrived, all I could think of was that I must now be more than halfway to my death. It seemed that I had done nothing of any importance in that half of my life. I had won a few inconsequential battles with pirates and raiders, I had fathered a few children, and I had spoken in the City Council on such matters as rebuilding wharves and buying arms. The pirates and raiders survived and will doubtlessly return; my children will grow old and die; my speeches will be forgotten. What was worse, I saw no prospect of anything better in the future. I would grow old and die without ever having done anything to make a mark upon the world. In a century or two, no one would remember that I had ever existed. I did not want that to come about, but I could think of no way to avoid it."

"No one looks forward to death," Galt said.

Garth glanced in the direction of the Forgotten King, but did not deny Galt's statement. Instead, he said, "I know, I know, it is the way of things. I was not satisfied with that, however, and resolved to change it, if it could be changed. I went to the Wise Women of Ordunin and asked, first, whether there was anything I could do that would alter this way of things, some act of cosmic significance I could perform that would change the nature of life. They told me that was beyond the power of mortals. I had expected that. I then asked if there was any way that I could be remembered forever, so that, if I had to die, at least my memory might survive."

The innkeeper arrived with Garth's second ale; he drank it and handed back the mug. Before he could resume his narrative, Saram asked, "Who are the Wise Women of Ordunin? You have mentioned an oracle of some sort, but you never told me much about them."

"Ao and Ta are sisters who live in a cave near Ordunin; both are ancient and deformed overwomen," Galt told him. "They have been there at least since the city was built during the Racial Wars. They will speak with certain people, but avoid all others by hiding in the depths of their cave. They answer questions. Although no one has ever known them to lie or to be wrong, they are fond of evasive and confusing answers."

"You trust them?"

"They have never been wrong and have never lied," Garth said. "I trusted them last winter. I am not certain I will trust them in the future."

"Go on, then, with your story," Galt said.

"When I asked the Wise Women how I might be remembered until the end of time, Ao told me that I must go to Skelleth, find the Forgotten King, and serve him without fail. She told me the name of this inn, and that he could be found here wearing yellow rags. I was sufficiently caught up in my search for eternal fame that I immediately gathered together supplies, armed myself, and came south on Koros — though I had not yet named it then; it was simply my warbeast. I told no one what I planned because I considered it wholly my own affair and did not want it known that I was coming to Skelleth. I feared that the City Council might consider such a venture potentially dangerous, since at that time we all still believed Skelleth to be a mighty fortress whence the humans might attack us at any time. I could not then truly explain why I was suddenly so concerned with being remembered, why I was obsessed with death, or what had brought on my depression; I still cannot. Whatever the reason, knowing I would be remembered seemed the most important thing imaginable.

"I knew nothing about Skelleth, of course, save for the old tales from the wars, and not much more about humans. When I saw that the walls were in ruins, I thought that the fortress must be deserted; therefore, I rode directly in, making no attempt at stealth. When I came upon people, it was too late to change my approach, so I continued on openly and asked directions to the King's Inn.

"Here I found the Forgotten King, exactly matching the description I had been given; he told me he could, indeed, guarantee that my name would be known until the end of time if I were to serve him, and if he were successful in some great feat of magic he had planned. I agreed to undertake an errand for him as a trial of sorts; I was to go to the city of Mormoreth, southeast of here, and bring back the first living thing I found in the crypts beneath the city. I did as he asked, but I was not pleased with the outcome. The only living thing in the crypts was a basilisk, a magical and incredibly poisonous creature, so venomous that its slightest touch or even its gaze was fatal. To capture it, I had to kill several bandits and a wizard, which I had no wish to do."

"In the course of attempting to deliver it, I encountered further difficulties; the Baron of Skelleth learned of the creature's existence, and desired it for use as a weapon of war. He took possession of it briefly, but I recaptured it and delivered it to the King. I didn't know what he wanted with it, or what he did with it, but it did not serve his purpose. When he had finished with it, I killed it, rather than let so dangerous a creature fall into the hands of the mad Baron."

"That enraged the Baron; he already disliked me because I had failed to cooperate with him, and being deprived of the basilisk seems to have caused him to hate me implacably."

"Meanwhile, I had reconsidered my bargain with the Forgotten King. I was dismayed at having accomplished nothing beyond several deaths in running his errand; when he pointed out that I would be remembered in Skelleth and Mormoreth for those deaths, I broke off our agreement. I was no longer so enamored of eternal fame as to wish to buy it through slaughter and servitude."

"The King, however, perhaps to soothe me, made a suggestion; he pointed out that, as I could see, Skelleth was no longer the unforgiving enemy of overmankind that it had once been, and that I might acquire some measure of fame and wealth by establishing trade between Skelleth and the Northern Waste. As you all know, I set out to do that. I found you, Galt, to handle the details of trade, that being outside my own knowledge, and brought you, Tand, and Larth back here to open up trade, only to learn that the Baron would not cooperate with the one who had deprived him of the basilisk and his hopes of becoming a mighty warlord. He set intolerable conditions on our trading in order to humiliate me. You know that, Galt; you were there. You know that he asked me to swear fealty to him, to become his vassal.

"Caught by surprise, I foolishly agreed to present his proposal to the City Council and, in fact, swore an oath to that effect. That was a bad mistake on my part; I concede that."

A third mug of ale arrived; Garth paused to drink, but did not gulp it down as he had the first two. He waved the hovering innkeeper away.

"It is difficult for me to explain exactly why I acted as I did. I had it fixed in my mind that the establishment of trade was an absolute necessity, both for the good of our people and for my own aggrandizement. I wanted to accomplish something that would be an unmixed blessing, that would be beneficial to all concerned, and the opening of this trade route seemed to fit. No one would die; I would be serving no mysterious old man. Still, I would achieve renown which, if not eternal, would at least be of a positive nature. Convinced as I was of the value, to myself and to Ordunin, of trade, I was ready to agree unthinkingly to almost any terms. It took the shock of the Baron's insults and arrogance to jar me out of that.

"By the time I realized what I had done in swearing that oath and accepting banishment, it was too late to retract. To have gone to the Baron and asked him to reconsider at that point would have been humiliating in itself. I wanted time to think, to see if there were any way to arrange matters more to my satisfaction. The oath I had sworn had a loophole – I had agreed to speak to the Council immediately upon my return to Ordunin, but I had not said when I would return. I decided, therefore, that I would leave Skelleth as ordered, but would not return home. Galt told you this, Kyrith, or part of it, but you chose not to believe him. I have treated you badly in giving you no explanation before this and I apologize for my negligence.

"Having decided that I could be in neither Skelleth nor Ordunin, I had nowhere to go. I could have gone to Kirpa, I suppose, or Mormoreth, but I had no reason to. The Forgotten King had expressed an interest in renewing our bargain and had even offered to change the terms, promising me not merely eternal fame but actual immortality if I would return to his service. I was not eager to accept; I'm sure you know tales of how a long life can prove more a curse than a blessing, and I had begun to suspect that the old man was practicing deceit. I was wary. However, I had nothing better to do, and he promised me that running his new errand would provide me with the means of avenging the slights I had received from the Baron of Skelleth. Therefore I agreed to attempt the task he set, though I made no promises that I would complete it. This task was to bring him whatever I found upon the altars of the seven temples of Dûsarra. I had no idea where Dûsarra was, or how long it would take me to rob the seven temples, or even whether I would truly go there; therefore I could not tell Galt when I would be back. I guessed that it would be by the end of the year and told him to tell you that, Kyrith. I should have told him more, explained the situation perhaps, but I was angry and slightly drunk at the time and in no mood to do so. I am sincerely sorry if I caused you worry."

He finished his ale and put the mug to one side. Kyrith nodded, as if accepting his apology.

"You still haven't explained the sword or the girl," Galt said.

"I'm coming to that. I did go to Dûsarra, you see; the task was an interesting challenge. I had a vague idea that if I found and brought back whatever it was the Forgotten King wanted, I could withhold it from him until he met whatever demands I might decide to make. He *is* a magician of some sort, there's no doubt of that.

"At any rate, I found Dûsarra and robbed six of the seven temples. Some were easy; others were not. I won't go into detail about what I found or what I did, but there are a few things worth mentioning.

"Dûsarra is the city of the dark gods, the seven gods of evil that humans believe in. Each of the seven has a temple and a cult – or had. One of the gods is Bheleu, the god of destruction; his temple was a ruin, his altar a pile of burning wood. The sword I brought back with me was on that altar. From the first moment I saw it, it seemed to have some sort of control over me; I felt a compulsion to take it from the altar, ignoring the flames, and to kill the worshippers of Bheleu with it. I did. It was involuntary on my part. As you have all seen at various times and in various ways, the sword is undeniably magical and powerful. It was also very useful; in the course of events in Dûsarra

I lost virtually all my other weapons, so that I needed it for my own protection. Therefore, dangerous as it was, I brought it back with me. That was obviously a mistake. I thought I had it under control, but I was completely wrong; it seized hold of me again and made me slay the Baron and start the battle. That did indeed gain me my vengeance upon the Baron, as the Forgotten King had promised, but the other results are less pleasant.

"After the battle, the sword had apparently exhausted its power temporarily; I awoke in an alleyway with it lying beside me, the red gem dark and no compulsion or anger working on me. I tried to break it, but could not. My attempt only caused it to glow again. Rather than permit it to dominate me anew, I fled and came here, leaving it where it lay."

Having completed his tale, he sipped his ale.

"You claim, then, that your apparent insanity was the work of this magical sword?" Galt asked.

"Yes, exactly," Garth answered.

"That alone?"

"I believe so – that is, if you refer to my actions since acquiring the sword. I have no good explanation for the depression that first drove me into venturing south after eternal fame."

"No, I can accept that; I have heard of such emotions before. It's not uncommon for overmen of your age. It's the sword that worries me. If it is truly what you say, was it wise to leave it lying about unguarded?"

"Perhaps not, but I had little choice. I dared not touch it again; the brightness of the glow assured me that it would seize control immediately."

"Would it not be better for you to handle it, now that you know of its dangers, than to leave it where any stranger happening along might pick it up?"

"Ah, but such a stranger could not pick it up. You saw, did you not, what happened when Herrenmer attempted to touch it?"

"My view was not clear," Galt began.

"I was not there at all," Saram said, interrupting. "What happened?"

"The hilt grew hot to his touch and burned him so badly that he could not pick it up. Yet a second later, I used it without taking harm. I have thought this over, considering as well the circumstances under which I came into possession of the sword, and have concluded that it cannot be used by humans. Therefore, we need only keep our own troops away from it to ensure that it will not be used."

"I am not sure, Garth. Perhaps we should test this."

Garth shrugged. "Perhaps we should, but to test it may be dangerous. If it worries you, then post a guard around the sword. That would ease my own mind as well."

"I find it hard," Galt said, "to accept your claims about the sword's power. I admit that it has magic to it, but it is merely metal; how can it have a mind and will of its own?"

"I don't say that it does; it may merely be linked to some great power. I am tempted to believe that it is in truth controlled by the actual god of destruction, whatever he may be. My experiences in Dûsarra have shaken my atheism; there are undoubtedly spirits and powers in the world beyond what we know."

"Could it not be, Garth, that something – perhaps the sword, which plainly is magical, or perhaps something else you encountered in your journeying – has driven you mad and caused you to *imagine* this controlling power?"

Garth considered this. "I suppose it could be," he admitted. "But I do not think it to be the case."

"We will have to investigate the sword further and test out what you have said."

"You are free to do so, but do not expect me to use it again. I ask only that you be very, very careful."

"Whether you are correct in your belief in its power, or merely deluded by madness, it seems to me that we cannot wholly trust you."

Garth shrugged. "I will not argue with that. I think you will see, in time, that I am again as rational and sane as you."

"That would seem to be settled, then."

Galt was interrupted by Kyrith; she touched his arm and then pointed at Frima. "Oh, yes," Galt said. "Who is this person, and why did you bring her here from Dûsarra?"

"Frima? That's simple. My task was to bring back whatever I found on the seven altars; at the time I arrived in the temple of Sai, the goddess of pain, her worshippers were in the process of sacrificing Frima. She was the only thing on the altar, so I took her and brought her back with me. Having done so, I had no further use for her and turned her free."

"It would seem you have, as you said, an explanation for everything – bizarre as those explanations may be."

"Yes. If you would like confirmation of some part of what I have said about the sword, Frima can attest to its effects upon my temper. She saw on the journey back here that, when the red jewel glowed, I became angry; when it dimmed, I remained calm."

Frima spoke for the first time. "That's right."

"Another question occurs to me," Galt said. "You were sent to fetch these things by the so-called Forgotten King; why, then, did you not deliver them to him?"

"He refused them. You will recall I said I robbed six of the seven altars. The seventh held nothing but a skull that was apparently part of the altar and which I did not trouble to pry loose. The old man, however, claims that the altar should have held a book, which was the only item he really needed. My failure to deliver this book angered him so that he marched off and left the other things in my possession. I regret that, since his magic seemed able to control the sword; had he kept it, today's battle might not have taken place."

"Curious."

"Perhaps not. The caretaker of the seventh temple, the shrine of The God Whose Name Is Not Spoken, told me that the god's true high priest was a mysterious ancient called the Forgotten King. The description was unmistakably of the same man. The King has not denied it. It is not so strange, then, that he would know what might be found in his own god's temple, and that he might wish to make use of it."

"I see. The underlying circumstances here remain unclear, but I begin to understand that they are in fact interrelated."

"My own thoughts are similar," Garth agreed, "and I want no further part of it. I have done with magic and gods and priests, I hope. For the moment, since you feel I cannot yet be trusted, it appears I am done with politics and diplomacy as well."

"Then we are agreed that Kyrith and I will retain command?"

"Yes. We cannot be sure that I am truly free of the sword's influence. From your point of view, we cannot be sure I am sane. I do hope, though, that you will permit me to advise you. I know more about Skelleth and the lands to the south from first-hand experience than any other overman living."

"True. What, then, would you advise us to do in the current situation?"

"The most important consideration is to establish peace with Eramma, but it is not, perhaps, the most immediately pressing. The need to provide some organization here in Skelleth seems more urgent. A human should be appointed to take charge of the surviving human population, as a sort of interim baron, under your command; the humans would not take well to the direct rule of our people, and we in turn do not understand how humans think, so that direct rule would be inefficient and unnecessarily galling. I would recommend Saram here for the position, since, as a former guardsman – and perhaps the only one surviving – he has some experience at organization. He was a lieutenant and therefore knows how to give orders. Furthermore, he is a human we are comfortable in dealing with, and one who seems comfortable with us, yet who is not outcast by his own kind."

Saram protested, "I don't want the job."

"So much the better; you'll be less tempted to abuse it."

"We can settle that later," Galt said. "What else?"

"Well, once some semblance of order is established, the human population should be set to rebuilding the town to suit themselves, while our people serve as garrison and administration and lend whatever aid we can. We now control Skelleth, but it remains essentially a human town and we should deal with it on that basis, allowing the humans to arrange it as they please."

"You imply that we should retain possession of it, however."

"Oh, yes; why give up a good bargaining point before we're even asked?"

"As a trader, I know that's sound. What else?"

"Word of events here must be sent to the City Council of Ordunin immediately, and their advice asked – but we must remember we are south of the border and outside their jurisdiction; and we are here on the spot and more knowledgeable than they, so that we must be willing to reject their advice, should it seem foolish."

"Would you set Skelleth up as a new nation, then?"

"No, not necessarily, but I would keep every option open for as long as possible."

"Is there anything more?"

"When the effort can be spared, an exploratory mission should be sent to the Yprian Coast. As well as establishing trade, such a mission should investigate the possibility that the overmen there will be willing to support us militarily against Eramma, should it become necessary."

"Now *there* you have a very good point."

"I envision that Skelleth may become a mixed community of humans and overmen permanently, equally part of Eramma and the Waste, serving as a center of trade between them and with the Yprians. I think such an outcome would be highly desirable. There is no reason that the memory of the Racial Wars should continue to blight all our lives."

"You are ambitious, Garth."

"I think such a scheme wholly practical, Galt."

"It may be. We will try it and see. I will admit I have no better suggestions."

"Good." Garth downed the rest of his ale and signaled to the innkeeper. He was pleased; even though he himself was now to be excluded from the mainstream of events – and thereby freed of aggravating details – things seemed to be working out well. The Baron was dead and gone, Garth's commitment to the Forgotten King was at an end, he was free of the Sword of Bheleu, and it seemed quite likely that everything could be worked out peacefully.

Oh, there were still loose ends – the Forgotten King yet lived, the sword still existed, and peace was not yet made – but it looked good. It looked very good.

Chapter Eleven

Dawn was breaking by the time Saram was convinced he should serve as acting baron until someone better could be found. Garth and the others decided that it was hardly worth trying to sleep before sunset. Garth had had his nap in the alleyway, but the others had not slept since before the battle. Galt had managed to sleep the previous morning, after standing the night watch, but his rest had been interrupted by Garth's return.

In short, all of them were exhausted, as were almost all the townspeople and overmen. As a result very little was accomplished beyond a good deal of bleary discussion.

At sunset nothing had been done about the Sword of Bheleu beyond posting two overmen to guard it – maintaining a safe distance at all times, since Garth insisted that, if they came close to the weapon, it might seize control of their actions. Nothing had been done toward the reconstruction of the village, except that the villagers had been divided into work parties of fifteen or twenty, each under the direction of a skilled craftsman. Ideally, each group would have been run by a master house builder, but the entire village had only a single journeyman in its surviving population; for decades there had been no need for new houses and few had bothered to repair the old ones.

The overmen had pitched their tents in the marketplace, as they had planned, but did not enjoy the privilege of occupying them; instead, preference was given to women and children, followed by the wounded – including the seven injured overmen – and finally by the feeble or elderly. That accounted for at least three people to a tent. The remainder of the population was left to take shelter in the ruins or do without.

The warbeasts were gathered together; after carrying out their attacks on the archers, some of them had been left undirected during the remainder of the battle and had strayed aimlessly through the town. They were fed with unidentified corpses or those with no surviving kin; the recognized bodies were spared to avoid offending their families. Some protests arose when it first became known how the overmen proposed to feed their animals, but were quieted when it was pointed out that if the warbeasts weren't fed they would seek their own meals, and that they preferred to take their prey alive. It was suggested that the town's livestock would serve, but the proposal was rejected on the grounds of unnecessary squandering of the available resources.

Garth refrained from taking any direct part in the day's activity, but watched carefully and offered occasional suggestions to Galt and Kyrith. Galt strove mightily to retain his civilized calm, but as the day wore on it grew ever thinner, allowing flashes of temper to show. Kyrith, handicapped by her inability to speak, gave up trying to give orders by noon and instead sat sulking in the King's Inn, deigning only to answer questions brought to her and allowing Galt and Saram to run the entire affair.

Saram, for his part, despite his show of reluctance, took to command immediately. He appointed temporary officials to ad hoc jobs at the slightest excuse, ordering each to fulfill a particular function without ever once explaining how the job should be done. Whenever he thought of something that needed to be done or had some matter brought to his attention, he named the nearest willing human as the minister in charge of getting it done. By the time new tasks stopped appearing, around midafternoon, he had at least fifty ministers under him, making up a good part of the surviving population.

The new officials, unfortunately, were not coordinated and were as tired as anyone else, so that very little was actually done as well as it should have been. Food and water were found for all the survivors, and the tents were distributed, but rubble was not cleared, no construction was begun, and the remaining fires were left to die on their own.

Still, Galt saw quickly that Saram had the humans in hand; even though they were accomplishing little, they were being kept busy, and had no time to think about the fact that they were now virtually slaves to an alien species in their own village.

Once he was convinced that he need not worry about a rebellion, Galt turned his attention to making use of his own warriors. Of the sixty overmen who had accompanied Kyrith and himself from Ordunin, eleven had died in the fighting – almost all from arrow wounds – and seven had been wounded in varying degrees, not counting scrapes and bruises. That left him forty-two. Besides the two he had assigned to guard the Sword of Bheleu, he posted two at each of the five gates and assigned ten more as their relief. That left him twenty. Saram assigned humans, mostly male teenagers who were eager to help but not otherwise much use, to guard the gates as well, so that each entrance to the town had four guards, two of each species, at any given time.

Galt had objected at first on the grounds that the duplication was an unnecessary waste of manpower, but gave in when Saram pointed out that if men and overmen were to live together they had best learn to work with one another. Furthermore, he pointed out that humans approaching Skelleth might be alarmed at seeing only overmen and might flee, while they would be only confused and wary upon seeing men and overmen together.

From the twenty remaining overmen Galt chose his apprentice, Tand, and four others, and assigned them to journey to the Yprian Coast as an impromptu embassy and trade mission. They were to depart the following morning and they spent the rest of the day gathering supplies and resting. They were to have two warbeasts – enough to carry them all in an emergency and adequate to defend them against almost any peril of the road, but not enough to deplete the force in Skelleth seriously. Galt held the remaining overmen in reserve in case of an attack by humans angered by the overmen's capture of the town.

A mission was also to be sent to Ordunin. At first Galt considered going himself, but he quickly realized that the only person he could possibly leave in command in his absence was Garth, and he did not feel ready to do that. Kyrith volunteered to go, but hesitated when Garth refused to accompany her; he insisted he still had business to attend to in Skelleth, primarily finding some permanent solution to the problem of the magic sword. At last, after some debate, she did agree to go, leaving immediately and taking three other overmen with her for escort.

That left twelve warriors, Galt, and Garth. The warriors were put to work pitching tents and carrying water. Galt was busy every minute overseeing the work. Garth watched as well, but without the, responsibility of command.

Frima, for her part, served as a messenger.

The King's Inn was used as a command post, but throughout the long, wearing day no one spoke with the old man in the back.

When at last the sun oozed down past the western horizon, the anger and fear of the battle were gone, replaced by fatigue and resolve. Garth, despite his weariness, felt peculiarly refreshed and clean as he settled down for the night on straw from the stable beside the King's Inn – which, like the tavern itself, had not burned. For more than a fortnight his dreams had been only of destruction, but he had spent this day obsessed with rebuilding – a welcome and healthy change. He was very pleased that he had managed to escape the spell of the Sword of Bheleu.

He was almost cheerful when he fell asleep.

Within an hour, though, his dreams began to trouble him. Images of blood and pain began to appear, and everything seemed washed in a red haze. He saw again the image of the high priest of Aghad whom he had fought in Dûsarra and again saw the Sword of Bheleu splatter the priest's brains and blood across the dirt of the Dûsarran marketplace. He saw himself slaughtering the entire cult of Bheleu with manic glee while thunder pounded overhead. He relived the battle just past and recalled in detail what he had done to Darsen. Finally, he found himself standing alone on a barren plain, holding the Sword of Bheleu before him. He tried to cast it away, but his fingers would not release the hilt; he tried again and became aware suddenly that there was someone behind him.

He knew, not knowing how he knew, that behind him was the sword's rightful owner, the one to whom he could give the weapon and be rid of it once and for all.

He turned around and saw himself, clad in a loose red robe over black armor, hand held out to receive the sword; his other self's face was twisted into a malign grin that suddenly poured forth mocking laughter.

With a grunt of surprise, he awoke.

He was no longer on his pile of straw but on his feet, facing the part of town where he had left the sword.

He shook his head to clear it and looked about. He had not gone far; his pile of straw lay a yard away. He settled down upon it once again and considered.

The dream did not seem wholly natural. It might, he thought, be a lingering remnant of the sword's influence. Or perhaps he was more vulnerable while asleep, and the sword or its master had sent the dream to him for some reason. Or, of course, it might be an ordinary dream – perhaps a bit more vivid than most, but that could be attributed to exhaustion and the excitement of recent events.

The oddest feature was that he had started to sleepwalk; he did not recall ever having done that before. That, more than anything else, made him suspect a magical influence. Perhaps the sword was attempting to draw him back, and the dreams had been his own attempt to resist.

Whatever had caused the dream, it made him uneasy and ruined his earlier contentment. It appeared that he could not be really sure he was free of the sword until it was destroyed. He would have to see to its destruction as soon as possible. He decided not to go to sleep again, but to stay awake until he could discuss the situation with Galt. Fatigue overcame him, however, and he dozed off and slept uneasily.

He awoke again as the first light of dawn painted the eastern sky with faded pink and lay for a moment watching the stars go out. He had dreamt again, but only in vague and muddled images – all unpleasant. There had been none of the eerie clarity of the first series; perhaps whatever power was affecting him had tired itself.

He had to destroy the sword. He dared not undertake any of the other tasks that he hoped eventually to complete while its baleful influence lingered. He could not, however, do anything with the sword without Galt's cooperation, as the guards posted upon it had been told specifically to keep Garth away from it unless Galt was with him.

At the first opportunity, he would have to take Galt out to the sword, convince him of its power, and then find a way to dispose of it once and for all. Until then, he could do nothing.

He sat back, leaning against the wall of a burned-out house, and did nothing.

When Galt awoke he was instantly besieged with decisions to be made, orders to be given, and work to be done; Garth waited patiently. The morning passed. Garth contrived to speak with the master trader turned commander as they ate their noon meal.

Galt agreed that the sword should be dealt with. He promised that at the first opportunity he would accompany Garth to deal with it. The organization and reconstruction of the village was of primary importance, however; he had to oversee that. When he could spare the time, he would.

Garth resigned himself to waiting. He waited through the afternoon and evening. That night he slept heavily and dreamed of death; he awoke to find himself standing amid the ruins a few dozen yards from the sword.

Galt was busy throughout the following day as well, as heavy rains came, flooding foundations, turning the streets to mire, and slowing down all work. Villagers jammed themselves into the tents and the few structures that still had roofs.

The rain was not wholly unwelcome, though; for the first time the smell of wood smoke subsided, and some of the soot and filth was washed from the ruins. Supplies of drinking water, which had grown scant, were replenished.

Garth spent the day in the King's Inn, speaking to no one, sitting in the front corner by the window, watching the people who crowded the room. He did not approach the Forgotten King. He did not see Galt at all. He noticed that Saram and Frima were together almost constantly and that the girl was now more of an aide than a messenger. On several occasions he noticed her staring at him; he guessed she was wondering at his inactivity or perhaps hoping he would return her to Dûsarra.

The third night after the battle, recalling his experiences of the first two nights, he moved his bedding further from the sword, up into the abandoned northeastern portion of Skelleth. He slept covered by a sheet of oilcloth someone had found in the rubble and felt the rain gathering in pools atop it.

He awoke several times, each time finding himself upright and moving south, the rain on his face. It was obvious that the rain had awakened him each time, and that only that had kept him from moving further. His dreams were jumbled images in red and black; he relived repeatedly all the bloodier incidents of his life. In stark contrast to the tedious hours he had spent doing nothing while he waited on Galt's convenience, his nights were full of fury and violence. He fought pirates and raiders on the coasts of the Northern Waste, killed bandits on the Plain of Derbarok,, and slaughtered priests and worshippers in Dûsarra. Throughout, whatever the actual circumstances had been, he found himself gleefully wielding the Sword of Bheleu, laughing as blood spattered about him, killing anything, friend or foe, that got in his path.

By dawn, he was resolved that he could not wait much longer. If Galt could not spare the time before sunset, he would leave Skelleth and try to get far enough away to escape the dreams.

Chapter Twelve

The village of Weideth lay in a small valley in the foothills below Dûsarra and consisted of perhaps two dozen homes and a single combined tavern, inn, and meetinghouse, all arranged around a crossroads. The West Road led up the slope to Dûsarra; the North Road led through the mountains to the Yprian Coast; the South Road led to the rich farming villages along the upper branch of the Great River; and the East Road led through the heart of Nekutta to the civilized lands of Eramma, Orûn, Tadumuri, Amag, Mara, and Orgûl.

Of late there had been a great deal of traffic coming down the West Road and leaving by either the East or the South. Those who had bothered to stop at all reported that they were fleeing from an outbreak of the White Death. There were also stories of great fires, riots, and a heightening in the city's perpetual internal conflict among the seven cults.

There had also been more overmen leaving Dûsarra than usual; the Yprian traders had cut short their visits and were turning back their fellows from approaching Dûsarra. No more caravans came down the North Road, and all those that had come before had already returned. It seemed likely that there was not a single overman left in the city.

The people of Weideth had watched the refugees go through, had offered what aid and comfort they could, and had accepted whatever payment was offered in exchange. They were practical people and saw no reason to refuse good money. The village was wealthy with Dûsarran silver.

It was three weeks since the plague's outbreak, and the number of people coming down the West Road had dropped from more than a hundred a day to a mere handful, when the girl in the black robe arrived in the nameless village inn.

She was young and walked with a limp, the Seer of Weideth noticed when she entered the public room. Her face was hidden by her cowl – that was typical of the secretive Dûsarrans. She carried no personal belongings that he could see; that was unusual for a refugee at this late date. There had been plenty of time now for anyone planning to flee to have gathered a few things together. Perhaps, he guessed, she had converted everything to cash and had the money hidden somewhere beneath her robe.

She paused just inside the door and looked about. He knew that she was looking for someone specific – he did have the true talent of a seer, though only weakly. That was very odd; how would a Dûsarran know anyone in

Weideth? There were no other city-folk in the tavern just then – only him and a dozen of his fellow villagers.

He was interested. Could it be that she was not a refugee after all?

The innkeeper had noticed her now and was coming over to speak to her. The Seer watched and had one of his erratic flashes of insight. She was looking for *him,* the Seer of Weideth. Before he could do anything about this sudden knowledge, she was asking the innkeeper, who pointed him out.

He put down his wine cup and considered her as she approached the table.

"I am looking for the Seer of Weideth," she said.

"I am he," he answered. "Have a seat."

Made awkward by her injured foot, she took a moment to arrange herself on the offered chair. The Seer looked her over.

She was olive-skinned, like most Dûsarrans, with thick, curling, black hair which she wore long; a few strands spilled out of her cowl, reaching down past her breast. She seemed pretty, but he could not see clearly the outline of her face. There was something out of the ordinary about her that he sensed rather than saw, an aura of perversity and twisted emotion.

"I am Aralûrê; I'm a wizard's apprentice. I was sent here with a message for you."

She was lying about her identity, but had indeed been sent to him. He nodded. If it was important, he could worry later about who she really was and why she was lying.

She hesitated. "How can I be certain you're really a seer?" she asked.

He shrugged. "Ask anyone in Weideth." He knew her uncertainty was due partly to the ease with which he had accepted her lie. When she still seemed unsure, he added, "Your name is not Aralûrê, and you are not a wizard's apprentice, but you do have a message for me. What is it?"

"How do you know who I am?"

"I don't, but I would be a very poor seer if I could not tell truth from falsehood."

That seemed to satisfy her. "I have been sent here to warn you and any other magicians I may find, of whatever discipline, of the actions of a certain overman."

"You refer, I suppose, to Garth of Ordunin, who caused so much havoc in Dûsarra."

"You know his name?"

The Seer was gratified by her surprise. "Oh, yes," he answered. "Am I not the Seer of Weideth?"

The girl eyed him dubiously. "How much do you know about him?"

"Tell me what you came to tell me."

The Dûsarran considered for a moment, then said, "As you will. It was Garth who loosed the White Death upon the city, you know. He killed a great many people in other ways as well, including several priests. He was responsible for the burning of the market place."

"I know all that, and I am sure you know that it is common knowledge. The refugees who have passed through Weideth have kept us well-informed, quite aside from my own abilities. We have an ancient prophecy here that when an overman comes out of the east to Dûsarra he will unleash chaos and disaster upon the world. It would appear that Garth is the overman described, and the White Death the prophesied disaster. What of it? Why have you come here to tell me what I already know?"

"You did not allow me to finish, my lord. Did you know that the overman is still spreading destruction? Three days ago he destroyed the fortress town of Skelleth, on the northern border of Eramma."

The Seer studied the girl. "How do you know that?" He could perceive beyond any doubt that she spoke the truth as she knew it. "Skelleth is a fortnight's ride from here."

"My master has methods of learning what goes on in the world."

"Your master is the one who sent you to me?"

"Yes."

"Who is he?"

"A wizard; he prefers not to give his name."

"He's no wizard. Is he a priest, perhaps?" He read in her face that he had guessed correctly. "A priest who seeks vengeance upon Garth?"

She nodded reluctantly.

He sat back. It seemed plain enough. One of the Dûsarran cults, unable to avenge itself directly, hoped to recruit his aid in pursuing the overman. He had little love for any of the vile cults of the black city, but if this Garth were in truth disturbing the peace of the world and causing further destruction, then the overman had to be stopped.

He wondered why the priest had chosen him to contact. Were there no wizards left in Dûsarra?

Perhaps there weren't; the plague might well have depopulated much of the city. Reports were vague and inconsistent, since even those still healthy remained in isolation in their homes for the most part.

Or perhaps this priest had an inflated idea of the Seer's own power; perhaps the, priest did not realize that the Seer's predecessor, a truly remarkable prophet of great vision, had died and been replaced by a much lesser seer.

Perhaps . . . but there was no need to wonder, when he could ask the girl. "Why were you sent to me?" he asked. "What can I do?"

"I don't know," she admitted truthfully. "My master did not say. He told me to seek you out, and to speak also to any and all other seers, or wizards or magicians I might encounter."

Perhaps this priest thought that the Seer would spread the word until eventually the news reached someone in a position to act upon it. That made sense, though he found himself resenting slightly the implication that he was a gossip. As a matter of fact, though there was no way the priest could know it, he would see that the news, once verified, did indeed reach those who could respond appropriately; he would send a message to the Council of the Most High, of which he was a very junior and peripheral member. No priest would know that the Council existed, though; it had been a lucky chance, he was sure, that brought this young woman – whoever she was – to one of the councilors.

Surely it could be nothing more than that.

"I see," he said. "Very well, then. You have done your duty." He wondered if he should pursue the question of her identity, but decided against it. Every sect in the city was dedicated to darkness, in one way or another, and every sect apparently had been affronted by Garth. It mattered little, he thought, which one had chosen to take action.

There was the question, though, of how word had been received from Skelleth in a fourth the time it took a man with a good horse to cover the intervening distance. Perhaps one of the priests had a hireling wizard with a scrying glass. That might be dangerous.

It wasn't his concern, however. He would contact the Council, tell them everything he knew on the subject, and let them worry about it. His place was here in Weideth, tending to the needs of the villagers, guarding and interpreting the prophecies of his forebears.

He downed the rest of his wine and rose. The girl rose as well. He nodded politely to her and turned to go.

The Aghadite watched the gray-robed man leave with her contempt scarcely hidden. The fool had hardly questioned her at all! He had asked for no proof, no details of Skelleth's destruction. He had not questioned her motives nor divined her identity. He had not even taken the trouble to ask her to show her face!

He was probably a worthless drunkard, she decided, whatever talent he might possess.

It didn't matter; all that mattered was that she had done what Haggat had ordered and delivered the message. Her part was finished. She could not imagine what good it could do to inform this third-rate oracle of Garth's actions – but she was still a novice in the ways of intrigue. Haggat knew what he was doing, she was sure.

And if he didn't, if the whole thing turned bad, that was all right, too; she would use the failure to ruin Haggat and enhance her own position in the cult. She could advance with equal ease, she knew, either by allowing herself to be pulled along in Haggat's wake or by stabbing him in the back.

And if the time came, she would enjoy stabbing the lecherous high priest in the back – either figuratively or literally.

Chapter Thirteen

It was mid-afternoon of the fourth day after the battle when Galt finally found himself with time to spare for Garth's obsession with the magic sword. As he had expected, he found the older overman in the King's Inn, sulking in a corner with a mug of ale.

"Greetings, Garth," he said, standing beside the table.

"Greetings, Galt. I don't suppose you have time to sit down."

"No, but I do have time to tend to the sword, if you like."

"Good!" Garth rose, a trifle unsteadily; Galt realized, with considerable misgiving, that the overman had been doing nothing but drinking since early morning. He knew that Garth would be offended if he suggested putting off the matter of the sword, and he was not sure how long he would be free of other concerns, so he said nothing, but followed as Garth led the way out of the tavern.

The fresh air seemed to help, Galt saw; Garth's step steadied quickly.

"Have I mentioned," Garth asked, "that I've been having strange dreams lately?"

The question caught Galt by surprise. It was not customary to speak openly of dreams; it was widely believed among overmen that, if properly interpreted, they revealed the inner truths of the dreamer's personality, so that learning the nature of another's dreams was a serious breach of privacy.

Besides, overmen only rarely remembered their dreams, unlike humans, who seemed to think that dreams showed the future and who therefore cultivated the art of remembering and interpreting them. They seemed undeterred by the usual failure of reality to fulfill the prophecies that resulted.

Startled, Galt said nothing.

"I have," Garth continued. "I have dreamed of blood and death every night since I abandoned the sword and I often awaken to find that I have arisen and moved toward it in my sleep. I think it's trying to draw me back."

Galt glanced at his companion, but said nothing. Such talk worried him. Surely Garth knew that dreams were wholly internal, he told himself. Was the prince really going mad?

"Had you not found time today, I had thought I might leave Skelleth for a time, and go further from the sword, to see if the dreams were lessened by distance. At the very least, I would then be assured that I could not reach it before waking."

"Garth, are you certain that the power that has influenced you is entirely in the sword? Perhaps some spell has affected you, some enchantment encountered in, your travels, and this obsession with the sword is a mere after-effect."

Garth considered this, then replied, "It could be, I suppose; I have had spells put upon me in the past, and they can be very subtle. I honestly doubt it, though; I think you're overcomplicating a simple situation. Wait and see what you think when you've handled the sword yourself."

"Speaking of the sword, would it not be useful for your demonstration to have other subjects besides ourselves? In particular, you claim that the sword behaves differently when handled by humans than when handled by overmen. Should we not take a human or two along to test this theory?"

"You have a good point. You run things here, Galt; where can we find a subject for such an experiment?"

The two had now reached the market. The square was still cluttered with tents, but the surrounding ruins had been cleared away, and low barriers erected to keep passersby from falling into the open cellars. Work crews were busy sorting out stones and fallen beams, dividing those that might be re-used from those that were nothing more than ballast or firewood.

"Humans are Saram's responsibility," Galt replied.

"Then let us ask Saram." Garth pointed.

Saram and Frima were leaning over the barrier that had replaced the threshold of the Baron's mansion, speaking quietly between themselves; Galt had not noticed them until Garth drew his attention to them.

Galt shrugged. "As you please," he replied.

The two overmen turned from their course and approached the two humans. Saram heard them coming and looked up as they drew near.

"Greetings, my lords," he said.

They returned his salutation.

"What can I do for you?" Saram asked.

"We are going to deal with Garth's magic sword," Galt replied, "and it would be useful to have a human along to test Garth's theory that only overmen can use his weapon. Who can you spare for such a task?"

Saram glanced around the square, then shrugged. "I'll come."

"No, you have to stay here and supervise," Galt protested.

"Do you see me supervising anything?" He waved to indicate the cellars he had been staring into. Garth smiled, amused by Galt's discomfiture.

"But . . ."

"Besides, I want to see this."

Galt gave in. "Very well, but do put someone in charge here."

"Certainly. Frima?"

"No, I'm coming, too. I don't trust that sword."

"All right. Ho, Findalan!"

A middle-aged man Garth recognized as one of the village's few carpenters looked up from assembling something.

"I'm going away for a little while; you're in charge until I get back!"

Findalan nodded.

"There. Let's go."

Reluctantly, Galt followed as Garth and Saram led the way. Frima brought up the rear at first, then ran forward to be nearer Saram.

As they made their way through the village and into the encircling ruins, Saram said, "We had an idea, Galt, that I wanted to discuss with you."

Galt made a noncommittal noise.

"Did you know there's a statue in the dungeons under the Baron's mansion?"

"No," Galt replied.

"It isn't a true statue," Garth said.

"No, but it will serve as one. That was our idea. Might we not hoist it out and set it up somewhere as a monument?"

"What sort of a monument?" Galt asked.

"That statue is a petrified thief, Saram, a half-starved boy. What sort of a monument would that make?" Garth asked.

"It would serve as a reminder of the cruelty of the Baron you slew, Garth."

"It would serve as a reminder of my stupidity in allowing a madman to gain possession of a basilisk, as well."

"I think it would make a good monument," Frima said. "He has such a brave expression on his face! You can see that he was scared but trying not to let it show."

Remembering what he had seen of the face in question, Garth could not deny the truth of her words. "Where would you put it?" he asked.

"We haven't decided yet," Frima answered.

"I'll consider it," Galt said, in a flat, conversation-killing tone.

A moment later they reached the nearer of the two guards. Garth stopped.

"It's all right," Galt said. "Let them through."

The guard nodded, but Garth still didn't move. "I think we should take one of the guards with us," he said.

"What? Why?"

"Because if the sword does take control of you or me, it will almost certainly require two overmen to restrain whichever of us it might chance to be. Saram may be strong for a human, but he would be of little help in handling a berserk overman."

"Oh." Galt considered that. "Very well." He motioned for the guard, a warrior named Fyrsh whom he knew only vaguely, to accompany them.

The five proceeded on. Galt found himself growing nervous. He felt as if he were being watched and criticized by someone.

Garth, for his part, felt an urge to run forward, to find the sword and snatch it up. The afternoon sunlight seemed to redden, and he found himself conjuring up mental images of blood and severed flesh, similar to those that had haunted his dreams.

"There it is!" Frima pointed.

The sword lay where he had left it, Garth saw, across the block of stone. The two halves of the broken stone that he had placed atop it lay to either side, and gravel was strewn about where the third stone had shattered. The hilt was toward him, and the gem was glowing vividly red.

"It's glowing," Frima said unnecessarily.

Her words penetrated the gathering fog in Garth's mind. He stopped. "Wait," he said. "Don't go any closer."

Galt stopped. He felt no attraction to the sword, but only the uncomfortable sensation of being watched. He wanted to get the whole affair over with, to convince Garth that he was ill and should go home and rest and not concern himself with Skelleth or the High King at Kholis or the Yprian overmen. "Why?" he asked.

"This is close enough for now; from here, only the person who is going to try and use it should approach any nearer."

"And if someone goes berserk, how are we to restrain him at this distance?" Galt demanded.

"I thought of that." Garth reached under his tunic – Frima had finally returned it when Saram had found her a tunic and skirt such as the local women wore – and brought out a coil of rope. "We'll put a loop of this around the neck of whoever goes to touch the sword, with one of us overmen holding each end. If there's any danger, we can jerk it tight before whoever it is can reach us with the sword."

"The person might choke to death."

"We'll be careful. When the person drops the sword, we release the rope."

Galt was still doubtful of the scheme's safety, but he was outvoted. Even Fyrsh sided with Garth. "I've been nervous ever since you posted me here, Galt," he said. "There's something unhealthy about that sword. We shouldn't take chances."

"Very well, then. Who is to make the first trial?" Galt asked.

"I will," Saram said.

"All right. Now, as I understand it, Garth, it's your contention that Saram will be unable to pick up the sword?"

"Yes. It will feel hot, too hot to handle, to any human." He hesitated, and added, "At least, I think it will."

Saram was already on his way toward the sword as Garth spoke. He slowed his pace as he drew near and then stopped. "We forgot the rope," he called back.

"I don't think we'll need it," Garth answered.

"It would be better to be cautious," Galt replied.

Garth shrugged, found one end of the rope, and held it while tossing the main coil to Saram. The man caught it, unwound several yards, and threw a loose loop around his neck. Making sure that it did not pull tight, he then tossed the free end back. It fell short; Galt stepped forward and picked it up. He and Garth each held one end now, while the central portion was wrapped once around Saram's throat.

Saram stooped and reached out for the hilt. His fingers touched it. Immediately there was a loud hissing, plainly audible to the four observers; smoke curled upward as he snatched back his hand, thrust his fingers into his mouth, and began sucking on them.

"It's hot!" he managed to say around his mouthful of singed fingertips.

"It is?" Galt was genuinely surprised. "Try it again."

Reluctantly, Saram obeyed, reaching out toward the sword.

The hiss was briefer this time; Saram had been better prepared and was able to pull his hand back more quickly. With his fingers in his mouth, he shook his head. "I can't touch it," he called.

"All right, then. Come back here and I'll try," Galt said.

Saram returned, looking slightly embarrassed. Galt handed his end of the rope to Fyrsh, then lifted the loop from around the human's neck and lowered it down past his own head onto his shoulders. That done, Saram stepped aside into Frima's considerate attentions, while Galt walked forward toward the sword.

He stopped when he reached the blade's side and called back, "As I understand it, Garth, you believe that I will be able to pick up the sword, but it will attempt to dominate me."

"I think so," Garth called back. "It can be subtle, though; it may just make you more irritable at first, more prone to react with irrational anger." He pulled in some of the slack in the rope he held.

Garth and the others watched intently; Saram, in particular, was curious as to whether Galt would be able to touch the sword without injury.

"I suspect that humans are merely over-sensitive to heat," Galt said, hesitating.

"It did not burn me at all," Garth replied, "save for the first time, when I pulled it from a fire."

Galt bent down and reached his hand slowly toward the hilt. As it neared, the black covering on the grip abruptly flared up in a burst of flame; as Saram had, Galt snatched back his hand. Unlike Saram, he immediately reached forward again. "It caught me by surprise," he called, "but I think it must be an illusion of some sort."

As the overman's hand neared it again, the flames died away to a yellow flickering. Galt ignored them and grasped the hilt firmly.

The smell of burning flesh filled the air and smoke poured from his hand; with a faint cry of pain he released his grip and looked at his scorched palm.

"I don't think it's an illusion," Garth said, "but I don't understand why it rejected you."

For a moment the five stood silently considering. Then Saram asked, "Guard, would you care to try?"

"I am called Fyrsh, human. Yes, I'll try it."

Galt returned and exchanged portions of rope with Fyrsh. The warrior had no better luck than his predecessors; like Saram, he touched the sword only lightly, with his fingertips, and received only slight burns. There was no flaring of flame, but the faint flickering remained.

"May I try?" Frima asked, when Fyrsh had rejoined the group.

There was a moment of surprised silence at this unexpected request. "Why?" Galt asked at last.

"Perhaps it only burns males – or perhaps only those who have not been in Dûsarra."

Galt looked at Garth, who shrugged. "I don't know," Garth said. "She could be right. My theory that it was attuned to overmen obviously wasn't. Let her try."

"Are you sure you want to?" Saram asked her.

She nodded.

"All right," Galt said. "Do you want the rope?"

"No."

"I don't think we need it," Saram said. "She's outnumbered four to one and outweighed at least six to one."

There was general agreement, and Frima approached the weapon unencumbered. She used only one finger for her experiment, and thereby escaped with the least injury of any.

She came running back into Saram's arms and held up her scorched finger for him to kiss.

"Perhaps," Galt suggested, "the sword has changed somehow – the time of year may have affected it, or some occurrence in the battle. Perhaps no one can now handle it.

Garth nodded. "I hope you're right; let us see if it will singe my fingers as it did yours." He picked up the rope and threw a loop around his neck, handed the ends to Galt and Fyrsh, and then marched toward the sword.

Almost immediately he felt the familiar urge to grab it up, to use it on his enemies. The red glow of the jewel seemed to fill his vision and flood everything with crimson.

As he drew near, any caution he might have felt faded away. He reached down and picked up the sword, easily and naturally, as if it were an ordinary weapon. The flames that had glimmered about the hilt vanished as his hand approached; the grip was warm to his touch, as if it had been left in bright sunlight for a few moments.

He lifted the sword, and the red haze vanished from his sight. The glow of the jewel faded. He felt none of the berserk fury that the sword had brought upon him in the past; instead he was strangely calm. He turned to face his companions. "You see?" he called. "It has a will of its own, and it has chosen me as its wielder."

"I see," Galt called back. "Now put it down again."

Garth nodded and tried to turn back.

The sword would not move; it hung in the air before him as if embedded in stone.

Garth tried to release his hold and drop it where it was; his fingers would not move.

"I think we have a problem," he called.

Instantly, Galt jerked the rope tight; with equal speed, the sword twisted, feeling as if it were moving Garth's hands rather than the reverse, and cut the rope through. Before Fyrsh could take any action with his end it flashed back and severed that, as well. The two overmen found themselves holding useless fragments, while the loop around Garth's throat remained slack.

There was a moment of horrified silence; then Galt called, "Now what?"

"I don't know!" Garth replied. "I can't let go!" He struggled, trying to pry his fingers from the grip, but could not move them.

He attempted to move his arm and discovered that he could now move it freely. He lowered the sword from the upright display he had held it in; there was no reason to be unnecessarily uncomfortable.

He tried placing his other hand on the grip and then removing it; there was no resistance. He then placed his left hand on the grip and tried removing his right.

It came away easily and naturally.

Now, however, his left hand was locked to the sword.

He switched back and forth a few times, and established to his own satisfaction that whatever power held him to the sword would be content with either hand or both, so long as he retained a hold suitable for wielding the thing. He could hold it with two fingers and one thumb, if he chose; that seemed to be the absolute minimum. Any one finger and both thumbs on the same hand would also work. A single finger and thumb, however, or just two thumbs, would not suffice; when he attempted to use such a grip, his other hand would not come free.

He was about to point this out to Galt as clear proof that there was a conscious power involved – after all, how could any spell, however complex, manage anything so subtle? Galt chose that moment to call, "Garth, stay there; I will return shortly."

For the first time Garth realized that while he had been playing with his fingers, the other four had been discussing his situation and had apparently arrived at some sort of a decision. Galt and Saram were leaving. Fyrsh and, oddly, Frima were staying. He called after the departing pair, "See if you can find a sheath that would fit this thing! I have an idea!"

It had occurred to him that, if it were sheathed, the sword might behave differently; it was certainly worth trying.

He was frankly puzzled by this new difficulty. He had never before had any trouble in releasing the sword.

But then, he told himself, he had never tried to destroy it before, or tried to abandon it.

Perhaps he could still destroy it, he thought. His previous failure might have been because the sword held some special relationship to stone; after all, he knew almost nothing about it. The standard method for breaking a sword had always been to snap it across one's knee; he could try that.

He turned back toward the stone blocks – the sword seemed to have no objection now that the rope was cut. He placed one foot on a block, raising his knee to a convenient height.

Ordinarily he wouldn't have done something like this without armor. Metal splinters might fly, and the broken ends could snap back and gash his knee badly. He thought such injuries would be worthwhile, though, if he could be rid of this particular sword. He placed it across his knee, his right hand holding the hilt and his left gripping the blade, and pushed down.

Nothing happened. The sword bent not an inch.

He pressed harder. It still did not give.

He put his full strength into it, so that the pressure bruised his knee and the palms of his hands; had it snapped, he knew he would have been thrown forward on the fragments and probably seriously cut.

It did not snap. It did not yield at all.

He gave up in disgust and looked speculatively at the stone block.

Raising the sword above his head in a two-handed grip such as he would have used on an axe in chopping firewood, he swung the blade down at the stone with all the might he could muster.

The stone block shattered in a spectacular shower of sparks, dust, and gravel.

He studied the blade and ran a thumb along it carefully. It was as sharp as ever, with no sign of nick or waver.

Destroying this thing would be a real challenge, he realized. It might take days or even months to contrive an effective method.

It was very curious, though, that it was allowing him so much freedom to try. He knew that it could cloud his thoughts and turn him into a mindless engine of destruction or move in his hands without his cooperation, yet it was doing nothing of the kind. Instead it had displayed this new talent, this refusal to come free of his hold. Why had it not done so before?

Perhaps it had felt no need. He had cooperated with it readily at first. Only after he realized how disastrous the consequences of the destruction of Skelleth might be had he seriously resisted. When he had actually managed to abandon it perhaps it had become frightened, aware that it might lose its control of him.

Could a sword be frightened? Or, if the sword were only a tool, could a god be frightened?

Frightened might be too strong a word; "cautious" would be better. If he could reassure the entity, whatever it was, perhaps he could contrive to slip away and abandon the sword for good. Once he was free of its hold, he would be certain never to touch it again.

If he could pick it up without touching it, with tongs perhaps, and transport it, he could find some way to get rid of it even if he couldn't destroy it. He could throw it in the ocean; no one would retrieve it from the bottom of the sea.

That assumed, however, that he would be able to get it out of his hands.

The Forgotten King would probably be able to make it let go. Judging by the ease with which the old man had darkened the gem and suppressed the sword's power before, he should have no trouble in doing so again. The only problem with that solution was that the King would almost certainly demand something in exchange, and Garth did not care to deal with him further.

Still, if he could not manage something else, sooner or later he might be forced to give in to the Forgotten King. Even that would be preferable to unleashing the sword again, he was sure. He had felt the sword's personality, if it could be called that, and he knew that it sought nothing but death and destruction. It was being canny now, biding its time, allowing him to think, but he was certain that soon its bloodlust would grow and more innocents would die, as they had died in Dûsarra and Skelleth.

Thinking of death, the sword, and the Forgotten King, he began to wonder at the exact nature of the King's immortality. What would happen if the old man were to have a blade thrust through him? Would he live on regardless? Could he bleed or feel pain? What if his head were to be severed? Surely, death-priest or no, he could not survive decapitation.

It might be, then, that he could not be decapitated, that any blade would break in the attempt. In that case, what would happen if he were to be struck by the unbreakable blade of the Sword of Bheleu?

This seemed a very interesting question. What would happen when the irresistible destructive power of the sword met the immortal body of the Forgotten King? One or the other would have to yield and perish.

If the sword were to break, then Garth would be rid of it.

If the King were to die – as seemed far more likely, more in keeping with the natural order of the world – then Garth would have performed an act of mercy, and would no longer need to worry about the old man's schemes. Unfortunately, he would also no longer have a means of last resort for disposing of the sword.

Perhaps both would be destroyed. That would really be the ideal solution.

He would have to consider this further, and perhaps attempt a few experiments. He might want to obtain some advice on the matter. He wondered if he could trust the old man to tell the truth; perhaps he would do better to go home and consult the Wise Women of Ordunin.

As he considered this, he saw Galt and Saram returning, leading a squad of half a dozen overmen and an equal number of humans. Someone was even leading a warbeast.

He wondered, out of a warrior's professional curiosity, whether the sword would be able to kill so many opponents before they could rip him apart. Without the warbeast, he suspected it would have no trouble. Warbeasts, however, were notoriously hard to kill and moved with a speed and ferocity that no overman could even approach, just as no human could equal an overman.

He hoped that he wouldn't have to put the matter to the test.

Several of the overmen, he saw, were carrying various ropes and restraints. Saram was carrying the same oversized, over-the-shoulder scabbard that had held the sword before.

That was encouraging, because it implied that they hoped to restrain him – and the sword – without harming him. Less pleasant was the fact that four of the humans carried crossbows. Galt apparently did not care to take too many chances. Garth hoped that those would be strictly a last resort and that the archers would not aim to kill.

The newcomers stopped where Fyrsh and Frima waited and spoke with them; Garth did not try to listen, but it was plain that Frima was protesting such extreme measures.

While the argument continued, Garth called, "Ho, Saram! Toss me that scabbard!"

The acting baron looked up and thought for a moment before obeying.

Garth picked up the sheath with his free hand and flung it back across his left shoulder. He managed to catch the lower strap with the fingers of his right hand, despite the sword's encumbrance, and to bring it up to meet the shoulderpiece.

It took several minutes and much fumbling, but he contrived to tie a reasonably secure knot. He wished that the thing had a buckle; he was sure he could have managed that much more readily.

When he had the scabbard in place, he tipped it forward and slid the blade into it. Then, slowly, he removed his fingers, one by one, from the sword's hilt.

They came away easily, and the sword fell back into place, slapping his back. It felt peculiar to be wearing the scabbard without armor; a two-handed broadsword was strictly a weapon of war, not something to be carried casually about the streets.

"There, you see?" he called to the watching crowd. He held up his hands, showing that they were free and empty. "All I needed was the scabbard."

Galt called in reply, "We see that you have released the sword, but has it released you? Can you remove the scabbard?"

"Of course I can, Galt, but I think I had best keep it with me for the moment. It's too dangerous to leave lying around." He lifted the sheath's strap up from his shoulder, to show that it was not adhering unnaturally. He had no problem in doing so. "See?" he said. "And the gem is dark. It's quiescent right now."

In truth, he did not believe that he could remove the sword and scabbard; he was sure that the knot would prove impossible to untie as long as the sword was sheathed. It was his own problem, though, and he did not want Galt and a bunch of ignorant helpers making matters worse. He was reasonably certain that the only way the sword would voluntarily let him go was if he were to be killed and that Galt's motley group would be unable to remove the sword against its will. He had no wish to die when they attempted to do so, nor to kill any of them.

He had some idea of how powerful the sword was, and they did not, as yet. He would be unable to convince them that the sword was more than they could handle without bloody experimentation. He therefore intended to convince them of the opposite, that the problem was already under control.

"Are you sure?" Galt asked.

"Yes, I'm sure. I've handled this sword for weeks, Galt. It's harmless right now." He reached up and grasped and released the hilt a few times to show that it was not spitting flame or grabbing hold. It remained cooperatively inanimate.

He had it partly figured out now; it was determined to remain in his possession, but it was intelligent enough not to waste energy in holding him any more tightly than necessary. As long as he kept it on his person, it didn't care how it was carried.

He pulled it out, then sheathed it again, demonstrating that it was behaving like any ordinary sword. "You see, Galt? I think it's worn itself out, at least temporarily."

"Very well, Garth. Carry it, if you please. I warn you, though . . ."

"I know, I know. You cannot trust me while I bear it with me."

"Exactly. I would ask, Garth, that henceforth you sleep well away from the center of town, lest it rouse in the night and drive you mad."

Garth shrugged. "As you please."

Reluctantly, Galt dismissed his dozen supporters; they trailed off toward the market, returning to whatever they had been doing previously. After a final uneasy glance in Garth's direction, Galt followed them.

Garth, in turn, followed; Saram and Frima joined him. Fyrsh turned, as if to accompany them, then stopped and said, "We forgot Pandh."

"Who?" Saram asked.

"Pandh. The other guard Galt posted here. If you're taking the sword, there's no need for him to stay here. He's still up the road; he probably hasn't noticed any of this."

"You're right," Garth agreed. "Go relieve him, then."

Fyrsh nodded and turned back down the street.

When he had gone, Garth remarked to the two humans, "I'm bound for the King's Inn; all this shouting back and forth has made me thirsty."

"We'll join you, if we're not needed elsewhere," Saram said.

"I'd be glad of your company." At least, Garth thought, they would be welcome while he quenched his thirst, which was quite genuine. His primary reason for visiting the King's Inn, however, was to speak with the Forgotten King, and he would prefer privacy for that. He hoped that Saram would be needed somewhere.

Chapter Fourteen

The Seer of Weideth had never acquired the knack of using a scrying glass and made do instead with an assortment of divining spells. Every spell he tried gave the same answer; the Dûsarran girl had indeed told the truth.

Garth of Ordunin had destroyed Skelleth for no reason. Furthermore, he had murdered the rightful baron of the village on only the slightest provocation, and killed a score of innocents with no cause at all. The girl had not mentioned that.

The overman had done this with the Sword of Bheleu, which was obviously an artifact of great power. The apparent level of arcane energy was, in fact, so great that no material force could possibly stand against it. There would be no point, therefore, in sending an army to Skelleth; only magic or stealth could hope to deal with such a menace.

The Seer wondered how so dangerous a weapon had been left lying about where any passing overman could pick it up in the first place; one of the Council's overseers must have been shirking his duties.

It was not, fortunately, his responsibility; he was only liable for the village and the surrounding hills. Since the matter had been brought to his attention, it was his duty to report it – and that was the entirety of his duty.

He gathered together the three village elders; his own powers were too feeble to reach more than a dozen leagues with a message-spell, and he judged that this matter was worthy of the immediate attention of the Chairman of the Council. That was old Shandiph, and a simple divination told the Seer that Shandiph was in Kholis, the capital city of Eramma, which lay more than a hundred leagues to the east. Communicating over such a distance would require three other minds working in concert with his own. He had worked with the elders before, and they had become reasonably adept at this sort of thing.

By the time he returned to the tavern's common room after divining the Chairman's location, ready to make the attempt at contact, the messenger from the city was long gone and the elders were waiting for him.

In Kholis, Shandiph was visiting with Chalkara, court wizard to the High King. The two were alone in Chalkara's velvet-draped chambers, playing caravanserai with an ancient set of hand-carved jade and ivory which the court wizard had inherited from her predecessor, and sampling a golden wine of unknown but venerable vintage that Shandiph had brought with him from a stay in Ur-Dormulk. Shandiph had had more than his share of the wine and was consequently a good sixty coins behind in the game when the image of the Seer of Weideth suddenly appeared on the tapestry Chalkara was leaning her back against.

Startled, the old man dropped his wine glass, scattering the green pieces in all directions and spilling yellow wine across the whites. For a moment both wizards were too busy picking up pieces and sopping up the spill with Shandiph's cloak to pay any heed to the message.

When some semblance of order had been restored, Shandiph demanded angrily, "What do you want?"

The Seer's image mouthed something.

"Oh, Regvos, the damnable fool hasn't got a voice; I have to do everything myself!"

Chalkara said soothingly, "I'll do it, Shandi." She reached up to an ornate silk and silver box on a nearby table and pulled out a gleaming amulet, then recited a brief incantation before slipping the golden trinket around her throat.

"Speak, image!" she commanded.

"I am the Seer of Weideth," the image said, "and I have an urgent and private message for Shandiph the wandering sorcerer."

"I am listening," Shandiph replied.

"Ah . . . it is not to be heard by any but Shandiph."

"Never mind that, Seer, just give me the message. I have better things to do."

"Oh, I'm sorry. Did I interrupt something?"

"Give me the damn massage!"

With much hesitation and awkwardness, the Seer explained about the visit from the Dûsarran girl and reported what his divinations had told him.

When he had finished, he waited for a response. Shandiph sat silently for a long moment, then said, "All right. You've delivered your message; you can go now."

The Seer's image vanished immediately.

In Weideth, the Seer relaxed. The matter was out of his hands. He thanked the elders for their assistance, then ordered a final mug of ale before retiring.

In Kholis, Chalkara looked at Shandiph, who was staring at the floor. "This could be serious," she said. "It could start the Racial Wars all over again."

"We'll have to make sure it doesn't," Shandiph replied. "Listen, I'm having trouble thinking clearly; have you got something that counteracts wine? I left all my potions in my own rooms."

"I think so." She rose gracefully, crossed to a cabinet against the far wall, and began rummaging through it.

"Do you think he's right about how dangerous this overman is?" The elder wizard scratched his balding head.

"I don't know anything about it, Shandi. I have never even heard of Weideth or its Seer, nor Garth of Ordunin, nor of the Sword of Bheleu. The only name I know from the whole affair is Skelleth; and even if Skelleth is a pesthole – it is, too – the High King won't be pleased to hear it's been destroyed. It's a bad precedent. Besides, the Baron of Sland is bound to make trouble about it." She pulled out a small brass bottle. "I think this will do; it's a cure for drunkenness and senility."

"I am neither drunk nor senile, woman, merely tipsy. Still, it should serve; pass it here."

Chalkara complied and told him, "The normal dose is three drops."

"One should do, then, but I'll make it two to be safe." He suited actions to words, then shut his eyes and mouth for a moment.

"It tastes awful," he said a moment later.

"Potions usually do," she replied.

"I know. You'd think something could be done about it."

"Right now, I think there are other things more important to do."

"You're right. I don't know anything about Garth of Ordunin or about Skelleth, and the Sword of Bheleu is legendary, which means the available information can't be trusted. I do, however, know the Seer of Weideth, albeit only slightly. It's a hereditary post, one of these odd little oracular talents that turn up here and there. Weideth is a village in the hills in the northwest of Nekutta, and its seers have certain undeniable gifts as long as they remain within the immediate area. The current Seer is no great prophet, but he can do a simple divination; I'm afraid there's no disputing his facts."

"Then this sword really is too powerful to defeat by mundane methods?"

"Oh, we can't be sure of that; a clever assassin might manage something. There could be flaws in the Seer's detail work in that particular conclusion. I would certainly agree that an army won't work; he couldn't have missed the mark by that much."

"Do you want to try an assassin, then?"

"Chala, my dear, *I'm* not going to try anything. I don't know enough about it. I'm going to get some expert advice first."

"What sort of advice?"

"Oh, I think I had best consult an astrologer and a theurgist, since there may be a god involved, and experts on swords and overmen and perhaps an archivist or two. I'll find a really good diviner to study the entire affair; I'm no good at that sort of work myself."

"Shandi, if you're going to do all that, wouldn't it be simpler just to convene the entire Council and turn the whole thing over to them at once? You know that you need approval from a quorum before you start commissioning assassinations or fooling with major arcana."

Shandiph considered this silently for a moment. The pleasant glow he had felt earlier was almost wholly dissipated now, and he found himself slightly irritable in consequence.

"You're right, Chala. Aghad take this overman, you're right. I *hate* convening the Council; there's always argument, and I always have to break it up. There's no getting around it, though; this is important enough for the whole Council. A border has been violated and the invaders are using magic. That's exactly the sort of thing that the Council is supposed to prevent."

"Well, at least if you turn it over to the Council, you won't have the entire responsibility."

"Oh, I don't mind the responsibility. It's better than having to listen to that fool Deriam and his idiot theories about the natural supremacy of Ur-Dormulk, or trying to keep peace between Karag of Sland and Thetheru of Amag. You know, I came down here early just to get away from Deriam and now I'm going to have to invite him here."

"I thought you came to see me!"

"I did, I did; after all, I could have gone anywhere from Ur-Dormulk, couldn't I?"

"I know, Shandi. I guess we won't be finishing the game, will we?"

Shandiph looked at the scattered caravanserai pieces. "I suppose not. And just when my luck was changing!"

"Ha! You would have been lucky not to lose a hundred coins!"

"Would I? We'll see next time, then!" He smiled, then frowned. "Right now, though, I had best go find the Charm of Convocation." He clambered awkwardly to his feet.

Chalkara began gathering up the carved tokens. "Shall I come with you?"

"You tempt me, but no. Only the Chairman is to see the Charm – another silly rule."

"In that case, shall I go and tell the King to expect company?"

"Yes, I think so; it is his castle, after all. He might get upset if three dozen magicians were to turn up on his doorstep without warning."

Chalkara nodded, and began placing the ivory pieces neatly into their places in the rosewood box.

Shandiph watched her for a moment, then said, "Gau and Pria bless you, Chala." He left, closing the door gently behind him.

That night each and every member of the Council of the Most High had the same dream, and each awoke knowing that he or she was to leave immediately for Kholis.

Chapter Fifteen

Saram was not called away immediately, but eventually, as Garth was beginning to feel rather soggy from the vast amount of ale he had consumed, someone came looking for the interim baron. A jurisdictional dispute had developed between two of his ad hoc ministers.

Garth watched him go, taking Frima with him, and marveled that he could walk straight. The human had consumed ale mug for mug with him, and if Garth was feeling the effects, then surely, he thought, the much smaller human should be staggering drunk. It did not occur to him that he had been drinking earlier as well, before picking up the sword, while Saram had not.

It was the middle of the evening and the tavern was crowded; nonetheless, as usual, the Forgotten King was alone at his table in the corner beneath the stairs. Garth seated himself opposite the old man.

For a long moment neither spoke; Garth was unsure how to begin, and the Forgotten King preferred to let the other speak first.

"I have questions I would ask you," Garth said at last.

The old man said nothing, but the yellow cowl dipped in a faint nod.

"You say that you cannot die by ordinary means. How can this be? What would happen if you were struck with a good blade? If your neck were to be severed, would you not die like any other mortal?"

"My neck cannot be severed by any ordinary blade," the King replied.

The hideous dry voice caught Garth off-guard; he had forgotten how unpleasant it was to hear. He hesitated before asking, "How can that be?"

The yellow-draped shoulders rose, then sank.

Garth felt a flicker of annoyance and immediately looked at the hilt of the Sword of Bheleu. The gem was glowing very faintly.

That was not necessarily bad, he thought. Perhaps if he were to allow himself to become angry, the old wizard would douse the sword's power as he had done before, and Garth would be able to escape from the weapon's hold without making any sort of deal at all.

He turned back to the Forgotten King and asked, "You say no ordinary blade can kill you; what of the sword I carry?"

"You are welcome to make the attempt," the old man replied.

Garth considered that.

If the result were the destruction of the sword, then all would be well, and his problems would be at an end for the moment. If the result were the death of the King, then he would have performed an act of mercy, but he might be stuck with the sword indefinitely. If both were destroyed, that would be best all around.

There was surely some other way of getting free of the sword. Perhaps, even if it were not destroyed, it would be sufficiently weakened by the effort to loose its hold.

One way or another, the odds appeared to be in his favor. He decided to risk it. He stood, reached up, and pulled the sword from its sheath, awkward in the confined space of the tavern. The tip of the up-ended scabbard scraped the ceiling as the blade came free. It was obvious that he would be unable to swing the blade up over his head; he would have to use a sweeping horizontal stroke instead.

There was a hush, and he looked about, realizing that the other patrons of the tavern had abruptly fallen silent. They were staring at him and at the great broadsword, wearing expressions that ranged from vague curiosity to abject terror.

"Have no fear," he called. "I mean none of you any harm. The old man here has challenged me to strike off his head. Haven't you, old man?"

The yellow-garbed figure nodded, and Garth thought he caught a glint of light in one shadowed eye.

The overman looked along the path he planned for the sword and saw that it would pass uncomfortably close to the humans at a neighboring table.

"Excuse me, friends," he said, "but I would greatly appreciate it if you could step back for a moment, to give me room to swing."

The humans quickly rose and backed away.

Satisfied that he would endanger no one but the King, Garth took a good two-handed grip on the sword and tried to swing it.

At first it moved normally, but as it approached the old man's neck it slowed, as if moving through water rather than air. From the corner of his eye Garth could see the red gem glowing fiercely, but he felt none of the roaring anger and exultant bloodlust that usually accompanied the glow.

Then the sword stopped, inches from the ragged yellow cloth, frozen in mid-air as it had been just before it severed the rope earlier that afternoon. He could force it no closer.

He strained, putting all the strength of his arms into driving the sword toward the old man's throat.

The blade did not move; instead it rang, like steel striking stone, and flashed silver. The hilt grew warm in his grasp.

That inspired him to push harder; perhaps he could force the sword to reject him.

The ringing sounded again, louder, like the sound made by running a moist finger along the rim of a fine crystal goblet, and this time it did not fade, but grew. The red glow of the jewel was brighter now than the lamps that lit the tavern, and the blade was unmistakably glowing as well. The hilt was hot, but there was no pain, no burning, and he knew that he could not release his hold any more than before he had swung.

The sword did not move, but remained stalled in midair, as if wedged in stone, a few short inches from the old man's neck.

Then, abruptly, it forced itself back, against his will.

Startled, he released his pressure and found the sword hanging loosely in his grasp, apparently quite normal. The ringing had stopped. The glow had vanished, and the hilt was cooling rapidly.

He was determined not to give in that easily. He swung the sword back and attempted another blow.

This time, as the blade approached its target, it veered upward, twisting in his hands, and cut through nothing but the air above the Forgotten King's head.

He stopped his useless swing and brought the weapon back for a third try. This time he found himself unable even to begin his swing; the sword was suddenly heavy in his grasp, impossibly heavy, and he could not lift it to the height of the old man's neck.

Annoyed, he applied his full strength and hauled the blade upward. It seemed to struggle, and he felt a pull, as if a great lodestone were tugging it away from the King.

He fought it, but could not bring the weapon to bear on the old man.

After several minutes of struggling, the Forgotten King's dead, dry voice called to him.

"Garth. Stop wasting time."

Reluctantly, he gave up and let the tip of the sword fall to the floor. It lost its unnatural weight, and he picked it up as if to sheathe it.

Then, abruptly, trying to take it by surprise, he yanked it around into a thrust toward the King.

It stopped short a foot from the tattered yellow cloak.

He gave up in disgust and sheathed the sword. It did not resist.

He seated himself again and asked, "Was any of that your doing?"

There was a pause before the King replied, "Not willingly. None of it was of my choosing, but it was as much my curse as the sword's power at work."

"Then an ordinary blade would behave similarly?"

"Not quite. It would break if forced, rather than fighting back."

Garth sat back, thinking.

He was unsure whether or not to believe that an ordinary blade would break. He was not even certain that he should believe the old man's claim not to have willingly interfered. Perhaps he had lied, lied throughout; perhaps he did not want to die. His claims might be camouflage for some deeper, more subtle scheme.

He could not be trusted.

He did, however, have the power to control the sword.

A vague, uneasy thought occurred to Garth; he considered it, let it grow and take form.

Perhaps it was in truth the Forgotten King who controlled the sword's actions entirely, and not the mythical god of destruction. Perhaps Garth's entire mission to Dûsarra had been an elaborate charade the old man had contrived for reasons that remained unclear.

Such a theory seemed unlikely, but could not be completely discounted.

Carrying his imagining a step further, Garth arrived at another possibility. What if the sword and the Forgotten King were both being controlled by some other unseen power? It might be Bheleu, The God Whose Name Is Not Spoken, or just some mighty wizard.

What if everything that had befallen him was part of some vast plot? Could his depression and resulting quest for eternal fame have been the result of some spell? Could the entire sequence of events that followed have been planned, his every action guided?

Had he ever had any choice at all in his actions?

He shook his head. This was all getting too complicated and far-fetched; he doubted that there was any such conspiracy at work. If there were, it was obviously far beyond his own capabilities to do anything about it.

"O King," he said, returning to the subject at hand, "I would like to make you a gift of this sword. It was at your request that I brought it from Dûsarra, and I feel it right that you should have it."

The Forgotten King said nothing.

"You will not refuse it?"

"I will not accept it," the King replied, "until you swear to serve me by bringing me the Book of Silence and aiding in my final magic."

"You have said that this magic will kill many people; I cannot in good conscience aid you in it."

"Then I will not accept the sword." He did not say anything more, but it was plain to both what was implied; while Garth kept the sword, he would be in constant danger of having further death and destruction on his conscience.

He faced a choice of two evils, neither clearly the lesser, and both, in fact, quite large.

Garth reached up to his breast and picked at the knot that held the scabbard on his back. As he had expected, he was unable to work the strands at all.

"Will you not reconsider?" he asked.

"Will you?"

Defeated for the moment, Garth sat back and thought.

It seemed clear that the Forgotten King would not help him; the overman had feared as much. The sword had not obliged him by driving him into a frenzy that the King would have been forced to quell; a glance over his left shoulder showed that the gem was glowing moderately, yet he felt no particular anger, no great compulsions. The thing was biding its time. Perhaps it knew something of the future and was waiting for something specific; perhaps it was aware of the Forgotten King and had learned that he was able to control it, and so was restraining itself.

Perhaps, should it attempt to wreak havoc in the future, he could contrive to bring it here and threaten the King, so that the old man would be forced to dampen its power in self-defense.

No, that would not work; what need did the King have to defend himself? He was immortal and wanted to die – at least, so he claimed.

That might be a bluff, Garth thought, to convince him that there was no point in threatening the old man. Next time the killing fury came, Garth decided, he would make an attempt to find the King and test out his invulnerability again.

For the present, though, there seemed nothing more to be gained here. He rose and left the tavern.

The streets were dark, but torches lit the marketplace directly in front of him on the far side of the cellars of the Baron's destroyed mansion. He paused and looked again at the knot that held the scabbard in place.

It was a very simple, rough knot; he had tied it himself and knew that to be the case. Ordinarily it would have been hardly adequate to hold the sword; normal jarring would have worked it loose in an hour or two. The sword's power, however, could apparently be spread beyond the weapon itself; the knot was tight and solid.

He picked at it again, but could not work the strands loose.

There was an ancient legend about a knot that could not be untied. The story was that after many wise men had tried to undo it, a simple warrior had cut it apart with his knife. If Garth could not untie the scabbard strap while the sword was sheathed, perhaps he could cut it.

He made his way around the cellars and approached the nearest overman he saw. It was Fyrsh, relaxing by a campfire after his supper. He had no objection to loaning Garth his dagger. "After all," he said, "you've already got that sword if you want to start trouble."

Garth agreed, smiling, and thanked him. Then he found a quiet spot to sit and tried to cut the strap.

It was difficult slipping the blade under the strap at all; where a moment before it had seemed comfortably loose, it was now drawn tight across his chest. Finally, though, he managed to force it in and turned the blade, working it against the leather.

The blade was notched almost immediately, as if meeting steel.

Garth shifted it and tried again, sawing at the leather.

The blade snapped off completely, gashing his chest with the broken edge and cutting a long slit in his tunic before falling to the hard ground with a rattle.

The broken stump was of no use. He returned the pieces to Fyrsh with his sincere apologies and promised to pay for a new one.

It was growing late, and he had no further ideas that could be readily tried. Disgruntled, he set out to find somewhere to sleep. He did not care to be near other people; he was afraid that the sword might make him murder them while they slept.

After much walking, he settled down for the night in the shelter of a relatively intact stretch of the town's wall, midway between the North and East Gates. His sleep was calm and dreamless.

Chapter Sixteen

The first to arrive at the High King's castle was Karag of Sland, which was somewhat surprising; Sland lay almost two days' ride to the west of Kholis, and Shandiph knew there were other councilors closer at hand.

Furthermore, Karag did not come alone. The Baron of Sland had accompanied him, with a party of half a dozen black-clad soldiers.

The presence of the Baron made the arrival a matter of state; the High King was roused and formal presentation arranged. While this went on, Chalkara reported to the Chairman that a ragged stranger dressed in brown and carrying a staff had arrived at the scullery gate, refusing to give his name but insisting that Shandiph had sent for him.

"That's all right," Shandiph told her as he watched the High King accepting Karag's obeisance. "That would be Derelind the Hermit; he lives just south of here."

"Why wouldn't he tell me that?"

"Oh, he's a secretive young fool. Don't mind him."

Karag was rising now, and the six soldiers were being presented, together with a list of names and the honors they had received. Shandiph wondered how warriors could acquire so many marks of distinction on their records when the kingdom had been at peace for almost three hundred years.

"Should I find Derelind a guest chamber?"

"I don't know; ask him. He would probably prefer to sleep on the kitchen floor with the lower servants, and we may not have enough rooms for everybody, if we get a good response to the call."

Chalkara nodded and slipped away.

She was back by the time the soldiers had finished their ritual presentation. Now, by custom, the High King and the Baron would retire to the King's private council chamber for a report on the state of the Barony of Sland, and Shandiph would be able to speak to Karag without the Baron's presence.

"Now, my lord Baron; I would hear how your lands have fared since last we spoke." The King recited the traditional request slowly and precisely; it was plain to all present that he really didn't care how Sland fared, but was merely fulfilling his obligations. That was no surprise; the current King was perhaps the most worthless to reign in Eramma to date.

Still, the ritual would proceed; to make it look good, the King and the Baron would have to stay in seclusion for at least a quarter of an hour. Shandiph suspected they would do little in that time other than drink a few toasts, but it gave him his chance to speak with Karag.

When the nobles had left the room, Shandiph started across the floor of the throne room. Karag met him halfway. Before Shandiph could begin a polite greeting, Karag snarled at him, "Have you gone mad, you old fool?"

Shandiph was taken aback. "What?"

"What in the name of all the gods did you think you were doing, summoning the Council to this castle?"

"This is a matter for the Council to discuss," Shandiph replied stiffly. Chalkara came up behind him as he spoke.

"So you blithely called us all here, to the castle of the High King at Kholis?"

"Yes, of course. Why not? I was here; as chairman, it is my prerogative to choose the meeting site. Further, Kholis is centrally located and has good roads."

"Does it mean nothing to you that our little group is supposed to be a *secret* organization, one whose existence is unknown to the world at large? For three centuries we have guarded that secret, and now you have virtually announced to the High King that there is an organization of wizards meeting here."

"I have done nothing of the sort. Is that why you came so promptly? To tell me this?"

"Yes, it is; I thought that, if I got here soon enough, I could talk sense to you and convince you to warn the others away. We have ridden night and day since half an hour after I received the summons."

"And you've brought the Baron of Sland with you."

"I had to; had I left without telling him, he would have had my head. I told him that I needed to speak with you immediately, and he insisted on accompanying me."

"And you call *me* a fool? Do you think he won't suspect that something out of the ordinary required such urgency?"

Chalkara interrupted Karag's sputtered reply. "Why did he come with you? Did you not tell him this was a matter involving only wizards and their affairs?"

"Yes, I told him; I think that's why he chose to come. He's been taking a great interest in magic lately, even asking if I could teach him a few simple spells."

"You haven't, have you?" Chalkara asked.

"Of course not! But as you have probably heard, it's unhealthy to deny Barach of Sland anything, however slight. I dared not argue with him about this trip as well."

"If there is anything that will reveal the nature of this meeting, Karag, it is his presence. The King pays no attention to what happens around him; he cares for nothing but wine, women, and old books. The servants and courtiers can be frightened or bribed into silence. The Baron of Sland, however, is not so easily handled." Shandiph tried his best to sound stern.

Karag paused for a moment, then said, with no trace of contrition, "Well, it's done now, and if we're to keep it secret you'll have to turn back all the others. I'm sure that the three of us can handle whatever this problem is by ourselves."

"The four of us; Derelind the Hermit is downstairs somewhere."

"Very well, then, the four of us. What is this world-shaking problem? Has someone stolen a love potion somewhere or caught a councilor kissing a baron's daughter?"

"The problem requires a quorum of the Council. An overman has gotten hold of a magic sword, a very powerful one, and has destroyed large parts of two cities. The Seer of Weideth has divined that he is beyond the power of ordinary measures. At the very least he'll require assassination, and we may need to be even more drastic. Now, Karag of Sland, do you feel I was unjustified in calling the Council together?"

There was a moment of silence.

"Are you sure of the facts?"

"The Seer of Weideth swore to them."

"Are you sure it was the true Seer?"

"No, but if it were not, Karag, then we have an even worse problem, do we not? The message was an image-sending; if it was not the Seer, then we have an enemy or traitor of unknown purpose and power to deal with."

"True. What cities were destroyed?"

"Shall we go somewhere more private?"

"Yes, of course. Chalkara?"

"There is my chamber; it has the customary wards upon it."

"Good." They retired to her quarters, pausing only to order a servant to send up Derelind, and any other enchanters who might arrive.

When Shandiph and Karag had settled on the velvet cushions in her sitting room, Chalkara found the remains of the golden wine that she and Shandiph had been drinking when the message first arrived and served it out to the three of them. They sipped it, waiting for Derelind.

When the hermit had arrived and refused cushions and wine, preferring to squat on the bare stone between rugs, Karag again asked, "What two cities were destroyed?"

"Permit me to explain, Derelind. The matter that I have summoned the Council to discuss involves an overman who has obtained a very powerful magic sword. He has already destroyed much of the city of Dûsarra, in western Nekutta, defiling most of its temples, burning the market and much of the surrounding area, and spreading the White Death, a particularly vile sort of plague. Dûsarra being what it is, I think we might forgive him that, but he has continued by laying waste to the bordertown of Skelleth and murdering its Baron."

"Murdering?" Derelind inquired.

"He was stabbed in the back, I am told."

"That would seem to be murder," Karag agreed. "What else?"

"He and a force of overmen have occupied Skelleth and are rebuilding it to suit themselves. It appears that they may intend to renew the Racial Wars. I need not remind you that it was those wars that created this Council in the first place; we were sworn to maintain peace by whatever means necessary."

"Is the High King aware of this invasion?" Derelind asked.

"No."

"You have not told him?"

"We would prefer to settle the whole matter ourselves. The Seer of Weideth tells us that armies would be of no use against this overman, and what other option would the King have, save to send an army?"

"What, then, do you propose instead?"

"I wish to send either one or more very good assassins, or to use magic of a level this sword cannot counter," Shandiph said.

"What magic did you have in mind?" Karag asked.

"You know what our great weapon is, Karag," Derelind said.

"Yes, and I also know that many people think it a panacea and wish to use it every time the least little difficulty arises."

"You exaggerate, Karag. It has been used only once in the last three centuries," Derelind said.

"That once was more than enough; were it not for the sorry state of trade in these decadent times, the news of that use would have been a world-wide legend by now."

"Would that be so harmful?" Chalkara asked.

"Our organization's existence is a secret," Karag stated slowly and precisely. "We want to keep it a secret. Only in secret can we continue to maintain peace and to manipulate the governments of the world so that there is no aggressive action taken. Only by acting in secret can we limit the knowledge of the arcane arts and prevent the magical battles that caused such catastrophes in the earlier ages."

"It seems to me," Chalkara said, "that we are getting ahead of ourselves. It is not our place to decide this; it is a matter for a quorum of the Council. I think we can all agree on that."

"There is no harm," Derelind said, "in planning ahead. I suspect that the Council as a whole will, in fact, agree that this situation may require drastic remedies – and quickly. Might I suggest that, as soon as someone with the requisite talents arrives, we should send a magical message to the keeper of the weapon? I know little about the spells involved in controlling it; do they require any preparation time?"

"I'm afraid I don't know either," Shandiph admitted. "That has always been left entirely to the keeper."

"I still think it's a mistake," Karag said. "Turning people to stone can't help but attract attention."

"We are only suggesting sending a message, to have it ready if needed. You know that Shang has orders to stay where he is and to ignore the summons I sent; we can't leave the thing unguarded."

"All right, then, send a message to Mormoreth. I still think, though, that using the basilisk is a mistake, and I'll vote against it in the Council."

Chapter Seventeen

Over the course of the next several days Garth attempted repeatedly to get rid of the sword. In doing so he broke two dozen assorted blades; hurt his jaw in trying to chew through the scabbard strap; burned his hand badly in a candle flame in the hope that sufficient heat or pain might cause the sword to lose its hold; cut the same hand and lost considerable blood in trying to pry his fingers open with a knife which eventually broke; and acquired several scrapes and bruises in using various blunt instruments to try to pry his fingers from the hilt.

He antagonized several people, both human and overman, by breaking their tools, wasting their time, avoiding their questions, and sometimes by accidentally inflicting minor injuries of the sort that had battered his own hands and chest. He also talked three individuals into burning their hands in varying degrees by trying to handle the sword, which continued to allow no one other than himself to touch it.

His own injuries were of no consequence, however, and in fact scarcely even rated as a nuisance, since every cut, bruise, burn, or scrape healed miraculously overnight. There could be no denying that the sword had its beneficial aspects.

Unfortunately, the injuries received by others were not so obliging, though the burns caused by touching the sword invariably turned out to be less severe than they first appeared and always healed quickly and cleanly.

His attempts to remove the sword were further complicated by the necessity of keeping them secret from Galt; Garth was quite sure that Galt would interfere if he realized that the sword did have a hold on Garth, and that any such interference would do far more harm than good.

Saram was more astute than Galt and quickly figured out the truth of the matter. Garth was able to convince him to say and do nothing about it.

Galt, fortunately, was too busy trying to organize and govern Skelleth and the warrior overmen to pay much attention to Garth – particularly since Garth was specifically excluded from any say in the new government.

Garth was amused by his observation of Skelleth's resurrection. He had plenty of time to play the disinterested observer, since he was the only person of either species not actively involved in it. He had nothing to do with his time except to eat, drink, sleep, think, try to dispose of the sword, and watch the events going on around him.

His amusement derived from the differing styles and results of Galt and Saram. Galt had thrown himself completely into a frenzy of planning and organizing, spending every waking moment hard at work on governing. Any dispute that came before him was given careful and detailed attention and settled logically after much thought and analysis.

Saram, on the other hand, spent as little time as possible in work of any sort; he often joined Garth in doing nothing but watching. He settled disputes by fiat, without discussion, or by vote of whoever happened to be present – assuming disputes ever reached him in the first place, as he had given his horde of ministers to understand that it was their responsibility to keep their people in hand and out of his hair. Only when an argument crossed jurisdictional lines or involved jurisdictional lines did it reach Saram's ear.

Galt's efforts had resulted in very little in the way of concrete accomplishments; he had not managed to set up any permanent housing for his overmen, despite the approach of winter, nor to establish any lower levels of governance that could function without constant supervision.

Saram, on the other hand, had been building houses out of rubble at the rate of almost three a day and had had the town's wells cleaned out and a rudimentary distribution system set up. His ministers had sifted themselves out into levels of importance; some had resigned, either because their jobs were done or because they felt that they weren't needed. Two had been fired for incompetence and replaced. In short, Saram was the head of a working government.

That was the situation that existed when the messenger from Ordunin arrived.

Garth was sitting on a block of stone in front of the hole where the Baron's cellars had been, the stone walls having been excavated for use in new buildings; he wore his quilted gambeson beneath his tunic to keep out the growing chill in the air. Changing his clothing while the sword retained its grip had proved difficult, but possible. He had exhausted every method he could think of for getting free of the sword's hold that did not involve either travel or giving in to the Forgotten King and was now trying to decide where he should go first – the nearest ocean, to see if salt water might have an effect, or Ordunin, where the Wise Women might be able to suggest a solution. He was no longer particularly concerned about his oath, though he had never been released from it, because it hardly applied to the current situation.

He was beginning to think that, after all, he no longer had much reason for staying in Skelleth. He had declined to accompany Kyrith because he had wanted to deal with the sword, which was then in Skelleth; now, though, the sword was wherever he was, and be could easily carry it to Ordunin and deal with it there. Ordunin was on the ocean, as well, though hardly the closest coast. Furthermore, if he were to travel, he would prefer to do so before winter closed in.

The only thing still keeping him in Skelleth – other than his interest in the rebuilding – was the presence of the Forgotten King, the one person known to be capable of controlling the sword.

There was a possibility that by taking the sword elsewhere it would stop being so complacent and again drive him into a destructive fury; that would be very unfortunate if it happened in Ordunin. But then, it might happen in Skelleth, which would also be unfortunate now that the rebuilding was well under way. His best course might be to head due east to the coast of the Sea of Mori; there were no towns along that route, nothing that he might destroy.

He reached up and pulled the hilt of the sword down so that he could look at the gem. Its glow was faintly visible even in the midday sun, yet he felt no anger nor bloodlust building up. The thing was being subtle, he was sure, planning something, waiting for something, or perhaps affecting him in some new way he hadn't yet detected.

As he stared at the red gem, he heard the rattle of armor and looked up. It came from somewhere behind him, to his right; he turned and saw three overmen approaching, with two men trailing along behind them. One of the overmen was riding a good-sized warbeast.

Garth recognized the humans and the two overmen on foot, but he could not place the mounted figure for a long moment.

As the party drew up near him, he finally realized who it was: Selk, one of the City Council's messengers. He had not been among the sixty volunteers.

This, then, he knew, must be the response to Kyrith's mission to acquaint the Council with the situation.

"Where is the master trader Galt?" the messenger demanded.

"He's in the King's Inn," Garth replied politely, ignoring the other's imperious tone.

"You, fetch him," Selk ordered one of the two overmen who had accompanied him. Garth realized that they and the humans must be those who had been posted to guard the North Gate.

The warrior hurried to obey, taking the direct route through the pit; earthen ramps had been built on both sides to aid in removing the stones.

"Have you come alone?" Garth inquired

"You're Garth, Prince of Ordunin?"

"You know who I am."

"I wish to be sure."

"Yes, I am Garth, and you are Selk, son of Zhenk and Valik. Did you come alone?"

"I am here alone."

"Kyrith did not come with you?"

"I have said I am alone."

Garth was dismayed by the messenger's surliness; it did not bode well for the message the overman carried. He rose to get a better look at Selk's face. The warbeast growled.

Surprised, Garth looked at it, rather than at its rider.

Like almost every warbeast, it was black; its eyes were green, and its belly-fur white. Its fangs were gleaming white, a sign that it was young and healthy, since the teeth tended to yellow with age. Perhaps, he thought, it still had some of the excitability of cubhood.

Its tail was lashing, and Garth realized that it was looking, not at him, but at the hilt of the sword that protruded up above his left shoulder.

This was something new; none of the warbeasts remaining in Skelleth had reacted to the sword before. He wondered if this beast might have some special sensitivity to magic, or if maybe the sword was doing something new that was perceptible to a warbeast but not to an overman.

Selk also looked at the sword, startled, and said, "It really does glow!"

It was the first thing he had said that had not been spoken as harshly as possible, Garth hoped that it was a sign that Selk was relaxing somewhat.

"Yes, it glows," he replied. "It also burns and does other unpleasant things. Did Kyrith tell you about it?"

"Kyrith said nothing – I mean, she wrote nothing of it in her statement. The others with her, however, did mention it."

"Did you doubt them?"

Selk did not answer immediately; when he did reply, it was only indirectly. "I have never encountered magic before."

"You have now. Be glad that you have not seen much, though; in my experience, most magic is very unpleasant."

Selk made no reply.

Before Garth had decided on his next remark, Galt and his escort arrived. In addition to the warrior sent after him, he was accompanied by three humans, including Frima, and another overman, a young fellow named Palkh. Garth had seen both the male humans before, but did not know their names.

"Greetings, Selk!" Galt called as he climbed up the ramp from the cellars.

Selk did not reply. Garth thought he glimpsed a trace of worry in Galt's expression at that. For his own part, Garth now suspected that either Selk's news was very bad indeed, or that the fellow was simply rude by nature.

When Galt had reached the top of the slope, Selk suddenly spoke, declaiming in a loud voice while he held up a golden rod that represented his authority to speak for the Council.

"Know all present that this is the decision of the City Council of Ordunin! I have been sent here to present this decision, and bear no responsibility for its content. I bear no malice toward any present, nor do I favor them. I speak as I have been commanded."

Several women and children who were gathered in the marketplace, trading salvaged household goods among themselves, stopped and turned to listen.

"Whereas it has come to the attention of the Council that the party of overmen of Ordunin under the joint command of the master trader Galt, son of Kant and Filit, and Kyrith, daughter of Dynth and Dharith, and commissioned to negotiate trade agreements with Doran, Baron of Skelleth, has exceeded its authority and committed acts of war against the Barony of Skelleth; and whereas these acts were committed under the direction of the aforementioned Galt and also Garth, Prince of Ordunin, son of Karth and Tarith, and a Lord of the Overmen of the Northern Waste, and resulted in unnecessary bloodshed and destruction; therefore, the City Council of Ordunin hereby disavows all responsibility for these actions."

Selk paused to catch his breath, and Galt started to protest. Garth silenced him with a gesture.

"Furthermore, inasmuch as the members of the party in question may have been unaware of the limits of the authority granted to their commanders, no blame shall be assigned to any person other than the aforementioned Galt, Kyrith, and Garth, if those other persons immediately remove themselves from the area of Skelleth and return to the Northern Waste. No charges shall be drawn up against these persons.

"Furthermore, the aforementioned Kyrith, by virtue of her avowed reluctance to participate in acts of war, and by virtue of her presence before the Council and arguments presented, is hereby pardoned, conditional upon her continued presence in Ordunin."

"Finally, the Council disavows all claim to any portion of the Kingdom of Eramma, or to any profits that may accrue from acts of war committed against the Kingdom of Eramma, and declares the aforementioned Galt and Garth to be outlaws, this information to be delivered to them as soon as circumstances shall allow."

Selk stopped speaking, returned the rod to its place beneath his tunic, and sat astride his warbeast, looking down at Galt and Garth. There was a moment of silence.

"They can't do that," Galt said at last.

Garth was unsure what to say. Palkh said, "It appears that they have done it, though."

The women who had heard the announcement suddenly began talking among themselves, discussing this unexpected news.

Garth felt anger growing somewhere within him; he did not bother to look at the red jewel. Whether this anger was wholly his own or not did not seem important.

"Selk," he said, "is that your entire message?"

"Yes, that's it, at least so far as you are concerned."

"What do you mean by that?"

"I am to carry the same message to the High King at Kholis, together with a formal apology."

Garth had reached the conclusion three days earlier that, through some great good fortune, the High King and the other lords of Eramma were as yet unaware of the sacking of Skelleth. Had they known about it, there would surely have been some sort of reaction by now, such as a formal demand for surrender.

This ignorance was very useful. It gave them time. The King would have to learn eventually, but Garth hoped that the news would be delivered at the right time and under the right circumstances for the maximum advantage of overmankind. Therefore, he did not want this messenger spreading the word prematurely.

"I can't allow that," he said.

"What?" Selk was plainly astonished.

"Garth, what are you doing?" Galt asked.

"I cannot allow any such message to reach the High King at Kholis at this time," he said.

"You have no authority to stop me," Selk answered.

"I need no authority. I am an outlaw, am I not? Dismount, Selk, slowly and carefully, and make no move toward your weapons."

Selk hesitated.

In a single fluid motion Garth unsheathed the Sword of Bheleu; the red gem was gleaming brightly, and the blade shone silver.

"Dismount, Selk."

The bystanders, including Galt, were drawing back, unsure what to do. Frima called, "Garth, is it the sword?"

Without turning his gaze from Selk's face, Garth answered, "I don't think so. This is really what I think best."

Selk looked about uncertainly and saw that no one was making any move to aid him. Garth stood ahead of him and to his left, five feet away, the immense broadsword clutched before him in both hands. Selk was not a warrior, but a messenger and a peaceful person, yet he dared not surrender; the Council would hear, and he would lose his position.

He could not fight and he could not surrender. That left flight. Trying to give as little warning as possible, he suddenly shouted the command to run to his mount.

Obediently, the warbeast surged forward; the Sword of Bheleu lashed out with preternatural speed and caught Selk across the chest. Garth had managed at the last instant to turn the blade so that the flat struck the overman, not the edge; the sword had fought the turn, but given in. Therefore Selk was not killed, but he was knocked backward off the beast's back, to lie stunned on the hard ground, his chestplate dented in more than an inch, his chest crossed by a great bruise, and two ribs cracked.

Garth started to lower the sword but found it resisting him; almost immediately he saw why.

The warbeast had been trained to protect its rider. As soon as it realized he was no longer in the saddle, it whirled to face Garth.

Everyone in the marketplace – the women, Frima, Galt, the three men, and the other overmen – immediately fled, amid a chorus of shrieks and shouting, leaving Selk lying on the ground and Garth facing the monstrous creature.

The warbeast roared deafeningly, baring fangs more than three inches in length, and charged toward Garth.

For an instant Garth was certain that he was about to die; he had seen warbeasts in action and knew that an overman was no match for one, regardless of what weapons he might hold. Spears and arrows could not penetrate the natural armor created by thick fur, loose, leathery hide, and layer upon layer of muscle that protected a warbeast's vital organs. A well-wielded sword might manage it, but only by luck; no other creature could move as fast as a fighting warbeast, or dodge with so much skill. A single blow from one of the great padded paws could tear an overman in half.

He forgot all that though, as the warbeast neared him. He forgot everything except that he held the Sword of Bheleu. It came up in his hands, hissing with flame and moving with blurring speed to meet the warbeast's charge.

The monster leaped upon him, and the blade met it in mid-air, at the base of its throat.

There was a sudden roar of flame, and Garth was smashed backward and down.

He came to a second or so later and found himself lying on his back on the ground, pinned beneath the immense bulk of a dead warbeast, both his hands still clutching the hilt of the sword. The blade had gone cleanly through the beast, its tip emerging between the shoulders, red with blood.

The air was full of the stench of scorched fur and burned flesh.

Garth found it hard to believe that he was still alive. How could the warbeast have died so quickly? Even had he struck it through the heart, which he had not, it should have lived long enough to tear him apart.

"Garth?" It was Galt's voice that called uncertainly. "Are you alive?"

"Yes," he answered. The effort was painful; the wind had been knocked out of him by the creature's impact, and one fang had gashed his cheek in passing.

"Can you move?"

Garth was not sure whether he could or not; he tried, shifting slightly, and discovered that he could not.

"No," he called, "I'm pinned here."

There were sounds, but no further words reached him.

Something occurred to him, and he called, "Don't let Selk escape!"

"He's not going anywhere," someone said grimly; Garth thought the voice was human, rather than overman. It was definitely not Galt.

Something else occurred to him, and he looked down at the hilt of the sword. He was unable to raise his head enough to see anything other than black fur; there was no way he could see whether the stone pressing into his belly was glowing.

Cautiously, he removed his left hand from the hilt; it came away easily, as he had expected. Then he tried to open his right hand.

One thumb and one finger came free, but the other thumb and fingers remained in place. The sword had not released its hold.

He lay back, disappointed.

A few minutes later, with much straining, Galt and a party of overmen managed to push the warbeast's carcass off him. He pulled the sword free, wishing he didn't have to, then staggered to his feet, the weapon hanging loose in one hand. The gemstone flickered dimly.

"Thank you," he said.

"Garth," Galt demanded, "why did you do that?"

Garth looked at him. The brief battle had tired him, and his entire body ached from the strain of supporting the warbeast's weight and from being slammed against the ground. A stray pebble had cut open the back of his head when he fell, and he felt blood dripping down his back, across immense bruises, as well as running down his cheek.

"Do what?"

"Why did you stop Selk from leaving?"

He stared at Galt in astonishment. Could the trader really be that stupid? "Galt," he said, "what would the High King do upon receiving such a message?"

"I don't know," Galt answered. "Send a polite reply, I suppose."

"Don't you think that he might send an army to recapture Skelleth, once he was aware that we had taken it and that Ordunin would not send any reinforcements to our aid or back us in any way?"

"But he wouldn't have to recapture Skelleth!"

"Why not? We happen to be running it right now."

"But we're leaving, aren't we? The Council has disowned our occupation; our troops will be going home to take advantage of the amnesty, and we'll either have to go back and plead for pardon or seek refuge somewhere."

"Galt, I am not leaving. The Council has declared us to be outlaws and renounced all claim to Skelleth. The rightful baron is dead, without heir. We are in control of the barony. It seems to me that we can do quite well for ourselves by staying here in control. If the High King believes us to be here with the approval of the Council and the Lords of the Overmen of the Northern Waste, he will negotiate with us to save bloodshed – I hope – and we can have Saram declared the new Baron, thereby ensuring us of a place here. The Council will not interfere; they have disclaimed the whole affair."

"I don't understand. What good will it do to stay here and have Saram made Baron? We will still be outlaws in both lands."

"No, we will not; we will be Erammans, able to establish trade between the two realms. Benefits aside, though, have you considered what will happen to Saram and his ministers if we leave? He will be tried for treason and beheaded for cooperating with us. Would you willingly allow that to happen?"

"I had not considered that. I find myself confused."

"And are you so certain that all our warriors will take advantage of the amnesty? Might some not prefer to remain here, outlawed or not? There are things to be done here and very little to be done in Ordunin. Here they are a powerful elite; in Ordunin they are nothing out of the ordinary."

"I don't know."

"Galt, if you wish, you can go home and plead for clemency, but I am staying here and intend to call for volunteers to stay with me. And so long as I stay here, I dare not let Selk deliver his message to the High King. Is that clear?"

"Clear enough. I will have to think this through carefully."

"In the meanwhile, what will be done with Selk?"

"He's under arrest, more or less; I'll keep him there until I decide."

Garth nodded; that would do for the present.

Things had changed suddenly, he realized; less than an hour earlier he had been thinking that he might return to Ordunin. Now he was absolutely refusing to do so.

The difference was in Selk's message. It had not occurred to him that the Council could be stupid enough to throw away its claim to Skelleth. The Council might be sufficiently timid to let Skelleth go for nothing, but Garth was not. He intended to hold it. If he was not to hold it on behalf of Ordunin, then he would hold it on his own behalf. He was sure that he could run it better than the Council could in any case. He found himself almost hoping that Galt would give up, go home, and leave him in charge. He would show the trader how a village should be run.

That was still to be decided, though. He stood and watched as Galt walked off, lost in thought, toward the King's Inn.

Saram appeared from somewhere; he had finally gotten word of the fight. He looked at the dead warbeast and called, "Find me someone who knows how to skin animals! We shouldn't let so fine a hide go to waste. Garth, will warbeasts eat their own kind? We've been running short of meat for them."

Garth's chain of thought was broken as he tried to recall whether he knew anything about cannibalism among warbeasts.

Resorting to experimentation after the fur had been stripped from the carcass, he and Saram learned that warbeasts had no objection to cannibalism.

When the warbeasts had stripped much of the flesh away, it also became clear how the Sword of Bheleu had killed the monster quickly enough to save Garth's life; the internal organs had all been burned to a fine ash.

Chapter Eighteen

The first arrival capable of sending a message to Shang was the sorceress Zhinza, an ancient, tiny woman who maintained a small farm a few leagues to the east. Despite her age, she was still cheerful and energetic. She gladly consented to make the attempt when Shandiph explained the situation.

Chalkara obtained the High King's permission to use the castle's highest tower, which Zhinza said would make her sending easier. The topmost chamber, which had been used for storage of old weaponry, was cleared out and furnished with a clean, new mattress and an assortment of cushions and hangings; that done, Zhinza was moved in and left in the privacy she demanded.

The dozen councilors present by this time had expected her to emerge with an answer within the hour; as the minutes crawled by, they became first impatient, then concerned, and finally worried. The minutes became hours, and finally a full day passed, during which Zhinza had had no food or drink.

The more impatient wizards finally convinced Shandiph that something must have gone wrong, that the strain had been too much for the poor old creature; a rescue party was on its way up the stairs of the tower when Zhinza finally emerged.

It was apparent that the sorceress had not slept or rested any more than she had eaten, and Shandiph arranged for her to have a good meal and a few hours rest before reporting her results to the members present.

By the time Zhinza felt sufficiently recovered to tell the gathering Council what had happened the members in attendance numbered fifteen besides herself, and Shandiph had finally found time to speak with the two astrologers present as well as the one theurgist. He had also, by compiling information brought him regarding the deaths of members, by accepting proxies granted, and by consulting the Council's by-laws, determined that the quorum necessary to conduct business was twenty-one members. A quorum required two-thirds of the total votes, but not all members were equal; he, as chairman, had five votes of his own and several by proxy, while the most junior members had only one. It was also required that a quorum be one of the numbers with mystical properties; twenty-one, being the product of the mystical numbers three and seven, as well as the recognized age of adulthood, met that prerequisite neatly.

No formal action could be taken until five more members arrived; nevertheless, to ease the impatience of many present, Shandiph officially convened the Council of the Most High. With the High King's permission, he had converted an unused gallery into a meeting chamber, complete with warding spells on each door and a row of three long trestle tables in the center.

The meeting was to have begun at noon; but as Shandiph had anticipated, it proved impossible to gather the entire group together on schedule. It was a good hour past midday when he finally rose at the end of the first table and called the meeting to order.

The gallery had a southern exposure and high, narrow windows; the sunlight from one of them lit Shandiph from head to foot, from the sweat glistening on his balding scalp to the sterling silver buckles on his black leather sandals. His remaining hair was thin and gray, his face broad and flat. He wore a tunic of black silk worked with silver that was cut to disguise his growing paunch, and soft gray breeches hid his thighs.

"Fellow magicians, seers, and scholars, I welcome you here and hereby convoke the session of the Council of the Most High," he said. "We are met to consider a matter that threatens to disrupt the peace of the world, which we are sworn to safeguard. A border has been violated, and magic of great power has been used."

"We all know that," Karag of Sland called. "Get on with it! What has Zhinza got to say?"

"Karag, I want to deal with the necessary formalities, if you don't mind, and get them out of the way. Now, is there anyone present who questions my authority to convene this Council or questions that I had sufficient reason to do so in this instance?"

There was a moment of silence; Karag was visibly restraining himself from interrupting again.

"In that case, is there anyone present who does not have a clear understanding of the situation we're here to discuss?"

This time there were muttered words and a few uncertain questioning noises. Shandiph gestured for silence, then began an account of what was known of Garth and the Sword of Bheleu.

"Reliable divinations have determined that this sword is in fact powerful enough that it could be used to defeat any army that Eramma might send against this Garth," he concluded. "Therefore, it falls to the Council to deal with this trouble maker and prevent a long and bloody war. We are considering both assassination by ordinary methods and the possibility of using the basilisk to turn this Garth to stone. Other suggestions will be welcome. For the present, though, we asked the sorceress Zhinza to contact Shang in Mormoreth, the keeper of the basilisk, and inquire as to the monster's readiness for use. I now ask Zhinza to report what she has learned."

He gestured toward the old woman, then sat down, glad to be off his feet.

Zhinza rose, looked around at the gathering, and cleared her throat. She was at least two inches short of five feet in height, thin, and frail; her face was narrow and wrinkled, her hair long and shining white. She wore a simple unbelted gown of white linen.

"Shang isn't there," she said.

There was a moment of silent surprise; before anyone could speak, she went on, "I mean, I can't find him. As a lot of you know, my specialty is the knowledge of other planes of reality and the conveying of messages through them or drawing knowledge and power from them. I think I know as much as anybody about communicating over long distances or through other realms, and probably more than any of you here. I used every bit of that knowledge in searching for any trace of Shang. I knew him when he was young and I know the shape of his thoughts and the image of his face. I couldn't find him – not in Mormoreth, not anywhere in Orûn or Derbarok, and not in any of the known planes that he might have been translated into. I think he must be dead. If he's not dead, then he's behind a warding spell the like of which I've never seen, or else has gone someplace completely beyond my knowledge. I think he's dead, and I wish he had carried a warning spell so we could be sure, but he didn't."

She paused, and then rushed on before anyone could interrupt, "And I can't find the basilisk either. After I couldn't find Shang I looked for the basilisk, and it's not there. I don't know its thoughts, but it has an aura of evil and death that's unmistakable, and there was nothing but the memory of it in the crypts of Mormoreth."

She looked around defiantly and then abruptly sat down.

There was a moment of babble; then Shandiph rose and silenced the meeting. "Let us behave calmly and rationally," he said. "Now, who wishes to speak? You, Karag, what do you want to say?"

Karag rose, impressive in his red velvet and black leather, his black beard bristling. He was not particularly tall or especially heavy, but he gave the impression of great strength nonetheless, for his every muscle was hard and tense.

"I would like to know," he announced, "how reliable this old woman's findings are. I do not deny that she was, in her time, a sorceress of great repute, but she must have lived three-fourths of a century by now, and even the mightiest of us is not immune to the effects of time."

"I'm eighty-six, but I still know more than you ever will, you strutting idiot!" Zhinza retorted.

Karag looked at her with manifest disdain, and Shandiph rose again. "Sit down, Karag," he said. A hand gestured for his attention, and he added, "Yes, Chalkara, what is it?"

The court wizard to the High King got to her feet; like Shandiph she stood in the direct light of a window, so that her long red hair and cloth-of-gold gown were as vivid as flame. Karag glared at her, then seated himself, though not before Shandiph had noticed for the first time that she stood slightly taller than Sland's wizard.

"I do not impugn Zhinza's knowledge or power, but the fact remains that we do not know what has become of Shang; as she says, he may be concealed by some warding spell of which we know nothing or hiding in a place of which we know nothing. Or it may be that something has deceived Zhinza, by means we do not know, and Shang and the basilisk remain in Mormoreth, as always. This is a matter that must be investigated immediately, and I suggest that we send someone in person to Mormoreth to inquire there what has become of our great weapon and honored colleague."

Karag objected. "If Shang is dead, then there won't be anyone in Mormoreth to ask!"

Without rising, Thetheru of Amag said, "If Shang is dead, then his killer will be in Mormoreth."

Karag whirled to face the Amagite and retorted, "Nonsense! The killer would have fled long ago!"

"We don't even know that there is a killer," Deriam of Ur-Dormulk interjected. "Shang may have gotten careless with the basilisk's venom."

"Shang was never careless," replied Lord Dor, Baron of Therin – or at least the avatar he had sent to the meeting, since Dor had developed the ability to reproduce himself in identical copies that shared his consciousness.

"Anyone can be careless once," Deriam insisted.

"Please, councilors!" Shandiph called as argument became general. He was answered, after some shuffling, by silence; Karag seated himself, having risen so as to be able to yell in Thetheru's face more easily. The old sorceress shifted in her chair, and Shandiph asked, "Is there something you wished to add, Zhinza?"

"There is someone in Mormoreth; I could see that when I looked for Shang and for the basilisk. There are several people, none of whom I could identify in any way, and none of whom were magicians, so that I couldn't communicate with them."

"There, you see?" Thetheru said; Karag turned toward him, his hand falling to the hilt of the dagger he carried on his belt.

"Silence!" Shandiph bellowed.

When he was satisfied that he had the full attention of those present, he went on, "It would appear that there are people in Mormoreth, whether or not they are connected with Shang's death. These people may know what became of Shang and of the basilisk. I think that it would, indeed, be a very good idea to send someone to investigate, particularly since we are still five votes short of a quorum to decide matters of importance and can therefore spare the time. I suggest we vote on that, here and now; no quorum is necessary for sending a messenger. All those in favor of sending an investigator to Mormoreth will signify their position by standing."

With much scraping of chairs, most of the members rose; Shandiph tallied up the votes, to make it official. Zhinza did not stand, nor did Deriam, nor did a blue-clad young woman Shandiph could not immediately place; all others had voted in favor. Karag and Thetheru were glaring at each other, obviously annoyed that they had voted the same way.

"Good," Shandiph said. "The next question is who should be sent?"

"With the Chairman's permission," Derelind the Hermit said, "I volunteer."

"Are there any other volunteers?"

There were several, and a disorganized debate ensued. It was finally settled in favor of Derelind when he explained his proposed mode of transportation, which none of the others could equal; he claimed to have learned the languages of winds and birds, and to be able therefore to fly to Mormoreth carried on the backs of eagles, his weight borne up by the west wind. He estimated the round trip at three days' travel.

Once that was settled, Chalkara suggested that no round trip was necessary to deliver information, since Zhinza should be able to communicate with him while he was still in Mormoreth. Derelind agreed, but asked that no votes for death be taken until he had returned.

When that, too, was settled, Derelind said, "By your leave, then, I will depart immediately."

Shandiph replied, "You may if you choose, but the meeting is not done; we have yet to hear the advice of the astrologers and our theurgist on the nature of the danger that Garth and the Sword of Bheleu present."

"I will forego that pleasure." He bowed his head politely and headed for the door. Deriam released the wards he had placed upon it, and Derelind stepped through, closing the door behind him.

When he had gone, Shandiph announced, "I will now call on Herina the Stargazer, one of our most learned astrologers and scholars, to tell us what she feels may be relevant in the motions of the stars."

Herina rose; she wore light blue that contrasted well with her butter-yellow hair. She was plump, but not distressingly so, and age had not yet done any serious damage to her figure or face – certainly no more than had her diet.

"Ah . . . it appears we have the misfortune to be living in evil times. The beginning of a new age is upon us; the familiar Thirteenth Age, which has lasted for three hundred years and is all any of us has known, is over. The Fourteenth Age began approximately a month ago, and I believe that all these events that we are here to discuss relate somehow to its advent. The Fourteenth Age is, according to the priests and scholars as well as to the more orthodox astrologers, to be ruled by the god Bheleu, Lord of Destruction, as signified by the presence of the three wandering stars in the constellation of the Broken Sword. It is therefore believed that this age, which is to last for only thirty years, will be an age of fire and blood, in which the wars that ended with the coming of the Thirteenth Age will return threefold.

"The ancient texts and prophecies include several descriptions of signs, omens, and warnings that will signal the onset of this great destruction. An overman will come out of the east to the city of the dark gods, according to one; this is obviously fulfilled by Garth's visit to Dûsarra. The worshippers of P'hul will honor the servant of Bheleu, says another; this is not confirmed, but it could be interpreted to mean Garth's alleged spreading of the White Death. The others I am familiar with do not appear to have been fulfilled as yet, though. There is mention of a slayer of monsters who shall come out of the north, and of storms of fire, and of various other portents. Since none of these has occurred, as far as I know, I don't believe that too much weight should be given to the seeming fulfillment of one or two of the prophecies. They're quite vague, after all.

"Regarding the Sword of Bheleu, that's not really within my area of expertise, but it seems to fit in with the start of the new age. I have no idea where it came from or what it is capable of."

She sat down.

Shandiph rose and said, "We have a second astrologer on hand; Veyel of Nekutta, have you anything to add?"

The old man robed in black shook his head. "No. She covered the general topic well, and I cannot deal with specifics without casting a proper horoscope of this overman, something I do not have sufficient information to attempt."

"In that case, I call on Miloshir the Theurgist to inform us regarding the nature of the Sword of Bheleu."

The theurgist was a middle-aged man wearing white and gold, of nondescript appearance except for his flowing brown hair. He got slowly to his feet, and spoke.

"I am afraid that we may be in serious trouble very soon. As Herina has told us, this is now the Fourteenth Age of the world, ruled by Bheleu, the god of destruction. Bheleu is the second most powerful of the Lords of Dûs, the evil gods, second only to The God Whose Name Is Not Spoken. Among all the gods, only the ineffable Dagha and the gods of life and death are reckoned his superiors, and Bel Vala, god of strength and courage, is his only near-equal. Furthermore, Bheleu is not a god who can be accommodated and lived with, as we have lived with the goddess P'hul for these past three centuries; he demands constant destruction, unlimited death and chaos. Herina said that this age would last for thirty years; my own studies indicate that it will last for only three, since it will take no longer than that for the world to destroy itself utterly under the influence of Bheleu.

"As for the Sword, every god, in his time, uses tools to work his will in our mortal world. Each deity has some token, some powerful magical object, through which his power is channeled and by which he dominates the age given to him. Each such token has existed, it is said, since the very beginning of time, when the First Age began, but each remains hidden and powerless until it is found at the proper time and used by the mortal being or beings chosen by the god to wield it.

"I am very much afraid that this overman, Garth, is Bheleu's chosen agent and has already found and begun using the sword that is the god's token. This means that he has at his command, should he learn to use it, the full might of the god and all the supernatural powers and abilities attributed to the god. While I might ordinarily suspect that this overman is a fraud and the sword a fake given a prestigious name – such hoaxes have occurred – I fear that is not the case here. You will recall, some of you, that idols of Bheleu always depict him as an overman, and that, as the astrologer mentioned, this Garth has already fulfilled at least one, and probably two or more of the relevant prophecies.

"As the agent of destruction, this Garth – or, if you prefer, the god Bheleu

– will be most eager to destroy the forces that help preserve order. The foremost force for order in this decadent world of ours is this very Council. Therefore, we will be one of his prime targets."

He stopped speaking. Karag asked, "Then do you say there is nothing that can be done?"

"Oh, no! I never said that. It is entirely possible that Garth can be defeated and much of the havoc he would cause averted. Only three of the gods are so mighty that they cannot be thwarted, and though Bheleu, in this age, is fourth among the gods, he is not one of the three. He can be defeated, his agent destroyed, and his token suppressed. However, any such action must be taken immediately, since the god's power will grow steadily for some time as the new age asserts itself."

"You are saying, then, that if we do not immediately destroy this overman, he will destroy us?"

"Yes, and the world with us. Exactly."

Chalkara said, "You spoke of tokens of all the gods. Could we find these other tokens and use them against this overman?"

"I suppose so, yes. Of course, the tokens of the Arkhein are of very little power and would be of no use at all against the Sword of Bheleu. I believe the tokens of the Lords of Eir may have been destroyed in the Eighth Age, when the balance first shifted in favor of the Lords of Dûs; I certainly know of nothing that would indicate that they still exist. That leaves us only the tokens of the other six dark gods. We already possess one of the six, and I know what the others are, but not where they might be found."

"We already possess one?"

Miloshir was suddenly hesitant and uncertain. He glanced at Shandiph. "I have spoken out of turn."

Shandiph rose again; his knees were growing tired. "That's all right. Yes, we already possess one; it was the Ring of P'hul that first permitted the Council of the Most High to gain what power we now hold, at the end of the Twelfth Age. It has been kept carefully hidden ever since, because it is far too dangerous to use; it was the Ring which caused the Great Plague that wiped out the Royal Eramman Army and thereby put an end to the Racial Wars before the overmen could be wiped out. It was the Ring that laid waste the Plain of Derbarok. It always did what was asked of it, but never in the way desired; it ended the Racial Wars only by killing the army and ended the war with Orûn only by ruining what both sides fought for."

"What are the others?"

Miloshir replied, "The White Stone of Tema, the Black Stone of Andhur Regvos, the Whip of Sai, the Dagger of Aghad, and the Book of Silence are the remaining five."

"And each of these is as mighty as the Sword of Bheleu, yet we know where none of these potential menaces are?" Karag demanded.

"Oh, no, they are not equally powerful; none of these is the equal of the Sword of Bheleu except the Book of Silence, which holds the fate of the world in its pages."

"But we know where none of them are?"

"That's right."

"Where does the basilisk fit into this?" Deriam asked. "Surely it's the equal of one of these mysterious objects!"

"Ah, there's debate about that. Some say that the basilisk is the true token of The God Whose Name Is Not Spoken, and that the Book of Silence is a lesser item, or a myth, or perhaps the token of Dagha himself."

"I can readily believe that that thing is the symbol of the death-god. If it is, then we possess two of the tokens, including one mightier than this sword; Garth stands no chance."

Miloshir looked at Deriam, and then up and down the tables at the thirteen other councilors present. "I hope you're right," he said.

Chapter Nineteen

It was plain that there would be no shortage of fuel in Skelleth that winter; partially burned beams and rafters were plentiful, and charcoal abounded. Nor was building stone lacking, since the ring of ruins provided all that might be needed. It was sound wood, for roofing, flooring, and furniture, that was most sorely missed. Ceilings could be constructed of arched stone and roofs made of thatch, but such work took vast amounts of time, as well as consuming great quantities of stone and requiring elaborate scaffolding.

There were no forests or even groves anywhere in the vicinity; firewood had traditionally been gathered from bushes by those fortunate enough to use wood at all, rather than dried dung. No building had been done in Skelleth since the completion of the Baron's mansion some two hundred years earlier. Prior to that, wood had been shipped in by caravan in great wagons, as had much of the stone and other material.

What wood could be salvaged was used, but the supply ran out when some twenty-odd houses had been erected and before any had been furnished.

There was talk of using the wood, chairs, and tables from the King's Inn, but that was quickly abandoned when it became clear that neither Garth nor the Forgotten King thought much of the idea.

Therefore, Saram decided that it was time to re-establish communication with the south, so that wood could be bought. He said as much to Garth.

Garth had been doing very little since Selk's arrival and the killing of the warbeast. He had made a halfhearted attempt to cut off his left hand while it held the sword; but as he had expected, the knife-blade broke before it had cut deeply, and the wound healed overnight. After that failure he had spent much of his time sitting and staring at the sword, trying to devise some way to get free of it without giving in to the Forgotten King.

Galt, after due consideration, had decided to stay; he realized that the City Council would almost certainly be willing to put him to death to appease the Erammans. They were unlikely to pardon him, since such an action would look very suspicious once the High King heard of it. Someone had to be the scapegoat, and he and Garth had been chosen.

Of the forty-one other overmen in Skelleth, fourteen had remained; twenty-seven, including all the wounded, had gone home when offered the choice.

Selk was being kept under guard in one of the upstairs rooms of the King's Inn; he remained fairly quiet, but complained at every opportunity that there was something unsettling about the room, something in the air that made his skin crawl. Garth and the others could detect nothing but an extraordinary amount of dust.

The overman guards at the five gates were withdrawn, due to the loss of so many warriors, leaving only humans.

Galt lost interest in governing his remaining party, leaving Saram in virtually complete control of the village. It was under these circumstances that Saram came to ask Garth's opinion about sending an embassy to Kholis.

Garth considered. "I think," he said, "that you may be right. It has been more than a fortnight since the battle, and we have heard nothing from anywhere south of here. I think that we can therefore tell them whatever we choose, and they will accept it. Furthermore, winter will be here soon – already the winds have turned northerly and cold – and the High King will be unable to send an army here without extreme difficulty once the snows begin."

"I hope he'll have no reason to send an army. I don't intend to tell him that you're an occupying force."

"That's good; what do you propose to tell him?"

"I've been thinking it over some, and I think this will hold up. I will send a message saying that the Baron, whom everyone knew to be mad, finally went berserk while speaking with a peaceful trading mission and set fire to the village. In the ensuing confusion many died, and much of the town was destroyed. The survivors joined together to rebuild, with the aid of your overmen, when it became clear that it was the Baron's insanity that began the fighting and fires, rather than any legitimate dispute or action of your party. We need not mention that your trade mission consisted of sixty warriors; we need not mention anyone but the sixteen of you still here. I exclude Selk, the seventeenth; he can be another little secret. We will ask for supplies to be sent so that we may survive the winter and for a new Baron of Skelleth to be named, and we will express our continued loyalty to the Kingdom of Eramma. How does that sound?"

"Good, very good; it puts all the responsibility for wrongdoing on the dead Baron."

"I thought you'd like it."

"If the King accepts it, then we can present the City Council with a whole new situation and ask them to reconsider."

"If you want to, yes."

"Why do you say, 'If you want to?' Why should I not want to?"

"It seems to me that your Council isn't very helpful; why not just forget about them?"

"I came here to establish trade between the Northern Waste and Eramma. I intend to establish that trade, whether the others involved want it or not; it will benefit both, whether the rulers have the wit to realize it or not."

"Oh. I see. Garth – whatever happens, whether you convince your City Council or not – you're welcome to stay here in Skelleth as long as I'm running it."

"With luck, though, that won't be long; the High King will be sending a new Baron."

"Ah, that's true. I'd forgotten." He smiled. "I'll be able to relax, then, and pay some attention to my wife."

"Your wife?" Garth was startled.

"Certainly."

"What wife?"

"Frima, of course."

"Oh." Garth considered that. "Are you two married?"

"More or less. The law says that a marriage is valid if approved by the lord of the region. As acting baron, I'm the local lord, and *I* say we're married. When we get a new Baron I may ask him to confirm it."

"I see. Congratulations, then."

Saram studied the overman's face. "Are you missing your own wives? Perhaps you could send for them."

"No. My kind is not as prone to loneliness as you humans are."

"You seem depressed, though."

"I am depressed, not by the absence of my wives, but by the presence of this sword, and by the stupidity of the Council."

"Oh. There isn't anything I can do about the Council, other than send my message to Kholis; is there any way I can help you with the sword?"

"I know of none."

"Let me see if I can pull your fingers free."

Garth cooperated, and a moment later Saram was stuffing burned fingers in his mouth.

"How can you *hold* that thing?" he muttered.

"I don't have much choice; I have even tried severing my hand, with no success."

"Shall I try?"

"If you wish, but I warn you, your blade will probably break."

"I won't try it, then; I like my sword."

Garth snorted.

"Listen, maybe you can burn the thing out."

"I don't understand."

"Maybe you can use up all its power. Then it would be too weak to hold you."

"I had considered that, but I could think of no way to do so without killing innocent people and destroying property."

"Why don't you go out on the plain somewhere, where there's no one to kill and nothing to destroy?"

"And what would I do then?"

"Can you direct the sword's power, as you did when it possessed you?"

"I don't know."

"Can you make it possess you?"

"I have tried without success."

"Well, I suggest that you go out on the plain, find a nice barren spot, and then try to make the sword burn, as it did when you slew the Baron. Try to burn the earth itself. See what happens."

Garth thought that over. His mind was not clear, and he could think only slowly and muddily; he knew, vaguely, that this was the sword's doing.

He could think of no objection to Saram's proposal. "I will try it," he said.

"Good. I have to go put together that embassy to Kholis," Saram said, rising, "but I wish you luck."

Garth watched him depart, then held up the sword and looked at it. The gem was glowing bright blood-red.

Nothing else he had tried had done any good, and he couldn't trust the sword to behave itself much longer. He rose, pulled the cloak he had borrowed from Galt more tightly around him with his free hand, and headed toward the West Gate; that direction led to the most desolate stretch of wilderness.

He could feel winter coming; the air felt thin and hard and chilled him, even through the cloak, tunic, gambeson, and his own fur beneath. Skelleth had no autumn in the usual sense, since there were no trees to drop leaves nor late crops to harvest – the hay was brought in late in summer – but it did have a brief period between the warmth of summer and the first snow, and that was what had arrived in the last few days. The only warmth Garth could detect anywhere in the world around him was the heat of the sword's hilt in his hand.

It was oddly comforting. He knew that he should be uneasy about feeling anything positive about the thing's power, but the warmth was welcome nonetheless.

None of the few people he passed on the way out of town paid much attention to him; they had become accustomed to seeing him wandering about the village, hoping to find some means of release from the sword's thrall. Even the guards at the West Gate did nothing more than nod polite greetings.

Out on the open plain the north wind drove through him; his right flank became so cold that his left seemed warm by contrast. The sword's hilt in his right hand burned like a live coal, but it was a good, soothing heat and did not cause him any pain.

He strode on across the wasteland. Skelleth was not considered part of the Northern Waste, but it was still harsh, barren country, little better than his homeland. The few farms that he passed or crossed were empty and silent; the hay had been cut and gathered a month before, and the farmers had taken their crops and their goats and gone to the village to take shelter for the winter when first the north wind blew down from the hills. Only the ice-cutters ventured out on the plains once the snows came, and then only in large groups.

At the end of an hour he had traveled something over four miles, a distance he thought should be sufficient. He stopped and looked around.

The plain lay, bleak and empty, in all directions. To the north it ended in low hills; to the east Skelleth was still visible as a line on the horizon; to the south and west there was nothing else for as far as he could see. He had left the old Yprian Road a hundred yards from the gate, and it was now lost in the distance.

He took the sword in two hands and stood for a moment feeling the warmth that now bathed them both; the left seemed to be thawing, though it had not actually frozen. He concentrated on the heat and let it flow up his arms.

He was not sure at first how to go about what he wanted to do. He recalled that, when he was possessed, he often lifted the sword above his head just prior to performing his magical feats; feeling slightly foolish, he raised the blade up.

Without any conscious volition, his hesitant gesture changed; he thrust the sword powerfully upward, pointing at the sky, until the red gem was directly before his red eyes, its glow as bright and warm as fresh blood. Overhead, the steely gray sky was darkened by wisps of black cloud.

The glowing jewel held his gaze. He stared at it in fascination for a long moment, and the clouds gathered above him. Thunder rumbled in the northern hills.

The sound broke his trance, and he looked upward.

The sky had not been clear when he left the town, but it had shown no threat. Now it was filled with blossoming thunderclouds. There would be a storm long before he could reach the shelter of the village walls.

He still held the sword before him, its point toward the sky; now, involuntarily, he thrust it up above his head, crying out, *"Melith!"*

The name was unfamiliar to him; it was answered by a flash of lightning and a low rumble of thunder.

He remembered suddenly that, when he had entered the temple of Bheleu in Dûsarra and first taken the sword, the sky had been full of thunder, and lightning had blasted the broken roof of the temple. Lightning had struck the altar and scattered the bonfire that surrounded it.

Lightning had struck the sword while he held it.

He realized suddenly that he was standing on a dead-flat plain in a thunderstorm, holding up six feet of bare steel. Lightning had an affinity for metal, as everyone knew, and was drawn as well to the highest objects in reach. Standing thus would ordinarily have verged on suicide.

This was no ordinary sword, however, and he began to wonder if it was an ordinary storm. Was it natural or had the sword summoned it? Had the storm that shattered the temple of Bheleu been natural?

He did not think he cared to try so dangerous a test of the sword's nature as to invite being struck by lightning. Merely because he had survived it once did not mean he could do so again. He yanked the sword down.

It resisted, but obeyed.

Immediately the seething clouds overhead stilled; where it had seemed that the storm would break in seconds and pour a torrent upon him, now the clouds were calm, and it seemed as if there were no storm at all. No lightning flashed. No thunder roared. Even the north wind died away to a breeze.

He recalled Saram's proposed test; would the sword burn the earth? He thrust it out before him, pointing at the ground a dozen feet away.

The gem flared up brightly, and a rumble sounded. At first he thought that it was fresh thunder, but then the ground heaved up beneath him, rolling under his feet. Staggering to keep his balance, his left hand fell from the hilt, while his right, holding the sword, swung out to his side.

The tremor stopped, and the earth was again as still and solid as ever.

He no longer felt the cold; the warmth of the sword's touch had spread through his body. As he looked at the blade and realized what had just happened, sweat broke out on his forehead.

He could not believe that the sword had caused an earthquake. He took it in both hands, in a reversed grip, and placed the tip on the soil at his feet.

Nothing happened.

He held it in that position, waiting and thinking. He realized that he did not *want* anything to happen. Perhaps that was affecting his experiment. He forced himself to stop denying the sword's power, and instead recited to himself, "Move, earth, I command it!"

The ground shook, roaring; he saw dust swirl up on all sides.

"Stop!" he cried.

It stopped.

Earthquakes frightened him. The uneasy movement of that most immovable of things upset his view of the way the world should be. Such displays undoubtedly consumed vast amounts of the sword's energy, but he could not bear to continue.

Storms, however, were something he was accustomed to.

He looked at the gem. It was glowing brightly, vividly red.

It could not be limitless, he told himself. It must exhaust itself eventually.

With that thought in his mind, he raised the sword above his head and summoned the storm to him.

The light of the jewel bathed him in crimson, and the blade glowed brilliantly white as the storm broke about him with preternatural fury. A bolt of lightning burned through the air over his head and shattered against the sword, bathing him in a shower of immense blue-white sparks, but he felt nothing but a slight warmth and a mounting joy in the power he wielded.

Another bolt followed the first, though Garth knew that was not natural; and then a third came. He was washed in white fire, and the ground at his feet was burned black.

Lightning continued to pour down upon him while cold rain beat against the plain around him. He stayed dry in the heart of the storm, for the lightning and the heat of the sword boiled away the rain before it could touch him, encircling him in steam and mist.

He discovered that he could steer the lightning away from him and direct it where he chose by pointing with the sword, as he had spread flame in Skelleth. He drew the sword's heat into him and thrust it upward, and the rain turned warm around him; then he sucked it back down and away, and the rain became first sleet, and then hail – though the frozen drops were smaller than natural hailstones.

He called aloud another strange name, *"Kewerro!"* The wind howled down out of the north, and the storm became a snowstorm, then a raging blizzard.

He was drunk and staggering with the power of the sword, and still the gem glowed as brightly as ever, the blade as gleaming white as the moon.

He sent the snow away again, turning the north wind back, and allowed the south wind to bring rain in its place. The sky was black, the sun buried in thunderheads; only lightning and the light of the sword lessened the gloom.

He drew the storm around him, whipped it into a howling maelstrom, and forced its winds to whirl faster, until his cloak was flapping with a sound like the breaking of stone; still the gem remained undimmed. Maintaining the roaring hurricane, he moved the earth as well, rippling it around him like a lake in a breeze. He pulled the rain from the sky in sheets, in streams, and pounded lightning on the shifting ground, surrounding himself in a halo of crawling electric fire.

Finally, he could stand no more; he fell to his knees. The earth stilled. One hand fell from the sword's hilt; the lightning stopped, and the wind dropped. In the sudden silence after the final thunderclap, he closed his eyes and heard the beating of the rain soften to a gentle patter.

He opened his eyes and looked hopelessly at the sword. His fingers adhered to the hilt as firmly as ever.

The gem glowed fiery red, and he thought he heard mocking laughter, his own voice laughing at his despair.

Chapter Twenty

The twenty-first councilor and Derelind's report from Mormoreth arrived almost simultaneously.

It was the Seer of Weideth, uncomfortable on a borrowed horse, who completed the Council's quorum; he arrived late in the evening while a light, chilling drizzle blew down out of the north, and his calls to the castle's gatekeeper went unheeded for fully fifteen minutes, unheard over the hiss of the rain and the mutter of the wind. There was only a single guard posted at the gate after dark and he was huddled well away from the window, drawing what warmth he could from his shuttered lantern and a skin of cheap red wine; finally, though, he heard something worth checking on and peered down to discover the Seer, shivering at the gate, wrapped in an immense gray cloak.

The gatekeeper was an honest man and not inconsiderate; he hurried to his winch and called down an apology as he cranked open the portcullis. That done, he rushed down the tower steps, stumbling in the dark and very nearly sending himself falling head-first, and opened the Lesser Portal. In daylight there would have been two other guards to share the task.

"My lord, I am very sorry, truly I am! I had not thought any would be out in such dreary weather!"

The Seer nodded, but did not manage to say anything. His home village was kept perpetually warm and dry by the heat of the neighboring volcanoes, and he was not accustomed to the damp chill of autumn rains.

"I should have known better, though, with all of you folk arriving for these past several days; I don't suppose you're the last, either. I guess the rain caught you already on the road, and you didn't wish to waste money on an inn with the castle so close; I'd do the same myself. It's damnably strange weather for this early in the year, too, my lord – far colder than any year in my memory."

The Seer looked at the gatekeeper and realized that he was a very lonely man, spending his nights sitting alone at the gate. He was unmarried, with no children, and his most recent woman had left him a few days earlier.

That was not his business, the Seer told himself. His gift sometimes told him more than he wanted to know – and then other times it wouldn't tell him anything. He wished it were more reliable. He didn't particularly care if he were ever a great prophet, but it would be pleasant, he mused, at least to be a competent one, rather than having erratic flashes of insight and foreknowledge.

It was the guard's loneliness, combined with his genuine contrition, that had brought on his little speech. He would go on talking until he got an answer.

"Oh, I'm all right," the Seer managed. "You mustn't trouble yourself."

"That's kind of you, my lord. Is there anything I can do for you?"

"Where can I put my horse?"

The gatekeeper replied with directions to the stable, instructions on whom to rouse and how, and warnings against trusting the worthless grooms.

"Thank you," the Seer replied. He rode on as directed, before the man could begin another speech.

At the stable he obtained directions to a hall where he might find someone who would know where he was supposed to be; following them, he got lost briefly in the maze of stone corridors. Eventually, though, by asking whomever he chanced to meet, he found his way to the upper gallery where the Council was gathering.

Chalkara noticed him as he reached the top of the stairs and recognized him immediately from his sending. "Greetings, O Seer," she said. "I hadn't known you were here. When did you arrive?"

The Seer held out a flap of his cloak so that she could see that it was still wet and answered, "Just now. What's going on?"

A stranger in a gaudy robe of purple velvet pushed past him and entered the gallery as Chalkara answered, "It's rather complicated to explain, and the meeting is about to start. Why don't you just come in, sit down, and warm up? If you have any questions, ask them as they come up."

Confused, the Seer let Chalkara shove him through the door. There were chairs inside, arranged around a row of three long tables; he was tired, and sank into one gratefully.

The room was lighted by several dozen candles in hanging chandeliers and standing candelabra, and a dozen or so men and women were already seated around the tables. Others were arriving as he took this in. Shandiph was seated at the head of the table he had chosen; none of the others were immediately recognizable. There was a tiny old woman seated at Shandiph's right.

A stout man not quite into middle age seated himself at the Seer's right and remarked without preamble, "You're wet."

"It's raining," he answered.

"Have you just arrived, then?"

"Yes."

"Who are you?"

"I am the Seer of Weideth."

"Ah, then it's you who started all this!"

"I suppose it is. Who are you, then?"

"You don't know me? I am Deriam of Ur-Dormulk, and probably the only wizard here who knows what he's doing." He gestured to take in the entire assembly.

The Seer decided that he didn't care for Deriam of Ur-Dormulk. He was trying to think of a polite way to break off the conversation when Shandiph rose and broke it off for him by calling the meeting to order.

"I see that we now have the necessary numbers," he said when the entire group was seated and silent, "counting Derelind. With this quorum, then, we are constituted an official gathering of the Council of the Most High, empowered to take action on behalf of the entire membership. I think that you will all agree shortly that some action must be taken, and quickly."

He paused dramatically, and someone in his audience snorted derisively. Shandiph ignored it.

"We have just received word, through the offices of the sorceress Zhinza, from Derelind the Hermit, who was earlier sent to the city of Mormoreth in Orûn to ascertain the status of our comrade Shang and the basilisk which had been placed in his keeping. I now yield to Zhinza, so that she may give Derelind's message herself." He gestured toward the ancient woman and then sank into his chair.

Zhinza rose and proclaimed, "Shang is dead. I was right."

Deriam muttered something into his beard.

"Tell them what Derelind said," Shandiph reminded her.

"Derelind said," she went on, "that he arrived safely and found that Mormoreth is now inhabited by the bandit tribe that formerly roamed the Plain of Derbarok. Being a wizard, he was easily able to convince the bandits to talk to him and tell him how this came about. They claim the city was given to them as a gift by the person who killed Shang, as a blood-price for several tribesmen he killed as well."

"All right, woman, who was it killed him?" Karag demanded.

"Shang was killed by an overman named Garth."

There was a moment of stunned silence as this news sank in.

"What about the basilisk?" someone called.

There was a hush as Zhinza looked about for the speaker and failed to locate her. Finally, addressing the group at large, she said, "Garth took it with him."

The ensuing silence was brief and followed by a babble of many voices. Shandiph let it go on for several minutes before demanding order be restored.

"You mean," Karag of Sland said, when he was reasonably sure he could be heard, "that our greatest weapon has fallen into the hands of the enemy even before we have begun to fight him?"

"That would appear to be the case," Shandiph said. "Before we begin debate, however, I would like to have all the available information laid out. We are fortunate in that Kala of Mara thought to bring with her a good scrying glass. At my request, she has been studying this overman. At this time, I would like to ask her what she has learned."

Kala was a young woman in a simple brown robe; she stood and said, "I haven't learned much, I'm afraid. It's very hard to use the glass on Garth of Ordunin; the sword resists the presence of all other magic, and he is never apart from the sword."

"Have you seen the basilisk?" asked Thetheru.

"No, I haven't. I haven't seen any trace of it anywhere in Skelleth. I don't know what happened to it, but I don't think it's there."

"That's good," Deriam said.

"What I have seen, though, is enough to frighten me badly. I cannot look at Garth directly; the sword will not allow it. When I attempt to force it, it retaliates by filling my crystal with its own hideous light, so that I can see nothing. I haven't the strength of will to fight it. However, I have watched the village of Skelleth and places around the overman. There have of late been several great storms in that area, as well as earthquakes; they have had snow and hail, as well as the rain and sleet that might be expected in this season, and winds sufficient to tear apart thatched roofs. I have glimpsed lightning storms that lit the night sky as if it were day. I think that Garth is somehow using the sword to create or summon these storms."

"You say that you haven't been able to watch the overman himself?" Karag asked.

"No, I haven't. I have also been unable to see inside the local tavern he frequents, whether he is there or not; I have no idea what this might mean."

"These storms," Karag asked. "Are you sure he's causing them? I've never heard of any such magic."

"I am not certain, but they are like no natural storms I have ever seen."

There was a moment of silence; then Thetheru of Amag said quietly, "Do we have any chance of stopping such power?"

"He has already taken our greatest weapon," Herina the Stargazer observed.

"Well, no," Shandiph said, "he hasn't, really."

There was another moment of silence; then Miloshir the Theurgist asked, "Are you referring to the Ring of P'hul?"

"Among other things, yes."

The Seer was confused. He had never heard of the Ring of P'hul. He looked about for Chalkara, but she was seated well down the table on the opposite side.

"What other things?" Karag demanded.

Shandiph sighed. "I was afraid this would happen sometime. A need was bound to arise."

"What in the name of the seven Lords of Eir are you talking about?" someone asked. The Seer was surprised to see that it was Chalkara; he would have guessed that she was privy to all the Chairman's secrets.

"Have none of you ever wondered at how little power our magic has? Haven't you all heard the tales of the great magicks used in the wars of the Twelfth Age and wondered what became of them?"

The other magicians were all staring at Shandiph now.

"They're just stories," someone said.

"No, I'm afraid they aren't."

"You mean that Llarimuir the Great really did move mountains? That he created the overmen on a whim? That Quellimour raised a city overnight and then sent it sailing in the clouds?" Karag's voice was openly sarcastic.

"Yes, they probably did just what you say," Shandiph replied mildly.

"Then what happened?" Miloshir asked.

"It was at the end of the Twelfth Age," Shandiph explained. "The world had been in a constant state of war for over a thousand years, probably more than two thousand – the wars destroyed all the records, so we can't be sure. The wizards of that age fought in those wars, using all the magic at their command; reading their descriptions, I find it miraculous that anyone survived at all. The seers and oracles helped by giving military counsel to the generals and warlords."

"But that's forbidden!" the Seer burst out.

"It is now, yes; it wasn't then. As I was saying, magicks mightier than any we can imagine were common and were employed without any compunction, not only in genuine wars, but in looting and pillaging at whim. The wizards themselves were among the most feared of the warlords. It was only the balance of power, the fact that each side could recruit and use equal amounts of magic, that kept the wars going – and it was probably that balance that kept most of the population alive. Each wizard, you see, defended his subjects, and there were protective spells as powerful as the destructive spells.

"At any rate, this continued throughout the Twelfth Age; but about three centuries ago, the surviving wizards grew tired of the constant conflict and gathered in council to arrange a peace. That was the beginning of the Council of the Most High. You've all probably heard that the wizards were advisors to the warlords, and some were, but most were the warlords themselves. It was agreed that all wars would stop at once, whether the other lords wanted them to or not; the Ring of P'hul was used to end the Orûnian War and the Racial Wars, and lesser magicks dealt with the lesser conflicts. It was then decided, when it was seen what the Ring and the other spells had done, that such powers were too dangerous to keep in use, and they were sealed away in a spot known only to the first Chairman of the Council."

"And I suppose the secret has been passed on from chairman to chairman, down to you?" Karag said.

"No, not exactly; not the secret itself, but only the means of obtaining it. I didn't know until an hour ago where the great magicks were, only that a certain spell would inform me. I used it when I first heard Derelind's message, before calling this meeting. The old magicks, those that survived, are in the crypts beneath Ur-Dormulk."

"They are?" Deriam exclaimed.

"Yes, they are," Shandiph replied.

"What of it?" Karag asked.

"Comrades, I think we could debate on this for hours or even days, but Miloshir tells us that time is precious, that the overman draws greater power from the Sword of Bheleu with every passing moment. Therefore, I would like to put this proposal to an immediate vote: that we should without any further delay send a party to Ur-Dormulk to acquire these ancient powers, whatever they may include, and then use them to end the threat posed by Garth of Ordunin and the Sword of Bheleu, thereby averting the coming Age of Destruction. If the vote does not show a clear consensus, I will open debate, but I hope that it won't be necessary."

It wasn't. There were three dissenting voices, for a total of only four votes.

Chapter Twenty-One

For three days Garth had tried to burn out the sword's power with storms and earthquakes, but had succeeded only in exhausting himself and disrupting the reconstruction of Skelleth. Finally, when the gem still glowed as brightly as ever at the end of the third day, he admitted defeat.

At least, he admitted temporary defeat; he had not yet abandoned hope, but only convinced himself that he could not exhaust the sword in such displays. He suspected that he might manage to free himself by allowing the sword a surfeit of killing, but that was not a method he cared to employ; it was to avoid unnecessary killing that he wanted to dispose of the thing.

He spent the following day sitting in the King's Inn, drinking and talking with Saram. The reconstruction was continuing, but only slowly; the cold had made work difficult, and materials were running low – stone excepted. The embassy had been sent to Kholis, as planned. The petrified thief had been set up in the center of the marketplace on an elaborate pedestal of stone blocks from the Baron's dungeon. Galt, Garth, and the other overmen considered this to be a mistake, but Saram and Frima insisted that the pitiful figure was appropriate and admirable.

Another petrified villager had been found in a ruin nearby; apparently someone had had the misfortune to look out a window while the basilisk was being moved through the streets. This figure was not to become a public statue; even had it not broken in half when the house it was in collapsed in flames around it, it was much less attractive. The person in question had been a plump matron, bent over to peer around a shutter.

No one had known that this second petrification had occurred until the rubble had been cleared from the house. The victim had been a recluse, little liked by those who knew her at all. Garth still thought it odd that her absence could have gone unnoticed for the intervening months.

"I had hoped," he remarked to Saram, "that the death of the basilisk would remove the spell that it had cast upon its victims."

"It would seem that magic is not as transitory as some tales would have it," Saram replied.

"I suppose that if it were, then Shang's death would have ended the usefulness of his charms, and thereby freed the basilisk from my control."

"And if that had happened, you might be a statue now yourself."

"But on the other hand, these two innocents would not."

"Oh, you can't be sure; what if the basilisk had begun roaming, once freed, and eventually reached Skelleth?"

"That seems extremely unlikely."

"Yes, it does. But then, the very existence of such a creature seems unlikely."

"It does, doesn't it? Everything that's happened to me since I first came south seems unlikely. One strange event has followed another, almost as if they were planned."

"Perhaps they were."

"Perhaps they were, but by whom and how? Is it all a scheme of the Forgotten King's contrivance? If so, how did he influence me to ask the Wise Women of Ordunin the questions that would send me to him in the first place? If not he, then who? Have I become a pawn of the god of destruction? Is there some other power manipulating us all?"

"Perhaps it's fate, or destiny."

"The Wise Women mentioned fate when last I spoke with them, fate and chance; I have never believed in fate, but only in chance."

"Yet now you say that events don't appear to be shaped by chance. That would seem to leave fate, if your oracle's words were complete."

"They probably weren't."

"You don't trust these women?"

"They're overwomen, actually, despite their name, and I am not sure whether I trust them or not."

"Perhaps you should go and speak with them again, and settle the matter once and for all. They might know how you can be freed of the sword."

"They might, at that. They are, however, in Ordunin, where I am now an outlaw."

"Do you know of any other oracles?"

"I'm not sure; I once met a seer, of sorts, and of course there is the Forgotten King, who knows more than he should. There was also a priest in Dûsarra who was said to have special knowledge. None of these are even as trustworthy as the Wise Women."

"I would say, then, that you would be well-advised to return to Ordunin, outlaw or not, and speak with your oracle. If you travel by night and stay clear of the city, can you not manage it?"

"Probably. I will think about it."

He did think about it and by morning he had resolved to make the attempt.

Unfortunately, by morning the winter snows had begun, blowing down from the northern hills. This storm was wholly natural, but fierce enough that he decided travel would be foolhardy. He would wait it out, he told himself.

It was only after two days of tedium, sitting in the King's Inn worrying about the warbeasts' food supply – five of eleven, including Koros, had stayed in Skelleth when the others had returned to Ordunin – that it occurred to him that, if the sword could create storms, it might be able to control natural ones as well.

It could. He ripped the storm into tattered shreds of cloud and sputtering gusts of wind in ten minutes of concentration.

A foot of wet snow lay on the ground, but he thought Koros could handle that without undue difficulty. He set about gathering supplies.

With the ground under snow, game would be scarce along the way, and foraging difficult; furthermore, he did not dare to visit his home, which meant that he needed supplies for a round trip. Saram was reluctant to part with so much of the village's meager provisions.

Garth also wanted another sword, a more ordinary blade that he could use without worrying about whether he was controlling it or it was controlling him, a knife for skinning and dressing whatever game he might find, an axe to cut firewood, and various other tools that were in short supply in Skelleth. His friendship with Saram did not provide unlimited credit, and he found himself spending part of the Aghadite gold to purchase what he needed.

It took another two days before he felt himself properly equipped, but at last, one morning, he mounted his warbeast and rode out the North Gate toward the hills that marked the border of the Northern Waste.

Chapter Twenty-Two

The party sent to Ur-Dormulk consisted of Deriam, since he knew his own city better than anyone else; Shandiph, since he alone could use the spell that would show them the way to the crypt that held what they sought; Karag, who insisted upon accompanying them; and Thetheru of Amag, who refused to remain behind if Karag went. The four rode the finest horses in the High King's stable; Chalkara, with the aid of a subtle spell, acquired retroactive approval for this from the King an hour or so after the quartet had slipped quietly out.

The stealth was considered necessary because of the presence of the Baron of Sland. He had already protested the existence of secret meetings of wizards in the High King's castle and tried to force Karag to tell him what was under discussion. Only the presence of the other wizards had kept him from resorting to violence.

Two of his six soldiers had vanished since their arrival, and Karag suspected that the Baron was keeping his own secrets. His men did not desert; they did not dare.

Therefore, the four wizards had begun their journey an hour before dawn, while the Baron and his men slept. A simple spell of drowsiness kept the gatekeeper from noticing their departure.

Once out of the castle, they rode night and day, using invigorating spells to keep their horses alive and moving. Such travel was hard on the older two, Shandiph and Deriam, but did not seem to bother Karag at all, and Thetheru concealed his own fatigue rather than admit that Karag was more fit. Ordinarily, each would have avoided the use of so much magic so quickly, but with such a threat hanging over them and such a promise of greater power before them, it seemed foolish to worry about conserving relatively trivial resources.

They were slowed by the necessity of crossing the Great River, which they reached early in the second day, but they nevertheless managed to arrive at the gates of Ur-Dormulk by the sunset following their ferry ride.

It then became necessary to conceal their haste, and they struggled to appear as if nothing unusual were taking place – as if the four of them had decided on a casual visit to Deriam's home. They received curious glances from pedestrians as they made their way through the streets, while Karag and Thetheru displayed their own curiosity in studying the city around them. Shandiph and Deriam were both natives of Ur-Dormulk, though Shandiph had left it as a child to become a wanderer, and they were accustomed to its peculiarities, but the other two had never before seen it.

The entire city was built of stone and was so ancient that the stone had been worn and weathered on even the newest buildings. The older structures did not have a single sharp corner remaining, and some resembled mounds or natural rock formations as much as they resembled anything man-made. The streets were all paved with great slabs of stone, yet there were grooves worn in them where countless cart wheels had passed, and wider, shallower depressions where the majority of the foot traffic had gone.

Deriam's home was a tall, narrow house on a busy avenue, of no special distinction save that there were gaps in its ancient granite walls where softer stones used as trim had been weathered away completely.

"We'll have to hide the horses," Deriam said as he dismounted at his door.

"Why?" Karag asked.

"There are no horses in Ur-Dormulk," Shandiph replied. "It was probably a mistake even riding them past the gate."

"What will happen if we just leave them here?" Thetheru asked.

"I don't know," Shandiph said.

"They'll probably be stolen," Deriam said.

"Then put a warding spell on them," Karag suggested. "Shandiph, you're good at that."

"I'm tired, Karag."

"It's a good thought," Deriam said.

"Then you do it," Shandiph replied.

Thetheru objected. "I think we should just hide them."

"We're wasting time," Deriam said. "Shandiph, put a ward on them and let's get on with it. You're outvoted, Thetheru."

Wearily, Shandiph assented, and cast a simple ward on the horses. The four then left them tied to the door handle while they entered the house.

"If we're in such a hurry," Thetheru asked, "why are we here instead of going directly to the crypts?"

"We *are* going directly to the crypts," Deriam said. "They can be reached through my cellars. There are easily a hundred entrances, and this is the one I know best. The crypts of Ur-Dormulk are a true marvel, you see; they extend . . ."

"Shut up, Deriam, we haven't got time for that," Shandiph said, made irritable by fatigue.

Offended, Deriam made no reply, but instead pulled a bell rope and called for his servants.

"You do well for yourself," Karag remarked. "I have no servants to wait on me."

"Ur-Dormulk is a rich city," Deriam replied. "And besides, I was not so foolish as to become a servant myself. I do not work for the Overlord here, but on my own behalf."

"I doubt that you suffer from your lack, Karag," Shandiph remarked. "After all, you have the run of the Baron of Sland's castle and staff, don't you?"

"More or less," Karag admitted. "I can command the household workers, but have no authority over the guards."

The conversation was cut off by the arrival of Deriam's retainers. He sent one to fetch food and drink, another to bring the keys to the cellars, and the third and last to take a polite greeting to the Overlord and tell him that his faithful Deriam had returned but was resting from the journey and not to be disturbed.

The three vanished without comment on their various errands, and the four wizards settled down to await the promised meal. "We shouldn't take the time," Shandiph said, "but I'm hungry."

"Yes, and cold and thirsty as well," Thetheru added.

While waiting, the newcomers looked over Deriam's parlor. It was lush to the point of ostentation, with thick patterned carpets overlapping to cover every inch of floor, rich tapestries covering every wall, and ornate carved frames around every door and window. The furnishings included a myriad of cushions of silk and velvet and an assortment of tables, chairs, pedestals, statuettes, display shelves, bric-a-brac, and general clutter, every item made of costly materials and showing elaborate workmanship. A few of the cushions had old stains on them, and one carving of a handsome young couple was chipped through the woman's arm.

When the servant he had sent for the keys delivered them, Deriam sent the youth after as many lanterns and torches as could be found in the house. "We'll need light in the crypts," he explained, "and there's no sense in wasting magic."

The food, when it arrived, consisted of a plate of fruit, nuts, and cakes; the drink was a decanter of yellow wine and a steaming pitcher of a brownish liquid Karag and Thetheru did not recognize.

"A discovery of my own," Deriam explained with an air of patently false modesty. "It's an infusion of herbs and spices in boiling water and it's really quite invigorating. Try it."

Karag refused the unfamiliar brew and confined himself to cakes and wine; Thetheru took a cup of the steaming concoction and an assortment of fruit and pronounced both to be good.

Both wine and herbal brew were warming and felt so good to the weary travelers that they made no effort to silence Deriam when he began a long description of the history of the crypts.

"They aren't exactly crypts in the usual sense of burial vaults or areas for underground storage," he said. "They're actually another city that used to stand on this same site. Ur-Dormulk, you see, is the most ancient city in all the world and has stood here for longer than any records have existed. It was once called Stur-dar-Malik, which means 'City of the Old Ones' in the language of the time. Even then it was old. The most learned scholars in the city, who are of course the wisest and most learned in the world, say that there must once have been a great catastrophe that destroyed much of the city, and the survivors built the new city upon the ruins without bothering to excavate them. The old cellars and passages were forgotten for centuries, until finally someone broke into them while digging a new wine cellar. That was, I have heard, in the Eleventh Age, about four thousand years ago. Since then they have been explored and extended and elaborated, until now they are so complex that no man living knows them all – and I personally doubt that anyone ever did. They reach under every corner of the city and extend out beyond the walls for miles in every direction, as well as continuing quite deeply down into the earth. There are said to be many strange and wondrous things in them, and there are tales of men and women who have become lost down there only to be preserved by the unnatural powers that lurk in the darkness, to wander about forever."

"That's a cheering thought," Thetheru said.

"Oh, it's just a legend," Shandiph replied.

"We thought that the great old magicks were just a legend," Thetheru returned.

"If the crypts are so extensive, how can we hope to find these magicks we seek?" Karag asked.

"There are signs," Shandiph replied.

"Signs? You mean that these carefully hidden things, too dangerous to leave where they might be misused, can be found by following signposts?"

"Not exactly. The signs can only be read by means of an enchanted glass."

"Where do we find this glass, then?"

Shandiph reached down to a pouch on his belt. "It's right here," he answered.

"Let me see it," Karag asked.

"Not yet," Shandiph replied.

Karag started to protest, then caught sight of Thetheru's smile and thought better of it.

They finished their repast in silence. As Deriam drank the last of the wine, his servant reappeared with a double armful of prepared torches and with four lanterns.

The torches were distributed evenly among the four wizards. Karag suggested that Deriam's servants accompany them, but Deriam overruled the notion immediately. "That is beyond their duties," he explained.

"Besides, we want to keep the whole thing secret," Shandiph added.

Accordingly, the servants stayed where they were, while the wizards made their way through Deriam's kitchen and down the stairs into his wine cellars. From there they descended another flight into a fruit cellar, where a trap door opened to reveal a ladder leading down into utter darkness. The light of the lanterns did not reach the bottom.

With the torches bundled on their backs, the four descended, Karag first, followed by Deriam, Shandiph, and Thetheru. The ladder swayed beneath their weight but did not break or fall. After what seemed an incredibly long time, they finally came in sight of the bottom.

When they stepped from the ladder, they found themselves on a flagstone floor buried in a thick layer of dust. At Shandiph's suggestion they lit one torch apiece to provide additional light.

They were in an immense chamber of stone; their footsteps echoed from the bare walls, which even the light of torches and lanterns combined revealed only as vague and distant patches amid the all-encompassing darkness. Three of the four stared about in uneasy surprise at the room's extent; Deriam remarked casually, "I haven't been down here in a long, long time; I'd forgotten just how big it is."

"Where's the door to the crypts?" Karag asked.

"We are *in* the crypts, Karag," Deriam replied. "This chamber has a dozen doors opening on various rooms and passages."

"Which way do we go?" Thetheru asked.

"I haven't any idea," Deriam answered.

Shandiph carefully placed his torch and lantern on the stone floor and fumbled with the pouch on his belt. He brought out a small sphere of yellow glass and held it up to his eye.

After a long moment he said, "I see nothing."

"What do we do now?" Thetheru asked.

"Pick a direction at random," Karag suggested.

Deriam shrugged, and led the party to the wall of the room, choosing his route by walking forward in the direction he happened to be facing.

The wall was bare stone and faintly dusty.

"Now," Deriam said, "I propose that we walk along the wall until we find one of the signs Shandiph mentioned."

No one objected, and the foursome moved along the wall.

Almost immediately, they came to an open doorway; Deriam looked at Shandiph, who shook his head. They moved on.

A second doorway was passed, and a corner of the room. At the third doorway Shandiph asked, "Does the pentacle above the door mean anything?"

"What pentacle?" Thetheru asked, holding up his lantern. The stone lintel was blank.

"I think we've found it," Karag replied.

Shandiph lowered the glass from his eye and stared at the lintel in puzzlement. "I still see the pentacle, though," he said. "Don't you see it?"

"There is nothing there, Shandiph," Karag replied.

"We see nothing but bare stone," Deriam added.

Shandiph looked at the glass, then back at the stone. "I thought I had to look through it," he said. "It appears I was wrong." With a shrug, he led the way through the door and into the passage beyond.

The passage was more of the dull gray stone, huge blocks of it stacked together without mortar, forming a corridor ten feet wide and twelve feet high. It sloped downward for a hundred yards or so and then ended in a T-shaped intersection. Karag had moved into the lead and now stopped, unsure which way to turn.

"The pentagram is on the left," Shandiph said as he came up. Karag immediately turned left, and the party advanced.

Following Shandiph's directions, the foursome made their way deeper and deeper into the crypts, through corridors and rooms that ranged from mere cubicles to vast caverns, up and down ramps and stairs, across bridges that spanned seemingly bottomless chasms, and past doors of wood, iron, and brass that stood ajar or were tightly sealed, with no discernable pattern. The first torches burned down to uselessness and were discarded, and the lanterns dimmed and died as they wound onward. There was no light save what they carried, and the only sounds were their own footsteps, their own breath, and occasionally the distant dripping of water. In one room they found a spot where drops of water fell and saw that it ran from the tip of a five-inch stalactite clinging to the low ceiling, to land with the smallest of splashes on a stubby projection from the floor. The chamber they were in was not a natural cave, but man-made; the water came through a crack between the stones of the ceiling.

The second set of torches died, and the third was lit; Deriam began complaining of the stupidity Shandiph had displayed in not bringing food and drink. Karag came to the Chairman's defense, pointing out that he had no way of knowing how long the search would take, while Thetheru remained silent. When Deriam demanded that the Amagite choose a side, he ended the argument by saying, "I'm too busy trying to remember our route."

"I hadn't thought of that," Deriam said after a moment of silence.

"I've been too busy finding our way forward," Shandiph said.

"Can you lead us back out?" Karag asked.

"I'm not sure," Thetheru admitted.

"Maybe we should turn back. Do we even know what we're looking for?" Deriam asked. "How will we know these wonders when we find them? Have they really survived for three hundred years in this damp darkness?"

"Darkness wouldn't hurt anything," Karag retorted.

"But we don't even know what we're looking for," Thetheru said.

"I assume that we'll find a few chests somewhere," Shandiph said, "and perhaps a shelf of books."

"I hope so," Deriam answered.

They were discarding the last of the fourth set of torches when Shandiph, who had moved on ahead while Karag lit the new torch from the stub of his old one, called out, "I've found something."

"What is it?" Karag called.

"This door has the pentagram sign on it, and another pentagram inside the first."

"Is it open?"

"No. It's locked."

The other three came up to join him and found that the Chairman was standing before a large oaken door bound in rusty iron; he was pulling and pushing at the great iron handle. The door did not move.

"Whatever we're looking for must be in there," Karag said.

"How do we get in?" Deriam asked.

"Break it down," Karag suggested.

Shandiph and Deriam looked at each other; Deriam shrugged, "Let him try; he's the strongest of us."

The other three stepped back, and Karag took a short run toward the door, slamming his shoulder against it.

Immediately, he was flung back against the far wall of the corridor in a shower of pure white sparks.

He lay stunned on the dusty stone. Thetheru said unnecessarily, "It must have a warding spell on it."

"I never saw a ward like that," Deriam replied. He was blinking, trying to help his eyes readjust to the dim yellow torchlight after the vivid brilliance of the sparks.

Shandiph looked at the door for a moment and then said, "I suppose they wanted to be sure that no one who just happened along could get in. We are the rightful heirs, though, so there must be some way we can annul the wards."

"There was no mention of this in your directions?"

"No. You have to understand, I know very little more than you do. When I became Chairman I was given the seal of office and a box of charms, and taught a spell that would tell me what each charm was for when the need arose; that spell told me that the yellow glass would show me the way through the crypts, but it said nothing of this door."

"Did you bring the other charms?"

"No. That shouldn't matter, though; I know what almost all of them do. Besides, if one was needed here, the spell should have told me before I left Kholis."

"Perhaps the spell has become muddled over the years."

"Aal and Amera, I hope not!"

"Is there some hidden instruction in the pentacle, perhaps?" Thetheru asked.

Karag was climbing to his feet once again. He said nothing, but stood unsteadily, staring at the door.

"Did you bring any magic besides the yellow glass?" Deriam asked Shandiph.

Before the Chairman could answer, Karag said, "I can see the pentagram now."

"What?" The others turned toward him in surprise.

"I can see the pentagram. But you said there was another pentagram within it, Shandiph, and it's not a pentagram, it's the Council seal."

"It is?" Shandiph also stared at the door; to him it still appeared to be a pentacle inside a pentacle. A possibility occurred to him, and he reached inside the neck of his tunic to pull forth the golden medallion that he as Chairman of the Council of the Most High, wore at all times. He placed it against the center of the pentagram and announced, "I am Shandiph, heir to Hemmaron, Chairman of the Council of the Most High, chief among the wise and first among equals!"

Nothing happened.

In desperation, Shandiph reached out and pushed once more at the iron handle. The door swung open.

The chamber beyond was utterly black, and the light of the torches did not penetrate. The four wizards stared into it for a long moment, none daring to step into the unnatural darkness.

"I think that magic is called for," Deriam said at last.

Shandiph nodded. *"Hoi, khiri! I'a angarosye t'aryo ansuyen, o mi alekye i zhure Leuk!"* he called. *"Hear me, spirits! I am an agent of the lords of demons, and with this talisman I invoke Leuk!"*

The room was suddenly flooded with golden light, and the four stared in astonishment.

The chamber was perhaps thirty feet wide, but so long that its far end could not be seen in the conjured light. The walls were lined with shelves of books, row after row of chests, hundreds of pegs from which hung amulets and talismans of every sort, and racks which held scepters, staves, orbs, jewels, swords, daggers, cups, plates, goblets, spears, stones, carvings, statues, sacks, pouches, jars, phials, and a hundred other implements and objects. More chests were lined up down the center of the room. Many objects glowed or glittered, and soft rustlings could be heard.

Directly before them stood an immense reading stand carved of some dark, rich wood, which held a great black-bound book.

Everything was brightly and clearly lighted for fifty yards of the room's length, but without shadows and with no apparent source of light.

"How did you do that?" Thetheru asked Shandiph.

"You mean the light? I learned a little theurgy years ago; it's a simple invocation. If you mean the door, I didn't do anything except what you saw. It must have been ensorcelled to recognize the seal of office."

"What *is* all this stuff?" Karag demanded, astonished.

Shandiph shrugged. "How should I know?" He stepped forward and looked at the lone book on the stand. "I think that this must be here where we see it for a reason." He opened the book at random and let the front cover fall back against the stand.

Pages flipped over without his touch; when they stopped, he read aloud, "This book is the true compendium of all arcane knowledge gathered in this room, compiled to guide those who come after us in the use of our arts."

"Useful," Deriam remarked.

"How can one volume explain all this?" Thetheru asked, gesturing at the thousands of books and tens of thousands of other objects.

Pages turned, and Shandiph read, "This book has been enchanted and will answer your every question. Speak, and you shall be answered; ask, and you shall know, that the glory of the Council of the Most High may be reborn upon the earth." He smiled. "So much for secrecy," he said. "It appears that our predecessors didn't expect it to last forever."

"Shandiph," Deriam said, "this is all too much for me. What are all these things? This is far more than I had imagined we would find."

A single page turned, and Shandiph read, "Gathered before you is every magical spell and power known to our members at the end of this Twelfth Age, save those thought too minor to waste space upon, and those that have been withheld by the power of the gods or reserved for the continued use of the Council's master."

"I think this is more than we can handle," Thetheru said. "I think we should contact the rest of the Council before we go any further."

A thick sheaf of pages flung itself over with an audible thump, and Thetheru looked at it in surprise. "I didn't ask a question," he said.

"The Greater Spell of Summoning has been embodied for your use in spheres of red crystal, stored in the first chest on your left," Shandiph read. "The shattering of one of these crystals in the heart of a well-drawn pentagram will bring you instantly whomsoever you shall name aloud while the smoke is thick."

"The thing dares to advise us!" Karag exclaimed.

"We should use it, though," Thetheru said. "Where is chalk for a pentagram?"

A page riffled over, but Shandiph did not bother to read what it said, as Deriam announced, "There is already a pentagram here, on the floor, inlaid in gold."

The other three looked, and Deriam was correct; a thin layer of dust had hidden the golden star.

Shandiph was already on the way to the chest indicated by the book by the time Karag and Thetheru had convinced themselves of the pentagram's reality. He opened it and found that a dozen identical spheres of red crystal, each the size of a clenched fist, were arrayed in a tray at one end. The rest of the chest held an assortment of other fascinating devices, but he resolved to leave those for later. He picked out a single red globe and, with a careful toss, flung it into the center of the pentagram. It shattered spectacularly when it hit the floor, and an impossibly thick cloud of red smoke billowed forth.

"Chalkara of Kholis, Derelind the Hermit, Miloshir the Theurgist, Herina the Stargazer, Veyel of Nekutta, the sorceress Zhinza, the mage Ranendin, the Baron Dor of Therin, Kala of Mara, Sharatha of Ilnan," he recited quickly.

The smoke continued to roll outward in a solid, spreading mass, with no sign of thinning; Shandiph continued his listing. "Kubal of Tadumuri, Haladar of Mara, Sherek the Thaumaturge!" He was beginning to have trouble remembering which other councilors had been at Kholis. "Amarda the Blood Drinker! Linder the Nightwalker!"

Vague shapes were becoming visible in the seething red cloud, which had reached out far enough to surround the original party of four. "The Seer of Weideth!" Shandiph added. There were still one or two others, he knew. "The wizard Alagar . . ." Were there still more?

The smoke showed the first signs of dispersing, and it occurred to him that he need not restrict himself to those who had attended the meetings. He remembered one more who had been at Kholis, though, and named him first, saying, "Phamakh the Wise!"

Abruptly the red fog thinned and vanished, and the room was suddenly crowded. Every person he had named was present, jammed together in the area around the golden pentagram; all were looking about themselves with varying mixtures of surprise and fear.

Shandiph realized that he had missed an opportunity to settle Shang's fate definitely once and for all by summoning him as well, or he might have called for someone who could provide a firsthand account of recent events in Dûsarra. He considered using another of the crystal spheres, but decided against it.

There was a sudden babble of voices as the new arrivals all began to talk at once; the only question that was decipherable in the confusion of noise was one that was repeated by several speakers, though the pages of the guidebook riffled wildly in trying to answer every startled query.

"Where are we?" was the one question that could be understood.

"Fellow councilors!" Shandiph called. "Your attention, please!"

The questions ceased, the book's pages lay still, and the entire group turned to face him.

"You are in the vault where our ancestors placed much of their magic for safekeeping; you were brought here by an ancient spell because we felt that the unexpected wealth of this lost magic was more than we four could handle by ourselves. If you will look around you, you will see that there is far more here than was anticipated; every single thing in this chamber is magical, it appears, and every book here contains arcane knowledge. As may be determined by the ease with which you were brought here, using a single, simple device – beware that you don't step on those shards of glass – much of this magic is extremely potent by our standards. We thought that all of you should have some say in the management of this treasure trove."

"*You* thought so, Shandiph, you and Thetheru," Karag said. "We four were appointed as representatives, and I see no need to waste time in further debate. We were sent to find powerful weapons to use against the overman Garth, and there are undoubtedly powerful weapons here around us. I say that we should find them, using that guidebook, and then go and deal with this overman and his magic sword before he becomes any more dangerous than he already is."

There were a few calls of support from the gathered crowd and several shouted questions; once again, the guidebook tossed pages back and forth, attempting to answer them all at once.

"Shandiph, where are we? Where is this vault?" someone called over the general din. Shandiph looked for the speaker and tried to call an answer.

Deriam and Thetheru were each beset by two or three of their comrades demanding explanations; most of the others crowded around Shandiph, barraging him with questions and opinions. Karag, too, drew his share of attention; the wizard Alagar and Kubal of Tadumuri, both old friends, came toward him. One or two individuals wandered off down the long room, looking at the thousands of trinkets and talismans.

Karag saw an opportunity in this complete disorganization and made his way to the reading stand, where he asked in a low voice, "What are the most powerful weapons in this chamber, and where are they to be found?"

Alagar and Kubal watched with him, saying nothing, as the pages turned and revealed a long list – much too long to be of use.

"Which of these are the three mightiest and most effective?" he asked.

Two pages flipped back, and Karag read, "The Ring of P'hul, on the Chairman's ring finger; the Great Staff of Power, first in the third rack of staves on the right-hand wall; and the Blood-Sword of Hishan of Darbul, fifth in the second rack of blades on the right-hand wall."

"We can't use the Ring," Alagar whispered.

"You both intend to join me; then?"

"Yes, of course," Kubal replied. "These fools will be arguing for hours. They'll thank us when it's done."

"True enough. All right, book, what is the fourth most powerful among the weapons here?"

The book turned a few pages. "The Sword of Koros," Kubal read. "I'll take that."

"I'll take the other sword," Alagar said.

"And I'll take the staff," Karag agreed.

"Karag, what are you doing?" Shandiph called. He had finally noticed that the other was using the guidebook.

"I thought that the book might be able to advise us on how to proceed."

"Has it?"

"No, not yet; give it a few more minutes."

"Well . . ." Shandiph was uncertain. Karag was impetuous, he knew, but usually meant well. Several of the newcomers had given him news that directly concerned Karag, but he was distracted by another question about the guidebook's working before he could tell Karag. He decided to trust Karag for the moment and to wait before telling him that his secret departure from the High King's castle had led to a dispute between the King and the Baron of Sland. Chalkara said that the Baron had accused the King of kidnapping Karag to deprive the Baron of his services. There was a great deal of acrimonious talk going on, though no action had yet been taken.

While Karag and Shandiph spoke, Alagar had been using the book; when Karag looked down again it was to find complete instructions for the use of the three weapons chosen. He read through them quickly, as did Alagar and Kubal.

Shandiph remained distracted; the Baron of Therin had been conjured in his true person, rather than the simulacrum that had come to Kholis, and was therefore able to relay information. The disappearance of the other magicians was creating quite a stir, and Dor's other self, together with Sindolmer of Therin, who had arrived after the foursome had left and therefore been excluded from Shandiph's listing, were trying to calm matters. The coincidence that both the apparent survivors were from Therin did not make their task easier.

Deriam had become entangled in a debate concerning the nature and origin of the crypts, and Thetheru was explaining the red crystal spheres to Sharatha and Miloshir. No one paid any attention to Karag, Alagar, and Kubal.

"What is the quickest means by which we three may be transported, with our chosen weapons, to wherever we may find Garth of Ordunin?"

Karag read the answer, and then closed the book.

"It is yours, Shandiph, to do with as you please," he called.

"Thank you, Karag. I'll want to speak with you in a moment."

"You have no objection if we look around, do you?"

"No, not if you're careful." Shandiph was too busy to be really suspicious; he was trying to answer questions about the vault room even as he asked his own about the Baron of Sland and affairs at the High King's castle.

Moving casually, so as not to draw attention, Karag and his two comrades gathered their chosen weapons, ignoring the questions and comments of the other wizards. When they were armed, Karag opened the first chest on the right and took out a blue crystal sphere very much like the red one that had summoned the majority of the Council.

At that point it became impossible to hide their actions and intentions any longer, and Kubal and Alagar, brandishing their swords, ordered that the pentagram be cleared.

Startled, the other councilors obeyed.

The three stood in the center of the golden star, and Karag announced, "We are going to do what must be done, without wasting any more time. We go to face Garth of Ordunin!" With that, he dropped the blue sphere.

It exploded in a cloud of bright blue smoke; when the smoke cleared instants later, the three wizards were gone.

Chapter Twenty-Three

As Koros reached the top of the first low ridge, Garth turned for a final look at Skelleth. The town's silhouette was subtly changed from the last time he had seen it from this spot, when he had ridden down from Ordunin with his little trading party; a few of the old rooftops were gone, lost to the fires he had spread, and had not been rebuilt. None of the new structures were high enough to be seen from this distance.

The snow, too, changed the outline, blurring the lines and bleaching the surfaces to an even white that made the shadows stand out more sharply.

When last he had ridden the Wasteland Road he had been accompanied by Larth, Galt, and Tand; now Galt was an outlaw and Tand had not yet returned from the Yprian Coast. He wondered what had become of his double-cousin Larth; he had not been among the sixty volunteers. He was probably living safe at home, going about his business as always, never questioning the wisdom of the City Council.

Garth turned his gaze forward once again, then cast a quick glimpse over his left shoulder. The sword's gem was glowing more brightly than usual, he thought. He wondered why; was it pleased to be leaving Skelleth?

There was little he could do about its glow; there was no guarantee that turning back toward Skelleth would make any difference, and he was determined to speak with the Wise Women of Ordunin.

He looked at the road before him – or rather, at the ground ahead of him. He could not be sure that Koros was actually following the Wasteland Road; the snow made it impossible to see where the road lay. He was heading in the right direction and knew the landmarks; he was not concerned about becoming lost.

There was a dip, and then a second low ridge ahead; after that, the road veered to the right somewhat, to follow the lay of the land and avoid the steeper slopes. The snow was smooth and unbroken; no one had passed this way of late.

There was a curious bluish mist hanging in the air above the second ridge; as he watched it seemed to thicken.

It was definitely unnatural, he decided as Koros reached the bottom of the slope. It was a small cloud now, and an utterly impossible shade of blue.

Then, abruptly, the haze was gone, and three men stood atop the ridge looking down at him.

He leaned forward and spoke a quiet word in the warbeast's ear; the beast stopped dead.

He studied the three men. One was tall and thin, with light brown hair, and carried a strange curved sword; he wore a thin gray cloak that flapped open in the breeze, revealing richly embroidered garments underneath. The second was of average size for a human, with thick black hair and beard, and wrapped in a heavy black cloak; he carried a staff of carved wood trimmed with bright metal. The last was large, with a dark complexion and very short, very black hair – and no beard, which struck Garth as odd indeed. He had never seen an adult male human without any beard at all. This last man wore no cloak, but a tunic of black leather trimmed with silver and breeches also of black leather; he carried a cross-hilted broadsword.

The third man fascinated Garth; aside from his beardlessness, this was the second human he had seen with skin as dark as an overman's, or nearly so. The first had been the wizard Shang, in the city of Mormoreth, who had been even darker than this newcomer or than Garth himself.

Judging by the manner of their appearance, at least one of these three was evidently a magician of some sort; Garth wondered whether wizards had some special predilection toward dark skin. Or perhaps there was a land somewhere inhabited by dark-skinned humans, whence many wizards came.

The three men were looking about them, as if unsure where they were and why they were there; Garth watched without moving.

Then the tallest of the three, the one with the curved sword, pointed at him. Garth could not hear his words over the intervening distance, but there was no doubt he was calling his comrades' attention to the overman and warbeast.

Garth had no reason to believe the strangers to be hostile, but he found his right hand reaching up toward the hilt of the Sword of Bheleu. He stopped it and considered.

The sword obviously wanted to be drawn, as he had made no conscious decision to move his hand toward it and would have preferred to use his more ordinary blade. The thing had demonstrated in the past that it wanted to protect him and keep him alive for its own reasons – but it had also demonstrated an incredible bloodlust and eagerness to kill anyone within reach.

These strangers were obviously here by magic; the only explanation for that blue smoke was magic, even if it had been nothing but a means of covering their appearance over the top of the rise, and Garth thought it more likely that the smoke itself had somehow materialized them from thin air. The three men might be wielding the magic themselves, or might be innocent victims – but would innocent victims be carrying drawn swords? And that staff that the center one carried looked very much like a magical device of some sort.

The only defenses Garth had against magic were the feeble natural resistance of magically-created species such as overmen and warbeasts to other magicks, and the much more powerful magic of the Sword of Bheleu.

He decided that his own survival was more important than any danger these three strangers might face from the sword. After all, they were in the Northern Waste, which was overman territory; the accepted border ran along the top of the first ridge. As invading enemies, their deaths would be acceptable. Garth drew the great sword.

He hoped that there would be no deaths.

The man with the staff was moving; he drew a circle in the snow around himself and his companions with the metal-shod tip as Garth watched, and then held the staff horizontally before him, gripped in both hands.

This looked more and more like magic at work, Garth thought; he lifted his own magical weapon in both hands.

The black-bearded man was speaking now, calling out words that reached Garth despite the fifty yards and wind between.

"Yahai Eknissa eknissaye!"

Garth knew that Eknissa was the goddess of fire, and assumed that what he heard was an invocation of some sort; he did not recognize the other two words. He had little time to worry about them before being distracted by their result.

A wall of flame had sprung up from the circle the staff had drawn in the snow, and was spreading outward with incredible speed. It roared up from the snow, melting it instantly as it marched, and reached a height of ten feet or more. Even before it came within twenty yards, Garth could feel its heat.

He raised the sword and summoned a storm to blow out the flames or drive them back toward their creator. He had had considerable practice in summoning storms in his attempts to burn out the sword's power.

The wind rose to a howling gale immediately, and clouds gathered overhead; the flames grew taller, and their advance slowed – but only slightly. Garth watched in dismay as they continued to approach.

The clouds were not yet thick enough to summon lightning, so he could not blast the wizard's staff – and there was no guarantee that that would stop the wall of fire; the death of the basilisk had not reversed the petrifaction of its victims.

The flames were within a dozen feet when he finally allowed the sword to act on its own. It had been tugging at him, but he had resisted it; he did not trust the thing. Now, with the heat beating against him as if he stood opposite the bellows in a blacksmith's forge, he let it have its way.

It twisted in his grip and pointed directly at the advancing barrier. The snow erupted into a second sheet of flame.

For a few seconds Garth did not understand how the sword hoped to save him by starting its own fire; then he saw that the ring had stopped expanding. It could not pass the new fire his sword had started.

The sword's fire spread; when it met the stalled ring, it vanished with a great roaring rush of hot air – and with it, several yards of the wall of flame vanished as well.

With the mystic circle broken, the remaining flames sank down and became nothing but flickering natural fires; when the sparse damp grass that had been under the snow was burned, they died into sputtering remnants, then went out completely, leaving charred earth behind.

The snow was gone and the ground blackened in a broad circle around the three human enchanters, and the heat had melted much of the ground cover well past Garth's own position, but the circle where the wizards stood was still untouched, their feet sunk past their ankles in snow. Garth could not see their faces clearly over the fifty yards distance, but he was sure that they were surprised by the failure of their attack.

Koros growled, and Garth allowed the warbeast to advance. It stopped of its own volition when it reached the edge of the scorched area; the ground was still hot and its paws were sensitive.

There was no need to risk the warbeast, Garth decided; as long as it remained within earshot, he could summon it if he needed it. He prepared to dismount and then stopped, one foot out of the stirrup.

The central wizard was wielding his staff again. Holding it as he had before, he called aloud, *"Yahai Sneg ghyemye, yahai Srig srigye!"*

The final word Garth recognized; it meant "cold."

He had no desire to waste time fighting off one assault after another; he raised the sword and cried aloud his own invocation. *"Melith!"*

Lightning flashed overhead, and thunder exploded deafeningly. He realized he had forgotten to direct the lightning; it had struck nothing. He was still inexperienced at wielding magic.

He had seen no new ring appear when the wizard spoke his spell, but the air about him was suddenly cold, much colder than it had been before the humans had appeared, colder than it had any right to be so early in the season. He ignored it and willed another bolt of lightning into existence; it struck with a blinding brilliance and earth-shaking roar at the feet of the three strangers.

"That was a warning!" he bellowed, slackening the gale he had conjured so that he could be heard. "Annoy me no further!"

"Surrender yourself and your sword, and we will let you live!" shouted back the man with the staff.

Garth began to consider whether he might, in fact, be wise to surrender or at least to inquire about exact terms, but then dropped the idea as a rush of anger flooded through him. He was dimly aware that it was the sword's doing, but that did not give him the power to resist it.

"I am Bheleu!" he screamed. "I surrender to no one!"

The storm roared into redoubled frenzy, and twin lightning bolts bracketed the three wizards. Garth swept the sword through the air above his head, leaving a trail of flame glowing in the air. With a word he sent Koros charging toward them, though his left foot was still out of the stirrup.

He was within a few yards before the wizards could manage any reaction beyond cringing in fear; but before he could strike at them, the central human raised the staff again. This time his invocation was in everyday speech, not archaic phrasing, as he called, "By all the gods, help!"

The staff suddenly blazed with light and Garth was himself again, free of Bheleu's control, though the sword still flamed in his hands. He held the sword in one hand while he used the other to slap Koros on the neck, turning its charge aside before it trampled the wizard into the little patch of snow at his feet. He called for the warbeast to halt.

The other two wizards had turned and fled as the warbeast approached, but the man with the staff had stood his ground.

"Yield, Garth of Ordunin!" he cried.

"Don't be a fool," Garth replied. "You're no danger to me; why should I yield? Who are you, anyway?"

"I am Karag of Sland, and I hold the Great Staff of Power, lost these three centuries!"

Garth looked the man over carefully and decided that even Karag wasn't entirely sure if he was bluffing. Whatever this staff was, Garth guessed that he hadn't had it long.

"Why did you attack me?"

"You have taken the Sword of Bheleu and destroyed Dûsarra and Skelleth with it; you must be stopped before you usher in the true Age of Destruction!"

Garth was grateful that the man's desperate invocation had apparently had the unintentional effect of freeing him temporarily from the sword's control. He might, he thought, be able to settle this peacefully.

"I don't want an age of destruction any more than you do," he replied mildly. "If that staff is as powerful as the sword, though, what do you have to worry about?" As he spoke he tested his hands, and discovered that though his mind might be free, his fingers were not. He regretted that; he had hoped that this over-eager wizard might have solved all his problems for him without meaning to.

His conversation was interrupted abruptly by the return of the tall, brown-haired human, who came lurching back out of the surrounding storm. With a hysterical scream of "Die, monster!" he swung his strange curved sword at Garth's waist; mounted as Garth was, his neck was well out of the man's reach.

With one hand, without thinking about it, Garth brought the Sword of Bheleu around to fend off the attack. The two blades met in a spitting shower of red and white sparks; then the wizard's sword exploded into glittering shards that stitched red gashes across the man's face and chest. Garth was unharmed. He felt a twinge of annoyance and then a renewed surge of fury; the sword was winning out over whatever had restrained it.

He lifted the blade to the sky and lightning blazed down around him, wrapping him in blue-white fire for a brief instant and then jumping to the broken hilt of the Blood-Sword of Hishan of Darbul – though Garth did not know that was its name. The tall human staggered, his mouth open as if to scream, though all sound was lost in the booming torrent of thunder; the blood boiled from the wizard's wounds, and he fell in a charred heap at the warbeast's feet.

The fit of rage passed and, hoping that this death might serve him, Garth tried again to drop the sword. It still held him.

He did not even notice that he was in the center of a blazing pyre; there had been so many pyrotechnic displays in the last few minutes that he had lost track of them. Koros growled, and he looked up from the glowing red jewel.

He was surrounded by flame, but he felt no heat and remained unharmed; something held it back, protecting both him and his mount.

He waved the sword, and the flames parted before him. He found himself looking at the man who called himself Karag of Sland; the man stood, the staff in his hands and the blood draining from his face, directly in front of the warbeast and its rider.

Then, suddenly, red mist swirled out of nowhere and wrapped around the wizard. There was nothing Garth could do in time to stop it, other than slaying the man where be stood, which he chose not to do. He looked around and saw that a similar fog was appearing around the other two wizards, both the live one who was still fleeing some two hundred yards away, and the smoldering corpse.

As he watched, the red stuff vanished again, taking the three humans with it. He had almost expected that to happen.

He gazed around at the area where the battle had occurred. There was a large ring of blackened earth which had now frozen hard, pocked with small craters where lightning bolts had struck. The central circle of snow was mostly a puddle. A few glittering fragments of sword were visible, and a few traces of bright blood.

New snow would come and cover the signs, he knew, but come spring it would be months before anything grew here. It was only a minor work of destruction and a single death, but still he sighed. It seemed that even when the sword did not force him to destroy of its own volition, other forces drove him to destroy in self-defense.

No, he corrected himself, most of this destruction was not his doing, but that of the wizards. He was simply the focus for it. The death, though, was his doing; he regretted that.

This was a new complication in his life. He wondered whether it justified changing his plan to consult the Wise Women. If wizards were to pop out of nowhere everywhere he went, he could hardly keep a visit to Ordunin a secret.

He would move on slowly, he decided; if there were further attacks, he would turn back.

That decided, he took a moment to get his foot securely back in the stirrup and urged Koros forward.

Chapter Twenty-Four

The councilors all stared in horror at the charred corpse that had appeared on the edge of the pentagram, almost ignoring Karag and Kubal.

"What happened?" Shandiph asked at last.

"He can control lightning," Karag answered. He was shaking, the staff that was still clutched in his hands fluttering like a bird's wing.

"How did you survive, then?"

"I don't know. Kubal fled, and I tried to ward him off with the staff. I think it worked, at least temporarily."

"Then the sword is not unbeatably powerful!" someone exclaimed.

Karag shook his head. "I have never seen so much power. I don't mean just the sword, but the staff as well. It felt like a live thing in my hands. Without the magicks in this room, we wouldn't have a chance. He made a storm from nothing with a single gesture, and directed the lightning wherever he chose; the sword burned and spat fire. The staff made a wall of flame that consumed everything it touched, until he turned it back with the sword's flame. He rides a great black monster with fangs as long as my fingers."

Kubal nodded agreement. "We didn't know what we were doing; I didn't know he could be so powerful. I didn't believe Kala when she said that he could summon storms."

"The three of you were all acting stupidly," Shandiph said. "The essence of magic is not power, but subtlety and deception, and poor Alagar paid for your rashness in not thinking of that. As additional folly, you alerted the overman."

"He is no wizard, though," the Baron of Therin said. "He won't know how to defend himself against us. Karag made a natural mistake in thinking that three wizards could handle him, magic sword or no."

"I do not say that they underestimated the overman, but that they underestimated the sword," Shandiph replied. "We need to use subtler methods, methods that the sword cannot counter directly."

"What did you have in mind?" Chalkara asked.

Shandiph replied by crossing to the guidebook, opening it, and asking, "Are there magicks in this chamber that can kill a foe from afar?"

The book turned to a page very near the front, which said, in large, ornate runes, simply, "Yes."

"What are the dozen most effective that can be used without great preparation, how do they work, and where can they be found?"

Pages turned, revealing a list.

"Kala, ready your scrying glass, so that we can see what happens."

"I don't have my glass; it was left in Kholis."

Disconcerted, Shandiph admitted, "I hadn't thought of that."

"There must be a scrying glass here somewhere," Chalkara said. "Ask the book."

A glass was found and given to Kala; she wandered several yards down the room and found a suitable spot to work in.

The magical light Shandiph had conjured was beginning to fade, which suited her well; it was easier to use a glass in dim light. She attempted to summon up Garth's image, and found it impossible. The sword's power still blocked her.

She said as much to the others, who had gathered together most of the devices and spell books the guidebook had listed as necessary for the dozen death-spells.

"I forgot about that entirely," Shandiph said. "I suppose we'll just have to try these, and then go there and see."

"If he resists other magic as well as he resists a scrying spell, I think we had best go prepared for battle."

"I fear you're right," Shandiph agreed. "Let me ask the book what other weapons we might take."

"I already asked that," Karag said. He was beginning to regain his composure. "We took three of the four most powerful – the Great Staff of Power, the Sword of Koros, and something the book called the Blood-Sword of Hishan of Darbul. The book said it was the third most powerful weapon here, after the Staff and the Ring of P'hul, but the Sword of Bheleu shattered it instantly."

There was a glum silence in response to this news.

After a pause, Shandiph asked, "Book, what would you recommend we use against the Sword of Bheleu?"

The page revealed bore a single sentence, which Chalkara read aloud over Shandiph's shoulder. "There is no power in the Council's possession that can withstand the Sword of Bheleu."

"You say there is nothing we can do?"

With a thump, pages turned back to reveal the single ornate word.

"Is there no power that can defeat the wielder of the sword?" Chalkara asked.

"There are two; the Book of Silence and the King in Yellow," Shandiph read.

"Who is the King in Yellow?" Thetheru asked.

A single page turned, and Shandiph said, "I knew this already. It says, 'the immortal high priest of Death.'"

"Where can we find him?" Chalkara asked.

No pages turned, but Shandiph replied, "We don't want to find him; he would be worse than the overman. He is the agent of Death as Garth is the agent of Bheleu."

"Then what of the Book of Silence?" called someone from the back of the little crowd.

"Do you know why it's called the Book of Silence?" Miloshir replied. "To speak aloud a single word written therein will kill anyone but its rightful owner."

There was a somber silence. Herina spoke up at last. "We could draw lots, and the loser would use the Book . . ."

"No, it won't work. The loser would die before completing the spell. It would take one of us for each word of the spell, and I have no idea how long the incantation we want might be."

"Can we find the rightful owner and ask his aid?"

"The Book belongs to the King in Yellow."

"It would seem we are defeated before we have begun," Derelind said.

"We must *try*, at the very least," Veyel replied.

"We must and we will. We will try each of these twelve spells the book led us to. It may be that the book is not infallible and has overestimated the power of the sword; it may be that Garth is not yet fully attuned to the sword's power. We still have a chance."

"Attuned?" Karag snorted. "The overman can summon storms from a clear sky and steer the lightning! How much more control over the sword's magic can he possess?"

"Much more, Karag. The sword's power is virtually limitless."

Kubal shuddered at that.

The discussion broke down after that into several groups of two or three, each working on one or two of the long-range spells. One by one, the death-spells were worked, amid strange chants, evil-smelling smoke, eerie lights, and other by-products of magic. The golden light vanished completely, and lanterns were found to replace it. Several of the councilors had become hungry, and Deriam used the book to locate a bottomless purse that could be made to produce an unlimited supply of biscuits and cakes and a wine flask that never ran dry.

"This is a very useful thing," he remarked as he gulped down the red wine, "though it's hardly a great vintage. I wonder why it was sealed away here?"

Shandiph was watching the last death-spell being worked, which involved an elaborate dance with a very sharp knife. Chalkara was the dancer. He answered absentmindedly, "Someone must have thought it was dangerous."

"How could a wine flask be dangerous?"

"Oh, easily enough, I think."

"How?"

"You could drown someone, I suppose," Amarda the Blood-Drinker suggested, "or flood out a place." She was nursing cuts on her palms from the spell she had helped with and licking off the blood with disconcerting relish. Deriam glanced at her, then quickly looked away again.

"I hadn't thought of that," he admitted.

At that moment the Baron of Therin distracted Shandiph from the dance. "I have news from Kholis," he said.

The Chairman turned and asked, "What is it?"

"An embassy from Skelleth has arrived and is at this moment speaking with the High King; my other self has just entered the audience chamber to hear what they have to say."

"What are they saying?"

Dor paused for a moment, as if listening, then answered, "They say that Skelleth has been burned and many of its people slain as a result of the dead

Baron's madness. They say that a peaceful trade mission of overmen was attacked by the Baron's guards without cause, and the ensuing battle ended with the guardsmen and the Baron all dead, and many others as well."

"That is not what the Seer of Weideth said had happened."

Dor shrugged. "The ambassador is undoubtedly lying. Now he is explaining that the overmen stayed to aid in the rebuilding, and that a man named Saram, once a lieutenant in the Baron's guard, organized the survivors."

Shandiph glanced at where Chalkara was whirling, her knife glinting in the lantern light, and then looked about "Where is the Seer?"

The man from Weideth made his presence known from somewhere behind the Chairman.

"Ah, there you are. Can you say anything of the truth or falsehood of what Lord Dor is telling us?"

"Lord Dor speaks the truth as he knows it, my lord, but of course, that is to be expected, and says nothing about the truthfulness of the ambassador from Skelleth. I cannot know what is true at secondhand, like this."

"You said that the Baron of Skelleth was murdered."

"Oh, yes, he was! I tested that by three separate divinations; he was stabbed from behind without warning, by the Sword of Bheleu, while unarmed."

"Then this ambassador is lying."

"Yes, I suppose so."

"What is he saying now, Dor?"

"He is explaining that Skelleth hasn't enough wood or food to last the winter and asking that the High King send aid and name a new baron, so that the town will flourish as before, despite this unfortunate incident."

"Skelleth hasn't flourished in two hundred years!" Deriam said.

"True enough," Dor agreed. "I merely repeat what I hear."

"Now what's happening?"

"Barach of Sland has interrupted the ambassador's speech; he says that the man is obviously a lying blackguard, and asks that the High King send him to Skelleth to learn the truth of the matter."

"The Baron of Sland *wants* to go to Skelleth?" Thetheru was plainly astonished. He could not imagine anyone wanting to go to such a place.

"That's no surprise," Karag replied. "He has always liked the idea of acquiring a second barony, and was rather annoyed when Skelleth went to someone else – when was it? – twenty-three, twenty-four years ago."

"Even if we do dispose of the overman, it appears that we may have to settle other matters regarding Skelleth," Shandiph observed.

"I would say so," Dor agreed. "The High King has just said that he sees no reason to disbelieve the ambassador and will send what aid he can. He is naming this man Saram as the new Baron of Skelleth, pending his formal presentation at Kholis for confirmation. Barach is raging mad. He's storming out now, calling for his men."

"We will have to patch up this quarrel when time allows," Shandiph said.

"Shouldn't we see to it immediately, before anyone does anything foolish?" Deriam asked.

"No," Shandiph answered, "I think we should tend to what we've begun first and deal with the overman. He's the more dangerous problem." He gestured at Chalkara, who was nearing the end of her ritual. "If these spells have worked, any of them, we should be in plenty of time. If they haven't, then it's all the more important that we handle Garth immediately."

Chalkara completed her dance with a final flourish and flung the dagger to the floor between her feet. According to the book that contained the spell, the blade was supposed to penetrate any floor, even stone, easily and draw blood. The blood would be that of the intended victim.

The knife struck, ringing, and stuck into the stone floor as intended, but only the tip had penetrated; no blood flowed.

"I don't think it worked," Kubal said.

"It may be that the overman was already dead," Derelind said. "After all, we have tried to kill him a dozen times over. We have burned him, choked him, stabbed him, flayed him, smothered him, poisoned him, and sent birds to tear him to pieces."

"I hope that's it," Shandiph said. He leaned on the reading stand and asked the guidebook, "Is Garth of Ordunin dead?"

Pages turned, and he read aloud. "This book is not a true oracle, and answers only questions about magic and arcane information known to the Council of the Most High at the close of the Twelfth Age."

"Try your scrying glass, Kala," someone said.

There was a general chorus of agreement, and Kala withdrew into the darkness with a single candle she had found. The candle came from a chest of similar candles, each of which the book said held a minor fire-elemental; this was supposed to allow it to burn for several days before being consumed.

The others spoke quietly among themselves for several minutes while Kala struggled with her glass. Most consciously did not look at her, but Karag could not resist; he watched and saw the crystal globe glowing a vivid red.

Then Zhinza, who stood nearest Kala, remarked, "I smell cooking meat." An instant later Kala cried out and dropped the sphere. It exploded, and gobbets of semi molten glass spattered in every direction.

Most of the councilors were unhurt, since Kala had stayed well away from the crowd, but Zhinza and Kala received several cuts and burns, and a glowing shard had cut open Sherek's arm. Derelind used the guidebook to locate a healing spell, which Chalkara applied.

The spell stopped the cuts from bleeding and eased most of the burns, but did nothing for Kala's scorched palms.

When that emergency had been dealt with, the twenty councilors looked at one another in the lantern light, each waiting for someone else to speak, until at last Chalkara said, "Now what? The overman is still alive, or else Kala's glass would not have exploded. None of our spells touched him, apparently. What do we do now?"

Shandiph, for once, had no reply; it was Karag who finally answered slowly, "I think I have an idea."

Chapter Twenty-Five

Garth was considering his situation as he rode northeastward along the narrow valley.

He was beginning to doubt that he would find any way out of his dilemma. It looked very much as if the only way to free himself of the Sword of Bheleu was to swear to serve the Forgotten King. After all, he knew that the King was someone unique and uniquely powerful; it might well be that there was nothing and no one else who could control the sword. The three wizards had certainly not given it much of a fight.

If it did finally come down to a choice between the King and the sword, he was unsure which he preferred. Either choice would lead to several unwanted deaths; he knew that he could not hope to restrain the sword forever, and the old man admitted that his great magic would kill many people besides himself.

Of course, the Forgotten King's spell would be a single event, while the sword was an ongoing problem. Furthermore, it was possible that Garth would not live long enough to fetch the mysterious book the King wanted. The book might have been destroyed or irrevocably lost long ago.

If it came down to a simple final choice, then, Garth would choose to serve the Forgotten King again, although he was not happy with that decision, since he did not like or trust the old man. He felt that the King was manipulating him, controlling him as if he were a mere beast of burden, to be ordered about or coerced into obedience when it proved reluctant.

Even that, though, was preferable to being possessed outright by the sword's malevolent power, whatever it was.

He might never find the Book of Silence. His oath to the Forgotten King might lead to nothing. He could not believe, however, that possession of the sword would lead to nothing.

He might somehow contrive to avoid delivering the book, if he did find it. If he worded his oath carefully, he might manage that – or if he broke his oath. He stopped his chain of thought abruptly at that point, and looked at that idea.

No overman, it was said, had ever broken a sworn oath, in all the thousand years since the species first came to exist. Garth certainly had not, though he had taken advantage of poor wording on occasion and events beyond his control had sometimes betrayed him.

To break an oath was said to be an offense against the gods – not just whatever gods one might swear by, but any others that might be listening. Garth would once have dismissed this as superstitious human nonsense; now that he was no longer firm in his atheism he considered it, but dismissed it eventually anyway. Surely the gods had better things to do than to interfere in mortal affairs over mere words.

Furthermore, he had already defied and offended several gods – Tema, Aghad, Andhur Regvos, Sai, and even The God Whose Name Is Not Spoken. He had defiled their temples and slain their priests, yet no harm had befallen him as a result. He did not need to worry about offending gods, he was quite certain.

But to break an oath would be to destroy his own honor, his family's honor, and the honor of his clan and of his entire species. Never again would anyone trust him, nor would he deserve trust. He would be outcast forever from Ordunin and all the Northern Waste, a disgraced exile. That is, this would be so if it became known that he had broken his word.

Even if it did not become common knowledge, though, *he* would know. His honor would be gone. He would be nothing; he would be no true overman. He would be no better than the lowest human in the alleys of Skelleth.

Ordinarily, he would never even have considered such an action. When the only other choices he faced involved nothing but widespread death, however, he had to consider the possibility. He owed it to the innocents that he might be consigning to death. Was his personal honor worth more than their lives?

Tradition said it was; the legends and tales he had heard in his youth said that nothing was more important than honor. There were stories of overmen and even humans who had died rather than be dishonored, who had allowed friends and family to die, who had slain friends and comrades, all in the name of honor.

It was still too early to be so pessimistic, he told himself. He would first ask the Wise Women what he could do to free himself of the sword. If they told him that only the Forgotten King could free him, then he would swear the oath – and most probably, he would keep it. He could not go against all he had been taught.

He hoped, though, that Ao would tell him of another way in which he could be free.

He studied the hills to his left; he was nearing the point at which the road turned northward again, leading over the next few ridges into a much wider valley, beyond which he would have to cross another, higher range of hills – a range that came much closer to being mountains.

The snow hid the details of the ground, but he was fairly certain he recognized an irregular peak ahead. His turn was just to the nearer side of that.

The sun was low in the west. He would have to consider making camp soon; the daylight had faded sufficiently for the glow of the sword's gem to be visible without turning his head. It seemed to be flickering oddly.

It had been a very strange day. First the three wizards had appeared and then vanished after a brief battle; then later a flock of ravens – unusual in itself, since in his experience ravens tended to be solitary – had swooped down within inches of him before veering off and fleeing, in what he suspected was an omen of some sort. He had felt a series of minor discomforts, which he thought might be unpleasant side-effects of the sword's hold on him; there had been a brief choking, a slight fever, and various prickings and pricklings. Each time the sword's glow had brightened briefly. Each had passed quickly, however, without harming him.

Koros growled faintly, and Garth looked carefully at the surrounding terrain. A faint blue mist was forming ahead of him.

He called a command, and Koros stopped.

The blue fog thickened into a sphere of solid smoke and then spread out to either side. Garth watched and saw vague figures within it.

The smoke continued to spread, and Garth realized that he was not going to be facing three wizards this time, but a small army. Already he could see at least a dozen humans.

Then suddenly the smoke cleared, and he had no time to count his attackers. Without knowing how it came to be there, he saw that the great broadsword was in his hand, and a ball of orange fire was coming directly toward him.

The sword moved in his hands, and the ball was consumed by a greater burst of flame.

More attacks were coming at him, several at once; there was a drifting black smoke, another ball of fire, and a shimmering transparent something that slid down the air toward him. The sword blazed into white flame in his hands and twisted to meet each one.

Overhead clouds gathered. Thunder rumbled in the distance.

A dark exultation grew within him with each threat he met and countered; when he sent a fourth fireball bouncing back toward its creator and skewered a whimpering batlike thing, he could contain it no longer and burst into roaring laughter. Lightning spilled across the sky above him, and thunder blended with his mirth.

Still the attacks came; the staff that he had fought earlier was sending wave after wave of flame toward him, while other magic tore the air around him and shook the ground beneath his feet.

He laughed again. Didn't these fools know who and what he was? As ravens dove out of the sky at him, to be incinerated by the sword's fire, he bellowed, "I am Bheleu, god of destruction! Death and desolation follow me as hounds; cities are sundered at my touch, and the earth itself shattered! Who are you that dare to affront me thus?"

His warbeast was shifting beneath him; the unnatural assault had upset it. With a wave of the sword he absorbed its consciousness into his own, making its body a part of him.

"I am Shandiph, Master of Demons, Chairman of the Council of the Most High!" someone answered him; the words were almost lost amid the roar of flame and thunder. "We have come to take the Sword of Bheleu from you, Garth, and thereby prevent the Age of Destruction!"

"Garth?" The overman-thing laughed, and the warbeast growled. "I am Bheleu, fool! Garth is nothing. Garth is my tool and nothing more. He was born that I might live through him. My time is come at last, and nothing can prevent it!"

"You are Garth of Ordunin, an overman who had the misfortune to acquire a sword you could not control, and we are here to take it from you!"

Garth heard the wizard's words, somewhere beneath the conscious self that called itself Bheleu. He struggled to regain control of his body; the god did not even notice.

"I am Bheleu, the destroyer, and I will destroy you all!"

The wind screamed, and the entire world seemed to vanish in a blinding flash of blue-white light. When Garth could see again, Bheleu's hold on him seemed weaker. He looked around and saw that there had been some sort of immense discharge of energy; several wizards were down, injured or dead.

He struggled again to regain control, vaguely aware that around him the surviving wizards were shouting, screaming, and crying.

The outside world vanished again, this time in blackness. He was floating somewhere in infinite empty darkness, and before him was a vague outline of a figure.

It opened baleful red eyes and spoke to him in his own voice, magnified somehow so that it resounded from the very bones of his skull.

"Garth, why do you resist me?"

Confused, uncertain what, was happening, Garth did not answer.

"It does you no good to defy me, Garth. You are my chosen vehicle. I created you in my own image, formed you from conception to birth, shaped your body to house me. You are destined to wield my sword and wreak my will. I have waited since the beginning of time for my age of dominion, and you cannot deny it to me. You will serve me, willingly in the joy of power and destruction, or unwillingly in bondage, for the thirty years I am to rule. The choice is yours. Do you still defy me?"

Garth stared in horror, unable to answer. He had caught a glimpse of the thing's face.

"I have been benevolent so far. I have refrained from destruction on your behalf and allowed you to waste time in useless attempts to free yourself from my power. You still resist, and thus I have deigned to speak to you. I could smash your will and force you to submit, and I will do so if you do not cooperate, but I would prefer to have you savor my triumph with me. You are my chosen; do not make me destroy you."

"I . . . I must think," Garth replied, stalling for time.

"I give you until dawn."

The blackness vanished and the world returned, but Garth could still see, in the back of his mind, the red eyes of the god.

They were his own eyes. As Bheleu had said, Garth was created in his image. The god had Garth's face, distorted somehow into an insane thing of terror.

The wizards were still attacking him, despite the carnage they had suffered. Eldritch flashes of light and color sparked up on every side, and a shimmering golden pentagram had formed in the air around him. The thing was of no consequence; pentacles could bind demons, but not gods.

One of the humans had crept up behind him, and he saw from the corner of his eye that it was the dark-skinned wizard, flinging a blue crystal sphere at him; he swung the sword to meet it in mid-air. It shattered, and blue smoke poured out.

"Twenty leagues due north of Lagur!" someone called, his voice cracking.

The blue smoke expanded and began to wrap itself around Garth. He laughed and blasted the smoke away with a twitch of his blade.

"You sought to dump me in mid-ocean?" He laughed again; he was a mix of both selves, Garth's consciousness with Bheleu's power and knowledge – which he needed to carry on the fight. "Is that the best you can do?" he asked mockingly.

Kubal, still standing where he had crept to fling the teleporting crystal, stared up at the overman. Karag's scheme had not worked. The overman had resisted the spell. Half the councilors were dead already, and the overman was laughing.

Kubal fainted.

Bheleu laughed and brought the sword around, intending to incinerate the unconscious wizard.

Garth fought him. The man had battled to prevent destruction; Garth could do no less. There was no need to kill him.

The sword wavered.

"Perhaps I was too generous. I may not wait until dawn," a voice within Garth said. He alone heard and understood the words.

Bheleu was threatening him. The god did not care to be thwarted. He wanted to kill this feckless wizard here and now, regardless of Garth's reluctance and his avowed intention of allowing Garth freedom to choose his fate.

Garth realized that he could not give in to the god; his choice was no choice at all. He could fight and have his own personality destroyed, or he could acquiesce and cooperate – which would require him to act in a manner alien to him, taking pleasure in killing, surrounding himself with death and chaos. If he chose that course, he would no longer be himself any more than if he forced Bheleu to blot his consciousness out of existence. He had a choice of quick destruction, or slow, subtle, but equally sure destruction.

He had to free himself of the god's domination, and he had to act immediately. Bheleu had given him until dawn, so that was the maximum he could hope for, but it was plain his time might be even shorter; the god did not seem to feel any obligation to live up to his offer, should Garth continue to resist in the interim.

He wished he had never left Skelleth; he might be able to call upon the Forgotten King and surrender to him before Bheleu could prevent it. Here, in the wilderness, he appeared to be doomed.

In despair, he chose to proclaim his defiance rather than yield willingly. There was always a chance that some miracle would save him. He called, in the same voice Bheleu had used, "I would rather serve the Forgotten King and Death himself!"

The sword turned and pointed at Kubal's prostrate form, but before it could spit forth its flame, a bony hand reached up and grabbed the overman's wrist.

"Swear, Garth," the familiar hideous voice said, plainly audible in a sudden silence that descended upon the battlefield.

Garth stared at the hand and the tattered yellow cowl that flapped in the dying wind. He swallowed and realized he could detect no trace of Bheleu's influence upon him. The fire in the sword was dying away, the red gem's glow dimming.

The gem went black.

Garth remembered that the old man had always seemed to know more than he should. He must have known what was happening here. It was nevertheless a mystery how he had appeared, unscathed, in the midst of the battle, at exactly the right moment. Garth realized that there were still attackers on all sides and said, "The wizards . . ."

"They will not harm us," the Forgotten King replied. "Swear that you will fetch me the Book of Silence."

Garth looked down at Kubal. He knew nothing about the man, save that he was a wizard who had come to halt the Age of Bheleu. He would die if Garth did not swear the oath asked of him.

All the wizards would die and hundreds more in time. Bheleu had said that his age would last for thirty years. Garth had not thought of it in those terms; he had thought of the duration of the sword's control as indefinite and vague. Thirty years was definite, and far longer than anything he had thought about.

Thirty years with no control of his own actions; thirty years of killing anyone who opposed him, rightly or wrongly – thirty years of aimless, wanton destruction and death! Garth could not face that. Anything was better than that. He had killed too often already, ended too many lives that were not his to end.

He would not give in to either destruction or death; he would not betray himself and others in that way.

"I swear," he said, "that if you tell me where it can be found, I will bring you the Book of Silence."

"After you bring it, you will aid me in the magic for which I require it. Swear!"

"I will aid in your magic."

The old man's other hand reached up and plucked the great sword casually from Garth's numbed fingers. "I will keep this," he said, "as a token of your good faith."

The words stung, but Garth nodded. He looked around at the wizards.

They stood, motionless, about him.

The Forgotten King held up the Sword of Bheleu and said, "I send you to your homes."

Blue mist gathered around each of the living wizards, thickened, and then vanished, taking them with it and leaving several corpses strewn across the valley, sprawled on the blasted earth. The snow had been melted away for well over a hundred yards in every direction.

"Won't they just return?" Garth asked.

"No. They have the war between Sland and Kholis to keep them busy, and they have been sealed away from the old magicks."

Garth had no idea what the old man was referring to. He gazed about regretfully at the dead. They had brought matters to a head sooner than he had wished; he had never had the chance to ask the Wise Women whether he had another course of action available. He was free of the sword now, but at a price to himself that seemed terrible indeed.

He had sworn an oath he had no intention of fulfilling; his honor was gone.

Chapter Twenty-Six

Haggat put down his new scrying glass and stared at it thoughtfully. He was not entirely pleased with the course events had followed, but it would do. The Council of the Most High had suffered badly, though it was not destroyed. The overman Garth yet lived, but he no longer possessed the Sword of Bheleu and could therefore be dealt with by the cult's ordinary methods. That was all satisfactory.

The yellow-garbed figure might be a problem, however. Haggat did not know who or what he was, but he obviously controlled considerable power, judging by the ease with which he had taken the sword from Garth and apparently rendered it harmless. The scrying glass would not show him directly, any more than it had been able to show Garth while the sword's power shielded him, but Haggat caught glimpses while watching Garth's slow journey back to Skelleth. The man in yellow tatters had walked at his side the entire distance and occasionally come partially into view. His face had never been visible at all, not even for the briefest of glimpses. He carried the sword as if it weighed nothing and seemed unbothered by cold or fatigue from the long walk – though it was hard to be sure from such fleeting images.

He probably wasn't anybody important, Haggat decided finally. He was some obscure wizard who had chanced upon a spell that could control the sword, at a guess. He was nothing to worry about.

Anyway, it was Garth who concerned the cult. The death of the former high priest had yet to be avenged. Something would have to be done about that.

Shandiph was a wanderer and had no true home of his own; he materialized in Chalkara's chambers in Kholis, side by side with the court wizard, and then collapsed onto the rug. He had survived the great blast, but his injuries were serious. He had remained upright, casting spells, only through force of will.

Chalkara was unhurt; she bent over him and tended to his injuries as best she could, while shouting for the servants.

"Where are the others?" he managed to ask.

"I don't know," she replied. "That . . . that whatever-it-was said it was sending us home; perhaps the others are in their own homes now."

"They aren't all dead?"

"No, no. They're not. I saw that many still lived."

"That's good." His head fell back on the cushion she had slid beneath it.

"Shandi . . . who *was* that? How could he do all that?"

"I think it was the King in Yellow," Shandiph answered.

"He has the sword now."

Shandiph shook his head slightly. "He can't use it. Only the god's chosen one can use it."

"Then it's all over?"

He nodded, weakly.

A servant appeared in the doorway, staring in astonishment.

"Don't just stand there," Chalkara snapped, "Go find a physician!"

The girl nodded and vanished, her running footsteps echoing in the stone corridor.

Chalkara remained, kneeling over Shandiph's body, praying to the Lords of Eir that he wouldn't die.

There was shouting outside his door; Karag dropped the last splintered fragment of the Great Staff and worked the latch.

Servants and guardsmen were hurrying past; he reached out a soot-blackened hand and stopped a rushing housemaid.

"What's happening?" he croaked.

"Oh, my lord wizard, you're back!"

"Yes, I'm back. What's going on?"

"The Baron has just returned from Kholis, my lord, and they say he's angrier than anyone has ever seen him! The High King has again denied him the Barony of Skelleth, he says, and kidnapped his wizard – he means you! Oh, you had better go and see him at once!"

Karag nodded. "I will go immediately." He released the woman's arm, and she ran off.

He looked down at himself. He was filthy, his cloak was in tatters, but he was unhurt; the staff had protected him. Then that great burst of light had shattered the staff, and he had been certain he was about to die. He remembered that.

Kubal had crept up behind the overman, as his plan called for, while Chalkara drew the pentagram, and he had used the transporting spell, but it hadn't worked; the sword had absorbed it somehow. The overman had laughed; Karag remembered that with painful clarity. The overman had laughed at his scheme.

Then there had been a stranger in a ragged yellow cloak at the overman's side, taking the sword from him – and then he was here, in his own room.

It didn't seem to make much sense.

There was more shouting somewhere, and he decided against taking time to clean himself up. The Baron would be mad enough with him as it was. He joined the hurrying crowd in the passageway and made his way down to the great hall.

As he walked in the door, the Baron, standing on the dais, immediately caught sight of him.

"There you are, traitor! Have you returned to beg my forgiveness?"

"What have I done, my lord? How did I come here?" He had decided instantly upon his approach; he would claim to remember nothing of the last few days. Let the Baron think he had been kidnapped.

The Baron glared at him for a long moment, then said, "All right, I will accept you back, and you will tell me later what became of you. Right now I have more important matters to attend to. I have abrogated the covenant and declared war upon the Baron of Kholis, who calls himself King. My men are preparing to march even now, and the messengers I sent back from the false king's castle have had siege engines built. You, wizard, will aid me in this war with your spells."

Karag stared up at his master in dismay.

Garth sat quietly at the Forgotten King's table in the King's Inn, staring at his mug of ale. He and the old man had traveled all night and half the following morning to return to Skelleth, and Garth had then slept away the rest of the day. When he awoke, the King was back in his corner as if nothing had happened. There was no sign of the sword.

Garth had gotten his ale and seated himself, but neither had spoken.

Finally, the overman said, "It would seem that the Age of Destruction is averted; what does that do to the reckoning of time?"

"Lessened, not averted," the old man replied.

"Only lessened?"

"Yes. Already the Kingdom of Eramma is destroyed by civil war."

"It is?"

The old man nodded.

Garth wondered at that. He saw no sign of any war, and no news of one had reached him since his return to Skelleth. Still, he knew that the Forgotten King had knowledge beyond the ordinary.

"That's unfortunate. Wars are wasteful and unnecessary."

The King did not reply.

There was a moment of silence, and then Garth asked, "Who were those wizards? Why did they attack me?"

"The Council of the Most High, as they call themselves, is sworn to preserve peace," the old man answered.

"Will they stop the war, then?"

"They will try and fail."

"Might they not attack me again – or you?"

"No. They have no magic powerful enough, and are scattered and weakened."

"They seemed powerful to me."

"They drew upon the vault where their ancestors stored away much of their power. I have sealed the vault against them."

"Might they be able to stop the war, if they had this old magic?"

The Forgotten King shrugged.

Garth sipped his ale, then asked, "When will you send me after the Book of Silence?"

"When I remember where it is."

"When you remember? Then you knew once?"

The King nodded.

Garth sipped ale again, and asked, "Have you any idea how long it will take you to remember?"

The King replied, "I know that it was I who moved the book from its place in Dûsarra, because no one save you and I can carry it and live. That is all I know. I may recall where I left it tomorrow, or not for thirty years. Until I do, do not bother me. You are free to do as you please, so long as you do not leave Skelleth for any extended period of time, until I remember. Now go away."

Garth kept his face impassive as he picked up his mug and moved to another table. When he was sure that the old man could not see him, he allowed himself a bitter smile.

The King had made an unusually long speech and an unusually careless one. He had failed to say what an extended period of time was, and Garth found no problem in thinking a year or two would not be excessive. The old man himself had freed Garth from much of the restraint his oath would have placed upon him; no one need know he was forsworn for some time yet.

Anything might happen before the Forgotten King remembered; he might die, Garth might die, or the oath might be renounced. Garth's false semblance of honor might be retained for years, perhaps even for the rest of his life.

He knew it to be a false semblance, for he had given his oath in bad faith. He gulped down the rest of his ale and signed to the innkeeper for another.

He wondered whether there might not be a higher honor in sacrificing his name and good word for the lives of others.

No, he told himself, he would not delude himself with such false excuses.

The innkeeper approached with a fresh mug, but before he could place it on the table a sudden loud noise drew the attention of both overman and servitor. There was a burst of shouting and much rattling and thumping somewhere outside the King's Inn.

After a moment of ongoing racket, the unmistakable roar of a warbeast sounded, and the taverner dropped the mug in surprise, denting the pewter vessel and spattering cold ale across the floor and Garth's legs. The overman paid no attention; he shoved back his chair, rose, and strode to the door to see what was happening, while behind him the innkeeper wiped at the floor with his apron.

Garth had a moment of fear that a new battle had begun and that Skelleth was perhaps to be destroyed all over again. Could the King have been wrong about the wizards? Were they attacking anew?

He dismissed such pessimistic thoughts almost immediately; the sounds were not those of battle, nor of any destructive magic he had yet encountered. There was a cheerful note to the shouting.

He paused in the doorway and looked out. Directly before him was the dark hole where the Baron's mansion had stood, but beyond it the marketplace was bright with torches and crowded with people and animals. The sun had been down for the better part of an hour, so this gathering was no ordinary trading.

There were men, women, and overmen in the market, as well as several warbeasts and oxen. Most of the people, of whatever species, appeared to be clustered about a pair of warbeasts and a small group of overmen.

Curious, and with nothing to prevent him from doing as he pleased, he marched down the ramp into the cellar pits, across the floor, and up the opposite slope toward the square. As he emerged he spotted Saram in the midst of the mob, looking about wildly; Frima was near him, and Galt was approaching from the opposite direction.

Garth looked over the central grouping; with a start, he recognized the warbeasts and one of the overmen. Tand and his party had returned.

The apprentice trader looked exhausted, and at least one of his companions wore a bloody bandage. Behind him, Garth realized for the first time, were several overmen he had never seen before, wearing strange and outlandish attire – bright cloaks, enameled armor, flaring helmets. Most of them stood quite tall, taller than Garth or most other overmen of the Northern Waste. There were men as well, dressed similarly, and the oxen he had noticed before he now realized formed a line, drawing carts and wagons.

Tand's mission to the Yprian Coast had obviously been successful; he had brought back a full caravan. Garth's bitter gloom dissipated in pleased surprise; he had held little real hope for Tand's errand after his own plans had been shattered by the Sword of Bheleu, the City Council's disavowal of his actions, and the disastrous battles with the wizards. He had somehow assumed, after all that, that nothing could ever go right again.

Saram had spotted him and was calling and waving; Garth could not make out any words over the general hubbub, but it was plain that Saram wanted to speak with him. Accordingly, he shoved his way into the crowd, bellowing, "Make way! Make way!"

Boots alternately sticking and sliding in the snow and mud underfoot, Garth finally managed to come within earshot of the acting Baron of Skelleth.

"Garth!" Saram called. "Do you have any money?"

"What?"

It was Tand who replied. "These people have brought stocks of food, furs, and other goods, but they demand to see payment before they will allow any to be unloaded. There is nothing in Skelleth they wish to trade for; I promised them gold, told them that Ordunin was rich in gold."

"Aye!" a new voice said in a harsh and alien accent. "The lad said there was gold to be had!"

"There is!" Garth called back. He turned back toward the King's Inn and bellowed at the top of his lungs, "Ho! Koros!"

He had left the warbeast in an alley at one side of the Inn; there were still too few buildings under roof in Skelleth to permit the stables to be used for mere beasts rather than homeless humans. Koros answered with an audible growl and emerged into the light of the market's torches.

Garth called again, and the monstrous beast trotted forward. Disdaining the earthen ramps, it leaped down into the cellar pits and then out again on the market side and made its way across the square toward its master.

The crowd parted before it, and it walked in silent majesty down a broad aisle to Garth's side.

He took a sack from behind the saddle and pulled out a handful of Aghadite coins that glittered rich yellow in the firelight.

Somewhere someone in the crowd applauded loudly, and the faces of the Yprians, half-hidden beneath their curious helmets, broke into smiles.

"You see?" Tand said with perceptible relief. "I did not lie."

"You did not lie, little one," agreed the Yprian spokesman. "Let the bargaining begin!"

Garth lost track of what was happening for several minutes as the crowd gathered around the ox-drawn wagons with much loud talking. He made his way nearer; the presence of Koros at his heel meant that he need not fight the throng, which parted before the warbeast's fangs like snow before flame.

When he reached the caravan he saw that the villagers were unloading grain, furs, and other goods from the wagons, with Yprian humans keeping careful tally of what was taken, and the Yprian overmen overseeing the operation, making certain that everything went smoothly and no pilferage occurred. As each cart or wagon was emptied of what the people of Skelleth wanted, the man who had been watching it brought the listing of what had been taken and what was left to the group by the warbeasts where Tand, Saram, and several Yprians took note and added the items to their own listings. Galt had made his way in from the other side of the crowd and was watching with evident interest.

Frima was shut out, being far too short to see above the shoulders of the traders; she came over, eyes shining in the torchlight, to speak to Garth.

"Isn't it wonderful?" she exclaimed.

"It is, indeed," Garth agreed.

"There's enough here to last half the winter!"

Garth could not help wondering aloud, "But what of the other half?"

"Oh, don't worry! We'll manage something! Saram won't let Skelleth starve."

Garth noted where she put her trust. "You seem pleased with Saram's company," he remarked.

"Oh, I love him! He's so kind and gentle! Thank you, Garth, for rescuing me from Dûsarra and bringing me here!"

Garth found himself amused by her shift in loyalties, but before he could reply, Saram, Tand, and an Yprian suddenly drowned out other conversation, debating the value of Yprian wine in belligerent shouts. Saram, quickly outmatched by the superhuman bellowings of the two overmen, dropped out and tried to settle grain prices with another of the caravan's attendants.

Galt noticed Garth's presence and came over to speak.

When the debate died suddenly with Tand's concession that even such a poor vintage was worth a pennyweight of gold for every twenty skins to a starving village, Galt remarked, "We are doing well. Our gold buys here seven times what it brought in Lagur."

"Fortunate indeed, since my supply is not unlimited; Tand has just sworn away half a pound of gold on wine and spices, if I heard right."

"Yours is not the only gold in Skelleth; we'll take up a collection when time permits. And do not think Tand wastes the gold; we can send some of Saram's people to Ordunin with those wineskins and spice jars and bring you at least triple your money. You've got the trade you wanted, Garth."

Garth nodded and watched.

Half an hour later the trading was finished; the Yprian oxcarts were mostly empty, and Garth's gold was approximately halved. Skelleth's people were scattering to wherever they currently made their homes, makeshift for most, permanent for a lucky few; the food and goods purchased were being stored in one of the new houses, under the supervision of several of Saram's ministers, for later distribution, save for furs and warm clothing that had been handed out to the old, the ill-clad, and the children of the village. The Yprians themselves made camp in the market, where they could keep a good eye on their profits and their remaining goods. Garth, Tand, Galt, Saram, and Frima gathered in the King's Inn for a round of drinks to celebrate the evening's events before retiring.

There was much congratulation of Tand and his fellows, and the apprentice trader remarked in reply, "It was mostly luck; they were eager to trade. In fact their leader, Fargan, tells me he's planning a second expedition, to be made with sledges instead of wagons, now that the snows have come."

"We can use it," Saram said. "And we'll want to buy some of those sledges, or build our own, and send them up to Ordunin, Galt tells me."

"There would be a fine profit in it," Galt agreed.

"I might send a party to Ur-Dormulk as well," Saram mused.

No one answered him; they were all tired and thirsty and preferred to drink.

Garth leaned back in his chair, which creaked warningly beneath his weight, and sipped wine. He smiled to himself.

False oath or no, and whatever the state of his personal honor, there was no denying that he had done at least some good here. The gold he had brought from the temple of Aghad and the knowledge of overmen on the Yprian Coast acquired in Dûsarra had saved Skelleth from starvation. The trade he had sought was at last a reality, and Ordunin would be free of Lagur's monopoly. He was himself free of the Sword of Bheleu. His enemies were defeated, and the Baron of Skelleth dead.

Things might be better, but for the present they would do.

Book Four:
The Book of Silence

Chapter One

The last caravan had departed ten days before, and the next was not expected for at least a fortnight. Skelleth's market lay still and almost empty in the watery sunlight of early spring. No merchants or farmers disturbed its silence, though a few loafers and strolling pedestrians were in sight. On the east side of the square the door of the new Baron's house was closed, indicating that its occupants were not to be disturbed. Garth, one of only two overmen still in Skelleth, sat in the King's Inn, staring out the window at the lifeless market, with nothing to distract him from his own sour mood and gloomy thoughts.

No news had come down from the Northern Waste since the last snows had melted. That meant that Garth had received no word of his family, nor a report about his latest petition to the City Council of Ordunin, asking that his sentence of banishment from the Waste be revoked. He was still an exile from his homeland, stranded in Skelleth for lack of anywhere better to go.

From the overman's point of view Skelleth was not a particularly pleasant place to dwell, but it did have certain advantages. First, it was on the border, the closest human habitation to his native city of Ordunin; therefore, his family could visit him more easily here than elsewhere, and his petitions and letters to the Council could be delivered more quickly.

Second, he was on good terms with the local rulers. Saram, Baron of Skelleth, before being elevated to his present position, had been the closest thing Garth had to a human friend. The Baroness Frima was the only other person who might possibly be considered for that title; Garth had brought her to Skelleth himself, after rescuing her from a sacrificial altar in her native city of Dûsarra. It was he who had introduced Frima to her husband.

Furthermore, the Treasurer and Minister of Trade was the former master trader, Galt of Ordunin, the only other overman still in Skelleth. Garth had brought him down from the Waste to aid in opening trade between Skelleth and Ordunin. That trade was flourishing now, despite the fact that Galt, like Garth, was under sentence of exile.

Third, although the local populace did not, in general, like or trust Garth, it had learned to accept his presence. The people of other human towns might not be so accommodating. Three centuries had passed since the Racial Wars between human and overman had dwindled away to nothing, but hatred, Garth knew, could linger long after its cause was forgotten.

Fourth, at least at the moment, Skelleth was at peace, and that was an increasingly rare distinction. Although the news from the lands to the south and east and west tended to be muddled and sometimes contradictory, Garth knew well that most of the world was at war. No one, including the Eramman barons themselves, seemed to have a clear idea which side any given baron was on in any given war, yet by all accounts that uncertainty had not impeded the fighting one whit. The greater wars provided the excuse for settling old border squabbles or for simple raiding and looting. The civil war in Eramma, begun almost three years earlier when the Baron of Sland rebelled against the High King at Kholis and declared him to be a false king and foul usurper, had settled down into an apathetic lack of cooperation after Sland had been defeated in a long and messy battle. The war between Eramma and Orûn, which had been launched by the opportunistic King of Orûn in hopes of taking advantage of Eramma's seeming dissolution, appeared to have reached a bloody stalemate along a front somewhere to the southeast of Skelleth. Despite the justification of an ancient border dispute, the war was not popular in Orûn and had created such discontent that there were now rumors of impending civil war in that land as well.

Vague reports came in of wars in the western realm of Nekutta, though no one seemed to know who was fighting whom, and no word at all reached Skelleth from Mara, Amag, Tadumuri, Yesh, or the other lands of the far south.

A possible fifth reason for Garth to stay was a result of the fact that Skelleth was peaceful and in a far happier state under Saram than it had ever been under his predecessor. With so many of the world's trade routes disrupted by war and insurrection, Skelleth's very worthlessness had helped to make it a center of commerce. No conqueror in his right mind would bother with so desolate a piece of land, so far from all the traditional caravan roads; that left Saram and his patchwork government free to pursue untraditional trade wholeheartedly and unhindered. The merchants of Skelleth, with their lord's active encouragement, dealt impartially with the men of Eramma, the overmen of the Northern Waste, and the mixed society of the Yprian Coast. With no assets but peace, a willingness to trade, and a manageable location, the town had grown prosperous for the first time in mortal memory.

It had also, in Garth's opinion, grown placid and boring.

No one else seemed to share his feeling. Galt was too busy buying and selling, planning new routes and new methods, or setting prices and taxes and tariffs to be bored. He had become far wealthier than any other overman since the Racial Wars, yet he appeared interested only in expanding trade, enriching the treasury, and acquiring still greater wealth.

Saram seemed content to enjoy the rewards of his new position as Baron while others did the work. He held elaborate feasts to greet every new envoy or caravan master, dressing himself in fine furs and embroidery – overman work, imported from Ordunin – and growing steadily plumper, thus losing the trim fighting form he had had when he served as a lieutenant in the guard under the last hereditary Baron of Skelleth.

Frima didn't appear to mind her husband's added weight. She had arrived in Skelleth with nothing; even the clothes on her back had been borrowed from Garth. She had been no one of importance, a tinker's daughter who worshipped the night-goddess Tema and was kidnapped by the rival cult of Sai, goddess of pain. Garth had rescued her and brought her to Skelleth against her will, leaving Dûsarra, long the greatest city of Nekutta, devastated by fire and plague. He had not wanted the inconvenience of caring for her and had turned her over to Saram. That had led to their marriage, and thus to her present position as Baroness. She seemed far more grateful to Saram, who had taken her in, than to Garth, who had saved her life. Though she still treated Garth as a friend, her primary interests in life now were pleasing Saram and enjoying their sudden wealth. Despite certain disappointments – her only child so far, a son, had been born dead – she was happy. She did not find her new station at all tedious or boring.

The other humans of the village might have been bored, but Garth ignored them entirely. They, in turn, avoided him for the most part. They could not forget that it was Garth who had murdered the old Baron some thirty months earlier, Garth who had led a company of overmen in the sacking and burning of the village. Men, women, and children had died. All the Baron's guardsmen had perished except the disgraced Saram, who had been removed from the guard for refusing to kill Garth in a previous confrontation. It had been this elimination of all other candidates, rather than any real qualifications for the job, that had made Saram the new Baron of Skelleth.

Galt had gradually been accepted and forgiven; his part in the battle had been small, and his trader's expertise had so benefited the village since its reconstruction that he was now something of a hero. Garth, however, remained an outcast.

At first there had been others among the surviving overmen who had chosen to stay in Skelleth after its destruction, and even after the rebuilding had been completed, but they had gradually drifted away with the passing months. Some had returned home to the Northern Waste and been pardoned for their part in the attack, though the Council steadfastly refused to pardon Galt and Garth, the two supposed leaders. A few had gone to explore the Yprian Coast and had not returned. One had been sent a special envoy to the court of the High King at Kholis, whom Skelleth's government still recognized as the rightful lord of all Eramma.

At one point there had been talk of using the overmen as the nucleus of a new company of guardsmen, but nothing had come of it; Skelleth had no military at all at present, save for the handful of warbeasts that the overmen had brought. The great animals were now tended by a special contingent of the Baron's staff, an entirely human contingent. Garth believed this to be the first time in history that warbeasts had been under human care.

He had considered demanding that he be put in charge of the creatures, on the grounds that it was not fitting for warbeasts to be tended by mere men and women, but he had never actually done so. He had feared that he would be turned down, as he had been turned down for every other duty in Skelleth. To be refused a position as a keeper of beasts would be too much for his pride; he preferred not to risk it. There had been enough blows to his self-esteem already.

The aversion to his presence that the townspeople displayed did not bother him; he was accustomed to it, could understand it, and furthermore cared very little for the opinions of most humans. There were, however, other matters.

His three wives, one by one, had come to Skelleth to see him, once the City Council had revoked his chief wife Kyrith's house arrest, imposed for her part in the sacking of Skelleth. Each had come, but each had refused to give up her home in Ordunin to join him in exile.

His children had visited as well, accompanying trading caravans, but he had not even troubled himself to ask them to stay; they were old enough to fend for themselves and make their own homes without his meddling.

Overmen did not have the strong family ties that humans had, but the triple rejection by his wives, and the failure of any of his five offspring to volunteer to settle in Skelleth, still hurt.

The City Council had refused petition after petition, so that he could not rejoin his wives in Ordunin. The councilors had, in truth, not even taken the time to consider his requests; they were too busy trying to deal with the worsening depredations of human pirates along their coasts and could spare no time from that obsession to discuss clemency for a troublesome renegade prince. Garth had tried to argue, by proxy, that he had fought pirates before and could be of sufficient value in fighting them again to make his pardon a real public benefit, but the Council had continued to ignore him nonetheless.

Things had started to go wrong when he found the so-called Sword of Bheleu in Dûsarra. Until then his word had been good and his actions his own, but at his first sight of the weapon he had begun to lose control. He had taken it from the altar of Bheleu, god of destruction, without any conscious decision to do so, and thereafter had been seized every so often by fits of what appeared to be a form of bloodthirsty madness. He had gradually come to realize, though, that some external power was possessing him, using the sword as a conduit. Even knowing that, he had been unable to free himself.

As the power had gained in influence and clarity, it had declared itself to him, claiming to be Bheleu himself, come to assert his dominance over the dawning Fourteenth Age, the Age of Destruction, through his chosen mortal host.

Garth had declined to serve willingly as host to the god, if god it truly was. His refusal had done little good; the god had controlled him anyway, and he had been unable to put down the sword.

While under the sway of the god and his sword, Garth had slain the previous Baron of Skelleth and destroyed much of the village.

In the days that had followed, as he became more aware of the sword's nature and seemingly limitless magical power, his companions had grown to trust him less and less. That had been the period when Skelleth's new government had taken shape, and Garth had been excluded on the basis of the madness the weapon had induced. He had not argued with that decision; he had been conscious of his own erratic behavior and therefore had been far more concerned with freeing himself of Bheleu's control than with village politics.

The sword was a magnificent weapon, a great two-handed broadsword with an immense red gem in its pommel. It was supernaturally indestructible, able to cut through stone or metal with ease, and could control the elements, summon or disperse storms, even shake the very earth. It gloried in fire and could burn in a hundred strange ways without being consumed. Had it not been under the evil aegis of Bheleu, dedicated to wanton destruction, Garth would have been proud to be the chosen wielder of such a thing.

As it was, though, he had wanted nothing but to free himself and he had at last done so. He no longer had the sword. The sword alone had been responsible for his madness, so that with its loss he was himself again; for these two years and several months past, he had been as sane and trustworthy as ever in his life, yet he was still not allowed to hold any post in Skelleth's little bureaucracy for fear he would again turn berserk. He resented this exclusion.

Perhaps the deepest hurt to his pride and self-esteem, however, was a personal matter, one closely tied to the malevolent power of the Sword of Bheleu and to his freedom from that power. The voice of the professed god of destruction had told him that he, Garth, had been born to serve Bheleu; indeed, he alone had been able to wield the sword, and on his own he had been utterly unable to resist its hold.

He had not freed himself alone.

Just to the north of its market square Skelleth had an ancient tavern called the King's Inn, and in this tavern dwelt an old man who called himself the Forgotten King. It was the presence of this individual that, more then anything else, made Skelleth a center for important events.

Garth was not entirely sure whether, on balance, the King's presence was good or bad.

He had originally come to Skelleth seeking the King, because an oracle had told him that only the Forgotten King could grant him the eternal fame he had, at that time, thought he wanted. He had returned to Skelleth a second time, after getting over that particular aberration of desire, because the King had pointed out the possibility of trade. He had gone to Dûsarra at the behest of the mysterious old man and had brought back Frima, now the Baroness, as well as the Sword of Bheleu and the knowledge of trading prospects on the Yprian Coast. His life, and the influence he had upon Skelleth, seemed to have been inextricably linked to the old man since Garth first left Ordunin.

In Dûsarra he had learned something of the King's history; the old man was apparently the one true high priest of the god of death, the chosen of The God Whose Name Is Not Spoken, just as Garth was the chosen of Bheleu. As such, the King could not die; he had lived through several ages and now desired nothing but the death that was denied him.

In pursuit of his own destruction, the Forgotten King had sent Garth on several errands. He sought to perform some great suicidal magic; from various clues, Garth had tentatively decided that the old man hoped to manifest the Death-God himself in the mortal world, so that the King might renounce the bargain made so long ago. The problem was that the proposed magic, whether Garth had correctly determined its nature or not, would involve many deaths, by the King's own admission. Garth did not care to contribute to unnecessary deaths and had therefore refused to aid the King further.

Then, though, the Sword of Bheleu had possessed him, and there was no power Garth could find that could free him from it, save the power of the strange old man. Of all the Lords of Dûs, the dark gods, only the god of death was more powerful than the god of destruction; thus only the chosen of the Final God, in his own right perhaps the most powerful wizard who had ever lived, could break the link between Bheleu and his chosen one.

To free himself, therefore, Garth had sworn to aid the Forgotten King. He had promised to fetch for him the final item needed to complete his magic, an object of great arcane power that he called the Book of Silence. Garth had sworn that oath knowing he had no intention of keeping it, and the suppressed knowledge that he was an oathbreaker, a being devoid of honor, in thought if not yet in deed, had gnawed upon him ever since.

As an injured man would probe at an open wound, fascinated by the pain, Garth found himself haunting the King's Inn and watching the Forgotten King for hours on end. The King had told him, when first he swore his oath, that he was free to roam, as long as he checked back every so often. The old man had not yet told him where the mysterious Book of Silence might be found; he said that he had left it somewhere, centuries ago, and was trying to recall where. When he did remember, Garth would be sent to retrieve it. Until the memory returned, Garth could do as he pleased.

There was nothing else, however, that he felt any need to do, and so he stayed in Skelleth, alternately wandering aimlessly through the streets and sitting silently somewhere, glowering at the village, as he now sat in the King's Inn and glowered at the quiet marketplace.

The Forgotten King was there as well, seated at his usual table. His presence there, at almost any time the tavern was open for business, was so reliable that he was thought of by the villagers not so much as a regular patron, but as a permanent fixture, like the dark wooden paneling of the walls or the heavy oaken tables. Day after day the old man sat alone, unmoving and silent, in the back corner beneath the stairs, wrapped in his ragged yellow mantle, his face hidden by his tattered cowl.

As he had a hundred times before, Garth turned away from the window and its view of the square and stared instead at the ancient human.

The King gave no sign that he was aware of the overman's scrutiny, but Garth had no doubt that he knew he was being watched.

Half a dozen more ordinary humans were in the tavern and they had all certainly noticed the overman's presence. Most had seen him turn away from the window as well. Overmen were unmistakable, and highly distinctive in Skelleth. Garth's size, quite aside from any other details, marked him as something different from the common run of humanity; he stood almost seven feet in height, but was so heavily muscled as to look almost squat. He dwarfed the chair he sat upon and seemed out of proportion with the entire taproom, though in truth he was of only average size among his own species. His eyes were large and red, the oversized irises bright blood-red, though his pupils were as round and black as any human's. Unlike human eyes, no white showed, only black pupil and red iris.

His hair was dead straight, dead black, coarse, and thick; it reached his shoulders and no farther, though he had never cut it. Sparse black fur covered his entire body, save his hands and feet and face. Where no hair or fur hid it, his skin was leathery brown hide, like that of no other species that ever existed and certainly unlike anything human.

His face was as beardless as a woman's; overmen grew no facial hair, and his body fur stopped well short of his chin. His cheeks were sunken by human standards, normal to his own kind. He had no nose, but two close-set slit nostrils. To human eyes, a healthy overman bore an unsettling resemblance to a human skull; the hollow cheeks, missing nose, great red eyes, high forehead, and hairless jaw all contributed.

Garth's hands, too, were unlike a human's. Rather than having a single thumb at one side, his hands had both the first and fifth fingers opposable, making possible acts of manipulation that humans had trouble even imagining.

It was hardly surprising that men and women feared overmen, as they feared anything that seemed monstrous and strange. Nor was it startling, therefore, that the other patrons of the King's Inn should glance occasionally in Garth's direction, wary of what he might do. Garth in particular, of all overmen, they feared; the possibility of a new berserk rage such as those brought on by the Sword of Bheleu was always at the back of the villagers' minds.

When he turned away from the window, therefore, to look across the taproom at the yellow-clad figure at the back table, what little conversation there had been faded and died. The townspeople watched, to be sure that the overman was not looking at any of them.

Garth rose, and even the rustling of clothes and the bumping of chairs ceased.

His gaze wandered for a moment from the old man to the great barrels of beer and ale along the western wall. His mug was empty; he picked it up, made his way through the tables and chairs, and drew himself afresh pint. The innkeeper, a plump, middle-aged man, stood nearby and silently accepted a coin with a polite nod.

Garth sipped off the top layer of foam, then let his gaze wander back toward the Forgotten King's table, where it settled once more on the silent old man. Without quite knowing why, he moved in that direction.

When he reached the table, he thumped his mug of ale down and seated himself across from the King, as he had done so very many times in the past three years.

"Greetings, O King," he said.

The old man said nothing.

Garth looked him over, as he also often had done. He noted again that the old man's eyes were invisible, lost in the shadows of his ragged yellow hood. No one, as far as Garth knew, had ever seen the Forgotten King's eyes. A thin wisp of white beard trickled from his bony chin well down his yellow-wrapped breast. His hands lay motionless on the tabletop, things of bone and wrinkled skin more like those of a mummy than the hands of a living man. The scalloped tatters of his robe hid the rest of him from sight, so that little else could be said of his appearance with any assurance, save that he was thin and seemed tall for so aged a human, though still shorter than any grown overman.

Garth wondered, once again, why the old man wore rags and why they were always yellow. Garth had heard him referred to as the King in Yellow, so it was scarcely a temporary or recent habit, yet there seemed no reason for it. The old man had money, the overman knew, and power, yet he spent his days in this ancient inn and wore only tatters. When Garth had first sought eternal fame, the Wise Women of Ordunin had described the yellow rags to identify the Forgotten King.

Garth had long ago lost interest in the pursuit of undying glory that had originally brought him to the King; the price had been too high and the rewards, upon consideration, too intangible. He no longer had a single goal he was consciously pursuing. In fact, he did not know any more what he wanted from his life, though he was sure of certain elements. He wanted to go home. He wanted the respect of his fellows, and to be rid of the stigma he now bore of being known as subject to fits of madness. Beyond that, he was unsure.

He did know, however, that he wanted nothing from the old man, unless it was the spontaneous renunciation of his oath. The King's gifts and bargains always seemed to have unwanted strings attached; Garth's dealings with him had been full of unspoken words and hidden meanings.

Still, Garth found himself at this back-corner table more and more often.

It was, he told himself, a natural curiosity in the face of the old man's enigma that drew him, that and the lack of anything better to do. He was without family or friends and had no job to occupy his time; why should he not take an interest in such a mystery? He could speak to the old man without making bargains, without being sucked into his plotting and planning.

If the thought had ever occurred to Garth that he sought out the King because the old man, alone in all of Skelleth, had absolutely no fear of Garth or the Sword of Bheleu, he had dismissed the idea as absurd and irrelevant.

He gulped ale, then said, "Greetings, I said."

The King moved a hand, as if to wave the overman away.

Garth was not willing to be turned aside that easily. He knew something of the King's background and had some idea of his immense power, but he was not frightened. Very little could frighten Garth; he would not allow himself such weaknesses as unnecessary fears. He shrugged at the old man's gesture and drank ale.

The King sat unmoving, watching with hidden eyes.

Garth finished the contents of his mug, motioned to the tavernkeeper for more, and stared back.

The King was old, Garth knew, older than anything else that lived in the world. He had survived for more than a thousand years at the very least, perhaps for several thousand. He had been in Skelleth since its founding three centuries earlier. He could not die in the natural way of things. It was hardly surprising that his behavior should be strange.

As Garth had pieced together the story, the King, in the dim and ancient past, had made a bargain with The God Whose Name Is Not Spoken, Death himself. The King had then been a monarch in more than name, the wizard-king of the long-lost and forgotten empire of Carcosa. He had sought immortality and agreed to serve as the Final God's high priest in exchange for eternal life. In time he had come to regret his bargain and had forsaken the god's service, only to find that he was unable to die. Blades could not cut him, blows could not harm him; the petrifying gaze of a basilisk had left him untouched. He still possessed knowledge and magical power far beyond anything known since the fall of Carcosa, but he had no call to use it, for it could not get him the one thing he wanted.

One great magic could attain his death, a mighty spell requiring both the Sword of Bheleu and the Book of Silence. He had the sword, but lacked the book. Garth had sworn to fetch the book in order to be free of the sword, but he did not intend to fulfill his vow.

As far as Garth was concerned, that put an end to the matter, save for one detail. He had not been called upon to carry out his promise; he was not yet truly forsworn. He was able to maintain a pretense of honor – a pretense he knew to be false – as long as the King did not demand that he fetch the book.

The King had not made that demand yet only because he had not recalled where, several centuries earlier, he had left the book. Garth hoped that the memory was lost forever; then he might never be forced to break his sworn word.

At the same time, though, he found himself wishing that the affair were over with, that the oath were broken and done, rather than still hanging over him.

He leaned back, his chair creaking a protest beneath his inhuman weight, and could not resist asking, "Have you remembered yet, O King?" His voice was expressionless, for overmen's emotions were displayed differently from humans'. The mixture of bitterness over his false oath and anticipation of its final ruination that had prompted the question was so well hidden that Garth was not really aware of it himself.

The King said nothing; his head moved very slightly, almost imperceptibly, to one side and then back.

"You must tell me where it is, old man, if you want me to fetch it."

The King did not reply and moved not at all. Garth felt a surge of anger at this silence.

"Speak, old man," he said.

No answer came. Garth's annoyance increased.

"Has your tongue shriveled in your head, then, O throneless King? Are you trying to imitate the corpses you resemble, since you cannot rightly join them? Have you now forsaken speech, the better to serve your foul black god?" He did not shout; his voice was flat and deadly, a dangerous sign among his kind.

The Forgotten King moved slightly, as if emitting a faint sigh, but still said nothing. Garth drew breath for another question, but was distracted by the arrival of the innkeeper with a fresh mug of ale. The overman snatched it from him, swallowed half its contents at a gulp, and then ordered, "Be off, man!"

The taverner risked a glance at Garth's baleful red eyes and inhuman face, then hurried away, wondering if it would be safe to cut the overman's next serving of ale with water. He knew the signs of Garth's anger; rudeness to underlings like himself was one such indication. He did not want to worry about dealing with an overman in a drunken fury – but an overman enraged at being cheated might be equally bad. He looked at Garth's mail-covered back and decided, at least for the moment, that his reputation for honest measure and good drink was worth preserving. He could only hope that the old man would calm the overman down.

Garth was in no mood to be calmed down. When the innkeeper had moved away, he asked, "Why do you not speak? Is it perhaps that I am unfit to address you, O King of an empire long since dust, monarch of a dying memory, lord of a realm unknown? Is the Prince of Ordunin, a lord of the overmen of the Northern Waste, suited only to serve your whims, but not to speak with you?

Does the master of ashes and woe, wearing rags and tatters and dwelling in a single dim room of an ancient inn, not deign to answer the exiled killer, the disgraced berserker? Will the servant of Death not choose to acknowledge the pawn of destruction?" His voice was calm, as still as water pooled on black ice, and laden with far more threat than any shout as he said, "Answer me, old man."

The old man answered. "Garth," he said in a voice like ice breaking, "why do you disturb me? You know I prefer not to waste words in idle chatter."

The overman was wrenched momentarily from his anger by the sound of the old man's voice, a sound unlike any other, dry and brittle and harsh, so unpleasant to hear that it could not fully be remembered. He regained his composure quickly, however, and replied, "Is everything I say idle chatter? Have I not the right to an answer when I ask a polite question?"

"Hardly polite," the old man demurred. "I will answer, however. No, I have not yet recalled where I left the Book of Silence in those ancient days when last I held it."

"So I must linger here, still waiting?"

"Garth," the old man replied, "you are bored, frustrated by inactivity. You are a warrior, given to violent action, not to sitting about a peaceful village. I have told you from the first that you are free to leave Skelleth and that your oath does not hold you here, as long as you return at intervals to learn whether or not I have recalled where the Book of Silence lies. Why, then, do you not find yourself some task to occupy your time, rather than remain here disturbing my contemplation?"

So long a speech was unusual for the King, and Garth knew it well. He realized that he must have seriously annoyed the old man. His own anger, however, had not faded.

"And what task shall I pursue, then? Where am I to go? I am forbidden the Northern Waste and therefore cannot aid my homeland against the human pirates who assail it. What other task awaits me? I have little taste for roaming aimlessly, particularly when the world is strewn about with wars and battles that do not concern me. I have no reason to side with any human faction and no desire to kill merely for my own amusement, so I will not join in these wars. I am welcome no place outside Skelleth. I have seen Mormoreth and left it in the hands of men who comrades I killed in self-defense; will they greet me as an old friend? I have visited Dûsarra and left it aflame and plague-ridden, its every citizen my enemy. The other lands and cities of the south are unknown to me, and overmen are unwanted strangers throughout. Where, then, shall I go?"

"What of the Yprian Coast?"

"And what might I do there, but find another tavern wherein I might sit and be bored? I am no trader, I know that now; I have no desire to seek out new markets and new routes."

"Think you that is all that may be found there?"

"What else might there be? Farms and villages, markets and men and overmen. The caravans have told us what may be found there, and it does not interest me. Others have gone before me as well; where might I explore that they could not have preceded me?"

"Must you be first, then, as you were first in coming to Skelleth, first to think that overmen might trade here?"

"For all the good that did me, yes. What point is there in doing what has been done before?"

"I think, Garth, that you resent the ingratitude of those who have benefited from the trade you began."

"Perhaps I do, old man; what of it? Does it matter to either of us that I am scorned by those I have made wealthy? Or that my old companions allow me no responsibilities in the village I gave them? They are no concern of ours. I am sworn to aid you in your death-magic, O King; that is what concerns us. I am waiting for you to tell me how I may fulfill my oath."

"I have told you that I have not yet remembered."

"Then I must wait until you do."

"And plague me with angry questions?"

"Should I so choose, yes."

The King did not reply immediately; during the pause, Garth drank the rest of his ale and decided against ordering another.

"Garth, I would have you leave me in peace," the old man said at last, "so that I might be able to think more clearly and recall more easily what I wish to recall."

The overman shrugged. "I care little what you would have, old man. I am not sworn to heed your every whim, only to fetch your book and aid you in your magics."

"You are bored. What if I gave you a task that could harm no one, but would result in great benefit for many innocent people?"

Garth stared into the depths of his empty mug, then looked up, gazing across the table into the shadows that hid the old man's face.

"What sort of a task?"

"Slaying a dragon that has laid waste the valley of Orgûl."

Garth considered. His anger was fading, but his mind was slightly hazed with liquor. "A dragon?"

The old man nodded, once.

Garth thought it over. He was bored. He was irritable from inaction. It would be good to travel again, to see new places, to spend each night somewhere different from the night before. It would be good to get out of Skelleth, away from so many unpleasant memories. It would be good to accomplish something useful, and there could be little doubt that killing a dragon was useful. He had never seen a dragon, but he was familiar with the stories and legends about them. All agreed that the creatures were huge, dangerous, and phenomenally destructive. He himself had been a destroyer far too often in the past, he felt; here, then, he might find a chance to make up for some of that by destroying a menace worse than he had ever been.

In a way, it might be a step toward avenging himself on Bheleu. The god of destruction had used Garth as a puppet, and the overman resented that. He felt that it might be a small sort of retaliation to kill a creature that could be considered one of Bheleu's pets.

He nodded. The more he thought about the proposed adventure, the more it appealed to him. "I think I'd like that," he said.

The Forgotten King's mouth curved into a faint smile.

Far to the west, in a windowless chamber draped in black and dark red, a man stared at the image in his scrying glass and smiled as well. The image had been exceptionally clear and detailed, and he had been able to read the overman's lips. He had only the tail end of one side of the conversation, but it was obvious that Garth was being sent on an errand of some sort. That should provide an excellent opportunity for actions long delayed. Nearly three years had passed since the overman had defied the cult of Aghad, smashed the god's altar, and slain his high priest; much had happened during that period, but the cult had not sought vengeance. Haggat, the present high priest of Aghad, was a patient man, and had taken his time in gathering power and planning his actions. He had wanted to be sure that nothing would interfere with the proposed revenge. Now, at last, everything was ready.

He put down the glass, blew out the single candle that lit the chamber, and went to give the order that would set the prepared machinery in motion.

Chapter Two

Garth was unsure just where, amid the hills and mountains, he had crossed the border between the Eramman Barony of Sland and the independent region of Orgûl; if there were any signposts or markers, he had missed them in the dark. Shortly after dawn arrived, however, he topped the crest of the final encircling ridge to see the valley of Orgûl spread out before him, its fields and forests a thousand shades of green, its rivers gleaming blue and silver in the morning sun. He saw no traces of the draconic ravages he had been led to expect.

In fact, he thought as he looked out across the countryside, Orgûl appeared far richer and more peaceful than the lands he had traversed to reach it.

For the first three days after leaving Skelleth he had ridden at a leisurely pace across flat plains brown with mud, traveling openly by day and stopping freely at the very few inns and taverns along the way. He had been turned away once simply because he was an overman, but had met no other serious inconvenience or opposition until the third evening, when, amid the smoldering ruins of a farm that chanced to lie between disputing baronies, a human soldier took a shot at him with a crossbow. The quarrel missed its target, and the man fled when Koros, Garth's warbeast, bared its fangs and roared; Garth himself did not even have to draw his sword. Still, he knew he had been lucky that the bolt had missed; he had not seen the man crouching behind a broken wall.

After that he had traveled by night, sleeping by day in whatever cover he could find. The land had grown ever richer as he moved south; though he could see no color by night, at sunset and dawn the earth was lush and green – where it hadn't been burned black.

That first burned-out farm had not been unique; as he continued on to the south he found many others, usually in clusters along the invisible lines between baronies. Nor were farms the only things destroyed; he passed an inn that was reduced to charred timbers, and a gallows nearby held three rotting corpses. On one piece of prime land the blackened crops were still smoldering. Some fields had been destroyed not by fire, but by marching feet, and one had apparently been the site of a recent battle; it had been churned into a muddy waste, strewn with broken links of mail and scraps of cloth spattered with dark blood. Everything of value, every weapon that might be reforged or melted down, had been removed, though Garth suspected that had been the work of looters rather than the contending armies.

He rode by still more farms, some abandoned, some where families cowered behind barricaded doors, and others where the doors were wide open in welcome, on the assumption that resistance to the whims of soldiers would be fatal. Garth avoided villages and towns and castles, giving them all wide berths, and dodged any armed men he spotted in time. No unarmed humans were to be found abroad after dark.

Those few patrols and sentries that he could not avoid, for whatever reason, invariably let him pass unhindered after the warbeast clearly indicated that it was ready to defend its master. Only rarely did Garth feel it necessary to draw a blade or speak a serious threat. He considered himself fortunate that he had not encountered any company larger than a patrol squad, nor any other sniping bowman with a grudge against overmen.

Eramma, in the throes of internal war, he had seen as a patchwork of the land's natural wealth and the barren leavings of battle.

The last portion of his journey had been the worst. The fighting had begun when the Baron of Sland had attacked the High King at Kholis, and although the High King had never managed to restore his full authority, several barons had helped him make sure that Sland would no longer be a threat. The troublesome Baron had been assassinated after his defeat on the field of battle, and his successor had made peace with his Eramman neighbors – though Garth had heard rumors that the new Baron had designs on the lands beyond his western border, outside Eramma's limits. Unfortunately, by the time this peace had been established, much of Sland was a burned-out desert. The land showed some signs of recovery after a year of peace, but was still largely desolate and empty. Garth had been relieved to get up into the hills, into the forests where he was not surrounded by mud and ash.

And now, as he emerged into the valley of Orgûl, the warm, green vista before him was a staggering contrast.

It was very odd. He had spoken with people along the way, wherever it had seemed safe to do so, and those who had heard of Orgûl at all had also heard of the dragon; they had described the valley as a scorched wasteland. Even in Sland, the survivors, racked by hunger and disease, had considered themselves more fortunate than the people of Orgûl. They had spoken of burned crops, seared fields, empty, ruined villages, and whole populaces devoured or destroyed.

That description did not accord with what Garth now saw. He wondered briefly if somehow he could have gotten turned about in the forest's darkness and wound up in the wrong valley. The sun was where he had expected it to be, and he had noticed no other trails as he had ridden, but he resolved to ask the first person he found.

If he was lost, he had no idea where he might be or how to get to the real Orgûl. He had little choice but to assume that he had indeed reached his destination and that the stories of the dragon's depredations had been exaggerated. He wondered whether the Forgotten King had known more of the situation than he had said; Garth hoped that he was not once again becoming entangled in some labyrinthine scheme the old man had concocted.

With an almost imperceptible shrug, he urged the warbeast forward. The spire of a small temple gleamed golden above the trees before him, not more than two or three leagues away at most; he was sure that he would find a village there, and someone from whom he could ask directions. If there were no one in the temple or village, then it was a safe assumption that he was in Orgûl and that the dragon was real and terrible.

The ride down the hillside was pleasant; the highway wound down from the promontory through a final patch of forest before opening out into farmland, and the morning sun poured through the leaves in a spatter of honeyed light. Birds sang on either side. A deer wandered across the narrow road, then turned and fled at the sight of the warbeast. Off to the left Garth heard the splashing of a rocky stream, its cheerful burble accompanying him down the slope. He glimpsed a hawk overhead, soaring in graceful, wide circles.

It seemed utterly incredible that this peaceful valley could harbor a dragon. Dragons were said to be the most formidable and destructive creatures in all the world, and the dragon of Orgûl, Garth had been told along the way, was the most ferocious dragon ever known. Something here was not as it seemed, and his mistrust of the King's motive for proposing the mission steadily increased. Having come this far, however, he was not inclined to turn back.

The road he followed was little more than a narrow trail at this point, but it was not seriously overgrown; Garth wondered what traffic it bore that kept down the weeds and grasses. He had been told that no outsiders dared venture into Orgûl and he decided that the Orgûlians themselves must be responsible. This implied that they still conducted a minimum of trade with the outside world, which did not quite accord with the stories Garth had heard. The people of Orgûl had been described to him as a dwindling handful of humans who lived constantly in hiding and in perpetual fear of the monster that ruled their land.

Obviously, if this valley was Orgûl, all the stories were greatly exaggerated.

The exact details were immaterial, however. He had come to dispose of the dragon once and for all, regardless of the extent of the damage it caused. A single unnecessary death was enough to justify his task.

It struck him as odd that the Forgotten King should allow him to risk his life in such an altruistic venture – if altruistic it actually were. He grew more certain that the old man had some ulterior motive, some subtle and selfish reason for sending Garth off on this journey.

His thoughts were interrupted by a growl from his beast; he glanced down at the creature's flattened ears, then at the road ahead.

A figure was emerging from one side of the forest and waving desperately at him. Whoever this person was, he evidently wanted the overman to stop. Garth spoke a word to his mount, and the warbeast came to a smooth halt a pace or two away from the man.

The overman glared down at the human. He was aware that his appearance, particularly when mounted upon Koros, was impressive and even intimidating; he made good use of that fact at times.

The man hesitated, gazing up at the huge, dark form of the overman. He had heard of overmen, but had never seen one before. Descriptions had not done them justice, and he was certain of Garth's species only because he knew of no other large humanoid beings.

Koros he could not place at all; he simply stared.

Two pairs of inhuman eyes stared back, one set golden and catlike, one red as blood and whiteless, but otherwise almost human.

He himself stood a little over five feet tall and was thin; the overman, he judged, was nearly seven feet in height, were he to stand on his own booted feet. He was not standing, of course, but was seated atop an immense and frightening animal, black as the heart of a cave and resembling an oddly proportioned, long-legged panther.

The man had never seen, nor heard of, a panther eighteen feet long and five feet high at the shoulder. The warbeast looked *down* at him, and he was not accustomed to having animals look down at him. Its rider, noseless, dark-skinned, black-haired, and beardless, towered above him as if he were no more than a crawling infant. Still, he finally managed to gather himself together sufficiently to stammer out his message in the face of these awesome intruders.

"Turn back, my lord! Do not venture further, I beseech you!"

Garth stared down a moment longer; then, without moving, he demanded, "Why not?"

Momentarily cowed still further by Garth's bass rumble of a voice, the man had some difficulty in continuing, but at last got out, "The dragon, my lord! The dragon has once more awakened, after a month's sleep, and is very hungry! I fear that this time the entire valley is doomed!"

After a brief pause, intended for dramatic effect, Garth asked, "This is Orgûl, then?" He wondered about the mention of a month's sleep; could that account for the valley's green richness? No, he decided, it could not. He had ridden through parts of Eramma that were not yet recovered from mere human battles after a year's respite; how, then, could the devastation caused by a dragon vanish in a mere month?

"Yes, my lord," the man said, "this is the accursed valley of Orgûl, home of the great dragon."

"I have come to kill this troublesome beast," Garth remarked casually.

"Oh, my lord, it cannot be done! His hide is like steel, his fangs like swords, his talons like scythes! He can outfly a hawk, and his breath is flame hotter than any forge!"

Garth saw that the man was almost trembling, but could not guess at the reason. He supposed that it might be fear of the dragon, or fear of Koros, or fear of himself, or some other emotion entirely. Even after living among them for three years, he still did not fully understand humans and knew that he did not.

"You think to frighten me, little man," he replied. "Know, though, that I am Garth, Prince of Ordunin, Lord of the Overmen of the Northern Waste. No beast lives that might defeat me." This was not exactly true, he knew; he would not care to tackle a hungry warbeast, and a dragon might also prove too much for him. Still, a little boasting was expected from a warrior. His statement was not quite an outright lie; had he kept the Sword of Bheleu and allowed himself to become the pawn of the god of destruction, he could easily have butchered any dragon that might exist.

He did not have the magic sword, but only an ordinary broadsword of good steel; even so, he thought he would be able to deal with the monster.

The man tried again, saying, "Please, my lord, turn back; the dragon is no ordinary beast!"

He was clearly desperate, and Garth hid some small surprise. Why, he wondered, was this fellow so concerned? Even if he was completely convinced that the dragon would kill both overman and warbeast, why should that upset him so? He had given his warning, done what he could to prevent a catastrophe; why should he be so distressed at Garth's determination? In Garth's experience, humans did not worry much about what befell overmen.

"Do you fear that I shall enrage the dragon?" he asked. "Is that why you seek to turn me aside?"

"No, no, my lord, I am concerned only for your own safety! Other heroes have come, and all have died beneath the dragon's flames and claws."

Garth shook his head slightly, mentally dismissing the man's actions as incomprehensible. "Stand aside, little man," he said, "lest Koros trample you." He signaled to the warbeast and rode on, ignoring the continuing protests and warnings that the man shouted after him.

It was not much later, and the sun was still low in the east, when Garth rode into the village that clustered about the temple spire he had seen from the slope. The shrine itself was an open pavilion, ringed with pillars that supported its spiraling cone of a roof; it faced onto a small plaza from which five roads led off in various directions. A handful of small, tidy, thatch-roofed cottages stood on each of the roads, and a larger structure that might have been an inn, with a roof of red tile, occupied one corner.

The plaza was paved with tessellated stone, and a small fountain played in its center. As Garth's warbeast neared the pavement, a breeze tinkled its way through miniature bells that hung from the eaves of the temple, joining the hiss and splash of the fountain and the soft steps of sandaled feet.

The villagers stopped and stared at Garth's approach, and the footsteps ceased. Then someone turned and ran for the inn, and the streets cleared almost instantly.

Garth found himself alone in the center of the square, looking about at the five roads with no idea which one he should take. It was time, he decided, to ask for directions. Getting himself and his beast a meal wouldn't be a mistake, either, he thought. Koros was already drinking from the fountain, which reminded Garth that he, too, was thirsty.

He dismounted and stepped up to the fountain, where he filled his hands with water and drank.

A sound behind him caught his attention; he let the rest of the water drop and whirled, his hand falling automatically to the hilt of his sword.

The door of the inn had opened again, and several people were emerging. A white-haired man stepped forward from the group and addressed him.

"Greetings, my lord overman!"

"Greetings, man." This human, Garth thought, unlike the one he had met on the road to the village, at least had the grace to speak politely.

"My I ask, my lord, what brings you to our humble village?" The man's manner was almost fawning.

"I have come to slay your dragon, to save you from its depredations," Garth replied, making an effort to sound casual.

The spokesman hesitated, then said, "My lord, do not think us ungrateful, but we ask that you turn back. We do not wish to see another great man . . . ah, I mean, another great warrior such as yourself die fighting the monster. Too many have perished already."

"I have no intention of dying, man."

"Do you suppose that any of the dragon's victims did? Please, my lord, turn back. You can do nothing for us. You would only throw your life away."

Garth was becoming annoyed by this manifest lack of faith in his prowess. "My life is my own, to throw away should it please me to do so," he said. "I have come to fight your dragon and I am not to be turned aside so readily, frightened by mere words."

The spokesman bowed in acknowledgment of Garth's words, but said, "We do not seek to frighten you, my lord, only to advise you. It would be foolish to waste your life in battling the monster."

Garth's temper, already frayed, gave way. "You are the fools," he called, "to refuse a chance of freedom from this menace! I am Garth, Prince of Ordunin, Lord of the Overmen of the Northern Waste, who brought the White Death to the black city of Dûsarra, who stole the sword of a god, who has fought the beasts of Death himself! I have come here to slay the dragon and I will have no one tell me that I must not!" He realized, as he finished his speech, that without consciously intending to, he had drawn his sword and was flourishing it about.

The little group of humans had clustered together and backed away from him a step or two, toward the inn. The spokesman looked back at his companions for support and, finding little, said nothing further.

His anger spent, Garth returned his sword to its scabbard and added, "But first, I have not eaten recently and would prefer not to face death on an empty stomach. Is this building whence you all came an inn, where an overman can break his fast?"

The spokesman reluctantly admitted that it was.

The inn was called the Sword and Chalice, though its signboard had fallen years ago and never been replaced. Garth had a goat sent out to his warbeast while he himself consumed a hearty meal of roast beef, carrots, and ale. He ate surrounded by a ring of wary villagers, silently watching his every move. He steadfastly ignored their presence and made a point of paying no attention to their comings and goings.

He paused in the midst of his meal at the sound of women screaming in the plaza, but a quick glance out the door reassured him. The screams were in response to the warbeast's eating habits. Koros had killed the goat with a single blow of its paw and immediately devoured it, hair, hooves, and all, though the warbeast spat out the horns and larger bones. Those villagers who happened to be watching had been horrified to see a living animal reduced so quickly to a spatter of blood and a few scraps.

When Garth had eaten his fill he rose, tossed a gold coin on the table, and walked back out into the plaza. The circle of villagers parted before him, then coalesced into a single mass and followed him out – all save the innkeeper. He had not expected to be paid, and took a moment to hide the coin before joining his fellows.

Half a dozen villagers were watching in fascinated revulsion as Koros licked the blood from its paws. They were maintaining a safe distance, Garth noted; he was pleased by that. It showed that they respected the beast's power.

"Whose goat was it?" he demanded loudly.

A woman timidly raised a hand in an affirmative gesture. He tossed her another of his gold coins, which she caught deftly and quickly pocketed.

A boy at her side whispered something and was hushed. Garth noticed men and women staring at him, at the warbeast, and at the broadsword on his hip and the battle-axe slung on the saddle. He looked around, but the spokesman was nowhere in sight. Choosing a man at random, he remarked, "I take it you see few warriors around here and fewer overmen."

The man gaped at him, then gathered enough wit to reply. "Yes, my lord. Very few. The dragon keeps them away. No overmen, ever."

"I would think that many would come to try their skill at dragon-slaying."

His unhappy respondent glanced to either side, but saw no sign that any of his townspeople were willing to take over the burden of the conversation.

"No, my lord," he replied, "not anymore. Long ago there were some, but the dragon killed them all, and after a time they stopped coming. There were never overmen, though; only the men of the Baron of Sland, or roving mercenaries and adventurers."

"They stopped coming?" Garth said, encouraging him to continue.

"Yes, my lord. After all, there is no reward offered, no great prize to be won."

"Nothing but a chance for fame and glory, and the risk of death, more easily found elsewhere, to be sure." Garth nodded, then swung himself up into the saddle.

"Forgive me, my lord," the man said, gathering his courage, "but why . . . ah, why have you come here? Why do you bother with our accursed and wretched valley?"

"Your valley does not seem wretched to me, man. I have come here out of boredom, people of Orgûl; I grew weary of a life of quiet and decided, on a whim, to come here and aid those the dragon oppressed. I have lived for more than a century and adventured in many lands, but never before have those I came to aid tried so hard to turn me away."

"But, my lord," someone protested, "we seek only to prevent the loss of another brave –"

"Enough, human," Garth interrupted. "Tell me, now, which road is most likely to lead me to this vile monster?"

Reluctantly, the man pointed to the western road, and with a word in the warbeast's triangular ear, Garth rode on.

Chapter Three

The road he took from the plaza appeared to run through the village's commercial area; the houses on either side held small shops, displaying fine rugs and fabrics in their many-paned windows, or delicate carvings, or gleaming pots and kettles, or other goods. A blacksmith's forge trailed smoke into the blue of the sky, but the smith was not at work as the overman passed.

Even though the people he encountered shied away from him, averting their eyes and hurrying out of sight, he enjoyed the ride. This village, it seemed to him, was more the sort of place he might have liked to live in, if he were to live among humans, than the wastelands of the north. Skelleth might be flourishing, but it was still cold and dirty and gray, huddled on a barren plain against the long harsh winters; this village was bright and cheerful, trailing off without a border into the surrounding green of field and forest, rather than being chopped off short by a ruined city wall. The sunlight was warm on his back, the breeze fresh with the smells of abundant greenery.

Garth found it quite impossible to believe that this was the home ground of a dragon as terrible as the one he had heard described. He puzzled anew at the Orgûlians' insistence that he turn back.

Looking about, he wondered idly whether overmen had ever lived in this delightful valley, back in those long-lost legendary days before the Racial Wars, before his people were driven into the barren Northern Waste. For centuries the overmen of the Waste had believed themselves to be the only ones to have survived those bitter wars, but recently Garth himself had discovered that others still lived on the Yprian Coast, a region nearly as desolate as the Waste itself. Could there be more, scattered about the world? Might some still linger in the hills around Orgûl? Garth found that an appealing fancy; this country was one he would have enjoyed calling his home, and it pleased him to imagine that it might not wholly be wasted on humans.

His musings were interrupted when his eye caught a sudden movement in one of the village shops; he turned to see what had drawn his attention.

The last of the buildings that lined the street was a strange little shop on the left, its mismatched windows full of whirling, whirring clockwork toys. Fascinated, Garth stopped his mount, swung himself to the ground, and went over for a closer look. He was in no real hurry, he told himself; the dragon had reportedly gone its way for decades, and another few moments would surely make no difference.

The shop's display held dozens of intricate toys, full of gears and springs, which did amazing and delightful tricks. An armored warrior, with head and hands of china, swung a miniature sword in long, swooping strokes, narrowly missing the bent-over back of a mechanical smith striking sparks from a half-formed steel rake with a stone hammer – the head of which, Garth realized, must be flint, a clever method of creating the sparks that so resembled those of a real blacksmith at work. Nearby, a toy dog wagged its tail, its tongue moving as if panting, and a plaster witch stirred a tiny copper cauldron. Elsewhere dancers whirled, acrobats leaped, and animals paced, in a glittering festival of copper and brass and silver and ceramics. A few devices had no recognizable form, but were unabashed machines, tossing arms and gears about in complex and fascinating patterns.

Garth had never seen so fine a display of machinery; northerners, either the humans of Skelleth or the overmen of Ordunin, had little time for such inessentials. Clockwork was used for clocks on ships, which needed accurate timekeeping for navigation, but was seldom used elsewhere.

He could not resist a broad grin as he studied the things; he hoped that no one noticed it, lest it destroy the image he had been cultivating of the implacable inhuman warrior. Anyone who saw it, though, might not recognize it for what it was; humans were not always able to identify the expressions of overmen, being distracted from the fundamental similarities by the hollow cheeks, thin lips, and noseless slit nostrils. The two species reacted somewhat differently to various situations and emotions, furthering the confusion. To the uninitiated man or woman, Garth's happy smile might appear to be a ghastly grimace, his delight in the clever toys and machines to be bitter disgust.

The shop window was not lighted, and Garth's own shadow blocked out a measure of the morning sun; he peered in, trying to make out the shapes that flopped and fluttered in the dimness at the back of the display. A brass rooster crowed, with a flapping of wings, and he marveled anew.

"Would you like to buy one, my lord?"

Startled, Garth whirled to face the owner of the pleasant little voice that had interrupted his studies. A small, whitehaired man stood in the door of the shop, squinting and blinking in the bright light of day; he smiled, revealing a jawful of randomly assorted gold and white teeth.

The overman stared at the man for a moment, then back at the window, where the swordsman's blade continued to miss the smith's broad back and swinging hammer by the breadth of a few hairs, where the yapping dog bounced merrily along and the plaster witch grinned gruesomely.

"I think I might, yes," Garth said at last. "Are they expensive?"

"Oh, no," the little man replied. "I don't need much to live on. I have a pension of sorts – I suppose you could call it a pension. Enough to make do, at any rate. But it does get so dull! So I keep making these toys, to amuse myself. The children seem to like them. Have you any children, my lord?"

"Five; two sons. They're grown, though, old enough for families of their own."

"Grandchildren, then?"

"Not that I know of; I haven't been home lately." He smiled wryly to himself at that.

"A pity, a pity." The old man shook his head, looking downcast, as if it were the greatest tragedy of his life that this fine overman should have no grandchildren and should be so long away from home.

Garth's smile became a little less bitter; the man was amusing. "Did you say that you find this village dull? What of the dragon, then? Does it not provide enough excitement for you?"

"Oh, the dragon . . ." The man shrugged, as if the legendary monster were beneath his notice. "I meant that doing nothing for myself was dull, not that there had been no excitement in my life. I like to keep my hands busy when the dragon is not about, my hands and my mind." He gestured, wiggling his fingers to show that they were still agile.

Garth decided that he liked this fellow. "Have you children yourself?" he asked.

"Oh, all long since grown, like your own, my lord; even my grandchildren are married now, some of them." He glanced at the shop window. "Tell me," he said, "which do you like the best?"

Garth turned back and studied the collection; his gaze wandered over ships and horses, men and castles, women and machines. The swordsman had run down, frozen in midstroke with his sword thrust out before him.

"I cannot say," Garth replied. "I have not seen them all run. Some are not displayed to their best advantage here."

"Come inside, then, and I will show you more closely any that interest you." The toymaker grinned and beckoned, and Garth followed him.

The building's interior was dim and smelled strongly of metal and oil and herbs. A narrow passage led between two great tables that held the two window displays; beyond, a fair-sized room contained a fireplace and oven, a table, a few chairs, and a workbench. The last was cluttered with gears and wheels and snippets of copper, chisels and scissors and knives, powders and pastes, jars and vials, a potter's wheel, and a pedal-driven lathe. At the rear another door stood slightly ajar.

Garth looked over the two tables; dozens of toys were displayed, perhaps a hundred or more. The toymaker wound up a spider that danced in circles as the cauldron-stirring witch ground to a halt.

Everything was a maze of arms and legs and wheels, plaster faces staring in the waxed-paper windows of wooden castles, and Garth could not imagine picking a single favorite from the muddle. He let his eyes roam, and found himself staring at a glistening copper shape that gleamed in one corner.

"What's that?" he asked, pointing. The object stood out because of its smooth, curving surface, unbroken by flailing arms or whirling gears.

The old man followed his pointing finger and fetched the object in question out into the light that poured through the window. It was a copper sea gull; two eyes of smoky quartz stared unseeingly from its tapered metal head, and its wings were polished to mirror brightness. "Ah, my lord," the old man said, "you have excellent taste."

"What does it do?" Garth asked.

"Why, what else would a bird do but fly?" He pulled a silver key from somewhere, inserted it in an opening in the mechanical gull's back, then gestured for Garth to follow him back outside. "Let me show you."

The overman followed and watched as the toymaker turned the key. With a small click, the key stopped; the old man pulled it out and, with a proud smile, cast the gull away.

Garth instinctively reached out to catch it, to keep its graceful curves from being scarred or broken by its fall, but it did not drop into his waiting hands. Instead, its metal wings caught the breeze and flapped once, twice, lazily, with the languid grace of a living sea gull, and it swooped away. Riding the wind, it glided upward, then looped back and circled slowly overhead. Garth gaped in astonishment.

For several long minutes the gull soared overhead, flapping smoothly now and then, gleaming golden in the morning sun; then, gradually, it settled lower and lower, until at last, with a rueful smile, the toymaker reached up and plucked it out of the sky.

Garth heard a click and a final soft whirr, and the gull was still.

Garth stared at the man with deep respect. "It is very beautiful," he said. "I was not aware that such things could be built of mere metal."

The toymaker looked down, obviously embarrassed. "Well, actually," he admitted, "they can't. I cheat. It's not just clockwork."

"It's not?"

"No. I use magic."

"Oh," Garth said knowingly. He had seen magic before, more of it than he liked. At least, he thought, this magic was harmless.

"I didn't originally – at least, I don't think I did. I started off using just clockwork when I was an apprentice, but I found right from the first that I could make machines that no one else could understand, things that worked when by all rights they should not have. Even when I built my clocks and toys in the usual ways, mine would run far longer and more smoothly than any of the others. I got better and better at it, too, until I was doing things that were plainly impossible to do with just clockwork. I had no idea how I did what I did back then; it simply came to me, as naturally as breathing, without my ever thinking about it. When I realized what was happening, I studied sorcery briefly; even though my teacher said I had a real talent, I didn't care for it. It seemed too dangerous, too uncertain. I went back to clockwork, but now I know a bit more about what I'm doing. I even use spells intentionally now, though I still make them up, rather than follow the old formulae. As I said, I have the knack for it. A fellow who came through here last year, fleeing from Sland, a wizard by the name of Karag, told me that it wasn't anything to be concerned about. He said that there are a lot of minor magical talents like mine scattered about; probably one of my ancestors back in the Twelfth Age, when magic was widespread, was a wizard of some sort, and I inherited a bit of his lingering power without knowing it."

"I had no idea it could work that way," Garth said.

"Neither did I when I was young, but it seems that's just how it *does* work. That gull wouldn't fly if anyone else had made it. I've shown other tinkers and craftsmen how to make flying toys, and they've done them just as I do, but theirs don't fly at all, they just fall."

Garth reached out, took the gull from the toymaker's hands, and turned it over, studying it. "Magic or not, it's a beautiful thing," he said.

"Yes, it is," the toymaker agreed.

"Do you wish to sell it?"

"Of course; I have no use for it. Besides, I have others and I can always make more. Would you like it?"

"Yes, I think I would; it's a wondrous device, whether clockwork or magic. What is your price?"

The man named a figure; Garth declined politely. After a brief and mild bout of bargaining, a price was settled upon as fair to both parties.

"Will you take it with you now, then?" the toymaker asked.

"No," Garth answered, handing it back, "I think not. I am seeking after the dragon at present; were I to take the gull, I fear that it might be broken in the fight. I will stop here and buy it on my way back, at the price agreed upon, if that will suit you." After a second's pause, he added, "Assuming, of course, that I come back; the stories I have heard of the dragon imply that I may not."

"The dragon?" Surprise and concern were plain in the toymaker's face. "You've come to slay the dragon? Oh, dear. That's most unfortunate."

"Is it?" Garth asked as he moved to mount his warbeast. "It may prove unfortunate for the dragon; it has never faced an overman before."

"Well, that's true," the old man admitted, "but still . . ." He fell into a confused silence and stood watching, the metal bird in his hands, as Garth rode on past him and out of the village.

Chapter Four

Garth rode for an hour through peaceful groves and flourishing farmland; on all sides blossoms were giving way to budding fruit and grain, and it was obvious that, barring some disaster, there would be an abundant harvest at summer's end. He could still see no sign anywhere of a dragon or a dragon's depredations. He did see, to his surprise, recent footprints, all human, on the road he followed; they were wide-spaced, as if the men who made them had been hurrying. They all seemed to run westward, the same direction in which Garth was bound. He wondered if the makers of the marks had been fleeing from the dragon. The villagers had seemed quite certain that it was awake and active and somewhere west of the town; perhaps they had seen it pursuing some of their countrymen along this highway.

There was no trace of the dragon itself, however. Garth scanned the horizon.

To the north and east he saw nothing but trees. To the south a few clouds hung in the sky above green fields. To the west the hills reared up before him; the valley was narrow at this, its northern end, and he had already crossed half its width.

To the southwest a thin trail of smoke was curling upward, blue smoke almost invisible against the blue of the sky.

He signaled Koros to stop, to allow him a better view; the warbeast obeyed, and Garth stared at the faint wisp. It seemed to be growing thicker as he watched.

Dragons, it was said, breathed fire. Garth had never taken that aspect of the monster's description very seriously; legends tended to be distorted in the retelling. Still, there was general agreement that much of a dragon's destructiveness resulted from fires. Garth had assumed heretofore that the creatures might produce some sort of highly combustible substance, a venom or vapor, perhaps.

If they actually did produce flame, however, then the smoke he now saw might be coming from the monster.

Of course, it could also be coming from village cook fires and hearths, but he saw no sign of a town in that direction – no temple spires or roofs showed above the treetops. If there were a village, though, perhaps the people would be able to direct him to the monster's current location.

He pointed toward the smoke and called a command to his mount. With a growl, the warbeast turned off the road and began running cross-country toward the thickening column.

Koros' normal pace was almost unnaturally smooth and silent, far more comfortable for its rider than that of any other mount Garth had ever ridden; but when running, even though it was loping along well below its full top speed, Koros bounded up and down in such a manner that Garth was forced to cling precariously to its harness, rather than risk being thrown.

The beast's long strides ate up the distance, carrying the overman over farmland and meadow with phenomenal speed. Animal and rider passed through an orchard, then a patch of pine forest, then out into a new stretch of meadow. Beneath them the ground began to slope upward, and Garth saw that the smoke was rising from just beyond the crest of a grassy hillock.

If he were to ride on directly over that rise, he realized, he might find himself face to face with the dragon without any time to prepare; the monster could easily be lurking in ambush.

He called a command, and Koros came to a sudden stop. Garth gathered himself together and looked at what lay before him.

He was on an open expanse of grassland, unfarmed and apparently wild; ahead the land rose into a sort of mound, and the smoke behind it streamed upward in a single thick column. It did not look like the dispersed traces of smoke from a village or the thin mark from a farmhouse chimney. Some farmer might be burning debris, or a cremation might be under way, but Garth thought that caution was called for in any further approach.

Beyond the rise the ground sloped downward again, into a riverbank; he could not see the stream itself, but the broad cut into the earth that extended in either direction beyond the hillock could be nothing else.

The nearest cover was a patch of forest that he had passed through on his approach; it lay a hundred yards behind him.

He had, he judged, four choices. He could head on directly over the mound, he could circle it to the northwest, he could circle to the southeast, or he could retreat into the woods.

He glanced down at the warbeast's harness, making sure it hadn't been loosened by the fast ride he had just finished, and considered. Remaining where he was did not seem prudent; he was out in the open, an ideal target. If he advanced, he did not know what he might be facing. If he retreated, the dragon might depart – assuming it was there at all.

He would have to face the unknown eventually; he decided to advance. If he looped to the northwest his shadow would be away from whatever awaited him, but the sun would be in his eyes when he turned south again on the far side of the mound. If he went southeast, his shadow might signal his approach.

He had just resolved to head on directly over the mound, slowly and cautiously, when Koros let out a growl that he recognized as indicating surprise. He looked up from the harness and found himself staring straight at an immense red-gold dragon that was sailing down at him on huge, batlike wings.

It had made no sound, no bellow of challenge, no great flapping, but now that he was alerted he noticed a faint hissing that he had not heard over the breeze rustling the grass.

The creature was at least a hundred feet long, with a slender, graceful tail winding out behind it and a long, arching neck. Its wingspan was even greater than its length, easily fifty yards, perhaps sixty or more. Its hide was covered with glittering scales that flashed like golden coins in the sun.

Its head was a thing of horror; its gaping jaws were black, and long, curving teeth lined both top and bottom like rows of knives. The great heavy-lidded eyes were faceted ovals, as red as Garth's own but without white or pupil. Smoke billowed from its flared nostrils and streamed back behind it.

Seeing it, Garth realized for the first time that perhaps he might not defeat the creature. It was much bigger than he had expected and had the advantage of flight, and was armored as well. It really did breathe flame, apparently. He understood now why the villagers had despaired of ever killing such a monster; it moved with sure grace and calm power, a truly awesome sight as it swooped down, gleaming in the sun.

He drew his sword and waited for its attack.

It swept past him, out of reach overhead, enveloping him in a cloud of black smoke; he fought down the need to cough, but blinked frantically to clear his eyes. The hissing grew, crescendoed, then faded as the monster drew away. The smoke stank; it was greasy and vile, and the smell of it filled his nostrils.

When he could see again, he looked up; the dragon was looping about in the eastern sky, coming back for another pass. It had not actually attacked him, he realized, but merely spewed forth its smoke as if it meant to blind or frighten him.

He watched it, his face immobile and calm. It would soon learn that overmen, or at least Garth of Ordunin, could not be frightened easily.

He signaled for Koros to turn, so as to face the dragon's next pass, then stood in the stirrups and swung his sword as it rushed down at him.

He did not strike squarely, but the blade dragged along the side of one great, curved talon, making a harsh scraping sound. Again the monster did not actually attempt to hit him, but merely swooped by, leaving a trail of thick smoke behind.

He whirled when it was past and saw it swinging around toward him again. Its mouth gaped wider, and it roared, belching forth an immense cloud of smoke and fire.

Garth watched the monster spout yellow flame and black smoke and realized that he might do well to retreat, at least temporarily. The thing had been easy on him; it could have fried him on its first pass, yet it had not.

He wondered why. Perhaps it wasn't hungry, and merely wanted to drive him away without a fight. Or perhaps it was hungry and did not want to destroy its dinner. It probably preferred its food raw, not roasted.

Koros roared an answer to the dragon's bellow and turned to face it; the warbeast, at least, was still ready to fight. Garth decided against retreating; he had come to kill the thing and he would never kill it by fleeing.

The creature finished a long, slow turn in mid-air and came at him again, screaming this time like a maddened demon, its cry like nothing the overman had ever heard before. It tore past him, inches above his lowered head; he thrust his weapon upward, where it glanced ringingly off the creature's forelegs without seeming even to scratch them. Garth doubted the dragon had felt the blow through its scaly armor.

The monster wheeled about again, and again it rushed down the sky at him, even lower than before; he leaned sideways in the saddle, ducking out of its path, and struck upward again. The point of his sword bounced and scratched along the creature's belly, then rang metallically from a hind leg and was knocked aside. There was still no sign that the dragon had felt a thing.

If it came in any lower on its next pass, Garth knew, he would be unable to duck under it where he was. As it looped about with another roar, he prodded Koros' flank with his heel and shouted a command.

The startled warbeast broke into a run, moving forward under the dragon's next howling lunge. This time the monster spat forth a jet of flame that seared the grass where the warbeast had stood a moment earlier, and Garth congratulated himself on his decision to dodge.

He watched intently as the creature turned again; it moved smoothly and gracefully, but was not actually very fast in maneuvering. It seemed unable to bank more than a few degrees; Garth guessed that, perhaps due to its size, it was not as stable in flight as a bird. A sufficient tilt might bring it down. He wondered if there were any way to use that against it, then forgot about aerodynamics as it swept down toward him again.

He sent Koros sideways this time, turning the warbeast out of its path. He misjudged slightly, or perhaps the dragon had allowed for his motion, and he felt the heat of its fiery breath at his back. Koros roared in pain; the fur of its tail had been singed.

Garth patted the warbeast, apologizing, as he considered the situation. The traditional method of dragon-slaying, according to legend, was to find some minute chink in the creature's armor and strike at it. He had seen no sign of any flaw in this dragon's defenses – but then, he had been too busy dodging to study it very closely. Still, the armor on this monster seemed almost unnaturally perfect – countless rows of fine golden scales in flawless, gleaming array.

The dragon was not making another attack, he realized; instead it was circling, far out of reach. It appeared almost to be waiting for something, as if to see if the overman still intended to fight. Garth considered retreating, then dismissed the idea. When diving, the dragon moved with the speed of a falling stone, and it could probably catch him from behind before he could reach the forest. It might, he thought, be trying to coax him into just such a foolhardy maneuver.

He watched it wheel about, and an idea struck him. The thing was gigantic, and as it made the far part of its turn, he glimpsed its broad, smooth back, as wide and solid as the deck of a ship. If he could get atop it, he could hack at it at his leisure; with its limited aerodynamic ability, it might be unable to dislodge him. He had used a similar technique against a monster once before, the great worm that lived beneath Dûsarra, though that particular creature had not had the benefits of flight, flame, and armor.

The difficulty lay in getting onto the thing, but even that might not be impossible. He looked down at Koros' black-furred back, shoulder muscles rippling under its hide as it shifted its stance. He had seen the warbeast leap to and from low rooftops, and bound over crowds of humans. It could almost certainly manage the jump he wanted.

Of course, he was not at all certain that he himself could manage his part of the feat he planned, but if he did not, it would probably mean nothing worse than a long fall. He could take a fall. He could see little to be lost by trying; the dragon could slay him just as easily if he did not make the attempt.

The dragon still circled smoothly in the sky above the mound; he turned the warbeast toward it and gave the command to charge.

Koros roared, so loudly that Garth's ears rang, and began bounding up the slope. Seeing this, the dragon turned and came to meet the overman and warbeast, bellowing and screaming and smoking like a burning city. As they drew nearer to one another Garth gauged the distance carefully and, when he judged the moment to be right, shouted the command to leap.

Koros leaped, jaws wide and claws out, to attack the dragon; the warbeast was roaring with bloodlust. Garth felt the leap as a great surge upward; so smooth was the movement that he hardly realized when Koros left the ground. As the dragon loomed up before him, a gleaming coppery wall, he leaped himself, flinging himself upward from the saddle to grab at the monster's neck.

He struck hard against a shining red-gold flank and clung desperately, digging fingernails into the overlapping of the scales and scrambling upward with his feet.

His faithful mount, thrown off course by his own jump, hit the dragon full in the chest, then fell away, yowling with pain and anger, as its fangs and claws failed to penetrate and grip the gleaming armor.

Garth watched, concerned, as the warbeast fell. When Koros landed, catlike, on all fours and rose, apparently unhurt, Garth turned his attention back to his own situation with great relief.

He had a precarious purchase on the monster's shoulder, the wind whipping about him as the dragon sped through the skies. With all his superhuman strength, he forced himself upward against the hard scales and, with muscles straining, managed to haul himself up atop its back.

When he felt that he was reasonably secure between the mighty shoulders, he looked the beast over. He was surprised to discover that the scales felt fully as metallic as they looked.

The dragon seemed to be searching for something, looping back and forth across the mound and the meadow below, and Garth realized that it was unaware of his presence on its back.

It could feel nothing through its armor and thought that he, too, like Koros, had fallen.

He smiled, brushed aside a lock of black hair that had fallen into one eye, and drew his dagger. He had lost his sword in his leap, releasing it without conscious thought when he had to find a fingerhold, but his axe was slung across his back, and the dagger's sheath was secure on his belt. He set about prying at the scales on the back of the dragon's neck, wedging the point of the knife beneath their overlapped edges and working upward.

The scales tore loose and fell, tinkling down past the dragon's wings into space. To Garth's surprise, the monster did not react. He leaned forward to look at the spot of hide thus uncovered, as the wind of a high-speed turn lashed at him.

Beneath the scaly armor was a fine wire mesh, and beneath that, Garth could faintly make out a myriad of gears, chains, springs, and sprockets, ticking quietly.

He sat motionless for a moment, absorbing this discovery of the dragon's true nature. Quickly, he reached a decision; he could not kill this thing, obviously, and now he decided that he did not want to destroy it. He sat back and waited.

It was almost pleasant, crouching atop the broad metal back of the dragon as it swooped through the air. Garth had never flown before and found what little he could see from where he sat to be intriguing indeed. The wind was fresh and exhilarating when the monster was not in one of its sudden turns or dives, and the view was amazing.

He did not have to wait long; after a few more passes across the hillock and meadow the dragon looped back up across the riverbank, then soared gracefully down into the gaping mouth of a cave on the eastern shore, at the base of the hillock. It braked by cupping its wings forward.

Inside the opening, it folded its wings and settled neatly to the ground, landing with a heavy thud and a mild bump. Then, in a scant second, it froze into total immobility, losing completely its incredible semblance of life and becoming a mere metal construct.

Garth glanced up and about and saw that the entire inside of the mound was hollow. Nor was it a natural cave; stone arches braced the ceiling, and niches were occupied by flaring oil lamps. Three young men stood off to one side, well away from the dragon; they had not yet noticed its unwanted passenger.

The smoke that still streamed from the creature's nostrils suddenly thickened, and a loud hissing came from somewhere beneath the overman; then the smoke stopped entirely, leaving a thinning cloud to obscure the chamber's sooty upper reaches.

Garth leaned over the dragon's shoulder and watched as a door in its belly swung open, just barely visible to him beyond the curve of chest and foreleg. Three men crawled out, then two more, and finally two more still.

Garth lifted the axe off his back with his right hand, keeping his drawn dagger in his left, and vaulted down to the cave floor. He landed in front of the party of seven that had emerged from the dragon, with the other three humans to his right. The jump was longer than he had realized in the poor light, but he managed to catch himself and keep from sprawling, though it was not the dignified and dramatic entrance that he had hoped for.

The men froze, staring at him in astonishment. He stared back.

After a moment of stunned silence, Garth demanded, "So it was all a fraud?"

The faces of the men were blackened with some sort of gritty dust, but Garth thought he recognized one of them as a person he had seen in the village where he had eaten that morning. It was this man who answered. "No, no . . . I mean, not originally. There was a real dragon once, really there was."

"But he died," another man said.

"We fed him poisoned sheep," a third added. "It was really very simple. My grandfather told me all about it."

"And you built a new one, so that no one would know it was dead. Why?"

The men looked at one another; it was plain to Garth that they were terrified of him, overawed by this huge inhuman warrior they faced, and none wanted to be the first to give an answer he might not like.

"Why?" Garth demanded again, brandishing his axe.

There was a sudden babble of response as they all decided simultaneously that not answering might be even more dangerous than speaking unpleasant truths. "To frighten off outsiders and keep away invaders," one replied.

Garth lowered his weapons; everything was suddenly clear. Orgûl was a peaceful valley; any warriors it might once have had to defend it must have died fighting the dragon. Yet it was surrounded by avaricious warlords who would gladly turn it into a battlefield – the Baron of Sland, for example, would undoubtedly be delighted to have an undefended target for conquest that was not a part of the Kingdom of Eramma and thus not covered by the terms of his predecessor's surrender. While the dreaded dragon had lived, though, no one had dared to attack; the tales had kept potential invaders away, assuring them that the monster could destroy an army.

The Orgûlians had not meant to harm anyone, but merely to protect their homes. They had not slain Garth with their toy even when they had a chance. They could have burned him to death three times over, yet had not. He could not hold against them their desire to defend themselves and to frighten away a menace to their security.

It was impressive indeed, this device of theirs, and obviously a needed precaution; stories alone would not have staved off adventurers forever, but the sight of a dragon flying overhead, perhaps snorting fire and smoke, would deter all but a dedicated lunatic such as Garth.

He looked at the great machine and asked, "How does it work?"

The change in the human faces was dramatic as the tension suddenly dissipated. "Oh, it's most complex!" a young man, perhaps only a boy, exclaimed. "Come and see! There is a furnace for the smoke and flame, and one man works that, and there's one to each wing, while another serves to guide them. I control the tail, and Deg, here, controls the claws, and then there's a man in the neck. It's all most intricate, and all clockwork, all mechanical, machinery like no other. It takes all ten of us all day to wind it."

Garth nodded in response to the youth's enthusiasm, and a tentative smile appeared here and there among the humans. "Who made it?" he asked, though he thought he knew the answer.

"Why, old Petter, the toymaker, did most of it, designing and building most of the machinery. The smith built the framework, and the tinker and three apprentices made the scales. Gerrith the jeweler made the eyes, and the whole village worked on it where we could. Every town in Orgûl helps in mining coal for the furnace now."

Another man interrupted, asking desperately, "You won't tell anyone, will you? It's all that keeps the Baron of Sland away!"

Garth's grin faded. "I should tell the old man who sent me here – but no, I need not do that; I can tell him, truthfully, that the dragon is dead. I will say nothing to any other, and I think that you need not worry about the old man; he speaks little and will keep silent about it."

"That's all right, then," someone said. Relief was evident on several coal-darkened faces.

"Would you like to see inside?" the young man asked.

Garth nodded. "Yes, I would. But I must not stay too long; my warbeast must be found and its injuries tended."

"I don't think he's hurt much," one of the dragon's crew volunteered.

A roar from the mouth of the cave confirmed his opinion; Koros had had little trouble in tracking down the dragon. It stalked silently into the chamber to greet its master.

Garth made it welcome, then remarked to the man who had last spoken, "*It*, not *he*; only the neuters ever grow large enough to be ridden." He told the warbeast to behave, then followed the youth into the dragon's belly to study the workings of the great machine.

Chapter Five

Garth spent the night in a room at the Sword and Chalice, but the inn had no stable adequate to house Koros, so the warbeast stayed out on the plaza. There was little danger that anyone would try to steal it or any of Garth's belongings still on its back; the beast knew well who its master was, and would not accompany a stranger without Garth's orders, or permit anyone but the overman to disturb the supplies it guarded. No one in his right mind would argue with a warbeast. No one mad enough to try would survive the argument.

The overman arose late, a good hour after sunrise, and took his time in preparing for his departure. The afternoon, he knew, would be more than enough for him to find his way out of Orgûl; once he was in Eramma again he intended to travel by night, as he had done before.

When he had finished his packing, eaten a hearty breakfast, and made sure that Koros had been tended to, he swung himself into the saddle, ready to leave. Before Koros had taken more than a single step, however, he changed his mind and ordered the warbeast to turn west rather than northeast. He had no reason to hurry; no urgent tasks needed to be undertaken, no one eagerly awaited his return to Skelleth. It could do no harm if he lingered for a visit to the toymaker; after all, he had a purchase to make.

Koros had no objection; it strode silently down the western street and halted obediently at the door of the last shop.

The door was closed, and the curtains were drawn across the display windows; Garth saw no sign of the old man. He dismounted and rapped lightly, twice, on the wooden panels.

A muffled call answered him, and a moment later the toymaker emerged, blinking in the bright sunlight. He stared up at the overman.

"Oh, it's you," he said with an uncertain smile.

"Greetings," Garth said. "I hope I did not wake you."

"What? Oh, no; I was just eating my breakfast. Hadn't had time to open the shop yet." He blinked again and then said anxiously, "I heard about your fight with the dragon. I hope you didn't hurt it too much; I'm not sure whether I could fix any serious damage. It's mostly magic, you know, and magic is tricky stuff. I'm no wizard; I don't usually know how what I do works. I just build things and they work – or sometimes they don't. Did you do it much harm?"

"No," Garth replied. "I pried a few scales from its back and I might have scratched the belly a little. I think that hurt my sword more than it hurt the dragon – or maybe the blade was dulled when I dropped it." He had retrieved the weapon before returning to the village; it had not been bent, fortunately, but part of one edge, from the tip halfway to the hilt, had been ruined.

"What about yourself? Were you hurt?"

"No. My warbeast's tail was singed, I'm afraid, and it seems to have been bruised here and there."

"Oh, I am sorry!" The man stared past the overman at the beast, his face radiating sympathy.

Garth decided that it was time he got to the point. "I came for the gull," he said.

"Oh, of course!" the toymaker exclaimed. "Just a moment!" He vanished back into the shop, then emerged a few seconds later holding the metal bird. Garth accepted it, paid out the agreed-upon price of half a dozen silver coins, and placed it delicately on the saddle.

"You'll need the key," the old man reminded him.

Garth turned back and held out his hand; the toymaker dropped the silver key onto his palm, and he closed both thumbs over it. "Thank you," he said as he dropped it in his purse.

"Take good care of it," the man said. "It's one of my finer pieces."

"It is indeed," Garth agreed, gazing at the gleaming clockwork gull. "But not your finest," he added, with a nod to the west.

The toymaker smiled. "No, it's not my finest, but my very best is not for sale." He watched as Garth seated himself in the saddle, the copper bird perched before him, and gave a command to his mount.

Koros turned and headed back through the village, its smooth, silent progress carrying it and its master quickly northward out of Orgûl.

That steady stride seemed effortless, and the warbeast could keep it up for hours on end, perhaps days on end; Garth was continually impressed by the creature's incredible power and stamina.

It took them the remainder of that day and the following night to reach the northern edge of the Barony of Sland, moving along the foothills east of the mountains that formed Eramma's western border. Garth made camp atop a ridge overlooking the desolate site of a moderately recent battle.

His brief stay in Orgûl had put him in a state of mild euphoria. He had not fought and slain a monster, but instead had found that his real task, that of freeing people from the menace that beset them, had been accomplished long before by the threatened people themselves. That was heartening; only rarely in his long life had he seen much evidence of human competence. Even among his own species, it often seemed that the average mortal had no more ambition or wit than a lower animal had. Too many people were willing to suffer under various forms of oppression, rather than make the effort necessary to improve their lot.

No one among the overmen of the Northern Waste had attempted to come south overland for any purpose during the three centuries of relative peace that had followed the Racial Wars; they had been told that the border with Eramma was guarded night and day by ferocious human warriors and they had believed it until Garth made the journey to Skelleth himself, for reasons of his own, and discovered the pitiful state of the human defenses.

No overman had troubled himself to explore other kingdoms until Garth, on an errand for the Forgotten King, ventured into Nekutta and learned that there were other overmen still in the world, living on the Yprian Coast. And no attempt had been made to establish trade until Garth began it.

Among humans, the people of Skelleth had tolerated an insane baron without serious complaint, ignoring his bizarre behavior and occasional arbitrary executions, until Garth murdered him. In the Nekuttan city of Dûsarra the populace had made no protest against the domination of the cults of the dark gods, nor had it tried to halt the kidnappings and human sacrifices of the more vicious cults.

In Orgûl, though, when heroes had failed to kill the dragon, ordinary farmers had managed to poison it, and common village craftsmen had built and maintained a replacement to ward off other predators, more human but no less vicious.

That fact cheered Garth considerably.

His own behavior pleased him as well. For the first time he had ventured out into human lands beyond Skelleth, accomplished as much of his purpose as he saw fit, and headed homeward without killing a single person.

He was, he had been told, the chosen avatar of Bheleu, doomed to symbolize the Fourteenth Age, the Age of Destruction. Heretofore it had seemed that he was destined to bring chaos and disaster wherever he went; he had led the sacking of Skelleth, been responsible for bringing the White Death to Dûsarra, been involved in the death of the wizard who had ruled Mormoreth and killed its population, and, he suspected, somehow contributed to the collapse of the Kingdom of Eramma.

On this particular journey, however, he had not destroyed anything, nor killed anything more important than goats, and those only for food for his mount.

This raised his spirits so much that even the battlefields and soldiers he passed on his way north did not dissipate his good cheer. He moved on past Sland and along the mountains until he came within sight of the towers of Ur-Dormulk, where he turned east and circled around the city. He had traveled this far by night, but from here on, the population was thin and the land inhospitable; the war would therefore not be much in evidence. Furthermore, beyond Ur-Dormulk, overmen were no longer totally unknown; the Yprian caravans had been crossing these lands occasionally for most of the past three years, and the people were accustomed to them. Householders would not attack Garth on sight simply because of his species.

He could, if he chose, travel by day and use the highway to Skelleth openly.

Switching his schedule all at once, however, was not particularly convenient; instead, he lengthened each leg of it, riding on into the morning until he was too weary to want to go farther, then sleeping on past sunset until he awoke naturally and fully rested. He did, however, follow the high road; the plains were still muddy from melted snow and spring rain.

He finally came within sight of Skelleth around noon, but he had been awake since midnight, so that as far as he was concerned it was late in the day and he was ready to rest. He had bought a goat for Koros the previous morning and eaten well himself, at a small farm he had passed, but he had had nothing since save for a handful of dried fruit and salted beef; his provisions were beginning to run low. He was tired and hungry and looking forward to cold ale and hot food at the King's Inn, followed by a soft bed in the house he had rebuilt for himself from the ruins at the edge of town.

The prospect of a good rest, and his lingering good mood, put a smile on his face. He glanced down at the clockwork gull he kept on the saddle before him; he had not cared to pack it away where it might be damaged by bumping against his other belongings. It gleamed golden in the thin, dreary light that seeped through the thick clouds overhead. The weather had been good throughout his trip, but he knew that could not last much longer; indeed, the sky looked very much as if there would be rain before nightfall.

When he glanced up from the metal bird, Garth noticed that something or someone stood outside the town wall, beside the highway he rode upon. His smile faded. The last time he had ridden up this highway someone had been waiting upon it, an overman named Thord; he had been posted there as part of an inept siege laid by Garth's chief wife Kyrith, and it had been that siege which had led to the sacking of Skelleth. Garth did not much care to be reminded of that.

He wondered whom or what he was seeing; the distance was such that he could not yet make the figure out. He hoped that, whatever it was, it was not the harbinger of more trouble.

The thing stood about the height of an overman, Garth judged, or perhaps an unusually tall human, but the shape seemed slightly wrong. He rode on.

When he had drawn somewhat nearer, he saw that it was, indeed, an overman, or something very much like one, but slumped forward, and with something projecting upward at the back of its neck.

Another of the warbeast's long strides allowed Garth to determine that the overman, if such it truly was, was hanging from a post or stake, apparently lifeless.

Garth was confused; he had no idea what this thing could signify, what overman could be there, or why. He did not like it. The figure was utterly lifeless, and Garth wondered whether perhaps it was an effigy of himself, put there by some enemy, a townsman, perhaps, who had never forgiven him his part in Skelleth's destruction.

The other possibility, that it was a real overman's corpse hung up as a warning of some kind, was much less appealing.

He rode closer and began to perceive details. Black hair hung down limply, hiding the face; the hands were pulled back, out of sight, presumably tied to the pole or to each other. The figure faced directly toward him. A blue tunic covered the torso, and brown leather riding breeches the legs, with mudspattered boots on its feet. There was a disturbing familiarity to it.

The possibility that it was just an effigy grew dimmer with each step and vanished long before he reached the corpse's side.

The sensation of familiarity increased, and with it Garth's concern. By the time he told Koros to stop, he was seriously worried, convinced that he had come upon the body of someone he knew well.

He dismounted, and as he turned toward the suspended corpse he realized for the first time that it was female. Overwomen were not as clearly differentiated from overmen as women were from men; there was no difference in height, and both sexes were equally flat-chested, though males tended to be broader at the shoulder and narrower at the hip. The primary sexual distinction was in the odor.

With the realization of the sex of the corpse, he was suddenly sure of its identity; he ran to it, hoping that he was wrong, and lifted the drooping head.

He had not been wrong. It was Kyrith. Her red eyes were open, blank, and staring, and her leathery brown skin was cold and clammy; Garth could have no doubt that she was dead.

He was so horrified, so caught by her dead gaze, that he did not at first consciously notice the marks on her forehead. Like all their people she had a broad, high forehead, the skin drawn tight across the bone; now her brow was caked with dried blood, and blood had congealed in rivulets down either side of her face.

When Garth was able to turn his eyes from hers, he saw the blood and followed the dried streams to their source.

There were cuts in her forehead, many of them, but not mere random slashes; Garth did not immediately see the pattern, for the blood had blurred it, and shock had dulled his wits. As he continued to stare, however, he made out the nature of the marks. On her right side was a horizontal curl, and a diagonal, and then a long downstroke – the rune for A. Next was the upward curve, hooked downstroke, and downward curve of GH, then another A, and finally the short upright and long double curve of a D – except that here the curve was broken and awkward, more like a series of short slashes. Runes were meant to be drawn with ink on paper, not cut into flesh.

AGHAD.

Garth knew that name well. Humans swore by it, sometimes, and used it in jesting reference to liars or unfaithful spouses, but Garth knew it to be no joke. It was the name of the god of hatred and treachery, and of a cult he had defied and defiled when he robbed their temple and slew their high priest in Dûsarra about three years before.

The cult had made a habit of casual and gruesome murders, and had sworn vengeance upon him, but he had long since dismissed it from his thoughts. He had believed the cultists to be limited to their own city, far to the west, and had considered their threats merely human boastfulness.

He had, he saw now, been wrong.

No trace remained of his earlier euphoria, nor of the boredom and purposelessness that had driven him to undertake his errand to Orgûl. A cold, hard determination burned in his breast; he would destroy the cult of Aghad, and if the means could be found, he would kill the filthy god himself. Garth was an oathbreaker, forsworn, so he made no spoken vow, but his unvoiced commitment was none the less certain for that.

The initial astonished horror was fading, driven out by rage, and he looked over his wife's corpse.

A cord was wrapped around her throat, then looped back and tied around the stake. Wire bound her wrists behind the post so tightly that it had drawn blood, gouging deeply into the flesh. A third strand, this one of hideously inappropriate gold braid, passed across her chest, under her arms, and up to a spike driven into the back of the stake; it was this last that actually supported most of her weight and held her upright.

Garth drew his dagger and cut away the braid with a single short slash, then caught the corpse with his left arm as it started to slump. Another cut severed the line around the neck, allowing a small pouch he had not previously noticed to fall to the ground.

He ignored the little bag for the moment as, holding his dead wife with his left hand and body, he tried to pry apart the wire at her wrists. It resisted; although it had the appearance of cheap iron, the wire notched the blade of his knife when he worked the point underneath. Nor could he find any loose end whereby he might untangle it.

He lowered the body into a sitting position, the hands resting on the ground behind the stake, and considered. The followers of Aghad, he recalled, took a perverse delight in doing everything they could to infuriate their victims. They were also fond of mutilation. They probably intended to frustrate and annoy Garth with some manner of trickery, until he became sufficiently maddened that he would sever Kyrith's hand to free her from the post.

The wire, he decided, must be ensorcelled in some way. There was no point in struggling with it – yet he had no desire to gratify the Aghadites by dismembering his wife.

The problem could be handled in another way. He fetched his battle-axe from the warbeast's saddle and, with three blows, cut through the foot-thick stake just above Kyrith's sagging head. Having eliminated the spike that had held the braid, Garth was able to lift her easily, so that her hands slid up over the broken end and came free.

That done, he remembered the pouch that had fallen from the neck cord. He laid the corpse gently on the ground and looked for it.

The little bag lay where it had fallen, at the foot of the stake. He picked it up, opened it cautiously, and drew out the roll of parchment it contained.

He had heard of spells that worked through runes, of messages that could bind an unsuspecting victim to the writer's will, but he did not seriously consider it likely that this parchment was anything of that kind. He thought, rather, that it would be a threat or a boast, or perhaps both; the Aghadites had seemed to him the sort of vicious creatures who would not be satisfied with the mere fact of murder, or with the crude attribution carved on the corpse's brow.

He unrolled the parchment and read the following: "Greetings to Garth of Skelleth, once Prince of Ordunin. The righteous vengeance of Aghad has begun, and you will suffer a thousandfold for the affronts you have committed. For the desecration of the god's shrine and the murder of his chosen high priest, you will pay with everything you value. All those you care for will die horribly. Your sons will die slowly as you watch. That which you have built will be cast down and destroyed. That which you have opposed will be exalted. That which you own shall be taken from you. As your pain grows, know always that Aghad will take joy in it, and his worshippers will laugh at your agony."

There was no signature.

Garth crumpled the parchment in his fist and thrust it into a pouch on his belt. Before he could withdraw his hand, he felt a sudden warmth, and the smell of smoke reached his slit nostrils. Startled, he withdrew his hand and dumped the pouch onto a patch of bare earth.

Nothing remained of the note but smoldering ash.

He snorted. If the indestructible wire had not been proof enough, this little demonstration left no doubt that the cult was using magic against him. He looked up, glanced quickly around, but saw nothing. He had fought magic before, several times, and knew it to be a real and sometimes deadly force; he would need to keep a careful watch.

Someone, he realized, might be watching him even now, and he could no longer resist speaking. "Your god will not save you, filth," he said, his voice flat. "Your cult will die, to the last man or woman. My wife's forehead bears your death warrant." He picked up the axe he had dropped and, in a sudden display of fury, splintered the stump of the stake with a single blow.

In Dûsarra, in his inner chamber, Haggat watched the overman's actions and permitted himself a small, silent chuckle. Events were proceeding almost exactly as he had envisioned, though the failure of the wired wrists was slightly disappointing. It was still much as he had wanted. The stolen magics were working perfectly.

This might, he thought, be worth the long wait.

Chapter Six

His anger under control once more, Garth returned the axe to its place on the warbeast's saddle. He looked around at the scattered shards of the stake, then gathered up everything of possible value. That done, he picked up Kyrith's body and ordered Koros to follow him. Carrying his dead wife in his arms, he marched into Skelleth.

The manner of expressing certain emotions differed between human and overman. Overmen made no show of grief or anger on their faces, but instead displayed at such times an expression that in humans would appear to be one of utter disinterest. This was not a result of training in stoicism or any other cultural influence, but a difference in genetic makeup. An overman who seemed bored might be in a murderous rage.

A human guard was posted at the southwestern gate – not a professional soldier, but a volunteer, put there not so much for defense as to run ahead of an arriving caravan to inform Galt and the town's merchants of its approach. The man assigned to this job carried a crossbow and a short sword, more or less as a formality.

The individual who was on duty at the time of Garth's return from Orgûl had not heard the overman's approach, having dozed off in the shelter of a ruined wall. He had stirred slightly at the sound of the axe smashing the post, but did not come fully awake until Garth's footsteps had drawn quite near.

Startled, he got to his feet, his hand on the hilt of his sword, and prepared to call a challenge.

Garth's face was calm and still, but had the guard spoken, Garth would have taken delight in killing him, probably using only his bare hands. He was in no mood to deal with strangers, particularly human strangers; the cult of Aghad was comprised mostly of humans. Few overmen took an interest in anything so ethereal as religion.

Only the fact that the guard recognized both Garth and Kyrith saved his life; he was so shocked at the sight of the corpse that he could not speak at first, and when he had recovered something of his composure, a glance at Garth's bloodred eyes discouraged any questions he might have had. He stood back respectfully and let the burdened overman and riderless warbeast pass unhindered.

When they had moved on up the road he debated briefly with himself. He was supposed to run ahead of new arrivals and give warning of their approach;

Garth, however, was a resident of Skelleth, however unwelcome his presence there might be to some of the villagers. Furthermore, the overman did not look as if he would appreciate a welcoming committee.

The guard decided, with a glance at Garth's armored back, that he would prefer facing a charge of dereliction of duty to risking the overman's annoyance. He stayed where he was.

Most of the outer portion of Skelleth was a ring of uninhabited ruins, a reminder of the town's long decline; only the central area, around the market, was populated. As a result of this, Garth walked some distance on empty streets, between fallen stones and broken beams, before he was again seen by human eyes.

Like the guard at the gate, the villagers who saw his approach recognized him. Remembering the sacking of Skelleth and seeing the warbeast at his heels, they hung well back and let him pass without hindrance or comment. The traditional fear of overmen had been largely dissipated by three years of trade, but Garth's berserker reputation, the sight of the corpse, and the presence of the warbeast were enough to send even the boldest scurrying out of his path without concern for their dignity.

He reached the market unmolested, not having spoken a word since he entered the walls. There he lowered Kyrith's body to the ground, turned toward the new house on the east side of the square, and bellowed, *"Saram!"*

Windows opened instantly, and faces peered out. Saram's was not among them, but Garth recognized one that appeared on the upper floor of the Baron's house. He pointed at the girl and shouted, "You, there! You get Lord Saram out here!"

The girl, Saram's housekeeper, vanished inside.

A moment later the front door opened, and one of the Baron's clerks thrust her head out. "My lord Saram is occupied at present, my lord Garth," she said. "How may I help you?"

Garth's hand fell to the hilt of his sword. He replied, slowly and clearly, without shouting, "You will inform Lord Saram that if he is not out here within the count of twenty, he will not live to see the sun set today, and this stinking village will not see tomorrow's dawn."

The clerk's politely noncommittal expression vanished instantly, to be replaced with a gape of terrified astonishment. She disappeared back inside, leaving the door open.

Garth did not bother to count; as he had expected, Saram appeared on the doorstep within a few seconds, a napkin in his hand.

The Baron of Skelleth did not trouble to look about, but simply stared directly at the overman. "What is it, Garth?" he asked, a trace of annoyance in his voice.

Garth's reply was toneless and deadly. "Come here, human," he said.

Saram knew better than to argue. He came; halfway to where Garth waited, he suddenly noticed Kyrith's body and stopped dead. After a moment's hesitation, he continued on and stood a few feet away, staring down at the corpse in surprise.

"What happened?" he asked.

"You will tell *me* that, man, or I'll burn this town to the ground. How could

this happen?"

"I don't know, Garth, I swear by all the gods! She came into town two days ago, looking for you; she said you had sent an urgent message asking her to come to Skelleth. We told her it must have been a mistake, that you'd been gone for days, and that was the last we saw of her – until now. I thought she'd gone back north again, gone home?"

"She was last seen alive two days ago?"

"About that; 'twas midafternoon of the day before yesterday."

"She has been dead only a few hours at most, Saram. Where was she in between?"

"I don't know, I swear it." The Baron met the overman's gaze for a moment, then turned back to the corpse.

Garth reached out and grabbed the front of Saram's elaborately embroidered tunic. "What do you know about the cult of Aghad?" he demanded.

Startled, Saram looked up again. "What cult of Aghad?" he asked. "There isn't any, is there? I never heard of anyone outside Dûsarra who worshipped him or any of the other dark gods, and the White Death has destroyed Dûsarra."

"Look at her forehead, human." Garth released Saram's tunic and grabbed his neatly trimmed back hair, pulling his head down close to Kyrith's face. Saram looked, as Garth added, "There was a note as well, a magical one that destroyed itself after I read it. A cult of Aghad still exists, and his followers have killed my wife."

"I don't know anything about them," Saram insisted after Garth allowed him to straighten up. "Perhaps 'tis some other enemy of yours, trying to avoid the blame."

"What enemy?"

"How should I know? Maybe 'tis that bunch of wizards that tried to kill you three years ago."

"No; why should they kill Kyrith? Why would they not attack me directly? I am no longer defended by the power of the Sword of Bheleu; the wizards would surely know that. If they sought revenge they would simply slay me, attacking directly, as they attacked me before. No, Saram, this is cruelty for its own sake; this is the work of evil people, to kill an innocent like this just to get at me. It must be one of the cults I angered. The followers of Bheleu are all dead; the priest of Death is a harmless old man. I did nothing to anger the cult of P'hul. That leaves four: Tema, Andhur Regvos, Sai, or Aghad. Only Aghad takes pride in treachery; had one of the others slain Kyrith, that cult would have proclaimed itself openly. The followers of Aghad might have lied and blamed others, but no one would falsely accuse *them.* It is in truth the Aghadites who have done this, I am certain."

"Then what do you want of *me?*" Saram asked. "I am no Aghadite."

"You are the Baron of Skelleth. Whatever happens in this town and the territory surrounding it is your responsibility."

"I accept no blame for this murder, Garth."

"You have allowed the cult of Aghad to exist, to take action in your domain."

"I have not! I told you, I thought the cult was extinct."

"The cult is not extinct, Saram, but if you value your life, you will do what you can to see that it *becomes* extinct."

"Of course I will! Do you think I want more murders? Do you think I do not regret this one? Kyrith was my friend, Garth, and you are my friend as well. What has hurt you has hurt me. I wish that there were something I could do to undo what has happened, but I am as mortal as you; I cannot turn back time."

Garth did not reply; the phrasing of Saram's defense reminded him that he had other business to attend to. As Saram had said, he was merely mortal and could do nothing to restore Kyrith to life, any more than Garth could – but there was one person in Skelleth who was something other than mortal. The Forgotten King was the chosen of the god of death; he had lived for centuries, perhaps for millennia, and had powers and abilities greater than any ordinary priest or wizard.

He was also a treacherous old schemer. Garth did not say so to Saram, but he suspected that if anywhere in the world there was anyone other than the cultists of Aghad who was implicated in Kyrith's murder, it was the Forgotten King. His part in it, if he was involved, might have been anything from the most indirect sort of encouragement to planning and carrying out the whole scheme himself and falsely accusing the Aghadites. The old man could, of course, be innocent, but Garth would not take that for granted; the King had been entangled in Garth's life too often for the overman to dismiss the possibility of his complicity. It was the old man who had suggested that Garth should go adventuring and who had proposed his destination and thereby ensured a certain minimum travel time.

Perhaps the old man had planned the whole ghastly murder for some perverse reason of his own; perhaps it had been calculated to goad Garth into some action he would otherwise have avoided.

It was just as likely, though, that the cult of Aghad had simply seized upon the opportunity Garth's absence had presented and that the old man had had no part in it.

Garth had mulled this over while carrying Kyrith's body through the village to the market; the possibility of the King's involvement had been immediately obvious as soon as Garth had gotten over his initial shock.

It bore looking into, but he had wanted to acquaint himself with the available facts about Kyrith's return from Ordunin and whatever was generally known of her death. The Forgotten King, with his reluctance to speak, would have been of little help there. Nor had Garth wanted to waste any time in alerting Saram to the murder, the probable presence of the cult of Aghad, and Garth's anger.

He had done that; now he could turn his attention to the King.

Saram's words had also suggested a faint possibility Garth had not previously considered. The King, no mere mortal, had an undeniable connection with The God Whose Name Is Not Spoken; if there was anyone in all the world who might be capable of restoring Kyrith to life, it was he.

With that in mind Garth turned, leaving Kyrith's body on the packed earth of the marketplace, and marched toward the King's Inn. "See that she is not disturbed," he called back over his shoulder to the Baron, "and that the cult of Aghad is driven from Skelleth."

Saram stood in open-mouthed astonishment at this sudden change. Garth seemed to have abandoned the conversation in midstream and had simply walked off after dragging him, Saram, Baron of Skelleth, out of his home. Koros, too, was apparently caught by surprise; the warbeast gave a low, questioning growl, which the departing overman answered with an order that meant "stand and guard." Saram looked at the beast, noticed the gleaming metal bird on its back, and grew still more confused. What, he wondered, was that thing? He looked again at Garth, then back at Kyrith's body, and decided to stay where he was until he could get everything straight in his mind.

Garth stalked across the wooden weighing platforms that occupied what was once the site of the old Baron's mansion, across the narrow strip that used to be a back alley cut off from the square by the mansion, and through the open door of the King's Inn.

The tavern looked very much as it always had; there was no indication that anything within was not as it should be. The heavy, worn tables were in their accustomed places, the great brass-bound barrels still lined the west wall, and the vast stone hearth still took up most of the east. At the rear stairs led to the upper floor, and the Forgotten King's table stood in the corner beneath. Everything was clean, with the soft sheen that could only result from centuries of use and care.

The tavernkeeper stood by one of his barrels, a mug and a polishing cloth in his hands; two customers were conversing over wine. The Forgotten King sat motionless at his table.

Garth marched across the room. He did not bother to seat himself, but stood beside the King's table and demanded, "What did you have to do with it?"

The old man croaked, "Nothing."

"Is that all you have to say? Am I to trust you so readily?"

"I swear by my heart and all the gods, by the true name of The God Whose Name Is Not Spoken, that I had no part in your wife's murder."

Some portion of Garth's mind was aware that the old man was taking this seriously indeed, to make so long an answer so quickly, but his anger would not permit him to consider that. "And what good is your vow? How can it bind you? Death holds no terror for you, old man; you have little to lose in that regard. Nor have you shown any thought for your honor; what need have you of honor or trust, you who have incomprehensible power and no desire but death? You have abandoned the service of your god; can I know that his name still holds you?"

"You cannot be certain. Take my word or not, as you please." The old man's ghastly voice was as dead as ever.

Garth was by no means so calm; with a wordless bellow, he reached out and grabbed the King's throat in one huge hand. "Lying scum!" he cried. "Deathless monster! Do you dare to mock me at such a time?" In his rage, he cared little for accuracy or fairness and ignored the fact that, if any mockery had been spoken, it was he who had mocked the King and not the reverse. He squeezed.

His hand went limp and dead, falling with a heavy thud on the table.

"Your pardon, Garth. I lived for several years with a broken neck once, long ago, and I have no desire to repeat the experience."

Garth stared down at his hand. Sensation returned in a sudden rush of pain.

He had bruised several knuckles on the oaken tabletop.

The discomfort quickly faded to insignificance, but served to distract him from his anger long enough for his rationality to reassert control. As the incident had demonstrated, the King had power. Garth could not harm him, but he might be able to use him. After a moment's hesitation, he moved around the table and sat down opposite the old man.

"It is I, rather, who should ask for pardon, O King," he said. "Forgive me; I let my grief get the better of me. I came here not to challenge you, but to ask a favor. I do not know the limits of your power, O King; perhaps what I ask cannot be done. Still, I must make the attempt. Can you restore Kyrith to life?"

The King paused before he moved his head once from side to side. "No, Garth. I am sorry."

"It is not possible?"

"I cannot do it."

"Why not? You are the high priest of Death; have you no power over him?"

"You ask me to undo the god's work. Could you create with the Sword of Bheleu, restore what you had destroyed?"

Garth had to acknowledge that he could not have done such a thing; the very essence of the sword's power was destruction. He was not willing to give up completely, however. "What of your own spells? You were a mighty wizard in your own right, were you not? Knew you no magic to restore the dead?"

"If ever I did, it is centuries forgotten."

"Is there no talisman that can serve? Bheleu has his sword, and the Death-God his book; has the god of life no totem?"

"The totems of the Lords of Eir lost their virtue at the center of time, in the Eighth Age, when the balance first shifted against them. They have no power now, if they still exist at all."

"Is there no way to shift this balance again?"

The old man shrugged almost imperceptibly. "There may be; if so, it would be in the Book of Silence. That is not the totem of The God Whose Name Is Not Spoken, but of Dagha, god of time, the creator of both Eir and Dûs." He stopped suddenly, as if he had meant to say more and then thought better of it.

Garth, listening intently, noticed the peculiarly abrupt stop, but could read no meaning into it. He ignored it and considered instead the words that had preceded it.

He had taken it for granted that the Book of Silence was the totem of The God Whose Name Is Not Spoken; after all, the Forgotten King had obviously expected, three years ago, that Garth would find it on the Final God's altar in Dûsarra, as he had found the Sword of Bheleu on Bheleu's altar, and the Stone of Tema on Tema's altar, and the Stone of Andhur Regvos on the altar of Andhur Regvos. Furthermore, the book was needed for the King's great final magic, and Garth was fairly sure that that somehow involved conjuring the Death God into the mortal world. That, too, seemed to imply a link with the Final God. Garth knew relatively little of human theology, and most of what he did know he had learned on his trip to Dûsarra, but he had had the definite impression that Dagha had few dealings with mortals. He had never heard of any cult of Dagha, nor any temple dedicated to Dagha. Why, then, should so powerful a talisman be linked with this obscure deity?

It did not seem reasonable. He decided that the King was lying, hoping to trick Garth into keeping his oath and fetching the Book of Silence on the basis of a false hope that it might aid in the resurrection of his dead wife.

If he could expose this trickery, he might find himself in a better position from which to deal with the old man.

He reached this conclusion in barely three seconds; the pause in the conversation was scarcely noticeable before Garth said, "Indeed. Then what is the Death-God's totem? Surely you must have it, as his high priest and chosen vessel."

"I left it in Hastur, in my chapel." The King's voice was softer than usual, barely audible, a grinding, scratching whisper. He seemed not to be looking at Garth, though how Garth knew that, when the old man's eyes were as invisible as ever, he could not have said.

"Hastur?"

"Hastur, capital of Carcosa."

"Where was this place? Surely the chapel must be long gone; I have never heard of Hastur, and Carcosa has been forgotten for centuries by all save yourself."

"The barbarians took the city and it became Hastur-dar-Mallek, Hastur-of-the-Barbarians, but they could not have destroyed it, even had they tried. They buried it instead, Hastur below, Hastur-dar-Mallek above." There was a strange animation in the old man's tone.

"I have never heard of Hastur-dar-Mallek, O King."

"That was long ago, before overmen were first created; the name has been shortened to Ur-Dormulk."

"Ur-Dormulk? That was your capital?" Garth was astonished. He had heard the Forgotten King speak of his long-lost kingdom of Carcosa once or twice before, but he had not paid very much attention to the stories. He had never doubted that the old man had once been a true king, yet he had not seriously supposed that this vanished empire had had any connection at all with the world as it was in this, the Fourteenth Age.

Now, suddenly, he was told that Ur-Dormulk, the most ancient and independent of Eramma's cities and Skelleth's trading partner, which he had seen from afar on his trips to Dûsarra and Orgûl, was once the King's capital. This revelation provided a new and more definite link between his own era and the old man's vague past. Somehow Garth had always thought of them as two separate worlds, unconnected save by certain magical objects and by the King himself; it required a major readjustment of those thoughts for him to realize that it was all one, divided only by time.

There were a few seconds of silence as the overman absorbed this news. Then he thrust it aside; it was not relevant.

"You have not said what it was that you left in your chapel."

"I left them both there, the Pallid Mask and the Book of Silence, and I sealed the chamber with the Yellow Sign. I knew that the invaders could not pass that, and that they could not use the book or the mask if they did, but I posted a guard as a matter of form. I was still concerned with form then, and with my reputation as a great wizard."

"You remember, then? The Book of Silence is there? How very convenient that you should recall that just now!" Garth did not try to keep the scorn out of his voice; he was quite sure that it was no coincidence that the King's memory had returned just as he had suggested how the Book of Silence might be of use to Garth.

The old man seemed to be almost lost in reverie, quite oblivious of Garth's tone; he made no answer.

"Do you think, then, that I should fetch the book immediately, so that Kyrith might be revived?" Garth's tone was still sarcastic, but there was a sincere thread of hope in it.

The Forgotten King shifted suddenly, and the tattered edge of his hood flapped. "No," he said.

"No?" Garth's surprise was genuine.

"Your wife is dead, Garth," the King said, "and I know of no way she can be restored to you. Even were the cosmic balance shifted again, and the totem of the god of life found and used by its rightful master – for I promise you, we who are bound to destruction and death could not touch it – I doubt that it could turn the corpse into anything better than a half-rotted vegetable. Too much time has passed already."

"Is time, then, the crucial point? Could not the god of time be coerced, with the Book of Silence, into undoing what has happened?"

"No. I doubt that the book wastes space on anything so trivial."

"The reversal of time, the resurrection of the dead, are trivial? Why, then, have you recalled where it lies? What good can it do me now?"

"There was no deception in my sudden memory, Garth; your mention of the Death-God's totem, the Pallid Mask, reminded me. I had brought the book from Dûsarra so that I might have both my great devices in a single safe place."

"In three years, you did not recall so simple a fact?"

"In three centuries, three millennia, I did not. Perhaps I was not intended to; though I do not currently wield the mask directly, no greater power has freed me of my patron as I freed you of Bheleu. The Age of Death is not yet come, but Death holds sway in every era."

This presented Garth with another new concept. It had never occurred to him that the Forgotten King might himself be the victim of the machinations of the gods beyond the fact of his immortality. Garth had assumed that the old man had had no contact with the gods since he left the service of The God Whose Name Is Not Spoken, that he dealt with no being more powerful than himself. The suggestion that his patron deity was still affecting him, perhaps involving him against his will in some divine scheme, was unsettling.

The entire conversation was becoming unsettling; it was getting out of hand, Garth decided. He had come with the intent of asking a few simple questions and receiving a few simple answers. He had wanted to know what part the King had played in Kyrith's death and whether she might be brought back to life somehow. He had not wanted to listen to details of the King's past, or to anything about the Book of Silence that might remind him of his own false oath. The King was being more loquacious than ever before in the three years Garth had known him, but everything he said related to his own concerns, rather than to Garth's. In mixed anger and desperation, Garth declared, "I care nothing for that. Answer me my questions."

The King said nothing.

"Is there any way known to you, no matter how fantastical or difficult, in which Kyrith might be restored to life?"

"No." The old man chopped the single syllable off short, but it was unmistakable and definite.

"Have you any reason, however slight, to believe that there might be some way *not* known to you?" Garth was reluctant to give up until he had exhausted every possibility.

Again, the King said, "No."

That seemed final; Garth could think of no other approach. The old man might be lying, but if he were, Garth had no way of coaxing the truth out of him.

"You had no part in her death?"

"No. I am no oathbreaker."

The added phrase hurt, and Garth wondered whether the old man knew of his intended infidelity. It was only after a few seconds of silence that he realized that the King had had no need to mention his oath, for the King did not like to speak unnecessarily. Garth had no choice but to conclude that the King knew very well that the overman had sworn falsely when he agreed to fetch the Book of Silence and was reminding him of it as delicately as possible.

He was not at all sure why the old man should do so. Perhaps, Garth thought, the King meant to shame him into fulfilling his false oath. The overman leaned back, his chair creaking beneath his shifting weight, and thought in silence for a moment.

In Dûsarra, watching his scrying glass, Haggat decided that this was an ideal opportunity for his next planned event. He gestured to his waiting acolyte, who hurried off to tell a priest, especially trained for this coming performance, that it was time to begin.

A moment later, in the King's Inn, something flickered at the edge of the overman's vision. He whirled, startled, his hand already on the hilt of his dagger, since the table's presence would have made it difficult for him to draw his sword.

The glinting had not been, as he had first thought, the gleam of firelight on metal. There was no one behind him. The flash of light had come from something he could not identify, a blurry redness hanging in mid-air and glowing faintly.

It hovered at the level of his eyes, perhaps a foot wide and a foot and a half in height, a blot of color against the dark background of the taproom.

This, obviously, was magic at work. He kept his hand on his dagger, though he knew ordinary weapons would probably be useless against whatever it was. Various possible origins for the thing passed through his mind. It might be a manifestation of Bheleu, come to reclaim him with or without the sword. It might be a sending of the council of wizards that had sought to destroy him, as a menace to the peace of Eramma, three years earlier. It could be something the Forgotten King had contrived, for reasons of his own, or it might have been sent by the cult of Aghad as part of its revenge upon him.

He had, he thought, made altogether too many enemies in his life, and too many of them possessed of supernatural power.

The blot was changing as he watched; it swirled and roiled about, not like smoke or even liquid, but as if it were made of flowing light. It grew, and shadows appeared within it.

Red was Bheleu's preferred color, but that was the bright red of fire or fresh blood; this thing was of a duller, browner shade, like blood that had dried. The King was the King in Yellow, but could, of course, use any color he chose; the council wizards had employed a wide variety of spells. Still, Garth found that he associated the unhealthy hue of the thing with Aghad.

As he realized that, the thing suddenly resolved itself into an image. It was a face, a not-quite-human face, twisted and sneering, with curving fangs protruding from its upper lip. Garth stared; he knew he had seen it, or one like it, somewhere before.

He glanced around; the Forgotten King was paying no attention to this manifestation, nor to anything else for that matter, but the tavernkeeper was staring in horror. The other customers had departed.

Garth turned back; the apparition was still there, hanging motionless, as if waiting.

"What are you? Why are you here?" Garth demanded. "Speak, O vision, and explain yourself!"

The face grinned and replied, "Greetings, Garth. It is good to see you so untroubled that you can share a drink and pass the time with this doddering old fraud." The voice was a low rumble, lower than any human voice and not easy to understand; it spoke with an accent unlike that of Skelleth, but one that Garth had heard before.

"Who are you?" Garth asked.

"Do you not recognize me? Have you never seen my likeness?"

"You are familiar, but I cannot place you."

"Ah, so, feeble a memory, and in an overman! It is scarce three years since you invaded my home and destroyed my altar."

"Aghad!" Garth remembered now where he had seen that face; it had appeared on the small, carved idols sold in the Dûsarran market. The accent, too, was Dûsarran.

"You do remember! I am flattered!"

"Filth!" Garth spat. He did not give any serious consideration to the possibility that this might be the god himself; he was quite sure that it was some sort of trickery contrived by the cultists. He shifted, so that the table would not impede him, drew his sword, and rose to his feet.

"I had feared that you would be displeased by my paltry attempt to return the favor you did me, but I suppose you must have tired of your bitch years ago. Perhaps you would like to thank me for freeing you of her?" The thing grinned again.

Garth's sword came up and slashed through the image in a single smooth motion. It cut a narrow swath through the ethereal substance of the thing, but the speaker did not seem perturbed. In fact, it did not seem to notice his action at all. Garth had hoped for some sort of magical feedback.

"I notice that you haven't troubled to bury her; were you planning to feed her to your warbeast? You need not fear for its health; we used no poison. Nothing that could harm a warbeast, at any rate; we did not want to hurry her death. She took quite a long time to die; we found it very enjoyable. Would you care to guess whom we plan to kill next?"

Garth growled low in his throat and slashed at the image again, striking vertically this time. The sword passed through without resistance, leaving the floating image divided into quarters, but still unconcerned.

"You're not guessing, overman," the voice rumbled. "Will it be another of your wives? One of your children? Your cousins, or your uncle? Your friends on Ordunin's City Council? Perhaps the next won't be an overman at all; maybe we'll kill one of your friends here in Skelleth. The old man might do for a start. Or perhaps we might take the best of both worlds and kill your traitorous comrade, Galt the swindler. Will you guess, overman? Will you guess, or will you just wait and see?"

Garth hacked at the thing again, splitting it further and leaving six fragments. The face was no longer clearly visible; the edges of each segment were blurred, and the whole image seemed to be distorted.

It grinned and vanished completely, with a sound of fading laughter.

Garth stared at the empty air, then looked about, seeing no sign of any further supernatural manifestation. The sword still in his hand, he announced, "Hear me, Aghadite scum! I have had my fill of you. You owe me a life for my wife's death, and a hundred more for the manner of it. I swear that I will find you and destroy you, wherever you may hide. I will return to Dûsarra, smash your temple, and grind it into the dust. Your magic will not protect you; your god will not save you. I swear this, by everything I hold dear."

There was no answer but the silence of the almost-empty tavern.

Chapter Seven

After a long, wary moment, Garth finally admitted to himself that he could do nothing more immediately. He sheathed his sword, flexed the bruised knuckles of his right hand, and sat down again.

The apparition's words rankled, particularly the remarks about leaving Kyrith's corpse untended. One didn't bring a cadaver into a taproom, however, and he had hoped that the Forgotten King might resurrect her; that had seemed more important than providing the body with an appropriate rest.

He glanced at the Forgotten King. The old man wasn't going anywhere; Garth could come back here later if he decided he had to speak with him further. Without any more conversation, he rose and marched out the door. The King said nothing and made no move to stop him.

A crowd had gathered in the market, clustered about Kyrith's body. Garth was tall enough to see over their heads and noted that they were maintaining a respectful distance. A young boy had clambered up on the base of the statue that stood near the center of the market, a statue that had once been a young thief who had been petrified by a basilisk by the order of the previous Baron of Skelleth.

The crowd's presence irked Garth; it did not seem fitting that these members of an inferior species should cluster around Kyrith's remains like a pack of wolves around a dead warbeast. "Get away!" he bellowed. "Go home, all of you!"

Startled, the townspeople's faces turned toward him, but no one moved to depart until he picked up two women on the northern fringe, one in each hand, grasped by the shoulder, and placed them off to either side. They backed away, rubbing where his hands had gripped, and the rest of the villagers backed away as well.

"Go home!" Garth bellowed again; he drew his sword for emphasis, and people began vanishing into houses and down streets. A moment later no one remained in the square but himself and Saram, both standing over Kyrith's body. Koros stood nearby, as it had stood since its arrival in the market, the copper gull gleaming dully on its back.

Saram watched Garth closely, waiting for him to speak.

The overman spent a few seconds staring down at his dead wife's face. It was sinking in that she was really dead, gone forever. She had always been his closest companion in Ordunin, much more so than his two remaining wives; he regretted, now, that he had spent so much of the last few years away from her.

Word would have to be sent to Ordunin. She had kin there, not just her sister and co-wife Myrith, or her other co-wife Lurith, but two brothers and a few nephews and nieces. At last report, her mother was still alive. Kyrith, alone of Garth's wives, had no children; Garth had regretted that before, but now it seemed almost comforting somehow. Fewer people would grieve over her loss.

The overmen of the Northern Waste were not much given to elaborate ceremony and did not bother with funerals after the human fashion; since most had no belief in an afterlife of any sort, there was no religious necessity for them. The custom was, rather, to combine the disposal of the body with the division of property, whether by the reading of a will or by adjudication. The body itself was ordinarily sunk in Ordunin's ocean or buried in more inland regions, without fanfare, once the property settlement was announced and no doubt remained of the subject's identity and death.

That would not be appropriate here, Garth decided. Shipping the body home would be difficult and unpleasant, and the people of Ordunin would think it wasteful and eccentric, at the very least. Holding the reading of the will in Skelleth would seem equally bizarre to all concerned, since, save for himself, none of her heirs were present or likely to turn up; to the religious and sentimental humans, it might well seem callous and disrespectful.

There was certainly precedent for separating the ceremony from the burial; overmen who died at sea were simply tossed overboard, and the ritual of legacy was performed later on shore. A death in a foreign land, it seemed to Garth, would follow the same pattern. He would see the body interred in Skelleth, and Kyrith's other family would hold the ceremony in Ordunin, without either Garth or the corpse.

To keep up the dignity of his species among the humans of Skelleth, Garth knew that some sort of ceremony, though perhaps not a real funeral, would be in order. He would have to devise something.

For the present, however, there was no hurry. He knew that humans waited as much as two or three days before burning or burying their dead. He wanted to use that time to consider how best Kyrith's memory might be honored. He recalled what he had heard of human customs and broke the silence by saying, "She must lie in state."

Saram had been waiting for some such indication of Garth's plans. "I will have a bier prepared immediately, in my audience chamber," Saram said.

Garth nodded, and the Baron hurried away.

Once in his house, Saram summoned the nearest courtiers he could find and sent them to locate an appropriate platform and fine cloths to cover it.

He knew that running errands for the overman would not help his image as an authority figure, but he didn't much care. Garth was, after a fashion, a friend, and he had just received a terrible blow; one had to forgive him for failings of etiquette under the circumstances. Saram did not resent being manhandled and ordered about. He knew that he would behave no more politely or rationally if his own wife had been murdered.

The very thought of Frima's death gave him a moment's discomfort; he shook it off and began planning what he could do to eliminate the cult of Aghad from Skelleth.

In the square, Garth knelt and studied Kyrith's body. It was not immediately obvious what had killed her; the wounds on her forehead and bound wrists were quite minor, really. He felt her throat, and although it was bruised and lacerated, she did not appear to have been strangled.

He moved a hand to her chest and felt broken ribs.

He stopped, withdrew his fingers, and stepped back. He had decided that he didn't really want to know the extent of what the Aghadites had done to her; it was enough to know that she was dead and that they were responsible.

The marks on her forehead would have to be covered, he thought, while she lay on display in the Baron's house. The blood would need to be cleaned off her face. If he was going to subject his wife's remains to human ritual, he would do everything he could to ensure that the ceremony remained as dignified as possible.

Koros growled, and a shadow encroached at the edge of Garth's vision. He looked up to see a human, covered by a loose, heavy, red robe, face hidden by an overhanging hood, standing nearby. The overman could not tell if the figure was man or woman.

The people of Skelleth did not ordinarily wear robes or cloaks; the people of Dûsarra did, and this robe was the color of dried blood. Garth's hand fell to the hilt of his sword.

"What do you want here, human?" he demanded.

"Greetings, Garth," the creature said. Its taunting voice was male, Garth decided, and the man spoke in the guttural manner of the Dûsarrans. "I came to bring you a message."

"What message? From whom?" The overman wrapped his hand around the sword's hilt.

"We heard your oath just now, and your offer to come and visit us in Dûsarra."

Garth drew his sword, but did not attack; he was wary of unseen menaces.

"You will be welcome, of course. We would be delighted to have you stay with us; on your last trip you rushed off so quickly! This time you really must stay to dinner."

Garth saw no sign of any hidden threat, yet the Aghadite messenger simply stood, speaking calmly, ignoring the overman's bare steel.

He was probably armored, Garth reflected. He thought that padding and metal would protect him. The heavy robe was to conceal the helmet and gauntlets that would have been exposed by the sort of tunic normally worn in Skelleth.

"We have a request, though," the Aghadite said as he extended a long, bare finger and pointed it at Kyrith's body. "You bring the meat."

With a wordless bellow, Garth swung the sword.

The blade struck the man's robe and instantly exploded in a burst of red flame and splintered steel, leaving the overman clutching the useless hilt. The Aghadite laughed, but even in his state of unreasoning fury, Garth could detect the nervousness in that laugh, its forced quality. The man was not as sure of himself as he wished to appear.

Garth tossed the broken sword aside and reached for the Aghadite with his bare hands.

A wisp of red smoke swirled up from empty air between them; Garth ignored it as the man backed away hurriedly. The Aghadite was not yet running, merely stepping back, away from Garth's outstretched hands. Garth knew that he could catch the man; no human could outrun an overman. He grinned and advanced; the Aghadite continued to retreat.

The red smoke thickened and grew, gathering about the human, and Garth belatedly remembered seeing a similar mist once before. With a growl, he lunged forward, wasting no more time. His fingers closed on the edge of the red cloak, then passed through, holding nothing but air. The Aghadite had vanished.

Furious, Garth whirled, looking for other enemies, and with a cry of anguish saw Kyrith's body disappear in a red cloud.

He ran, but in the second or so that it took to reach it the corpse had vanished as completely as the Aghadite or the image that had spoken in the King's Inn.

He staggered to a halt in the center of the market, staring about wildly. Several of the people of Skelleth stood watching him, clustered in small groups in the streets that led out of the square. They muttered among themselves. Garth realized that they had seen the entire affair, had seen him humiliated, had seen Kyrith's body stolen. They had done nothing; no one had moved to aid him.

But then, he thought, why should they? He was not their kind, and the Aghadites were. At least none had joined in taunting him.

"Leave me!" he bellowed. "Get away from here!"

A few of the villagers obeyed, retreating out of sight; more did not. Garth glared at them, and a few more backed away; others met his gaze without flinching.

Seeing no practical alternative, he resolved to ignore them. He turned and stooped to pick up the stump of his sword. As he did, Saram came running from the door of his house. The entire altercation had lasted only moments, and he had not at first realized that the noises outside were of any real concern.

"What happened?" he called.

"Shut up," Garth replied.

Frima's head appeared in the doorway, but she said nothing. Saram came to a stop, looking about the market, his eyes returning regularly to the spot where Kyrith's body had lain. He glanced at Garth, but did not care to venture a question.

Garth stood, glaring at the hilt and the jagged shard that projected from it. Somehow the Aghadites had acquired powerful magic. They had apparently possessed some sorcerous devices or methods at the time of his previous encounter, in Dûsarra, but it had been his clear impression that they had relied primarily on trickery and simple machinery. Now, though, they seemed to be using real wizardry. The red mist that caused people to vanish had been used by the council of wizards he had fought, but never before by the priests of Aghad. The protective spell that had shattered his sword was nothing he had ever seen them demonstrate before, and the floating image that had spoken to him in the tavern was also new.

He knew that ordinary weapons were not enough against magicians. He had defeated the wizards only by wielding the Sword of Bheleu, and it had been the sword that he used to slay the high priest of Aghad.

He had given the Sword of Bheleu to the Forgotten King to free himself of its power, but now, he decided, the time had come to take it back. He would use it to destroy the cult, and then, he told himself, he would return it to the King's keeping. He knew that Bheleu would try to reassert his authority, try to take over Garth's body and possess him utterly, but he believed that he would be able to resist, to direct Bheleu's destructiveness, long enough to do what he had to do. The Aghadites had angered the chosen of the god of destruction, and they would be destroyed in consequence. Garth would use any means needful to make sure of that.

He obviously no longer needed to waste time on Kyrith's funeral arrangements, with her body stolen; he marched north across the market and into the King's Inn.

Behind him, Saram, Frima, and several other people watched him go. When he had vanished through the tavern door most of them went on about their business, but Saram and Frima followed him.

At his table in the rear, the Forgotten King sat exactly as he had sat when Garth left the inn. The overman made his way across the deserted taproom and seated himself, as if he, too, had never departed the place. Saram and Frima found seats at a nearby table, but did not intrude or do anything to draw Garth's attention.

The room was silent for a moment. Garth was aware of the two humans behind him, but did not care to acknowledge their presence. The King acknowledged nothing, merely stared at the table, as he usually did, his eyes fixed on the little spot of mismatched wood near the center. The Baron and Baroness watched, making no attempt to hide their concern for Garth; they watched, but said nothing.

Finally Garth spoke, addressing the yellow-robed old man.

"Greetings, O King," he said.

The King said nothing.

"I have come," Garth continued, "to ask that you free me from my oath, given three winters back. Return to me the Sword of Bheleu and release me from my commitment to aid you, and all will be as it was."

The old man gave no sign of replying, but Saram burst out, "Garth, have you gone mad?"

"Silence, human," Garth said without turning. "This is not your affair."

"Garth, that thing will possess you again and drive you mad! You might destroy Skelleth again, and that means it *is* my affair. I cannot allow you to take back the sword!"

"Silence!" Garth bellowed. "Saram, I need that sword to take my vengeance upon Kyrith's murderers; their magic protects them from ordinary weapons, and I have no other magic available."

"I cannot allow it," Saram insisted. "Not in my village, not while I am Baron."

Garth turned to face him and said, "I have no intention of staying in Skelleth with the sword. Once I have slain whatever Aghadites I may find here, I will go to Dûsarra to destroy their temple, as I have sworn to do. I may not return. If I do return, I will try my best not to bring the sword back with me. If I do bring it, rest assured, I will be doing everything I can to keep myself free of its control. I do not like the sword, but I need its power. Now, be quiet!"

Saram had half-risen as he protested, and would have stood and argued, but Frima was pulling at his embroidered sleeve, urging him to sit down again and listen. Reluctantly he yielded and sank back into his chair.

Garth glared at him for a second, to be sure he was done arguing for the present, and then turned back to the Forgotten King.

"Your pardon, O King. I ask again, let us abandon our agreement, and return to me the Sword of Bheleu."

The old man spoke, without looking at the overman. "No. You must being me the Book of Silence."

Garth hesitated. He could no longer agree and simply hope that he would not be asked to deliver; the King had remembered, just minutes earlier, where he had left the book, where it might be found and recovered. Garth had hoped that by taking back the sword he might avoid the problem and retain his pretense of honor; it now appeared that he was not going to be allowed that luxury.

Now that he took the time to think about it, even through the haze of his righteous rage, he realized that he had been ridiculously optimistic. The King had no reason to free him of his vow. He cared nothing about whether he had the Sword of Bheleu or not; he wanted only to have the Book of Silence.

No, Garth corrected himself, that was not quite right. The old man's greater magic required both the book *and* the sword, if the overman had understood him correctly. That made him even less likely to agree to give up both.

"Let us forget my oath for the present, then," Garth said. "I will not ask you to renounce it, but rather will ask simply that you return to me, only temporarily if you would prefer it so, the Sword of Bheleu."

"If you do not renounce your oath, then when will you fulfill it? I have told you that I know now where the Book of Silence is."

Garth struggled to keep his anger under control, not to lash out uselessly against the old man. His face was so slack and expressionless with rage that he appeared almost half-wilted, like a drunkard or one under the influence of narcotic potions. He still held the fragment of his sword; to dispel some of the tension in his body he rammed it down against the table. The jagged, broken edge bit into the oaken tabletop, scarring it, but did not embed itself as a real blade would. Instead, it turned and skidded across the surface, gouging up curls of wood. Garth's wrist was twisted painfully, and his sore knuckles scraped as well.

The pain added to his fury, and he lost control, blurting out the truth. "I have no intention of fulfilling my oath, foul deceiver. You extorted my agreement, knowing I had no choice. I would rather die in disgrace than aid you."

Behind him, he heard Frima gasp, and Saram draw breath.

The King lifted his head slightly and murmured, "Your word is not good? Your sworn vow means nothing?"

Feeling cornered, his fury subsiding as he realized his mistake, Garth replied, "No."

"The vow you swore in this place not an hour ago is meaningless?" The old man's voice was a low grating that tore at Garth's nerves.

Rage flowered anew, and Garth said, "I did not say that! I *will* destroy the cult of Aghad."

"Can one oath be binding and another meaningless, sworn by the same tongue?"

Garth, trapped, said nothing, and a moment of tense silence ensued. Saram and Frima dared not speak.

"Garth," the old man said at last, his voice more nearly normal, but with a trace of either sorrow or sarcasm in it, "I regret to hear this. If you are not bound by your oath, then I must propose a new bargain. You want the Sword of Bheleu so that you may destroy the followers of the god of hatred and those responsible for the death of your wife. I want the Book of Silence so that I may perform a certain magic that will cause many deaths, my own among them. I will not give you the Sword of Bheleu at present, but we both may yet have what we want. You want the Aghadites dead. I want to complete a spell that will kill them."

He paused, and Garth said, "What?"

The King lowered his head again and said nothing.

"Do you mean that your magic will destroy the cult?"

The old man nodded.

"Are you sure?"

The King shrugged.

Garth tried to think; it was difficult, for his mind was full of anger and confusion.

It had never occurred to him that the King's final magic might be guided, that the King might have some control over who died when it was performed. Garth had assumed that the spell would involve conjuring The God Whose Name Is Not Spoken into the mortal world and that, thus freed, the god would kill all those in the immediate area.

Perhaps this was not the case at all. Perhaps the god would demand a certain number of deaths, but this summoner could choose who would be sacrificed in order to banish him again. That seemed to be what the King was implying. There was no reason to assume that a god would be limited by distance or even by time; weren't gods supposed to be everywhere and nowhere all at once?

He did not trust the King, however.

Furthermore, there seemed to be something unsatisfying about the solution the King proposed. Garth wanted to kill the Aghadites *himself,* to see the color of their blood, to watch them die.

"I . . ." he began, then stopped. "I am not sure."

"Another bargain, then. Bring me the Book of Silence, and I will loan you the Sword of Bheleu. I must require it back from you eventually, but I am sure you will not object to being freed of the god's control."

Garth turned that proposal over in his mind and, awash in fury as he was, could see nothing wrong with it at first. He would have the Sword of Bheleu, and with it he could destroy the cult of Aghad. He dismissed without thought the fact that he would be giving himself over to the god of destruction rather than simply wielding a weapon; it did not occur to him that Bheleu might not be satisfied with killing only Aghadites.

He did, however, realize that he would be delivering the Book of Silence to the Forgotten King, and after planning for three years to avoid that, he was reluctant to give in so quickly simply because the King now claimed that the other victims of his magic would be Aghadites.

The old man might be telling the truth; it might be that delivering the Book of Silence to him would do no Harm to innocents. Although Garth had been fooled in the past by partial truths and things left unsaid, the King had never, so far as he knew, told an outright lie.

This was a matter that deserved more than a moment's thought, but there was no time to waste, he felt, in his pursuit of his wife's murderers.

That pursuit would go nowhere, however, without the Sword of Bheleu.

If he accepted the King's offer, he would be in possession, at least temporarily, of either the sword or the book, and it was his belief that both were required for the final magic. If he remained unconvinced of the King's intentions, he could always withhold whichever totem he had at the time; after all, he was already forsworn, in his heart, and had no more honor to lose by such treachery. It would, he thought, be a just repayment for the King's own deceptions and manipulations.

"Yes," he said at last. "I agree. Tell me where I may find the Book of Silence, and I will bring it to you."

"I left it in the royal chapel of my palace in Hastur. That palace is now a part of the crypts beneath Ur-Dormulk. Signs and portents will be sufficient to lead you to it." Something like glee was in the old man's tone.

"Will you provide me no further guidance?"

"You need none."

Garth found himself growing wary. He was beginning to realize that he was again trusting himself to the Forgotten King, again agreeing to perform an errand for the old man. Always before, such errands had had unwanted and unpleasant results. Even his journey to Orgûl, just completed that day, had ended in Kyrith's death.

An idea occurred to him, a strange idea. Always before he had set out alone, while the King stayed in Skelleth and awaited his return. Garth had been a messenger, a servant. What if the King were to accompany him this time? The old man's magic could protect them both from whatever difficulties they might encounter; they would travel as equals, rather than Garth's assuming the inferior's role again.

"O King," he said, "will you come with me?"

Behind him, Saram and Frima stared. The King was silent for a moment before replying, "No."

"Why not?" Garth demanded. "Why must I act on your behalf?"

"I cannot venture far from Skelleth. My power is centered here."

The old man's tone was final, but Garth was in no mood to be put off. "Why?" he persisted. "Because you have lived here for so long? Is it possible that you do not wish to discomfit yourself?"

"No," the King said, with perhaps a trace of anger in his voice.

"Then why? Why did you come to Skelleth in the first place? How did you become trapped here? Explain yourself!"

"This place is the center of power in this time, as Hastur was of old; the world's energies have shifted with the ages. I had no choice in my dwelling place once I had given up the book and the mask, but was compelled to live wherever the power's heart might be. Had I the book once more, I could go where I pleased."

"You left the village once, when I gave you the sword."

"Only a few leagues, and yet that was near my limit."

"What would happen to you, then, if you were to leave?"

"Garth, this is not your concern."

"What would happen?" the overman insisted.

"I cannot leave."

"What if I were to carry you?"

With apparent reluctance, the King admitted, "I would lose my strength, both physical and metaphysical. I would have no more power than a corpse, yet I would still live."

"You mean that you would be unable to work magic?"

"I would be unable to move or speak or see or breathe; I would be in appearance as ancient as I am in truth."

That explained, of course, why so powerful a being dwelt in this miserable border town and needed an ordinary overman to run his errands. For that reason, if for no other, Garth was willing to accept the King's explanation, at least for the present. He still hoped, however, to have some sort of further aid.

"Then can you give me no protection against the cult's magic?" he asked.

"No."

"You might loan me the sword now." That, of course, would be ideal; he could then simply renege on his agreement.

The King did not bother to answer. Garth knew that, quite aside from his own present trustworthiness, once he was beyond the King's power it might not be Garth but Bheleu who occupied Garth's body; no oath or power would be able to restrain the god or bring him back to Skelleth against his will, if the King's power were in truth limited to the immediate area.

"They have powerful magic," he said, as a last resort.

The King shifted slightly, but said nothing.

"The image of the god, for example. What am I to do if they attack me with such things?"

"That was a simple messenger image; it could not even speak until ordered to."

"What of the spell that shattered my sword?"

"A warding spell against metal, useless for any other purpose."

"The red mist that caused the Aghadite and Kyrith's body to vanish, then."

"A teleportation device taken from a dead wizard; they have few more and will not waste them."

"Surely, though, they have other magic and will not hesitate to use it against me. Can you do nothing to protect me?"

"Have you turned coward, then?" The King lifted his head, and though his eyes were still hidden in shadow Garth thought he saw a glint of light. The springtime warmth seemed to fade from the air of the tavern, replaced with a clammy chill. "Regardless of what magic they may possess, did they not say that you would see all those you care for die before your own time came to perish? They will not harm you directly, then, until they have carried out their threat. Now go! Fetch me the Book of Silence, and trouble me no more until you have it!"

Disconcerted by the King's sudden coldness, Garth nodded and rose to depart. Saram and Frima rose as well. The Baron began to speak, to make one more attempt at dissuading the overman, but Garth ignored him and stalked out into the marketplace, where a thin rain had begun to fall.

Chapter Eight

The eastern gate of the ancient walled city of Ur-Dormulk stood between two massive stone towers, set in a gap in the ridge that supported the eastern ramparts; the great valves themselves were carved from two immense sheets of ebony, bound in the brown-black hide of some extinct monster. There was no shining metal or bright paint anywhere on the gate or the somber gray walls to either side. The tower walls, Garth saw, were carven from roadbed to battlement with spidery runes of a tongue that he had never seen before.

Some of the runes seemed to have an odd familiarity about them that Garth could not explain to himself; he wondered idly what language they represented, and what they said. Perhaps they gave a history of the city's founding, he thought, or were protective incantations of some kind.

He was quite sure from the very first that they were not Eramman or anything like it. As a child he had come across other, older languages, all dead, and this strange script was none of them.

Of course, he told himself, Ur-Dormulk was very old. It had stood, much as it was now, before Eramma became a nation half a millennium ago. There had been plenty of time for the builders' native tongue to die out.

The whole matter was irrelevant, he told himself. He had an errand to perform. Despite the protests of the Baron and Baroness, and the arguments Galt had made when he had been informed of the situation, Garth intended to find the Book of Silence and return to Skelleth with it.

He was not completely certain as to exactly what he would do then, save that he would somehow pursue his vengeance against Aghad's followers. He was not sure whether he would give the Forgotten King the book or whether he would take the Sword of Bheleu, but he had not cared to say anything that might cause anyone to doubt his intention of honoring his agreement with the King.

Saram had gone so far in his concern for the overman as to offer to accompany him on his journey; Frima had protested, and Garth had turned him down. Saram had a barony to run, and could not go haring off on adventures without warning. Garth had no commitments, save his vows to fetch the Book of Silence and to destroy the cult and temple of Aghad. He did not want to involve anyone else in either of these.

As a compromise of sorts he had accepted a letter of introduction to the overlord of Ur-Dormulk, signed by both Saram and Galt. That had been his only concession, and it was a practical one. If he was going to search the city looking for signs and portents, he would very much prefer not to have to worry about explaining himself to guardsmen or homeowners while doing so.

His only other delays had been to make a few basic preparations. He had left the copper gull at his house, borrowed a sword, and bought a few supplies, but had been in Skelleth so briefly that this new journey seemed almost a continuation of his trip to Orgûl. The mood, however, was very different; this was a task of real personal consequence, not the casual lark his attempt at dragon-slaying had been.

Since he intended to introduce himself to the overlord or at least to his representatives, he had no need for stealth in entering the city. That was just as well, as he saw no easy way to pass the fortifications unseen. Unlike Skelleth's ruinous outer wall, these were intact and well maintained, extending quite some distance along the ridge top and then turning back westward out of sight.

Seeing no other entrance, he had ridden directly up to the huge gate, and now sat for a moment looking up at the black portal and rune-covered towers.

This was the sort of fortress the legends of Ordunin had described Skelleth to be, until he had ventured down and discovered for himself how greatly the stories had exaggerated. He wondered why he had heard no tales describing Ur-Dormulk.

It didn't matter, he told himself. He was stalling, putting off the necessity of announcing himself and having to deal with unfamiliar humans.

"Ho, the gate!" he bellowed, refusing to delay any longer.

An answering shout came, much more loudly than he had expected.

"State your business, overman!"

He looked, but could not see any face above the parapet, and the echo from the towers made it impossible to judge just where the sound had originated.

That, he decided, was probably intentional; the builders of this city had done their work well.

"I come from Skelleth on a personal errand; I bear a message, as well, from the Baron of Skelleth to the overlord of Ur-Dormulk!"

"Dismount and approach," the voice called. "Leave your sword and axe on the saddle!"

Garth realized that the voice was not coming from above, or at least not from very far above; the speaker was, therefore, not on the battlements at all. The only other place that he could be was in one of the towers, and the overman looked at the runes with new interest, noticing how deeply some of the symbols had been cut. Somewhere in those shadowy tracings were openings into the towers from which a man could peer out, or shout commands, or perhaps aim a crossbow.

It was a very clever device, he thought; it would be almost impossible to find the actual holes amid the myriad lines and curlicues. He would want to remember this for later, but for the present he had business to attend to. He swung down from the warbeast's back, checked the axe that hung on the saddle, then took the scabbarded sword from his belt – a sword he had borrowed from Galt, since he had not wanted to take time to have a new one forged after shattering his on the Aghadite protective spell, and since human-sized weapons were not suited to his grip – and hooked it through one of the straps that held the saddle in place.

He looked questioningly up at the nearer tower, his hand on the sheathed dagger that remained on his belt; no command or comment came. The knife was apparently not considered a serious threat. He shrugged, lowered his hand, and strode toward the gate, the dagger still in its place.

With a series of rattles and thuds, the bars were removed from the gate, and one side of the great portal swung slowly ajar. A guard in a peculiarly shaped brass helmet and dull green tunic leaned out through the opening.

"You have a letter?" he said. The voice was not the one that had called from the tower.

Garth said nothing, but proffered the folded parchment.

The guardsman took it, looked at the seal, and hesitated. "It looks genuine," he said, not to Garth, but addressing someone out of sight behind the gate.

A hand appeared, and the guardsman surrendered the letter.

A moment later a new voice called, "Let him in."

The guardsman stepped back and motioned for Garth to enter. The overman hesitated. "What of my weapons and my mount?" he asked.

"Your pardon, my lord, but we prefer to be cautious until we have established that you are what you say you are. Your weapons will be brought, if you like, and returned to you when your identity is confirmed."

"I would appreciate that," Garth said. "What about Koros?"

"Your beast? I regret, my lord, that no beasts of burden are welcome in the city, for reasons of sanitation and public safety. We maintain a stable outside the wall to serve visitors such as yourself."

Garth was not happy about that. The indomitable warbeast had served him well in human cities in the past when, on occasion, things had turned nasty. He was, however, on a peaceful errand, one that might well stay peaceful. To the best of his knowledge, even if the people of Ur-Dormulk knew that he meant to take the Book of Silence, they should have no reason to object; he had been told that no one but the Forgotten King could use it and that for anyone else even to handle it might well prove fatal – though his own undesired connection with Bheleu would be sufficient protection to allow him to transport it. Logically, nobody should mind if he were to remove so dangerous an object from the city.

He would just have to hope that nothing went wrong and that no one had any unreasonable objections.

"Do you know anything about handling warbeasts?" he asked the guard, certain of what the answer would be.

"No," the man replied. "I never saw one before."

Garth nodded; he had assumed that to be the case, since the creatures had been invented by the overmen of Kirpa, in the Northern Waste, too late to have been used in any number in the Racial Wars. Even three centuries after the wars ended they remained rare and valuable and were almost all owned by governments, as being too precious and dangerous to be left in private hands. Garth had one of his own only because he had accepted it in lieu of all further tribute that, under an ancient agreement, the people of Kirpa had owed to him as Prince of Ordunin.

"What sort of animal do you have in the stable ordinarily?" he asked.

The guardsman shrugged. "Horses, I suppose, and oxen; I'm no stableboy. Yackers, too, I think."

Garth glanced at Koros, standing motionless on the highway, triangular ears flattened back slightly, golden eyes half shut, three-inch fangs gleaming dully in the midday sun. The warbeast would have no objection to being stabled, but it wouldn't mind staying out in the open, either, as long as the good weather that had followed the brief rain held. The other occupants of the stable might not care for its presence; the smell of warbeast was not recognizable to most animals as that of a predator, due to its magical origin, but the sight of one tended to make many beasts understandably nervous.

More importantly, it was possible that Garth might find himself fleeing the city, and in that case he would not want to waste time finding the stable. Having the warbeast waiting right at the gate would be far more convenient.

"I think I'll just leave it where it is," he said.

The guardsman shrugged. "As you please."

The voice that had first answered his hail called out, "Did you say you're leaving that monster where it is?"

Garth called back that yes, he had said as much.

"Would it not be better if you were to move it out of the road?"

Garth realized that Koros might be a serious obstruction to traffic where it was. He bellowed a command, and the warbeast turned and padded off the highway. Once well out of the way, it stopped.

"Is that better?" Garth called.

The voice replied that it was.

"Good. Now, if one of you would fetch my sword and axe, as you suggested, I trust we may proceed. And might I suggest that you feed my beast a goat or a sheep or two; my business may keep me for some time, and I cannot speak for its behavior if it becomes hungry. Water, too, would be appreciated. I will pay the necessary expenses."

The guardsman at the gate nodded. "I'll have someone see to it." He swung the gate open a few feet farther, allowing Garth past him into a small courtyard enclosed by gray stone, its nearer side comprised of the great portal and its farther side occupied by another, identical barrier. Half a dozen men in green uniforms and brass helmets were scattered about the court; one had a golden plume that curled upward from one side of his helmet and was holding Garth's letter of introduction. The overman took him to be the officer in charge of the squad manning the gates.

As one of the others trotted down to fetch Garth's weapons, Garth called a command to the warbeast so that it would not rip the man apart as it would a thief; ordinarily it allowed no one but Garth to touch anything it carried. When the soldier had retrieved both sword and axe while evoking nothing more than a mild growl of displeasure from Koros, he started back, and Garth ventured to ask the officer, "Do you treat all your visitors like this?"

"No, of course not," the officer replied.

"What makes me worthy of such special attention, then?"

The human looked at him uncertainly, as if he suspected that the overman might be slightly insane, or perhaps attempting some sort of bizarre humor.

"We get very few armored overmen arriving unannounced, riding monstrous giant cats and asking to see the overlord," he said.

"Ah." Garth had to agree that the man had a point. "It's a warbeast, only partly a cat, despite its appearance. See the long legs? And I did not ask to see the overlord, but said merely that I carried a letter intended for him."

"Perhaps I misunderstood, then; would you prefer to wait here while I deliver the letter?"

Garth considered very briefly. "No," he said, after only a slight hesitation, "I would like to speak with him, if I may." Dealing with the head of state directly was bound to be more efficient than working with underlings.

"I think he may well wish to speak with you, as well. We see very few overmen here." The officer ventured a small smile.

The soldier bearing Garth's sword and axe had returned to the courtyard, and the other guardsmen were pushing the gate closed. Garth watched with casual interest, noticing from the corner of his eye that the man carrying his weapons was making a concerted effort to stay as far away from the weapons' owner as the small area between the gates allowed.

When the portal was closed and a half a dozen bars and locks were back in place, the inner gates were opened by men on the other side; to Garth's surprise, they opened away from the city, into the court where he waited. That was not the usual custom.

The officer gestured, and Garth found himself neatly surrounded, two soldiers before him, one on either side, and two behind, while the officer led the way and the weapons-bearer brought up the rear, several paces back. Garth had not realized there were as many as eight humans in the group; he wondered if more had joined them from the towers or behind the inner gate, or whether he simply hadn't been paying close attention.

At a command from the officer the little party marched forward; Garth cooperated, marching with them. His exact status here was unclear, perhaps intentionally; the men marched with hands on their weapons, but swords stayed sheathed, and the lances borne by the pair behind him were shouldered. He was not chained or hobbled, but he was disarmed. If he was a prisoner, then he was being treated with courtesy and a lack of caution; if he was a guest, he was being treated with great suspicion. The escort could be considered either an honor guard or a party of jailers with equal reason.

This uncertainty, he decided, accurately reflected the guards' attitude; he had committed no crime, and claimed to be a person of some significance, but they had seen no proof of his good intentions. They were not eager either to trust him or to offend him beyond what prudence demanded.

He was not particularly troubled by this. The thought did slip into his mind that, had he carried the Sword of Bheleu on this trip, he would have taken umbrage at such treatment and massacred the lot of them.

His first sight of the city of Ur-Dormulk distracted him from questions of protocol or concern over proper behavior. He had expected the inner gate to open onto a street of packed earth or mud, lined with houses of stone, wood, and plaster, such as he had seen in other human habitations; or, if not onto a street, then perhaps into a market square. Skelleth had been built of fieldstone and half-timbered plaster; the buildings of Mormoreth had been faced with white marble; Dûsarra was a jumble of gleaming black stone and more humble structures.

Ur-Dormulk was built of granite, and rather than on a street, he found himself at the top of a long staircase, easily half a hundred steps, whence he looked out at an array of towers and turrets. Crags of bare rock thrust up in the distance, reminding him that he was in the foothills of the western mountains.

He had noticed from without that the ramparts stood atop a ridge, and that the gate was set into the top of that ridge, so he had expected to find the city inside sloping downward from the heights; he had not expected to find the drop so sharp that steps were necessary, or so long that only the higher towers reached above eye level.

He had known that there were stone towers, and had even glimpsed them from a distance; he had known that they were old and weathered and strange, but now he could see that they were more bizarre than he had realized. The towers were not merely pitted and dull, but worn down to near shapelessness; not a single sharp corner remained anywhere in sight. Flat-topped or spired, each of the tall buildings seemed more like a rough mound than anything structured by man – save that they stood as much as a hundred feet above the city streets. Some were almost indistinguishable from the weathered humps of rock with which nature had ornamented the city.

Those outcroppings struck Garth as being slightly eerie, rising up in naked splendor throughout Ur-Dormulk, differing from the towers only because they were larger, windowless, and slightly more irregular. They seemed to form a rough line, beyond which he could see nothing of the city; he wondered if they formed part of its western perimeter and if they had been incorporated into the defenses as the ridge had been used in the east.

A cool, damp breeze brushed his face, and he blinked; then the soldiers were escorting him down the steps, and he was too concerned with his footing to look at the city further. The steps themselves were badly worn, polished by the passage of thousands, perhaps millions, of feet; the central portion had been smoothed down until it was almost a ramp, so that his guards directed him to one side, where the steps, though gleaming smooth and worn far below their original level, still had enough of an edge separating one from the next to make them more readily negotiable than the sheer slope.

When he was reasonably sure that he was not going to slip and tumble down the remaining length of the stair, he lifted his gaze from his own feet to the foot of the steps. They ended in a broad plaza, paved with the same gray stone that seemed to make up the entire city and as level as the plains of Skelleth. He was certain that that level surface was not natural, so close to the steep ridge.

He had at first been certain, also, that the gray stone was granite, a familiar substance in his homeland, but doubts began to creep in. Granite was a very hard stone, difficult to work, heavy and brittle – and it did not erode easily. He glanced at the steps again. There was an old granite wall in Ordunin, not far from his home, that had been erected when he was young, a century before; the edge that ran along its top was still sharp enough to cut an overman's finger. These steps, assuming that they had originally been level all the way across, had worn down a good eight inches in the center. If the stone were in truth granite, and had been eroded only by foot traffic, then its age must be incomprehensible.

The stone, he decided, must be something else, some substance that mocked granite in appearance, but which was far softer. Or perhaps water drained down the steps and had cut them away – though the fact that the wear was so broad argued against that, since water ordinarily cut a single channel, not a wide, uneven swath.

It didn't matter, he told himself.

He reached the bottom and looked around with interest. The plaza at the foot, though paved with this seeming granite, was worn down as well, with paths sunk inches deep into the stone showing where the merchants set up their booths on market day, where the traffic was heaviest, and what were the most popular routes across the square. The streets that led off in various directions were likewise paved and level, and likewise worn. Narrow parallel troughs indicated where carts had passed over the centuries, and broader depressions revealed where pedestrians walked. There were no gutters visible anywhere, save for these signs of wear, and no bare earth, and Garth realized why animal traffic was forbidden. Such streets would need careful cleaning; there was no natural drainage, since none of the streets sloped at all, and what drainage the paths provided would carry sewage directly to those areas that enjoyed the heaviest traffic and, therefore, the deepest wear. It struck him as odd that a city in the foothills should be so flat, save for the single ridge and the distant outcroppings. It was obviously contrived, and probably at great expense. He wondered why the builders had thought it worthwhile.

He wondered also, for perhaps a second, what pulled the wagons that had cut the parallel grooves he had noticed, but that question was answered by the sight of a young man pulling a small, two-wheeled cart, balanced on a single axle for ease in hauling.

The buildings that surrounded the plaza were all of the gray stone, ancient and worn. Most stood three or four stories in height, but were weathered into rounded, moundlike shapes, all corners erased by time. Any surface ornamentation that might once have existed had vanished long ago; only the size and location of doors and windows served to distinguish one from another.

He noticed that here and there gaps were visible, as if something had fallen away; here a door lintel was sunk back from the facade, there a few dark holes were arranged above a window. He realized that these must be where substances other than the gray rock had weathered away completely, and guessed that iron fittings had succumbed to rust – though if so, then it must have been a very long time ago, for all trace of rust had washed away.

The stone walls, he saw, were incredibly thick. They would have to be, to weather so badly and still stand strong.

The entire city gave the impression of something indescribably ancient, something that had stood so long that it had been accepted by the earth as part of itself, rather than being a mortal creation erected thereon.

The people of Ur-Dormulk gave no such impression; in contrast to their city, they wore gay silks and embroidered velvets in ornate and fantastical outfits. Garth saw no ordinary homespun anywhere; even the lowliest cart-hauler's garb was brightly dyed and embellished with colored threads. Red, green, blue, and purple – the streets were aswirl in color wherever the people of Ur-Dormulk went abroad.

There were no great crowds, but neither were the streets empty; strollers dawdled along, while others hurried about their business. Many glanced at the overman curiously, but none stopped to stare, and no one ventured too near the forbidding cluster of soldiery.

One figure, wearing a drooping hat and flowing tunic and cape all the color of dried blood, seemed to look at him for longer than most, and Garth was reminded very strongly of the magically protected Aghadite he had fought so futilely in Skelleth. He wondered whether the cult was active in Ur-Dormulk, whether it was an open, tolerated religion here or a secret society working underground.

He had not been molested by the sect since the incident in the market that had cost him his own sword, and his anger had therefore had a chance to cool slightly, but now it flared up again. He resolved that he would see that person who stared at him so insolently gutted by the Sword of Bheleu.

He turned his head to follow the red-garbed human out of sight and found himself looking at the profile of the soldier to his left. That reminded him where he was, and he fought down his ire. The human might not be an Aghadite, he told himself; the color might be coincidence, the gaze simple curiosity.

Or perhaps, his reasonable self had to admit, it was indeed an Aghadite agent, sent to watch him, or to taunt him with his or her presence – he was not certain of the creature's sex beneath the loose robe and overhanging hat. If it were an agent, then Garth had been meant to see him or her; why else would he or she wear the cult's color so ostentatiously?

This assumed, of course, that the cult had known he was coming to Ur-Dormulk, and it was not at all clear how they *could* have known. It would have required either magic or the presence of spies in Skelleth, and some way of sending messages faster than Koros traveled.

The cultists did have magic, of course; he knew that well. He knew also that they had not given up their plans of vengeance, however quiet they might have been during his preparations and journey. The figure in red might indeed have been an Aghadite. The overman would need to be very careful, here in a strange city.

His escort was conducting him up the widest and straightest of the streets that led westward from the market, and they were almost at the palace before Garth noticed that no one wore yellow. Every other color was represented, it seemed, but nowhere was there cloth-of-gold or yellow silk, no amber or straw, saffron or chrome. White and beige were in evidence, and he glimpsed copper or orange occasionally, but no hue that could truly be called yellow.

That struck him as very curious indeed. A tradition, he guessed, dating from some ancient respect for the King in Yellow.

The party of soldiers, with the overman in their midst, arrived at the steps of the palace that closed off the end of the avenue and marched without hesitation up them. Great doors sheathed in some metal blackened with age blocked their way; Garth wondered whether the covering might be silver. Flecks of gold clung to the upper portion, forming broken curves, as if a symbol had once been traced there but had worn away, until only these scant traces remained.

The doors opened as they approached, and Garth was led into an ornate tapestried hall. Two men and a woman, wearing vivid red robes, met the party there. As two of the soldiers closed the huge doors, the woman gestured toward a row of stone benches. "Make yourselves comfortable," she said. "We will announce you, and inform you of the prince's pleasure."

The officer nodded to his men; the six who had ringed the overman found themselves places and sat. After a moment's hesitation, Garth joined them, taking a bench to himself, with three soldiers to either side on adjoining benches. The weapons-carrier remained standing, moving to the far side of the room, where he chatted with one of the red-clad men too quietly for Garth to hear.

The officer and the other red-garbed man walked off through the arch at the inner end of the hall, into the interior of the palace. The woman stood off to one side.

After a moment, noticing Garth glancing about impatiently, she remarked, "The wait may be quite long, my lord; would you care for food or drink?"

Garth shook his head and sat there in silence.

Chapter Nine

Allowing for the slow passage of time when one was bored, Garth estimated that he waited half an hour in the antechamber before the officer returned, Garth's letter of introduction in his hand and the red-robed man at his heel.

He gave the overman the letter and announced, "Follow me; three guards. Bring the weapons."

Garth rose; after a few seconds of debate over who would go, so did three of the soldiers. They formed a cross, the overman in the center, a soldier on each side for the crosspiece, and the third behind, followed by the swordbearer, while the officer and the red-clad courtier led the way.

From the antechamber, which was gray stone hung with faded tapestries, they entered a long gallery of black and white marble, the floor made up of black and white diamonds of marble, the walls alternating white marble pillars with gold-veined, black marble slabs. Their footsteps echoed from the bare stone. Garth was impressed with the architecture.

An open door gleaming golden at the far end led into the overlord's audience chamber, a vast hall clouded with incense and decorated in gold and red. Lines of soldiery stood to either side, their dull green uniforms and brass helmets identical to those of Garth's escort. Two dozen courtiers stood casually at the foot of the dais; about half wore the brilliant red of the palace staff, while the rest were as variegated in their clothing as the people on the streets – more so, in truth, for one tall, red-haired woman wore a yellow gown beneath a knee-length, sleeveless vest of red velvet. She appeared to be staring at Garth with a strange intensity while she clung to the arm of an elderly man in blue; though it was only natural for the overman to be the center of attention, her gaze seemed unusually fixed.

The overlord himself wore black, glossy black velvet, unadorned save for a circlet of gold set with glittering gems that shone on his brow. He sat upon an immense throne of red plush and gold, raised up on a red-carpeted platform three feet high, at the top of a flight of six golden steps. He was a man in middle age, heavy but not really fat, with pale skin and dark brown hair that flowed down well past his shoulders. He wore a curious ring of carved and cracking wood on the fourth finger of his left hand. His face was broad, his eyes dark.

As Garth approached the dais, the officer stepped off to the right, the courtier to the left; the overman stopped at the foot of the steps and bowed politely.

There was a murmur and a moment of awkward silence; Garth suspected, too late, that some further form of abasement was customary.

A red-clad courtier stepped forward from somewhere and announced, "Behold, O supplicant, Hildarad, seventh of that name, Prince of Alar, Lord Dormulk, Master of the City, Conqueror of Hastur, supreme in Aldebaran and the Hyades! Speak, then, if you dare!"

Garth wondered what Aldebaran and the Hyades might be, and where Alar was, as he replied, "I am Garth, Prince of Ordunin, Lord of the Overmen of the Northern Waste. I come with a letter of introduction from Saram, Baron of Skelleth, to ask a favor of you, O Prince." He had almost addressed the overlord as "overlord," but caught himself at the last moment; the title of prince was more prestigious, and therefore more courteous. He had no idea if the overlord actually had a legitimate claim to it, but he did not care to risk any insult.

The overlord shifted slightly on his throne and said, in a conversational tone, "I have glanced through this letter you bring. My lord of Skelleth asks me to accept you as minister without portfolio in his government and to treat you with all respect due himself. If you are in truth Prince of Ordunin – and I do not question it – that might seem little favor, to give you the courtesy due a baron, yet the relationship between my own domain and the Baroney of Skelleth is most exceptionally warm, and I think that is what he had in mind. Therefore, I invite you to ask your favor, knowing that I look upon you as a good friend and ally."

"Thank you, O Prince," Garth replied. "I am seeking a book, an arcane volume known as the Book of Silence. I am told that it lies in or beneath Ur-Dormulk, most probably in what was the royal chapel of an ancient palace."

He had meant to continue with a few meaningless courtesies and then ask for assistance in locating the book, but he was distracted by the expressions on the faces of two of the overlord's courtiers. The woman in the yellow gown had turned pale, her face as bloodless and white as bleached wool; beside her, the blue-clad man's mouth was open, his eyes wide, his broad face flushed.

The overlord, looking at Garth and not to the side, did not notice. He remarked casually, "The Book of Silence? An odd name; is not a book meant to speak to its readers? I have never heard of it; my tax collectors will be grieved to learn that there is something of value within the walls that they had not discovered for me." He smiled at his jest, and Garth smiled in return; some of the courtiers chuckled politely.

The two who obviously *had* heard of the Book of Silence managed to compose themselves while their lord was speaking, Garth noticed, though the woman remained pale and unsteady. He wondered who they were. He was slightly disappointed that the overlord seemed unable to tell him where to find the book, but it looked as if this pair might be of help.

Serious again, the overlord asked, "Is this book some sort of grimoire or book of spells?"

"I don't know," Garth admitted. "I seek it on behalf of a wizard of my acquaintance, who has told me that he requires it to perform certain magics I wish him to perform." That was not quite the truth, but it was close enough to serve.

"And was it this wizard who told you the book was in Ur-Dormulk?"

"Yes," Garth replied. "He told me that it lay in an ancient chapel, or perhaps the ruins of one."

"I know of no such chapel, and this palace is the only one that has stood in this city in all its recorded history."

Garth shrugged. "I have said what I was told."

"This is all strange to me, and I fear I can be of little assistance. Is there any other way in which I might aid you?"

A trace of color was returning to the woman's face, Garth saw, and the man beside her had wholly recovered, pretending that nothing untoward had happened. Those two, Garth decided, were definitely worthy of investigation. He found himself thinking that there was something familiar about them, but dismissed it as overactive imagination.

That could wait, however. He had another concern he wanted to mention to the overlord, and another audience might not be easy to obtain, despite the man's expressed goodwill.

"O Prince," he said, "forgive my ignorance of your city, but is the cult of Aghad active in Ur-Dormulk?"

The overlord appeared momentarily startled. "Aghad? The Dûs god of hatred? There is a temple to him here, certainly, and it has, I suppose, its complement of priests and devotees. We of Ur-Dormulk pride ourselves upon the toleration of all faiths – or at least all save the most repulsive. The dark gods and their followers may be distasteful, but we permit them to remain and worship as they please, so long as they do not disturb the peace. One or two have, in truth, been banished for practicing human sacrifice, but to date, the Aghadites have behaved themselves. Why do you ask?"

"I have a personal interest in the cult of Aghad, O Prince. Its followers murdered my wife."

Garth's tone was flat and dull; the humans probably took it for the emptiness of grief rather than the seething anger it was. A few of the courtiers made vague, sympathetic murmurs.

The overlord was slow in replying. "I am sorry to hear of this," he said at last. "Why do you mention it? What would you have of me?"

"O Prince, I am sworn to destroy those who slew my wife, yet I do not wish to trouble your domain. The Baron of Skelleth, the people of Skelleth, and I would esteem it a very great favor if you were to expel the followers of Aghad from Ur-Dormulk, so that they might be removed from your protection." That seemed the most he could reasonably ask. He would have preferred to demand that the overlord send his soldiers immediately to burn the temple and kill its priests.

"I am reluctant," the overlord admitted. "It goes against the traditions of the city to banish any faith that has not directly harmed my subjects." He paused, then continued. "I will take what you ask for under advisement; I am well aware that it is to our benefit to respect Skelleth's wishes, yet this request is unprecedented. If you could identify any person who had a direct role in your wife's death, I might have him arrested and sent to Skelleth for trial – but to exile the entire sect! You ask much, and I must consider well before making my decision."

Garth bowed in polite acknowledgment. He had both feared and hoped that the overlord would refuse him. He was already planning a venture of his own into the temple. He knew, rationally, that to destroy the temple himself would antagonize both the overlord of Ur-Dormulk and the Baron of Skelleth and would make his life less pleasant all around. Emotionally, however, the prospect of wreaking havoc was very appealing indeed.

"Is there anything else, overman?"

"If I may, O Prince, I would like to consult with some of your advisers regarding the possible location of the Book of Silence, if there are any who might have knowledge of it."

The overlord raised a hand and gestured. "I have here with me two most excellent wizards; if this book is indeed magical, they might be of some assistance." He indicated the woman in yellow and the man in blue. "This is Chalkara of Kholis, Court Wizard to the High King at Kholis, retired recently and come here upon leaving the King's service; and Shandiph the Wanderer, a magician of some note and a native of Ur-Dormulk, returned home to join my court. There is also," he said as he turned and indicated an old woman in somber brown and burgundy velvet, "my court archivist, Silda; she knows more about this city than any other living person. They will accompany you to the Rose Chamber, where you may speak in comfort. Now, if you will forgive me, there is other business I must attend to."

Garth nodded. He had suspected that the pair might be magicians or seers of some sort and had hoped that the overlord would answer as he had. Only one more point remained to be mentioned before the end of the audience.

"O Prince, I thank you for your consideration; if I might trouble you just a moment longer, however, there is a detail . . ."

"What is it?" The overlord was becoming impatient and trying unsuccessfully to hide it.

"My sword." Garth pointed at the soldier who carried his weapons. "Will it be returned to me?"

"Yes, of course." The overlord waved a hand in dismissal. "When you leave the palace, your weapons will be returned." He gestured at the officer who had escorted Garth. "See to it."

"Thank you, O Prince. May your reign be long and prosperous," Garth said. He bowed, retreated a few steps, and looked about.

A red-clad courtier stood ready to guide him; wary and unsmiling, the three advisers stepped from their places at the dais and joined him.

The party made its way out of the incense-filled audience chamber through a side door, then down a long paneled corridor that seemed chill and empty by contrast, and finally into a small room that opened off to the right.

The walls of this room were lined with rose-colored velvet, and the floor was an elaborate rosewood inlay; chairs of rosewood and velvet were gathered around an ebony table that held a vase of fresh-cut white roses.

This was obviously the Rose Chamber, and Garth settled cautiously into one of the chairs, uncertain at first that it would support his weight. Shandiph took the place opposite the overman, while Chalkara seated herself on Garth's right and Silda on his left, so that each occupied a different side of the table.

The red-clad guide pulled the two superfluous chairs off to one side, out of the way of extended legs or stretching arms, and then vanished discreetly.

For a moment of awkward silence the four studied one another. Garth noticed that Silda seemed, if anything, slightly bored, but the two magicians were obviously nervous and ill at ease. Chalkara appeared almost desperate, he thought, while Shandiph, fumbling with something small and shiny, was only marginally calmer.

He wondered what had so upset them.

When the silence had dragged on uncomfortably long, Garth said at last, "I saw your faces." He was turned somewhat to the right, leaving the archivist out for the moment. "You two have heard of the Book of Silence."

The two wizards glanced at each other, then back at the overman.

"We have heard of it," Shandiph admitted.

"You seem reluctant to speak of it," the overman remarked.

After a moment's hesitation, Shandiph nodded without answering.

"Why?" Garth asked.

Again the two looked at each other before replying.

"Do you think we should explain?" Chalkara asked.

Shandiph nodded slowly. "I fear we must."

Chalkara turned away and studied the velvet walls. "You do it," she said.

Garth glanced at Silda; she looked very confused and was obviously not a party to whatever conspiracy was afoot.

"To begin with," Shandiph said, "we have met before, Garth of Ordunin, something over two years ago."

Garth gazed with new interest at the wizards' faces; that explained why he had thought they might be familiar. He had encountered various wizards in various ways, but he was fairly sure where he had met these two. They had almost certainly been among the group of fifteen or twenty that had attacked him, appearing out of thin air in the hills north of Skelleth. The Sword of Bheleu had turned back their every assault and retaliated; Garth had seen that several had been killed before the Forgotten King had stepped in and ended the battle by magically transporting the wizards to their respective homes. That was the battle that had driven him to swear his false oath; he was hardly likely to forget it, but in the red haze of the sword's power and the flare and shadow of spell and counterspell, he had not seen clearly the faces of all the wizards.

"I believe I recall the incident," he said.

"I thought you might," Shandiph said. "I hope you bear us no ill will for our attempts to kill you; it seemed at the time to be the only way in which untold destruction might be averted."

"I have wondered, since then, who you might be, why you chose the time you did to attack me, and why you made no further attempts after your initial defeat," Garth said in a tone of polite curiosity.

Shandiph glanced at Chalkara, then replied, "As for who we were, it doesn't matter any more; our organization was destroyed. The survivors of our conflict with you were scattered, and the wars that followed prevented all attempts to regroup from succeeding. We had attacked you in hopes of halting the onset of the Age of Destruction, which was heralded by your acquisition of the Sword of Bheleu. We made no further attempts after our initial failure because there was no reason to, even had our organization remained intact; you no longer had the sword, and it was obvious that, whatever your part in it might have been, the Age of Destruction had already begun. Eramma was destroyed by civil war."

Garth nodded, though he thought to himself that the destruction hadn't been very complete.

"Chalkara and I fled here, hoping that Ur-Dormulk, which has lasted so long with so little change, would remain safe. We had not expected to see you again. Your arrival was something of a shock – most particularly when you professed to be seeking the Book of Silence."

"And that," Garth said, "brings us back to the original question. What do you know of the Book of Silence?"

"Little enough. What do you know of it? Why do you seek it?"

Garth shrugged. "I agreed to fetch it for an acquaintance of mine. I assume it's a book of magic of some sort." He saw no reason to give any unnecessary details, but he could scarcely claim complete ignorance.

Chalkara asked, "Who is this acquaintance?"

"A wizard, of sorts," Garth replied.

"The wizard who took the Sword of Bheleu from you after the battle?" she persisted.

Reluctantly, Garth admitted, "Yes."

The yellow-gowned wizard exchanged glances with her companion.

The archivist broke her long silence and remarked in a slightly querulous tone, "I wish I knew what you three were talking about. What battle was this? Who is this wizard, and what is the Sword of Bheleu?"

Shandiph held up a hand. "Patience, Silda. Let us speak a moment longer, and I will explain it all to you when I can." He paused, and the woman settled back into her silent discontent.

When he was fairly sure that Silda would not make any further protest, Shandiph went on. "Garth, this wizard – the one we saw two and a half years ago. Is he the King in Yellow?"

Silda gasped. "The King in Yellow?" she blurted.

"Silda," Shandiph said. "Please!"

The archivist stifled another outburst. When order was restored, Shandiph repeated, "Is he the King in Yellow, Garth?"

The overman shrugged. "He's an old man who lives in Skelleth. He told me his name once, but I've forgotten it; it was hard to pronounce."

A glance around the table made it plain that both women were now struggling to keep from shouting at him. Shandiph sighed. "I wish you were more cooperative, Garth."

"My apologies, wizard, but I am not here at your convenience, to be interrogated as you see fit. *You* are here to answer *my* questions, are you not? That was the overlord's instruction."

"I know that. I'm sorry. This is very important, though, and very dangerous."

"Why?"

"Because of what the Book of Silence is, damn it!"

"Perhaps if you were to tell me what you believe it to be, we would both gain," Garth replied. This verbal sparring, each side trying to get the most information in exchange for its own, was beginning to annoy him, yet he was not about to end it by telling all he knew. Were he to do so, the wizards would have no reason to reveal their own secrets.

"It's death," Shandiph told him. "It's the end of everything."

One expression that was the same in both species was that of skepticism, and Garth looked openly skeptical.

"It's the totem of death," Shandiph insisted. "You know that the gods each have their unique devices; you must know it. You were the chosen of Bheleu, the one who bore his totem, who was to be his mortal incarnation."

Garth gave a noncommittal nod. "Go on," he said.

"I am no theurgist, no expert on dealing with the gods, but an old friend of mine was; he died in the hills outside Skelleth. He had no protective spells that could defend him against the Sword of Bheleu, though he knew what it was. He explained it to me, and I have studied further since then. Each of the greater gods has a period of ascendancy, an age in which the balance of power is tilted in his favor, and those things that please him are prevalent in our own mortal realm. Each of these ages has its particular herald, someone who wields the totem of the dominant god or goddess. When an age ends, the servants of the waning deity perform a service for the representative of the ruler of the new age, as a symbol of the shift in power. We are now in the Fourteenth Age, the Age of Bheleu, god of destruction, as you know only too well; you are Bheleu's chosen representative, though you have, with the aid of a power I do not pretend to understand, refused that role. I am not aware of the circumstances, but according to theory, a representative of P'hul must have done you a service of some sort, to mark the beginning of this era and the end of the Thirteenth Age, ruled by P'hul, goddess of decay."

Garth nodded. The cult of P'hul had, in fact, spread the White Death in Dûsarra when he had asked, in a fit of madness, for the city's destruction.

"Now, you see, the King in Yellow is the undying priest of The God Whose Name Is Not Spoken. It is a safe assumption that he will be the chosen avatar for the Final God when the Age of Death arrives. That means two things: he must have the totem of the god of death, and a representative of Bheleu must perform a symbolic service for him. Do you not see, then, why we cannot permit you – you in particular – to deliver the Book of Silence to the King in Yellow?"

Garth remained skeptical. "It has been scarcely three years since the Thirteenth Age ended; that is hardly an age."

"No rule is known that limits the length of each god's age, either maximum or minimum. Perhaps your refusal to accept your role, welcome though it is, has cut short the Age of Bheleu."

"Why are you so certain that I wish to take the book to the King in Yellow?"

"I saw that old man who took the sword, Garth, and felt something of his power. Who else could it be?"

Chalkara made a suggestion. "You do not trust us, Garth, but Silda, here, has heard of the King; let her describe him, and we will let you decide whether it is he you serve."

Garth was quite well aware that the Forgotten King was also known as the King in Yellow and that he was exactly what the wizards said he was, but the overman found himself wondering what the archivist knew. He would welcome any new information that might help in his dealings with the old man.

"Speak, then, archivist," he said.

Silda looked at each of the three in turn, then said in a precise voice, "The King in Yellow is a legend in the most ancient histories of Ur-Dormulk. I know of no connection between him and any deity, nor of any connection with a book, or with overmen, or anything else you have spoken of, save only destruction and death. He once ruled an empire from this city, long ago, when it bore another name; one version called it Hastur, another Carcosa. His origins have never been explained; in the very earliest records and even earlier myths, his presence is accepted as an ongoing thing since time immemorial. The legends are all vague as to who or what he was – many seem to assume that any reader will already know – but it is clear that he could not die, and that he was an object of terror throughout the world as these historians knew it. His visage was said to hold death or madness for all who met his gaze.

"Although he was once a king in fact, and a king whom emperors served, he gave up his throne to a successor who founded the ancient Imperial dynasty that the founders of the present Ur-Dormulk overthrew centuries later – yet it was said that in time the King would return and reclaim his rightful place, and when he did, the stars would fall and the earth shatter. He disdained all trappings of royalty and went about the world in scalloped tatters that were a strange shade of yellow – hence the name, the King in Yellow. His servants wore black. This is said to be why the lords of Ur-Dormulk wear black and the people of the city shun all shades of yellow."

Silda paused and shook her head. Chalkara glanced down at her yellow dress, and Garth was uncomfortably aware of his custom of wearing black armor.

Silda continued. "Such a bare recounting of the facts known to me does not convey the essence of what I have read and heard concerning him. Throughout all the city's recorded history, from times so ancient that we cannot interpret the dates and on until the chaos of the Twelfth Age, the shadow of the King hangs like smoke. In every account of tragedy he is mentioned, and in descriptions of more pleasant times there is always an air of foreboding associated with him. In the wars of the Age of Aghad the city was sufficiently disrupted so that the continuity was lost and the myths forgotten among the public. But there can be no doubt that, before that age, the tales of the King had persisted, at least among the learned, for more than ten thousand years. This, despite the fact that no historian or storyteller ever dared set down anything but veiled hints as to his true nature. I had thought that no one now alive had ever heard of him, save myself; that only in the ancient books and scrolls was he mentioned – books and scrolls that no one but me has read in three centuries or more. To hear you three speak of him as if he were alive today, as if you had seen him . . ."

"I *have* seen him," Shandiph said.

"He has been lost for more than a thousand years!"

"You said yourself that he could not die," Chalkara pointed out.

Garth said nothing. He was mulling over what he had heard.

He had thought of the Forgotten King's life span in terms of centuries, not millennia. He could not conceive of anything existing for eleven thousand years. He could not truly conceive of living even *one* thousand years. That would be seven times his own lifetime, roughly; eleven thousand years would be his years seventy-sevenfold. His species itself had not existed for much over a millennium.

For the first time he honestly thought he understood why the King wanted to die. The weight of so many years was surely more than any mind could bear.

He had known that the King had a sinister reputation among any who knew of him at all; Garth had attributed this to his position as the high priest of death, but here there seemed to be something more. Why were the city's histories silent on the exact nature of the King's menace? Why was it said that the heavens would fall if he returned?

Would delivering the Book of Silence truly begin an Age of Death? If so, what would that mean?

That, at least, was a question he might ask. "What would an Age of Death entail?" he inquired.

"Widespread death, obviously," Shandiph replied. "Just as the current age is one of war and chaos and destruction, and the last was a time of stagnation and decay."

"And after it, what?"

Shandiph shrugged. "Who knows? Perhaps nothing will survive the Age of Death, not even the earth or the gods themselves. Perhaps humanity will be destroyed but the rest of the world will go on, and your people will begin a new cycle of their own. Perhaps death will be limited, and many, even whole nations, will survive, and the lesser gods will have their turns as the rulers of the ages. I don't know. I do know that an Age of Death is not something I want to see."

Garth considered these possibilities, particularly the first and most horrific.

What if *nothing* were to survive the Age of Death? The world itself vanished, and the gods dead; would not even time itself cease to be? The end of time would be an actual fact, not just a poetical turn of phrase.

He recalled, with a growing apprehension, that when he had bargained with the King for eternal fame, the King had sworn that Garth's name would be known "as long as there is life upon this earth." When the King had offered him immortality – or so he had understood the offer – the old man had said that Garth might live until "the end of time" if he aided the King's magic. The King had said that his magic would cause many deaths, including those of the entire cult of Aghad. And perhaps most important of all, the priest of The God Whose Name Is Not Spoken in Dûsarra had told Garth that the Forgotten King was bound to live until the end of time. The King sought to perform a feat that would allow him to die.

It appeared very much as if the Forgotten King meant to bring about the end of time and the death of everything. He had meant to assure that Garth might live and be known until the end of time, not by extending the overman's life, but by destroying the world and time itself.

Chapter Ten

After a moment of silence in which Garth absorbed the basic concept that he might be aiding in the utter destruction of the world, he began to consider the possible ramifications and permutations of his situation.

One question came to mind immediately. It seemed reasonable to assume that the world could not end, and the King could not die, until the *end* of the Age of Death. Yet the old man had implied that his death would be immediately achieved by his conjuring. When Garth had believed that the method involved summoning The God Whose Name Is Not Spoken and renouncing his bargain, he had seen no contradiction there. He had thought that the King's offer of eternal life was based on substituting Garth for himself in the Death-God's power, but that no longer seemed reasonable. The offer had not been of eternal life at all.

"How long," he asked, "would the Age of Death last?"

Shandiph shrugged. "I told you," he said, "I am no theurgist, nor am I an astrologer or a seer. I don't know. I have heard philosophers say that the length of an age is subjective and cannot always be predicted or measured. Perhaps it will last a million years, until the sun grows cold and the seas run dry, or perhaps it will be over in an instant, and the world will vanish in a puff of smoke."

That was a very unsatisfactory answer, in Garth's opinion. "Wizard," he said, "I was told by Bheleu, in a vision he sent while I held the sword and he sought to dominate me, that his reign would last thirty years. Now you speak as if it might be over in just three. How can that be? Could the god have been wrong? That was not part of my understanding of the nature of a god. Might my refusal to serve him have altered that, when the god himself had once said it? I had thought that the ages were fixed in the stars, and that only failures of interpretation caused the uncertainty and disagreement among astrologers."

"I don't know," Shandiph admitted. "Perhaps the stars offer a choice; perhaps the god lied. My friend Miloshir told me that Bheleu's reign would last for either three years or thirty, but could not say which; it may be that his knowledge was lacking, or it may be that it had not yet been determined. Your refusal might in truth have been the crucial event; perhaps you ameliorated the Age of Destruction only to hasten the Age of Death."

Garth remembered the smoking battlefields and charred wastelands he had seen in his journey south through Eramma. If these were the scenes of a *mild* Age of Destruction, what would it have been had he not refused his role? That was a depressing line of thought.

The possibility that by limiting the destruction he had brought the end of the world half a generation earlier – or a full generation for humans – was even more disheartening. It appeared that he had faced a situation in which he would cause disaster, whatever course he might choose.

"You say that my actions might bring the Age of Death; how could that be prevented, if that is to be the next age? Must there be an Age of Death? Need it be the Fifteenth Age, and not the Hundredth?"

"Again, Garth, I cannot say with any certainty. Miloshir spoke as if there were to be fifteen ages to complete the current cycle, the first seven dedicated to the Lords of Eir and the last to the Lords of Dûs, while the Eighth Age was an era when light and darkness were in balance. Whether this scheme of being is truly fixed and immutable I do not know. If it is unalterable, then there will be a Fifteenth Age, a final age, an Age of Death, and it will occur immediately after our current Age of Destruction."

"It seems little to choose, between destruction and death."

Shandiph shrugged. Chalkara, who had been following the conversation closely, said, "I would prefer to live, however terrible the times in which I live, than to perish."

"Do you think that by stopping me from performing my errand you might avert this Fifteenth Age?"

"We feel we must try. It may be that it can be delayed for another twenty-seven years, or perhaps it can be weakened, as Bheleu's reign was, so that some might survive where they otherwise would not."

Garth sat back and thought for a moment. He was not happy about this new information. The possibility that the wizards were making it all up for reasons of their own did not escape him, but that seemed unlikely; it all fitted far too well with what he knew. The blue-clad man had suggested the end of the world as just one of several possibilities, which did not jibe with a lying attempt to frighten anyone; it was Garth's own knowledge of the Forgotten King that convinced him that that was exactly what was fated to occur.

The Fourteenth Age had lasted almost three years thus far; before it, the Age of P'hul had been three centuries, and the Twelfth Age was old when the first overmen were created a millennium ago, as he understood it, so it had lasted at least seven hundred years. The ages appeared to be getting shorter. The Fifteenth might be three days, or three hours. The end of the world, and his own death, might be only a few days in the future.

This assumed, however, that the Fifteenth Age would really begin when the Forgotten King received the Book of Silence. Garth knew of a serious flaw in that theory.

"Would it lessen your concern," he asked, "if I told you that the Book of Silence is not the device of The God Whose Name Is Not Spoken?"

Shandiph considered for a moment, and then said, "Not really. If it is not, then what is? And you, Bheleu's chosen, will still be doing the King in Yellow a service if you bring him the book, even should it be the totem of another god. Miloshir told me that it might be the device of Dagha himself, god of time, the father of all the higher gods. But in that case, what is the totem of Death? He thought it might be the basilisk that dwelt beneath Mormoreth, but that seems unlikely; the creature died, did it not? And bringing the King in Yellow Dagha's totem might easily be as devastating as bringing him his own, whatever it might be."

Garth had to admit the logic in this speech; after all, he had taken the Sword of Bheleu from Bheleu's altar, and not from the followers of P'hul.

"Still," he said, "the Age of Death, as I understand it, cannot begin until *two* conditions are met; I must do the King a service, yes, but more importantly, he must acquire the totem of his god. Is that not correct?"

Shandiph nodded. "I would ask, though, how you know that the Book of Silence is not that totem, when you profess to know nothing about it."

"The King told me," the overman replied; almost immediately, he realized how feeble that sounded. Still, he believed the old man. He knew that the King was a schemer, adept at speaking half-truths and implying falsehoods without actually stating them, yet he had never heard him tell a direct and definite lie. The old man had said, in effect, that the Book of Silence was the totem of Dagha, not of Death. At the time, it had seemed odd that he had wasted so many words, rather than letting Garth believe what he chose, but now it appeared the King had foreseen a moment such as this, when Garth might be reluctant to fetch the book if he believed it to be the device of the Final God.

The Final God – that name suddenly seemed more appropriate, if his age was to end the world.

"You may have reason to accept his word," Shandiph said, "but we do not. Furthermore, how do you know that he does not already possess the symbol of the Unnamed God, whatsoever it may be?"

"He did possess it once, but left it here, in this city, with the Book of Silence."

"He told you this?"

"Yes." Garth remembered that the old man had said also that he was not wholly free of the Pallid Mask even when apart from it, but Garth suppressed the thought. He wanted to bring the Book of Silence to the King so that he might trade it for the Sword of Bheleu and kill Aghadites with the sword.

The thought of killing Aghadites, of watching them bleed and die, was so appealing that he let himself linger over it for a moment, and Chalkara's next question did not register at first.

"I said, what is the totem of Death?" she repeated.

Garth recalled himself and shrugged. "He called it the Pallid Mask."

The two wizards glanced at each other, then at the archivist.

"I never heard of it," Chalkara said.

"Nor I," Shandiph declared.

"I am not sure," Silda said. "It might have been mentioned in the tales of the fallen moons."

"That doesn't matter," Garth said. "I have no intention of bringing anything to the King but the Book of Silence. You have my word."

"I would rather have your word that you would give up this quest entirely," Shandiph said.

"I cannot do that. I need magic for my revenge, a magic that the cult of Aghad cannot counter."

There was a moment of silence. It was Chalkara who said at last, "You want the Book of Silence for *that?*"

"No," Garth replied. "I want the King's aid, which he has promised in exchange for the book." It seemed impolitic to mention that he meant to take up the Sword of Bheleu again; the wizards would surely oppose that as strongly as they opposed the Age of Death. The Fifteenth Age was a theory, but they had seen the sword's power and suffered under it.

"You would risk the lives of every man, woman, and child, every overman and overwoman, every bird and beast in the world, to avenge your wife's murder?" Shandiph asked.

Garth answered simply, "Yes." He did not think it worth pointing out that the cult of Aghad was a menace to all and had threatened further deaths, or that destroying it would be both an act of vengeance and one of prevention. Kyrith's death was reason enough.

Chalkara glanced at each of the others in turn, then whispered to Shandiph, "He's mad!"

She had not allowed for the keen ears of overmen; Garth heard what she said, but ignored it.

"Garth," Shandiph said, "please reconsider. We will aid your vengeance in every way we can, if you will not bring the King either the book or this mask, or serve him in any manner."

That was a tempting offer, but Garth reluctantly knew he had to refuse it. These wizards had little real power; much of what they had turned against him before, they had lost, either destroyed by the Sword of Bheleu or sealed away by the Forgotten King. They might be a match for an Aghadite magician in a fair contest, one against one, but the cult was clearly widespread and did not trouble itself with fairness; rather, it made a point of being unfair, treacherous, and hateful, in keeping with the nature of its deity. Furthermore, the full party of wizards that had fought him – and surely they had summoned their greatest strength for that combat – could not have exceeded two dozen, and at least one in four had died, perhaps half or more. That meant that far less than a score could have survived, while the cult might well number in the hundreds or even the thousands.

More importantly, he had sworn an oath. For two and a half years, the knowledge that he had made a false vow had eaten away at him, and that pain had finally been alleviated slightly when he undertook this journey. He did not care to let it return. He had regained some trace of honor, tarnished though it might be, and preferred to keep it for as long as he could.

"No," he said. "I am sorry." He rose, before any protest could be made. "I came to this chamber hoping that you might aid me in my search for the Book of Silence, perhaps tell me more of its nature. You have told me much, but it was not what I wished to hear. This conversation has been most enlightening, and I thank you for it, but still, I must pursue my original intention. I do promise you that I do not want to see the Age of Death begin and that I do not intend to aid in bringing it about, if I can avoid it and still meet my sworn obligations. It is plain that none of you would willingly help me in my search for the Book of Silence, and I will not compel you to do so; you act as you see best, as do I. For that reason, I believe there is no point in continuing this discussion." He nodded politely to each, then turned and marched out through the door they had entered by.

The paneled corridor was almost empty, but, half-hidden in a neighboring doorway, Garth saw a red-clad figure. "Ho, there," he called. "Can you show me the way out?"

In the Rose Chamber, the wizards watched him go and then turned to each other.

"We have to stop him, Shandi," Chalkara said.

"I know that, but what method would you suggest? I have no magic left that can kill from afar, and I see no other way of stopping him. And even if I had some, it might not work; true, he no longer carries the sword, but he is still the chosen of Bheleu."

"Is he really?" Silda asked. "You two and the overman seem to know a great deal more than I do about all this."

"Yes, he is. Everything we have said here is true."

Silda glanced at the door Garth had closed behind himself. "We should tell the overlord," she said.

Chalkara agreed. "She's right, Shandi. Garth hasn't got the Sword of Bheleu; ordinary soldiers should be able to kill him if necessary. At the very least, the overlord might insist that he leave the city; that would make it harder for him to find the Book of Silence, if it really is here."

Shandiph nodded. "I think you're right. If we act quickly, we might be in time to prevent the return of his weapons; even an overman would not be likely to put up too much of an argument at sword point when he's armed with nothing but a dagger."

Chalkara asked, "Who will speak to the overlord?"

"Speed is important, and we must impress upon him how urgent this is. We must all go, at once."

He rose, and Chalkara did the same. Silda got to her feet more hesitantly, then followed the wizards out of the room.

In the corridor they caught a glimpse of the overman vanishing into a side passage. Chalkara hesitated. "Should we pursue him? One of us, perhaps?"

"No," Shandiph said. "I'm sure that the overlord will have him followed as a precaution, and by someone less recognizable than we are. Let him go for now."

"He'll get his sword and axe back," Silda pointed out.

"He may be delayed, if he chooses to take advantage of the overlord's hospitality by accepting a meal or a drink, and we have no authority to prevent the return of his weapons without the overlord's word. You know that we are all three distrusted here, as wizards always are."

"I'm no wizard," Silda protested.

"You're a scholar, which is close enough for most people. You know things they don't. If we try to interfere without the prince's support, we'll be accused of conspiracy and treason, most likely. Better to risk Garth's arming himself while we talk to the overlord."

"We have no choice now," Chalkara said. "While we've been standing here debating, he's undoubtedly gotten that much farther away."

"True enough," Shandiph replied. "Let us waste no more time, then." He turned and led the way down the corridor toward the audience chamber.

Chapter Eleven

The overlord did not pay much attention when the archivist and the two wizards re-entered the hall; he assumed that they had finished their discussion with the overman and had come back to the audience chamber in case their prince might require their services. He was rather startled, therefore, when, instead of resuming their accustomed places, they stood before him and made the accepted ritual obeisance.

He had been chatting with his treasurer while the doorkeepers selected the next petitioner to be granted a hearing; during the time that the overman had been talking in the Rose Chamber he had settled a property dispute and refused to hear the appeal of a convicted thief, turning the man back over to the jailer for flogging. The day had been going well, and except for the arrival of the overman from Skelleth and his unorthodox requests, it had been routine.

There was nothing routine, however, in having three of the prince's advisers appear before him, uninvited, while he was holding court. They knew better, he told himself. If they had public business, it could go through the regular channels – though, of course, they would have fewer delays than outsiders would face – and if it was private, it could be handled informally after the day's work was finished.

He paused for a few seconds, letting the trio perceive his annoyance and grow a bit more nervous, then demanded, "Why have you come here? Speak, if you have any excuse for your action!"

With his head politely bowed, as protocol required in a petitioner, the male wizard said, "O Prince, we beg your forgiveness, but we have urgent business, very urgent indeed, and must speak with you immediately."

The overlord considered for a moment. The formalities and rituals of his life served a definite purpose, in that they made it easier for him to deal with the unending demands made upon him. Each piece of business, whatever its nature, was categorized and run through the appropriate ceremonies, delays, and sortings, so that only a tiny fraction of the whole ever needed to reach him at all; when it did, it was stripped down to the essentials, his choices laid out for him and awaiting a quick decision. Cutting through the rituals was a dangerous precedent; if he permitted the formal structure to weaken, he might be deluged in trivia. Only foreigners, who must be assumed to be ignorant of the usual procedures, were ever allowed to deviate from the pattern, and then only if it seemed a diplomatic necessity – as it had appeared with the overman.

On the other hand, he faced here not a single unknown individual, but three of his most learned counselors. He had not yet had time to become truly familiar with either of the wizards in the months since their arrival, but Chalkara had been the chosen magician of the High King at Kholis, despite her youth – if she was as young as she appeared, which was not something one could be sure of with wizards. She, in turn, deferred to Shandiph, so that he, too, must be considered worthy of respect – unless it was his age that engendered her deference. The vanished Deriam, the overlord's previous wizardly adviser, had spoken well of Shandiph; these two said that Deriam was dead, and the possibility of a magical feud had occurred to the overlord, but that did not detract from the pair's apparent worth. The archivist Silda had lived all her life as a member of the court, under first his father and then himself, but the prince knew less about her than he knew about the wizards; she seemed to care little for his company, or for that of any of his friends or informers. She was given to long historical discussions full of obscure references whenever he consulted her professionally; he suspected that she hoped to impress him with her erudition. He was not easily impressed, but he had to admit that she knew her job well.

These three, he thought, must honestly believe that their need was urgent, or they would not have interrupted the day's routine. Despite the unfortunate precedent it set, he decided to hear them out.

He would not do so publicly, however, whatever the matter might be. That would be too damaging to his aura of imperviousness.

In fact, as he prepared to speak, a way of settling the affair to his benefit occurred to him, a scheme that would make plain to all present that the overlord was not to be disturbed without good reason.

He waved an arm, finger pointing. "Guards! Take these three to the Black Hall, and summon the executioner! I will hear their plea, as I must in fairness do, but the penalty for usurping my attention thus and delaying the work of governance must be no less than death, if the cause is not sufficient!"

That, he thought, should impress any over-eager father wanting reimbursement for his daughter's lost maidenhood, or a householder demanding that his neighbor's hounds be silenced, enough to keep them out of his hair. He rose, watching as six guardsmen snatched the advisers up off the floor, a soldier at each arm. An officer had gone for the headsman; that was good. The prince led the way to the black and gold door, moving in his stately, slow walk, aware that the soldiers were bringing the three advisers along a few paces behind him.

A footman opened the door into the back corridor, then ran ahead to the black iron door of the execution chamber. The overlord entered the room, waited as the wizards and the archivist were brought in, then waved imperiously at the guards and servant. "Begone," he said.

The seven vanished, and he looked about for somewhere to sit. The room was empty save for the black stone platform in the center and the great block of ebony that stood upon it. The walls and floor were rough black stone; the ceiling was black-veined red marble, arched and vaulted. It was a thoroughly uncomfortable place, he decided as he settled on the edge of the platform.

The three counselors stood awkwardly, facing him, unsure whether to prostrate themselves, to bow, or just to stand there.

"Now," the overlord said, "what is it that's so urgent?"

"O Prince," Shandiph replied, "you must prevent Garth from. taking the Book of Silence!"

"Garth? The overman?" The overlord was puzzled. "Why?"

"O Prince," Chalkara said, "the Book of Silence is perhaps the most deadly object ever to exist. It is linked with the higher gods, the gods of life and death and even Dagha himself, it seems. Its arcane power is so great that ordinary wizards cannot use it, for to speak a single word from its pages would be instantly fatal." She paused to catch her breath.

The overlord remarked, "That would seem to make it one of the most *useless* of objects."

Shandiph demurred. "I fear not, my lord. As Chalkara has said, no ordinary wizard can use it, but Garth of Ordunin serves one who is not an ordinary wizard. The book was created to be used by a single individual, the immortal high priest of The God Whose Name Is Not Spoken. That is whom Garth intends to deliver it to."

"How do you know this?"

Shandiph asked, "Which part, O Prince?"

"How do you know whom the overman plans to give the book to? He mentioned a wizard, not a priest."

"We know him, Chalkara and I, from a previous encounter. We know that he is associated with the King in Yellow, as the high priest of Death was known of old, and with no other wizards. He admitted as much to us when we spoke with him just now."

"The King in Yellow?" The overlord looked at Silda. "I believe you've mentioned an ancient legend about someone with that description."

"Yes, my prince."

The overlord saw that the archivist had no intention of elaborating, and did not pursue the matter.

"Well, then, what if the overman does take this book to this priest? How will that harm us here in Ur-Dormulk?"

Shandiph answered, "We believe it will bring about the start of the Fifteenth Age, the Age of Death."

"You fear that? Are not the ages preordained and unchangeable?"

Shandiph hesitated, and Chalkara answered for him. "We do not know, O Prince. It may be that they are not."

"We are only in the third year of the Fourteenth Age; it seems to me that any worry, about the next age is premature."

"We do not know how long the Fourteenth Age is to be," Chalkara said.

The overlord nodded; he had heard the court astrologer bewailing that uncertainty. "Still," he said, "I cannot believe it will be so brief as that."

"We think that it may be," Chalkara insisted.

The overlord leaned back on his hands and looked at the three scholars. "*I* think," he said, "that you have all managed to frighten one another with old myths and vague suppositions until you have convinced yourselves that we are all in mortal peril, when in truth we are in no more danger from this mad overman than from the Emperor of Yesh." He held up a hand to forestall any protest. "Furthermore, I think you're missing a few essential facts in your worrying."

He shifted, leaned forward again, and held up a finger. "First, the danger you envision may not exist at all. Second, if it does, this overman may have nothing to do with it. Third, whatever else he may be, the overman is a representative of the Baron of Skelleth. You may not realize just how dependent we are upon Skelleth in these unsettled times. You may take seriously my magnificent titles and the splendor of this palace, but I know better; I may call myself a prince and be known throughout Eramma by the title of overlord, but the hard truth is that I'm nothing more than an Eramman baron. Those lesser lords in my court who give me the claim to be an overlord have no power at all, they are worth no more to me than the officers of my guard – probably less, actually.

"Maybe in ancient times Ur-Dormulk was a real nation unto itself and a power to be reckoned with; maybe Alar and Hastur and those other lands I claim really existed; I don't know and I don't care. All I rule is a walled city, a few miles of lakes and mountains, and a good-sized piece of plain that's totally impossible to defend, should one of my neighbors decide to invade. One of those neighbors is the Baron of Skelleth, and right now he's the only one who isn't at war somewhere and the only one conducting any trade at all. We haven't had a caravan in from Therin or Kholis in eighteen months; have you noticed what fresh fruit costs in the markets and shops these days? And what there is, is all our own, at that; I haven't seen a date or an orange in over a year, and if any were available in the city, I'd know it, I promise you.

"That may not mean much to you, but if we lost the trade with Skelleth, you'd know it and you'd feel it. I don't know where the goods are coming from, but we've been getting better furs and wool than we had in times of peace, pickled fish at half what we used to pay, and ivory and gold and a dozen other things – more than a dozen – scores, or hundreds! From Skelleth, which used to sell nothing but ice and hay! It was a gift from the gods that the new Baron began selling to us just about the time the other routes started to be cut, and I don't dare jeopardize that. The Barony of Skelleth covers half our borders, to the north and northeast, and if this Saram can bring us caravans out of nowhere, he might be able to bring armies with equal ease. Now he's sent us a representative, and an overman at that – where in all the world did he find an overman? I thought they were extinct, despite the stories we heard from the traders out of Skelleth. I was wrong. What's more, the gatekeeper tells me that the overman arrived riding a monster twenty feet long with fangs the size of a man's fingers.

"And now you ask me to throw away the goodwill of this overman, and with it the goodwill of the Baron of Skelleth, because of a vague legend. You ask me to risk losing our only remaining trade route, the richest I've ever seen. You ask me to risk an invasion, perhaps led by overmen on monsterback, like those in the tales of the Racial Wars. Why? Because you don't want a magical book no one can read to be taken to a mysterious wizard.

"And that brings me to my fourth, and most important, point. What makes you think that this overman will *find* this Book of Death, or whatever it is? He says that it's in the royal chapel of some palace. What palace? The only palace in Ur-Dormulk is this one, and I promise you all, on my soul and the shades of my ancestors, that there is no royal chapel here containing a mystical book no one can read! If this book exists at all, it must be in the crypts somewhere. Have you ever been in the crypts, any of you?"

The three advisers nodded in unison, like chastised children.

"All of you. Then you should know that you can't find *anything* in the crypts unless you know exactly where it is! They go on forever, in a maze, like a mass of worms tied in knots.

"So do you know what I'm going to do? I'm going to let this overman wander about the city all he likes, and if he wants to get himself lost in the crypts, I'll allow that, too. I'll even give him a guide, if he asks, one who will lead him in nice, large circles through the more familiar corridors. If he persists I'll let him wander all he wants. He can go explore the ruins between the lakes. He can kill a few Aghadite priests, if he does it quietly, and I won't do a thing about it. If he *does* find the book, or anything else of real value, I'll know it, I promise you. If that happens – *if* it happens – then I'll talk to you again, and maybe have it taken away from him if you can convince me it's really that important. *That's* what I'm going to do about this overman, and I hope it satisfies you, because I am *not* going to offend the Baron of Skelleth unless I really have to, for my own safety and for the safety of Ur-Dormulk. Is that clear?"

The three, overwhelmed by this lengthy speech, nodded again.

"Good. So if you want to make yourselves useful, you might apply your magic, you two, to help keep an eye on the overman. All three of you might want to see if you can get some idea where this book is, if it exists, so that we can get to it before he does – if we have to." The overlord waved a hand in dismissal. "So much for that. Now, about the matter of your barging into the audience chamber. As you may have guessed, I am not going to have you executed."

Silda was visibly relieved to hear this; Shandiph and Chalkara, who had never taken the threat seriously, were startled by its mere mention.

"However," the prince continued, "I am not at all pleased that you took it upon yourselves to interrupt my routine; therefore, you are all confined to the north wing of the palace until further notice. I don't want you in the hall with me, I don't want you in my apartments, and I don't want you in the front rooms. Is that understood?"

"O Prince," Shandiph began, "I think you underestimate . . ."

"Silence!" the overlord bellowed.

Shandiph subsided.

"That's better. If you do that again, wizard, you'll be a wanderer once more; I won't execute you, as that would be a stupid waste, but I won't hesitate to banish you from the city if you become more trouble than you're worth to me."

Shandiph bowed his head in acknowledgment.

"Good." The overlord got to his feet and brushed off his velvet robes. "Now let's get back to work." He gestured, and Silda opened the door.

The executioner, hooded and robed in black and yellow, stood outside, his axe in his hands. Behind him, a ring of nervous guards and footmen waited.

The prince spread his arms theatrically. "My thanks, my lord, for heeding my summons. I have decided, however, to be merciful; your services will not be needed."

The headsman bowed low, backed up a pace as soldiers scurried to clear a path, then turned and marched away without speaking.

The overlord spotted an officer among the clustered guardsmen and called, "Captain, if you would escort these three to their quarters, I would appreciate it. They are not prisoners and are not to be confined, but I think they would like to rest. They have been overexcited. See to them; I must return to my own business."

The officer saluted, setting the crimson plume on his helmet bobbing; he pulled two of his men off to one side as the others formed an honor guard around the overlord, then waited as servants, soldiery, and prince marched back into the audience chamber. When the black and gold door had closed behind the last footman, the officer gestured for the first of his two men to accompany Silda and for the other to guard Chalkara, while he himself escorted Shandiph. Thus arranged, he bowed politely and said, "At your service, my lord wizard."

Shandiph was in no mood for pleasantries. "Lead on," he said.

Together the party trooped up the corridor, past the golden door of the Hall of Promotion, and through the ornate gate at the end of the passage. All turned right, but Silda and her guard continued directly down the carpeted corridor, while the wizards and their unwanted companions headed up the gilded staircase. The archivist's apartments were on a lower level, near the archives themselves, which were in an upper part of the crypts. The wizards, in keeping with tradition, were housed on the topmost floor of one of the palace towers. Shandiph, not as young and spry as he once was, sometimes regretted that.

During the long walk along the length of the north wing, ascending each flight of stairs they encountered, neither Chalkara nor Shandiph spoke. Each observed the other, however. Chalkara saw Shandiph's fists clench and unclench, saw him biting back words. Shandiph saw Chalkara's eyes shifting, her face pale, with the look of a hunted animal in her manner.

They reached the spiral stair that led into the tower proper, and Shandiph broke his silence. "You need go no farther," he told the soldiers. "There's no reason to tire yourselves out by climbing all these stairs."

The captain stopped, glanced about, and nodded. "Very well. The prince said you were not under confinement, and at any rate, there is no other exit from the tower."

"Indeed," Shandiph said. "Thank you for your company, captain, and a good evening to you." He bowed slightly.

The officer saluted, but did not depart; instead he stood where he was and watched as the two wizards made their way up the staircase. Glancing back, Shandiph noticed, with some amusement despite his worry over Garth's actions, that the young guardsman who stood at his captain's side was not watching both wizards, but only Chalkara. Unaware that he was observed, the soldier stared at her hips as she climbed the steps. Shandiph was not surprised; Chalkara was worth staring at. He guessed that the youth was wondering whether the tales one heard in every barracks were true, that sorceresses are not like other women.

Shandiph turned away, resisting the urge to comment. The stories were not true; Chalkara was as human as anyone.

The curve of the stair took them out of sight before they reached the first floor of the tower; their own rooms were in the fifth and highest storey. Shandiph paused, out of breath, at the first landing, but then marched determinedly onward.

"Shandi, we . . ." Chalkara began as they rounded the next curve.

He waved her to silence and trudged upward.

At the third landing he stopped and listened; Chalkara came and stood beside him.

"I don't think they can hear us," he said, keeping his voice low. "Chala, do you like it here?"

"What?"

"Do you like Ur-Dormulk? Do you want to stay here?"

"I don't know. It's comfortable, even if it isn't home, and where else could we go?"

"Sland, perhaps; I understand that it's at peace now, and Karag fled years ago. There might be a place for a wizard or two."

"Shandi, what are you talking about? Why should we leave Ur-Dormulk? If the Fifteenth Age starts, it won't matter where we are."

"It might, but that's not my point. I want to know if you'll go along with me if I disobey the overlord and get us both exiled."

"Oh, Shandi, of course I will! We *have* to do something, whatever he says! The King in Yellow wouldn't have sent Garth here unless he knew the Book of Silence could be found!"

"We'll have to run for our lives, probably. The prince may decide to put us to death if we stay here."

"I don't mind. Maybe we should leave anyway, Shandi, even if he doesn't do anything. I want to see Kholis again; the fighting hasn't reached there yet, not all the way to the castle, and I'm sure the King is over his anger by now. I may not live long enough to go home if we don't stop the overman."

"Don't be so pessimistic, Chala; we'll stop him, at least for now. He's just one overman." Shandiph did not wholly believe that, even as he said it.

Chalkara did not believe it either, but she said nothing to contradict the older wizard. "What are you planning to do?" she asked.

"I'm not sure yet, but I have an idea. Can you make a golem?"

Chalkara considered, then shook her head. "No."

"What about illusions?"

"Oh, I can do those, but they aren't always reliable. What are you thinking of?"

"I'm thinking of ways of killing Garth. I don't have any spells that can do it anymore; do you?"

"No. At least, I don't think so."

"Well, I'm not about to go up and try to kill him in person; he's dangerous. That means we'll have to send someone else to do it."

"Shandi, should we do that? Isn't there any other way to stop him?"

"I doubt it. He's stubborn. I'm sure we can't destroy the King in Yellow or the Book of Silence, but we can probably get Garth killed."

"Should we consult with the rest of the Council?"

"Why bother? The Council is broken, Chala, you know that. We're not bound by its rules anymore. Besides, his death was authorized three years ago, by vote of the quorum."

"You're right. We'll kill him."

"*We* won't; the city guard will. Did you know that Sedrik has always hated overmen? One of his ancestors got butchered in the Racial Wars, I suppose."

"How do you know that?"

"I got him drunk one night; it's always a good idea to learn something about the people who run the place you're living in. I was hoping to find out who was intriguing against whom – there's always some of that in a palace – but instead I got a tirade about murderous inhuman monsters and a lecture about the cowardice of the Eramman nobility in not invading the Northern Waste and wiping the vermin out."

"I see; he'd love an excuse to kill an overman, then, and it's probably one of his men following Garth." Chalkara nodded.

"And if he should receive an order from the overlord himself, I don't think he'd bother to wonder why the prince changed his mind."

"From the overlord?" Chalkara looked puzzled for an instant; then comprehension dawned. "Oh, of course! A golem would be better, but an illusion should work if the light isn't very good."

"I hope so," Shandiph said.

"You start packing, Shandi; the overlord won't like this at all if he finds out. I'll need some things for the illusion, but you can pack up everything else." She hurried up the last two flights; Shandiph, still weary, plodded after her.

Ten minutes later, Sedrik, Commander of the Guard, Marshal of the City, was startled by the appearance of his lord and master in the door of the wardroom. The overlord's voice seemed odd, higher in pitch and not very clear. The corridor was dim and the wardroom's windows did not illuminate the doorway this late in the day, so the prince's black robes seemed insubstantial and almost blended into shadow. There was no sign of the prince's customary entourage. Still, there was no mistaking who it was that spoke to Sedrik, or what his orders were.

Sedrik was absolutely delighted.

Chapter Twelve

Garth acknowledged the return of his sword and axe with a deep bow, then turned and marched down the steps of the palace.

When he reached the stone pavement of the avenue he paused, unsure where to go. He had two goals to achieve and no clear idea of how to pursue either one. Somewhere in the city was the Book of Silence, and he had sworn to find it and bring it back to Skelleth. Somewhere in the city there was also a temple dedicated to Aghad, and he was determined to destroy it and kill the god's worshippers, regardless of what the overlord might say or do about it.

Finding the book, he decided as he slung the axe on his back, should come first; the overlord had expressed no objection to that, despite the misgivings of his counselors. The wizards might try to change his mind, but so far, at any rate, Garth had a free hand to do as he pleased with regard to the book. The cult of Aghad, on the other hand, was under the overlord's consideration. If Garth were to attack the temple now, the overlord might well take it amiss and try to have Garth killed or driven from the city.

Once he had the book he would have no objection to leaving Ur-Dormulk. Therefore, the book came first.

That settled, and with his sword on his belt once more, he looked about, trying to locate the signs and portents the Forgotten King had promised him.

The sun was halfway down the western sky, and the shadow of the overlord's palace stretched over him. To the east, much of the avenue was still brightly lit; citizens were bustling about the gray stone buildings in a flickering river of vivid colors. Streets branched off to either side in a variety of widths and angles.

As he turned to the southwest, looking toward one corner of the palace facade, a gust of cold, damp wind caught him in the face.

That seemed as good a sign as any; he strolled south and around the corner.

He did not notice the green-clad figure that followed him, nor the two in red – one in the brilliant carmine of the overlord's household staff, the other wearing the color of dried blood – that watched him closely but did not pursue.

He wandered along aimlessly, watching for other signs, yet found none save the occasional wet breezes. He gradually worked his way westward, noticing as he went that the number of people on the streets and the general noise of the city diminished steadily with his increasing distance from the avenue that connected the eastern gate and the overlord's palace. After some time spent thus, he rounded a corner and found himself looking out across a rift. The city appeared to end in a broad stretch of pavement running north and south along the edge of a valley or chasm; from where he stood he could not see what lay in the gap, but he could see the far side, a granite barrier topped with buildings. Something was odd about the view, but mists drifting up from the valley made it hard for him to decide just what he was seeing.

He walked onward, out onto the wide pavement, and noticed to his surprise that there were no people anywhere on it. This promenade was the first completely uninhabited place he had seen since arriving in Ur-Dormulk.

He made his way cautiously up to the edge, wary lest it crumble beneath him, though it looked as solid as any part of the city. When he had gotten as near to the precipice as he cared to, he gazed out beyond it again.

More than fifty yards below lay the smooth, dark surface of a lake, black and chill; thin clouds rolled across it in bands, like waves upon the ocean, and mist rose in dissipating plumes.

That, Garth told himself, explained where the cold winds came from.

He lifted his gaze, looking out across the lake; the mists blurred his vision, and he could not decide whether the barrier that reared up on the opposite shore was natural or man-made. The buildings atop it, he now saw, were ruins.

It occurred to him immediately that the Book of Silence was quite possibly buried somewhere in those ruins; that would explain why nothing was known of it.

The sun was behind the broken towers, which made it impossible for him to make out much detail, but he guessed that those towers had once been part of a palace or citadel, such as the Forgotten King must have maintained. He stared intently, but the shadows and mist prevented any clear view. The sun itself seemed distorted by the fine spray, broadened to almost twice its natural width.

He turned his eyes away and blinked, then looked at the gray stone pavement for a moment to rest them. As he did, he noticed two things.

First, the pavement here was not worn nearly so much as the city streets. He would have supposed that a lakeside promenade would attract strollers in the hot days of summer, or perhaps fishermen – someone, at any rate – yet there was no one anywhere in sight save himself, and the stone slabs were only lightly marked by the passage of feet.

The second thing he noticed was a sound, a very faint, deep, distant sound; he could not quite make it out.

Neither item seemed of immediate importance; he looked up once more, avoiding the sun for the moment, and scanned quickly around the edges of the lake.

It was long and narrow, with the city on one of its long sides and the ruins on the other. At either end of the promenade on which he stood walls of natural rock thrust up, raising the lakeside cliff to greater heights and cutting off the streets to the east, turning them back from the lake. Garth realized he had seen those stone barriers from the steps at the gate.

Similar outcroppings divided the opposite shore, but beyond and between them lay more ruins. The area directly opposite him was the largest, but there were four clusters of buildings in all on the western shore, each split off from the others by the masses of rock and connected to the rest of the city only by the lake. The ends of the lake, at north and south, were sheer cliffs, with no signs of human habitation upon them. He could not see if there were ruins or other inhabited areas elsewhere on the eastern shore; the outcroppings at either end of the promenade blocked his view.

Once, he guessed, the various enclaves must have kept in touch with one another by boat, so that all were part of a single great city. Now, though, there were no signs of docks or boats, but only the still black water, laced with mist and cloud, far below. He theorized that over the centuries the level of the lake had dropped, making such water travel more difficult, and finally impossible. The lake might be too shallow to navigate – though it looked infinitely deep.

He turned his gaze back to the ruins opposite his present position and noticed for the first time that mists seemed to be rising behind them as well as in front. He was unsure whether this indicated the presence of another lake, or whether it was merely an optical illusion.

With a sudden shock, he spied something very strange that could only be a trick of the mist; the sun had split in two, and twin crimson orbs, like baleful eyes, were sinking behind the towers into the mist of the farther lake – if such a lake was really there.

He blinked, but the illusion persisted, and it was only after a moment of staring that he realized how long he must have been wandering about Ur-Dormulk if the sun – or suns – was setting.

He wondered if this strange vision might be one of the signs he was to follow.

The sound he had noticed before impinged again upon his awareness, and he found himself trying to making out just what it was. It, too, might be a sign, he told himself.

It seemed to be coming across the lake, or up from the ground, rather than from the city behind him. He resolved to follow it if he could.

He still had no idea what it was; it was so low in pitch, so slow and drawn-out, that he could barely perceive it at all. Picking a direction at random, he turned right and strode north along the promenade, then paused and listened.

The sound had grown very slightly louder; he was going in the right direction. He marched on. At the northern end of the lakeside pavement, he stopped and listened once more.

The sound was once again slightly louder; he did not appear to have passed its point of origin. It seemed, more than ever, to be coming from the ground beneath his feet, still barely audible, as much felt as heard, and felt only as slow, crawling uncertainty. A cold wind brought a puff of mist swirling around him, chilling him even through his surcoat and armor.

The sound, or vibration, or whatever it was, was as slow as the turning of the universe, slow as no human-generated sound ever was; a vague foreboding trickled through the back of Garth's mind as he listened to it.

From where he now stood he could not go west, over the cliff into the lake, nor north, up the sheer stone face of the outcropping; south would take him farther from the sound. That left only east. Two streets led back into the city proper from the northern end of the promenade at diverging angles; Garth took the left-hand, more northerly route, hoping that it would bring him to the source of the mysterious low throbbing. If it did not, he told himself, he would have to find a way across the lake.

The route he had chosen was a narrow, winding street lined with an assortment of buildings. Garth recognized some as shrines, though they lacked the domes and spires he had come to identify with temples, by the scent of incense and the sound of chanting. He wondered if any were dedicated to Aghad; the thought triggered a rush of anger and adrenaline, and his hand fell to the hilt of his borrowed sword.

He saw none of the dark red robes he had learned to associate with the cult, however, and the name Aghad was not written above any doorways or audible in any of the prayers he heard. He gradually relaxed as he walked on.

Around him, in contrast to the deserted lakeside, large numbers of humans went about their business, going to and from the various shrines and shops. Their bright garments were lighted in fiery shades or lost in lengthening shadows as the sun sank farther in the west and the evening torches were set ablaze. No one interfered with Garth's progress, though several people stared, and almost everyone who saw him gave him at least a second glance. Overmen, he knew, were not seen in Ur-Dormulk.

The street curved to the north, following the contour of the upthrust rock, separated from the bare stone only by the row of buildings that lined the left-hand side. Other alleys and byways led off to the right, but to the left there was nowhere to go.

This road, like all he had seen in Ur-Dormulk, was paved with gray stone; the marks of wear clearly indicated the parallel tracks of carts and the wider pathways of the more common pedestrians. Branches led from this central route to each of the temples and shops and houses. Garth realized that he could judge the relative popularity of the various establishments by the depth of the path that led to each door.

He paused to listen for the sound; he had lost it among the noises of the busy street. As he listened, he noticed that one temple, nestled close up against the rock wall to the west, had no visible path at all. That struck him as curious. He watched for a moment and saw that not only did no one approach the shrine but some people actually veered away to give it a wide berth. The trough in the center of the street swayed to the right in consequence. This avoidance was obviously not of recent development.

His curiosity piqued, Garth approached the shunned building. He could see nothing about it that might inspire dread; it had a low, simple facade, a row of pillars supporting a narrow porch in front of a bare stone wall and a single open door. A central portion of the roof was raised up above the facade. There were no adornments of any kind; no incense drifted from the open portal, and no chanting could be heard. No bells chimed, no draperies rustled; the shrine appeared deserted.

Garth paused for a moment, then heard the dull sound he had been following, just barely perceptible over the pattering feet and flapping sleeves of the passing traffic. He was about to conclude that the temple was completely empty, perhaps a relic of an outlawed death cult, when he realized that the sound itself, that low, slow throbbing, seemed to come from the abandoned fane.

His red eyes fixed on the somber stone, he watched the temple for a long moment. He saw nothing, no sign of life; it was just a building – a row of pillars, a wall, and a roof, jammed in between two other buildings. The sound went on unchanged, and with each moment, each slow beat, Garth became more convinced that it emanated from the building he studied.

With a mental shrug, he took the few remaining steps across the street, up the single step onto the porch, and to the open door.

He paused there as he heard gasps behind him. He turned back for a quick look and saw that several passersby had frozen in their tracks to stare at him. It was obvious that there was something about this temple, about the thought of someone entering it – even an overman – that frightened them.

Superstition, Garth told himself. He turned back to the door and peered through it, into the gloom of the chamber beyond. The sound was louder than ever. He decided that it might not be wise to rush in. He backed down the step and out onto the street.

The people who had stopped to stare remained where they were, still staring. He looked about, picked out a man he judged to be intelligent in appearance, and called, "Ho, there! What is this place?"

The man was reluctant to speak, but those behind him thrust him forward, appointing him their spokesman.

"This is the temple of Dhazh," he replied at last.

"Dhazh? I have never heard of him," Garth said.

"His cult was outlawed for feeding people to the god; it is said that he takes the form of a great monster and still dwells within, asleep."

"What is that sound I hear, that seems to come from this place?"

"What sound?" The man seemed both frightened and genuinely perplexed. "I have never heard any sound here."

"A low, throbbing sound; do you not hear it?"

"I hear no sound from the temple," the man insisted.

"Listen, then; all of you, listen!" The overman held up his hand for silence.

The crowd that had gathered around him listened, and the street grew quiet, though beyond the immediate vicinity people still went about their business, talking and laughing and rattling things.

After a moment, a woman called, "I don't hear anything."

"Nor do I," someone else said, and a volley of agreement sounded.

"None of you? No one hears it?" Garth was surprised; he had heard the sound more clearly than before during the moment of listening.

He was aware that his hearing was somewhat keener than that of mere humans; overmen had several advantages, he knew. But the sound had seemed loud enough for even human ears. Perhaps magic was at work, and he alone was meant to hear the sound, whatever it was. If that was the case, it was almost certainly one of the signs the Forgotten King had meant him to find.

With that in mind, he dismissed the humans from his thoughts and turned back to the temple. There was said to be a monster in there, he reminded himself; he checked his axe, making certain he could get it free quickly if the need arose, then drew his sword and marched back up the step and into the abandoned shrine.

A few moments later, while the little crowd was still largely intact, a cluster of jabbering humanity discussing Garth's presence and actions, Sedrik and a small company of chosen warriors marched up the street.

It had taken Sedrik a quarter hour to find his men; he was not so foolish as to try taking on an overman single-handed, however much it might have suited him to do so. He had been ordered to kill the troublemaker, ordered personally by the overlord himself, and he knew that he would be derelict in his duty if he were to get himself killed in single combat, satisfying as that combat might be. He was responsible for making certain that the overman died, and for that a dozen men were wanted, the very best men he had.

Those he had chosen were now arrayed behind him, armed with sword and spear, four of them carrying crossbows as well, four with heavy shields, and four with maces. Sedrik himself carried an axe in addition to his sword; he hoped to be able to strike off the overman's head with it, as befitted a criminal.

Arming had taken more time, and then he had had to wait until the spies changed shifts and brought back news of the overman's whereabouts. He had marched his men out to the edge of the lake Demhe, only to learn that the overman had left. The commander had sent out the scout he had brought with him, and followed as soon as the fugitive's path had been reported. Now he saw no sign of the overman, but the cluster of people on the street seemed worthy of investigation.

Sedrik gave orders to his men, who formed a quick but effective block across the street, preventing the departure of the gathered citizens. That done, he marched forward and bellowed, "You, there! What is this?" He pointed his sword at the nearest person of responsible appearance. By chance, he had chosen the same man Garth had spoken with.

"My lord," the man said, recognizing the black plume that marked Sedrik as marshal, "an overman has come and entered the temple of Dhazh!"

Startled, Sedrik realized that he was standing before the forbidden shrine. He did not like the temple of Dhazh; to a man born and raised in the weathered streets of Ur-Dormulk the unworn condition of its step, and indeed of the whole building, sheltered as it was by the great rock barrier, appeared alien and sinister. Furthermore, he was an educated man, as the Marshal of the City had to be, and knew something of the cult itself, outlawed centuries earlier. Dhazh had been a demonic earth-god, and as such did not fit anywhere in the accepted Eramman theology. A destructive male earth deity seemed to contradict several basic tenets of the popular religion. No one had ever visited the shrine but a handful of hereditary priests and their unwilling sacrifices, even in its heyday, and Sedrik considered it a wise decision of an ancient overlord to have outlawed the cult and put its priests to death.

There was also the unpleasant myth of the god's heartbeat, a sound said to be heard by those the god had chosen as servants or sacrifices.

Sedrik's thought was echoed by the crowd's spokesman, who added, "He said he heard something!"

Sedrik glanced at the pillared facade. Perhaps there was some connection between the overman's presence in the temple and the order to kill him. The overlord might be worried that the overman would somehow restore the cult to life.

That was none of Sedrik's business; his duty was to obey orders, not to guess why they had been given. He had been told to kill the overman, and the overman was in the temple of Dhazh. Therefore, it was his duty to enter the temple and seek the criminal out. That such an action might serve to dispel some of the lingering respect accorded the demon-god was an added bonus, really. The more he thought about it, the more he liked the idea of entering and defiling the temple. It should have been torn down long ago, he told himself.

The thought of killing the overman was also pleasant; he found himself looking forward eagerly to the coming battle.

"All right, men," he called. "Follow me, arms at ready!"

With that, he marched up the step and into the temple.

After a moment's hesitation the twelve soldiers followed him, with varying degrees of reluctance. Each knew that he was one of the city's best, a chosen master in the art of killing, but the dark legends that clung to the temple lingered in each man's mind. The finest warrior was no match for an angry god.

Had one soldier hung back, others might have joined him, but none dared be first to be called coward, and all marched on into the forbidden temple, following their commander.

Chapter Thirteen

The only light in the temple came from the open doorway; the few clerestory windows were heavily curtained, and the prickets and sconces on walls and pillars held only melted wax, almost invisible beneath dust and cobwebs. There were no torches, no clouds of incense, no chanting priests; there was no sound at all, except for Garth's own footsteps scraping through the dust and the low, dull throbbing he followed. The fane was empty, save for a stone altar on either side of the single great hall that made up most of the building's interior, and dust lay thick everywhere. No carpets covered the stone floors; no tapestries hid the stone walls.

Garth stood still for only a moment as his eyes adjusted to the dimness; then he advanced into the room, sword ready. He saw no sign of a monster, and nothing that might be making the sound he pursued.

He found a large door, black with age, at the rear of the chamber; Garth pushed at it gently, hoping it was not locked, and it fell to dust beneath his hand.

He stepped through immediately, sword held before him, swinging the blade gently from side to side to help him feel his way; though he held his breath and blinked, the dust from the door stung his eyes and nostrils. The inner chamber was even dimmer than the main hall, due to the dust and the greater distance from the main portal, but once Garth had rubbed the grit from his eyes with the back of his free hand, he could see that the room was quite deserted.

The sound, however, was definitely louder here; he listened, trying to ignore the noise that still reached him from the street.

The vibration grew, then dropped, then sounded a long beat like a distant, rolling thunderclap, then began again, with a steady, ponderous rhythm, each cycle taking whole minutes. Hearing it more clearly now, Garth realized what it was, or at least what it seemed to be.

He was listening to a heartbeat, so slow, so deep, that he could only think it to be the pulse of the earth itself; no conceivable leviathan would be a fit possessor of that drawn-out throbbing.

As he listened, his eyes took in the details of the inner sanctum. He was in a small, bare chamber, with a thin trickle of light seeping around the curtain that covered a window high in one corner. There was no furniture, only dust, layered on the floor and drifting in the air around him. On either side of the room were open doors, the areas beyond them utterly in darkness.

At first glance, Garth saw nothing to choose between one door and the other, but a second's careful listening convinced him that the sound was slightly louder to the left. Accordingly, he turned left and stepped through the doorway.

The room beyond was totally black, and Garth found himself groping along cautiously; nonetheless, he almost fell when he reached the top step of a staircase leading down. He had been alert for walls, doorways, or living creatures before him; he had not been paying attention to the floor beneath him.

He caught himself at the brink and paused, hesitant to continue onward in the dark. If there was a monster in the temple, it would have the advantage of him in its lightless lair; he was unfamiliar with his surroundings, but any longtime inhabitant would be at home here.

A slight movement of the air distracted him. The sound was definitely coming up from below, he decided, and that was one attraction beckoning him on, but the faint breeze was strange. It took him a moment to realize what was odd about it.

A slight current could be felt coming from almost any cave or cellar at times, cool and moist, and he would not have been surprised by such a thing here, particularly since the chill water of the lake might seep in somewhere – but this breeze was *warm.*

That did not seem to make sense. The only places Garth knew of where underground chambers or passages were warm were volcanic, and he had thought that the mountains around Ur-Dormulk were no more prone to volcanic activity than the Yeshitic jungles of the distant south were prone to snow in midsummer. Furthermore, the air that he felt ascending the stairway was damp and slightly fetid, like the air of a swamp.

Fascinated, Garth was determined to investigate further, but the darkness still daunted him. He had flint and steel and tinder in a pouch on his belt, but nothing that would burn well enough to provide a reliable light.

It occurred to him that some of the melted candles in the main hall might still retain enough of their substance to serve him, but he dismissed the thought; he had no idea how far he might want to pursue this venture and he needed something that would last longer than a burned-out candle stub.

Surely, he told himself, the priests who had once used this shrine would have had some way of lighting the stairs. He reached out and felt along first one side of the room, then the other. His hand struck something metallic that rattled, and he heard a faint gurgling as well. He sheathed his sword carefully, reached up, and felt the object he had discovered.

It was an oil lamp, still partly full, hanging from a hook.

Once he had found the lamp, it was a simple matter to light it. The wick was still in place, but cut off from the reservoir by an airtight metal lid that had to be unscrewed; even after he had worked the lid free and dipped the lower end of the wick into the oil, it remained so dry that it ignited almost immediately, only to flare up and burn mostly away before any of the fuel caught.

The oil had thickened with age, and after the first bright flame died away the light was low and smoky, scarcely reaching above the remaining stub of the wick. Still, it was adequate for his purpose. He marveled that, even sealed, the oil had not all dried up long ago, and wondered whether the temple might not have been completely abandoned for as long as he had first supposed.

With his sword again naked in his right hand, and the lamp slung in his left, he began his careful descent.

The staircase was much longer than Garth had first thought, and after about fifteen feet the steps changed from the solid and unworn ones that he had expected from the condition of the street outside the temple to shorter, narrower treads worn to a slippery polish, sufficiently ancient and used that the center of each step was an inch or more below the ends. They were almost as difficult to negotiate as the steps at the city gate and made for very slow going.

Garth guessed that this change must indicate that he was below the city proper and entering the legendary crypts. When he finally reached the foot of the staircase he paused to catch his breath and shine the light around; as he did, he thought he heard sounds above him. He dismissed the idea as absurd. He had just come through the temple and seen it to be completely empty; if he was, indeed, hearing anything from above, it could only be street noise, reflected down to him by some freak of acoustics.

He was in a rectangular room, long and relatively narrow, with side walls that sloped inward at the top and curved over to blend smoothly into the ceiling; the comers of the chamber were also curved. The floor was a curious uneven inlay of several different varieties of stone, and the ceiling was low overhead.

The walls and ceiling were gray, and the floor a maze of dull colors half-hidden by dust. The sound of the monstrous heartbeat, if heartbeat it actually was, was louder than ever.

There was a door in the far end; Garth flashed his lamp around, but could see no other entrance or exit, save for the staircase and the single door.

He strode the length of the chamber and pushed at the door, halfway expecting it to crumble to dust as the one in the upper temple had done. It did not; with a high-pitched creak and a flurry of disturbed dust, it swung open, revealing another chamber.

Garth stepped through, lamp held high. This second chamber was identical with the first, save that the walls and ceiling were a dull red instead of gray.

He had now descended at least thirty feet below street level and moved more or less due west, with only the single jog to the left at the top of the stair, since entering the temple. A rough estimate told him that he had come at least a hundred feet from the front pillars – which meant that he was now in or under the great stone outcroppings, since the temple itself had been no more than sixty feet from front to back.

That was very interesting indeed, he thought. He wondered if he might find his way *under* the lake, to the ruins on the far side.

He proceeded through the second chamber and into a third, this one walled and ceiled in dead black, the floor again a dust-covered polychrome. The door at the end of this chamber opened onto another staircase leading down; he followed it without hesitation.

It seemed to run on forever. He had been in crypts before, in the Orûnian city of Mormoreth, but this stair appeared far longer than any he had previously encountered anywhere.

It was also straight, which might have added to its apparent length; the crypt stairs in Mormoreth had wound slightly back and forth, so that he had never been able to see their full length at one time. Here, though, he found it disconcerting to hold up the lamp and see step after step after step, stretching away into the distance both above and below him, both ends lost in the darkness beyond the reach of his feeble lamplight.

Finally, as the lamp swung forward, he glimpsed the lower end; he increased his speed as much as he dared, for the steps were as treacherous as the lower portion of the first set.

The stair ended in a short corridor, and that in turn led to another stair, this one ascending. Garth wondered whether he would find himself in the midst of the ruins beyond the lake.

He did not; the upward-bound steps ran only a tiny fraction of the distance he had just descended. Almost as soon as he reached the first step, he glimpsed the upper end.

A moment later he emerged into another room, away from the confining stone walls of the stairway, and paused to catch his breath again.

Again, he thought he heard noise behind him, but now it was almost drowned out by the slow beating ahead of him, a sound that had acquired a sinister, menacing note as he drew nearer its source. Something about it made him nervous.

He had not yet given much thought to what the beating might be; he had decided that it was a heartbeat without considering what that might mean. Now, as he stood in a passage that he judged to be several hundred feet below the level of Ur-Dormulk's streets, he wondered what he might find if he went on. *Could* there be a monster with a heart so great? If so, he would stand no more chance against it than a beetle. A mere mechanical dragon had been capable of killing him; how could he think to face a creature whose heartbeat could be heard half a mile away?

On the other hand, why would such a monster even notice him? He need not worry about being devoured; an overman could scarcely begin to feed the appetite of such a thing, and he could easily retreat into places where a behemoth could not reach him.

The idea of such a creature went against all his instincts, and he decided that it was far more likely that the sound was being artificially produced by some lost remnant of the outlawed cult, for reasons of its own. In any case, he was not about to turn back at this point. He held up the lamp.

He was in another long, narrow, low-ceilinged room, longer than the three on the upper level and walled in gray stone. Again there was a single door at the far end, yet this one was not a simple portal in a post-and-lintel frame, but an elaborate carved construction of several different woods, hung in a red stone arch embellished with golden tracery.

Garth approached cautiously; the ornate door, so different from the others, seemed almost threatening. He paused when he had reached it and put a hand to one of the wooden panels. It vibrated beneath his fingers with the slow, slow beating.

For a third time he thought he heard something behind him, the sound only detectable in the interval between beats, and lost thereafter in the throbbing he had followed for so far. He turned and looked back at the stairs, but saw nothing.

This new portal did not yield to a simple push, but the latch handle still moved freely; he lifted it and shoved the door wide.

Beyond lay a chamber unlike the others; although the walls curved into the ceiling in the same fashion, this room was circular rather than oblong. The walls were black, and the floor here was also black, made up of stones arranged in a spiral leading in toward the room's center.

It was what stood in the center, however, that was most different. A column of horn or ivory projected upward from the floor, yellowed with age but still almost white, tapering from a diameter of eighteen inches or so at the base to about a foot where it was cut off, three feet above the floor, to form a slanting surface. In the center of this tilted top, a single drop of some reddish-black substance was very slowly oozing forth.

A circular trough surrounded this strange column, and Garth saw that there was a trickle of the red-black goo down the side of the column and a shallow pool of it in the trough.

He saw no way in or out of the chamber save for the single arched door. Garth entered cautiously, lamp and sword both held high.

There was nothing to look at but the column and its curious issue, so he studied that. As he watched, a fat black drop rolled sluggishly from the center of the column's top to the edge, joining the slow trickle. Its separation from the central spot coincided exactly with the end of one of the vast heartbeats, Garth noted idly.

Another drop began to grow as Garth studied the walls, looking for concealed openings. He turned back as a beat ended and saw the new drop follow its predecessor.

That the first drop had happened to fall in time with the sound had struck him as nothing but coincidence, but the second one made it seem more than that. He listened, watched, and soon reached an inescapable conclusion: the sound he had followed came from the base of the mysterious shaft. Furthermore, it was somehow connected with the oozing fluid.

It occurred to him that it might be the vibration that caused the drops to fall in synchronization with the beating, rather than any more direct connection. It did not seem reasonable that so great and ponderous a throbbing should do nothing but pump out a stream of blackish goo. He looked for some secret opening or lever on the column or in the trough surrounding it, being careful to touch nothing, lest he trigger a trap.

His investigation of the small metal pipe that allowed the excess fluid to drain off when the trough was full ceased abruptly, however, when for the fourth time he heard sounds other than the beating, coming from somewhere outside the arched doorway.

Once, perhaps twice, he could dismiss this as illusion, or the action of overwrought nerves, but now there was no chance at all that noise might be reaching him from outside the crypts. No vermin would be audible over the great throbbing, yet the sound was there once more. It was closer than before, and he did not lose it again after the first hearing. Now that he was no longer moving deeper into the catacomb, whatever made the noise was gaining on him quickly. After listening carefully for a few seconds, he thought that it was the rattle of armor.

He dropped the lamp where he was; it flickered, but stayed lit, as it bounced once and came to rest on the stone floor at a sharp angle, tilted up on the curve of its metal oil reservoir and prevented from rolling by the thick dust.

The circular chamber offered few places of concealment, with no corners, alcoves, or hangings that might hide him. The looming shadow of the central column, stretching up the wall opposite the spot where the lamp had fallen, would provide some cover, but Garth decided against it, preferring the more obvious place behind the only door. Whoever was approaching would probably not realize immediately that he had reached a dead end in the little room. The person would wonder why the lamp was there, certainly, but would probably not think to check behind the door before entering. Putting out the lamp would leave Garth in total darkness, and he did not care for that idea; let his pursuer wonder, then.

Besides, he had no time to think of a better plan.

The sounds were drawing nearer; in the pauses between beats, he could make out footsteps and the rasping breath of human exertion. He pressed up against the wall behind the carven door, sword ready in his right hand, axe swung around within reach, awaiting whoever might come.

Chapter Fourteen

Sedrik's pursuit of the overman was delayed slightly by the darkness of the temple; he had assumed that he would find his quarry on the streets or in some well-lighted shop and had not bothered to equip his men with lanterns. When it became clear that Garth was not to be found anywhere in the dim precincts of the temple proper, and giving due consideration to the fact that the overman was a newcomer to Ur-Dormulk who could scarcely have known of secret exits, Sedrik had no choice but to conclude that Garth had taken the stair to the crypts. Sedrik had his orders, and his own hatred as well, and was eager to follow – but no glimmer of light indicated the overman's presence; surely he would not have ventured into the depths without a light of some kind! Sedrik had to assume that Garth had either built up a considerable lead, or turned corners, or passed through doorways. To pursue him in total darkness would be reckless to the point of abject stupidity. Therefore, lights were needed, and Sedrik had to wait with half his company at the head of the crypt stairs while the other half returned to the street to fetch torches or lamps from the surrounding shops.

As he waited, the faint, fetid warmth that drifted up from below made his skin crawl.

Finally all his men were together again, torches in hand. No lamps or lanterns had been secured, but a plentiful supply of torches intended for lighting temples and storefronts had been available; the rightful owners had been willing to give them up without payment beyond a promise of government recompense later. The possessors of other means of illumination had not been so obliging, and the soldiers had not cared to argue.

With one man in four carrying a lighted brand, Sedrik and his party descended the steps, following in Garth's wake. Sedrik, in his impatience at the delay and in his eagerness for battle, tried to hurry the soldiers along, but with limited success. The worn steps, the evil reputation of both the temple and the crypts, and the unsteady torchlight all served to keep the pace down.

At the foot of the first flight, some of the men sighed audibly with relief; Sedrik paid them no mind but moved forward more briskly, now that the floor was solid underfoot.

They passed through the gray room, the red, and into the black; here one of the men whispered, "Shh! I think I hear something!"

Sedrik gave the command to halt and held up a hand for silence. His men obeyed, and all listened.

Uncertain, they looked at one another.

"Do you hear it, commander?" one murmured.

Sedrik nodded, reluctantly.

"What is it?" another asked.

Sedrik shrugged.

"'Tis the heartbeat of the god!" someone said.

"Dhazh?"

"That's only a myth!"

Sedrik spoke at last. "This sound is no myth; we all hear it. Perhaps it is what first gave rise to the tales of Dhazh's existence. I suspect it to be an underground waterfall; after all, we must be near Demhe here, and no one knows where its bottom may be, or where its waters come and go."

"I don't hear anything," a soldier at the back confessed.

"Then it's your hearing that's at fault, for the sound is there," one of his comrades retorted.

"Whatever it is, men," Sedrik said, "it is no concern of ours, wherever it comes from. It may well be beyond the walls of the crypts entirely. I doubt that anything could fit into these rooms that we would not be able to handle; certainly the monster-god of the old legends could not squeeze beneath this roof!" He gestured at the low ceiling; someone chuckled, which pleased Sedrik. He saw about an even mix of smiles and worried looks; that was worse than he had hoped, but better than he had expected. Even the best fighters could be discouraged by empty darkness and narrow passages.

"We go on," he said. "We have an overman to catch."

They moved on down the length of the black chamber in formation, six ranks of two, with Sedrik to one side of the second rank. At the door at the inner end, the first rank balked. The foremost torchbearer, in the second rank at Sedrik's elbow, held his light high and forward, its flame spattering on the ceiling, its smoke lost against the black stone, its light spilling down the second stair.

"I cannot see the bottom, commander," the torchbearer reported.

Sedrik stepped forward and peered over the shoulder of one of the first pair. "And I cannot see the overman, nor have we seen anywhere he might have turned. We go on." He noticed, but did not mention, that the faint roaring – the god's heartbeat – seemed to be coming up the stairway from somewhere below.

"We don't know what's down there!" another soldier protested.

"The overman is down there!" Sedrik said, repressing the urge to bellow as if on a parade ground; there was no knowing how far an echo might carry, and he had no desire to alert Garth to his presence. "I see no sign of any danger, save that one of you clumsy fools might stumble and crack his skull on the steps." Despite his anger, Sedrik immediately regretted those words; they would only serve to make his men more nervous, which would in turn make their descent still slower and more cautious. "We have orders, from the overlord himself, to hunt down and kill this inhuman foreigner. He's somewhere below, and I intend to find him. Now, come on!" He pushed past the leaders and started down, thinking to himself that he should have taken the lead position right from the first.

Reluctantly, his men followed.

The length of the stair eventually became daunting even to Sedrik; he heard his men muttering unhappily when the rearmost torchbearer had lost all sight of the top, but he forced himself onward, determined to show no fear in front of his subordinates, and resolved that he could face any dangers that an overman could face. The distant rhythmic rumble became more distinct as they went on; Sedrik had hoped that they would pass its source and lose it, but so far there had been no sign of that happening.

It was fortunate, he thought, that the stair remained barely wide enough to march two abreast; had they been forced into single file, he knew that his men would have been even more anxious.

At last the company reached the short corridor and, with visible relief, continued on, up the ascending steps beyond. They emerged into the long gray room at the top of the final stair, and the beating sound was clearly audible even over the rattle of armor and their heavy footsteps. Sedrik stopped and raised his hand for silence; the men stopped, the first rank just inside the chamber, the rest still arrayed upon the stairs.

He was not absolutely certain, but Sedrik thought he had at last glimpsed a dim light somewhere in the darkness ahead. He pointed to the torch nearest him and made a passing motion; its bearer understood and obeyed, passing it back to the men farthest down the steps, who held it and the two other torches down low so as to disturb the darkness at the far end of the chamber as little as possible.

Sedrik stared into the gloom, shading his eyes against the glare from behind, and made out that there was indeed a light ahead, just beyond a wide doorway.

The light was not moving; whatever the overman had come for, he had presumably found it. Sedrik did not think he had merely paused to rest; the natural place to do that would have been at the foot of the long stair, or the top of the last.

Unless, the commander thought, yet another stair lay beyond the door, and the overman had paused before tackling it.

Still a third possibility occurred to Sedrik. The overman might have brought more than one light and abandoned this one when it burned low. Staring at it, Sedrik observed that it was low, far dimmer than any of his own three torches, which had burned almost to stubs.

"Change torches," he whispered, reminded of their state.

Word was passed down the steps, and three new torches were lighted, flaring up brightly; the old were stamped out and cast aside.

The presence of the doorway was not helpful; Sedrik had no way of knowing what lay beyond it. Marching his men in without further investigation would be stupid and reckless. He was tempted to go forward himself and scout it out, but that was not a commander's job, and he knew it. If he were to stick his head through the door and be slain, his men would flee; if another were to do the same, Sedrik knew he could fire up the survivors with a lust for vengeance and lead them to the attack.

Reluctantly, he signaled for one man to step forward.

"Nalba," Sedrik whispered, "I want you to go and see what's beyond the door there." He pointed. "Be careful about it; I don't want you killed. If the overman's in there and you have a chance, jump him and call for help; we'll come. If you don't think you can get him, or if he sees you coming, you come back here and tell me. If he's *not* there, come back and report; don't do anything foolish." Sedrik pointed to the mace on the soldier's back. "Use that if you can; it's harder to parry than a sword, and overmen are strong. You're more likely to keep him busy with that than with your sword, even if you can't kill him. Have you got all that?"

Nalba nodded silently, then crept cautiously past his commander and down the length of the room, unslinging the heavy mace as he went, so that it was ready in his hand when he reached the arch.

He peered through, and saw the lamp flickering on the floor. He glimpsed the tapering column and thought for an instant that it was the overman, crouched to spring. He swung back out of the way; then, when no attack came, he inched forward again.

This time he made out the column's nature more clearly and determined that it was not an immediate threat. He advanced, slowly and carefully, into the room.

Behind the door, Garth watched and waited.

Nalba paused a few paces in, just short of the trough encircling the central pediment, and peered around into the darkness. He saw nothing – no overman and no way out of the room.

A chill ran through him, despite the chamber's muggy warmth, as the notion arose that the overman they pursued had vanished by means of sorcery.

His first thought was to run back and tell the marshal that the overman had disappeared into thin air. He stopped himself, however, and tried to think it through.

It was undeniable that, as far as he could tell, the room was empty of everything but dust, shadows, and the abandoned lamp; but he could not see *all* of the room. Sedrik would be disappointed in him if he were to turn and leave now, and if it were later discovered that the overman was hiding behind some secret panel lost in the gloom.

Besides, he saw no actual danger.

Mace held out before him, Nalba began to make his way around the room, poking his weapon at the wall every so often and peering into the shadows. He came at last to the deep darkness behind the broad door and paused; any concealed opening there would just lead back out into the long chamber, but he knew he should check it for the sake of completeness. Something about it made him nervous; he thought he saw something glinting, or heard something breathing, or perhaps both. He could not be sure of his sight in the unsteady light and clinging darkness, or of his hearing while the dull throbbing pounded on his ears, or of his thoughts in the foul, moist air of the chamber.

If the overman were hiding there behind the door, Nalba told himself, he would have jumped out and cut my throat long ago. The soldier prodded with his mace.

Steel flashed, and the tip of a sword slipped between his chin and the throatpiece of his helmet.

"One word, human, and I sever your head," Garth warned.

Nalba froze, fighting a sudden urge to swallow, his teeth clenched to hold in a scream.

"Put the mace down, slowly and quietly," the overman said.

Nalba tried to obey; he lowered the head, but was unable to handle the weight of the weapon. The metal ball struck the stone paving with an audible thud, and the terrified soldier discovered that he could not reach down any farther to place the handle on the floor. If he dropped it, it would rattle; if he bent down, the sword would be forced into his gullet.

Garth grasped the situation and said, "Drop it." He did not see how it could matter; anything listening would have heard the sound of the mace's head falling.

Relieved, Nalba dropped the mace; the handle rolled down and clicked against the stone.

That done, the two stared at each other, Garth seeing a shadowy backlit figure wearing the green uniform and bronze helmet of Ur-Dormulk's soldiery, while Nalba could see nothing but a great black shape holding a sword at his throat. A few inches of the blade caught a stray glimmer from the fallen lamp, and the soldier thought he could make out something shiny and red where his captor's eyes should have been.

At the head of the stair, Sedrik had been watching Nalba's actions as best he could. He had seen the soldier begin his circuit of the chamber, vanishing to one side, returning to visibility for a brief moment as he crossed back into Sedrik's line of sight to the rear wall, and then disappearing again along the other side.

Nalba seemed to be taking plenty of time to search the second side, Sedrik thought; then he heard the thud, just barely audible over the steady beating sound, of the mace hitting the floor.

Something was wrong, Sedrik was sure. He did not know what, but one possibility was obvious: the overman had been hiding there and had caught Nalba by surprise and cut his throat so quickly that he had no time to cry out. The monster had not managed to catch the mace before it fell, though, and that might prove his undoing.

Sedrik knew there were other explanations available, but he was certain that this was what had happened. He ordered his men, "Weapons at ready!"

Swords slid from scabbards, shields were raised, the thongs of maces were looped around wrists, crossbows were cocked and loaded, all as silently as the dozen men could contrive. Sedrik unslung his war axe, hefted it with his left hand, and drew his sword with his right. The deep throbbing covered much of the noise they made.

Still, Garth heard something other than the beating. He had intended a leisurely questioning of his captive, using long pauses to increase the man's nervousness, but he suddenly realized he might not have time for that.

"Are you alone?" he asked.

Nalba stared, petrified, unable to nod, not wanting to shake his head in a truthful answer, lest it enrage the monster that held the sword.

In the long hall, Sedrik whispered, "Something's gotten Nalba; it must have surprised him somehow. I don't know if it's the overman or not, but it probably is. I don't want him to surprise *us.* If we charge in there at full speed, we may startle him out of attacking; then we'll be able to see where he is and fight him fairly. Understood?"

Most of the men nodded; he ignored those who did not. They would follow along and do well enough, he was sure.

"We want to catch him off guard, so no yelling until we're through the door; then you can bellow your lungs out if you want. We're going to run in there and kill him before he knows what's happening. Right?"

This time almost all of his men nodded.

"Good. On the count of three, then. One . . ."

Garth pressed the point of his sword forward slightly, forcing Nalba's head back. "You're not alone, then. How many of you are there?"

Nalba moved back a step, but the gleaming blade followed, keeping the pressure on his throat. His head was tilted so far back that the base of his helmet was digging into his neck.

"How many?" Garth insisted. "Five? Ten?"

Nalba managed to shake his head.

Sedrik advanced a step, allowing the rest of his men to come up off the stair and into the room. He half-turned toward the door beyond and raised his sword. "Two," he said.

"Twenty?" Garth demanded, his voice slipping into a growl.

"Three!" Sedrik breathed. He charged toward the open door.

Nalba was trying to take another step back, his head forced up by the sword so that he could no longer see the floor, when one of the slow beats ended, allowing both Nalba and Garth to hear the clinking of metal and the pounding of booted feet running toward them. Hoping that the overman – if it was indeed an overman that held the blade to his neck – would be distracted, Nalba groped for the hilt of his sword and tried to twist aside.

Garth was not sufficiently distracted to forget his prisoner; he saw the hand reaching for the belt, though he could not clearly see what weapon hung there. He knew that the man might be of value as a hostage, but he might also be dangerous, since Garth had no time to bind him. The overman could not afford to divide his attention. Unhappily, he rammed his sword forward, through the human's throat; it scraped past the spine and thunked against the back of the bronze helmet.

The soldier died without a sound; Garth pulled the sword out and sank back into his shadowy corner, letting the corpse fall to the floor with a sodden thump. The helmet bounced off and rolled noisily to one side.

An instant later a stream of men burst into the chamber, steel blades flashing in every direction; the first stumbled over the lamp and sent it spinning away toward the far wall.

Startled by the number of foes, despite what Nalba had indicated, Garth did not wait for them all to arrive and surround him; he braced his back against the wall behind him and kicked out with all his strength at the carved door.

It squealed in protest, but slammed with satisfying force into two of the humans; one went sprawling off to the side, within the circular chamber, and the other was knocked back against his advancing companions, gashing himself on an upraised sword.

A second kick closed the door, and Garth braced himself against it, knowing as he did so that a solid blow of an axe from the other side might injure or even kill him.

Not counting the bleeding corpse on the floor, six or perhaps seven men were in the room with him; the shadows made an exact count very difficult. One held a smoldering torch. All carried weapons. One was down for the moment, bowled over by the door; he had dropped a crossbow, but still gripped a sword.

Three held swords and shields, one had a mace and a sword, another bore a mace and the torch while a sword hung on his belt, and the last – there were seven, Garth realized – was coming at the overman with a raised axe.

Garth had no time for finesse; he raised his sword and lunged forward, meeting the axe-wielder's attack with his own. The blade slid between the man's ribs and stood out from his back, gleaming wetly red in the flaring torchlight.

Sedrik had underestimated the overman's reach, and had not been aware of his superhuman speed at all until it was too late. He felt the sword go into him above the belly, and knew he had misjudged. His mouth gaped open, blood from a pierced lung gurgling in his throat, and he made a desperate try with his axe, swinging wildly. His right arm fell aside and went limp; his sword clattered to the floor.

The arc of the axe brought it down across Garth's sword arm, grazing it, but doing little real damage; then Sedrik sagged and fell.

Garth pulled his blade free in time to face the charge of a mace-wielding soldier on his right and a shielded swordsman on his left. He ducked back and to the left, letting the mace slam into the wooden door, hoping the spikes would become caught; splinters flew, but the mace scraped onward.

The swordsman was being cautious, his shield limiting his movement, and missed an opportunity to strike at the overman as Garth slid back off the door and around to the soldier's right. Startled by the overman's speed and fooled by the common human idea that large size meant slow reactions, the swordsman was still turning to face his opponent when Garth gripped the axe in his left hand and brought it around.

The soldier flinched back and the axe missed his right arm, but his sword was knocked from his grasp. The axe continued on and bit into the side of the shield with a loud thunk.

Seizing the opportunity, Garth used the axe to force the shield down and ran his sword into the man's face.

The mace was coming down for another blow as Garth yanked his sword from the shield-bearer's eye; the overman met the descending weapon with his blade.

The parry was successful, but Garth could see that the sword was badly notched – Galt's sword, he remembered, not his own – and he could feel the metal straining as he forced the mace back. He pulled at his axe, using his left knee to knock the shield away. The other two shieldmen were advancing on his left, he saw; he turned, and a crossbow quarrel whirred past his face, then went spinning from the wall beyond. The fallen bowman had recovered his weapon.

Garth did not worry about that; the man would have to reload before he could fire again, and reloading a crossbow was slow work, particularly when lying on the floor. The weapon was designed to be held between the knees and braced against the ground, with the feet holding down the crosspiece.

Someone was banging and calling on the other side of the door; Garth ignored that as well. Three men were down, dead or nearly so, but five were still trying to kill him.

A small part of his mind, unconcerned with the battle, wondered who these men were and why they had come after him and tried to kill him. All wore the uniform of the city guard; that worried him. Temple guards or warrior priests he might have expected, but this party looked official. He hoped that the overlord had not sent them. He had no desire to antagonize Ur-Dormulk's ruler. Perhaps, he thought, it was all a misunderstanding.

The two surviving shieldmen were advancing, confident of their safety behind their heavy protection, and Garth decided that they needed a demonstration of his strength, something that would damage their confidence and thereby diminish the threat they presented. He moved left, away from the mace and its wielder. The shieldmen turned and kept their swords weaving, looking for an opening; the man with the mace stumbled when a swing met no resistance and stepped back to recollect himself.

With him out of the way for a few seconds, Garth held one shieldman back with his sword and brought his axe down on the other in a long overhand smash, like the swing of a sledgehammer, with as much of his strength behind it as he could muster. He had to angle the blow to avoid hitting the low ceiling.

The axe split the man's sword in two, the tip spinning away to the side, the hilt dropping from impact-numbed fingers, and drove on downward, hacking into the riveted steel shield as if it were rotten wood. Had the soldier not had it securely strapped to his arm, he would have dropped that, as well.

Disarmed and terrified, the man fell back, wrenching his shield off the axe and saving Garth the trouble of having to free his embedded weapon. That left the other shieldman's right flank unguarded. Garth sent the axe chopping sideways, behind the shield. It scraped across mail, but did not cut.

Still, the shieldman was disconcerted now. He turned his arm to fend off the axe, and Garth's sword slid into his left armpit, making good use of the overman's superior reach and speed.

Behind Garth, the door started to open again, and he slammed it shut with his foot, throwing himself off balance for a moment, unable to pursue the momentary advantage he had gained. The mace-wielder came at him again; Garth turned, parried the mace with his axe, met sword with sword, and drove both back by sheer strength. When he had forced the soldier's arms up so that the man had to retreat or fall backward, Garth pulled the axe down the shaft of the mace and twisted, yanking the mace from the human's weakened grip.

While he did this, however, his left side presented an open invitation to the two shieldmen; the one who still held his sword gathered enough courage to accept and lunged forward.

Garth dodged, so that the blade scraped across his back, gouging him slightly but not penetrating deeply. He brought his left arm swinging back and caught his attacker on the right shoulder. The man withdrew, wary of losing sword, sword arm, or both.

That permitted the overman to force his way past the guard of his now-maceless opponent and drive his sword into the man's shoulder. The soldier gasped as Garth's blade withdrew and blood spurted; he fell back, dropping his own remaining weapon.

Garth was working himself up into a state of unreasoning fury; in consequence, when he saw the unarmed maceman fall back, he gave no thought to subtlety, but swung around to face the shieldmen – and the other mace-wielder, now advancing to join the'attack-head on. "Fools!" he shouted, breaking his silence.

"Inhuman monster!" someone replied.

The crossbowman was still on the floor, apparently just watching; the injured maceman was upright but unarmed and also seemed content to play spectator. The axeman, the first shield-carrier, and the original advance scout were all down for good. That left Garth facing three opponents, one of them twice wounded, with no reinforcements ready to jump to their aid.

That meant he no longer needed to be cautious; no one was going to sneak up on him unexpectedly. He roared wordlessly and brought his axe arcing overhead, barely missing the low ceiling, to smash through a human skull. The man tried to parry the blow with the sundered shield he bore, and his arm met Garth's in mid-air. The soldier's forearm broke under the impact; Garth received a bruise, but the axe continued on and splattered blood and brains across the next man over.

The shieldman dropped, and Garth faced two terrified opponents. The fight had gone out of them; they were retreating, staying out of his reach. To one side, the unarmed soldier was struggling to open the door and escape. The crossbowman had finally gotten to his feet, but showed no interest in anything but flight.

Garth took a step forward, pursuing the enemy. They stepped back; one stumbled over the trough around the central column and dropped the torch. The flame flickered and went out as the burning tip landed, hissing, in the dark fluid. The only remaining light was the faint glow of the oil lamp, still burning where it lay against the far wall.

Garth tried to lift his foot to take another step forward, but something prevented him; something was gripping his ankle. He looked down.

Sedrik was not dead; he supported himself on one elbow, his axe clutched in that hand, while his other clutched at Garth's leg. Blood was seeping from his closed mouth. He was trying to lift himself up and raise the axe to strike, his movements uncoordinated and feeble.

Garth stared at him in surprise for a second, then decided that, mortally wounded as he was, the man was of no consequence. He thrust his foot forward despite the encumbrance upon it.

Sedrik's grip did not loosen; instead he was dragged forward, and Garth turned again to look at him.

The maceman who had dropped the torch saw his opportunity; he danced in and made a desperate, wild, sideways swing. The heavy spiked ball caught Garth's sword where it had been notched, snapping the blade off.

Garth whirled back and roared in anger. That was not his sword! Galt would be annoyed, he knew. He swung his axe and saw it bite deep into the soldier's chest, grating against bone.

It did not come free when he tried to pull it back. He attempted to step forward, the better to brace himself, and found that Sedrik was still clamped onto his ankle. Enraged beyond all thought, he released his axe, letting the dying soldier fall to the ground with the weapon still in him, then flung aside the broken hilt of Galt's sword, reached down with both hands, and yanked Sedrik free.

The man's mouth opened and blood spilled out. "Monster," he tried to say; the word emerged as a croaking gurgle. He struggled to lift and swing his axe.

Garth saw that the man was obviously dying, too weak to be anything but a minor annoyance; infuriated, he flung Sedrik away in the general direction of the surviving soldiers.

At that instant the door burst open and light poured in from the remaining torches, allowing Garth to see clearly what next took place.

Sedrik's body slammed against the central column, his arm flopping and the blade of the axe bit into the yellowed substance of the thing, the cut penetrating the tubule whence the black fluid oozed. Three great drops spattered forth across the steel head of the weapon, and the beating stopped.

For a moment nothing more happened; the combatants, human and overman, in the inner chamber or the long hall, all froze in astonishment.

"Gods," someone said.

A low rumble sounded, far different from the earlier sound, and the beating returned – but not as the tortuously slow thing it had been before. The new sound was higher in pitch, but still bone-shakingly deep; it was much louder, and faster as well, a single beat now taking no more than a few seconds.

One of the soldiers in the outer room turned and ran; Garth heard others moving uncertainly.

A new sound added itself to the racket, a loud rumble; Garth felt the floor vibrate beneath him. Somewhere, something broke with a sharp cracking. The wounded maceman Garth had disarmed screamed and ran, and others followed him.

More rumblings sounded, and the throbbing grew still louder and faster, as if whatever creature possessed the mighty heartbeat were awakening from sleep. The floor shifted, then seemed to drop a few inches beneath Garth's feet; he saw that the column was sinking downward out of sight.

Then it paused, with only the uppermost foot still showing, and the rumblings subsided for a moment; the heartbeat continued unabated. Garth had a sensation of knowing that something was about to occur without knowing what it would be.

The remaining soldiers who were still capable of fleeing did so during this brief interval, but Garth resolved to stay where he was. He had come to this place seeking a magical device of great power, and it was possible that the shaking of the earth and the mighty rumblings and beating were somehow connected with it.

At his feet lay three corpses; just ahead lay Sedrik, still twitching slightly, his eyes open and staring at the overman. The various movements of the room had left him lying on the floor, free of the strange column, his axe still clutched in his hand.

Then the rumbling began again. With an immense crashing, the column thrust upward, splitting the floor of the chamber into scattered shards and sending Garth back against the wall. The wall itself turned and gave, and he fell back into dark emptiness; all around him, he could hear the grinding of stone on stone and the sound of breaking rock. Hot, fetid air rushed past him. He had a final glimpse as he fell of a vast monstrosity rising up before him, its hideous visage twenty feet across. Flat, golden eyes gleamed from sunken black sockets on either side of a great curving nose-horn, its tip broken and oozing dark fluid. Garth recognized that horn; its upper end had been the mysterious column. Here, then, was the beast whose heartbeat he had followed, awakened and unleashed.

A piece of rubble smashed against the back of his head, and he saw nothing more.

Chapter Fifteen

Garth awoke with sunlight warm on his face, and with no idea of where he was. He lay sprawled across a small heap of rubble, a sharp stone digging into the back of one thigh, his head hanging down off the edge of something, his whole body tipped at an uncomfortable angle.

He lifted his head with effort, closing his eyes against the glare of light, and shifted his leg off the point that gouged it. With a little struggling, he managed to get himself sitting upright, then opened his eyes and looked about.

He was perched on a slab of broken pavement – or perhaps a broken wall – that lay atop a mound of debris, three or four feet high. This pile was one of many, in varying sizes, scattered across a broad stone floor. Most of the wreckage was also stone, but Garth saw metal scraps, shards of tile, bits of wood, fragments of furniture, the remains of various tapestries, drapes, carpets, and hangings, and at least one human body, that of one of the soldiers he had fought, half-buried in a pile near his own. He and the heaps of rubble were all scattered about an immense chamber, but most of the walls were lost in shadow, and he could not guess what the chamber might be, or where. Only one section of the far wall was in full sunlight, a small area centered on an arched doorway. A yellow symbol gleamed brightly on the black door; it seemed familiar, but

Garth did not recognize it.

The uneven light and drifting dust made it difficult to judge the size of the place, but Garth estimated that it was a good fifty feet to the far wall.

He turned around to see what lay behind him and discovered that he was only a few feet from the wall. He saw no door, no windows, and wondered where the sunlight was coming from. He looked up.

The room extended upward incredibly far, easily a hundred feet; graceful columns soared out from the walls into elaborate vaulting, the details lost in distance and shadow. Much of that vaulting was in disarray; a large section of the roof was missing and, Garth realized, a large part of the wall directly behind him was gone as well. He had not noticed it sooner because the wall was intact to a height of twelve or fifteen feet, but from that point up, most of it was gone.

That explained where most of the rubble had come from.

The sunlight was spilling in through the break, and the steep angle indicated the middle part of the day – though Garth could not be certain which day it was. Dust was drifting everywhere, sparkling and blurring in the beams of light; surely, Garth told himself, it would have settled if more than one day, or at most two, had passed since the wall was shattered.

The overman considered his situation. He had no clear idea where he was; he could not even be certain he was still in Ur-Dormulk, but the presence of the dead soldier implied that Garth was still wherever he had fallen when the immense horned monster had burst up from beneath. It seemed reasonable to assume that the break in the wall and roof had been made by the creature. Of the beast itself, however, there was no trace, save a faint, lingering, unpleasant odor; the sound of its heartbeat was gone. The silence, in fact, was nearly total; Garth felt as if he could hear his own breathing, his own heartbeat, and perhaps even the faint hiss of the dust sifting down onto the stones. The air, too, was almost still; no wind could be heard blowing around the broken columns overhead.

That did not necessarily mean that he was safe from the monster; it might be lurking just beyond the walls.

Almost anything might be out there, Garth thought. He had no way of knowing that there had been only one monster. Even leaving monsters aside, he could reasonably assume that any humans he might find would be hostile. After all, he had been attacked for no reason he knew of, and now any survivors might consider him responsible for awakening the creature – though Garth was sure it had been the blow of the human's axe on the thing's horn that had done that.

He could not in good faith deny *all* responsibility. He had been investigating where he was not welcome, and perhaps he had interfered in things best left alone. He had not, he had to admit, known what he was doing. He had apparently been the indirect cause of more destruction; it seemed that ever since he had first touched the Sword of Bheleu, he brought destruction wherever he went.

That was not of immediate concern, however. He had no desire to sit where he was all day. The sun was reassuringly warm. He was stiff and sore, with several minor wounds, but he was well rested and thirsty. It was time to be up and about.

Garth stretched, hoping that the movement would not reopen any of the cuts he had received in the fighting and his fall, and climbed down off the slab.

He looked himself over carefully; he still wore his mail, which was dented and twisted here and there, with several broken links. The black metal was stained brown in several places, but Garth did not think any of the blood was his own.

His breeches, too, were bloodied but intact, though no one would ever again take them for new. One leg had come untucked from his boot top; he stuffed it back in.

The boots themselves seemed sound, but something had gashed one of them across the instep; Garth doubted it was still watertight.

His sword, axe, and helmet were gone, but his belt was still in place and his dagger still in its sheath; he was not completely unarmed. He recalled that the sword – Galt's sword – had been broken. That was unfortunate.

Nothing remained of his surcoat but tatters; he removed them. His cloak was missing.

He glanced around, seeing nothing but broken stone, scattered debris, drifting dust, and sunlight. There was no sign of life, nothing that could be considered threatening. He decided to take a complete inventory. Slowly, he removed his coat of mail.

The gambeson beneath was filthy, soaked through with sweat and blood, and pierced in several places, though Garth could not remember feeling anything stab through it. He untied it and began to peel it off.

Blood had clotted inside it, and yanked painfully at his fur and flesh as he tore the garment away, but at last he managed to get it off.

He looked himself over, tugging here and there at matted patches of his sparse black fur. He found half a dozen scratches, none of which he could remember receiving. All were healing adequately, though he had reopened at least one when he removed the gambeson. Bruises were more numerous; one arm in particular ached.

He had nothing to clean his wounds with, save his own saliva; he moistened one of the scraps from his surcoat in his mouth and then dabbed at the cuts with it. He had kept medicinal salves in a pouch on his belt, but that was missing; he was not sure what had happened to it. Only his dagger remained on his belt; the pouch and his purse were gone. A wild slash might have cut the pursestrings and the strap that held the pouch, he thought; he had been fortunate that such a blow had not done far worse, if that was what had occurred.

Though the sun had seemed almost hot on his face when he first awoke, he found himself growing chilly with only his fur protecting his chest and back; reluctantly, he donned the stiff, stained gambeson again and pulled the battered mail back on.

That done, he considered his next step.

He had several things he wanted to do. He wanted to find the Book of Silence, do whatever he could to damage the cult of Aghad, and see what had become of the monster, whether it had gone on a rampage or just settled down quietly somewhere. He felt responsible for it and hoped that it had not done too much damage. He had caused more than enough death and destruction already, without the aid of any monsters. He might also want to investigate the attack on him, to find out whether the overlord had sent those soldiers. If he had, retaliation might be called for. Garth had come to Ur-Dormulk on a peaceful errand – relatively peaceful, at any rate, vengeful though it was – and the trouble had begun only when he was attacked without warning or cause.

If the monster was on a rampage, he might want to do something about that, too – but he was not about to try to defeat anything that large without a great deal of help, preferably magical.

All of that could wait, however, because his first priority, as always, was survival. He did not know where he was; he was stranded here without food or water or decent weapons.

Water seemed like the most important concern. He had the dagger and no visible foes, so weapons were not urgent, and if he grew sufficiently desperate for food, there was the corpse of the soldier. He hoped that it would not come to that. He had never eaten human flesh, nor wanted to; no overman had, so far as he knew, despite what some of the nastier human legends suggested. The idea of eating what had once been a fellow sentient being was slightly revolting. Still, if it came to a choice of that or starvation, he did not intend to starve.

Water, then, was what he had to find.

If he was still where he thought he was, in Ur-Dormulk, then water should be available one way or another. He had not forgotten that lake.

He saw no sign of water in the vast chamber about him, however. He would have to find a way out.

He looked up at the broken wall and the missing section of roof. He could, if he had to, leap high enough to pull himself up to the bottom of the opening – but he was not at all sure that he wanted to. He could not be certain that he would be able to go much farther from there. Furthermore, if there were enemies or monsters anywhere about, they would, he thought, probably be in that direction.

The door on the far side of the room looked more promising. He had no idea where it led, but at the very least it promised a more complete shelter than the great, broken chamber. It was a sign of civilization, and civilization could not exist without water.

It occurred to him that he was far below the level of the city streets – assuming that he had awoken where he had fallen. He had been deep in the crypts beneath and behind the temple and had, he was sure, fallen still farther. This door, then, whatever it was, was also part of the crypts rather than part of the city.

He wondered whether he was below the level of the lake; he had descended a goodly distance, but the lake itself had been sunk down far beneath the city. If he was below the water line, then it would be wiser to turn and head upward; the monster might have damaged the walls enough for water to find its way through the ruins at any time, and he might be trapped and drowned.

Even as he thought of this possibility Garth dismissed it, without knowing exactly why. He intended to investigate the door. He felt himself drawn to it by something more than simple curiosity.

Besides, he told himself, if the chamber did flood, he would be able to swim out through the break in the wall, and at least he would not die of thirst.

He began picking his way cautiously across the pavement, dodging the scattered heaps of rubble and watching for any place that looked as if it might crack beneath his weight; the thought that the monster might have damaged the structure of the crypt made him suddenly very suspicious of its stability. He looked up at the vaulting overhead, and around at the walls, trying to learn as much as he could about this place where he found himself.

The hall was square, or nearly so, and about sixty feet on a side, he judged. The walls began curving inward about a hundred feet up, and the peak of the central vault was another twenty or thirty feet above that. The broken side appeared to have been smashed outward all at once – undoubtedly by the horned monster. Garth regretted that; it was one more act of destruction that could be laid to his account.

The architecture was rather odd, in that there was no ornamentation above eye level save the vaulting – if that could be considered ornamentation; it was not needlessly elaborate. There were no galleries, no sign that there had ever been hangings or any other display. The room was bare and coldly functional, which seemed very peculiar in so vast a space. A chamber this size was surely built to be ostentatious, Garth thought, yet it showed no sign of ostentation beyond its size.

As he passed the center of the chamber he noticed that the floor seemed slightly warmer there, and the air fouler, with a vague fetidness about it. That was, he guessed, because the leviathan had stood in this spot while it slept, presumably throughout the city's recorded history.

With that, it seemed plain that this immense hall had existed solely to house the creature; it had been the cage wherein the creature was pent. That would explain its dimensions and architecture; nothing else Garth could think of would do so as well.

Realizing this, Garth grew slightly uneasy. What if, after so long a residence here, the monster considered this its home? How would it deal with any piddling little pest, such as an overman, that it found here upon its return? Most likely, Garth thought, it would stamp him flat, if it had feet in proportion to its head. He felt instinctively for his weapons.

Sword and axe were gone, as he already knew; he had only the dagger on his belt.

It didn't matter, he told himself. The monster would barely notice his best blow with either axe or broadsword. Human enemies he could handle with the dagger or whatever weapons he might find, if there were not too many of them at any one time, and the monster he couldn't handle at all with any ordinary weapon. He glanced back at the breached wall, wondering what the creature had done to Ur-Dormulk and what had become of the city's people.

Whatever had happened, there was nothing he could do about it. He stepped forward and studied the door he had come to investigate.

It was not large; he would have to duck to pass through it. It was made of some dull black substance, not ebony, though it appeared to be wood. The yellow symbol, only a single character, was etched upon it in bright metal – not pure gold, Garth was sure, as the hue was more vivid than gold. It was no metal he recognized, and the symbol was also strange – yet somehow familiar.

He had an uneasy feeling that he had seen it before and that it had not boded well. He realized he was staring at it and turned his gaze away.

His hand was on the latch, though he did not remember putting it there. It was a very curious latch, made of a metal that gleamed like silver, yet had no trace of tarnish, though surely it had been centuries since any mortal hand had touched it. There was no simple lever to lift, no bolt to draw, but a handle that Garth gripped and squeezed, without having consciously figured out the mechanism.

He felt the latch release and pushed on the door, only belatedly thinking that he was being incautious.

The door gave with a hiss of air, then swung silently back. It did not squeal or creak, but moved as smoothly as if the hinges had just been oiled.

Finally growing wary, Garth hesitated on the doorstep. Something had drawn him here, something beyond his own curiosity. He did not like being compelled; he tried to resist the impulse to step into the room he glimpsed through the open portal.

Perhaps, a part of his mind whispered, this compulsion was one of the signs the King had spoken of; perhaps the power of the Book of Silence, eager to be released, was drawing him to its hiding place. That was what he had come for, and he should follow the urging and seek out its source.

The logic of this swayed him, and he took a step forward into the dim interior. He found himself in a small chamber, about twelve feet wide and twenty feet long; thick, dark carpets, coated with dust and moldering with age, covered the floor, while the tapestries that had draped the walls had fallen to pieces beneath their own weight, leaving only faded tatters on their supports. At the far end a black stone oval hung on the wall, with the same sign etched in gold upon it as ornamented the door. Below it stood a small altar of finely wrought gold; to either side of the altar stood tall candelabra, holding nothing but low stubs of wax lost in dust and cobwebs. There were no windows, and the only light was what poured in through the door. Garth's shadow lay across much of the floor, and the altar was buried in gloom, but the overman could see something gleaming palely upon the altar's upper surface.

Trying to retain some semblance of caution, yet strongly drawn, Garth made his way slowly toward the altar, pausing after each step, weighing his own wishes and his own will against the force that pulled at him, and allowing himself to yield.

The thing upon the altar, he saw when he had crossed half the length of the room, was a mask, of a size to fit a human face. He tried to see what it was meant to represent, but with each step its aspect changed. At first he had thought it was simply a human face with a peculiarly hostile expression; next it seemed to bear a strange and bitter smile; seconds later, it was not the visage of a living man but the white, drawn features of a corpse. At his next step it showed the marks of advanced decay, swollen and bloated, with remnants of flesh drawn back from teeth and eyes; then it became the face of a mummy, its dry and wrinkled skin drawn tight over the bone beneath.

Finally, as he stood over the altar and looked down full upon the mask in the shadows of the chamber, it was plainly a representation of a naked skull, distorted so that it might be worn by a human over a living face.

Whatever the thing was, Garth did not like it, yet he found his hand reaching out for it. He drew back, and for an instant the object seemed not a mask at all, but the face of the Forgotten King, its eyes lost in shadow, the wisp of beard trailing from its chin, its skin shriveled but still alive.

Then it was a skull once more.

A vagueness seemed to be invading Garth's thoughts, not totally unlike the sensations he had sometimes felt when holding the Sword of Bheleu, and he guessed that this must be a similar object of power – presumably the Pallid Mask, totem of the god of death.

The aversion that should have accompanied that realization did not come, and it took a ferocious effort of will to draw back his hand and keep from stepping forward and picking up the ghastly thing.

He was not the chosen of The God Whose Name Is Not Spoken; he knew that and asked himself why he should be drawn to the mask. He wondered if he could handle it at all; ordinary people were unable to wield the Sword of Bheleu, and he had seen Galt seriously burn his hands just trying to touch its hilt.

Perhaps, Garth told himself, the Death-God knew that he would be returning to Skelleth in time and seeing the Forgotten King. Perhaps, as the chosen of Bheleu, he could handle the mask without harm, as the King said he could touch the Book of Silence.

Or perhaps the Death-God was hungry and wanted him to pick up the mask and die. The overman was quite sure that its mere touch could be fatal if the god so chose.

A sudden wave of revulsion swept over him; he kicked out at the altar, hoping to smash it and lose the hideous mask in the dust.

The golden framework tilted back, wobbled, rocked forward, and then fell back on its side. The mask slid off into the dust, as Garth had wanted, but he hardly noticed. He was staring at the space where the altar had stood.

The floor beneath the altar was bare stone, made of cut blocks arranged in neat rows, and one block, directly beneath the center of the altar, was missing. In the gap it left lay a book.

The compulsion that had drawn Garth before was as nothing to the force that seized him now; he lunged forward and pulled the thing from its place of concealment totally without thought or volition of his own. As soon as his fingers touched it, he felt an electric tingle run up his arm, and the room seemed alive with eerie colored light. The mask no longer concerned him; he all but forgot its existence as he lifted the Book of Silence.

It was miraculously light, weighing no more in his hands than a single straw. The binding was of some hide that at first glance appeared black, but had a subtle sheen to it in which other colors could be seen as it was moved; it had a faint oiliness to it. Garth stared at the book, running his hands over its surface, and only realized that he had turned and found his way out of the chapel when bright sunlight washed over the cover, sending a wave of iridescence across it.

He forced himself to pause. He had been seeking water, not the Book of Silence, and had found this thing almost against his will. It would seem that the chamber, the mask, and the book were in all probability the royal chapel, the Pallid Mask, and the Book of Silence – but could he be sure that everything was what it seemed? He had been led here by mystical force, yet had no assurance that this was what the Forgotten King had meant by his signs and portents. This was obviously a book of great power, Garth told himself, but could he be so certain that it was the Book of Silence? He took it in one hand and reached out with the other to open it.

A sudden foreboding swept over him, and his hand drew back. He paused again.

The thing was playing with him, manipulating his emotions, making him do whatever it pleased, rather than what he wanted to do. A surge of anger seethed up within him; he reached out and opened the book.

As he lifted the cover, the characters seemed to writhe on the page beneath, and he felt a cold breeze, as if it issued from the book.

The symbols were as stationary as any ordinary writing when he looked directly at them, each lying sedately on the page and forming neat blocks that were words and rows that were sentences. The runes, however, were totally alien, like nothing he had ever seen before, and he could not read a single word or recognize a single letter. The shapes hinted at meanings somehow, sinister and cold meanings, and Garth repressed a shudder.

He was unsure how long he stood staring at the incomprehensible runes, with their subtle suggestions of dark power and evil truths; finally, though, he tore his eyes away.

His gaze came free of the book only after considerable effort; he felt as if there were some physical connection between his eyes and the page, some powerful force keeping his head turned toward the text. When at last he managed to pull away, he suddenly realized that he was walking, not standing still as he had thought. He had moved away from the chapel door, across the chamber toward one of the far corners; furthermore, he saw with a shock that the sun now hung well to the west of where he had last seen it. The patch of sunlight no longer brightened the black door; it had swung over to what he judged to be the northeast corner of the hall, where it illuminated a low-relief carving so worn with age that its subject could not be determined with any certainty.

Garth had apparently walked so as to keep pace with the sun; he still stood in its full light. Frightened, he closed the book without daring to look at it again.

When it was safely shut but still held securely in both hands, he glanced about. Nothing in the great chamber had changed except the light. The scattered piles of debris were undisturbed, and the broach in the wall was just as he remembered it. The door to the chapel was closed again, though he had no recollection of shutting it. He no longer doubted that the room behind him was the Forgotten King's royal chapel and that he held the Book of Silence. The circumstances fitted too well for anything to be otherwise. He remembered the King's mention of posting a guard – for the sake of form – and knew that that guard had been the monster he and his attackers had awakened. This vast chamber had been built around it to hold it.

He wondered for a moment that the leviathan had left as it had, but then realized that its job was done; the old man had sent him to fetch the book and had freed the creature of its charge. The Forgotten King had planned the course of events somehow, Garth was sure. Signs and portents, indeed!

The carved panel in the northeast corner caught his eye; when he had entered the chapel it had been lost in shadow and effectively invisible. He had thought the walls blank, as most of them were.

He studied the surface, but could not make out what the scene was intended to represent; there were two figures in it, one tall and straight, the other short and stooped, standing against what had once been a detailed background but was now just a maze of broken lines. So blurred were the edges that Garth could not say whether the figures were even meant for humans, let alone their age, sex, or station. He supposed that the carving was much older than most of the chamber, to be so badly worn.

At one edge, however, one detail remained sharp and clear; a circle was incised deeply into the stone, and the hand of one figure was stretched out toward it.

Curious, Garth reached out and felt the knob of stone isolated within the circle; it gave beneath his fingers.

Startled, he drew his hand back, but a moment's thought convinced him that this must be an ancient, secret door and that the knob was the trigger whereby it might be opened. He had no idea why such a door should be here, but it seemed very promising; after all, he had no idea why most of what he had encountered in Ur-Dormulk should be what it was. He did not particularly want to go clambering about the wreckage beyond the broken wall, and he had seen no back door in the chapel; this appeared to be the only other way out of the creature's chamber.

He wondered if the Book of Silence, or the power controlling it, or perhaps the Forgotten King, had led him here intentionally. He guessed that the chamber had been designed in such a way that when the monster broke out, the afternoon sunlight would fall upon this door; he could only imagine what the ancient builders had been capable of in the way of prophecy, planning, and engineering. They might well have foreseen everything that had befallen him since the behemoth awoke.

At any rate, he determined to take advantage of his discovery; he reached out and pressed the stone knob.

Something clicked, and the whole panel swung back beneath the pressure of his hand. He peered through at the tunnel beyond.

Chapter Sixteen

The need for light, far more than simple caution, was responsible for Garth's decision to gather what supplies he could from the debris in the huge chamber. The passage he had found, unlike the stair down from the abandoned temple, was not conveniently equipped with lamp or torch; he was forced to rummage about in the wreckage for something that would serve. He had an idea that he might recover the battered oil lamp he had had with him in the round chamber, and therefore began his searching in the general vicinity of the dead soldier, on the assumption that the man had not been very far from the lamp when the floor erupted, and that the two might not have become far separated. Only after several minutes of unsuccessful exploration did it occur to Garth to investigate the corpse itself.

The soldier's belt held flint and steel and a small flask of something oily. Garth was not quite sure what the stuff was, but after a broken length of wood was soaked in it and then wrapped in strips of cloth from the overman's surcoat, similarly soaked, it made a thoroughly adequate torch.

Before venturing into the tunnel he also took the opportunity to appropriate the soldier's only remaining weapon, a sword that was ludicrously short for Garth's use, but still better than his dagger. He also gathered up pieces of cloth, scraps of wood, and other items that he thought might prove useful and wrapped them all in a torn tapesty, which he knotted and slung over his shoulder. The Book of Silence he tucked under one arm.

Thus prepared, he marched on into the passageway, his makeshift torch held high.

The tunnel was not straight; it wound sinuously back and forth, but seemed to run generally in one direction, which Garth judged to be east or slightly south of east. Doors lined either side, and side passages occasionally headed off at various angles, but Garth ignored those. He was not eager to get lost in the crypts, and the simplest way to avoid getting lost was to keep his route simple. Furthermore, he theorized that the exit from the monster's chamber had been set up intentionally for the use of someone such as himself, someone who could not be expected to know his way around the crypts. Such an individual would not be expected to make the correct decisions at every crossing or doorway unless those decisions were so obvious as to be unavoidable – and that meant, in Garth's opinion, continuing straight ahead.

Whether his theories were correct, or whether by chance, he eventually came to a set of steps leading upward, just as his improvised torch, which he had moistened and rewrapped until both oil and scraps of fabric had run out, began to burn low. He gazed at the staircase with relief; he had been planning to start tearing strips from his fragment of tapestry, and he was not sure that those would burn well without oil, quite aside from leaving him without his bundle. He started up the steps eagerly.

He had forgotten how far he had descended; his torch flickered and died while he was still out of sight of the top. He made his way on in the darkness, moving entirely by feel. Fortunately, this flight of steps was not worn as badly as the others he had encountered in Ur-Dormulk, and his footing remained secure.

Finally, his outthrust hand struck an obstruction; he stopped and felt it carefully. His hand came across a latch; he lifted the lever and pushed.

It did not yield.

He had a brief moment of uncertainty before it occurred to him that doors could open either way. He pulled at the latch.

The portal swung inward with a dull grinding, and disappointment seeped into Garth's breast as he saw darkness beyond. It was not the total, absolute blackness of the tunnel and stair he had just traversed, but it was obviously not the daylight he had hoped for, either.

Nonetheless, he saw little choice. He stepped forward through the door.

To his surprise, he felt a cold, damp breeze on his cheek and realized that he was, indeed, out of the crypts and on one of the stone-paved streets of the city. The darkness was the darkness of night; he had taken longer than he had thought to find his way through the underground passages. Low-hanging clouds obscured the moon and stars, but enough diffuse illumination reached him from the surrounding city to let him make out the immediate area.

He did not recognize the street he was on; there were no lighted torches or bright windows to help him in making out details. The area was quiet and seemed utterly deserted. Since he was unsure of the hour, he could not be sure whether this atmosphere was natural and ordinary.

It occurred to him that he might have come up into one of the ruinous districts, but what little he could make out of the buildings around him displayed no signs of decay or abandonment. Doors were all secure on their hinges and tightly closed, save for the one he had just emerged from, which was located near the corner of a large old house. Looking back at it, Garth guessed that, when closed, the door would blend in with the ornate stonework and appear to be just part of the wall. He stepped out onto the street, away from the shelter of the wall, and looked about.

An orange glow lit the sky in several places above the surrounding rooftops; Garth could not decide whether it was the normal torchlight of the city going about its business, or something brighter and more sinister. It was the only sign of life he could see; the street he was on was dark and empty for as far as he could see – not that that was very far, since, like most human streets, it curved out of sight in a block or two in either direction.

Sounds reached him, sounds he could not readily identify; he heard a distant crashing, and what might have been voices shouting somewhere, and beneath it all a dull, low-pitched rumbling.

He turned, listening, and decided that the rumbling and crashing came primarily from what he judged to be the northwest, while the voices were on several sides. Furthermore, the rumbling seemed to be approaching; at any rate, it was growing louder.

He wondered what was going on. Did this eerie situation of deserted streets and strange sounds relate to the freeing of the monster? Might it have something to do with the Book of Silence? It seemed ominous; although he saw no obvious damage to the buildings around him, he suspected that, once again, he had triggered widespread destruction. He hoped that there were Aghadites among the victims.

Now that he was aboveground again, and fairly certain that he could find food and water, he was curious. He suppressed his thirst, tucked the book more tightly under his arm, then turned and headed north, toward the rumbling.

As he did, he realized that he was actually very thirsty indeed, and hungry as well, but he did not turn aside. He might obtain food and water by breaking into one of the buildings, but he was not yet desperate and preferred to obtain them legally. Where there was sound, there was life, as a general rule, so he hoped that he would be able to find someone who could feed him if he headed toward the rumbling.

With that in mind, he quickened his pace, so that it took him a moment to stop when he turned a corner and found himself facing a scene out of a nightmare.

The city was ablaze ahead of him, or as much of it as could burn in a community built primarily of raw granite. Towering over the burning buildings stood the monster from the crypts, upright on two legs, with a wagonload of screaming hogs clutched in its claws, the traces whereby the wagon had been drawn dangling from one side. As Garth watched, the behemoth jammed the animals into its gaping mouth and bit down; the remaining fragments of the wagon fell out of sight with a distant crashing.

The horn on the creature's nose gleamed a sickly reddish yellow in the firelight, a thin line of black trailing down one side where its ichor ran. Its eyes blazed golden and seemed to Garth to be alight with madness. Its hide was wrinkled and black, its body shaped like nothing the overman had ever seen before. It was vaguely humanoid, in that it stood upright and used its forward limbs to grasp, but it had a hunched, ugly shape, its body proportions closer to those of a bull than to those of a man – though no bull had ever stood upon such hind legs, each as thick around as a castle tower, and no bull had such talons, long, agile fingers ending in vicious, curving claws.

The thing stood easily a hundred feet high; in fact, Garth estimated that it must have had to crouch down, badly cramped, to fit into the chamber that had held it for so long. The rumbling sound that had drawn him issued from the creature, though whether from its heart or its belly Garth was unsure.

With the hind legs of a pig still trailing from its jaws, the monster turned and reached down toward something Garth could not see over the intervening buildings. It seemed to struggle, like a man pulling at a stubborn root; then, with a tearing, crumbling roar, it lifted up the complete upper floor of a house.

The stones held together for a brief moment, then crumbled and fell through the creature's claws like sand through the fingers of a child, leaving it holding a pitiful assortment of roofing tiles, bedroom hangings, and broken furniture. It flung them aside and reached down again.

Garth had seen enough. He could do nothing at all against this monster by himself; it would take magic to destroy it.

He was determined, however, that it had to be destroyed. He had not seen it kill anyone since it first burst up through the floor, but it was doing incredible amounts of damage, and he could scarcely doubt that it had killed any number of people, perhaps without even meaning to, in making its way through the city. The creature was his responsibility, the overman told himself; he had ventured where he should not have gone, and it had been awakened as a result. He had brought destruction again, as he always did when he agreed to aid the Forgotten King.

He knew what could destroy it, he was sure; nothing could stand against the Sword of Bheleu. That would be fitting, using the tool of the god of destruction to kill such a destroyer. That would not atone for freeing the thing in the first place, but it would put the Sword of Bheleu to constructive use. If for any reason the sword should fail, the Forgotten King might well be able to use the Book of Silence against the monster.

He, Garth, could not use the book; he could not read it. He did not have the sword. The sword and the one who could read the book were both in Skelleth. Any doubts he had about swapping the book for the sword had vanished. He was still concerned about the possibility of the King's bringing on the Fifteenth Age, but that was mere theory, while this rampaging beast was a fact. Furthermore, he was certain that the King required more than the Book of Silence for his final magic.

He had to get to Skelleth without delay. His campaign against the cult of Aghad could wait; this monster was a far more immediate threat to the safety of innocents. The time he had spent in making his way through the crypts, or in his leisurely exploration of the creature's prison, or in the King's little chapel, now seemed to have been horribly wasted; the monster had probably killed dozens or even hundreds of people during that period. Even the time he had lain unconscious now seemed unforgivable.

He wondered how he could have been so thoughtless as to have not given the monster's whereabouts and behavior his immediate attention. Even as he spun and headed eastward on a side street, he berated himself for allowing such destruction.

He did not know the city, nor where in it he had found himself, but he knew that the gate where he had left Koros was near the easternmost extremity; for that reason, he kept heading east whenever possible. Almost immediately he passed through an area where the creature had obviously already been; many of the buildings were stamped flat, the rubble ground into powder against the granite streets. In places, the streets were indistinguishable from the buildings. Garth marveled that none had collapsed into the crypts which, he knew, honeycombed the entire area beneath the city.

He passed several fires, varying from a few smoldering curtains thrown in an alley to conflagrations consuming entire blocks. Only very rarely did he see any humans, and then it was merely a fleeting glimpse of someone vanishing behind a closing shutter or fleeing around the corner of a building. Nowhere were the streets lighted by the usual torches or lanterns, and the shops and houses were dark.

This both reassured and disturbed him; most of the population had obviously fled from the city, which was probably a very good thing, but why, he wondered, were the few stragglers avoiding him? Did they assume him to have some connection with the monster, or to be a threat in his own right by virtue of his species?

Finally he reached the steep slope that led up to the eastern wall of the city, but he had not managed to arrive at the gate. After some study of the surrounding buildings, the firelit rooflines and the parapet of the city wall in particular, Garth decided he was north of his intended destination and turned right.

A walk of four blocks south, complicated by dodging around in the tangled web of streets, brought him to the central avenue and the remembered steps. There, however, he stopped, hanging back out of sight around a corner.

The steps were not deserted, as the streets had been. Instead, what looked like the entire city guard was ranged on them, illuminated by hundreds of torches. Perhaps half were just standing and looking watchful, while the other half were coming and going and bustling about. Garth could not decide what they were doing; part of it seemed to be gathering in stragglers and escorting them up to the gate, but that did not account for all the movement.

Crowds of civilians were still in the area; the overman noticed them streaming in and out of one large building, under the gaze of a row of torch-bearing soldiers.

Whatever was happening, there seemed to be a fair measure of order and organization to it; Garth saw no signs of screaming panic and no bodies lying in the streets. That was promising.

It was important that there should be order, because this was the only way he knew that would get him out of the city; he would have to pass through that array of soldiery and do it peacefully. Had it been a desperate mob, that would have been virtually impossible. They might well have panicked at the sight of him.

Having assessed the situation, he saw no reason for further delay. He stepped from concealment and marched purposefully toward the gate.

As he had half expected, several people noticed him immediately, and a cry went up. "An overman! There's an overman here!"

To Garth's dismay, he could also make out shouts of "Kill the overman! It's another monster!" Other voices muttered and babbled, and he was sure that, despite the outward semblance of calm, this crowd could easily degenerate into a raging mob.

Several of the soldiers had noticed him as well, and one, an officer, was approaching.

"Ho, there!" Garth called. "How goes it?"

"Who in hell are you?" the soldier replied.

"I am Garth of Ordunin; I was a guest of your overlord, but became lost and have only now found my way here."

The man looked uncertain. "What do you want?" he asked.

"To pass through the gate."

The soldier nodded, as if that were what he should have expected. "You'll have to wait your turn," he said.

That was disconcerting. "I think," Garth said carefully, "that it would be wise to let me through immediately." He did not want to seem arrogant, or to take any action that might start trouble, but he also did not want to wait in line; every minute he was delayed from returning to Skelleth meant another minute of the monster's rampage.

"You can wait like anybody else, damn you," the soldier replied.

Garth started to protest, but a call from the dark at the top of the stair interrupted him.

"Have you got an overman down there?" someone yelled.

Startled, the soldier who had stopped Garth turned and looked. The call was repeated.

"We've got an overman here, yes," the officer called back.

"Is it the one who owns this damned animal out here?"

The soldier started to turn back to Garth, who said, "That is my warbeast, yes. I left it there because it was not allowed in the city."

"He says it's his," the soldier bellowed.

"Then get him up here and tell him to get the thing out of the way! It won't move, and it's slowing up the whole evacuation!"

The officer turned back toward Garth with a sour expression. The overman tried to smile ingratiatingly and avoided saying anything that might annoy the soldier.

"Go on up," the man said, waving him on.

Garth obeyed with alacrity, bounding up the worn steps as fast as he dared. At the top he was waved through, and another officer pointed out the warbeast, standing quietly in exactly the spot where Garth had left it.

The problem was that the entire eastern side of the ridge, from the wall down to the plain, was ablaze with torchlight and jammed with people – except for a wide circle, perhaps thirty feet across, around Koros. That circle happened to take in the only easy path around the south tower, and its north edge skimmed the main highway.

"Can you get it out of here?" someone asked.

Garth nodded.

"Then do it, please."

Garth nodded again, then paused. He was rather overwhelmed by the vast crowd of people; he had never seen so many individuals of any major species gathered together before. He had known, in an intellectual way, that Ur-Dormulk held tens or perhaps hundreds of thousands of people, but that had not prepared him emotionally for seeing most of the population packed together on a hillside at night without shelter or much of anything else but a few personal belongings.

"What are you going to do with them all?" he asked the officer.

"How should I know?" the man replied. "I just follow orders. With any luck we'll be able to start letting them back into the city by daybreak."

"You will?" Garth was startled. "How can that be? What of the monster?"

"The court wizards are trying to drive it into one of the lakes, I understand – probably Demhe, but Hali if they have to. I doubt anything that big can swim."

"How can they do that?"

"How would I know? I'm no sorcerer. They've kept it from chasing the crowds so far; they should be able to handle it."

Garth was far less optimistic, but did not say so. Instead, he asked, "These wizards – do you speak of Chalkara of Kholis and a person called Shandiph?" He had forgotten the cognomen attached to the latter name, if he had ever in fact heard it.

"Those names sound right," the soldier replied. "The two from the prince's court, whoever they are. They were about to flee the city themselves, I hear, when they got ordered to deal with the thing." He was obviously not interested in such details. "Now, could you move your animal?"

"Yes, of course," Garth said. He considered telling the man that he would be returning shortly with the means of dispatching the monster, but decided against it. This fellow did not appear to have much authority, and even if he had some, what good would such a message do? Besides, the possibility of something going wrong was always present; Garth might be delayed or might have difficulties with the Sword of Bheleu, or with the cult of Aghad, that would prevent his return. There was no point in raising hopes that might go unfulfilled.

He said nothing, but marched down to the side of the waiting warbeast. The crowd parted reluctantly before him, pressing back upon itself.

He stowed his possessions, including the Book of Silence, and made certain they were secure. A moment later he was in the saddle again; he shouted a warning to the people gathered before him, then gave Koros the command to advance.

Those immediately in the beast's path moved back as quickly as they could, eager to stay out of its way, but the resistance of the mass behind them ensured that Garth's progress remained slow until the crowd thinned out, a hundred yards farther down the slope. At that point Koros began picking up speed, and when rider and mount passed the line of soldiers that marked the outer perimeter of the clustered refugees, Garth gave the warbeast the order to run.

Koros obeyed magnificently, hurtling forward so fast that the overman's eyes stung and watered with the wind of their passage. He was able to do little but cling desperately to the harness, casting an occasional glance back to be sure that the pack behind the saddle that held the Book of Silence remained secure.

He rode on thus for hours, pausing only at a roadside tavern for a long-overdue drink and a hearty meal.

It was this scene, of Garth bent over his warbeast's neck, charging onward at top speed, that Haggat conjured up in his scrying glass when he found time to check again on the overman's whereabouts. He was startled; he wondered what urgency drove Garth to maintain such a pace. He had not bothered to follow events in Ur-Dormulk personally, relying instead on reports from the cult's many agents there; half a dozen had been equipped with the communication spells acquired from murdered wizards, which provided almost instant news – a great improvement on the old system of relays and carrier pigeons that they had relied upon before the breaking of the Council of the Most High.

No reports had reached him from Ur-Dormulk, which could mean many things; he told himself that he would have to look into that later.

For the present, Garth was obviously returning to Skelleth with all possible haste, and if the cult were to maintain its image and its hold upon him, then a greeting of some sort would have to be arranged. The overman's homecoming – Haggat thought of Skelleth as Garth's home, even though Garth did not – could not be allowed to go unheralded.

The high priest had already considered this matter in his planning and had devised two possible unpleasant surprises. The better one, unfortunately, was the more difficult and time-consuming, and at the rate Garth was moving, it might not be ready in time; therefore, the other would have to do.

Haggat paused before giving the signal, however, and studied the image in the globe thoughtfully. The warbeast had to be taken into consideration. He was determined that his people would maintain an appearance of total invulnerability, and the warding spells that he had provided his last group of tormentors would not serve against so powerful a creature as a warbeast.

Well, he told himself, he had a device that would. It was one of his most prized possessions, acquired by careful planning and considerable craft from the wizard who had pocketed it in that mysterious vault beneath Ur-Dormulk, whence so much of the cult's pilfered magic was derived. It was truly a shame that the chamber was lost and that all attempts to locate it had failed; if a score of magicians had brought out so much worthwhile magic just by retaining what they had casually picked up in a few hours' stay, what other treasures might still lie there, undiscovered?

One of Haggat's dreams was to find and reopen that vault; another was to obtain and use the Sword of Bheleu. Accomplishing either feat would give him, he was sure, mastery of the entire civilized world. He did not wholly understand why he had made no progress toward either goal. Divinations that were usually infallible came to nothing; spies vanished mysteriously and were never heard from again; healthy agents died of sudden heart failure while climbing the stairs of the King's Inn. It was obvious that some other power was blocking him. He was determined not to be thwarted; once Garth had been dealt with, he would track down and destroy whoever was responsible for the interference.

First, though, he had to deal with Garth, and for that, he wanted to provide the appointed agents with an infallible protection. He had only one, apparently unique in all the world, a simple metal rod that could, if properly used, temporarily render up to half a dozen people immune to all harm. After taking it from Haladar of Mara he had intended to keep it solely for his own personal use, but this situation was special, and called for special measures. He would, he decided, loan it to the chosen cultists.

That, he was certain, when combined with the other magic at his disposal, would ensure that Garth received the greeting the followers of Aghad thought he deserved.

Chapter Seventeen

After further hours of traveling at high speed, with its rider clinging to its neck, Koros slowed as it approached the crumbling walls of Skelleth. Garth rose from his crouch into a more comfortable and dignified posture; thus he was able to see clearly, in the gray light of morning, what awaited him at the gate. He had time, also, to hide his shock and dismay.

Three red-robed figures were slouched comfortably on the broken battlements, gathered around a pole that stood ten or twelve feet high, leaning at a jaunty angle and topped with Kyrith's severed head.

Lying crumpled against the wall below was the dead body of the man assigned to guard the southwestern gate; a long, crooked streak of blood ran from his slit throat down his arm to the ground.

Garth was as much appalled by the pointless murder of the sentry as by the defiling of his wife's corpse. After all, Kyrith had already been dead, insensible to further indignity. Even though she was his own species and his own family, the awful waste of killing the man simply because he was in the way – and Garth was quite sure that was the only reason the Aghadites had slain him, to remove him from the chosen site for their little display – was sickening.

As Garth fought to keep his anger leashed until he knew what he faced, one of the loungers called, "Back again?"

"We've been waiting for you," another said; his accent was Dûsarran. "We didn't want to kill anyone else important while you were off adventuring; that wouldn't be fair. So we've just been playing games." He waved casually at the gory trophy.

Garth growled involuntarily, as much at the calm dismissal of the guard's death as unimportant as at the taunts, and drew the undersized sword he had picked up in Ur-Dormulk.

The Aghadites laughed.

Enraged as he was, Garth remembered what had happened before when he struck at one of his red-clad tormentors. He saw no point in breaking another sword, even so poor a one as he now carried – but he was not sure that the protective spell worked against other weapons. The Forgotten King had called it a warding spell against metal. The overman leaned forward and whispered a word in the warbeast's ear.

Koros roared in reply and plunged forward, fangs bared and claws out. With a bound, it landed atop the three – and slid off, scrabbling for a hold it could not find. It was as if the Aghadites were sheathed in indestructible glass. They obviously had more protection than a ward against metal.

Garth lost his balance and slid from the saddle as the warbeast writhed about, trying to get at its indicated targets; he landed with a heavy thump on a patch of bare dirt, the wind knocked out of him, but not otherwise injured.

When he had regained his breath, he clambered to his feet to find himself facing a truly bizarre tableau. The three humans were sitting where they had been, trying desperately to look unconcerned, while Koros, standing awkwardly upon its hind legs, wrapped its immense forepaws around one man and tried to bite his head off. Garth could hear the grinding of teeth against something impervious.

The warbeast twisted its head for a better grip, but had no more success. The other two Aghadites wore ghastly, contrived smiles; the beast's intended victim was frozen with fear, despite his magical defenses, and his expression was one of sick terror as three-inch fangs skidded across his throat like fingernails on marble.

Garth took a great deal of pleasure in seeing the Aghadites discomforted, even though he realized that he could do them no real harm. He did nothing to interfere; something else had occurred to him. He stepped forward, sword in hand, climbed atop a pile of rubble, and, leaning over the head of one of the trio, swung the blade against the wooden pole.

As he had hoped, the protective spell had not been extended that far. The wood splintered gratifyingly, and the upper portion toppled over. Before any of the Aghadites could recover, he had stepped over and scooped up his wife's head.

The two not involved with the warbeast called out in protest; Garth ignored them. He watched for another few seconds as Koros continued trying to gnaw off the other's head and wished that it were possible for the beast to succeed. It would have been an appropriate retaliation for the desecration of Kyrith's corpse and the murder of the guard. He regretted leaving the man's corpse where it was, but did not want to burden himself with it and perhaps give rise to unpleasant speculation in Skelleth as to how the guard had died. He doubted that the Aghadites would bother to desecrate the corpse; they were, he suspected, sufficiently ignorant of overman psychology not to realize that Garth would care about the man at all.

Reluctantly, he at last called the warbeast away, afraid that, in its mounting frustration, it might damage its teeth.

The two unmolested Aghadites had gone into a huddle, conferring with each other; they made no move to interfere with Garth as he led Koros onward into the town. The intended victim had fainted; when Koros released him, he tumbled to the ground in a heap.

After the overman had moved on out of sight of the Aghadites, he paused for a moment to wrap the head in his tapestry bundle, dumping unceremoniously the assorted litter that he had gathered and transferring the few items he still thought might be useful to the pack behind the warbeast's saddle. He checked to be sure that the Book of Silence was still secure, then continued on his way.

He ignored the townspeople he encountered on the streets and marched across the marketplace without glancing to either side. At this point he was not concerned with anyone in Skelleth save for the Forgotten King and the Aghadites. He intended to spare a few minutes, once he had the Sword of Bheleu, to kill his three tormentors before returning to Ur-Dormulk to deal with the monster. This latest meeting with the cult, he thought, had come out a draw; he intended to be victorious in the next one.

He wondered if Chalkara and Shandiph actually had any chance of getting the awakened creature into one of the lakes and whether that would be enough to kill it. Drowning such a thing would require a very deep lake indeed; he doubted that the one he had seen in Ur-Dormulk would do the job.

The monster might, however, be unable to climb out, given the long drop that surrounded the lake on all sides. If that happened, Garth was sure that the people of Ur-Dormulk would be glad to have it destroyed, rather than have it remain as a perpetual nuisance.

And, of course, if the wizards failed, Garth would have to kill it to prevent wholesale slaughter. Ordinary soldiery, however successful it might be in defending the city against human foes, could do nothing against such a creature.

The thought of soldiery reminded him that the men guarding the eastern gate of the city and serving to control the crowd of refugees had not tried to kill him, nor had hindered him in any way; he wondered again why the party that had pursued him into the crypts had done so. Had they been given orders to slay him, orders that were never spread to the other troops? Or had their commander taken it upon himself to kill the intruding overman?

It was all rather confusing, and Garth decided that none of it really mattered. All that mattered was getting and using the Sword of Bheleu to avenge the wrongs done him by the cult of Aghad and to destroy the monster he had unleashed.

That thought was uppermost in his mind when he reached the door of the King's Inn, but he paused for a moment before entering. He carried the bundle containing Kyrith's head in one hand, intending to keep it with him so that the Aghadites could not recover it once more to taunt him anew. The Book of Silence, however, was in a pack on the warbeast's back. He debated leaving it there; the Forgotten King would not be able to take it from him as readily if he left it outside while he spoke with the old man. On the other hand, thieves might happen along. Koros could easily dispose of most threats and guard anything it carried from them, but if the Aghadites with their protective magic should chance upon it, could the warbeast prevent them from taking the book?

In the interests of at least knowing what became of it, should anything go wrong, he removed the book and tucked it under his arm. Then he ordered Koros to wait by the door and strode into the King's Inn, marching directly for the table in the back corner.

He was halfway across the room before he noticed that though the old man sat in his accustomed place, something new had been added. The Sword of Bheleu lay across the table, the hilt pointing straight at Garth. The immense gem set in its pommel was not the dead black it had been when last he saw it; instead, it was murky and dark, its dull reddish hue seeming to shift as the overman approached, as if something were seething and swirling within it.

The sight of the sword gave him pause; his stride faltered, and his thoughts grew muddy and unclear. He slowed and stopped, still several feet away from the weapon's waiting hilt.

The great jewel seemed to flicker; Garth, staring at it, was now quite sure that something was moving within it. He had an unpleasant feeling that he was being watched by the power that lurked in the sword, and fancied that he could make out the image of a baleful red eye in the strange stone.

The idea of handling the thing was suddenly far less appealing, as he remembered the sick joy and dull thoughtlessness that he felt while wielding it. He started to take a step back, then stopped, angered by his own cowardice. Irritated, he tried to stare back at the stone, to confront directly the hostile power that dwelt therein.

After a second or two of motionless glaring, he realized he must look like a fool, watching an inanimate stone as he would a deadly foe. His annoyance grew.

He knew, vaguely, that he should not let himself be angered so easily, and that only enraged him still further. Confused and furious, he was tempted to step forward and snatch up the sword; that would settle the whole affair. His free hand reached out.

The Forgotten King's hand moved as well, a subtle shifting of the fleshless fingers, and the gem went black. Garth's anger vanished, and his mind was clear again.

The anger and confusion, he knew, had been caused by the sword. He raised his gaze from the now-dormant gem to the withered face of the old man.

The King had intentionally let the sword affect him, that was obvious. He seemed to be able to damp its power effortlessly whenever he chose and for as long as he saw fit, yet he had let it affect Garth.

Even then, though, he had kept it weak, kept the stone dim; he had not wanted it to seize full control of the overman.

Realizing this, Garth felt a surge of his own authentic, self-generated anger. "Why did you do that?" he demanded, striding up to the table.

"A reminder," the old man replied in his hideous, dry voice.

Garth hesitated. The sound of the Forgotten King's voice was always disconcerting; no matter how often Garth reminded himself that it was horribly unpleasant, it always came as a surprise. Memory and imagination could not live up to the reality.

"A reminder of what?" he said at last, his tone less belligerent.

He did not really need to hear the old man's answer. The King had ways of knowing of events without seeing them; Garth was certain that the human had known he was coming to the King's Inn with the intention of taking the Sword of Bheleu and had staged the brief incident to remind Garth what the sword did to his mind and emotions.

As it happened, the old man did not bother to answer at all; he merely shrugged once, almost imperceptibly.

But why, Garth asked himself, would the King want to remind him of the sword's dangers?

Obviously, the old man did not want Garth to take the sword; that was the only explanation that seemed reasonable.

And why would he want to keep the sword?

Garth thought he knew the answer to that. He recalled that when he had first brought his booty from Dûsarra, the Forgotten King had dismissed most of it as junk, but had been pleased to see the Sword of Bheleu. Later, he had agreed only to *loan* it to Garth in exchange for the Book of Silence, but not to trade it outright. The wizards in Ur-Dormulk, in their theory that the King sought to bring about the Fifteenth Age, the Age of Death, had said that he required a service from the servants of Bheleu. Garth was, as far as he knew, the only servant Bheleu had alive; had events followed their predicted pattern, he would have the Sword of Bheleu.

He believed, therefore, that the old man's final death-magic, the spell that Garth thought would destroy the world, required the sword as well as the Book of Silence – and presumably the Pallid Mask as well. It would do the King little good to acquire one of the tools he needed if he were to give up another in exchange. He was therefore, Garth guessed, trying to coax Garth into giving him the Book of Silence without taking the sword.

Or perhaps it was something subtler than that. Perhaps the old man did not mind giving Garth the sword, but feared that after the overman took it, he would renege on his side of the bargain and keep the book. After all, Garth had admitted that his word was not good. In that case, the King presumably sought to frighten Garth out of taking the sword, so that the only way in which the magically protected Aghadites, or the monster in Ur-Dormulk, could be slain would be by the old man's use of the book.

It might even be that he sought to anger the overman into thoughtless defiance, and then Garth would snatch up the sword immediately. That didn't make very much sense, however, as surely the King could achieve the same result simply by letting Bheleu's power go free, so that it would suck Garth in.

If that last possibility was the truth, Garth decided, the old man might yet have his wish, because Garth was now more determined than ever to take the Sword of Bheleu and use it against the Aghadites and the leviathan. If the Forgotten King wanted to keep the sword, it was almost certainly in the best interests of all mortals for Garth to take it away from him.

As he arrived at that conclusion, Garth reached down toward the hilt of the sword.

The old man's hand shot out with unbelievable speed and grabbed the overman's descending wrist. To Garth's astonishment, he found himself unable to pull free or move the hand either nearer to or farther from the sword. It was as if the bony fingers were solid steel – and a very good grade of steel at that, to resist an overman's full strength without yielding the slightest fraction of an inch. The wrinkled skin even felt cool and dry, like metal.

"Why do you stop me?" Garth was now sure that the old man did not want him to take the sword, but thought it unwise to admit his belief.

"Give me the Book of Silence." Again, even after so brief an interval, the King's voice was shockingly ugly.

Garth struggled to free his wrist; the old man gave no sign he was even aware of the overman's efforts. Finally, after several seconds of useless strain, Garth conceded defeat. "Take the book, then, if you want it," he said.

The Forgotten King rose, the tatters of his yellow mantle rustling. He reached out his free hand, plucked the volume from beneath Garth's arm, and held it before him, but did not loosen his grip on the overman's wrist.

"Release me," Garth said, mustering as much dignity as he could in so awkward and embarrassing a pose. To be held so easily by a mere human, even one as unique and powerful as the Forgotten King, shamed him.

"My reminder, Garth," the King warned. "Bheleu is insidious and powerful and can dominate you with ease, perhaps without letting you know he is doing so. Remember, though, that I can free you of his influence as easily as you can blink an eye. You must serve one of us. The choice of masters is yours. Now, take the sword, if you want it, but remember, I lend it, I do not give it." The bony grip was gone, and Garth watched as the old man, the great black book clutched in both hands, turned away and moved across the room and up the stairs.

When the Forgotten King had vanished into the gloom at the top of the stairs, Garth looked down at the sword.

It lay, untouched, on the table; the gem remained black and lifeless.

Had that, then, been the purpose of the King's actions – to remind Garth that he would never again be free while both the Sword of Bheleu and the King in Yellow existed?

But then, with the Book of Silence in the King's possession, how much longer would he exist? He sought his own destruction and needed the book to accomplish it. Perhaps Garth was wrong about the other elements required, and the old man was even now weaving his final spell, a spell that would destroy the cult of Aghad and perhaps all the world as well.

No, that could not be. The old man had not said it, but he had definitely implied that he would live for some while yet, long enough to require Garth's services. Furthermore, the overman was certain that either the Sword of Bheleu, the Pallid Mask, or both were needed. Other things might also be required; he recalled that the Forgotten King had made him swear, almost three years ago, that not only would he fetch the book but he would also aid in the final magic.

Garth shook his head, dismissing all such considerations as not immediately relevant. He had more important concerns than maybes. He had his wife's murder to avenge, Aghadites to kill, and a monster to dispose of.

He reached down and grasped the sword's hilt; as his fingers closed on the black grip, the gem blazed up a fiery blood-red, washing the overman in crimson light. Savage joy and a blinding fury burst into being within him, and somewhere mocking laughter sounded.

Chapter Eighteen

At first the surge of emotion was too powerful to allow any conscious thought or awareness of the external world at all. For three long years Bheleu had been suppressed, held down, his control of his chosen mortal form cut off; now that he was free once more, he reveled in it. The sword crackled with eldritch energy, and the air around the overman's body glowed redly.

Garth's own consciousness was lost for a long moment. He felt himself cut off, drifting in a formless nowhere of red and black, and he struggled desperately to regain his body. He fought to contain the all-consuming bloodlust that possessed him. The initial wave of ecstasy, the emotional overflow from Bheleu's relief, passed away. Anger remained, but as he pushed his way to the surface, he managed to redirect it, to channel it against the usurping presence in his body and mind.

"Bheleu!" he tried to call. "Listen to me!"

He knew, even in his confused state, that the words had not been spoken, that his lips and tongue had not obeyed him; nevertheless, he heard his own voice, made terrible by the god's power, answer him.

"Why do you call me, Garth? You have taken up the sword again, of your own choice, and freed me from all restraint. Now you will serve me in destruction, as you were meant to serve me. What need is there of words?"

"I want to make a bargain," Garth managed to say – or at least to communicate, though he knew he had still not spoken aloud.

The god did not reply in words; instead, Garth felt a wave of contempt sweep over him, felt his consciousness slipping into darkness, and he struggled to retain what feeble control he had.

"No, wait! Bheleu, you are not free yet! There are terms to be set!"

"I am free," Bheleu replied.

"No!" Garth insisted. "You must meet my terms, or the Forgotten King will stop you again as he did before!"

There was a pause that seemed to stretch for hours, a timeless waiting while Garth's awareness drifted in nothingness and Bheleu considered.

"What are your terms?" Bheleu said at last.

Garth did not allow himself to feel relief yet, though he was sure that the god's willingness to listen at all proved that the point had been won, at least for the moment. "I took the sword back for a reason," he said. "I have enemies and I wish to destroy them." He felt a surge of hunger, of desire, as he said that. "They have the means of defying my own strength, so I need the sword and the power that goes with it."

"I am that power," Bheleu said, fury and bloodlust seething.

"I know," Garth answered, struggling against the overwhelming force of the god's driving emotions. "And I'll allow you freedom to destroy my enemies, but no others."

"You would use me, the destroyer god, as a tool for your own vengeance?"

Garth was almost swept down into nonexistence by the god's wrath, but managed to answer, "I would use anything I found necessary. Were you not planning to use me for your own ends against my will?"

"I am a god, Garth; you are nothing."

"I am a nothing who knows how you can be stayed; I am the chosen of a god. Is not the freedom to destroy my foes better than no freedom at all?"

"What do you propose?"

"I propose that you leave me in control of my own body and my own mind; in exchange, I will allow you free rein to work your will upon my enemies. If you refuse, you will surely be restrained again."

There followed another timeless pause; then, abruptly, Garth found himself fully conscious once again, albeit dazed and awash in unreasoning anger. He stood in the King's Inn, the sword clutched in one hand, its blade dripping red fire. The floorboards were scorched beneath his feet, in a circle a yard across, and a line had been burned across the top of the King's table where the sword had rested, obscuring with char the line he had gouged with his broken sword before leaving for Ur-Dormulk.

He could detect no sign of Bheleu's presence save for the heat of the sword, burning without harming him, and the eerie flame that flickered from it. His thoughts seemed slow, but unnaturally clear; a fierce joy suffused him at the realization that he had won his argument, and righteous wrath filled him at the thought of Aghadites lurking somewhere in Skelleth waiting for him to come and kill them.

No one else was in the tavern; the innkeeper and the handful of other patrons had vanished while he debated with Bheleu. He did not concern himself with their whereabouts; they had, he told himself, undoubtedly fled before his manifest power.

He strode out the door, the sword's fiery aura gradually fading, and mounted his warbeast. With a word, he directed it back the way they had come, out toward the southwestern gate, hoping to find the three Aghadites. The Forgotten King had told him that the red-mist transporting spells were rare and precious; surely, then, the trio would not have wasted one, but would be moving on foot.

By the time Koros reached the south side of the marketplace, the sword appeared to be ordinary steel, though the black grip was hot in Garth's hand.

He found the three robed humans perhaps halfway to the gate, walking toward the center of town. They saw him at almost the same instant that he spotted them; one turned to flee, another hesitated, while the third fumbled with something beneath his ruddy robe.

Garth bellowed, urging Koros into a charge.

The fumbler stopped his actions and stood up straight, defying the warbeast and overman. "Ho, Garth!" he began.

Then the Sword of Bheleu struck his neck; with a roar and a sheet of flame, the blade passed through the protective aura and into the Aghadite's throat. Blood spurted, and the man's severed head rolled forward, tottered grotesquely, and fell to the ground as his body began to crumple. White sparks spattered from the dripping blade, and something hissed fiercely.

The man who had hesitated had no time to react before the sword swung around in a gleaming arc and beheaded him as well, spraying blood and fire across the packed dirt of the street.

Before the second corpse could fall, Garth twisted the sword back and impaled the dead man, holding it upright, the blade thrust through the chest – though the head had fallen to one side, where the overman ignored it. He was not willing to let both these foes escape with so quick and clean a death as simple decapitation.

The third Aghadite was still fleeing; Garth urged the warbeast after him, dragging the headless corpse alongside with the sword.

He gained on the human rapidly, despite the encumbrance of the dead body, but not rapidly enough; he saw wisps of red vapor gathering about the man's head, staying with him as he ran. With a growl, Garth tore the sword from the corpse's chest, letting the body fall aside, and urged Koros to greater speed.

It did no good; the Aghadite vanished before Garth could reach him.

The overman bellowed in rage and frustration. The man had escaped him!

Haggat was standing by the pentagram when the cult's surviving agent reappeared in a cloud of mystic vapor; he had given up trying to follow events in Skelleth. The Sword of Bheleu had the capability of resisting any attempt at scrying spells, should it choose to do so; Aghad's high priest had learned that fact almost three years earlier, at the cost of a good glass. On this occasion he had not bothered to try to observe the overman at all, after the image distorted and vanished at the instant that Garth's hand touched the sword's hilt. Instead he had followed the actions of his three cultists, keeping one of his wizard-acolytes ready with one of his handful of transporting crystals. Even that image had been lost, however, when the overman attacked the threesome, and Haggat's brief resulting confusion had given Garth time to kill the two who had chosen to rely on the protective spell.

It was of interest, Haggat thought, that the spell, which he had believed quite potent, had been unable to resist the Sword of Bheleu for as much as a second. The sword was obviously a weapon well worth having, and a very serious threat in Garth's hands.

He had not thought that the overman would take the sword back from the strange old man in rags. That, it seemed, had been a miscalculation, one that had cost the cult two good men already and that might prove disastrous.

Garth had sworn to return to Dûsarra and wipe out the whole sect; now that he had the sword in his possession once more, there was a chance that he might actually manage it. Haggat considered it essential to distract the overman, to harry him, to do whatever could be done to keep him busy until defenses could be prepared.

With that in mind, Haggat signaled for his advisers and assassins to attend him. Obediently, a dozen red-robed figures clustered around him.

While the Aghadites were gathering about their master, Garth sat astride his warbeast, roaring with anger and swinging the Sword of Bheleu in circles over his head. Streaks of shimmering white fire hung like smoke, emitting waves of intense heat. Thunder rumbled in the distance, drawn by the sword's power.

The human had to be somewhere, Garth told himself. The red mist was merely a transporting spell, nothing more. It did not create people out of thin air, nor snatch them into nothingness. The Aghadite was still alive somewhere, perhaps nearby, perhaps laughing at his escape.

Wherever he was, Garth would find him; he would find him and cut him apart, watch his blood pour out, watch him suffer and die. He promised himself that, ignoring the tiny inner voice that protested this open bloodlust.

Koros had slowed and stopped when its prey vanished; now, at the urging of its rider, it turned back toward the inhabited portion of Skelleth. As it passed by each of the headless corpses, Garth thrust the sword out casually and set both afire with the weapon's supernatural flame.

That done, he rode on, considering his next move.

His first thought was to return to the marketplace and begin searching for the escaped Aghadite there, but that, he decided, would be a mistake. The man was almost certainly hiding somewhere in the ruins, where no stray villagers would wonder at mysterious colored smoke or strange noises. Garth had lived in Skelleth for almost three years and had not seen anyone wearing the distinctive red robes between the time of his giving up the Sword of Bheleu and his finding of Kyrith's body – yet now these three had turned up suddenly. None of the faces was familiar; he could not recollect having seen any of them in other garb. Therefore, he guessed that they had only recently arrived in Skelleth – and since newcomers, other than caravans, were rare enough to excite a great deal of comment, Garth thought he would have heard of them if they were living openly in the inhabited part of the town.

Therefore, he concluded, they had been living in concealment somewhere in the ruins, and it was in the ruins that he must search for the survivor, and any others who might have taken part in Kyrith's murder.

Somewhere in the back of his mind, he remembered the behemoth destroying Ur-Dormulk, but somehow it seemed far less important than dealing immediately with the cult of Aghad.

Besides, he told himself, surely he couldn't object to destroying ruins, and that would keep the sword busy and Bheleu happy.

That thought troubled him somehow; something seemed wrong with it, and perhaps with his other decisions as well. Something appeared to be clouding his thoughts.

The idea refused to come clear, so he dismissed it. He had an enemy to hunt down and destroy; that was what mattered. He turned Koros off the road leading into the market and set out instead into the ring of ruins that encircled Skelleth's inhabited core.

The town had been built as a border fortress, and its houses were constructed mostly of stone as a result, so that they would not burn readily. After three hundred years of neglect, many houses and buildings had lost roofs and floors, and some walls had fallen, but many still stood, making the streets a maze, with some routes blocked by rubble, others still open, and all divided by crumbling buildings.

Garth, armed with the Sword of Bheleu, did not bother to find his way through this labyrinth; instead, he dismounted and marched in a straight line, Koros trailing behind. Whenever he found his way blocked by a standing wall or a pile of debris, he blasted it apart with the Sword of Bheleu; only open pits were sufficient to turn him aside. When he came across those, he would pause and send a wave of flame down into them, to incinerate any Aghadites who might be lurking therein.

The use of the sword's power, he found, came very easily, almost without any thought or effort at all; the god's long restraint had not affected the increase in power that accompanied the establishment of the Fourteenth Age. Garth discovered quickly that all that vast resource was at his command, ready and eager to be applied.

When he had held the sword before the Age of Bheleu had been just beginning. The god's power had been erratic, sometimes manifesting itself unbidden, other times appearing only after great mental effort. That was no longer the case. Now, Garth had almost infinite energy literally at his fingertips.

He had been cutting a swath through the ruins for an hour or so, enjoying the exhilaration of battering down the empty houses until he had almost forgotten what he was looking for, when a red-clad figure appeared, perched precariously atop a wall off to his right.

Garth did not notice the human's presence at first; he was basking in the delight of shattering a foot-thick stone pillar with a single blow of his sword and therefore did not see whether the man had arrived magically or had simply climbed up the other side of the wall.

"Ho, Garth!" the human called.

Startled, Garth lowered the Sword of Bheleu and turned toward the source of the voice.

"You'll never find us that way!" the Aghadite said.

With a growl, Garth swung the sword about, pointing it toward the human. After an hour of practicing with the sword's power, he had no intention of wasting time in unnecessary pursuit. He had learned better.

"We've got a surprise for you in town," the man began; then the sword spat flame toward him, blazing across the intervening distance in an instant. Immediately, red mist gathered about him, but Garth listened with satisfaction to the Aghadite's screams as the sword's fire reached him first. The spell would deliver a burned corpse.

It did exactly that; Haggat stared in dismay at the smoldering remains. He had been using up transporting crystals far faster than he liked, and to little effect. He had lost another good agent. He had not expected the overman to react so quickly.

At least, however, Garth was still searching Skelleth and was not on his way to Dûsarra. The cult would have time to devise an effective strategy.

That assumed, of course, that any strategy could be effective against the Sword of Bheleu. Haggat was not sure that was the case. He began to wonder whether the cult might have done better to have forgotten permanently about its vengeance against Garth.

It was too late now, though.

Perhaps the overman would think that he had succeeded in killing all his wife's assassins, as in fact he had, and would abandon his retaliation,

Somehow, though, Haggat doubted that, in light of both Garth's oath to destroy the cult's temple and what awaited him in Skelleth's marketplace. The high priest wondered if committing another atrocity might have been a mistake.

He looked down at the blackened, crumbling heap in the pentagram and hoped very much that Garth would be satisfied by the three cultists he had killed.

Garth *was* satisfied, but only for a very brief moment, as he thought of the transporting spell dumping a flaming ruin before Aghadites expecting a living man.

That very thought, however, gave him pause. If he had killed the man, who had completed the spell? Somebody had, apparently, because the red smoke had gathered, thickened, and then vanished, taking the burning Aghadite with it. By the time he disappeared, the man was almost certainly already dead.

Had the human set up the spell in advance so that he would not need to complete it, but only to set it in motion? Garth wished he knew more of the exact mechanism involved.

And whether the man had worked the spell himself or not, could Garth be sure that there were not still more Aghadites lurking in Skelleth? He had, as far as he knew, encountered only the three he had slain, but that did not mean that there were no others.

That corpse had gone somewhere, he was certain of that.

Had he killed all those directly involved in his wife's death, the desecration of her corpse, and the murder of the guard at the gate? Others might still be hidden. For that matter, he could not be sure that these three had actually killed Kyrith at all.

He had every intention of returning to Ur-Dormulk and killing the monster, then proceeding from there to Dûsarra to fulfill his vow to destroy the headquarters of Aghad's cult, but he wanted to be certain first that he had dealt with the sect's outpost in Skelleth and with those who had actually taken part in Kyrith's murder.

He tried to think, to marshal what information he had, in hopes of finding some clue that would tell him what he wanted to know. His thoughts seemed vague and elusive. He wondered if he had been hasty in killing the last of the trio so quickly, rather than taking him alive and interrogating him.

The man's last words had been about a surprise of some kind – "in town," he had said.

That, Garth was sure, meant in the inhabited portion of Skelleth; most likely, he thought, he would find whatever it was right in the marketplace. Perhaps that would provide the clue he needed to lead him to more Aghadites.

He was vaguely aware that the surprise might be unpleasant, but that seemed unimportant. With only the prospect of more enemies to kill in his mind, he turned and headed toward the square. He told himself that he had no time to pick his way through the winding streets and marched straight ahead, continuing to cut through every obstacle with the Sword of Bheleu.

It took a severe conscious effort to restrain himself when he reached the first of the occupied houses, but he managed it; from that point on, he found his way through the streets, forcing down the bloodlust, forcing himself to be calm. Koros followed him placidly, undisturbed by the sword's fiery displays of power and seemingly indifferent to the route it followed.

Garth was still a few short blocks from the market, his anger faded to insignificance under the steady pressure of his will, when he heard the wailing begin.

It was an eerie sound, a wavering, high-pitched note that went on and on interminably. It sounded like a human voice, but not quite natural, somehow; it grated on his nerves and made him feel uneasy, despite the aura of invincibility the sword bestowed upon him.

If it was a human voice, Garth told himself, then whoever was wailing had to be in a state of indescribable emotional upset. He had heard men scream and bellow and whimper, but he had never heard a wailing like this. It was not a scream or an ordinary cry; it had no words, no rhythm, no break in the constant stream of sound.

Unsettled, he hurried forward, Koros following at his heels.

He entered the marketplace from the northwest, waving for Koros to stay back out of the way, and found himself at the rear of a silent crowd. The wailing came from somewhere on the far side, near the door of Saram's house.

He glanced back, to be sure that Koros was staying behind; it was standing in the mouth of the street and glancing about as if the sound made it uneasy, too. Reassured that the warbeast would cause no trouble, Garth peered over the heads of the gathered humans.

Something dark was hanging in the open doorway of the Baron's house; shadows and distance hid the details, but Garth felt a sick certainty that this was the Aghadite surprise. The crowd faced toward the thing in the doorway, but had left an empty semicircle around it, and the wailing seemed to emanate, not from the house, but from somewhere in that semicircle.

Determined to find out what was happening, Garth marched forward and began shoving his way through the crowd; people parted readily when they saw him and almost seemed to be hurrying him onward. He crossed the square as quickly as if it were empty and emerged at last into the little cleared area.

He found there that the wailing was coming from Frima, who knelt facing the door of her home, her head thrown back, her arms limp at her sides, her eyes shut and her mouth open, pouring forth her grief.

Garth would not have guessed that such a sound could come from a lone woman, particularly one as small as Frima; he stared at her in helpless astonishment for several seconds before thinking to look up at the cause of her despair.

The ghastly thing that hung suspended in the doorway by its outstretched arms was all that remained of Saram, Baron of Skelleth. His wrists had been nailed to the doorframe with heavy metal spikes. His eyes were gone, leaving bloody sockets, and more blood spilled from his open, tongueless mouth. The front of his embroidered robe had been cut away and strips had been peeled from his chest, forming four red runes that spelled out AGHAD.

Grief and rage mingled with a feeling of helplessness before such savagery; Garth felt a need to do something, anything, to react to this new abomination, to help the woman who knelt, keening, before him. Fighting down a boiling wave of anger, he suppressed the urge to send forth white-hot flame to destroy everything before him. That would do no good, he told himself; it would only leave Frima still more bereft.

"You," he called, pointing at the nearest man who looked strong enough to be of use, "get him down from there!"

The man hesitated; Garth growled and lifted the Sword of Bheleu. "Help him," Garth ordered, pointing to two more villagers. "You women, prepare a place for him to lie." He spotted Saram's housekeeper in the crowd and called to her, "Find something to dress him in!"

The villagers did not move quickly enough to please him; he struggled against the urge to blast them all. Frima's keening bit through him, adding to his irritation, until he could not tolerate it further. He reached down, grabbed her shoulder roughly, and dragged her to her feet.

She refused to stand on her own; he supported her with one hang as he barked at her, "Listen to me, woman!"

Her wailing died away as the overman shook her; her head fell forward and her eyes opened, but then fixed on her husband's mutilated corpse. She did not speak and would not meet Garth's gaze.

"Listen to me!" Garth insisted. "Your husband is dead; there is nothing that anyone can do about that. It does no good to bewail his death like this. You do yourself only harm by kneeling here and screaming."

Frima hung limply in his grasp, and a sympathetic murmur ran through the crowd. The villagers were all watching intently every second of the drama taking place in their midst.

"Stand on your feet, woman! Do not let the scum who did this see how much they have hurt you!"

Frima met Garth's eyes for an instant, then turned her gaze back to the doorway. The man Garth had chosen was trying to pry out a spike, using a knife someone had handed him. He was making a mess of the wooden frame, but carefully avoiding any contact between the blade and Saram's dead flesh.

The Dûsarran swallowed and twisted her dangling feet about so that she could stand. Garth loosened his grip, and she did not collapse.

"The cult of Aghad has killed your husband and vilely abused his body; stand strong now so that they will not have harmed his dignity as well," Garth muttered in Frima's ear.

She nodded.

"You are the Baroness of Skelleth," Garth reminded her quietly. "You must behave accordingly."

Frima nodded again, then demanded hoarsely, "Where are they?"

Startled, Garth asked, "What?"

"Where are the filth who murdered him?"

"I don't know," Garth admitted. "I killed one of them just a few moments ago, when he came to boast to me of this latest crime, but there must have been others. I have sworn to destroy them all when I find them, and the temples and shrines of their foul god with them."

"I'm coming with you," Frima said.

"There is no need," Garth told her. "Saram's death will be avenged. I swore to destroy the cult for what it did to Kyrith, and this new butchery strengthens my resolve beyond what I can express in words. I will make them all pay for this."

"I am coming with you," Frima insisted. "They killed my man."

Garth thought it best to shift the grounds for argument. "You still live, my lady, and are still the Baroness of Skelleth. You have other concerns."

"They don't matter. Are there any Aghadites in Skelleth, or will you be going to Dûsarra?"

The first spike came free, and the men struggling with it hurried to catch Saram's body as it fell. While two held the corpse, a third began working on the other spike.

"I don't know where they are," Garth replied, "but I will find them."

"We will find them."

Garth could not think of any good way to deal with this. He turned from the intense, fixed stare that Frima was giving him and watched as the workers freed Saram's other wrist.

They stood for a moment holding their lord's body, uncertain what to do next.

"Take him inside," Garth said. "The housekeeper will find a place for him."

Two of the men earned the corpse out of sight while the third closed the doors.

Reluctant to meet Frima's gaze again, Garth looked about and realized that the market was still crowded with onlookers. A surge of irrational anger at their gawking boiled up within him.

"Go home, you people!" he called. "There is nothing more to see!"

He was answered with muffled voices and shuffling feet, but the villagers seemed reluctant to depart.

"Go away, I said!" he bellowed, raising the Sword of Bheleu in one hand. The blade glowed white, crackling with chained energy, and the crowd melted away rapidly before the implied threat. In a moment the square was empty of all save the overman, the new widow, and the warbeast that waited at the northwest corner.

Garth glanced about again, trying to decide what to do with Frima; he did not think it would be wise to send her home, into the house where her husband's mangled corpse waited. He was unsure how humans dealt with the deaths of those they loved.

"Are there any rites you must perform?" he asked.

"No," she replied. "We don't bother with fancy funerals in Dûsarra. When the other cults kill someone, the body usually isn't found; we grieve, but hold no ceremonies. The people of Skelleth can attend to the ceremonies. We have to go avenge him." She looked about the square and noticed Koros, waiting patiently, at ease now that the keening had stopped. Without hesitation, she slipped from under Garth's hand and began walking unsteadily across the marketplace toward the warbeast.

Garth followed. He could easily have stopped her, but was not sure how she would react.

Halfway across the square, she stumbled; he lunged forward and caught her before she fell. They stood for a moment while she regained her balance.

"Garth," someone called, in a hideous dry croak.

The voice was instantly recognizable. Garth turned, astonished, and saw the Forgotten King standing in the doorway of the King's Inn, the Book of Silence tucked under one arm.

"There are no worshippers of Aghad in Skelleth," the old man said. "Their transporting spells are not affected by distance; they have been striking directly from their temple in Dûsarra."

Garth stood dumbfounded by this unexpected speech. He knew that the Forgotten King never volunteered information without a reason.

"Then we have to go to Dûsarra," Frima said calmly.

The Forgotten King nodded, moving his head very slightly beneath the concealing hood of his robe.

"Why are you telling us this?" Garth asked.

"So that you will not waste time."

"Will you swear it to be true, by The God Whose Name Is Not Spoken, at the cost of all oaths I have made to you if you lie?" Garth could think of nothing more binding; he knew that the old man would not be eager to give up the vows Garth had sworn. He was startled by his own cleverness in coming up with such a promise so readily; his thoughts had not been very clear of late.

"I swear it," the King replied.

Garth looked at the shadows that hid the old man's eyes, and at the firm line of his mouth, set in dry, wrinkled skin above the thin white beard that trailed from his chin. He glanced at Frima, who was obviously waiting for him to accompany her in pursuit of revenge, and at Koros, still standing patiently, and finally at the Sword of Bheleu, which dangled from his right hand, its tip almost dragging in the dust of the market, the red gem in its pommel flickering faintly. He still did not know why the Forgotten King should volunteer such information. Perhaps, he thought, the old man was eager to get the sword back, lest it gain too strong a hold upon Garth; he would want the overman to go about his errand as quickly as possible, so that the sword's return would not be delayed. That would be in Garth's own interest as well.

"Very well," he said at last. "Then I will go to Dûsarra and I will destroy the cult of Aghad there. I swore I would and I will honor that oath. But I go alone."

"No!" Frima cried. "I'm coming with you!"

"I do not want to endanger you, Frima, and the journey will be very dangerous. You must stay in Skelleth." His major concern was that the Sword of Bheleu might usurp control of him and cause him to kill any traveling companions, but he did not care to explain that. It would be too much like admitting weakness to say that he feared he would be unable to control his own body.

"I have to avenge Saram! There's nothing I want in Skelleth. Besides, you'll need a guide; you don't know your way around Dûsarra as I do. I grew up there."

"No," Garth began, but before he could continue, Frima interrupted.

"Besides, do you think I'm safe here? You heard what the old man said; the Aghadites can strike anywhere, and they've just heard you say that you don't want me hurt. I'm a target now. If you don't take me with you, I'll follow you on my own."

The overman looked at the human's face and decided that she meant what she said. She had a good point about being in danger in Skelleth, and also about her utility as a guide. She would certainly be safer guarded by Koros and himself than trying to traverse Nekutta on her own.

"Very well," he said. "We will go by way of Ur-Dormulk, however; I have something I must do there." The monster had waited too long already. Garth found himself wondering how he could have delayed so long.

"All right," Frima agreed.

"We'll need supplies," Garth said, his practical instincts coming to the fore.

"We can forage on the way," Frima replied. "I don't want to wait."

"I will provide for your needs," the Forgotten King said.

Startled, Garth turned to look at him. "You will? From here?"

The old man moved his head to one side, then the other, in so brief and smooth a movement that it could hardly be described as shaking his head.

"I will come with you," he said.

Chapter Nineteen

As the little party made its way toward Ur-Dormulk, Garth found himself feeling that he had been rushed into action against his will. He had not intended to dash so precipitously out of Skelleth. Within half an hour of discovering Saram's death he had ridden out the southwestern gate, Frima perched behind him, the Forgotten King walking alongside.

He told himself that every minute saved meant that much less destruction the monster in Ur-Dormulk could cause, and that he had already wasted far too much time destroying empty ruins. Still, he felt unprepared and harried.

Thinking back, he wondered at his own willingness to delay in order to knock down buildings, compared with the insistent hurry of both his companions. He suspected that the sword had had something to do with his dawdling, and also with his eagerness to come to grips with the Aghadite assassins. Whatever the cause, he had behaved stupidly.

If he had not delayed, the cultists might not have bothered to kill Saram. He was sure that Saram had been alive when he slew the first two assassins. Had he left Skelleth immediately, the Aghadites might not have returned and the Baron might still be alive and well, his wife secure and happy at home, rather than perched on a warbeast seeking revenge. Instead of leaving, though, Garth had gone smashing about the ruins, wasting time and giving the worshippers of Aghad the chance to carry out another of their ghastly murders.

Could it be, he asked himself, that Bheleu had diverted him intentionally, to further the cause of his brother deity? Might Aghad himself have affected him somehow? Or had it just been the workings of chance?

Had the Forgotten King been involved? He had certainly appeared in the doorway at an opportune moment, with exactly the information that would send Garth and Frima on their way without hesitation.

The overman glanced to the left, where the yellow-clad figure strode along as smoothly and silently as the warbeast itself. The Book of Silence was still held under the old man's right arm, and Garth reminded himself that the totem was what enabled the King to travel freely. He would no longer need an overman to run his errands for him.

What benefit could the old man have gained from Saram's death? For that matter, what could Aghad or Bheleu gain from it? Garth would have gone to Dûsarra soon enough without this added impetus, and the King could have accompanied him or followed him. Saram's murder had increased his hatred of the cultists, if that was possible, and had impelled Frima to accompany him, but that was little enough. What good would it do anyone to have Saram's widow come along? How much difference could the increase in his fury make?

Garth could see no purpose in it and concluded, reluctantly, that it had been chance, rather than manipulation, that had led to the Baron's murder. That meant that his own weakness in yielding to the whim to search the ruins had been the indirect cause; he was at fault. Once again he had brought destruction, this time to an innocent friend.

The cult of Aghad would pay for that, he promised himself, and if he could ever contrive to accomplish it, the gods themselves, both Aghad and Bheleu, would suffer as well for what they had done to him.

He rode on, silently mulling this over.

Haggat watched the little group as best he could, trying desperately to think of some way of diverting them. He could not focus the scrying glass on Garth while the overman held the Sword of Bheleu, nor on the old man in yellow at all; he had to satisfy himself by following the warbeast's pawprints, or by close scrutiny, just barely possible despite the sword's influence, of the girl's face and the reflections in her eyes of the surrounding countryside.

The high priest had thought that Garth would be searching Skelleth for days, time which the cult could have used to lay false trails and arrange diversions; instead he had set out immediately, and there could be little doubt that he was bound for Dûsarra.

Haggat did not understand what had happened. Something was interfering with his plans. He suspected that it was the mysterious old man. The overman had apparently spoken with him in the market and decided then and there to leave Skelleth without further delay.

Who, Haggat wondered, *was* the man? He could be glimpsed only briefly, and even then not clearly, in the glass; most of what Haggat knew of him came from the reports of spies or from his occasional reflection in windows and in the eyes of others. Once before he had become involved in the cult's affairs, when he had put an end to the carefully contrived battle between Garth and the Council of the Most High, saving the lives of several councilors and taking the Sword of Bheleu away from the overman. That had apparently worked to the cult's benefit in the long run, though its followers had been slow to take advantage of it, by rendering Garth vulnerable and by allowing them to track down, rob, and murder several of the surviving wizards.

Now, though, the old man had given the overman back the sword and seemed to be leading him in his attack on the sect.

That was not to be borne.

All three of the party would have to be killed. The cult could neither afford further delays nor waste time on any more such pleasant preliminaries as the murders of Garth's wife and the Baron of Skelleth.

Only four of each variety of transporting crystal remained in the cult's cache of magic; they were not to be squandered. Furthermore, the Sword of Bheleu was a formidable protection against any assault, magical or mundane.

Haggat could not afford another failure. He glanced at the scarred face of his personal acolyte; he was well aware that she would be glad to replace him as high priest, should he allow the cult's prestige to suffer.

He needed to think out exactly what to do. He recalled all too well that, three years earlier, the full power of the Council of the Most High had been unable to do anything against the might of the overman and his damned sword.

Some time did remain, however; the journey from Skelleth to Dûsarra was at least a ten-day ride. Perhaps his best course would be to use every moment of that time to prepare an ambush.

At any rate, although he would want to keep a careful eye on the progress of the approaching party, Haggat decided that he would not waste any of the cult's hoard of magic in tormenting them along the way, nor in abortive attacks that the Sword of Bheleu could easily counter. At least, he would not do so until he had devised something more subtle and effective than a direct assault.

Perhaps the three would lower their guard if left alone, he thought, or would decide that Garth had killed all the cultists involved in the murders after all and turn back.

Haggat wondered again who the old man was and why he had given the sword back to the overman.

As he first came within sight of the walls of Ur-Dormulk, Garth was surprised to see motion along the battlements. The distance was such that he knew he could not be observing any ordinary patrolling sentries, nor even major troop movements.

When the party drew nearer he realized that he was seeing the head of the monstrous creature, projecting above the ramparts; the movement was its impatient marching back and forth. The wizards had obviously not succeeded in driving it into the lake.

The slope below the walls was still thick with people, though they had spread out considerably from their earlier close-packed arrangement. Tents had been erected, made from robes or overcloaks draped across walking sticks or scraps of wood. The perimeter was still patrolled by brass-helmeted guardsmen; more soldiers were posted along the base of the wall and clustered around the gate, their metal headgear gleaming in the midday sun. The sparse grass of the hillside had vanished into the dirt beneath the tread of so many feet.

The great beast prowled behind the battlements, but the people seemed to pay it little heed; they had already grown accustomed to their situation. Garth wondered at that.

He also wondered why the monster stayed behind the wall when it was obviously eager to leave the city. Surely, he thought, it was capable of breaking through the stone barrier, as it had broken out of its own chamber and had broken apart the buildings of the city.

Then he remembered the long slope on the other side of the wall. The creature might be unable to climb it; the natural barrier could confine it, where the man-made one could not.

There were also the two wizards. Garth saw no sign of them; they had plainly been unable to drive the leviathan into either of the lakes, let alone destroy it, but perhaps they were able to keep it from breaking out of the city.

That assumed that they hadn't been squashed in their attempts to defeat the thing.

The soldiers posted around the ramshackle encampment saw the party approaching while it was still some distance away. That was hardly surprising; the mounted overman, towering far above the tallest of the crops that lined the roadsides, was visible for a thousand yards or more across the flat plain. Had the guards not seen him, they would have been derelict in their duties.

Garth knew he had been seen, but was unconcerned. He had no need for stealth; he had come to perform a vital service this time. He watched as soldiers ran hither and yon, obviously carrying news of his coming up to the gate, and orders back down in response. A party began to form on the road, presumably to greet him and his companions, and to stop them if necessary.

In keeping with his idea of the dignity appropriate to his position, Garth pretended not to notice them, but rode directly forward, head held high, until he came within a dozen yards.

At that point he deigned to react visibly to the presence of an obstruction in his path and spoke a command to the warbeast. Koros could, he knew, have gone straight through the little cluster of men without even slowing down, whether they resisted or not, but that would scarcely have been diplomatic. Instead, at his order, the warbeast stopped dead, and Garth stared balefully at the party before him.

He felt a twinge of familiar bloodlust, an urge to order Koros forward and strike out with the Sword of Bheleu, but he fought it down.

"Greetings," he said.

An officer with a golden plume on his helmet replied, "Greetings, overman."

"May I pass?"

"That depends. As you can see, the situation in Ur-Dormulk is very unsettled at present." The man gestured, taking in the crowded hillside. "A monster," he said with a wave toward the ramparts, "has driven us from our homes. What business brings you here?"

"I have come to rid you of this troublesome creature."

The officer stared up at Garth for a moment, then looked down, turned to one of his men, and muttered, "He's mad."

The soldier nodded agreement. Garth wondered just how poor human hearing was; he had made out the remark without straining.

There was a pause in the conversation; the officer was obviously considering how best to handle an insane overman. He glanced at Garth again, then said, "Forgive me for the delay, overman, but I must confer with my superiors."

"Soldier," said a croaking, hideous voice. Startled, the officer seemed to notice the presence of the Forgotten King, standing beside the warbeast, for the first time.

"Let us pass," the old man said. "What harm can it do if the overman wishes to destroy himself?"

The officer stared for a second, then turned away, uncomfortable with looking at the King. He shrugged. "As you say, old man. Go on, then."

Garth was at least as startled by the old man's intervention as the soldier had been. The Forgotten King was becoming positively chatty, it appeared. He wondered if this was a result of traveling, of leaving his familiar surroundings, or was perhaps some side-effect of possessing the Book of Silence. Perhaps the seeming nearness of his long-sought goal had cheered him out of his usual gloomy taciturnity.

If so, he would be disappointed, because Garth had no intention of aiding the old man any further.

The party of soldiers divided in half, allowing the warbeast and its two riders to pass between, and the Forgotten King to follow in the animal's wake. Garth urged Koros forward. Behind him, he could feel Frima shifting uncomfortably.

The officer signaled, and the two groups of soldiers marched alongside, escorting the overman and his party to the city gates.

Once there, they were passed over into the care of another officer and his own command of a dozen green-garbed men, who guided the travelers through the double gates and to the top of the staircase that led down into Ur-Dormulk.

Garth stopped his mount at that point. The soldiers hurriedly departed and closed the gate behind them, leaving the overman and his companions inside the city, face to face with the monster.

The creature was watching the new arrivals with dull interest showing on its immense and ugly face. It stood a hundred yards or so to the north, at the far side of a block of buildings it had trampled flat, and at the foot of the slope below the wall.

Garth looked out over the city and was appalled by what he saw. The monster had torn up or smashed down a significant portion of the buildings, leaving a crisscrossing maze of rubble. Once or twice, Garth saw, it had broken through the streets and cellars into the crypts, leaving great pits partially filled with the remains of the structures that had stood above them. A dozen fires flickered in the daylight, combining with others less visible to draw thirty or forty lines of smoke across the sky.

He was relieved to see no corpses in the streets and no circling carrion birds; the people of Ur-Dormulk had apparently had sufficient time to escape. Nonetheless, the destruction was startling and saddening; less than a week before, he had stood in the same spot and seen an intact and vigorous city where he now saw ruins.

What made it worse was that his own actions had caused this. He had been responsible for freeing the monster.

He turned back to face his foe. It was still standing and studying him; it had not moved.

He paused, unsure just how he was going to deal with the creature. He was quite certain that the sword had the raw power necessary to kill the thing, but he had not decided how best that power might be applied.

Probably, he thought, it would be wise to approach the monster on foot. He turned away and dismounted, a bit awkwardly due to Frima's presence on the back of the saddle.

Reminded of the Dûsarran's existence, he considered what to do with her and decided to leave her where she was, astride Koros. The warbeast was the best protection she could possibly have, short of Garth himself.

He glanced up at her; she sat motionlessly and stared back, her lips drawn tight. The hurried, high-speed trip from Skelleth had told on her, Garth was sure; she was obviously tired, but still determined. She said nothing.

Garth shrugged and looked about; he realized for the first time that the Forgotten King was not close at hand. Startled, he spotted the old man at the foot of the steps, walking calmly down the avenue and into the shattered heart of the city.

The overman stared after him for a moment, then turned away. The old man could take care of himself; it was not Garth's concern if he went off on his own. Garth reached up and pulled the Sword of Bheleu from where it had been strapped onto the warbeast's harness, along Koros' flank.

Immediately the blade flared up into a bright white glow, and the red gem in the hilt dripped crimson fire; Garth felt a surge of joyous strength, of riotous enthusiasm and vigor. He had not been wholly free of the sword during the journey, but now its power washed over him unhindered. He threw his head back and roared with laughter. The King, Saram's widow, and the warbeast were all forgotten; nothing mattered but the sword, its power, and his intended target.

Frima watched the blazing sword with apprehension; she was exhausted from the ride, still dazed with the shock of her husband's death, and slightly nauseated, but alert enough to recognize the danger the weapon represented. She slid to the front of the saddle and leaned forward, ready to command Koros to carry her to safety, should Garth appear to be running amok.

On the city's ramparts, struggling to maintain the warding spells that kept the monster from climbing up the slope and smashing the wall, Chalkara and Shandiph were suddenly startled by a vivid flash of white light somewhere off to their left. As they glanced at each other in surprise, the sound of inhuman laughter reached them.

"What's that?" Chalkara asked.

"I don't have any idea," Shandiph replied. "I think we had better investigate."

Hesitantly, Chalkara nodded in agreement. The two abandoned the pentangle they had etched in glowing blue on the stone of the battlements and leaned out between the nearest merlons.

Garth, or whatever was using Garth's body, saw them but paid no attention; he was interested only in the monster.

Frima glimpsed a lock of Chalkara's hair as it blew out from the wall for a moment, but mistook it for a military banner accidentally left flying.

The creature itself stood motionless, as if hypnotized, watching the overman with the glowing sword march diagonally down the steps toward it. It seemed unaware of the two wizards who had done so much to thwart it.

When Garth judged that he was close enough, standing on level ground not far from the bottom step and perhaps a dozen yards from the monster's gigantic feet, he raised the sword, gathered his will and the sword's energy, and sent flame ravening forth.

The glare blinded the wizards temporarily; they moved cautiously back, feeling their way, blinking and trying to restore their vision.

Frima, too, blinked and turned her head aside, but could not retreat out of sight so easily. She was farther away and had not been looking directly at the sword; when the initial flare had faded somewhat, she looked back, peering between two close-set fingers, and watched.

The first burst of fire caught the monster full in the chest and splashed upward around its chin; any sound it might have made was lost in the roar of the flames.

Frima, squinting, could see little detail, but it seemed to her that the flame was not so much burning anything as it was washing away the monster's flesh, like a spray of water washing away mud. Swirls of fire spattered in every direction, setting the air shimmering with heat and creating howling, fiery whirlwinds that seemed to pull and tear at the monster's limbs.

The creature clutched at its chest, and the flame swept across its claws, scorching away the talons, melting away their substance and leaving bare bone.

The monster staggered, leaned forward, but did not fall; it was as if the torrent of pale fire pouring from the sword were supporting the leviathan even as it destroyed it.

Its eyes had lost their glowing appearance at the first flash of the sword's power, paling in comparison to the weapon's glare, and now, as Frima watched, the yellow orbs glazed over. The monster was obviously dying, but could not fall.

The flames subsided for an instant, and Frima saw that the creature's lower jaw had been stripped clean of its flesh, leaving gleaming bone that shone white in the sword's bleached, colorless light. No blood or ichor flowed; the heat had cauterized wherever the fire touched.

The girl shuddered at the thought of the pain the thing must be feeling, if it were mortal enough to feel pain at all; her stomach twisted in empathy. Then, as she watched, the behemoth finally fell, not so much forward as into itself, the neck collapsing, the skull sliding down into the cavity where its chest had once been.

She turned away, sickened, while Garth continued to spew forth the sword's destructive fury, stripping meat from bone, wiping the monster out of existence.

Frima closed her eyes against the light and refused to look back. Worn out by the long ride and the ghastly events that had befallen her, she dozed fitfully, leaning forward on the warbeast's neck, her gaze averted and her eyes closed.

On the city ramparts, it was several minutes after the initial flash before the two wizards could see again, and even then they dared not return to their earlier vantage point, for the white glow brightened and dimmed erratically as Garth wielded the sword.

When at last the light died away completely, Chalkara advanced cautiously to the break, motioning for Shandiph to stay where he was.

Although the light was gone, she was almost blinded anew by flying dust; a fine gray powder was being whipped about by a small but powerful whirlwind, forcing her to turn away and wipe her eyes clear with a corner of her sleeve.

She looked at the residue that clung to the fabric; it was white ash.

Wary this time, she again approached the opening and leaned out, squinting to protect her eyes.

She saw no sign of the monster. The whirlwind was dying down, and the swirling cloud of ash that it carried was slowly subsiding. Blinking, her eyes watering painfully, Chalkara looked down to see what remained of the overman and where the monster's trail led.

Garth was still where she had last seen him, but rather than standing with the glowing sword raised, he was kneeling, leaning heavily on the hilt of a sword that Chalkara did not recognize at first as being the same weapon. This sword was black, from the obsidianlike stone in its pommel to the midpoint of its tarnished blade; the remainder of the blade, from midpoint to tip, was buried in a mound of debris that held the weapon upright. The overman's arms were draped across the quillons, his eyes half-closed, his mouth half-open; a perfect portrait of exhaustion.

Where the monster had stood was only the seething ash; Chalkara stared at it, puzzled. As the cloud sank, something white protruded from its heart, and the wizard realized with a shock that it was the end of an immense thighbone.

Fascinated and repulsed, Chalkara watched as the dust cloud sank down to nothing, revealing a pile of dry, white bones, half-buried in ash, that were obviously all that remained of the leviathan that had terrorized the city. The upper portion of the skull stared with empty sockets at the afternoon sky from atop the heap, a few of the longer bones leaning up against it; with the great teeth buried in ash, and the broken-tipped horn lost in a tangle of ribs, it seemed almost pitiable.

"Shandi," she called.

The older wizard joined her and stared down, as fascinated as she.

"I think we should leave," she said.

He didn't answer.

"I think we should get out of Ur-Dormulk and not let anything stop us this time. We should get out of here and keep away from anywhere else Garth is likely to be."

Shandiph nodded, blinking away an errant flake of ash.

"We can visit Kholis, but I think we should keep going – head south, perhaps. Maybe to Yesh. They worship different gods in Yesh. Maybe Bheleu has no power there."

"The gods are the gods, Chala; only their names change."

"How do you know that? It's worth trying, isn't it?"

"Yes, it's worth trying. You're right. It's certainly better than staying here; I've been in one place too long. It's time I wandered again."

"It's time we both wandered. I don't think I care to be Chalkara of Kholis anymore; I don't think it's safe. Chalkara the Wanderer sounds better."

Shandiph nodded again. He did not believe that anywhere was safe, but thought better of saying so.

Chapter Twenty

Garth was not aware of having lost consciousness, but he realized from the altered light that he must have. It had been shortly after noon when he had attacked the monster, with the sun bright overhead, and now the sun was in the west, the shadows as long as the things that cast them. He had been standing, and now he knelt, leaning upon something. The sword had been hot in his hands, and now his hands hung empty, the palms stinging with mild burns. The pain reminded him of the various injuries he had received during his first visit to Ur-Dormulk, and he realized they were gone; he had forgotten until now that the Sword of Bheleu had healing properties as well as destructive ones.

He blinked and leaned back, off whatever had been supporting him. He felt drained, but managed to rise to his feet only through a concerted effort. Once he was upright he looked about, trying to assess his situation.

He had been draped across the hilt of the Sword of Bheleu, which was burned black and thrust two feet or so into a pile of dirt and ash. He stood now in a wide circle that had been blasted flat and carpeted with fine gray ash, extending from the bottommost step of the climb to the wall out across most of a city block. Its even surface was broken by three things: himself, the mound that held the sword, and a great heap of ash and bone that sprawled across the farther side, directly in front of him.

The bones were unbelievably large; had he never seen the monster whence they came, he would have been certain that they were fakes made of stone or plaster. A thighbone that leaned up against the half-buried skull was taller than he, and as thick through as he was in full padded armor.

Whatever else they might be, the bones were clear proof that he had succeeded in the task he had set himself. The monster was destroyed.

Furthermore, he was free of the Sword of Bheleu, and this without the Forgotten King's intervention. Destroying the leviathan had at last burned out the sword's power – though only temporarily, he was sure. Even now he thought he could see a faint stirring in the black gem, a distant flickering of dull red.

He was not sure whether he wanted to keep the sword or not; he stepped back out of easy reach to consider the matter.

He still intended to take his vengeance upon the cult of Aghad, and it was undeniable that the sword would be useful against the god's followers – but it was also true that the weapon had a continuing influence on his thoughts and behavior, despite Bheleu's acceptance of his terms. He did not know whether the god was attempting to deceive him or was unable to prevent the effects, but he was quite certain that it had been the god of destruction, and not Garth himself, who had wanted to go walking off through the ruins in Skelleth, blasting everything in sight, while the monster trampled Ur-Dormulk. He was convinced that the god had influenced his thinking and his actions, and he did not like that idea.

He stood a few steps away, at the edge of the flattened circle, staring at the sooty sword and trying to decide what he should do. A faint rustling attracted his attention.

Startled, he turned to see the Forgotten King standing three paces away on the worn stone pavement of the nearest street. The old man's tattered yellow mantle flapped in the damp breeze that blew from the lakes, his cowl pulled well forward about his face, a bundle wrapped in black silk beneath his right arm.

The bundle caught the overman's, attention immediately. The Book of Silence had not been wrapped up, and this thing was irregularly shaped and larger than the neat rectangle the book alone would form.

"What's that?" he asked.

The Forgotten King ignored his question and stood watching.

Garth glanced back at the Sword of Bheleu and then at the bundle again.

"What have you got under your arm?" he asked. He had a suspicion that he knew what it was, and a cold knot of dismay formed within him.

"Are you done with my sword?" the old man asked. His awful voice seemed to blend with the wind that stirred in the rubble, but that made it no less horrible.

Without meaning to, Garth replied, "No!" He paused; the King gazed calmly, expectantly, at him out of his shaded and invisible eyes.

Garth looked away, at the heap of bones, at the sword itself, at the devastated cityscape and the high slope that led to the city wall. He saw no cheer anywhere, only destruction or failed protections. The monster's release and its death had both been his responsibility, and he felt sickened by the resulting chaos. He did not want to allow more of the same, but he was unsure how best he might prevent it.

The dangers of taking up the sword again were obvious; he had lived with that before. He had forgotten in his years of freedom what the hold and the power of the sword were like; he knew now that he would never be able to restrain completely Bheleu's personality while he drew upon the god's power, and that he could not carry the sword without wielding it.

On the other hand, he did not want the King to have the sword. He was certain it was necessary to the magic the old man planned, magic that, Garth was sure, would bring on the Fifteenth Age and spread death throughout the world, even if it did not actually bring time to an end. Garth tended to think that the spell would destroy the world itself. Therefore, as long as Garth kept the sword away from the King, he was preventing such a disaster – but would instead find himself compelled into destructive acts of his own on a lesser scale.

He remembered that he had previously excused himself for bringing the old man the Book of Silence on the grounds that the King would not have the sword or the Pallid Mask and would therefore be unable to bring about the Age of Death – yet now that bundle was tucked under the King's arm, and Garth was sure of what it held.

That, he was certain, was the Pallid Mask. The chosen of the god of death had reclaimed his master's totem.

To give that person the Sword of Bheleu as well would be to give him all the power and every tool he might need. That was obviously unconscionable. Arriving at that conclusion, Garth started to reach for the sword.

He paused with his arm outstretched. Could he be sure he was doing the right thing? He was acting on a series of assumptions and deductions. He had no objective proof that the Forgotten King intended to destroy the world and needed only these three items to accomplish that goal.

He quickly reviewed what he knew. The King had admitted that his magic would cause many deaths. Further, the old man had expressed interest in the Sword of Bheleu. Garth did not know that the sword was actually a necessary component of the King's great magic, but it seemed almost certain. He knew that the King was the chosen of The God Whose Name Is Not Spoken, of Death incarnate. He knew that the wizards said that the next age, the Fifteenth Age, was to be dominated by the Final God. He knew that it was said that the Forgotten King could die only at the end of time, and that the old man said he wanted to die.

It all added up. Garth still could not know that he was right, but he made his decision. A period of such destruction as the Sword of Bheleu might cause, even as much as thirty years of it, could not possibly be worse than the end of time itself and the accompanying extinction of all life. He grasped the hilt of the sword.

The gem flared up redly, and the blade seemed to move of its own volition as it slid from the heap of debris. White light flashed, and the soot that had coated it vanished, leaving the blade gleaming silver, the jewel glowing the color of fresh blood. A wave of heat swept over the overman.

The Forgotten King watched silently, and the initial burst of warmth and bloodlust passed away quickly beneath his cold stare. Garth stared back, the sword in his hands. He knew that Bheleu had again tried to assert himself, but had backed down before the threat of the King's power. Garth realized that he could control the sword only as long as he remained near the King, keeping that threat viable. Were he to become separated from the old man, Bheleu would be able to dominate him easily.

He was, he saw, trapped, worse than he had ever been before. He needed to keep the sword to prevent the King from obtaining it, yet he also needed to remain near the King to prevent the sword from controlling him completely. He could not be sure that he would be able to prevent the King from taking the sword away from him, should the old man ever choose to exert his own considerable power, now augmented by both the Book of Silence and the Pallid Mask.

What was perhaps as disheartening as the situation itself was the knowledge that Garth had brought it on himself. He had chosen to go to Dûsarra and bring back the Sword of Bheleu. He had chosen to go to Ur-Dormulk and fetch the Book of Silence. He had willingly given the King the book, which had made it possible for the old man to move freely and get the Pallid Mask for himself.

Now Garth found himself in a precarious balance between the power of Bheleu and the power of the King, each determined to wreak havoc, with only Garth's refusal to cooperate preventing the unleashing of those powers.

Furthermore, he did not know if he could maintain that balance forever. In fact, he realized that he definitely could not, unless Bheleu, like The God Whose Name Is Not Spoken, bestowed immortality upon his chosen agent.

That was a possibility, as the god did seem to make Garth invincible and invulnerable, but it was not really an appealing prospect. Surely, the longer he held the sword, the greater Bheleu's control would become. The god was insidious.

Garth stared at the blade before him and understood that he was doomed. He could see no way out of his predicament, and if the theology of the humans was correct, insofar as he understood it, then there was no way out, no possible solution. His end, and the end of the world, were foreordained and could be no more than delayed – and then only for as long as he was willing to wield the Sword of Bheleu. Even a miracle would not change the terrible circumstances, for miracles were sent by the gods, and the most powerful of the gods were those who had trapped him. Ever since he had first consulted the Wise Women of Ordunin in his quest for eternal fame, he had been guided toward this hopeless situation; and furthermore, he realized, the Wise Women had known it. He recalled the reluctance Ao had displayed so long ago, when first she told him of the Forgotten King. Surely that had been because she had known what would, in the end, result.

He had not thought this through before, had not considered the long-term consequences of the events that surrounded and involved him. Now that he did, anger flared up within him.

He made a brief, desultory attempt to suppress it, knowing that it was as much Bheleu's doing as his own, but without success. He found himself furious, eager to lash out at something. The gods had brought him to this – Bheleu, Aghad, the Final God, and the other Lords of Dûs – but there was no way he could strike directly at any of them. The Forgotten King, too, had worked to enmesh him in the workings of destiny, to drive him and the world to destruction. He lifted the sword high and strode toward the old man, his anger mounting.

The King stood his ground as the overman approached, and even through the cloud of rage, Garth remembered his previous attempt to kill the old man with the Sword of Bheleu. He had been totally unable to harm him.

Still, as his fury grew, he found it impossible to believe that a weapon that could reduce so vast a monster to ash and bone could not kill a scrawny human. He slashed out viciously, aiming for the old man's throat.

The blade left a trail of sparks. Despite Garth's efforts to keep it on course, it sheered wildly upward, skimming over the Forgotten King's head.

Frustrated, Garth spun it back and struck again, this time slanting downward. Again the sword refused to cooperate, curving down and to the side, veering away from the old man without touching him.

Garth growled.

"Stop it, Garth," the old man said. "I am not so easily destroyed as Dhazh. You cannot do it like that."

The overman fell silent and lowered the sword, his red eyes flat and dead with rage. He could not kill the King any more than he could strike at the gods.

Perhaps he could strike at one god, though – not directly, of course, but through his followers. He struggled to think, but his mind seemed hazy and slow. He had already slaughtered the cult of Bheleu, when first he took the sword, and The God Whose Name Is Not Spoken had no servants except the King and one or two decrepit priests. But the cult of Aghad still flourished, and more than any other had driven him into his current predicament. He had sworn vengeance upon that god's worshippers, sworn to destroy them. Somewhere in Ur-Dormulk was a temple dedicated to Aghad, he remembered; he looked out across the battered city.

"Where is it?" he muttered, half to himself.

"What?" The Forgotten King's question was calm and indifferent.

"Where is the temple of Aghad?"

"The center of the cult is in Dûsarra."

"They have a temple here, in Ur-Dormulk. Where is it?"

"It is unimportant."

"Where is it?" Garth's tone was flat and dangerous. The King scarcely needed to beware of the overman's anger, but he chose not to argue further.

"I will show you," he replied. He turned and walked down the street.

Garth followed him through the ruins, through sections where buildings stood relatively undamaged, past smoking pits that had once been cellars or crypts, until the pair arrived in front of a low stone structure tucked up against one of the great outcroppings of rock that studded the city.

The King stopped and gestured at the nondescript building.

"This is it?" Garth asked. The temple was nothing like the one he had robbed in Dûsarra. There was no metal gate, no courtyard with poisoned fountain, no names etched in the stone walls, but a simple single story of weathered granite, with a few narrow windows that peered out, black and empty, upon the deserted streets. The windows flanked a heavy wooden door.

The King said nothing, but nodded once.

Reassured, his anger driving away any lingering doubts, Garth marched up to the entrance and swung the sword against it.

The heavy wooden door burst outward in a shower of splinters and dust, with a sound like sudden thunder.

Garth stepped through into a small, bare anteroom and looked about in the unlit gloom. Three other doors led further into the depths of the building; he chose one at random and smashed it down with the sword, sending shards rattling against the walls on all sides.

Beyond lay a small room hung in dark red and richly carpeted in soft gray; near the far wall stood a metal altar, and upon the altar lay a woman's corpse, partially disemboweled. Garth stepped closer.

A curtain plummeted down before him; with a growl, Garth hacked it apart in time to see the altar sink into the floor, taking the corpse with it.

This sort of mechanical trickery was similar, indeed almost identical, to what he had encountered in Dûsarra. Any further doubts he might have had were dispelled by his final glimpse of the dead body.

Runes had been carved into the woman's chest, four runes, spelling out AGHAD.

Satisfied that he had found the right place, Garth lashed out with the sword and blasted apart the sliding stone that moved into place to hide the sunken altar and its grisly burden. Without bothering to consider that the victim might deserve better, he then sent a burst of white flame that utterly consumed the corpse, leaving a thin layer of ash. That done, he set about serious destruction, shattering the ceiling and the roof beyond and working his way down the walls.

When at last he was satisfied that the job was done he stood at the bottom of a great pit, amid a heap of rubble, where no stone larger than a man's body remained and no stone stood intact upon another. He had found and destroyed hundreds of concealed machines and mechanisms, a dozen or so hidden bodies, a handful of dangerous beasts, and a vast armory equipped with everything from siege engines to endless shelves of varied poisons. The single floor aboveground had stood atop three levels of cellars and dungeons that extended out beneath the buildings on both sides and across the street into the house opposite.

Half a dozen doors led from the cellars into the crypts, but he did not bother to investigate those after blowing the doors themselves apart. He knew, even in his rage, that there was no point in destroying the entire system of crypts, and that to do so would mean destroying the entire city he had slain Dhazh to save. He drew the line at the point where the architecture and the texture of the stone changed, revealing the difference between the ancient buried tunnels and the far newer temple built to take advantage of them.

Nowhere in the entire structure were there any living humans.

In Dûsarra, Haggat watched, worried, as the temple in Ur-Dormulk crumbled. He was unable to focus his scrying glass on the overman or the sword and could not watch the destruction directly as a result, but he was able to see the remains. It distressed him to see so powerful an outpost of the cult, second only to its heart in Dûsarra, reduced so quickly to worthless rubble, but he knew he could do nothing to stop the demolition.

He could, however, save the cultists who had used the shrine. The overman's next step, obviously, would be to pick the Aghadites out of the crowd that waited outside the city gates and kill them; Haggat did not want that to happen. He abandoned the scrying glass for the moment, to order his disciples to send a message of warning.

When Garth climbed out of the hole he had made, he found the Forgotten King waiting, motionless, in the street.

"Are there any Aghadites in the city?" the overman demanded.

"No," the old man replied.

Garth was glad of that; he had not relished the thought of hunting them down in their hiding places, one by one. Far easier and more satisfying to blast the lot of them at once! He would divide them out from the crowd as the citizens were readmitted to the city, standing at the gate and stopping them as they passed. He did not consider how he would recognize them; he was sure he would manage it. The old man was apparently in a cooperative mood, having led him to the temple and now having answered his question directly; perhaps he would be willing to point them out.

There would be time for that later. His next step was to return to the gate and arrange with the authorities for permission to dispose of the Aghadites. It seemed a very minor demand to make in exchange for slaying the monster that had done so much damage to their city.

The sun was down, and Garth lit the way back to the gate with the glow from the Sword of Bheleu. Fires still flickered in the distance, but in a city so largely built of stone most were rapidly dying out.

Frima and Koros still waited atop the stairs at the gate, just as Garth had left them, save that Koros was now asleep and Frima awake. As a result of her rest, awkward as it had been to sleep in the saddle, she was alert and eager to pursue her vengeance against the worshippers of Aghad.

She had awakened feeling ill shortly before; after she had vomited, she had felt somewhat better and had noticed that Garth was missing. She had not been seriously concerned by his absence; she knew he would return for Koros, if for nothing else, and she had correctly concluded that he had gone in search of their common foe.

"Are there Aghadites in this city?" she asked as Garth and the Forgotten

King climbed the last few steps.

"No," the overman replied. "But there are many, I am sure, in the crowd outside the gates. I have just destroyed their temple here; now we must search them out from the other humans."

"No," the old man said unexpectedly. "They have fled."

"What?" Garth demanded. Frima stared silently.

"They are gone."

"They can't be," Garth insisted. "I have to kill them."

"They were warned magically and have fled."

"Are you sure?" Frima asked.

The King nodded.

"They're really gone? You swear it?" she persisted.

The King nodded again.

"Where did they go?" Garth asked.

The old man shrugged.

"To Dûsarra, perhaps?" Garth guessed.

The old man shrugged again.

"To Dûsarra, then," Garth said. Frima nodded agreement.

The conversation had awakened the warbeast; now, at the overman's urging, it turned and followed its master out the city gate and into the torchlit night beyond, where the people of Ur-Dormulk waited to reclaim their city.

Chapter Twenty-One

Garth and his companions stayed the night on the hillside by the gate, ignoring a thin drizzle that began around midnight. They kept a careful watch on the line of men, women, and children moving slowly back into the city, while guards stood nearby. A few reports came in of people who had vanished around sunset, wandering off in one direction or another, confirming the Forgotten King's claim that the Aghadites had been warned of their danger. The soldiers had generally not tried to prevent these people from crossing the perimeter; that was not what they had been posted for. Their orders were to keep dangers out, not to keep their own people in, and if a score or perhaps two dozen had chosen to depart for destinations unknown, it was no part of a soldier's duty to stop them. Garth, angry as he was at the escape of the Aghadites, had to admit that that was reasonable.

He and Frima, as well as large numbers of guardsmen, observed the whole re-entry operation, and nowhere did Garth see the dark red robes of the worshippers of Aghad. He knew, of course, that the cultists might well be disguised and that he had no reliable means of spotting them in the horde of muddy, bedraggled citizens who wound their way up the hill and through the gates. Still, he was sure that most, if not all, of those people reported missing had been the god's followers in Ur-Dormulk.

Around dawn, it was noticed that the two wizards could not be found. Garth wondered briefly if they might have been Aghadites, or whether they might have been devoured by the monster the Forgotten King called Dhazh, or whether they were simply lost somewhere. Eventually he decided that the matter did not concern him.

The overlord and his court had gathered in one particular area of the hillside and established themselves in charge of the return to the city, giving orders to the military and generally taking credit for the organization soldiers had imposed. This kept them busy running about, looking very out of place wearing their gaudy robes in the rain and mud. It seemed to Garth that such bright attire would look out of place anywhere other than in a palace – which might well have been exactly what was intended.

Despite the disappearance of the wizards there were enough witnesses, and enough evidence, to establish to the satisfaction of all concerned that Garth had, indeed, been responsible for the monster's destruction. The overlord's courtiers made at least a pretense of gratitude, confused and wet as they were, and their orders enabled the overman's little party to make a good breakfast from stocks of food brought out of the city by the more foresighted refugees. A fat sheep was found to feed the warbeast, and a few supplies were laid in for their coming journey, all at the city's expense. Someone even managed to dig up a sheath large enough to hold the Sword of Bheleu from an obscure armory in the city wall, and Garth strapped the weapon on his back rather than continuing to carry it naked in his hand.

Finally, at mid-morning, when Garth was convinced that it would do no good to watch the remaining population return to the ruined city, he and his party gathered themselves together and departed for Dûsarra.

By then the hillside was almost free of humanity, but had been left a littered expanse of churned mud, where makeshift tents flapped forlornly in the warm breeze.

Garth found himself alternately slipping and sinking in the muck, and rather than struggle on, he climbed astride Koros. The warbeast did not seem to notice the mud at all, and the Forgotten King walked on as smoothly and tirelessly as the beast. Frima had been in the saddle to begin with and stayed there, perched behind the overman.

Garth wondered idly for a moment how soon and how well the people of Ur-Dormulk would rebuild their homes. He doubted that any of them had ever had any experience in building; he had seen no structure in all the city that could have been less than several centuries old.

It occurred to him that it might not matter for long whether they rebuilt or not. If the world were to end, it would make little difference if the citizens of Ur-Dormulk died in the streets or beneath new roofs.

With that thought, his attention returned to his own situation, to the task that lay before him, and the presence and nature of the Forgotten King. He glared at the old man, without effect, and wished that he had never met him.

From Ur-Dormulk their route led southwest along the foothills, then west across a pass in the mountains into the land of Nekutta, across a broad valley, Around the southern end of another mountain range, and across another plain to the foothills of a third mountain range, this last one volcanic. There, perched on the side of a volcano, stood the black-walled city of Dûsarra, where the cult of Aghad was centered.

Dûsarra's name meant "gathering place of the dark gods," which was a fair description; each of the seven Lords of Dûs, despised elsewhere for the most part, had a major shrine there, serving as the center of his or her cult. In other lands the Dûs were considered to be wholly evil, and their worship an aberration, at best – though the more decadent and tolerant permitted that worship to continue, as it had in Ur-Dormulk.

In Dûsarra the dark gods were dominant; no other deities were worshipped, as far as Garth had been able to learn during his stay there or in discussions with Frima in the subsequent months, save for a few minor affiliated gods, such as Bheleu's son Koros, god of war, or Tema's servant Mei, goddess of the moon.

Elsewhere, people would have said that since the Lords of Dûs were evil, a society dedicated to them must also be evil and must therefore quickly destroy itself, by the very nature of evil, yet Dûsarra had survived for centuries, perhaps millennia. Garth was not sure how the Dûsarrans had managed it.

Garth's previous visit had brought fire and plague upon them, and at last report the city was in a state of chaos, yet the cult of Aghad remained active. Garth was not sure how to explain that, either – but he intended to put a stop to it.

From Ur-Dormulk, however, the journey to Dûsarra would require at least ten days.

It occurred to him that the Aghadites, with their teleporting magic, could cover the distance almost instantly and that the Forgotten King had pronounced their spells to be trivial. Did that mean, then, that the Sword of Bheleu, or the Book of Silence, or the Pallid Mask, or perhaps the King's own personal magic might serve the same purpose?

"King," he demanded without preamble, "can you transport us more quickly?"

The old man did not trouble himself to look up, but merely shook his head negatively.

Garth was not satisfied by that reply. It did not seem reasonable that this party should have such great magical power at their disposal, yet be unable to perform a feat the Aghadites managed with far feebler resources.

He recalled that the King had been confined to Skelleth for centuries and wondered if perhaps the old man wanted to see something of the world before attempting to destroy it and himself. The King was not making any visible effort to study the scenery, marching on steadily without turning his head, but it was a possibility.

Perhaps the powers they carried were too specialized, too strongly dedicated to death and destruction.

Whatever the reason, Garth regretted the delay; it meant that much more time for the cultists to strike against his family and surviving friends. Galt, back in Skelleth, was almost certainly in danger, as well as Myrith and Lurith and Garth's children.

He could think of no way to compel the Forgotten King or anyone else to speed them magically on their way, however, and could merely plot, plan, and worry as Koros strode onward into the mountains.

Behind him, Frima was slowly recovering from the shock of Saram's death. Her initial reaction had been wordless grief, which Garth had transformed into a cold, bitter hatred and a driving need for revenge with the words he had spoken to her in the market. Hatred and anger, however, had to be sustained by something outside oneself in order to dominate one's thoughts over an extended period of time. Had she stayed in Skelleth, Frima would have been reminded repeatedly of Saram's murder by the simple fact of his absence, by the empty side of her bed, by the unused or perhaps usurped baronial seat in the hall, where someone else might be giving orders, or merely by the old familiar places where she had seen him so often and the ordinary objects he had handled so frequently.

Here, though, as she clung to Garth with her arms and to Koros with her legs, riding for days on end through strange country and suffering from a vague illness that came and went, those reminders were lacking.

The sight of Saram's murderers, or any sign of their presence, would have served to sustain her craving for vengeance, but the mountains they crossed, and the plain beyond, were unmarked by any trace of Aghad or his followers. They passed small farms, stone cottages, and other human habitations, but nothing that could stir her dwindling fury. Instead, she found herself distracted by new sights and experiences.

This had begun with the burning of Dhazh. Seeing that had provided a countershock to Saram's death; it had been the first thing she thought about other than death and revenge since she had seen her husband's mutilated corpse.

Now, as she rode behind the overman across the rolling countryside of eastern Nekutta, she was able to think clearly again, her thoughts no longer smothered beneath an unbearable load of grief and rage. For the first time, she began to consider her situation now that Saram was dead.

Was she still the Baroness of Skelleth? She had no idea. She had held the title only by virtue of being Saram's consort, but since both he and his predecessor had died with no other heirs known, that claim might be sufficient to entitle her to rule in her own name. Had the stillborn son she bore almost two years earlier lived, he would have been the new Baron, and she the dowager and probable regent – but he had not lived. Nothing of Saram lived on; he had had no brothers, no sisters, no living family at all. Even his friends had mostly perished in the sacking of Skelleth three years ago.

That thought upset her anew, that there should be nothing left of the man she had loved, and she reaffirmed her vow of vengeance.

It was not fitting, she thought, that so fine a man should die so young and with no offspring – though it occurred to her that she had not known just how old he was. Older than she, certainly. Nor could Frima be certain that he had not sired children; she had not been his first woman, she knew, though she was his only wife.

Still, he had no legitimate heir – and she had no child to ease her loneliness.

She remembered her recurring illness and wondered if she might be wrong about that, but she suppressed the thought as mere wishful thinking. She did not want to fill herself with false hopes, and her bouts of nausea were far more likely to be caused by grief, or the rigors of travel, than by pregnancy.

Perhaps she should have stayed in Skelleth and tried to learn whether Saram had children whom she might claim and raise as her own. She would never have asked so improper a question while Saram lived, of course, but it occurred to her that Garth, who had known Saram before she met him, might know something. She inquired timidly, "Garth?"

The overman did not answer, but glanced back.

"Did Saram have a lover before I met him?"

Garth shrugged. "I don't know," he said. "I never saw any evidence of one." He turned his attention forward again, to the trail ahead, wondering what quirk had brought Frima to be questioning her dead husband's past at this late date. It was an almost-welcome distraction from his own gloomy, repetitious thoughts, which ran over and over again along the same deadend paths, considering ways out of his predicament that he already knew would not work.

Frima reminded herself that she was not totally alone; she had friends, or at least acquaintances, back in Skelleth, and she was sure that they would not desert her if she returned there. She had Garth, who had agreed to help her in her revenge and who still seemed to feel some obligation toward her from earlier events. She had her father and siblings, perhaps, though she could not be sure that any of them had survived. She had not thought much about them in almost three years, not even long enough to send them a message reporting her own survival and her improved estate as the Baroness of Skelleth, but surely, if they lived, they would welcome her back.

She felt suddenly guilty that she had never told them that she was still alive. They must, she realized, believe that she had died on Sai's altar long ago – unless her father or brother had been in the mob in the marketplace when Garth slew the high priest of Aghad. They would have seen her there and known she still lived, but would have no idea what had become of her after she fled the city.

Of course, if they had been present, they might well have been among the first to contract the White Death, which was invariably fatal. And if the plague had not killed them, the fires she herself had set, and the chaos that ensued, might well have caught them.

Her younger sisters would have been safe at home, she was sure – but the fires and plague and rioting might have found them even there. And if their father and brother had died, how would they have survived? Most probably they, like herself, would have wound up on a sacrificial altar somewhere, but without a strange overman to rescue them.

She was suddenly impatient to see Dûsarra again, to discover how much the stories of its destruction had exaggerated. She wanted to know whether her father, her brother, and her two sisters still lived. What remained of her father's shop? Were any of her old friends still there? Was the cult of Tema still active? She remembered the priestess Shirrayth, who had tried to teach Frima some of the mysteries of the goddess in hopes of recruiting her as an acolyte, and wondered what had become of her. She remembered the magnificent stone idol in the temple's domed chamber, which had awed and comforted her as a child, and longed to see it again. She was certain that it must still be intact; the goddess would protect her own image, Frima was sure of that.

She remembered how she had been consoled by a priest – she had never known his name – after her mother's death and how she had prayed to Tema and sensed her presence in the night sky in response. The knowledge that the goddess watched over her followers had eased Frima's mind many times when she was young, yet during her stay in Skelleth she had neglected her religion completely.

She tried to excuse herself on the grounds that Tema was a Dûsarran deity, not to be found in strange eastern lands, but she knew that for the lie it was. Tema was the goddess of night, and the night came everywhere, not just to Dûsarra.

She had not kept up her childhood faith; she had lived mostly by day, for convenience, since the people of Skelleth, unlike her own, were wholly diurnal. She had relinquished her ties to the night.

That was not right.

Had she remained steadfast, Frima thought, perhaps Tema might have warned her, or protected Saram somehow, or turned away Aghad's followers – or at the very least, eased the pain and grief.

Perhaps the goddess had watched over her family and she would find her father and siblings waiting for her in the tinker's shop, untouched by the catastrophes that had struck the city. They, surely, had remained faithful.

No, she told herself, that was going too far, believing that anyone who worshipped Tema would be preserved against the wrath of the other gods, for it was P'hul and Bheleu who had caused Dûsarrans suffering, at Garth's behest. Tema was the least of the seven Lords of Dûs, unable to stand against any of her six siblings. If P'hul's plague, or Bheleu's flames, or the machinations of Aghad had been directed against Frima's family, then they surely would have died. She could only hope that they had been fortunate.

It would do no good to pray to Tema that they had been spared, for not even the gods could alter the past, except perhaps for the being called Dagha, who had created the gods themselves. If her family still lived, she would find them when she reached Dûsarra; until then, it would do no good to worry about them.

Nonetheless, she worried.

She wanted them to be alive, for there to be someone she could go to, now that Saram was dead. She wanted to return to the comforts of her childhood, to the relative security she had known before her kidnapping.

With that in mind, as the party was coming within sight of Nekutta's central mountain range, she leaned forward and asked Garth, "Don't you think we should travel by night?"

The overman glanced back at her and asked, "Why?"

"Wouldn't it be safer?"

The overman looked out across the peaceful landscape of green pastures, grazing cattle, and occasional houses or plowed fields scattered along the roadside. Nothing within sight seemed in the least threatening.

Still, he remembered that reports had reached Skelleth describing wars and other disturbances in Nekutta. He had seen no evidence to support the stories – but caution would do no harm.

So far, the party had been spending long days on the road, traveling on well into the evening every day, and rising again before dawn to get an early start. Garth had no intention of slowing the pace, but he saw no reason not to move the sleeping period from nighttime to day. It might, he thought, provide a small decrease in the chance of danger.

"Old man? Do you have any preference?"

The Forgotten King shook his head and walked on, tirelessly, without looking at the overman. He had no trouble in keeping up with the warbeast. An ordinary man would have been left far behind in a single day, or else would have collapsed from exhaustion, but the King marched stolidly and silently onward, his pace always steady and matching the warbeast's own. It was one more little demonstration of his strangeness, but one that pleased Garth because it meant faster travel.

"Very well, then," Garth said. "Tonight we ride until dawn."

Frima smiled; she was returning to the night, where she belonged.

The habits of years were not so easily broken, however, and she dozed off shortly after midnight, only to be awakened half an hour later by the cessation of movement.

Startled, she opened her eyes and saw that Koros had stopped and was standing motionless in the middle of the road. No inn was in sight, and the eastern sky was still black and strewn with stars.

"What's happening?" she asked.

"Silence!" Garth warned in a low voice.

"Why?" she whispered. "What's happening?"

"I see campfires ahead, where none should be," Garth replied.

Frima lifted herself up on her hands and stared over the overman's shoulder. As he had said, several lights were visible on the hillside ahead of them.

"Couldn't it just be a caravan?" she whispered.

"It could be," Garth admitted, "but I think it is not. Look how many fires there are."

Frima peered into the darkness and tried to count the flickering lights; her hand slipped before she had finished, and she bumped down onto the saddle, losing her place.

She didn't need to finish her count, however; Garth's point was obvious.

"I estimate thirty fires," the overman whispered. "At the least. And assuming ten humans to each, that means three hundred people are camped there. I have never heard of so large a caravan. Raiding parties, however, are often such a size."

"Maybe the caravan set extra fires to scare away bandits," Frima suggested.

Garth did not bother to reply to that.

"What are you going to do about it?" Frima asked.

"I have not decided," he replied.

His first impulse had been to make a detour around the encampment, but the thought of going out of his way, even so briefly, annoyed him. He was tempted to ride straight through, as if nothing were out of the ordinary – and if anyone in the camp tried to stop him, well, the Sword of Bheleu could deal with such interference.

In fact, he thought it might be fun to destroy the camp, whether he was bothered directly or not; after all, the fools had settled themselves on the highway, obstructing traffic, and deserved whatever response travelers might be able to make.

He found himself considering with anticipation just how he would go about it. He might burn down the tents first – assuming there were tents – and then hunt down anyone who got out in time. He would pursue them individually, he decided, and skewer each one on the sword, so that he could watch the blood run up the blade and spatter across the ground.

"Garth?" Frima's voice was worried.

He ignored the girl; nothing she could say would be of interest.

"Garth, the jewel is glowing," she said.

He glanced up and realized that she was correct. The red light that had tinged the edge of his vision had been neither his imagination nor the approach of dawn, but the glow of the gem.

An instant's worry vanished. What did it matter, he asked himself, if the stone were to glow? He had made his bargain with Bheleu, and the god would not dare to interfere with his thoughts. The urge to destroy the camp was entirely his own, he told himself.

All the glow did was remind him of the sword's readiness and waiting power. It occurred to him that he might be able to use it to keep his prey from fleeing. A good thunderstorm would douse the fires and drive the people under shelter, making it more difficult for them to escape his anger. He reached up for the hilt projecting above his shoulder.

"Garth!" Frima said, her voice loud and unsteady.

"Silence, woman!" Garth growled in reply. His hand closed on the sword's grip, and he felt a surge of strength.

"Old man!" Frima called. "Stop him!"

Garth bellowed and tried to draw the sword; Frima pressed up against his back, holding the scabbard down so that he could not pull the blade free.

Enraged, Garth tried to twist away while simultaneously reaching up with both hands to lift the blade out of its sheath hand over hand.

"King! Help!" Frima called.

The glow of the gem suddenly died, and the stone turned black, darker than the night sky above.

Garth stopped instantly; his hands fell, and the sword slid back into place. His irrational anger had vanished, and with it all thought of assaulting whoever blocked their way. He felt as if a haze had cleared from his thoughts, a haze that had been present in varying measure ever since he had picked the Sword of Bheleu up off the table in the back of the King's Inn. Even when the sword had been black with soot and unable to hold him directly, he realized, his thoughts had been tainted and muddied by it. Perhaps the most frightening of the sword's effects was that he was not even aware of its influence until it was broken; it made him believe Bheleu's reactions and emotions to be his own.

Now, though, he was free again, at least for the moment.

"Thank you," he said.

"Bheleu is not to be trusted," the old man's hideous voice rasped from the darkness. "He would have delayed us here for no good reason, and I do not wish to be thus delayed. Further, I prefer your company, poor as it is, to his."

"I won't give you the sword," Garth insisted. He was wary, and his thoughts had not had time to reorder themselves fully, so he stated his position directly to avoid confusion, on either the King's part or his own. The old man had made a longer speech than usual, which was, in Garth's experience, often a sign of trouble. The extra words might be part of a subtle scheme, or a result of the old man's excitement – and anything that excited the Forgotten King was likely to be unpleasant for mere mortals.

"As you please," the King replied.

Garth relaxed very slightly. It could be, he told himself, that the old man had spoken the exact truth and that his motives were just as he said – but why had he bothered to explain them?

Frima did not worry herself about that. "Are you all right?" she asked.

"Yes," Garth answered, though he was not yet completely certain himself.

The party had continued onward as these events had taken place; when Garth had reached for the sword, he had urged Koros forward, and the warbeast had obeyed, undisturbed by the actions of its riders. The Forgotten King had marched alongside. Now, Garth realized, they were drawing near to the most easterly of the campfires; furthermore, they had been shouting at one another.

"Wait," he called softly as he signaled the warbeast to stop.

Koros stopped. Garth looked off to the side and saw no sign of the King's yellow mantle. He looked back, in surprise, wondering where the old man had gone.

Something rustled; he whirled to face forward once again, and found himself looking down the shaft of a spear.

Chapter Twenty-Two

"An overman!" exclaimed an unfamiliar voice very near at hand – the voice, Garth was sure, of an overman, deeper and more resonant than any human's.

"Who are you?" Garth demanded. He looked up from the spear poised at his throat and saw that it was clutched in double-thumbed hands below a noseless, red-eyed face. Two other figures stood nearby, one of overman size, the other smaller; both held their weapons ready.

"Who do you *think* we are, idiot?" the smaller figure asked in unmistakably human tones.

"More importantly, stranger, who are *you?*" the overman with the spear inquired.

Garth considered his situation and decided that he did not care to admit his identity yet. "I'm just a traveler heading west. Why does it concern you?"

"You travel at night?"

Garth shrugged. "Why not? It's cooler. I mean you no harm, whoever you are. If you prefer, I will go around your camp, rather than through it. It matters little to me."

"It may be that you won't be going anywhere for some time," the overman who had not previously spoken remarked.

"Why not? Who are you?"

"Who do you think we are?"

"I don't know," Garth said. "I didn't think there were any overmen in Nekutta. Either I was wrong or you have come here from somewhere else – but I have no idea where or why." This was not exactly true, of course; it did not take much intelligence to guess that the camp was a raiding party from the Yprian Coast, and that these three had been sent out to investigate the noise on the road.

"We didn't think there were overmen native to Nekutta, either, which is why you still live," the second overman said. "You may be a spy, perhaps a loner hired by some village to direct us away from it – but we have not previously encountered such a thing. Why would humans hire an overman, when surely they know we have both species among us? And I might suspect you to be a scout for one of our rivals, save that we had thought ourselves the most easterly party; why, then, would you be approaching from the east? Did you circle around unseen, and then become careless on the way back? It seems unlikely. Therefore, stranger, we are puzzled, and want to hear your explanation of yourself before we do you any permanent harm."

"And I want to know," the human interjected, "what that thing is you're riding, and who that is behind you."

"The animal is a warbeast," Garth replied, unsure how much of the truth it would be wise to admit. "The girl is Dûsarran and has hired me to escort her home." That story seemed as good as any and certainly more acceptable than the truth. He could not know what attitude this group had toward the cult of Aghad.

"Ah," the second overman said. "And who is this Dûsarran? Who are you, that she should trust you enough to hire you?"

"Her name is Frima, Baroness of Skelleth," Garth answered. He hoped that the title would impress his questioners. He did not care to reveal his own name yet; they might have heard it one way or another. "As for why she should trust me, that is her own concern – but I have been known to her for some time, and my word is good." He felt an uncomfortable twinge at that last statement, knowing it to be less than the truth.

"Skelleth?" the spear-carrier and the human exclaimed in unison.

"I think we've got a real prize here," the overman added.

"Think what a hostage she'll be, if she's really the Baroness!" the human said.

Garth had not considered that. He had assumed that these Yprians would not want to interfere with the friendly relationship between Skelleth and their own land.

"That would not be good for trade," he said.

"That, fool, is the whole point!" the human declared.

The second overman held out a hand, gesturing the human to silence. "I think I understand," he said. "You aren't Yprian, are you?"

"You mean he really *is* Nekuttan?" the human asked, surprised.

"No! Silence!" The overman's hand struck the human's helmet with a dull clunk. Turning back to Garth, he asked, "You're from Eramma?"

"No," Garth replied. "I come from Ordunin, in the Northern Waste."

"Ah, yes. That explains everything."

Annoyed, Garth said, "Perhaps it explains everything to you, but it does not to me."

"No, of course not. Come, then, and I'll explain." He sheathed his sword and held out a hand in friendship.

Hesitantly, the human returned his own sword to its scabbard, while the first overman lowered his spear.

At the second overman's urging, Garth dismounted and led Koros, with Frima still astride, into the camp. There was still no sign of the Forgotten King.

Once inside the circle of light from the nearest fire, Garth was able to get a good look at his captors. As he had thought, they were obviously Yprian, wearing the brightly enameled, flaring helmets and gaudy, enameled armor customary on the Coast.

They were not, however, exactly like the Yprians who had traded in Skelleth. The designs and colors on the armor were different, the accents, he realized, subtly altered.

When they had drawn near the fire, Frima was lifted off the warbeast, and both she and it were placed under polite but thorough guard – though Garth was sure that the Yprians were underestimating the warbeast's strength and that Koros could easily leave anytime it chose.

Garth himself was treated solicitously, led to a comfortable folding stool by the fire, and offered a cup of mulled wine. Wary of drugs, he refused the beverage, but seated himself and waited politely while the other overman made himself comfortable.

When both were settled, the other began his explanation. Garth, upon seeing the differences between this group and those who had come to Skelleth, had already guessed part of it.

The Yprian Coast, it seemed, was not a single united region living at peace with itself, but rather a patchwork of squabbling tribes, some human, some overman, most mixed.

For the last century or two, the situation had been relatively stable; each tribe had its area staked out, and borders were only rarely violated. Raids were not unheard of, by any means, but full-scale wars were a thing of the past. The tribes traded with one another and formed elaborate networks of allies and trading partners, the better to get what they needed. Goods not obtainable on the Coast were bought from the most southwesterly tribe, the Dyn-Hugris, who traded with Dûsarra, and who were consequently the most powerful of the various groups. The Dyn-Hugris, however, were kept in check by an alliance of half a dozen other fairly large and wealthy tribes in the central part of the region. All in all, there had been a stable balance of power and an acceptable division of the available wealth.

Then, almost simultaneously, two things had occurred to disrupt this situation.

Dûsarra had been stricken by plague, its marketplace and warehouses burned and much of the city evacuated. Trade had collapsed. The Dyn-Hugris lost their power base overnight; their control of the trade routes to Dûsarra was suddenly worthless.

In the east, a party of traders had come through the badlands from Eramma and offered to trade with anyone who was interested. The first tribe they encountered had been little more than a small company of bandits, but the second had been the Chuleras, a large and ambitious group previously limited by their poor location and meager resources.

Now, abruptly, the Chuleras had gold, large amounts of it, and were able to hire mercenaries, bribe allies, and generally assert themselves. They had done so with none of the tact the Dyn-Hugris had developed over the centuries and were in the process of driving the six Alliance tribes out of their central homelands.

Even without the resources of Dûsarra, the Dyn-Hugris were a formidable enemy, so instead of retreating westward the six tribes had come south, making the hard trek over the mountains, looking for new homes, new lands, and new wealth.

The Dyn-Hugris, not to be outdone, had sent armies south along their now-useless trade routes.

The old alliances had collapsed under the new strains; now the six tribes, and the Dyn-Hugris as well, were all rivals, gobbling up as much of Nekutta as they could. It had been a pleasant surprise to find it all so poorly defended. Usually a company of Yprians could take over as much land as they pleased by simply moving in and declaring themselves the owners. The local inhabitants, mostly farmers, rarely dared protest.

Conquest was so easy, in fact, that the Yprians became nervous, certain that there had to be a catch somewhere, some dire threat that would arise to thwart them. So far, no such thing had appeared – but Garth's arrival had been very suspicious. The camp was the foremost outpost of the army of the Khofros, most easterly of the six tribes, and just recently come around the central mountains hoping to claim the entire eastern region of Nekutta. The presence of an overman to the east of them was an unwelcome surprise.

Garth listened to this explanation silently. He realized that he, virtually single-handed, had managed to disrupt completely the society of the Yprian Coast and had thereby caused the invasion of Nekutta by these semibarbaric tribespeople. Both the destruction of Dûsarra and the rise of the Chuleras had been his doing.

Once again, actions he had thought beneficial had led to mass destruction. He wondered if it was possible for him to do anything significant at all that Bheleu and fate would not twist and pervert.

The Yprian, done with his story, asked, "Is that girl really the Baroness of Skelleth?"

Garth had been waiting for this question. "I wanted to impress you," he replied. "I thought the whole Yprian Coast traded with Skelleth, not just one tribe."

"Is she the Baroness?" the other persisted.

Garth realized that he was not going to be allowed to dodge the question. "Not anymore," he said. "She was the Baroness; her husband was recently murdered by his enemies. I doubt that anyone would care much about the widow of a deposed baron. There were no children to claim the title; she was left alone and decided to return to her home in Dûsarra rather than risk her life by staying in Skelleth."

He hoped that the implication that Frima had been exiled by a rival faction would be accepted. If the situation on the Coast had in fact been as the Yprian had described it, such things would probably have been common and familiar.

"Ah," the Yprian said. "A pity, if true."

"It is true." Garth spoke as if offended, his voice flat. As it happened, most of what he said was indeed accurate. It was the way it was said that gave a wrong impression, by implying that the enemies who had murdered Saram had been usurpers in Skelleth, rather than outside foes.

"A shame; she would have been such a good hostage in dealing with the Chuleras."

Garth shrugged. "I am sorry she is of no value to you. She has some worth for me; I am to be paid by her family upon her safe delivery to Dûsarra"

"That seems very odd, you know. Dûsarra is largely deserted now. And how did a Dûsarran ever come to be married to the Baron of Skelleth?"

"I do not know the details; she turned up in Skelleth almost three years ago. The dead Baron was something of an adventurer, you know; he took the title for himself, rather than inheriting it. His predecessor was murdered, as well."

"You still haven't told me your name."

"Thord," Garth said. "Thord of Ordunin, son of Dold and Sherid."

"I am Chorn of the Khofros."

"What do you plan to do with me?"

"I have not decided."

"I would like to point out that I will put up serious resistance if you do not release me very soon. Besides myself, the warbeast is a formidable threat. I do not think it worth your while to keep me here or to kill me. Far better to let me go in peace."

"You have a good point there. I will keep it in mind while I discuss this with our elders." The Yprian rose and signaled with one hand.

Three guards, all overmen, stepped forward and kept Garth under close watch while Chorn strode off and vanished into a large tent. They made no attempt to disarm Garth; he guessed that they judged the great two-handed broadsword too awkward a weapon to be much of a threat in such a situation.

Were he to reach for it, he could be killed long before he could get it free of its scabbard – or at any rate, he could have been killed if it were an ordinary weapon, rather than the Sword of Bheleu.

Garth was pleased that no one touched the sword; he was unsure how it might react, even when its power was damped by the Forgotten King. He sat waiting patiently for several minutes.

When Chorn finally emerged again he was smiling. Garth did not know how to interpret that until he saw the Yprian gesture for the guards to depart.

They obeyed, vanishing into the darkness beyond the fire's light.

Garth rose as Chorn dismissed the watch on Frima and Koros.

"Our apologies, Thord, for detaining you," he said. "You understand our situation, I'm sure."

Garth nodded.

"You are free to go, and we hope that you will speak well of the Khofros in the future. We bear no malice toward any people in Eramma or the Northern Waste, nor even in Dûsarra, and would welcome peaceful contacts with them. I am sorry that we were not more hospitable, but in war the amenities are neglected."

"Thank you," Garth said, still slightly suspicious.

No one interfered as he mounted the warbeast and helped Frima up behind him; no one attempted to stop them as they rode on westward through the camp and out the far side, past the sentries.

The stay among the Yprians had delayed them for something over an hour, but Garth was not excessively annoyed. He knew that it could have been much worse. He was relieved that the Khofros had apparently decided that they did not need anymore enemies.

He was not sure, however, whether he was pleased or dismayed at the Forgotten King's disappearance; he was still debating the point as he rode out past the final sentry, whereupon it became moot. The old man was walking alongside again as soon as they were out of sight in the darkness, as if he had been there all along – and Garth was not entirely sure he had not been. Invisibility could well be one of his wizardly talents. The overman decided not to mention it, and the old man did not volunteer any information.

Frima, however, was not so reticent. When she noticed the King's reappearance, she demanded, "Where were you?"

The Forgotten King did not reply.

After she had repeated the question three times, each louder than the last, and had finally been hushed by Garth, while the King remained obdurately silent, she gave up. Instead, she asked Garth, "Why didn't they kill us?"

"Why should they?"

"We might have been spies."

"We weren't."

"But we *might* have been."

Garth shrugged.

"*I* think they should have killed us."

"You would prefer to be dead?" Garth inquired politely.

"I didn't mean it that way – though I don't know, really. Maybe when I die I'll see Saram again."

Garth did not like the trend of that thought. "They did not kill us because it was not worth their trouble. Koros and I would have put up a good fight, and they would have lost several warriors before they could kill us – if they could kill Koros at all," he said, hoping to direct Frima away from thoughts of an afterlife. Even though he had come to believe in the existence of gods, or at any rate of supernatural powers, he had not accepted the human superstition of life after death. He did not want to risk saying anything that might tempt Frima to commit suicide, or to permit herself to be killed at what might be an inopportune moment.

"I suppose that's true," Frima agreed. There was a brief silence before she asked, "Who were those people?"

"Yprians," Garth replied.

"What were they doing there?"

Garth explained the situation, repeating points every so often, clarifying what Frima did not immediately comprehend, and admitting ignorance when she asked questions he could not answer.

When at last she was satisfied with his explanation and convinced that the whole camp had not been put there by the cult of Aghad, she fell silent.

Garth glanced back and noticed that the sky was beginning to lighten in the east. They would be resting soon.

That, he was sure, would do them all good.

He had been thinking over recent events while answering Frima's questions; one subject was Frima herself. She was talking again, as much as she ever had. Garth took that as a sign that she was getting over the shock of Saram's death and wondered whether she still grieved.

She was certainly more entertaining, if sometimes exasperating, as her normal talkative self than she had been during her long spell of silence. Traveling by night could be boring, with the scenery obscured by darkness, if one's companions refused to speak.

He began looking for somewhere they could take shelter for the day. It would not do to be caught unawares by another party of Khofros, or by any other Yprian tribe.

They found an abandoned, partially burned farmhouse shortly after sunrise, its former owner's skull on a stake by the door. A message was scratched on the wall with charcoal: "This is the fate of our enemies. This land belongs to the Khofros."

Frima was reluctant to enter the ruin, but Garth was insistent, despite the ash and odor. It was shelter, burned or not.

They spent the day sleeping peacefully; no one found them. Garth awoke in midafternoon and found the King sitting, fully awake, on the one intact chair at the unscathed kitchen table. The overman smiled at the familiar pose in the incongruous setting. He said nothing, but roused Frima, and the party set out anew.

Having learned from their first encounter, Garth carefully avoided all contact with humans or overmen thereafter, circling wide around the camps and outposts they encountered, sleeping in ruins, caves, or other places of concealment, and stealing supplies rather than buying them. They passed several Yprian encampments of varying sizes, and Garth tried to distinguish the various tribes by the differences in their armor and accouterments; he was fairly certain of some identifications, less confident of others. Since they were avoiding contact, they never learned the names of the five tribes between the Khofros and the Dyn-Hugris, but Garth was reasonably sure he saw representatives of at least three of them.

The sword's gem remained black throughout, to Garth's relief. He had no desire to defend Nekutta by destroying the invaders; after all, many of the Yprians were his own species, which the Nekuttans were not.

As well as the invading armies, they came across camps of ragged humans, mostly unarmed, whom Garth guessed to be refugees. Many of the inhabitants of these camps wore the traditional hooded robes of Dûsarra; others wore the homespun tunics of farmers.

Checkpoints had been set up at several places along the road; circling around them became enough of a nuisance that Garth gave serious consideration to Frima's suggestion of abandoning the road altogether, before finally rejecting it. He had traveled this route once before, but he was by no means sure that he would be able to find Dûsarra if he left the highway.

They were, by Garth's estimate, about a day's travel – or rather, a night's – from Dûsarra, with the mountains visible on the western horizon, when their rest was interrupted early one afternoon.

They had taken shelter in an orchard, hidden from view by the thick foliage of the apple trees. Garth did not expect anyone to trouble them unless the owner of the grove should turn up, and a farmer or two was a threat the overman knew he could handle easily.

It was not a farmer, however, who coughed politely to awaken him. He rolled over, reaching automatically for the Sword of Bheleu, and found himself looking up at a man of indeterminate age, muscular in build, and clad in a gray robe and hood.

There was something familiar about him, Garth realized as his hand closed on the hilt of the sword.

"Greetings, Garth of Ordunin," the man said. "I come in peace; you will not need the sword."

The fact that the man recognized him somehow did not surprise Garth; he was certain that they had met before, though he could not recall when or where.

"Greetings, man," he said.

"You don't recognize me?"

"No."

"I am the Seer of Weideth; we met three years ago, on two occasions."

"I recall only one," Garth replied. He had run afoul of illusions sent by the Seer and the village elders of Weideth when first he traveled to Dûsarra. He remembered the incident well and saw that this man was indeed the one who had called himself Seer on that occasion. On the way back to Skelleth he had passed through Weideth without incident, and without meeting the Seer again.

"I was one of the Council that fought you in the hills north of Skelleth," the gray-robed man explained.

"Oh, yes." Garth had not realized that the Seer had been included in that group, along with Shandiph, Chalkara, and a score or so of others whose names he did not know. There had been so many in robes, the traditional garb for a wizard, that he had not noticed the Seer among them. "Why are you here?"

"I have not come to interfere; it's far too late for that. You need not worry. I just wanted to see you and look at the sword that has caused so much destruction and meet the King in Yellow while we both still live."

There was a sadness in the Seer's tone, and something else Garth did not recognize; overmen were not prone to wistfulness, so Garth was not familiar with it. He saw no harm in the man.

"Here I am," he said, "and here is the sword. The King is the old man in rags over there."

"I know." The Seer looked down at the sword Garth held and remarked, "It's hard to believe that that thing can hold so much power."

The overman shrugged.

"And you have the book and the mask, as well. Do you know how long the spell will take?"

"I know nothing about it," Garth replied.

"O King, do you know?"

The old man had been sitting quietly, ignoring their visitor, but he answered, "Three days."

"And you have a day's travel remaining – four days in all. Why, then, can I not foresee my death? Is my gift *that* weak?"

The Forgotten King said nothing.

"You seem certain that the old man will be allowed to work his magic," Garth said, irked. "I am not so eager to see him succeed."

The Seer looked sideways at him. "What can you do?"

"I hold the Sword of Bheleu – and I intend to continue to hold it."

The King stirred, and the gem in the sword's pommel suddenly flared up, vividly red. A wave of unreasoning fury swept over the overman; he propelled himself to his feet, the sword ready, its blade glowing white.

Then the glow died, the stone blackened, and the King muttered, "Do you, Garth?"

"If it is the only way to prevent you from bringing on the Age of Death, yes, no matter what it may cost me." The rage had vanished as quickly as it had come, leaving his head feeling light; his right hand was warm, almost hot, where the sword's grip pressed against it.

"You swore to aid me in my magic."

Garth did not know how to reply to that at first, but finally said, "I did not know then what was involved."

"Do you now?" the Seer asked, openly curious.

"Do you?" Garth countered.

"In part. I have spent much time in study since last we met, learning more of what was to come. My own gift of prophecy is feeble, but it was sufficient to make clear the writings of others."

"Then tell me, Seer, what I am involved in. What is this magic the King pursues? What will it do? What is the Fifteenth Age to be?"

"The Fifteenth Age is the Age of Death; it will last no more than three hours – perhaps less – bringing time to an end. The gods themselves will die, and the Forgotten King with them. It will be brought about when a ritual from the Book of Silence is performed in the place of Death, a ritual requiring the totems of death and destruction as well as the book itself."

"And the world will be destroyed as a result?"

"I would think so," the Seer replied. "How can anything exist when the gods are dead and time has ended?"

"The spell requires the Sword of Bheleu?"

"Yes."

Garth turned to the Forgotten King and smiled. "I think that I may stave it off for some time yet," he said. "Can even the King in Yellow, high priest of Death, take the sword from its chosen bearer against his will?"

"You have seen, Garth, how easily I restrain its power," the old man said.

"True, O King, but you have not restrained me. I am still an overman, while you are only human."

"Do you think my powers so strained by confining Bheleu that I cannot use them upon you?"

"If that were not the case, O King, then why have you relied upon more mundane methods of bending me to your will these past three years? Why did you not simply compel me to do what you wished me to do? Why did you allow me to return to Ordunin after slaying the basilisk? Why did you not send me directly to Dûsarra? I think that, mighty as you are, you cannot directly force me to act against my own judgment. I don't know why this should be so, but I believe it is. If I am wrong, then I have lost, and the world is doomed, and you have but to command me to give you the sword to prove it."

The King did not answer immediately. At last, he shrugged slightly and said, "I have waited for seven ages; I can endure further."

Elated by what he took as an admission of defeat, Garth grinned. He was still trapped between Bheleu and the King, but he saw now that his position was, perhaps, not absolutely hopeless. He might find some solution if he could hold the King off long enough and remain sufficiently free of Bheleu's influence to think rationally about it.

It did not occur to him to wonder why the King should continue to suppress the god of destruction when Garth had openly announced his intention not to cooperate.

The overman turned back to the Seer and said, "There, you see? Your doom has been delayed."

The Seer nodded, but asked, "For how long?"

Annoyed at this ingratitude, Garth replied, "For as long as I can prevent it."

"And how long will that be? Will you live forever? I cannot foresee your death, any more than I can my own, but my power of foresight is weak, particularly when far from home."

"I expect to live for many years yet, human, and perhaps in that time I will find some other way of forestalling the end."

"I can only wish you well, overman."

Somewhat mollified, Garth relaxed slightly. He stood silently for a moment as the Seer gazed dolefully at him, then at the sword he still held.

Feeling that the silence was becoming uncomfortable, Garth asked, "How is it that you are here, rather than in Weideth? If you came to see us, would you not have done just as well to wait at home? Our route passes through your village."

"Weideth is gone," the Seer replied. "It was taken by a Dûsarran army over a year ago and destroyed a month later by advancing Yprians. Many of us fled, in small groups. I am the only survivor of my company and I have lost contact with the other parties. I've been living alone, a few leagues south of here."

Reminded anew of the chaotic conditions in Nekutta, Garth was uneasy. "I am sorry to hear it," he said.

The Seer said nothing.

"If you wish to join us, you would be safer than while traveling alone."

"Thank you, but no. I couldn't stand it. Sooner or later I would take up the sword, or look at the mask, or touch the book, and I would die, even before the world ends. I prefer to live out whatever time remains to me without facing such dangers."

"As you wish, then," the overman said. He watched as the Seer departed, walking away slowly until he was lost to sight among the close-packed trees.

Chapter Twenty-Three

Haggat had planned it all carefully. The cult's best assassins and most powerful magicians would be employed systematically, one after another or in small complementary groups, until one or another managed to get through. The overman was to be their primary target; the old man came next, and then the warbeast. The girl was of no importance; she might wind up on a sacrificial altar, as she had once before, but with no rescuer this time.

He was aware of the Sword of Bheleu's power, but he could not believe that it was omnipotent and impregnable. He had gathered all the most potent death-spells the cult could devise or steal, all the most deadly killers, and had laced every water supply between Dûsarra and the plains with the most lethal poisons at his disposal. He had devised stratagems and diversions, methods for separating the overman from his sword, methods of disposing of both simultaneously. He had thought of little else for almost a fortnight. For three days he had not even taken the time to use his scrying glass, save for a quick daily check on the overman's progress each morning. He had forgone the nightly sacrifices and neglected the cult's other business. He had eaten hurriedly, if at all, and had not touched his acolyte – though she remained always close at hand, translating his commands from sign language or writing to spoken words, carrying messages, running errands, and generally attending to his needs.

He had not given her presence much thought; he had been too busy to bother himself about her.

Now, though, all was ready. The killers were in place. The overman and his party were in the foothills, advancing along the highway, and Haggat watched his glass avidly. Unable to observe the overman or the old man directly, he had focused upon the road before them.

He was so involved that he neglected one of his customary precautions and allowed his acolyte to remain in the black-draped chamber with him. She stretched up on tiptoe to peer over his shoulder at the glass. Together they watched as the warbeast's forepaws rose and fell, always at one side of the image, moving along the highway toward the crossroads.

Garth remembered the narrow defile that led straight into Weideth; it was a welcome change from the winding of the road through the outer foothills. He judged that they would reach the gates of Dûsarra shortly after dawn; the eastern sky was just beginning to turn pink behind them.

When he had first ridden this road, Weideth had vanished before his eyes almost immediately after he turned the last corner; that had been the doing of the Seer and the village elders, using illusions in hopes of diverting Garth from his path. On this second journey there was no such magical trickery. Nothing disguised the devastation that had befallen the little town.

Where once an inn and a dozen houses had clustered around the crossroads, there were only heaps of ash and jutting, blackened timbers. Stones lay scattered about, strewn across the roads and hillsides. Garth remembered a small stand of trees that had adorned one slope; nothing remained but scorched stumps. Weeds grew thick in what had been tidy little gardens, and here and there white bones showed in pale contrast to the smoky darkness left by the destroying fires, catching the pale predawn light.

It was a depressing sight, and the overman wished that it *would* vanish, leaving his memories of the village untarnished.

The Forgotten King's voice interrupted his thoughts.

"Garth," the old man said, "be ready."

Puzzled, Garth glanced at the King, but saw no sign that would tell him what he should be ready for. The old man was walking along as calmly as ever.

A red glint caught his eye, and he realized that the gem in the pommel of the sword was glowing. With the realization came an uneasiness. He twisted around to look at the jewel, then looked back at the King.

The old man nodded and kept walking.

Confused, but trusting for the moment in the Forgotten King's supernatural knowledge, Garth reached up, leaning forward so the blade would not smack Frima, tipped the scabbard up over his shoulder, and unsheathed the sword.

The hilt felt warm and comforting in his hands.

"What's happening?" Frima asked. "Why are you doing that?"

Garth did not answer; he was too busy enjoying the mounting rush of strength and bloodlust that swept through him as he held the sword. The grip was hot in his hands, the gem glowing brightly, the blade shining faintly in the dim morning light. The sooty ruins of Weideth no longer saddened him; instead, the vista seemed almost inviting, the evidence of destruction somehow satisfying, even though it had been caused by hands other than his own.

There were enemies here, he knew, many of them, hidden away among the heaps of rubble, some concealed by magic, others by natural means.

This, he thought, would be fun.

Something twanged; he whirled the sword about to meet the crossbow bolt that flew toward his head. Sparks trailed from the blade, bright in the half-light, and the quarrel shattered spectacularly against the gleaming metal, sending a shower of splinters to rattle against the rocks beside the roadway. Frima yelped as a stray sliver pierced her arm.

Garth's buoyant energy turned suddenly to rage as he saw the blood trailing down the girl's sleeve; the sword blazed up in a burst of white fire that snatched the pale colors from the landscape around them, stretching sharp-edged bands of light and long black shadows out in all directions.

"I'a bheluye!" the overman screamed as he brought the sword sweeping back before him. Flame erupted wherever it pointed, in great rushing waves, and the screams of dying men mingled with the roar of the fires as crouching Aghadite assassins were caught in the blaze.

Something flashed crimson, and Garth laughed horribly as he felt the sword fend off a death-spell. Slung stones whistled past his head or exploded into dust against the sword's edge; arrows of every sort were diverted or destroyed by the blade's coruscating energy. Colored smoke arose from a dozen attempted spells, only to be dispersed and driven away by the force of the supernatural flames. The overman did not bother to locate his attackers, but simply blasted everything in sight, destroying anything that might conceal a foe. The piles of ash were swept away in whirlwinds, the burned timbers powdered by fiery bursts; the ground shook, sending rocks tumbling and bouncing like the spatter of rain on flat stone. The light of dawn was first lost in the more vivid light of the sword and then buried in clouds as Garth gathered a storm about himself. The fire of the sword was joined by flashes of lightning.

Long after the attacks upon him had ceased, Garth drew on the sword's power to keep the earth dancing and to send bolt after bolt of electrical fire onto every available target.

When at last he allowed the fury to subside and the clouds to part the sun was bright gold above the eastern horizon, but lit only blackened earth and drifting ash. No trace remained of Weideth or the assassins who had lurked there, save for scattered fragments of bone, shards of scorched metal, and a thin layer of cinders. The surrounding hills themselves had been gouged deeply and reshaped into stark, angular new forms.

Amid this devastation, Garth and Frima sat astride Koros; the Forgotten King stood alongside, untouched by the havoc the sword had wrought. Frima had closed her eyes and kept her head down throughout the conflagration; now she stared about in stunned disbelief, ignoring the blood that trickled from her single wound. Koros growled uneasily and shied away from the heaps of ash that still smoked. Even Garth, who had caused it, seemed impressed by the result of his actions.

The Forgotten King alone remained unperturbed and calm.

In Dûsarra, Haggat stared in disbelief at the final image that filled his glass in shades of gray. He realized, with a sick certainty, that he had done everything he could to destroy the overman and had failed utterly.

That was the last thing he thought; the acolyte who stood at his shoulder throughout had seen the truth as well and knew that Haggat's power was broken. She chose her spot carefully, making certain her thrust slid cleanly between his ribs and into his heart, forgoing the pleasures of a slow death to be sure that the high priest would not live long enough to retaliate.

She smiled as she drove the knife into his back.

Chapter Twenty-Four

The gates of Dûsarra were closed and barred; that came as something of a surprise to Garth. It was not, however, much of an obstacle. The gem in the sword's pommel still glowed red, and a single blow sent the splintered remnants of the massive city gate slamming back against the neighboring walls while showering the marketplace that lay just beyond with chips, sawdust, and ash.

Garth had dismounted to wield the sword and remained on foot as he marched into the city. Koros padded along close behind, Frima on its back, and the Forgotten King brought up the rear, the Book of Silence and the Pallid Mask in a bundle beneath one arm.

The overman stopped in the middle of the square, and the others drew up behind him and joined him in looking about.

The market was not as Garth and Frima remembered it. When Garth had first arrived in Dûsarra the square had been lined with merchants' stalls, shaded with canvas and lighted with torches; it had been swarming with people in robes of gray and red and blue, buying and selling and going about the business of the city. Now the sides of the square were bare stone walls, the black stone stained with smoke. Several of the buildings had obviously been gutted by fire; the charred ends of timbers projected, the windows were empty, blackened holes, and the doorways yawned empty. In some cases daylight was visible through the openings, showing plainly that in those buildings the roofs were gone.

The market was totally deserted, and the entire city seemed abandoned; Garth could see nothing alive and could hear nothing stirring, save for his own little group.

"Now what do we do?" Frima asked.

Garth considered that. His ultimate goal, of course, was the temple of Aghad, on the Street of the Temples in the northeastern part of the city. They had, however, been traveling for quite some time, having set out late the previous afternoon and it being now midmorning. For his own part, he was not particularly tired; his use of the Sword of Bheleu had left him feeling more invigorated than drained on this particular occasion. He did not understand why that should be so, yet it was. His companions, however, might not feel up to further activity.

Given that they were to rest, he was unsure where to go. From the appearance of the marketplace, he doubted very much that the Inn of the Seven Stars, where he had stayed before, would be open for business.

"What do you suggest?" he said at last.

Frima gazed about at the desolate market that she herself had set afire so long ago and said, "I want to go home." She was weary and distressed and, at least for the moment, more concerned with her own security than with avenging her murdered husband.

Garth mistook her meaning. "We have come to destroy the cult of Aghad and we are not returning to Skelleth until that has been done. Would you have this whole journey go to waste?"

"I don't mean Skelleth, I mean my *home,* Garth!"

"Oh," the overman said, realizing that he had misunderstood. "Where is it?"

"We lived above my father's shop, on the Street of the Fallen Stars," Frima replied, pointing off to the northwest.

Garth nodded. That seemed as good a course as any; the girl's home would provide lodging and a base from which to work. He would be able to plan his course of action, rather than simply charging in blindly.

Of course, this delay would allow the cultists time to plan as well, and to lay traps – but they had had ten days and nights already since he left Ur-Dormulk, and the result of all their planning had been the ambush he had destroyed in Weideth. He doubted that they could contrive anything more effective in one day. If they did attempt another, similar surprise, it would most probably give him a chance to kill more of their number.

If they chose to hide, another day could make little difference, since surely they would already have spent considerable time upon their preparations.

Better, he decided, to allow them that time, while he, Frima, and Koros rested and prepared, than to march up to the temple now, in broad daylight, and begin blasting away.

"Lead the way," he said.

Frima leaned forward and spoke a word in the warbeast's ear; she had, by listening, learned most of the commands it was trained to obey.

The beast growled and looked at Garth, who nodded and waved it along.

With a muffled snort, it strode forward, letting the girl direct it by twisting at the guide handle attached to its harness. The overman walked alongside.

The Forgotten King did not; instead, when the warbeast headed for the northwestern corner of the market, he began walking toward the northeast.

Garth, glancing back, noticed this divergence.

"Where are you going?" he called.

The King did not answer.

Annoyed, Garth lifted the Sword of Bheleu, which he had not sheathed after breaking in the gate, and set the ground in front of the old man afire.

Without even pausing, the King made a subtle gesture with his free hand. The flames vanished with a rush of air, and the gem in the sword's pommel went black.

Something whistled past the overman's ear.

Startled, he whirled in time to glimpse a human head ducking down below a burned-out window.

"Wait," he ordered Koros. Sword in hand, he ran toward the window. Again something whizzed past his ear; this time he saw it was a dart and realized that it came from a totally different direction. He spun about, but did not see the source.

He was unsure just what was happening, but he found it very inconvenient to have the sword's power repressed at this particular moment. He had come to rely on the weapon.

"I regret, O King," he called, while he kept moving to remain a difficult target, "that I so rashly annoyed you. I beg your forgiveness and ask that you release the sword from your restraint." It had been stupid, he knew, to have tried using the sword against the old man in the first place. His power was able to stifle the sword's greatest fury with ease and had protected the entire King's Inn from destruction during the sacking of Skelleth. It had been foolish for Garth to think that the old man would be hampered by a simple supernatural flame. Furthermore, causing him any offense at this point was probably a mistake. Garth's regret was completely genuine. Most of all, he regretted that he tended to behave stupidly when the sword's gem glowed.

Still walking northeasterly, completely unperturbed, the King waved a hand in dismissal, and the jewel flared red once more.

Awash in power and his mind hazy with rage, Garth promptly turned back and blasted to powder the wall that had concealed his first attacker, revealing nothing but the burned-out shell of a small shop. The assassin had escaped.

Garth could find no trace of whoever had thrown the second dart; he, too, had fled.

Annoyed, but struggling to force his anger down and to maintain careful control of himself, the overman again ordered Koros to wait and then ran after the Forgotten King.

He caught up to the old man half a block away, in a street leading out of the market, and slowed to a walk alongside the King. When he had composed himself somewhat, he said, "Your pardon, O King, for my lack of manners. However, I find it disturbing that you should choose to part ways at this point. I respectfully ask to know where you're going and why you do not accompany us."

"I go to the temple of Death," the old man replied, "to restore the Book of Silence to its proper place, in preparation for my final magic. That was my purpose in coming here. You have your own purposes to pursue. Go pursue them, and leave me to mine."

Garth was unsure how to reply to this; he began to phrase another question, then broke off as he realized that he had stopped walking and that the Forgotten King was moving on ahead of him. He tried to walk, but found that his feet would not obey him. He stood and watched as the old man marched on up the street, around a corner, and out of sight.

A red fury seethed through him, but he knew that there was nothing he could do. He struggled to fight down his irrational anger.

The King could do nothing, either, he told himself. He did not have the Sword of Bheleu, and Garth had not done him the service he had sworn, to aid in the final magic. The Fifteenth Age could not begin while those conditions remained unmet – or perhaps it could begin, since the King had the Pallid Mask and Garth had done him the service of bringing him the Book of Silence, but it could not end, the world could not be destroyed. Let the old man go and make his spells, speak his incantations; they would be nothing without the sword!

That, at any rate, was what Garth told himself, yet even when his anger had subsided, when he had fought down his rage sufficiently to dim the vivid glare of the sword's jewel, he worried. Why should the old fool be so confident, if his magic was useless without the sword? Did he perhaps know something that Garth did not, something that would deliver the sword into his hands?

If that were the case, Garth asked himself, what could he, Garth, do about it? The King's powers had stopped him in his tracks here and could surely do so again. He could only go on, ignoring the old man and dealing with new threats as they arose, relying on the deduced fact that, for some reason, the King seemed unable to take the sword from him without his consent.

With that decision, he sheathed the sword and turned back toward the market. His feet moved normally once more; he had no trouble in retracing his steps and rejoining Frima and Koros.

With Frima pointing the way, they made their way onward into the streets of the city, away from the shattered gate. They were less than a hundred yards from the market when they passed the first skeleton. It lay on one side of the street, partially buried in the dirt; it had obviously been there for some time and had sunk into the mud after a rainstorm. No flesh remained; the skull gazed up from empty sockets.

Frima shuddered and looked away. Koros ignored it completely. Garth gave it a look, then dismissed it as unimportant. It had undoubtedly been a victim of the White Death.

Of course, the presence of an unburied skeleton was a sign that the city was nowhere near recovery. Dûsarra was not wholly dead, since the cult of Aghad still remained alive and active, but any town where the dead were allowed to lie in the streets indefinitely was far from healthy.

They saw more skeletons as they proceeded into the city, but fewer burned buildings; the fire had not spread more than a few blocks to the northwest of the market. Most of the houses and shops were intact, but looked deserted. Some doors stood open; a few had been broken in. Fallen roofing tiles lay in the street here and there, and scraps of rotting cloth could be found in places, as well as scattered bones. There were no people to be seen anywhere; the resulting silence in the center of the city was eerie and unsettling.

Eventually they reached what Frima proclaimed to be the Street of the Fallen Stars and found her father's little shop. The door was closed and the windows intact, but Garth was not very optimistic about finding anyone alive within. The stone doorstep was dusty; no one had gone in or out recently, he was sure. Besides, they had seen no one alive since leaving the marketplace, and Garth thought it very unlikely that, in this dying, abandoned city, they would find the handful of people they sought still living in their old home as if nothing had happened.

Frima did not bother to think logically about such things. She hurried to dismount and ran eagerly up to the door, ignoring the dust on the stoop and windows. She knocked loudly; no one answered. She tried the latch. It clicked, and the door swung open. She stepped in, Garth right behind her.

The shop's interior was dim, and dust lay everywhere; human and overman both left clear footprints. To either side stood wooden display racks, from which hung pots, kettles, ladles, and tin vessels of every description. On shelves behind them were arrayed plates and tankards of pewter, copper bowls, and other implements. The tin and pewter were gray and dusty; the copper was dull and beginning to show flecks of green corrosion.

At the back of the shop stood the tinker's worktable, four feet across and ten feet long, a few tools laid out in a row near one corner, other tools hanging on the wall behind. Scraps of metal lay scattered about.

Sprawled across the center of the table were the bones of a man's arms, his skull grinning between them, his other bones in a heap on the floor behind the table.

Frima was horrified; she froze, stared, and stifled a scream.

Garth waited, ready to lend any help he could, but his assistance was not needed. The girl closed her eyes and fought down her trembling, forcing herself under control.

The overman decided not to ask if she could be sure it was her father. *He* was sure that it was; who but the tinker would be found at the tinker's bench? He saw no point in raising false hopes. Instead, he said, "We should look upstairs."

Frima nodded, took a few steps toward the curtain that closed off the back of the building from the public part of the shop, and then stopped. "You look," she said. "I can't."

Garth nodded. He had lived long enough among humans to understand how strongly they became attached to their homes, and to realize that Frima could not bear the thought of finding more dead in what should have been her sanctuary. He had no idea how large a family she came from; perhaps she was afraid of finding the remains of her mother or stepmother or siblings.

He moved cautiously through the curtain into the back room, and from there up the narrow staircase to the upper floor. Everywhere lay a thick carpet of dust. Cobwebs adorned the corners of each of the three small beds he found upstairs. A metal bowl on a small bedside table, now dry as the dust, had obviously been left full long ago; the bottom had corroded and sprung a leak, and the table had rotted where the water had dripped.

There were no more bones, no corpses, no sign of any other inhabitants.

When he had satisfied himself that no unpleasant surprises lurked in wardrobes or under the beds, he returned to the shop to find Frima standing over the table, studying her father's skull.

"Are there any others?" she asked.

"No," Garth replied.

"Good."

"Did you have any other family?"

"Two sisters and a brother."

"Perhaps they escaped, then, and are still alive somewhere."

"Do you really think so?"

Garth hesitated, then lied. "Yes, of course."

Frima stared at the skull. "Are you sure this is my father's?"

"No," Garth said. "How could I be sure? I never met him, after all."

"I know, but can't you tell? I've been looking at it, and I can't be sure. It doesn't look like him. There's no hair, no eyes; it could be anybody's."

"I know no more than you," Garth answered. "But who else could it be? Who else would be sitting here at your father's table?"

Frima shuddered and turned away. "Get it out of here," she said.

Garth obeyed, gathering up the skull and several bones and carrying them out into the street.

He returned to find Frima huddled in a comer, weeping. Quietly, he gathered up and removed the remaining bones, placing them in a corner out of the wind, where they were unlikely to be disturbed, between the shop and the house beside it.

When he had finished he went upstairs, cleared away the dust and cobwebs from one of the beds, tested it, and found it marginally usable. Then he returned to the shop, led the girl upstairs, and put her in the bed.

She went willingly and quickly fell asleep.

Garth watched over her briefly, then went downstairs again, found a water pump in the back, and filled one of the larger vessels with water for Koros. That taken care of, he settled himself on the floor of the shop and slept.

Outside, Koros stood guard, dozing occasionally, but always alert enough to warn away with a growl any Dûsarrans who ventured near.

Chapter Twenty-Five

Garth was awakened by the roar of a warbeast. Startled, he sprang to his feet and hurried to the door of the shop. There he paused, waiting, the Sword of Bheleu in his hand.

The roar was not repeated; instead, he heard an unfamiliar voice calling his name.

"Garth! Garth of Ordunin! We would speak with you!"

Puzzled, and without opening the door, he bellowed back, "Who are you?"

"I am Uyrim, a priest of Aghad; I have been sent to seek a truce!"

Garth considered that. His immediate suspicion was that it was some kind of trick, an attempt to lure him into a trap, but after further thought he decided that the offer might be genuine. After all, although he had suffered at the hands of the cultists, losing his chief wife and his best human friend, they had suffered worse in return. Perhaps they had had their fill of sending assassins to be fried by the sword; perhaps they did not want to see their temple reduced to ash, as the remnants of Weideth had been.

He lifted the latch and swung the door an inch or so inward, so that conversation would be more convenient, but he did not emerge, nor present any part of his body as a target. "I am listening," he called.

"Haggat, who set assassins upon you, who had your wife killed, who had the Baron of Skelleth slain, who sent the Council of the Most High against you, is dead, and his killer is the new high priestess of our sect. We wish to start anew. We are willing to forgo our rightful vengeance for the killing of Haggat's predecessor if you, in turn, will consider your own vengeance accomplished in the deaths you have already brought upon us. You have slain eighteen trained assassins and our fourteen magicians and cost us almost all our magical arsenal. You have destroyed our temple in Ur-Dormulk and eliminated our influence in Skelleth. Leave those of us who yet survive in peace, and we will, in turn, leave you and yours in peace. Swear that you will accept this offer, and we will swear in return, and you may leave Dûsarra unmolested. Refuse us, and we will strike against you in whatever way we can. We know now that we cannot kill you while you bear the Sword of Bheleu, but we can kill those you care for. For every member of our sect you slay from this moment on, a member of your family in Ordunin will die. Those, O Garth, are our terms."

"They're lying," Frima said close behind him. Garth started; he had been so attentive to the Aghadite's words that he had not heard her approach. The warbeast's roar of warning had awakened her as it had the overman, and she had made her way carefully down the stairs in time to hear most of what the priest had said.

"How can you know that?" Garth asked.

"They *always* lie," she said.

"They lie when it serves their purposes and tell the truth when that would serve better. Perhaps this is such a time," Garth said.

"They aren't going to give up their revenge. Aghad is the god of hatred, remember? And besides," she added, her expression turning hard and fierce and a hand going to the crudely bandaged wound on her arm, "I'm not going to give up *my* revenge."

Garth considered that and quickly agreed that the Aghadites could not be trusted. Still, the offer of peace might be genuine; he had, he knew, cost the cult heavily.

That did not necessarily mean that he should accept the offer. After all, if the cult could thus change direction once, it could do so again, when next its leaders felt they had the upper hand. The fact that they were offering a truce now implied that Garth currently had the advantage – and the essence of tactics was to pursue every advantage. If he were to attack now, he suspected that he could destroy the entire sect; if he accepted their truce and thereby allowed them time to rebuild, they might find some way of attacking him successfully while he was off-guard. Quite aside from his desire for revenge, the cult, by its nature, was a menace not just to himself, but to anyone else who encountered it, for so long as it existed.

By the priest's own admission, Garth had destroyed the cult's influence in Skelleth, and he could not believe that they had ever been strong in the Northern Waste – after all, he had seen no Aghadite overmen, save the high priest he had killed in Dûsarra's market three years before, who had almost certainly been Yprian; and had they not had to lure Kyrith south before they could kill her? Therefore, if he were to wipe them out *now,* they would be unable to carry out their threat to destroy his family and friends, whereas if he were to wait they might well manage some retaliation.

There was no question in his mind as to whether or not they deserved to die; these people were, by their own boast, dedicated to hatred and treachery. They had butchered Kyrith and Saram. They had insulted and reviled him, attacking him repeatedly. They deserved to perish, and he deserved the pleasure of dispatching them.

The thought of spilling Aghadite blood was warm and comforting; a pleasant reddish glow seemed to suffuse his thoughts. He did not notice the literal, physical existence of that glow, emanating from the gem in the sword's pommel.

Frima noticed it but, knowing it to be directed against the followers of Aghad, chose not to point it out.

"Who are you, to offer me terms?" Garth called through the crack in the door. "You are a priest of Aghad, you say, and you speak of a high priestess, and of someone named Haggat. I know nothing of any of you. You say that it was the dead Haggat who sought to harm me; why should I believe that? Your cult has acted against me, not as individuals, but on behalf of your god. I do not defy you, or your high priestess, or your dead Haggat, whoever he may have been if he truly existed at all. I defy your god himself. I spit upon your deity. I denounce Aghad as the filth he is. He has defied his brother and superior, Bheleu, god of destruction, and must pay for that affront." An inspiration came to him, and he called to Koros the command that meant, "Attack!"

The warbeast roared in response. An instant later Garth heard the sound of something being crunched, followed by human screams. He swung the door wide and stepped out, the Sword of Bheleu ready in his hand, glowing white and dripping hissing white flame.

The screaming stopped, and he saw Koros standing in the alley across the street, gnawing on the bloody remains of a red-garbed dead man, while another broken corpse lay sprawled nearby. A sling was draped across one limp hand, and half a dozen darts were scattered in the black dust of the street.

Something moved, and Garth swung the sword, spraying flame, only to find that he had roasted a plump rat, drawn by the scent of blood.

It seemed unlikely that the party sent to negotiate a truce had been only two men; Garth looked warily about for more, but saw none. If there had been others, they had slipped away unseen.

Frima emerged from the shop to stand behind the overman; her father's sword, taken from its place behind the curtain, was naked in her hand. Here, in her home city, however changed it might be, she was no longer content merely to watch Garth kill her foes for her. She was determined to kill a few herself, and her father's sword seemed an appropriate weapon. She wished she had thought to bring Saram's blade; that would have been still more fitting.

She knew, however, that she was no swordswoman, and the sling in the corpse's hand caught her eye. She picked it up, gathered up the darts, and tucked them into the pouch she wore on her belt in imitation of Garth and defiance of Dûsarran custom.

That done, she looked about and saw no enemies to attack, only the warbeast devouring its prey and the overman standing warily nearby.

"Now what do we do?" she asked.

"We attack," Garth replied without thinking.

"Attack the temple?"

Garth glanced at her, his red eyes ablaze in the afternoon sun. "Yes," he said.

"Good," Frima said. "Let's go."

Garth turned, looked about, then reluctantly turned back to the girl and asked, "Which way?" He was almost totally unfamiliar with this part of Dûsarra.

Frima suppressed a giggle at the helplessness of the god-overman who needed to ask directions of a tinker's daughter. "This way," she said, pointing.

Garth nodded, signaled Koros to accompany him, and followed as Frima led the way through the maze of the city toward the Street of the Temples and the temple of Aghad.

In a red-draped room beneath the temple, the new high priestess was arguing with some of her congregation who considered her sudden self-proclaimed elevation and subsequent policy to be faulty. The discussion had been going nowhere; Haggat's former acolyte had an irrefutable claim to her new position by virtue of being the only surviving person who knew all the cult's secrets, and she was utterly unyielding in her determination to abandon any attempt to kill the troublesome overman.

The objectors were equally adamant in their insistence upon following more traditional rules of succession and in pursuing the cult's ancient policy of unrelenting vengeance. There was nothing unorthodox in moving up through assassination, and they agreed that Haggat had deserved removal for his bungling, but the post of high priest was not to be taken by a mere acolyte with no grounding in theology. They argued that the high priestess should immediately begin training a proper priest in the inner mysteries of the cult's workings and return to her own rightful position as first among acolytes –

though they were willing to guarantee her accession to the priesthood shortly after that return.

She knew just what such promises from priests of Aghad were worth. After coming into her post as Haggat's acolyte she had maneuvered for three years to obtain power, and was not about to relinquish it now to please a bunch of doddering traditionalists. She was saying as much, thickly laced with invective, when a messenger arrived, gasping from his long run.

"Your pardon, O priestess, chosen of Aghad, blessed of the darkness, mistress of treachery, but I bear urgent news," he said.

"Speak, then," she commanded.

"Garth refused the offer of truce and sent his warbeast against us. Uyrim and Hezren were slain; the rest of us escaped."

"Aghad devour you!" the priestess shouted. "Why? What went wrong?"

"I don't know, O mistress. Uyrim spoke well, I thought, yet the overman refused to parley. He said that his quarrel was not with Haggat, but with Aghad himself."

"That's idiocy! It was not Aghad who slew his wife, it was men, men acting on Haggat's orders. Haggat was a fool, attacking the overman openly; the essence of Aghad's power is deceit and coercion, not magic or brute force."

"Yes, mistress," the messenger agreed; the gathered priests remained silent, but many wore expressions approving the priestess' words.

"Did Uyrim warn him of reprisals?"

"Yes, mistress."

"He must know how weak we are in the east, that he does not fear such a threat. We'll have to show him that we are not so weak as he believes. He has two more wives; I want them brought here as quickly as possible, alive and intact." She turned to the closest thing the cult still had to a wizard, an apprentice who had been given charge of the few remaining magical devices. "Do we have any means of teleporting them?"

"No, mistress," the girl replied. "The last were used in Weideth."

"Oh, gods, may Haggat's soul be Sai's plaything forever! Do we know where more such magic may be found?"

"No, mistress – at least, I do not."

"Then we must do it the hard way and hope that we can hold out until the overwomen are brought here. That could be a month." The high priestess had a tendency to think out loud, now that she was free of her master. Haggat had been unable to speak, having had his tongue cut out in punishment for killing his own master long ago, before he had joined the cult, and in consequence had been resentful of those who spoke freely around him. His acolyte, who had always been near him, had learned quickly to keep her mouth shut. Since killing him, she had taken much pleasure in being able to speak as often as she wanted and for as long as she chose.

She turned back to the messenger. "Does the overman still have the Baroness of Skelleth with him?"

"Yes, mistress."

"He treats her well?"

"Uh . . . I am not certain, mistress."

"He seems to care for her, doesn't he? And she's not protected by the magic sword. And the strange old man is no longer with them to protect her. We'll have to make use of what we have. She won't be as good a hostage as Garth's wives would be, but she may serve, at least for a time." She paused and was about to speak again when another messenger entered the room and prostrated himself before her.

"Your pardon, O priestess, chosen of Aghad . . ." he began.

"Speak, messenger," she ordered impatiently.

"The overman is on his way to the temple, with his sword blazing and the warbeast beside him."

"You're certain?"

"Oh, yes, mistress."

"P'hul!" the high priestess spat. "Tell everyone. We can't face him yet."

"What?" one of the older priests protested. "You can't mean to abandon the temple?"

"You are free to stay here and die if you choose, Sherrend, but I, and anyone else with any wits, will be hiding in the tunnels. Nothing can stand against that sword of his. I saw in the scrying glass what it did, and our surviving scouts have told all of you. You heard what it did to our temple in Ur-Dormulk. Only a fool would stay here to face it." She ignored the priest's sputtering objections as she climbed down from her cathedra and announced, "Gather everything of value and make sure everyone is armed; we leave immediately. And I still want people sent after those overwomen, and after that woman he has with him."

The messengers and the wizard's apprentice bowed obediently; the priests squabbled among themselves, some bowing and hastening to obey, others staying to voice protests that the priestess ignored.

Even the stodgiest, however, had some sense of self-preservation, and within minutes the room was empty as the Aghadites prepared to evacuate their stronghold.

Garth was completely unaware of this activity. He reached the Street of the Temples as the sun was sinking behind the western mountains, washing the shrines in shadow. The topmost edge of the silvery gate of Aghad's fane caught a stray beam and glinted brightly as the overman drew near.

Garth smiled, and the Sword of Bheleu blazed up whitely, chasing away the shadows and drenching the metal gate in its own sickly glow.

The valves of the gate were worked into ten-foot-high runes, two to each panel, spelling out AGHAD; the top of the GH rune was still dented where Garth had struck at it three years before. The walls of the temple were built of blocks of stone, each block carved into those same four runes, a myriad reminders of his enemy's name.

When last he had been here, he reminded himself, he had been unable to deal with the trickery of the Aghadites. His sword had broken against these gates. Now, though, he carried the Sword of Bheleu. He swung the blade up and brought it crashing down against the top of the gleaming metal valves.

The blade sheared through the metal as if it were paper; it could just as easily,

Garth knew, have exploded the gates into shards. That was not what he wanted; he wanted to destroy this place slowly, at his leisure, and enjoy each step of the process.

He slashed again, cutting away a triangular slice of the second A rune. Another blow removed the top of the GH, and another cut apart the D.

Half a dozen blows reduced the gleaming gates to scrap, and Garth stepped through into the courtyard beyond, leaving Koros and Frima waiting in the street.

The colonnade that ran around three sides of the court was dark, the torches mounted on its columns unlit; the fading sunlight did not penetrate its gloom. The fountain in the courtyard's center gurgled, but Garth could not see the spray; it was hidden behind a barrier of rotting severed heads, stacked up like bricks around the fountain's rim, five deep. None were of recent origin, that was obvious; the bottommost tier was comprised mostly of almost-bare skulls, and those in the top rows were sufficiently decayed for the worst of the stink to have passed.

Although the majority were human, of both sexes, the skull that faced him most directly on the lowest level was that of an overman.

Revolted, Garth swung the sword up and sent a bolt of crimson flame at the grisly pile. The heads scorched, blackened, and crumbled to ash, revealing the bubbling spout of the fountain.

When Garth had first visited this place the fountain had pumped clear, clean water, liberally laced with poison; now, the fluid that pumped forth was thick and red. He did not care to investigate further, but simply reinforced the sword's power and reduced the stone and metal of the fountain to powder, boiling away whatever liquid it had held.

He paused and considered his next step. It occurred to him that no one had, as yet, opposed him; no voice had addressed him from the shadows. In fact, there was no sign that anyone was in the temple at all. That worried him; was it possible that the Aghadites had seen him coming and had fled, giving up their sanctuary?

Wasting no more time, he began blasting away at the temple itself, slicing the columns that supported its porches, breaking down the walls beyond. Masonry fell roaring, and the temple crumbled about him. He marched forward into the rubble, continuing to blast at the walls that still stood.

In the street that fronted the shrine, Koros and Frima waited, alert for an attack. Frima was eager to spot and kill any Aghadite who might flee from the destruction; Koros, as always, was not concerned with the reasons for its master's orders, but was ready to obey them and slaughter anyone who came near.

No one came. Walls tottered and fell, sections of roof caved in spectacularly, stones shattered, but no one emerged from the temple of Aghad.

Garth's rage grew steadily as he broke into chamber after chamber without finding a living foe. Clouds gathered in the sky above him, lightning flashed, and the earth shook beneath his feet, breaking open the extensive temple basements.

He continued to wreak destruction, working his way down beneath street level into the catacombs under the shrine. He found corpses, some of them fresh, some ancient, but none wearing the dark red robes of the cult, none that were still warm. He found animals – bats, serpents, great cats, and others – and slew them, but he found no humans. He saw machinery and smashed it, but saw no one operating it.

At last, as he had done in Ur-Dormulk, he found himself standing in a great pit where the temple had been, a pit that was as empty and lifeless as the one in Ur-Dormulk. His foes had escaped him. He had destroyed their stronghold, but they had escaped.

He bellowed with rage, the sword swinging in circles above his head; thunder rumbled, and lightning flickered through the clouds, as if reflecting the streak of fire the blade left hanging in the air.

He lashed out in frustration, blackening the smoking rubble and cutting a groove in the stone that surrounded him. The ground trembled below him.

A pile of debris tumbled aside, revealing an opening into the black, volcanic bedrock; the flame from the sword sliced through a stone slab, uncovering another. Alerted, Garth hacked away at the walls of the pit and found several such openings, thirteen in all, ranging from broad passageways skillfully concealed behind camouflaged stone doors to narrow crawlways, too small for an overman to enter, that had been hidden by the heaped rubble.

Here, then, were the means by which his enemies had fled. He could pursue them, overtake them, destroy them; he needed only to learn which of the passages they had taken.

He growled in frustration; there was no way he could know which routes they had chosen. He pointed the sword at the nearest and sent a gout of flame into it, illuminating the dark stone with an orange glare, but he could see no sign that would tell him whether the tunnel had been used or not. No dust lay on its floor; no footprints showed.

Enraged, he sent the flame winding on into the depths, out of his own sight, a writhing serpent of living fire.

A moment later he heard an immense explosion, and shards of stone and wood spattered across the rubble from somewhere well beyond the edge of the pit, hidden from his view. Gobbets of flame flickered across the night sky, and he knew that his fiery messenger had reached the end of the tunnel.

He also knew that it had not found any Aghadites.

"Garth?" Frima's voice called from the edge of the pit, at the spot where the silvery gates had once stood.

He growled a wordless response.

"What happened? A house up the street burst apart; did you do that?"

"Yes," he said. He struggled to think, to plan; the raging fury in his head made it difficult to do so. "Did you see anyone leave that house?" he called.

"I don't know; I might have," Frima answered. "There were some people on the street just after we got here."

Garth growled. "Those were Aghadites," he said. "I'm sure of it. They had a dozen escape routes here. They could be anywhere in the city by now." He realized, as he spoke, that they might even have left the city. A party might well be on its way to Ordunin, to carry out the god's vengeance against Garth's family. Quite aside from his desire for revenge, the cultists were an ongoing threat to innocent people everywhere, and Garth was more determined than ever to destroy them all.

"Oh," Frima said.

"We will hunt them down, wherever they hide," the overman said as he turned the sword's flame against one side of the pit to carve himself a way out.

Chapter Twenty-Six

The logical place for someone to hide, Garth and Frima agreed, would be in one of the temples. Each one had its secret entrances and hidden chambers, or so the legends said, and each was suitable for fortification.

They resolved to explore the nearest first; that was the temple of Sai, goddess of pain, Aghad's twin sister.

Garth blasted open the spike-steel gate with the Sword of Bheleu and, remembering what had happened to his boots when last he had entered this shrine, he melted smooth the jagged, broken obsidian courtyard. That done, he marched on into the temple, Frima at his heels, Koros waiting outside.

They found no one in the sanctuary. Garth was ready to give up and go, but Frima, recalling her own uncompleted sacrifice, pointed out the secret doorway through which she had been brought up from the vaults below.

Garth agreed that the vaults were worth exploring – a decision he found himself regretting a few hours later, when an extensive search had turned up no Aghadites, but an impressive array of dungeons and torture devices, as well as a handful of half-starved, desperate worshippers of Sai who had taken shelter there when the plague began, three years earlier. Despite a surge of bloodlust, Garth did not kill these people, but instead drove them out into the streets. They promptly headed toward the market, obviously intent on leaving the city.

By the time he and Frima had investigated all the corridors and rooms beneath the temple of Sai and radiating out from it under the surrounding buildings, it was almost dawn, and Garth was tired. He had used up a great deal of the sword's energy in blasting the temple of Aghad, and the expenditure was telling upon him.

Neither Garth nor Frima saw any point in returning to Frima's old home; instead, they broke in the door of a convenient house and made themselves comfortable there. Frima found a store of preserves in the kitchen, and dried salt beef that had not yet spoiled; the wine cupboard included several bottles that had not yet turned to vinegar, though Garth was not impressed with any that he sampled.

At last, when they had both eaten their fill, the girl and the overman found beds and went to sleep.

Garth did not sleep very well; the bed was far too small for him. Around noon he gave up and moved to the floor, which served him better.

He awoke again well after dark to find Frima hacking off strips of beef for their breakfast.

They debated what should be done next. Garth suggested the temple of P'hul as their next target; Frima objected that no Aghadite would venture into that disease-ridden pesthole. That, after all, was where the White Death had come from in the first place.

Garth had to concede the truth of her argument.

He then considered the temple of Bheleu, but dismissed that immediately; it was a ruin, with no roof and an earthen floor. Where could anyone hide in there?

The last temple on the Street of the Temples was the temple of Death. That, Frima insisted, would be the very surest place. Any Dûsarran would consider himself safe from pursuit there, as no one would dare to enter it looking for him.

Garth doubted this hypothesis. Would not the Aghadites, he asked, be at least as frightened by The God Whose Name Is Not Spoken as by their pursuers? After all, the cultists knew that Garth had entered the temple once before and emerged alive, the first person not a devotee of the Final God to do so.

Frima agreed with this reasoning finally. That left the two temples located in other parts of the city – those dedicated to Tema and to Andhur Regvos. Accordingly, the little party headed for the temple of Andhur Regvos, god of darkness.

Here Garth did not waste time in exploring every nook and cranny; instead, he simply used the Sword of Bheleu to blast the domed pyramid into rubble, as he had done to the temple of Aghad.

As with the temple of Aghad, however, he found no trace of any Aghadites in the wreckage. The sanctuary held the desiccated remains of a dozen people, all dead for quite some time; Garth guessed them to be the blind priests of the god, slain by the plague three years before. Nowhere else in the maze of chambers and tunnels did he find anything that might have been alive recently.

That left the temple of Tema. Garth proposed to treat it much as he had the shrines of Aghad and Andhur Regvos, but Frima protested violently. After some argument, the overman gave in. The followers of Tema had not done him any real harm, unlike the Aghadites.

He did not like the delay, which would allow the surviving Aghadites that much more time to devise new schemes and for their emissaries to travel toward Ordunin, but he decided that he could live with it.

It was well after midnight when he and Koros, with Frima on the warbeast's back, reached the steps leading to the temple's entrance. He helped the girl off the beast and then led the way to the door, up between the serpent-carved balustrades.

To his surprise, the door swung open as he approached.

He entered the antechamber and stopped. Frima proceeded on past him toward the concealed inner door, but before she reached it, a voice said, "Please wait, girl."

Startled, Frima stopped.

A blue-robed, white-haired priest emerged from the darkness into the sword's light, blinking in the vivid glare. "Your pardon, but we have grown cautious in these unhappy days. We cannot admit you to the sanctuary until you give an account of yourselves, and swear that you do not carry the White Death."

"We do not carry the plague," Garth said, "and I will swear that however you like. We have come seeking the Aghadites who fled the destruction of their temple."

"There are no Aghadites here," the priest said patiently. "This is the temple of Tema, goddess of night."

"You will forgive me if I insist upon investigating for myself," Garth replied.

The priest hesitated, and the overman held up the glowing sword; it dripped streamers of white flame. "You will, I think, see that I have the means of enforcing my wishes. I intend to search this temple without delay, and if you or anyone else should oppose me, I am afraid that I will feel it necessary not only to kill you, but also to destroy this entire building, lest my enemies escape me."

The priest stepped back and said reluctantly, "As you wish." The inner door swung open, and Garth stepped through it into the great domed sanctuary.

This chamber was the first place he had seen since returning to Dûsarra that could be called crowded; fifty or sixty ragged people had made themselves at home here, sleeping or sitting on beds made of bunched rags, each with a few meager possessions clustered about. Many of them glanced up at the new arrivals, then stared at the strange, fiery sword the overman carried.

Garth looked at the motley collection of humans and demanded, "How long have these people been here? Did any arrive within the last two days?"

The priest at Garth's elbow shook his head. "Oh, no," he said. "You are the first newcomers in half a year."

The overman swung the sword around and held it at the man's throat. "Will you swear to that, by your goddess and all the other gods?"

"Oh, yes, my lord," the man said, not nodding for fear of cutting or burning his throat on the sword's point if he moved his head. "I swear it, by Tema and by all the gods! These people have been here for months."

Garth decided that he could trust the human. He lowered the sword, ignoring Frima's loud protests regarding his treatment of a holy man.

Again he looked over the great hall, noticing that in the sword's light the stone idol was rather less impressive than he recalled. It stood against the far side of the chamber, the goddess' cloak stretching up to cover most of the dome. It was still a fine piece of sculpture, beautiful and comforting, but he could see the marks of the carvers upon it, which he had not seen in the dark; its ethereal quality was gone.

He spotted dark stains on the wall near the door, but did not inquire after their origin. He was afraid that they might be from his own previous visit, when he had killed a priest very near to the spot where he now stood.

Escorted by the priest, with Frima trailing along behind, Garth made his way around the room, investigating every place that looked as if it might conceal a doorway or niche. From the sanctuary he moved on into the vestry, and from there to the refectory and the dormitory, and finally into the crypts below.

Nowhere did he find anyone in a red robe, or anyone out of place. All those who wore the blue robes of the priests of Tema also had the red eyes and white hair required of her servants, and he could imagine no way in which the Aghadites could have disguised themselves to pass as such, unless they possessed some magic of a sort he was totally unfamiliar with.

He passed the remainder of the night searching the temple, and on into the morning, until at last, around midmorning, he was satisfied that no Aghadites lurked anywhere in the great edifice.

He apologized, more or less, to several of the priests and took his leave, Frima still trailing after him.

Koros was waiting at the foot of the steps, and together they found themselves a new resting place where they might spend the day. Tired as they were, they did not bother about searching for food.

Garth awoke around sunset, ravenously hungry, and discovered that the house they had chosen to sleep in had nothing edible left in it. He began smashing in back doors and investigating the neighboring homes, and eventually came across a wheel of cheese that was still good, and a keg of ale that had almost gone flat but was still more or less potable. He brought these finds back, and found Frima awake and hungry.

When both had eaten he asked whether the girl had any suggestions, since none of the temples they had explored had yielded anything.

Frima suggested returning to the Street of the Temples and looking into the remains of the temple of Aghad again, in hopes of finding a clue that might lead them to the vanished cultists.

Having no better suggestion to offer, Garth agreed, and by the time the last trace of twilight had faded in the west the two were standing at the rim of the pit, Koros close behind.

They found nothing of any conceivable use. Garth had been thorough in destroying the shrine, and no papers or documents of any sort remained, nothing that might provide any information except for the tunnels themselves. Garth explored a few of those, but all came to the surface relatively near at hand, and none showed any sign of continued habitation.

The overman stood, at last, at the edge of the hole, looking up the Street of the Temples toward the shadowy blankness at its northern end that hid the entrance to the temple of Death. He found himself doubting his own logic in dismissing the underground temple as a possible hiding place. The Aghadites were the disciples of hate, and the high priest he had slain had said that self-hatred was the most basic of all the things that an Aghadite must possess. Such people might well be willing to hide in a place where no sane Dûsarran would go. Furthermore, they might follow his own earlier line of reasoning through to its conclusion and decide that, because they would be expected to be more frightened of it than Garth would be, the temple of Death would be the one place where the overman would never bother to look.

This convoluted thinking seemed exactly the sort of thing he had come to expect from the followers of Aghad, and the temple entrance was only a short stroll away. It was certainly worthy of investigation, he decided; he led a rather startled Frima northward, up the Street of the Temples.

Along the way, however, he found himself distracted by the ruins of the temple of Bheleu. The skeleton of the ancient dome was gone, but the jagged fragments of the wall that had supported it still remained. A wide gap indicated where the door had once been, and a heap of ash in the center was the last trace of the burning altar whence Garth had drawn the sword.

It occurred to Garth that there was something unnatural about that pile of ash. Surely, after three years, it should have been buried or scattered by the wind.

He had taken the sword from that spot; he had come full circle in the three years since that moment.

It had been three years almost exactly, he realized. He tried to calculate the interval, but could not do so; his memory was not sufficiently precise. He was not even absolutely certain of the present date, let alone when he had taken the sword. Still, within a margin of three days or so, it had been exactly three years since he first touched the Sword of Bheleu.

He wondered whether he might be able to leave the sword here, replacing it whence it came. It seemed worth attempting. Furthermore, an Aghadite or two might have decided to take shelter here – what shelter there was. He stopped at the entrance, startling Frima anew.

"What is it?" she asked. "What are you doing?"

"I want to look in here," Garth said.

Frima peered into the darkness within the stone circle. "Why?" she asked.

"It is a temple, is it not? You thought that the Aghadites might take shelter in the temples."

"Not *this* one!" she protested, obviously having forgotten her earlier suggestion.

The overman did not bother to argue further, but simply marched into the temple, the sword lighting his way. Frima and Koros followed, Frima reluctantly, Koros with its usual calm.

Garth strode unhesitatingly across the earthen floor, directly to the little gray mound in the center, where he stopped. He looked down at the heap, then reached out with the sword to stir the ash.

A sudden warmth surged up through the hilt, through his arm, and into his mind, and he was no longer in the eerie gloom of the broken temple, but floating in a crimson void flooded with ruddy light.

He froze, waiting for whatever would happen next.

"Garth," said the voice so like his own, the voice he recognized as the thing that called itself Bheleu. *"Why have you come here?"*

Garth could not answer that; he was unsure of his own reasons. He had entered the temple on a sudden impulse, thinking two contradictory thoughts – that he might find Aghadites here and slay them with the sword, or that he might be able to free himself of the sword here without the Forgotten King's intervention. He was not sure which was his true desire. He had been carrying out his revenge against the cult of Aghad, but it was, so far, unsatisfying. There was no pleasure, no recompense, in the sight of a dead cultist or a blasted temple. The only pleasure came in the instant of destruction, and that was a fleeting and unhealthy passion that he did not believe was truly his own. He still felt driven to destroy the cult, but he no longer found any real value in that destruction, nor any easing of his own mind.

He wanted to be free of the sword, he knew. Despite his bargain with the god, he knew that his thoughts were tainted, that he had become an unclean, irrational thing, and that he would remain such as long as he wielded the sword. Yet he wanted the sword's power, the ability to strike down whatever affronted him, and he feared what might happen if the weapon should fall into the hands of the only other earthly being who had demonstrated the capacity to handle it safely: the Forgotten King.

He did not know how to answer the god's question.

"Garth, my time is drawing to an end, and you have denied me my freedom throughout what should have been my reign over the mortal realm. You have cut my age to a tenth of its anticipated length. There is nothing left to me but the last destruction, the end of myself and my fellow gods. If you wish, I will free you of the sword and relinquish all claim to you; you need but thrust the blade into the ash and leave it there, and there will be no more little destructions by your hand, but only the final cataclysm, when the time for it has come. Decide now; I will not allow you another chance. Take the sword and go on as my emissary, or leave it and be free."

Garth struggled to think, to weigh his decision logically. He wanted to leave the sword, to leave behind all his involvement in supernatural events; if he still planned further acts to avenge Kyrith and Saram, he could carry them out with his own abilities. He had done well enough for over a century without any divine assistance. He released his hold on the weapon, and it seemed to float motionlessly in the void before him.

On the other hand, Bheleu's mention of a final cataclysm frightened him. He tried to convince himself that a god would see time differently and that this last destruction might still be millennia away, but he could not bring himself to believe it. He knew that somewhere in the city the Forgotten King was preparing magic that was meant to destroy the world, and he was absolutely sure that if he were to leave the sword in the temple of Bheleu, it would find its way to the old man and the final spell would be completed.

He could not allow that to happen. "I will keep the sword," he said. His hand closed on the hilt.

He had expected the god's mocking laughter, but there was only silence; the red light faded, and he was in the ruined temple again.

Frima had watched with concern as her overman companion had walked up to the pile of ash, poked the sword into it, and then frozen. "What is it? What's happening?" she called, but Garth did not answer; he stood staring off into space. She came nearer, waved her hand before his face, but got no response. Worried, she fished the sling she had appropriated from the dead Aghadite out of her pouch.

Garth released the Sword of Bheleu suddenly; it wobbled, but remained upright, held by the mound of ash. Its glow died away, from a vivid white light to a pale yellow flickering, but Garth did not move or speak. He still stared ahead blindly.

Something appeared off to one side; Frima whirled, a dart in the sling, and let fly.

Not one dart but two rattled off stone; her own had struck the broken wall near where she had glimpsed the movement, and another had whizzed past Garth's head and hit the far side of the chamber. "Koros!" Frima called. "Kill them!"

The warbeast looked at her, as if debating with itself whether or not to obey someone other than its master. Another dart flew, ricocheting from Garth's armor with a sharp ringing, and Koros decided; with a roar, it leaped toward the hidden attacker.

Garth remained unmoving. Frima had another dart in her sling and was crouched, ready and waiting, glancing warily about.

Someone screamed, the cry mingling with the warbeast's growl and ending in an unpleasant bubbling. Frima could not see what was taking place in the darkness, but it was obvious that Koros had found its prey.

Again something moved, and she turned to see a dark shape approaching with sword held high. She flung the dart in her sling, and the figure staggered and dropped.

Light flared up; Garth held the Sword of Bheleu once more, the blade burning brightly with its unnatural white flame. The overman was moving as well, turning away from the ashen remains of the altar. He and Frima gazed with almost equal surprise at the red-robed man who lay, his fallen sword nearby, midway between the Dûsarran girl and the temple's entrance.

The man was not dead, but only stunned. Garth picked him up with one hand, the sword blazing in the other, and demanded, "Where are the rest of you?"

Koros emerged from the shadows, its jaw smeared with blood. The Aghadite stared in terror, first at the warbeast, then at the flaming sword, and finally at the grim overman.

"I don't know!" he cried.

"Yours is the god of treachery, filth; betray your comrades!" Garth demanded.

"I can't," the man insisted. "I would, I swear to you by Aghad, but I can't!"

"You swear it, by all the gods?"

"Yes!" The man was nodding and weeping. "Yes, yes, I swear it!"

Disgusted and enraged, Garth flung the human aside; his head hit the stone wall with a sharp cracking sound, and he slumped in a heap at the base.

Garth had not intended to kill the man, but he did not doubt that he had done so and he did not regret it. "There may be more," he said.

"Koros got one," Frima told him. "I haven't seen any others."

"We'll search," the overman said.

They did search, going over the entire temple area carefully. Frima stopped and became ill when she saw what Koros had left of the sling-wielder. They found no more Aghadites, though, nor any evidence that others had been there.

When Garth was satisfied, he led the way back out onto the street and onward toward the temple of death. Frima followed reluctantly, Koros beside her. Garth did not look back, but he did find himself wondering whether he had done the right thing in keeping the sword.

That might, he realized, have been his last chance to get rid of it; still, he resisted the urge to run back and try to bargain with Bheleu. If he released the sword, the Forgotten King would get it, he was certain. He could not allow that, now or ever. He marched up the street, sword held up before him to light the way.

The city seemed deserted; nothing moved on the Street of the Temples save himself and his two companions. He wondered if anything still lived in Dûsarra other than the Aghadites, the huddled people in the temple of Tema, and his own little group.

At the end of the avenue the glow of the sword revealed black volcanic rock forming a narrow defile that led into a cave; the sword's light did not penetrate the shadows of the cave's entrance, visible as a deeper blackness amid the surrounding stones.

A human corpse lay sprawled half in, half out of the shadows. That was hardly surprising in this city of death, where Garth had found himself almost tripping over bare bones at every turn. This body, however, was still fresh; it had not yet begun to rot. Garth could detect only the faintest scent of incipient corruption and judged that it had been dead no more than three days at the most.

The remains were those of a very old man; Garth paused to study them, and recognized who the man had been.

He was clad in a robe of so pure a black that the sword's light, or any other light, was not reflected at all, making the corpse seem almost a heap of tangible shadow. It was small and frail, with one leg twisted and shrunken, one hand missing, half the face hidden beneath a purplish growth, one eye long gone and the other buried beneath white cataracts.

This pitiful thing had been the caretaker of the temple of Death.

The overman glanced around warily, but saw no sign of anything that might have killed the ancient priest. It was entirely possible that age had caught up with him at last. Even the priests of Death died eventually – with one exception.

It was very near this spot that the overman high priest of Aghad, whom Garth had later slain, had once taunted him from concealment. One of the tunnels leading from the temple of Aghad might, Garth guessed, come up in this vicinity. He peered at the surrounding rock, but could see no sign of human presence.

"What happened to him?" Frima asked, staring at the corpse.

"He died," Garth said. After a pause, he added, "Probably of old age."

"Oh," Frima replied, suppressing a shudder. She found so fresh a corpse, dead so mysteriously, to be far more unsettling than the less recognizable remains of the plague's many victims.

Garth was no longer interested in the body and felt reasonably certain that no assassins lurked in the immediate area. "Come on," he said.

"That's the temple of Death," Frima said, not moving.

"Yes," Garth agreed, "it is."

"I don't want to go in there," she said.

"Why not? You suggested before that Aghadites might hide here; are you frightened of them? Have you decided to abandon your vengeance?"

"No, that's not it!" she cried. "I'm frightened of Death!"

"I am here to protect you," Garth replied. "I have been here before and emerged alive. I have the power of Bheleu to defend us. However, if you prefer, you may wait here while I investigate the temple."

Frima hesitated, but finally said, "All right. I'll stay here if you leave Koros with me."

Garth had no objection to that; he had not intended to take the warbeast into the temple in any case. He was not sure the huge creature would fit through the entry passage.

He ordered the beast to guard the girl, and then strode onward into the cave.

Chapter Twenty-Seven

The floor sloped gently downward; there was no gate or door, but the corridor narrowed slightly at one point. Thereafter it gradually widened, opening at last into a large chamber, the heart of the temple. Although the passageway was entirely natural, this main room had been artificially enlarged, the floor smoothed and leveled, the walls carved into elaborate friezes separated by columns, and the ceiling around the sides ribbed with carved vaulting. The central portion of the ceiling remained rough, natural stone, and beneath this stood the altar, cut from a large stalagmite and carved in the form of a lectern, with a strange horned skull riveted to its upper edge.

The glare of the sword was not the only light here; a sullen red glow came from the tunnel that led down and away from the far side of the chamber. The carvings and the altar cast strange double shadows in this eerie illumination.

Garth paid no attention to any of this. He had expected the temple to be deserted; he had completely forgotten, in the press of other concerns, that the Forgotten King had announced his intention of coming here and beginning his magic. The overman had dismissed that, convincing himself that the King could do nothing without the Sword of Bheleu, and had somehow assumed that the old man was lurking somewhere in the city, waiting for Garth to relinquish the sword to him.

He had been wrong. The Forgotten King stood before the altar, his back to Garth, chanting something unintelligible. The Book of Silence lay upon the altar, open, and it was evident that the old man was reading from it.

The sound seemed to reverberate from the stone walls, turning the Forgotten King's already-hideous voice into an unspeakable cacophony. Garth could not recognize the language of the spell, save that it bore no resemblance to his own tongue. The words were harsh and sibilant, with unpleasant combinations of vowels, and consonants that seemed to be all either hissing or guttural. Words and phrases ended in the wrong places, and the rhythm was broken and hard to follow, but the King appeared not to notice; he chanted on, the words spilling forth in a constant stream.

Garth watched for a long moment, unsure what to do. He knew that he did not want the King to complete his spell, but he did not know whether it would be safe to interrupt it.

The chant ended abruptly with a high-pitched grating sound, and without hesitation or pause the King said, "Greetings, Garth." He did not turn.

"Greetings, O King."

There was a moment of growing silence as the last echoes rebounded, faded, and died.

"What are you doing?" Garth asked at last.

"I prepare the final magic," the King replied.

The overman stepped forward, circling wide to the left so that the old man would not be able to reach out and snatch the sword away from him. "How can you do that," he asked, "without the Sword of Bheleu?"

"The sword is required only in the final stage, at the end of the three days, a point that will arrive shortly. I can prepare the magic, but I cannot complete it without both the sword and your assistance."

This answer troubled Garth, not so much because of what was said as because it was given so freely and seemed so cooperative a response – totally out of character for the old man. Something about him had changed; Garth guessed that having begun his spell, after so long a wait, had affected him.

The overman took another few steps and looked at the old man's face.

For a moment he did not realize what he was seeing, but only that something was wrong. The King's face seemed to shimmer and alter as the overman watched, distorting itself, and after several seconds Garth realized that the old man was wearing the Pallid Mask. The mask had fitted itself to the contours of the King's face, but remained smooth and pale and metallic, retaining its unsettling ability to shift its appearance inexplicably. The old man's long wisp of beard was caught up inside the mask's chin, out of sight, and the eye sockets were less sunken than his own – though his eyes remained invisible, hidden now, not by the shadows of his cowl, but by the mask.

"You will not receive my aid." Garth said. "It may be that you will somehow get the sword from me, but I swear I will never help you to destroy all the world just so that you may die."

"No, perhaps you will not – but might you not destroy all the world so that your enemies, the followers of Aghad, will perish with it?"

"No."

"Do not speak so quickly, Garth. Think first. You seek to slay them all; you have sworn to destroy them. How else can you do this? With the Sword of Bheleu you can destroy the entire city of Dûsarra, it is true – but to do so will take time, and in that time many will be able to escape, to flee elsewhere. Some may already have done so. Will you hunt them down throughout the world, one by one? Do you expect to live forever, then? Are you ready to devote centuries to this pursuit? It will take centuries to find and kill them all, Garth. You cannot destroy each of them that way. Nor can you use the Sword of Bheleu to destroy every place that they might hide; the sword's power is not great enough to destroy all the world. Together, though, we might send them all to their deaths with a single simple spell, this same spell that I have almost fully prepared."

"And in so doing, consign the rest of the world, as well, to destruction, myself along with it."

"Would that really be so unbearable? A moment, and it would all be over. Is your life so pleasant, then, that you must cling to it so tenaciously? Would it not be a comfort simply to let go, to let yourself fall into the nothingness of death? I have sought for that peace for long centuries now; can you find it so repulsive?"

"My life is my own, old man, and none of your concern. I do not want to die, nor to be responsible for the deaths of millions of innocent people."

"Innocent? Who, Garth, is innocent? The overmen of Ordunin, who exiled you for aiding them and refused even to consider your pardon? Your family, who refused to leave a frozen wasteland to join you? The Yprians, perhaps, who squabble among themselves and have invaded, without cause, the lands of their neighbors? The Erammans, who have turned the richest empire in this decadent world into a chaos of civil war, who drove your people into the wilderness to die? The Orûnians, who tried to take advantage of their neighbors' internal strife? The people of Skelleth, who despise you even after three years, despite all you have done for them? The people of Ur-Dormulk, what few remain, who sent soldiers to kill you? Who among these is worthy of your consideration? Where are the people who deserve to live so much that you would give up your just vengeance and go on living a life that has become a burden to you, merely so that they might survive a few years longer amid war, plague, and famine?"

"You distort the truth with your words, old man," Garth said, resisting an urge to give in, to admit that the Forgotten King was right. He was uncertain whether this impulse came from himself or from Bheleu or from some magic wrought by the King, the book, or the mask. Whatever it was, it was powerful, almost hypnotic; his gaze was fixed on the Pallid Mask, white and gleaming, and he found it hard to think of resistance. "What of Frima?" he asked, grasping at the first memory he could dredge up. "She has done nothing to deserve death. Surely there are millions more like her."

The old man did not answer; instead, he leaned his head forward and began chanting again.

Garth remembered suddenly why he had come to this place and demanded loudly, "Old man, are there any Aghadites here?" He doubted that there were. The Forgotten King would not care to be disturbed by their presence, and Garth knew that the King was capable of enforcing his whims.

The chanting broke, and the King said, "We are alone here, Garth, alone with our gods."

The overman, refusing to trust the old man, tried to figure out some way in which this pronouncement could be interpreted that would allow for the presence of cultists. He could think of none; after a moment's hesitation he nodded and turned to go.

The King was chanting again, but his voice was suddenly drowned out by another sound, distorted by the echoes of the passageway and by the distance, but still, unmistakably, the roar of a warbeast.

Startled, Garth froze, staring into the shadows of the entry passage; then, with the glowing sword held out before him, he broke into a run.

Chapter Twenty-Eight

Blood spattered across his face as he emerged from the cave. Garth blinked and raised his free hand to shield his eyes. His ears were filled with human screaming and the roaring of the warbeast.

His first impulse was to strike out with the Sword of Bheleu, blasting whatever stood before him, but he restrained himself. Koros and Frima were around somewhere, and he did not want to harm them. The sword's power was not selective enough to leave them unscathed in a blind attack.

After the first shower of blood across his face nothing more struck him, although Garth did not yet realize what had actually hit him. He lowered his hand and opened his eyes.

Koros stood before him, fangs bared and dripping blood, several mangled corpses beneath its massive paws, others flung up against either side of the defile, weapons scattered on all sides. Its roar had died to a sullen growling.

Garth wiped at the liquid on his face, looked at the residue on his hand, and then understood that blood had been flung upon him by the warbeast's attack on the last of the Aghadites. It was, he was sure, human blood.

The warbeast was not uninjured, however. Three crossbow quarrels protruded from one shoulder, and a fourth from one of its forepaws. Something had gashed it across the face, narrowly missing one of its great golden eyes.

No further threat remained. There could be no doubt that every human in sight was dead.

With that thought, Garth became aware that Frima was not there. He looked over the bloody bodies, but saw none that might have been his Dûsarran companion.

The sound of screaming was still continuing, he noticed, coming from somewhere beyond the rocks to his right. Koros was looking in that direction, apparently trying to locate the sound's source. It was only then that Garth realized he was hearing, not the wordless yelling of dying men, but a human female calling, "Koros! Koros!"

It was Frima's voice, but no sooner had Garth recognized it than it fell silent.

"Frima!" the overman bellowed.

There was no answer; his cry echoed from the surrounding rock and was followed only by silence.

"Frima!" Garth called again. Koros growled; there was no other response.

It was obvious that the Aghadites had gotten her, separating her from the warbeast somehow, and then killing her. Garth felt his anger mount. He saw the glow of the sword deepen to red and brighten to a ferocious glare. The Aghadites would pay for this, he promised himself. They would all die, every one of them, no matter where they might hide. They had destroyed an innocent girl and they would regret it – if they lived long enough to know what happened.

He remembered the Forgotten King's words, and his own reply. Frima was gone now, and with her his concern for the world's inhabitants. The world might be full of innocent victims, he told himself, but if he didn't destroy them, someone else would.

"I'a bheluye!" he cried. "Aghad, I will destroy you!" He turned and strode back into the temple of Death.

Watching from their concealed vantage point at the mouth of a tunnel in the surrounding stone, the high priestess of Aghad and two of her companions saw the overman's magic sword blaze up a baleful red, and heard him proclaim his anger.

"I think," the high priestess said, "that we should wait until he's had some time to calm down. If we try to bargain with him now, he's liable to fry us all before we can speak a dozen words; he's too mad to worry about the girl. When he's had more time to think, we should be able to make a deal."

Her companions made noises of agreement, peering warily out. Farther down the tunnel, a loud thump sounded, followed by muffled cursing.

"Be careful with her!" the high priestess warned. "She may be the only thing that keeps us all alive!"

"I beg your forgiveness, mistress," someone answered. "But she fights like a mad creature. She chewed through the gag already, and we had to drop her to prepare another."

The priestess turned away from the tunnel opening and stared down at the struggling form of their captive, barely visible in the light of the single shuttered lantern allowed so near the entrance. "You can hurt her if you need to," she said, "just as long as you don't kill her or cripple her."

Frima thrashed harder and tried to scream; one of the Aghadites jammed another wadded cloth into her mouth, stifling the sound.

Garth did not hear Frima's struggles, and would not have paid enough attention to recognize them for what they were if he had. He was convinced that she was dead. Whenever someone else had fallen into the hands of the Aghadites, he or she had died. Kyrith had died and Saram had died; Garth saw no reason to think that Frima had fared any better. He expected to be confronted with her mutilated corpse when next he emerged from the temple of Death – if he ever did emerge.

He strode down the passageway with the sword blazing before him, the glow feeding on his anger and stoking it as well. His rage, or the combination of his own despair and rage with the malign influence of Bheleu, had driven all conscious thought from his mind, save the necessity of destroying the cult of Aghad, regardless of the means or the cost. He stormed into the inner chamber of the temple just as the Forgotten King's chanting paused.

"What must I do, old man?" Garth demanded.

"You will know when the time comes," the Forgotten King replied. He began to chant again.

Garth was in no mood to wait, but he forced himself to stand behind the King, awaiting the instructions he was sure would come. The old man would give him a sign, some way of knowing what was expected of him, and he would act; the spell would be completed, and the world would end.

His enemies would be destroyed – the cult of Aghad would be wiped out to the last stinking, treacherous member. The city of Dûsarra, which had so blighted his life, would vanish. The gods themselves, the foul Aghad and Garth's own unwanted master Bheleu among them, would die. The Forgotten King would perish, and his Unnamed God with him.

Garth himself would die, but what of it? He had little enough left in the world. His people had scorned him, Kyrith and Saram and Frima had been murdered, and his world had sunk into an era of chaos and destruction.

The old man would have his wish; his life, which had lasted so impossibly long, would be over.

Everything would end.

Everything.

Koros would die – both the warbeast and the god it was named for. It was hard to imagine the animal dying. The sun would go out, or so he assumed; there would be nothing left for it to shine upon. The green fields of summer would never be again; sun above and earth below would both be gone. The farmers in the fields would be gone, human and overman alike.

There would be an end to war and hatred and death, Garth told himself.

Yes, and an end to love and life as well. The destruction would swallow up the good with the bad, and there would be no more world, no more time, no chance to make anything right. He would never again feel the wind in his face or the sun on his. back, not only because he would be dead and beyond all feeling, but because there would be no more wind, no more sun, ever again. Fish would no longer swim in the sea, for the sea would be no more, and birds would not fly. No new year would ever follow this one, no autumn would supplant this final summer – all because he, Garth of Ordunin, had defied the gods and lost. He had been defeated by Aghad, Bheleu, and Death; he had lost himself in the anger and despair that the dark gods sent. He was allowing the gods to manipulate him.

This must not be.

The Forgotten King's harsh voice cut through to him, raised suddenly to a new pitch and volume, wrapped around the massed consonants of the chant, and Garth felt magical power seething around him.

He wanted to stop, to retreat, to reverse his decision. He did not want the world to end, did not want to aid in its destruction, but he could not move. He felt a fierce compulsion to give in, to do what the old man wanted, to serve the gods who had shaped the world in this one final act, and he fought desperately against it.

The chanting stopped, and the old man turned to face him, the mask gleaming dully in the red light of the sword, as if washed in blood.

In desperation, struggling to destroy the compulsion that he felt overtaking him, Garth lashed out with the Sword of Bheleu, striking at the old man, hoping to disrupt the spell before his part in it was needed. He thrust the glowing blade against the King's chest, expecting it to be turned aside and to receive a backlash of magical force, a resistance that would break the web of power that held him.

The blade sank easily through the old man's frail body with a sound like a soft sigh, emerging a foot or more from his back and scraping against the stone of the altar. Thick, dark blood oozed slowly forth onto the shining metal.

The Forgotten King smiled, the Pallid Mask twisting to fit his face, and Garth realized, even before the first rumbling began, what his part in the final ritual had been. He had been destined, all along, to plunge the Sword of Bheleu into the heart of the King in Yellow.

He stared in horror at the mask. Something was happening to the King; his blood was evaporating from the sword, and his body was fading, thinning away to nothing. The mask was melting into the flesh of his face, blending with it, reshaping itself; it sank back against the bone of the old man's skull, pulling itself tight.

The King's yellow mantle fell open, and Garth tried to scream at the sight of what lay beneath, but something had happened to the flow of time; he was unable to move normally. An eternity wound itself past him and through him as his mouth came open.

The King in Yellow turned insubstantial and seemed simultaneously to grow and shrink, departing from Garth's presence in some impossible direction. He was no longer more than a vague caricature of a human being. His head was a fleshless, grinning skull, the mask indissolubly joined; his fingers were gleaming bone, his whole being somehow smoky and indistinct.

Then he was gone, and Garth remained frozen in an instant of distorted time, waiting for his own death.

The Sword of Bheleu was still held out before him, impaling the space where the King had been; and now, as Garth watched, his mouth still opening in his need to scream, the blade puffed away in glittering, luminous powder, and the gem in the pommel burst into a shower of crystal, light, and blood. The grip crumbled away, and his hands were empty.

He became aware of a deep rumbling all around him.

He felt himself standing in the temple, suddenly conscious of every instant, of every action of his body. He felt his heart pumping blood, an age passing between each beat, felt his muscles contracting, and waited for it all to stop, waited to die.

It did not stop. Time dragged on, horribly elongated. He felt eldritch energy whirling about him, filling the air.

Then, abruptly, it was over – but he was not dead.

He stood in the cave that had been the temple of Death, his mouth open as if to scream, but the need to cry out had passed. His mind was clear and calm. The air was still, and the forces that had filled it with tension were gone. The sword of the thing that had called itself the god of destruction was gone.

The old man who had called himself the Forgotten King was gone. The strange pale mask was gone, and the old book on the altar as well. Nothing remained but a hollowed-out cave, its walls carved into ugly friezes. A dull rumbling still persisted.

Behind him, a voice said, "So it's finally over."

Chapter Twenty-Nine

Garth whirled, reaching automatically for the dagger on his belt.

An old woman stood in the entryway; she wore heavy robes, their color indistinguishable in the dim red glow that lit the cave – a glow that seemed brighter than Garth remembered it. He attributed that to the distorting effects of whatever he had just gone through.

The woman smiled cheerfully at him, looking utterly harmless despite the eerie light, but Garth was not comforted by her expression. He noticed, rather, that he was unable to focus clearly upon her face. Her features appeared to shift subtly as he watched.

"Who are you?" he demanded.

"I am Weida, goddess of wisdom and learning," the old woman replied, crossing her arms over her chest – or perhaps they had already been crossed, Garth could not be certain. He wondered if something was wrong with his vision, or if the weird events of the last few moments had addled his brain. Nothing else was affected; the walls were as solid as ever. It was only the old woman whose appearance was uncertain.

Even so, he relaxed somewhat. She might be a wizard of some sort, but she was obviously mad, and probably harmless. He guessed that she was a survivor of the plague who had wandered into the temple by accident. The absurdity of her presence was such a relief after the terrifying experience he had just undergone that he smiled broadly.

"I really am Weida," the woman insisted. "Observe."

She vanished.

Garth's smile vanished as well.

She reappeared again, seeming to coalesce from motes of dust. "I know," she said. "It's a trick any good magician could probably have managed a few days ago, but honestly, I really am Weida, and I am one of the Arkhein, what you would consider a minor goddess."

"If you are a goddess," Garth asked slowly, though he was still not ready to accept the idea, "then why are you still alive? Did not Bheleu and all the others perish? What else could it mean, when the Sword of Bheleu crumbled and the Book of Silence vanished?"

Before the woman could speak, he added, "For that matter, why am I still alive?"

"Why shouldn't we be alive?" She smiled, her face shimmering as she did, and for an instant Garth thought he saw the image of Ao, one of the Wise Women of Ordunin. Before the overman could protest, she went on. "No, never mind. I know what you're thinking – that's my province, after all. You thought that all the world would end, all the gods would die, when the King in Yellow completed the ritual. The King thought so, too. It may be that he convinced himself that would be the case, back when he first realized he would prefer death to unending life; he couldn't stand the thought of anything living on after him."

That sounded plausible, but Garth objected. "What about all the prophecies? Everyone agreed that the Forgotten King would live until the end of time! That was the bargain he made with the gods!"

"It was the bargain that deceived the oracles and prophets. The bargain was fulfilled, in a way, and the Forgotten King did live until the end of time. The problem lies in the exact meaning of that phrase. You must understand it, not in mortal terms, but in the way the gods meant it. It is not 'the end of time,' where 'time' is a common noun, but 'the end of Time,' where 'Time' is a proper noun, the name of a god. The King could not die so long as the gods that had given him immortality still lived – all three of those gods. He was not given eternal life by the Death-God alone, nor even by Death and Life in partnership, but by Death, Life, and Time – the god you knew as Dagha. It was Dagha-Time that created the Lords of Eir and Dûs, who in turn created the world and everything in it – myself included, and much less directly, you as well. And it was Dagha that ended when the King completed his spell."

Garth grappled with this explanation for a moment, then asked, "But how can the world exist if time is no more? How can I move? How can we speak?"

"*Time* still exists; it is *Dagha* who is no more. Dagha created time, but does that mean that the two must perish together? When a house-carpenter dies, do all his houses fall in? We are more than the dreams of the gods; though they created the world, it has an existence of its own. Dagha, itself, misunderstood this; it was incapable of conceiving of our world continuing after the fourteen gods who had created it ceased to be."

"The fourteen gods are truly gone, then?"

"Oh, yes; they had no real independent existence of their own. They were not so much Dagha's dreams, perhaps, as parts of itself – concepts that Dagha split off from itself. They couldn't exist beyond Dagha; each merged with his or her opposite and returned to the nothingness that brought them forth."

Garth considered this. "But then why," he asked, "do you still exist, if you're a goddess?" He was beginning to believe the woman's claim to divinity; her knowledge of the King's passing, and the calm rationality of her explanations, did not accord with his theory of a mad wizard.

"Dagha didn't create *me* from nothingness, Garth; Leuk and Pria did. Dagha, self-obsessed and self-contained, could not create anything directly that could have an independent life of its own, but the fragments it broke off and gave names to were not so restricted, being already incomplete and out of balance themselves. Dagha didn't create the world, either, nor living beings such as yourself; it was the fourteen beings Dagha had created who, in their turn, did that. We were all started by the Lords of Eir, and Dagha thought that, in balance, we'd all be finished off by the Lords of Dûs – but Dagha got that one wrong. Its playing at creation threw the balance out. I wasn't sure, though, to be truthful, how much of our little world would come through intact."

A sudden cold uncertainty soaked into Garth's thoughts.

"How much *did* come through?" He had visions of finding nothing but space outside the temple cave; perhaps nothing remained alive anywhere save for himself and this peculiar self-proclaimed goddess.

"Oh, almost everything; you need not worry, Garth. A few stars may be missing, a few things may be changed in how the world works, but in general, Garth, everything remains as you knew it."

"You're sure?"

"Oh, yes. I'm a goddess, Garth, and the goddess of knowledge, at that. I know a very great deal. We are not alone. The world remains much as it was; most people are probably unaware of any change, save a brief spell of dizziness."

"And you knew that the world would survive?"

"Well, as I said, even I was not certain until right at the end."

"How could you know what the other, greater gods did not?"

"Because I am what I am, Garth, the goddess of wisdom. I saw through the deceits and partial truths that Dagha used to fool itself and its constituent deities. I knew from the start that it had done more than it knew in creating our world, creating something so removed from itself." She smiled wryly, and for a moment her face seemed solid and normal. "I must confess, however, that I had my doubts. I saw the pattern of time that Dagha had set up, and saw how neatly the world followed along its set path, and feared that it might all end as Dagha had planned. It was not until you refused the service of Bheleu, three years ago, and thereby cut short the Age of Destruction, that I could be certain the pattern was broken. That act, more than any other in all the fifteen ages, threw the world aside from its predestined course and assured it of continued existence when its creators had gone. You disrupted the whole cosmic balance, Garth, by favoring life over death."

Garth was falling behind in following the explanations.

"But why are you different from the other gods? Did all the lesser gods survive, whatever they're called?"

"We are called the Arkhein, Garth, and I am not yet certain whether we have all survived. Some of us were closely tied to our creators; others, like myself, were more independent. I am not bound up in the time that Dagha controlled. The Eir and the Dûs were all predestined, with no say in their own existence; each took his turn for an age, tied to the scheme that Dagha had set up. The order of the ages was established from the beginning and the nature of each predetermined. Each had its rules, symbols, totems, and intended duration, all part of the pretty pattern that Dagha had designed for its little creations to dance through. When the pattern was finished, so were they. The Arkhein, however, were not part of that grand pattern. We were free to do as we pleased, pretty much – or at least most of us were. Dagha hadn't made us, didn't control us, and had no place for us in its designs. It hadn't made the world and it didn't control that; surely you knew enough theology to know that nobody bothered praying to Dagha, since it never did any good."

"Yes, I knew that," Garth admitted.

"Garth, if it confuses you so, don't worry about reasons and explanations. Just accept the situation as it is. The fifteen higher gods are gone, but the world continues. We're all free now, coasting on, as it were. There are no more predetermined ages – you survived the Fifteenth Age in the three minutes it took the higher gods to die. Nothing is set anymore; there is no more predestination. You are no longer the chosen of Bheleu, but merely an overman. There is no more Bheleu."

Garth thought that over, watching Weida's shifting features. The rumbling grew louder, and the floor trembled beneath his feet. The red glow appeared to brighten.

"What is that sound?" he asked. "It seemed to start during the King's spell."

"That's the volcano. Dûsarra was built on an active volcano, you know, and the priests of the seven dark gods worked a great spell to restrain it. Now that the gods are dead, the magic they powered won't work anymore. Major theurgy is a dead art – and nobody ever called on us Arkhein very much. Most magic drew on the higher gods, either Eir or Dûs, and when they died all their magic went with them. Their totems all burned out during the Fifteenth Age; the dying gasp of the fifteen gods, I suppose you might call it. You saw three of them go yourself. And because the magic is gone, the volcano is free; it's been pent up since the city was founded back in the Eighth Age, so I suppose it will erupt any minute now. This cave is one of its old exhaust vents; it will probably fill up with lava quite quickly."

Garth turned around and stared apprehensively at the brightening red glow. "Wouldn't that kill us both?" he asked.

"Oh, I suppose it will kill *you*, but it will take more than a volcano to harm a goddess."

The overman turned back, enraged – and relieved to realize that it was wholly his own anger, untainted by Bheleu's malign influence. It was a clean and simple feeling, very unlike the seething, perverse fury the god's power had engendered so often. "Why didn't you warn me sooner?" he demanded.

"Why should I? What does it matter to me if an overman dies?"

"If you don't care what happens to me, why are you here? Why have you manifested yourself and spoken with me?"

"Ah, you've seen through me. I do care, Garth, at least somewhat. I wanted to watch the fireworks, to see the end of our old order. I wanted to speak with the mortal involved, and to congratulate you on the part you've played in everything. Most of all, I was curious; it goes with wisdom. Only the curious ever learn much. That's why I alone am here, of all the Arkhein. But that's all done now, and it's not the place of a goddess to become too attached to a mortal. You must die eventually, after all – and have I not now warned you?"

Garth heard the rumbling grow louder, and the stone floor shook from a sudden shock far below. He glanced back at the red glow, which now seemed dimmer.

"You have a few minutes yet, Garth," the goddess said.

"A moment," Garth said. "If the god of death is gone, can I still die?" He wondered if the goddess, if she was in fact what she claimed to be, might be amusing herself at his expense. Could it be that he had inadvertently obtained immortality, not just for himself, but for all the world?

"The old god of death is gone, The God Whose Name Was Not Spoken, who was a Lord of Dûs and a part of Dagha, but there is still death. There must always be death. We have a new god of death now, one that you helped to create."

"What?"

"Certainly. You didn't see the King in Yellow die, did you? You were watching; he changed, and moved out of your realm of perception, but he did not die. He merged with the Pallid Mask, assuming the power it signified, and became Death himself. You saw it happen."

Garth remembered what he had seen beneath the King in Yellow's mantle and knew that Weida – if it was Weida – spoke the truth. A perverse amusement twitched his mouth into a smile. "Then after all that, he didn't die? His great spell was for nothing?"

"Hardly for nothing, Garth. The human part of him perished utterly, and Yhtill of Hastur is no more. The King in Yellow no longer has any material existence, but he still goes on, the embodiment of the power and concept of Death."

Half a dozen other questions came to mind while Garth puzzled this over, but the rumbling changed again, with a deep, slow, grinding sound, and the overman decided that any further inquiries were inessential. He ran toward the entrance.

Weida might or might not have stepped aside to let him pass; he was not sure whether she did, or whether he passed through her, or some impossible combination of both. Disconcerted, he stumbled against the wall of the passage and glanced back.

The woman was gone – or the image, or goddess, or whatever it had been.

The voice, however, lingered, calling, "I think you had better hurry, overman."

Garth righted himself and hurried on. While moving, he asked aloud, "How is it that you materialized here before me in this cave? None of the other gods I was involved with ever did that, not Aghad, nor Bheleu, nor any of them. Bheleu could only speak to me in visions."

"They were Dûs, Garth, and not tied to this world as we Arkhein are," the voice said quietly, speaking from the air near his right ear.

"All right, then, if the Arkhein can manifest themselves where the Eir and Dûs could not, why have I never heard of it happening before?"

"The rules are different now," the voice replied. "We were restrained by Dagha's rules, confined by the power of the higher gods even while we drew much of our own power from them. Now things have changed. *Everything* has changed. Even I don't know all the differences yet; I have never been so free before and have not yet had time to learn what this freedom means."

A brutal shaking distracted Garth from the conversation; he staggered up the dark passageway, grateful that there were no branches where he might make a wrong turning. Ahead, he glimpsed a pale gray glimmering; he moved onward and saw that it was the first faint light of dawn.

Chapter Thirty

Frima had been blindfolded as well as bound and gagged, and did not see what happened to her captors. She heard a rumbling, then a crashing, and then the deafening roar of an angry warbeast, mixed with human screams. The hands that had held her fell away, and she tumbled heavily to the floor, bruising her elbows on the stone. She tried to call out, but the gag stopped her voice. She struggled with her bonds in an attempt to work the loops of rope and fabric down over her hands.

She heard thrashing sounds and the scraping of stone on stone in those brief instants between the warbeast's growls and roars; the screaming of its victims was almost constant. At least once she heard a crunching she knew to be the splintering of bones. Something warm and wet sprayed across her legs where they protruded from her disarrayed robe.

Finally, when the roaring seemed to be almost upon her, the screaming faded and died.

The roaring, too, died in its turn, and she heard a harsh, inhuman breathing. Something viscous and unpleasant dripped onto her face.

She managed to work one hand free, thanking Tema and the other gods for giving her such small, delicate hands. Saram had complimented her on them more than once. She reached up and pulled away the blindfold, both hopeful and afraid.

Koros looked back at her, its golden eyes gleaming strangely in the faint dawning light that filtered into the Aghadite tunnel. She saw, behind the beast, that a large part of one wall of the tunnel had been broken away; Koros had obviously managed to track her down and come to her rescue, letting nothing bar its way.

That moment of realization seemed to stretch on forever; time distorted and slowed, and she felt herself drawn out across an eternity, staring into the warbeast's eyes for endless eons.

This was more frightening than anything the Aghadites could have done to her; the three-minute piece of warped and broken time was utterly beyond her experience or conjecture, and she was certain, while it was occurring, that the universe had come to an end for her, that she was dead or dying. She could think of nothing but death that might be so unlike life as she had known it.

Then, abruptly, time returned to normal. She wrenched the gag from her mouth and called, "Koros!"

The warbeast growled a greeting in reply, and she noticed for the first time that it was standing astride a disemboweled corpse, and that the substance dripping upon her face was blood from the creature's jaw.

"Get me out of here!" she cried, still unsure what was happening, but eager to be away from the dead and mangled Aghadite, away from the place where she had felt reality coming apart around her.

Koros seemed to understand; it backed up into the opening it had smashed through the stone wall of the hiding place, ignoring the ruined corpses it trod underfoot as it moved.

Frima reached down and struggled with the ropes that bound her ankles, getting them free after a few moments of tugging. She staggered to her feet, pulling at the bindings that still remained, and tottered after the warbeast, out onto the Street of the Temples and into the light of dawn.

She realized for the first time that the rumbling she had heard was still continuing, even growing. She had thought it to be caused by some Aghadite machine, but now discovered that it was coming from the earth beneath her feet, and that the ground was beginning to shake. She didn't like it.

She was unsure what to do; she did not know where Garth had gone, whether he was still in the temple of Death, whether it would be safe to enter the temple. She stood for a long moment, glancing about indecisively, trying to decide upon a course of action.

Finally, as she was about to try to coax Koros into hunting down its master for her, Garth emerged from the shadows of the temple cave, running unsteadily. She let out a glad cry at the sight of him, happy to see him still alive, and then noticed that the Sword of Bheleu was gone. She started to say something about it, concerned lest it fall into the wrong hands.

Garth ignored that; he stopped, stared in surprise at the sight of Frima alive, saw Koros, and called, "Mount up! Quickly!"

Confused, Frima obeyed; she had learned not to argue with Garth when he gave her direct orders so urgently. She clambered awkwardly onto the warbeast's back.

An instant later the overman leaped up behind her and called a word to the beast. Koros growled in response, then bounded forward and set out at full speed for the city gate. It seemed unhindered by its recent injuries, or by the two crossbow quarrels that still protruded from its shoulder. One had come free from the shoulder, and Koros had worked out the one in its paw, leaving an oozing wound.

For a long moment Frima had no time to do anything but hang on, as Koros moved at incredible speed through the city's deserted streets.

The rumbling sound grew and deepened, and she could feel the ground shaking whenever the warbeast's paws touched it for more than an instant. The air had turned very hot and dry and was full of sound and vibration; black dust was rising from the ground and vibrating off the buildings on either side.

Something terrible was obviously happening, or perhaps was about to happen, but she did not know what it was.

The street in front of them cracked open, and a stone house at one side fell inward with a roar; undaunted, the warbeast leaped the crack and bounded onward. It seemed untroubled by the trembling of the earth. When it reached the open ground of the market, it charged across at a speed that forced Frima to close her eyes and gasp for air.

Then they were out of the city, past the broken gate, and still Koros ran, headlong down the slope of ancient black lava.

Finally, when they had left the stone surface behind and reached the end – or the beginning – of the highway that led eastward through the site of Weideth, Garth leaned down and signaled to the beast with a blow on its flank. It slowed to a limping walk, its head low. Even its huge supply of energy was not inexhaustible. Frima struggled up into a sitting position, releasing her armhold around its neck, and peered back under Garth's arm.

A column of thick black smoke was pouring up from Dûsarra, from every part of the city, as if the black walls were the rim of a vast chimney; an orange glow lit the sky. More smoke and more of the orange light streamed from the crater above the city. As Frima watched, she saw one of the temple towers sway and then collapse. The rumbling was now a steady roar, but comfortingly distant.

Nobody emerged from the gate. She watched, expecting a fleeing multitude, but no one appeared; instead, the walls on either side of the ruined gate abruptly tottered and fell inward. Something red and glowing poured forth where they had stood, and she realized at last that the volcano had awakened and was consuming Dûsarra.

Garth glanced back at the crumbling black city and the lava that was devouring it. "So much, then, for the cult of Aghad," he said.

"Do you think they're all in there?" Frima asked.

Garth shrugged. "Enough of them are. Their god is dead and their temples destroyed; I won't trouble myself about any who may have survived." Without the Sword of Bheleu driving him on, he was no longer obsessed with the cult's destruction to the last man. He had his revenge.

Frima looked up at the overman's leathery, noseless face, then back at her vanishing birthplace. She did not understand what Garth meant about the god; gods did not die, she told herself.

Still, she, too, felt that she had had her fill of vengeance. She was ready to begin finding herself a new life. She suspected, as well, that she might be carrying more than her own life; she was beginning to notice other indications, in addition to her bouts of nausea, that she might be pregnant. The prospect delighted her. She turned away from Dûsarra and looked eastward toward the rising sun.

Appendices

About the Appendices:

The following appendices have been collected from all four volumes of the earlier Wildside editions and edited to remove duplicate material, with a few words of new material interpolated. All historical materials (Appendices A through D) were added for the Wildside editions, while the linguistic and religious material (Appendices E through G) was in the original Del Rey editions.

Appendix A: *The Origins and History of "The Lords of Dûs"*

The "Lords of Dûs" series consists of the four novels in this volume: *The Lure of the Basilisk, The Seven Altars of Dûsarra, The Sword of Bheleu,* and *The Book of Silence.* There are no published spin-offs or related series outside the four novels, nor are any presently in the works, but the possibility of adding more eventually hasn't been ruled out.

It seems to me that a brief account of the series history is in order, and here it is.

In February 1974 I flunked out of Princeton University's architecture department, and rather than go home in disgrace I wound up living in a run-down apartment in Pittsburgh's Oakland district, upstairs from an ice cream shop. I had no job, no money, no prospects, and was living off what little money I could cadge out of my disappointed parents. (While I am not proud of sponging off them, please note that I did pay them back every cent a few years later.)

So what did I do with myself? Did I go out looking for honest work? Did I apply to another college?

Hell, no. I intended to get readmitted to Princeton. The rules at the time allowed this, but required that the would-be reapplicant spend at least one full year off-campus – to get his/her head together, I suppose. So I wanted something I could do for about a year and a half.

I wasn't interested in a mere job, something to pay the bills but that wouldn't go anywhere, and I couldn't very well start an actual career if I intended to cut it off short in sixteen months or so.

And there was this anecdote I'd heard – I still don't know if it's true, and I suppose I should ask Larry Niven about it the next time I see him. The story was that when Niven decided as a young man that he wanted to be a writer, he gave himself a year – did nothing but write for a year, while living on his family's money. If he hadn't sold anything by the end of that time, he promised himself, he'd give up and get a real job.

Obviously, since he went on to a successful writing career, toward the end of the year he started selling his stories.

I'd always wanted to be a writer, ever since my second-grade teacher complimented a story I wrote, and I had sixteen months, so I decided to attempt the same feat. I'd spend my time until my readmission writing and trying to sell what I wrote. If I didn't sell anything by the time I went back to Princeton (assuming I did go back), I'd give up the idea of a writing career and concentrate on other things; if I did start selling, I could go on while in school and get serious about it after graduation.

So the next obvious question was, What should I write?

There I was in my picturesque garret, with an electric typewriter and plenty of time and motivation, trying to write to sell. What to write?

Well, what did I *want* to write? What did I like to read?

Sword and sorcery, that's what. I'd discovered Robert E. Howard's Conan not long before, and Moorcock's Elric, and Lin Carter's "Flashing Swords!" anthologies. I decided to take all the stuff I liked and put it together in my own series of sword and sorcery adventures.

Oh, I wrote other stuff, too, but my major project was to be a series of swashbuckling fantasy adventures.

For that, I needed a hero. I liked Moorcock's use of a not-quite-human hero, but thought his Melniboneans were too effete, so I invented overmen – which were, incidentally, based more on having read Desmond Morris' *The Naked Ape* than on Nietzsche. I took my hero's name and noselessness from Simon Garth, the title character in Marvel Comics' black-and-white TALES OF THE ZOMBIE.

One of the other early inspirations for Garth and Koros was Frank Frazetta's painting, "The Death Dealer." That was what decided me to provide my hero with a ferocious mount and an axe, and give him baleful red eyes.

So I had a protagonist, but then I needed something for him to do. I decided that I wanted a series of errands, not unlike the labors of Hercules, but that meant he had to have someone telling him what to do. So I added a mysterious mentor figure, swiping the King in Yellow from Robert W. Chambers for the job.

Then I needed an errand for my first story. Dragon-slaying is the traditional one, but I thought dragons were passé; I wanted some sort of monster that hadn't been over-used. I considered manticores and gryphons and the like, but settled pretty quickly on the basilisk, which just impressed the hell out of me with its lethality. Petrifying gaze, toxic breath . . . perfect! A basilisk was a little-used monster with the potential to be genuinely creepy and a real threat to my characters.

But even so, killing it was too easy, so I decided I'd have Garth capture it alive!

And there I was with the premise for a story. I sat down and started writing, without any clear idea where I was going – certainly without any real outline.

The result was a 10,000-word novelet entitled "The Master of Mormoreth," which had largely the same plot as the first nine chapters of *The Lure of the Basilisk*, but rushed through it headlong.

I sent that out to FANTASTIC, the only sensible market at the time for short sword and sorcery, and went on working on other stuff, including several more stories about Garth.

"Master of Mormoreth" didn't sell – I got a note from the first reader saying he liked it and had sent it on to his editor (that first reader was Moshe Feder, who I later dedicated the novel to, by the way), but I never heard back, and when I finally contacted the editor he swore he'd never seen the story. I suspect he just lost it.

Anyway, I didn't worry about it too much; I was writing a lot of stories, not putting all my eggs in one basket. I wrote four complete Garth stories and several fragmentary ones, and a couple of dozen assorted other stories.

I hadn't waited for a decision on that first 10,000-word novelet before continuing the series; I had followed it up with another novelet, 12,500 words, called "The City of Seven Temples." I wasn't being very sophisticated about this; I was setting Garth a bunch of tasks, that's all. The Forgotten King had him running errands. I knew what the Forgotten King wanted, and that made it fairly easy to figure out what sort of stuff he'd send Garth after. "The City of Seven Temples" was a pretty straightforward follow-up to the King's implied failure at the end of "Master of Mormoreth." When the basilisk didn't work out, he upped the stakes and went for the power of the dark gods themselves.

As for who those gods were, Appendix F describes them, but some explanation of how I created them, and for that matter the Eramman language described in Appendix E, seems in order.

The religion at the center of the story began as a reaction to the author's note in Philip K. Dick's science fiction novel, *A Maze of Death.* Dick says that the elaborate trinitarian religion described in the novel was the result of discussions with friends about what a truly logical religion would be like.

Fascinating as I found the novel and the invented religion, I thought this was pretty annoying, as the invented "logical" religion came out looking far too much like ordinary Christianity for my liking. I decided I wanted a logical, sensibly-structured *polytheistic* religion, and tried to devise one.

To create names for my gods and goddesses I hauled out my copy of *The American Heritage Dictionary of the English Language* and turned to the appendix of Indo-European roots, figuring I would find words that sounded natural and appropriate to English speakers. I had to modify some of them considerably, but eventually I had a list I was happy with. I also had the basis for a lot of the Eramman language, modifying the Indo-European roots to fit.

And then the Forgotten King sent Garth to steal from the dark side of my new pantheon, and I had the basis for "The City of Seven Temples."

Since I'd borrowed from Frazetta once before, I didn't hesitate to include another Frazetta-inspired scene, this one based on a painting entitled "Against the Gods."

I was pleased with how the story came out, but I never managed to sell it in its original form.

Altogether, I completed four Garth stories before deciding to switch to novels – the two novelets already mentioned, and two short stories, "The Eyes of Kewerro" and "The Dragon of Orgûl." I also began several stories that I never completed, as described in Appendix C.

Eventually I put aside the idea of a series of shorts and turned "The Master of Mormoreth" into *The Lure of the Basilisk* as the first step in switching over to a series of novels – but I'm getting ahead of myself.

Counting the four Garth stories, I wrote over two dozen short stories and novelets in 1974 and 1975. Out of that, I sold one short story in that time I'd allotted myself – a short-short entitled "Paranoid Fantasy #1" sold in October '74, and was published in August '75. That was enough to justify further attempts later on, but not enough to launch a career.

My application for readmission to Princeton, which was accepted, was accompanied by seventy-one rejection slips, to demonstrate that I was serious about writing and not just playing the artiste.

When I went back to Princeton in September of '75 I didn't think much about writing for awhile, but then, in 1976, I began to look seriously at the business end of it, and concluded that (a) all the money was in novels, and (b) short sword and sorcery was dead, dead, dead, but fantasy novels were doing okay.

And in May 1977 I dropped out of college to get married. This time I left for good – or actually, I theoretically took an indefinite leave of absence that's still going.

And again, rather than get a real job, I set out to be a writer – after all, I had that short story sale and a few articles to my credit, and my new wife had enough faith in me to support me for awhile. I'd written a complete novel during the summer of '76 (which turned out to be a first draft for *The Cyborg and the Sorcerers*), and that was out making the rounds, but I wanted to write another novel, and I looked through my stack of ideas and unsold stories.

"Master of Mormoreth" still looked pretty good, and it occurred to me that I could rework the Garth series of short stories into a series of books . . .

So I did. I finished *The Overman and the Basilisk* (as it was then known) in April 1978, but didn't get up the nerve to submit it anywhere until August, when I mailed it to Del Rey Books, which was then clearly the top fantasy market in North America.

I submitted that early version of *The Cyborg and the Sorcerers* at the same time; it came back, rejected, right around Christmas. *Basilisk* didn't come back, but after a couple more months I decided it must've gotten lost, and I was never going to make it as a writer and I'd better find another way to make a living. So I gave up writing and set myself up in the mail-order comic book business.

And on May 10, 1979, I got the acceptance letter from Lester del Rey, offering to buy *The Overman and the Basilisk* if I'd make a few minor changes, including a new title. I happily made the changes.

And by the way, Lester wanted to know, was I planning a sequel?

The Lure of the Basilisk was a good solid start for my writing career, and I think it was a decent adventure novel. Looking back at it now, I see flaws – I think I could write the story much better now – but all in all, it turned out well.

When Lester asked for a sequel it wasn't hard to figure out what to use; I hauled out "The City of Seven Temples" and expanded it to novel length.

Expanding 12,500 words to novel length was amazingly easy. The first three chapters had been one page in the novelet version. All I did was treat the novelet as an outline and flesh out all the incidents.

Except the result was still a bit short, and Lester had some major problems with the structure, so I wound up cannibalizing "The Eyes of Kewerro" and adding that material in as Chapters Four and Five. (Those chapters are about half the short story.)

That took care of it. Lester wanted a new title, on the grounds that the word "city" sounded too science-fictional, so *The City of Seven Temples* became *The Seven Altars of Dûsarra.*

In preparing for reprinting I found myself thinking that *The Lure of the Basilisk* really showed how much of a beginner I was when I wrote it, but *The Seven Altars of Dûsarra* seemed far more polished, and while I see a few places I'd have written it a little differently now, I'm still quite happy with it.

By now it was obvious that Lester wanted the whole series, so I sent him a proposal for a third novel. I had planned to have the third volume be a collection of short stories, but I didn't *have* any short stories ready to go, and Lester wanted a novel, so I came up with a novel.

There were four major sources for that next volume. Three of them were stories in my original series outline, back when I thought Garth would be the hero of a series of short works.

In my original plans most of the stories were intended to be about Garth running various errands for the Forgotten King, but there were two that were not. These two were instead going to center on other people reacting to Garth's actions and the Forgotten King's plans.

One of them, "Skelleth," would have dealt with the Baron of Skelleth learning that there's a powerful overman running errands for a mysterious magical character in his village, and wanting a piece of the action.

The other, "The Decision of the Council," would have dealt with the other magicians in the world responding to the discovery that someone is upsetting, stealing, destroying, or destabilizing various important magical artifacts.

Another story, "The Fall of Fortress Lagur," would have involved Garth running an errand, but would also have included material about the relationship between Garth and the City Council of Ordunin.

The actual impetus for what became *The Sword of Bheleu,* though, was the way *The Seven Altars of Dûsarra* had worked out. In writing the novel I had made the Sword of Bheleu more powerful than I had originally intended it to be, and had thrown in a bunch of background that all fit in with what I'd planned, but which wasn't part of the scheme I'd started with. The system of ages, the identity of the Forgotten King, the vendetta by the cult of Aghad – that had all been added, and once I'd set it up I couldn't really ignore it. It was obvious that the third book in the series had to deal with the Sword, and with Garth's relationship to the gods – and it made sense to me to take those three stories about Garth's relationships with other powers and add them to the mix, combining everything into a single package.

So I did. *The Sword of Bheleu* starts off with a blend of what would have been "Skelleth" and "The Fall of Fortress Lagur" – though I completely removed Lagur itself, and the errand the King would have sent Garth on – and then segues into "The Decision of the Council" to finish out the book. The working title was, in fact, *The Decision of the Council,* partly because I thought calling a fantasy novel *The Sword of* [invented name] was a dreadful cliché, but Lester was of the very definite opinion that that "Sword of" formulation had become a cliché because it *works*, and that *The Decision of the Council* was static and dull. Thus, *The Sword of Bheleu* it became, even though nobody can pronounce "Bheleu." It is, in fact, the only one of all the hundreds of names I've invented that *I* invariably have trouble pronouncing correctly.

A few quick notes on obscure sources for some of the details in the story:

The name "The Council of the Most High" was inspired by a Jefferson Airplane song called "War Movie" that contains a line, "Call high, to the Most High Directors!" I liked the sound of that, and in the earliest part of the very first draft my magicians were "The Council of the Most High Directors." I quickly shortened it to something I thought was more appropriate, though.

There is a formula Bheleu recites a couple of times: "I am Bheleu, god of destruction! Death and desolation follow me as hounds; cities are sundered at my touch, and the earth itself shattered! Who are you that dare to affront me thus?" This was inspired by a recurring line in Sapir and Murphy's early novels in the Destroyer series: "I am created Shiva, the destroyer; death, the shatterer of worlds, the blind night tiger made whole by Sinanju. What is this dog meat that stands before me?" I thought that was a neat gimmick, giving a superhuman hero a ritual introduction like that, so I swiped the idea. The Destroyer's version is in turn based on a line from the *Bhagavad Gita*, one of the Hindu scriptures; the same line in a somewhat different translation was quoted by Robert Oppenheimer on the occasion of the Trinity test in 1945, the first man-made nuclear explosion: "I am created Death, the shatterer of worlds . . ."

My own copy of the *Bhagavad Gita* has a completely different and far less poetic translation, by the way.

The name Saram is shortened from Saram-Silva, the name of the character played by my friend Keith Bass in a *Dungeons & Dragons* campaign I ran when I was in college in 1976. I have no idea where Keith got it; I assume he just made it up. My character is nothing at all like his, not even the same species; I only borrowed the name.

Speaking of people I knew in college, at least one old friend accused me of basing the Baron of Skelleth on him. The Baron of Skelleth actually *was* partially based on someone I knew in college – but not him. I had a heck of a time convincing him, though. I learned my lesson from that, and have never since consciously based any of my characters on my friends or relatives. If you're an old friend and think you recognize yourself anywhere in my work – you're wrong. (Well, unless you're the guy I *really* based the Baron of Skelleth on, and I haven't heard from him in twenty years.)

Chalkara of Kholis, while not based on a real person, was deliberately written as someone I'd like to meet.

There's one other major source I was drawing on in writing this series, but it really only became central to the story when I went to wrap up the whole thing in the fourth volume. I'll explain that, along with the other sources *The Book of Silence* came from.

The first and most obvious source is simply the need to finish up the series and tie up everything I had set up in the first three volumes. I always knew I was going to end the series with the events of Chapter Twenty-Eight of *The Book of Silence* – I won't be more specific in case you've skipped ahead to read this. In the very earliest version, believe it or not, that was just going to be an epilogue tacked onto the end of the planned collection of short stories, but I quickly realized that was a stupid idea; I needed to build up to it more than that.

It's almost tempting to include that original epilogue here – yes, I wrote it – but I'm going to resist the temptation. I was nineteen when I wrote it, and I wrote about as well as you might expect a reasonably-bright nineteen-year-old obsessed with sword and sorcery to write, which is to say, badly.

At any rate, I realized early on that I needed to do the ending right, in a climactic story describing Garth's last errand for the Forgotten King, and that was to be a novelet called "The Last Quest," in which Garth would fetch an item of great magical power from the crypts of Ur-Dormulk and bring it back to Skelleth for the Forgotten King. The central menace was to have been the monster-god Dhazh; back then the cult of Aghad, which wound up the major villain for this part of the story, had not yet developed into anything like its final form, and I had not yet worked out any details of the Age of Destruction. The nature of the desired object was not yet determined; I think my preferred theory at that point was that it would be some of that blood oozing from Dhazh's truncated horn. I'm really not sure when it became the Book of Silence.

And the final scene – the epilogue – would have taken place in the King's Inn, rather than in Dûsarra.

When I revamped the whole project to be mostly novels, I decided that this should all be combined with "Return to Dûsarra," which was to have been the story tying up all the loose ends from "City of the Seven Temples," such as dealing with the cult of Aghad. The two stories blended nicely, becoming what wound up as Chapters Five through Twenty-Eight of *The Book of Silence.*

When I gave up the idea of including *any* short stories in the series, the already-written "The Dragon of Orgûl" became Chapters One through Four and part of Five – well, except that the scenes involving Haggat were added later.

And Chapters Twenty-Nine and Thirty were added when Lester del Rey pointed out that ending the series with Chapter Twenty-Eight would be a really bad idea – bad enough that he wouldn't buy the novel if I stopped there. That was a very, very convincing argument, especially since I had largely outgrown my adolescent morbid streak by the time I got around to actually writing the book.

So those are the sources in my own plans for *The Book of Silence*, but there was another source for the whole series that had been just background before, but came to the fore in this volume. I refer to the works of Robert W. Chambers and Ambrose Bierce, specifically the collection *The King in Yellow* and the short story "An Inhabitant of Carcosa."

This all starts with the Bierce story. "An Inhabitant of Carcosa," written in 1887, describes a citizen of the great city of Carcosa who finds himself in an unfamiliar place that he eventually recognizes as the ruins of Carcosa, where he finds his own gravestone. It's a nice little ghost story that somehow caught the fancy of several later writers, most notably Robert W. Chambers, who in 1895 published a collection of short stories under the title *The King in Yellow.* Several of the stories in the collection, though not all of them, were tied together by mention of certain mysterious objects, apparently all related, chief among them a blasphemous, madness-inducing play entitled "The King in Yellow" and a strange symbol called the Yellow Sign.

And the play, "The King in Yellow," is set in Carcosa, and mentions several of the names Bierce invented for his story. We get tantalizing hints of the play's setting, characters, and content, but never anything even remotely resembling an actual explanation. Chambers (perhaps deliberately, perhaps not) appears to be not entirely consistent with Bierce's story; for example Bierce created the name "Hali" but applied it to a person (or perhaps a deity), while Chambers applies it to a lake.

At least two other writers then borrowed from Chambers, much as he had borrowed from Bierce; H.P. Lovecraft's Cthulhu mythos drew heavily on the horrific aspects of Chambers' creation, while Marion Zimmer Bradley adapted the hinted court intrigues and psychic powers from "The King in Yellow" into her Darkover series. (In case you've ever wondered why, for example, the name Hastur appears in those very dissimilar works, now you know – they both got it from Chambers.)

Right from the very start, I borrowed Chambers' King in Yellow as my mysterious mentor figure, the Forgotten King; as the series progressed, though, I decided that I would borrow considerably more than that. I went through *The King in Yellow* end to end, noting every detail, every name, every vague hint Chambers gave about the play, the Yellow Sign, and all the rest of it. I assembled all this into my own grand theory of just what the heck was going on, and then used that as the background for my own story.

I had already created my own gods and my own maps, but Chambers had never dealt with those, so there was no contradiction. I decided that the play, "The King in Yellow," was set during, and written during, the Eighth Age of my invented chronology, the age when light and darkness were in balance, and that it was the events described in the play that tipped the balance and began the world's long, slow, inevitable slide into despair, destruction, and death.

And I went to great lengths to make my descriptions of the city of Ur-Dormulk match the descriptions Chambers gave of Carcosa – or rather, what his Carcosa would have been if it were sacked by barbarians, left in ruins as Bierce described, and then rebuilt atop the ruins. The strange deep lakes, the mysterious fogs, an illusion of twin suns, doors sealed with the Yellow Sign . . .

It was great fun working all this in – and I'm sure the vast majority of readers never noticed.

Oh, lest anyone wonder about plagiarism, it's certainly not an issue legally, since *The King in Yellow* went into the public domain long before I was born; ethically it's perhaps slightly less clear-cut, but building on the work of previous authors is a tradition going back millennia. Had Chambers still been alive I would have asked his permission, but he was not.

Other influences on the series that I should probably mention, as long as I'm at it, would include Michael Moorcock's Elric and his sword Stormbringer; I admit that the Sword of Bheleu owes something to Stormbringer. Fritz Leiber's stories of Fafhrd and the Grey Mouser were part of the inspiration for the crypts of Ur-Dormulk, and specifically for the pillar/fountain, which was my own version of the fountain in Lankhmar's Plaza of Dark Delights.

Leiber's didn't have a monster under it.

By the time I completed the fourth volume I had clearly finished the story, and I was tired of Garth's whole entanglement with the King and the gods – but I still liked the world of Eramma, and thought it might be interesting to tell more stories set there, perhaps focusing on other characters instead of Garth.

I also thought, though, that it might be nice to do something entirely different. I had developed another fantasy world, called Ethshar, that I wanted to write about. Garth's adventures had tended toward melodramatic gloom and doom, where Ethshar was meant to be much lighter in tone, and I was looking forward to that change of pace – but I wasn't sure I wanted to abandon Eramma entirely. . .

In the end, I decided to leave it up to others. If Del Rey asked me for a fifth volume, or if I was deluged with fan mail asking for one, I would write it. Otherwise I wouldn't.

Del Rey never asked, and by the time a trickle of fan mail developed – it was never a deluge – I had put the whole thing behind me and moved on.

So that's it – four novels, now assembled for the first time into a single volume.

Appendix B:
A Publication History of This Series

The Lure of the Basilisk was first published March 1980 by Del Rey Books, ISBN 0-345-28624-3. The original cover art was by Darrell K. Sweet. The Del Rey edition went through at least eight printings – second printing was dated March 1984, fourth November 1985, fifth (labeled third, but it's the fifth) March 1987, seventh June 1988, eighth February 1990. All Del Rey printings had cover art by Darrell K. Sweet, but there are two different paintings – Del Rey decided the first was too dark, so from the second printing on it's the second, largely yellow one. The book finally went out of print in 1994.

The Lure of the Basilisk was quite successful commercially. In addition to the American and British editions, it's been translated into German, Polish, Spanish, Italian, Hungarian, and Japanese – details of the foreign editions are on my webpage.

The Seven Altars of Dûsarra was first published June 1981 by Del Rey Books, ISBN 0-345-29264-2. The original cover art was by Michael Herring, but Lester wasn't happy with it, and replaced it with a Darrell K. Sweet cover on the five (or more) subsequent printings.

The second printing was dated March 1984, the third June 1984, the sixth October 1986.

The novel has been translated into German, Polish, Spanish, and Italian – though I don't consider the German translation satisfactory; even with my limited German I can see that it seems pretty unimaginative, sticking too close to the literal English rather than using idiomatic German.

The Sword of Bheleu was first published January 1983 by Del Rey Books, ISBN 0-345-30777-1. The original cover art was by Laurence Schwinger. There were at least five Del Rey printings. The novel has been translated into German, Spanish, and Italian.

The Book of Silence was first published January 1984 by Del Rey Books, ISBN 0-345-30880-8. The original cover art was by Darrell K. Sweet. There were at least four Del Rey printings. The novel has been translated into German,

Spanish, and Italian.

All four Del Rey editions went out of print in the 1990s, and I reclaimed the rights; in 2001 I signed a contract with Wildside Press to publish this new edition, both in four separate volumes and this omnibus edition.

In preparing the Wildside Press editions I've gone back to the original 1978 manuscript of *The Lure of the Basilisk* and gone through it carefully, reviewing editorial changes made in the Del Rey edition. Some I have kept, but I have always believed that some of the changes Lester made were mistakes. In this edition I have removed the editing I disagree with, and returned to something closer to the original text. These differences between the two editions are all minor, but if dedicated readers spot small discrepancies in the first novel, no, it's probably not your imagination, nor a typesetting error.

Lester's editorial hand was much lighter in the other three novels than on *The Lure of the Basilisk*, so I saw no need to review every single page against the original manuscript. A few typos and other small errors have been corrected, and I've modified some punctuation I thought was off, but no significant editing has been done on them.

The map in the Del Rey edition, although based on my own original map, was drawn by Chris Barbieri, and Wildside was unable to obtain the rights to it. I have therefore redrawn the map – the original was lost twenty years ago – and Alan Rodgers at Wildside has adapted it into publishable form. This new map includes areas that Chris Barbieri had trimmed away in order to better fit the page, and is slightly more accurate in other ways, as well. I'm afraid it's a little uglier, but one can't have everything.

While *The Seven Altars of Dûsarra* and *The Sword of Bheleu* included the appendices on linguistics and religion, all the historical material in these appendices is appearing for the first time in the Wildside editions, most of it written in 2001 and 2002.

Lawrence Watt-Evans
Gaithersburg, MD
March 2002

Appendix C:

The Histories of Garth of Ordunin, Written and Unwritten:

The original 1974 plan for the Garth series was for twelve stories, ranging from 3,300 words ("The Dragon of Orgûl") to novel length (*The Lady in the Jewel).* In chronological order, they were to have been:

1. "The Master of Mormoreth"
2. "City of the Seven Temples"
3. *The Lady in the Jewel*
4. "The Scepter of Dor"
5. "The Eyes of Kewerro"
6. "The Dragon of Orgûl"
7. "The Decision of the Council"
8. "The Fall of Fortress Lagur"
9. "Skelleth"
10. "Return to Dûsarra"
11. "The Jungle by Night"
12. "The Last Quest"

"The Master of Mormoreth" was to start with a prologue explaining the series premise, and "The Last Quest" would end with an epilogue wrapping the whole thing up. The theory was that these could eventually be gathered into two volumes – a collection and a novel. Or possibly, if they ran longer than expected, two collections and a novel.

All the stories except "Skelleth" and "Return to Dûsarra" were begun; four of the first six were completed, but never published.

In 1975 or early '76 the plan was modified slightly – "The Decision of the

Council," "The Fall of Fortress Lagur," and "Skelleth" were to be combined into a novel called *The Decision of the Council.*

In 1976 I decided that I should focus on novels, and the list was revised again, becoming primarily a series of novels. The first, *The Overman and the Basilisk,* incorporated "The Master of Mormoreth," but expanded and extended the story, and was completed in 1978. The other novels were left unwritten until the first sold.

In 1979 *The Overman and the Basilisk* sold and was retitled *The Lure of the Basilisk,* and the series was continued, now planned as five volumes:

1. *The Lure of the Basilisk*
2. *The City of Seven Temples*
3. *The Eyes of Kewerro & Other Stories* (short story collection)
4. *The Decision of the Council*
5. *The Last Quest*

The Lady in the Jewel was dropped from the series as no longer really fitting in properly; the possibility of inserting it somewhere later was kept open.

The proposed novel version of *The Last Quest* would combine "Return to Dûsarra" and "The Last Quest."

The second novel, *The City of Seven Temples,* was written, expanding the 12,000-word novelet "City of the Seven Temples." Lester del Rey was not satisfied with it, and felt that it was too slow in getting to any sort of action or magic, so it was extensively revised, incorporating a piece of "The Eyes of Kewerro" into an early portion of the novel, resulting in *The Seven Altars of Dûsarra.*

That also resulted in rethinking some of the series structure, since there were loose ends in *The Seven Altars of Dûsarra* that were to be tied up in *The Decision of the Council,* and waiting an entire volume to address them seemed to be a mistake. Besides, the intended title story of the collection had been cannibalized and was therefore no longer available.

The revised plan was this:

1. *The Lure of the Basilisk*
2. *The Seven Altars of Dûsarra*
3. *The Decision of the Council*
4. *The Dragon of Orgûl & Other Stories*
   (short story collection)
5. *The Last Quest*

The Decision of the Council was written in 1981, and retitled *The Sword of Bheleu.* Its resemblance to the original fragment from 1975 was very faint, and although much of the intended plot of "Skelleth" did wind up incorporated into it, virtually no trace of "The Fall of Fortress Lagur" remained. In fact, by that point I think I'd forgotten "Fall" had ever existed, though one or two minor elements survived.

And after that was done, I looked at what I had left to work with, looked at the short fantasy markets, thought about how the series had developed, and decided that the only short story I still cared about at all was "The Dragon of Orgûl," which could hardly be a fourth volume all by itself.

So it was expanded into the first four and a half chapters of *The Last Quest*, which was retitled *The Book of Silence*, and the series was completed in four volumes, rather than five.

The astute observer will have noticed that this means the following stories were not included anywhere in the final version: *The Lady in the Jewel*, "The Scepter of Dor," "The Fall of Fortress Lagur," "The Jungle by Night," and a fraction of "The Eyes of Kewerro."

"The Fall of Fortress Lagur" and "Eyes of Kewerro" could still have fit into the series reasonably well; the other three just didn't belong in Garth's adventures as they eventually developed. I may yet re-use some of the premises, though.

Here are quick summaries:

The Lady in the Jewel: The Forgotten King wants a sorceress named Sharatha, who rules the city of Ilnan, removed from the world. Garth initially assumes that this means she must be killed, but learns that in fact she is from another universe, a world inside a magical gem, and was exiled to Garth's world by her enemies. He agrees to escort her home, but finds himself entangled in the same web of feuds and power struggles that caused her exile in the first place.

The link to the main story arc of the series was to be that the Forgotten King could not carry out his plans for Garth's world as long as beings from other worlds lived in it; thus, he demanded that Sharatha be removed.

"The Scepter of Dor": The Forgotten King wants a magical scepter that's in the possession of Dor, Lord of Therin. Dor has no intention of giving it up while alive, and Garth discovers that Dor is very hard to kill – he has multiple bodies sharing his consciousness.

"The Fall of Fortress Lagur": The heavily-fortified port city of Lagur, Ordunin's major trading partner, is one of the magical keystones holding Garth's world safe; the Forgotten King wants it destroyed, so Garth raises an army of overmen to attack it. Frankly, I think I abandoned this one because it was such a boring premise. Another fantasy siege – big deal.

"The Jungle by Night": Garth is passing through the jungles of Yesh, far to the south of Eramma, on an errand for the Forgotten King, and trespasses on the tribal lands of the Kikoru, who decide that an overman's hide would make a good trophy. The Kikoru are fierce, and the tribe's shaman is a formidable wizard, so the result is an impressively bloody sword-and-sorcery battle. This one had some nice cultural details for the Kikoru, but was very short on actual plot.

"The Eyes of Kewerro": Kewerro is the Arkhein god of the wind. In order to locate certain items the Forgotten King wants the Eyes of Kewerro, magical gems that allow their owner to see anything, anywhere in the world, that's touched by the wind. These gems are sealed in a tomb on the uninhabited polar continent, and Garth fights his way through various menaces in order to rob the tomb. About half of these menaces wound up guarding the village of Weideth in chapters 4 and 5 of *The Seven Altars of Dûsarra.*

And that was the whole thing as originally planned back in 1974.

Later on, as the series developed, a couple of other possibilities emerged – novels I might yet write someday, though I'm not planning to any time soon.

First, there's *A Handful of Gold.* Early in *The Lure of the Basilisk* Garth, ignorant of how highly humans value gold, grossly overpays a stable-boy. Later on it's mentioned that the stable-boy used that gold to buy a share in a caravan headed south. At one point I desperately wanted to tell the tale of that boy's adventures as he makes his way to Kholis, seeking his fortune, while Garth's actions are altering the familiar world around him. I never found the time for it, and eventually the enthusiasm faded.

And second, I have never ruled out the possibility of sequels, describing Garth's adventures (and Frima's – she's a character introduced in *The Seven Altars of Dûsarra)* after the end of *The Book of Silence.* I plotted two of these, but then got busy with other projects and never wrote them, or seriously proposed them to a publisher. One would have been called *Skelleth,* and would have concerned control of that increasingly-important town; it would not be the same as the never-written ninth story in the original series outline. It would have included a role reversal – Frima would have been the protagonist, and Garth her sidekick.

The other sequel was to be called *After the Gods Died,* and it would have been about certain people seeking vengeance on Garth for events in the first four books.

I could have written these two sequels in either order, since the outlines were still vague.

Every so often readers ask me if I'm planning to write any more about Garth or his world, and the answer is no, I'm not *planning* it, but it might happen someday.

And that's all there is to the series. Thank you, dear reader, for keeping it alive.

Lawrence Watt-Evans

Appendix D:
Ancient Fragments

While the original Garth stories from 1974 are sufficiently amateurish that I would prefer not to see them published – after all, I was only nineteen or twenty when I wrote them – I thought readers might be interested in a couple of samples:

Series Introduction, intended to accompany each story if it appeared out of context:

It is a strange bargain that was made in the King's Inn of Skelleth, made by two strange beings for their own reasons.

Garth, the great lord of overmen north of Skelleth, a head taller than any man, red-eyed and black-haired, leather-skinned and fur-chested, swore ever to serve the Forgotten King, so long as he should live.

The yellow-garbed bargainer, a figure in many a dim and evil legend, older than any man knows, swore in exchange that Garth's life would not pass unnoticed; that so long as anything shall live upon the earth, his name would be remembered with awe.

Such was the bargain.

Original prologue to
"The Master of Mormoreth":

Garth the overman rode into Skelleth alone, his battle-axe in hand, his armor gleaming; his blazing red eyes gazed ever straight ahead, ignoring the curious townspeople who stared at him from street and window.

Well might they stare, for only rarely were overmen seen in human realms, and Garth was impressive even for one of his race. He stood six feet ten inches tall and was proportioned to match, with broad, well-muscled shoulders and chest; his skin was the inhumanly tough, leathery brown typical of his kind, his nose nonexistent, his huge eyes vivid crimson; his black hair, never cut, reached little past his shoulders, while his unshaven jaw was as innocent of beard as a newborn child's.

Under his armor his hair was thick indeed, almost deserving the name fur; it was black, soft and silky as a panther's pelt.

Never before had Skelleth seen his like; as he wound his way through the dusty streets a crowd of children followed wonderingly behind his great black beast.

He alighted at the King's Inn, and gave his animal into the care of a stablehand; axe still in hand, he strode silently into the tavern-room, surveying the scene. A dozen tables, each designed to accommodate four diners, occupied most of the floor-space; three of them were occupied. Opposite the door he had entered by was a large stone fireplace, with a log burning pleasantly; down the left-hand wall ran a counter, with a plump man behind it polishing plates. The wall behind him held a large, many-paned window, while the right-hand wall was mostly taken up with a staircase to the upper floor.

The table nearest the counter held three scruffy-looking farmers, drinking heavily; one in the niche beneath the stairs served a pair of soldiers, swords nearby, who were engrossed in a game of dice; and lastly, a table just to the left of the fireplace held a single robed figure, his face invisible beneath his yellow hood. Garth crossed immediately to this last, and sat down opposite the hidden man.

They sat without speaking for a long moment; then Garth said, "Hear me, old one."

"I will hear you." The voice was little more than a whisper, dry as autumn leaves.

"I am called Garth. I am chief among the overmen of all the lands north of Skelleth."

The other made no reply.

"I seek the Forgotten King."

"I am he."

"So I had hoped."

"Why do you seek me?"

"O King, I am weary of life as it has been. I have lived long, as do all my kind, yet I have done little, it seems, and nothing of import."

"Such is the lot of all, be they man or overman."

"I would not have it so. O King, I know my place in the cosmos, I know that I shall never cause the stars to change, nor shall I alter the fate of the world; but I would have an influence upon the dwellers in this world, I would have it that my name be remembered throughout all the future of this planet, as long as anything that speaks shall live upon it."

The figure in yellow stirred. "Why would you have this?"

"O King, it is vanity. Though vanity is reputed not a good nor manly trait, it yet lives within me; I cannot rid myself of it."

"You know then that that is all? You do not make pretense to any other purpose?"

"There is no other purpose possible to such a desire."

"Think you not that your desire exceeds reason, even in vanity? What will it profit you that you be remembered when dead?"

"None. But I would know, while I yet live, that I shall be thus remembered; for this knowledge will comfort me when it comes my turn to die."

"So be it, Garth of the overmen; if you serve me without fail for as long as you live, I promise you that your name shall ever be known, as long as there shall be life upon this earth."

"I shall serve you, O King."

"Then listen; this is the first errand I set you . . ."

– Pittsburgh, PA
1974

Appendix E:
Notes on Language and Pronunciation

The reader should remember throughout that the characters do not speak English, but a language which, if pressed for a name, they would call "Eramman." All dialogue must be considered as translations from the Eramman, and all names as approximate transcriptions. An attempt has been made to keep all names as easily pronounceable for speakers of English as possible; since Eramman is an Indo-European tongue, reasonable accuracy is possible as well.

However, a rough guide to pronunciation seems advisable.

Accents: There are two different rules to be followed in regard to where stress falls; in Nekutta (including Dûsarra), Orgûl, Amag, Tadumuri, Mara, and almost all of Eramma, the accent always falls on the next-to-last syllable in any word, regardless of how many syllables there may be. In Orûn, the Northern Waste, the Yprian Coast, and in personal names but no other words in parts of northern Eramma (including Skelleth), the accent always falls on the first syllable, regardless of the length of the word. Thus Garth, being from the Northern Waste, pronounces the name of his home city OR-duh-nin, while the people of Skelleth or Dûsarra would pronounce it Or-DOO-nin.

The Plain of Derbarok, lying as it does between Eramma and Orûn, has no set rule; its inhabitants vary their pronunciation at whim, and there is no consensus as to whether the correct pronunciation is DER-ba-rock or Der-BAR-ock.

Phonetics: The Eramman language has seven basic vowels, which are represented in transcription by *A, E, I, Y, O, U,* and *Ü*; most have two pronunciations, depending on whether they occur in an accented syllable or an unaccented one.

A is always pronounced like the *a* in *era.*

E in an unaccented syllable is pronounced like the *e* in *get.*

E in an accented syllable is pronounced like the *é* in *passé.*

I in an unaccented syllable is pronounced like the *i* in *bit.*

I in an accented syllable is pronounced like the *ee* in *bee.*

Y is a sound which does not occur in English; regardless of accent it is pronounced like the Russian ы; best approximated as something between the accented and unaccented *I*.

O is always pronounced like the *o* in *got*; there is no long O in Eramman.

U in an unaccented syllable is pronounced like the *oo* in *book*.

U in an accented syllable is pronounced like the *oo* in *boot*.

Ü in an unaccented syllable is pronounced as in German; in an accented syllable it falls somewhere between the German *ü* and *ö*.

The use of a circumflex indicates that a vowel in an unaccented syllable is pronounced as if accented (e.g., Orûn and Dûsarra, pronounced OR-oon and Doo-SAR-ra). One-syllable words are always considered accented, but a circumflex may sometimes appear as a reminder.

Diphthongs are common in Eramman, especially *AI*, pronounced like the English word "I," and *EU*, which does not occur in most forms of English, but closely resembles the Cockney pronunciation of the long-O sound.

Consonants are pronounced much as in English, except *R*, which is trilled or "flipped" slightly (not rolled). The following combinations should be noted:

TH is always as in *thin*, never as in *there*.

DH represents the voiced *th* as in *there*.

BH represents a sound somewhere between *b* and *v*, as in the Castilian Spanish pronunciation of either.

PH represents a sound somewhere between *p* and *f*; in the combination *P'H* the apostrophe has no sound or value whatsoever except to indicate that the *P* and *H* are both pronounced individually and not as a single phoneme. *P'hul* is one syllable.

CH is pronounced as in *church*.

J is pronounced as in *jar*.

G is always as in *get*, never as in *gem*.

KH represents a voiceless gutteral, like the German *ch* in *ach*.

GH represents a voiced gutteral; it sounds rather like gargling.

SH is pronounced as in *sheep*.

ZH is pronounced like *z* in *azure*.

A final note on the names of the gods: Eramman is a declined language with seven cases; all nouns will ordinarily have an ending indicating their case and what part of a sentence they are. Names, however, do not have endings, ever. The names of the gods are, for the most part, simply words indicating their provenance with endings removed. Thus *aghadye*, the nominative form of the word for "loathing," becomes *Aghad*, and *bheluye*, meaning "destruction," becomes *Bheleu* (yes, it should be *bheleuye* or *Bhelu*; a few centuries earlier it was *bheleuye*, but pronunciations change).

Native speakers would not find this confusing, nor tend to identify a god too strongly with the single trait his name represents, because they are accustomed to names with root meanings that may not have much to do with the things named. For examples of similar attitudes among speakers of English, consider the names Grace and Victor; no one assumes that every woman named Grace is in fact graceful, or that every man named Victor is a successful fighter. How many people, upon hearing the name New York, even remember that there *is* an old York?

Furthermore, many of the root-words have changed meaning or dropped out of common usage; *regvosye,* meaning an unwillingness to understand, is extremely archaic, and no longer used as the ordinary word for blindness. That is just one example of many.

Appendix F:
Notes on Eramman Myth and Theology

In the beginning, according to the myths of Eramma and Nekutta, there was nothing at all except Dagha, and a nothingness far more complete than is ordinarily considered. There was no time, no space, no matter, no energy, no life, no death, nothing at all. Dagha, existing without these things, is therefore totally incomprehensible; it is customary to refer to Dagha as "he," but actually there is no way of saying whether he is male, female, neither, or both.

In some way, this incomprehensible being created time and space; however, being outside time himself, he could not directly interfere or manipulate anything within the space he had created. For that reason, there is no cult of Dagha, no worship, and no prayer to him.

Not satisfied with an empty cosmos, Dagha also created beings that could manipulate it, beings that were within time and limited by it, but were still immortal and unconfined by space. These beings were the gods.

Since they were created from nothing, they were of necessity created in pairs, each the negation of its twin. In each pair there was a god dedicated to the elaboration and ornamentation of the cosmos, and another dedicated to returning to primordial nothingness. Dagha created seven pairs in all; the seven dedicated to creation are known as the Lords of Eir (from an archaic word meaning both "tree" and "vitality"), and their seven foes are known as the Lords of Dûs (from *dusye,* meaning "death" and also "darkness").

The first pair created are usually referred to by their attributes rather than their names, Life and Death; they do have names, however. The role of Ayvi, the god of life, is frequently misunderstood; he is not in any way a preserver of life, but merely its bestower. He brings the first spark to each seed or embryo, but nothing more; and the Final God does nothing but remove that spark.

The next creation was of four gods rather than two: Aal, god of growth and fertility, countered by P'hul, goddess of decay; and Bel Vala, god of strength and preservation, countered by Bheleu, god of destruction. Aal is generally given precedence over Bel Vala, but P'hul is considered inferior to Bheleu; the reasons for this apparent contradiction are unclear.

The next creation was again of four gods, but this time there was no confusion in rank; Aghad, god of hatred, fear, and loathing, and his sister Pria, goddess of love, peace, and friendship, are universally acknowledged as mightier than Sai, goddess of sorrow and despair, and Gau, goddess of pleasure and delight.

These ten are the High Gods; their four younger siblings are considered lesser, but therefore more accessible, deities. The sixth pair is Leuk, lord of light and bringer of inspiration, and Andhur Regvos, the god of darkness and blindness.

The seventh and final pair of Eir and Dûs are Tema, goddess of night, and Amera, goddess of the day. With the creation of these two Dagha either exhausted his power or lost interest.

These fourteen gods amongst them created the world, to provide themselves with an arena in which to manifest themselves; and in the early days of their creation, in emulation of their master, they created lesser gods.

All the various cults of Nekutta and Eramma agree thus far, with the exception of a few outcast religions and followers of obscure deities; however, there is virtually no agreement as to the existence, number, and nature of these lesser gods, who are actually the objects of most worship, the Eir and Dûs being considered too powerful to waste time on mere mortals.

Most of the lesser gods are collectively classed as Arkhein, a word of unknown origin, and there are dozens, perhaps hundreds, of them, including among the more prominent Savel Skai, the sun-god; Mel, goddess of the moon; Eramma the earth-mother; Koros, god of war; Melith, goddess of storms and lightning, and her brother, (or half-brother, or son, or cousin, depending on which cult one adheres to) Kewerro, the god of wind and air, particularly the north wind and storms at sea. Others range down through such minor powers as Eknissa, the fire-goddess, to the obscure and pointless, such as Quon, god of dogs, and Bugo, god of masculinity and petty aggression.

A popular pastime in some areas is to debate the pedigrees of the various Arkhein, a diversion not readily exhausted, since despite the sexes generally attributed to the various deities it is assumed that any Eir or Dûs can mate with any other and produce offspring, or that any one can by himself or herself produce a child. Furthermore, the Arkhein themselves are fertile; Eramma is generally considered the mother of most of the minor nature-gods, though their paternities (if any) are debatable.

It is no wonder that, confronted with such a tangle, most overmen prefer to assume that no gods exist at all.

Appendix G:
Glossary of Gods Mentioned in the Text

(There are four classes of deity in Eramman theology. Dagha is in an unnamed class by himself, above all others. The other major gods are divided into the seven Lords of Eir, or beneficent gods, and the seven Lords of Dûs, or dark gods. Finally, there are innumerable Arkhein, or minor gods, who are neither wholly good nor wholly evil, but cover a broad range between. This glossary is arranged alphabetically, disregarding these distinctions and the elaborate hierarchy within each group, but each god's listing specifies in which of the categories he belongs.)

Aal: Reckoned either second or third of the Lords of Eir, Aal is the god of growth and fertility; he is worshipped widely, being the special favorite of farmers and pregnant women.

Aghad: Fourth among the Lords of Dûs, Aghad is the god of hatred, loathing, fear, betrayal, and most other actively negative emotions. He is widely sworn by, but worshipped only by his relatively small cult.

Amera: Goddess of the day, Amera is seventh and last among the Lords of Eir. She is worshipped widely nevertheless and revered as the mother of the sun.

Andhur: One of the two aspects of Andhur Regvos, sixth Lord of Dûs, Andhur is god of darkness. He is extremely unpopular.

Andhur Regvos: See Andhur and Regvos.

Ayvi: First of the Lords of Eir, Ayvi is the god of life and conception. Since he is ruler only of the creation of life, and not its preservation or improvement, he is prayed to only by would-be parents and breeders of livestock. His name is rarely used; like his dark counterpart, The God Whose Name Is Not Spoken, he is usually referred to by description rather than by name, e.g., Life, the Life-God, the Birth-God (inaccurate but common), the First God.

Bel Vala: God of strength and preservation, Bel Vala is rated either second or third among the Lords of Eir. He is a favorite god of soldiers and warriors, and supposed to be of particular aid if prayed to in times of dire stress.

Bheleu: God of chaos and destruction, ranked second among the Lords of Dûs. Bheleu is worshipped only by a very few people since Garth's killing of his Dûsarran cultists, mostly the more deranged and violent lords and warriors.

Dagha: In a class by himself/herself/itself, Dagha is the god of time and the creator of the Lords of Eir and Dûs. Dagha is the only deity not assigned a gender, though he is customarily referred to in the masculine form for the sake of convenience. Believed to be above all mundane concerns, Dagha is not worshipped or prayed to.

Dûs, Lords of: The dark gods: Tema, Andhur Regvos, Sai, Aghad, P'hul, Bheleu, and The God Whose Name Is Not Spoken.

Eir, Lords of: The gods of light: Amera, Leuk, Gau, Pria, Bel Vala, Aal, and Ayvi.

Eknissa: Arkhein goddess of fire, worshipped mostly by barbaric tribesmen.

Eramma: The Arkhein earth-mother goddess, for whom the Kingdom of Eramma was named, since the kingdom's founders intended it to take in all the world, a goal that it never came close to achieving. The worship of Eramma is considered old-fashioned, but still lingers among farming folk.

Gau: Fifth among the Lords of Eir, Gau is goddess of joy and pleasure in all its forms, including eating, sex, and strong drink, as well as the less earthly delights of humor and good company. Worshipped everywhere, in various and sundry ways.

God Whose Name Is Not Spoken, The: This term is used to refer to the first of the Lords of Dûs, the god of death. He does have a name, known to a very few, but it is popularly believed that any person speaking the name aloud will die instantly. He is sometimes referred to simply as Death. He is not worshipped, but shunned everywhere, feared even by the caretakers of his temple in Dûsarra. Various circumlocutions are used to avoid mentioning him; he is known as the Final God, the Death-God, and other such things.

Kewerro: A very ancient Arkhein god identified with storms and the north wind. Placatory sacrifices are common, but he has no real worshippers.

Koros: Arkhein god of war, strife, and battle, often considered to be Bheleu's son and servant. Worshipped by the more fanatical soldiers and warriors.

Leuk: Sixth of the Lords of Eir, Leuk is the god of light, color, and insight.

Melith: Arkhein goddess of lightning.

Mori: Arkhein god of the sea, worshipped by sailors everywhere. The Sea of Mori is believed to be the god's particular home.

P'hul: Third among the Lords of Dûs, P'hul is the goddess of decay, disease, and age. She is worshipped only by her small cult in Dûsarra, but is widely prayed to in hopes of warding off her touch.

Pria: Fourth among the Lords of Eir, Pria is the goddess of love, friendship, and peace, and of beneficial emotions generally, the exact opposite and counterpart to Aghad. She is one of the most popular deities.

Regvos: The more popular of the two aspects of Andhur Regvos, sixth Lord of Des, Regvos is the god of blindness, ignorance, stupidity, and folly.

Sai: Fifth among the Lords of Dûs, Sai is the goddess of pain and suffering. Where her brother Aghad dominates the actively negative emotions, Sai is the ruler of the passively negative: despair, sorrow, acquiescence, masochism. She is secretly worshipped by those with a sadistic streak throughout the world, since physical pain is within her province.

Savel Skai: Arkhein god of the sun; the name means "the bright shining one." Popular to swear by, but not seriously worshipped by civilized people.

Sneg: Sneg is god of the winter, one of the four Arkhein falling into the subcategory of Yaroi, or gods of the seasons. He is worshipped only by those who depend upon him, such as ice-cutters.

Srig: Arkhein god of cold, usually closely associated with Sneg.

Tema: Seventh of the Lords of Dûs, Tema is the goddess of the night and its creatures. She is the patroness of most of the population of Dûsarra and much of the rest of Nekutta as well.

Weida: Arkhein goddess of wisdom, Weida is worshipped by scholars and seers everywhere.

About the Author

Lawrence Watt-Evans is the author of more than two dozen novels, more than a hundred short stories, and assorted other works. Further information can be found on his webpage at http://www.watt-evans.com/.

www.ingramcontent.com/pod-product-compliance
Lightning Source LLC
Chambersburg PA
CBHW030823310726
48980CB00006B/615/J

* 9 7 8 1 5 8 7 1 5 6 6 5 6 *